*Jane Austen*

**2 Books in 1**

# Emma

# &

# Pride & Prejudice

*A Wilco Book*

Outstanding works of universal interest

This Omnibus edition printed in 2006

ISBN NO.: 81-8252-236-6

Jane Austen

Emma &

Pride & Prejudice

Complete and Unabridged

*Published by*
WILCO PUBLISHING HOUSE
33, Sri Saibaba Marg, Kalaghoda,
Mumbai - 400 001. INDIA
Tel: (91-22) 22041420 / 22842574
Fax: (91-22) 22041429
E mail: wilcos@vsnl.com

About the Author

# JANE AUSTEN

(1775-1817)

The youngest of seven children, Jane was born to George and Cassandra Austen, a Kentish family, in December 1775. Her early childhood was influenced by her father's parsonage and close companionship with elder sister Cassandra. After schooling at Oxford, and on recovering from a bout of long illness, Ms Austen began writing, initially as an entertaining pre-occupation; and gave up formal education. She never married, was adept at good house-keeping, embroidery, sewing, and actively followed the lives of her family members. Her exposure to the contemporary middle class society sharpened her imagination and enabled her to produce parodies and sentimental fiction. Mostly a home lover, she travelled sparingly, yet her works refreshingly embody the wit and the modern thought.

Her six famous full-length novels have given her immortality in the world of English Classics. Of these, *Emma* was written in 1815. Her first novel *Lady Susan,* however, was penned in 1793, at the age of 18, never to see the print during her lifetime. Jane Austen suffered failing health in 1816, resulting in rapid deterioration to the point of physical invalidity in the following year. She barely managed to complete her next novel *Persuasion,* which was to be her last. She died at a raw age of 41, in July 1817. Curiously, Ms Austen chose to be anonymous while publishing her superb novels that have, down the ages, entertained millions of readers, and have spurred numerous Jane Austen Fan Clubs and active Web sites.

# EMMA

# Chapter 1

EMMA WOODHOUSE, handsome, clever, and rich, with a comfortable home and happy disposition, seemed to unite some of the best blessings of existence; and had lived nearly twenty one years in the world with very little to distress or vex her.

She was the youngest of the two daughters of a most affectionate, indulgent father; and had, in consequence of her sister's marriage, been mistress of his house from a very early period. Her mother had died too long ago for her to have more than an indistinct remembrance of her caresses; and her place had been supplied by an excellent woman as governess, who had fallen little short of a mother in affection.

Sixteen years had Miss Taylor been in Mr. Woodhouse's family, less as a governess than a friend, very fond of both daughters, but particularly of Emma. Between *them* it was more the intimacy of sisters. Even before Miss Taylor had ceased to hold the nominal office of governess, the mildness of her temper had hardly allowed her to impose any restraint; and the shadow of authority being now long passed away, they had been living together as friend and friend very mutually attached, and Emma doing just what she liked; highly esteeming Miss Taylor's judgment, but directed chiefly by her own.

The real evils, indeed, of Emma's situation were the power of having rather too much her own way, and a disposition to think a little too well of herself; these were the disadvantages which threatened alloy to her many enjoyments. The danger, however, was at present so unperceived, that they did not by any means rank as misfortunes with her.

Sorrow came – a gentle sorrow – but not at all in the shape of any disagreeable consciousness. Miss Taylor married. It was Miss Taylor's loss which first brought grief. It was on the wedding day of this beloved friend that Emma first sat in mournful thought of any continuance. The wedding over, and the bride people gone, her father and herself were left to dine together, with no prospect of a third to cheer a long evening. Her father composed himself to sleep after dinner, as usual, and she had then only to sit and think of what she had lost.

The event had every promise of happiness for her friend. Mr. Weston was a man of unexceptionable character, easy fortune, suitable age, and pleasant manners; and there was some satisfaction in considering with what self-denying, generous friendship she had always wished and promoted the match; but it was a black morning's work for her. The want of Miss Taylor would be felt every hour of every day. She recalled her past kindness – the kindness, the affection of sixteen years – how she had taught and how she had played with her from five years old – how she had devoted all her powers to attach and amuse her in health – and how nursed her through the various illnesses of childhood. A large debt of gratitude was owing here; but the intercourse of the last seven years, the equal footing and perfect unreserve which had soon followed Isabella's marriage, on their being left to each other, was yet a dearer, tenderer recollection. She had been a friend and companion such as few possessed: intelligent, well informed, useful, gentle, knowing all the ways of the family, interested in all its concerns, and peculiarly interested in herself, in every pleasure, every scheme of hers – one to whom she could speak every thought as it arose, and who had such an affection for her as could never find fault.

How was she to bear the change? It was true that her friend was going only half a mile from them; but Emma was aware that great must be the difference between a Mrs. Weston, only half a mile from them, and a Miss Taylor in the house; and with all her advantages, natural and domestic, she was now in great danger of suffering from intellectual solitude. She dearly loved her father, but he was no companion for her. He could not meet her in conversation, rational or playful.

The evil of the actual disparity in their ages (and Mr. Woodhouse had not married early) was much increased by his constitution and habits; for having been a valetudinarian[1] all his life, without activity of mind or body, he was a much older man in ways than in years; and though everywhere beloved for the friendliness of his heart and his amiable temper, his talents could not have recommended him at any time.

Her sister, though comparatively but little removed by matrimony, being settled in London, only sixteen miles off, was much beyond her daily reach; and many a long October and November evening must be struggled through at Hartfield, before Christmas brought the next visit from Isabella and her husband, and their little children, to fill the house, and give her pleasant society again.

Highbury, the large and populous village, almost amounting to a town, to which Hartfield, in spite of its separate lawn, and shrubberies, and name, did really belong, afforded her no equals. The Woodhouses were first in consequence there. All looked up to them. She had many acquaintance in the place, for her father was universally civil, but not one among them who could be accepted in lieu of Miss Taylor for even half a day. It was a melancholy change; and Emma could not but sigh over it, and wish for impossible things, till her father awoke, and made it necessary to be cheerful. His spirits required support. He was a nervous man, easily depressed; fond of everybody that he was used to, and hating to part with them; hating change of every kind. Matrimony, as the origin of change, was always disagreeable; and he was by no means yet reconciled to his own daughter's marrying, nor could ever speak of her but with compassion, though it had been entirely a match of affection, when he was now obliged to part with Miss Taylor too; and from his habits of gentle selfishness, and of being never able to suppose that other people could feel differently from himself, he was very much disposed to think Miss Taylor had done as sad a thing for herself as for

1 Parochial about his health.

them, and would have been a great deal happier if she had spent all the rest of her life at Hartfield. Emma smiled and chatted as cheerfully as she could, to keep him from such thoughts; but when tea came, it was impossible for him not to say exactly as he had said at dinner:

"Poor Miss Taylor! I wish she were here again. What a pity it is that Mr. Weston ever thought of her!"

"I cannot agree with you, papa; you know I cannot. Mr. Weston is such a good humoured, pleasant, excellent man, that he thoroughly deserves a good wife; and you would not have had Miss Taylor live with us for ever, and bear all my odd humours, when she might have a house of her own?"

"A house of her own! But where is the advantage of a house of her own? This is three times as large. And you have never any odd humours, my dear."

"How often we shall be going to see them, and they coming to see us! We shall be always meeting! *We* must begin; we must go and pay wedding visit very soon."

"My dear, how am I to get so far? Randalls is such a distance. I could not walk half so far."

"No, papa, nobody thought of your walking. We must go in the carriage, to be sure."

"The carriage! But James will not like to put the horses to for such a little way; and where are the poor horses to be while we are paying our visit?"

"They are to be put into Mr. Weston's stable, papa. You know we have settled all that already. We talked it all over with Mr. Weston last night. And as for James, you may be very sure he will always like going to Randalls, because of his daughter's being housemaid there. I only doubt whether he will ever take us anywhere else. That was your doing, papa. You got Hannah that good place. Nobody thought of Hannah till you mentioned her – James is so obliged to you!"

"I am very glad I did think of her. It was very lucky, for I would not have had poor James think himself slighted upon any account; and I am sure she will make a very good servant: she is a civil, pretty spoken girl; I have a great opinion of her. Whenever I see her, she always curtseys and asks me how I do, in a very pretty manner; and when you have had her here to do needlework, I observe she always turns the lock of the door the right way and never bangs it. I am sure she will be an excellent servant; and it will be a great comfort to poor Miss Taylor to have somebody about her that she is used to see. Whenever James goes over to see his daughter, you know, she will be hearing of us. He will be able to tell her how we all are."

Emma spared no exertions to maintain this happier flow of ideas, and hoped, by the help of backgammon, to get her father tolerably through the evening, and be attacked by no regrets but her own. The backgammon table was placed; but a visitor immediately afterwards walked in and made it unnecessary.

Mr. Knightley, a sensible man about seven or eight and thirty, was not only a very old and intimate friend of the family, but particularly connected with it, as the elder brother of Isabella's husband. He lived about a mile from Highbury, was a frequent visitor, and always welcome, and at this time more welcome than usual, as coming directly from their mutual connections in London. He had returned to a late dinner, after some days' absence, and now walked up to Hartfield to say that all were well in Brunswick Square. It was a happy circumstance, and animated Mr. Woodhouse for some time. Mr. Knightley had a cheerful manner, which always did him good; and his many inquiries after "poor Isabella" and her children were answered most satisfactorily. When this was over, Mr. Woodhouse gratefully observed:

"It is very kind of you, Mr. Knightley, to come out at this late hour to call upon us. I am afraid you must have had a shocking walk."

"Not at all, sir. It is a beautiful moonlight night; and so mild that I must draw back from your great fire."

"But you must have found it very damp and dirty. I wish you may not catch cold."

"Dirty, sir! Look at my shoes. Not a speck on them."

"Well! that is quite surprising, for we have had a vast deal of rain here. It rained dreadfully hard for half an hour while we were at breakfast. I wanted them to put off the wedding."

"By the bye, I have not wished you joy. Being pretty well aware of what sort of joy you must both be feeling, I have been in no hurry with my congratulations; but I hope it all went off tolerably well. How did you all behave? Who cried most?"

"Ah! poor Miss Taylor! 'Tis a sad business."

"Poor Mr. and Miss Woodhouse, if you please; but I cannot possibly say 'poor Miss Taylor.' I have a great regard for you and Emma; but when it comes to the question of dependence or independence! At any rate, it must be better to have only one to please than two."

"Especially when *one* of those two is such a fanciful, troublesome creature!" said Emma playfully. "That is what you have in your head, I know – and what you would certainly say if my father were not by."

"I believe it is very true, my dear, indeed," said Mr. Woodhouse, with a sigh. "I am afraid I am sometimes very fanciful and troublesome."

"My dearest papa! You do not think I could mean you, or suppose Mr. Knightley to mean *you*. What a horrible idea! Oh no! I meant only myself. Mr. Knightley loves to find fault with me, you know – in a joke – it is all a joke. We always say what we like to one another."

Mr. Knightley, in fact, was one of the few people who could see faults in Emma Woodhouse, and the only one who ever told her of them: and though this was not particularly agreeable to Emma herself, she knew it would be so much less so to her father, that she would not have him really suspect such a circumstance as her not being thought perfect by everybody.

"Emma knows I never flatter her," said Mr. Knightley, "but I meant no reflection on anybody. Miss Taylor has been used to have two persons to please; she will now have but one. The chances are that she must be a gainer."

"Well," said Emma, willing to let it pass "you want to hear about the wedding; and I shall be happy to tell you, for we all behaved charmingly. Everybody was punctual, everybody in their best looks: not a tear, and hardly a long face to be seen. Oh no; we all felt that we were going to be only half a mile apart, and were sure of meeting every day."

"Dear Emma bears everything so well," said her father. "But, Mr. Knightley, she is really very sorry to lose poor Miss Taylor, and I am sure she *will* miss her more than she thinks for."

Emma turned away her head, divided between tears and smiles.

"It is impossible that Emma should not miss such a companion," said Mr. Knightley. "We should not like her so well as we do, sir, if we could suppose it; but she knows how much the marriage is to Miss Taylor's advantage; she knows how very acceptable it must be, at Miss Taylor's time of life, to be settled in a home of her own, and how important to her to be secure of a comfortable provision, and therefore cannot allow herself to feel so much pain as pleasure. Every friend of Miss Taylor must be glad to have her so happily married."

"And you have forgotten one matter of joy to me," said Emma, "and a very considerable one – that I made the match myself. I made the match, you know, four years ago; and to have it take place, and be proved in the right, when so many people said Mr. Weston would never marry again, may comfort me for any thing."

Mr. Knightley shook his head at her. Her father fondly replied, "Ah! my dear, I wish you would not make matches and foretell things, for whatever you say always comes to pass. Pray do not make any more matches."

"I promise you to make none for myself, papa; but I must, indeed, for other people. It is the greatest amusement in the world! And after such success, you know! Everybody said that Mr. Weston would never marry again. Oh dear, no! Mr. Weston, who had been a widower so long, and who seemed so perfectly comfortable without a wife, so constantly occupied either in his business in town or among his friends here, always acceptable wherever he went, always cheerful – Mr. Weston need not spend a single evening in the year alone if he did not like it. Oh no! Mr. Weston certainly would never marry again. Some people even talked of a promise to his wife on her deathbed, and others of the son and the uncle not letting him. All manner of solemn nonsense was talked on the subject, but I believed none of it. Ever since the day (about four years ago) that Miss Taylor and I met with him in Broadway Lane, when, because it began to drizzle, he darted away with so much gallantry, and borrowed two umbrellas for us from Farmer Mitchell's, I made up my mind on the subject. I planned the match from that hour; and when such success has blessed me in this instance, dear papa, you cannot think that I shall leave off match-making."

"I do not understand what you mean by 'success,'' said Mr. Knightley. "Success supposes endeavour. Your time has been properly and delicately spent, if you have been endeavouring for the last four years to bring about this marriage. A worthy employment for a young lady's mind! But if, which I rather imagine, your making the match, as you call it, means only your planning it, your saying to yourself one idle day, 'I think it would be a very good thing for Miss Taylor if Mr. Weston were to marry her,' and saying it again to yourself every now and then afterwards – why do you talk of success? Where is your merit? What are you proud of? You made a lucky guess; and that is all *that* can be said."

"And have you never known the pleasure and triumph of a lucky guess? I pity you. I thought you cleverer for, depend upon it a lucky guess is never merely luck. There is always some talent in it. And as to my poor word 'success,' which you quarrel with, I do not know that I am so entirely without any claim to it. You have drawn two pretty pictures; but I think there may be a third – a something between the do nothing and the do all. If I had not promoted Mr. Weston's visits here, and given many little encouragements, and smoothed many little matters, it might not have come to any thing after all. I think you must know Hartfield enough to comprehend that."

"A straightforward, open-hearted man like Weston, and a rational, unaffected woman like Miss Taylor, may be safely left to manage their own concerns. You are more likely to have done harm to yourself, than good to them, by interference."

"Emma never thinks of herself, if she can do good to others," rejoined Mr. Woodhouse, understanding but in part. "But, my dear, pray do not make any more matches; they are silly things, and break up one's family circle grievously."

"Only one more, papa; only for Mr. Elton. Poor Mr. Elton! You like Mr. Elton, papa, I must look about for a wife for him. There is nobody in Highbury who deserves him – and he has been here a whole year, and has fitted up his house so comfortably, that it would be a shame to have him single any longer, and I thought when he was joining their hands to day, he looked so very much as if he would like to have the same kind office done for him! I think very well of Mr. Elton, and this is the only way I have of doing him a service."

"Mr. Elton is a very pretty young man, to be sure, and a very good young man, and I have a great regard for him. But if you want to show him any attention, my dear, ask him to come and dine with us some day. That will be a much better thing. I dare say Mr. Knightley will be so kind as to meet him."

"With a great deal of pleasure, sir, at any time," said Mr. Knightley, laughing, "and I agree with you entirely, that it will be a much better thing. Invite him to dinner, Emma, and help him to the best of the fish and the chicken, but leave him to choose his own wife. Depend upon it, a man of six or seven-and-twenty can take care of himself."

## *Chapter 2*

MR. WESTON was a native of Highbury, and born of a respectable family, which for the last two or three generations had been rising into gentility and property. He had received a good education, but, on succeeding early in life to a small independence, had become indisposed for any of the more homely pursuits in which his brothers were engaged, and had satisfied an active, cheerful mind and social temper by entering into the militia of his county, then embodied.

Captain Weston was a general favourite; and when the chances of his military life had introduced him to Miss Churchill, of a great Yorkshire family, and Miss Churchill fell in love with him, nobody was surprised, except her brother and his wife, who had never seen him, and who were full of pride and importance, which the connection would offend.

Miss Churchill, however, being of age, and with the full command of her fortune – though her fortune bore no proportion to the family estate – was not to be dissuaded from the marriage, and it took place, to the infinite mortification of Mr. and Mrs. Churchill, who threw her off with due decorum. It was an unsuitable connection, and did not produce much happiness. Mrs. Weston ought to have found more in it, for she had a husband whose warm heart and sweet temper made him think everything due to her in return for the great goodness of being in love with him; but though she had one sort of spirit, she had not the best.

She had resolution enough to pursue her own will in spite of her brother, but not enough to refrain from unreasonable regrets at that brother's unreasonable anger, nor from missing the luxuries of her former home. They lived beyond their income, but still it was nothing in comparison of Enscombe: she did not cease to love her husband, but she wanted at once to be the wife of Captain Weston, and Miss Churchill of Enscombe.

Captain Weston, who had been considered, especially by the Churchills, as making such an amazing match, was proved to have much the worst of the bargain; for when his wife died, after a three years' marriage, he was rather a poorer man than at first, and with a child to maintain. From the expense of the child, however, he was soon relieved. The boy had, with the additional softening claim of a lingering illness of his mother's, been the means of a sort of reconciliation; and Mr. and Mrs. Churchill, having no children of their own, nor any other young creature of equal kindred to care for, offered to take the whole charge of the little Frank soon after her decease. Some scruples and some reluctance the widower-father may be supposed to have felt; but as they were overcome by other considerations, the child was given up to the care and the wealth of the Churchills, and he had only his own comfort to seek, and his own situation to improve as he could.

A complete change of life became desirable. He quitted the militia and engaged in trade, having brothers already established in a good way in London, which afforded him a favourable opening. It was a concern which brought just employment enough. He had still a small house in Highbury, where most of his leisure days were spent; and between useful occupation and the pleasures of society, the next eighteen or twenty years of his life passed cheerfully away. He had, by that time, realised an easy competence – enough to secure the purchase of a little estate adjoining Highbury, which he had always longed for – enough to marry a woman as portionless even as Miss Taylor, and to live according to the wishes of his own friendly and social disposition.

It was now some time since Miss Taylor had begun to influence his schemes; but as it was not the tyrannic influence of youth on youth, it had not shaken his determination of never settling till he could purchase Randalls, and the sale of Randalls was long looked forward to; but he had gone steadily on, with these objects in view, till they were accomplished. He had made his fortune, bought his house, and obtained his wife; and was beginning a new period of existence, with every probability of greater happiness than in any yet passed through. He had never been an unhappy man; his own temper had secured him from that, even in his first marriage; but his second must show him how delightful a well-judging and truly amiable woman could be, and must give him the pleasantest proof of its being a great deal better to choose than to be chosen, to excite gratitude than to feel it.

He had only himself to please in his choice: his fortune was his own; for as to Frank, it was more than being tacitly brought up as his uncle's heir, it had become so avowed an adoption as to have him assume the name of Churchill on coming of age. It was most unlikely; therefore, that he should ever want his father's assistance. His father had no apprehension of it. The aunt was a capricious woman, and governed her husband entirely; but it was not in Mr. Weston's nature to imagine that any caprice could be strong enough to affect one so dear, and, as he believed, so deservedly dear. He saw his son every year in London, and was proud of him; and his fond report of him as a very fine young man had made Highbury feel a sort of pride in him too. He was looked on as sufficiently belonging to the place to make his merits and prospects a kind of common concern.

Mr. Frank Churchill was one of the boasts of Highbury, and a lively curiosity to see him prevailed, though the compliment was so little returned that he had never been there in his life. His coming to visit his father had been often talked of but never achieved.

Now, upon his father's marriage, it was very generally proposed, as a most proper attention, that the visit should take place. There was not a dissentient voice on the subject, either when Mrs. Perry drank tea with Mrs. and Miss Bates, or when Mrs. and Miss Bates returned the visit. Now was the time for Mr. Frank Churchill to come among them; and the hope strengthened when it was understood that he had written to his new mother on the occasion. For a few days, every morning visit in Highbury included some mention of the handsome letter Mrs. Weston had received. "I suppose you have heard of the handsome letter Mr. Frank Churchill has written to Mrs. Weston? I understand it was a very handsome letter, indeed. Mr. Woodhouse told me of it. Mr. Woodhouse saw the letter, and he says he never saw such a handsome letter in his life."

It was, indeed, a highly-prized letter. Mrs. Weston had, of course, formed a very favourable idea of the young man; and such a pleasing attention was an irresistible proof of his great good sense, and a most welcome addition to every source and every expression of congratulation which her marriage had already secured. She felt herself a most fortunate woman; and she had lived long enough to know how fortunate she might well be thought, where the only regret was for a partial separation from friends whose friendship for her had never cooled, and who could ill bear to part with her.

She knew that at times she must be missed; and could not think, without pain, of Emma's losing a single pleasure, or suffering an hour's ennui, from the want of her companionableness: but dear Emma was of no feeble character; she was more equal to her situation than most girls would have been, and had sense, and energy, and spirits that might be hoped would bear her well and happily through its little difficulties and privations. And then there was such comfort in the very easy distance of Randalls from Hartfield, so convenient for even solitary female walking, and in Mr. Weston's disposition and circumstances, which would make the approaching season no hindrance to their spending half the evenings in the week together.

Her situation was altogether the subject of hours of gratitude to Mrs. Weston, and of moments only of regret; and her satisfaction – her more than satisfaction – her cheerful enjoyment, was so just and so apparent, that Emma, well as she knew her father, was sometimes taken by surprise at his being still able to pity 'poor Miss Taylor,' when they left her at Randalls in the centre of every domestic comfort, or saw her go away in the evening attended by her pleasant husband to a carriage of her own. But never did she go without Mr. Woodhouse's giving a gentle sigh, and saying:

"Ah, poor Miss Taylor! She would be very glad to stay."

There was no recovering Miss Taylor – nor much likelihood of ceasing to pity her; but a few weeks brought some alleviation to Mr. Woodhouse. The compliments of his neighbours were over; he was no longer teased by being wished joy of so sorrowful an event; and the wedding-cake, which had been a great distress to him, was all eaten up. His own stomach could bear nothing rich, and he could never believe other people to be different from himself. What was unwholesome to him he regarded as unfit for anybody; and he had, therefore, earnestly tried to dissuade them from having any wedding-cake at all, and when that proved vain, as earnestly tried to prevent anybody's eating it. He had been at the pains of consulting Mr. Perry, the apothecary, on the subject. Mr. Perry was an intelligent, gentlemanlike man, whose frequent visits were one of the comforts of Mr. Woodhouse's life; and upon being applied to, he could not but acknowledge (though it seemed rather against the bias of inclination) that wedding-cake might certainly disagree with many perhaps – with most people, unless taken moderately. With such an opinion, in confirmation of his own, Mr. Woodhouse hoped to influence every visitor of the newly married pair; but still the cake was eaten; and there was no rest for his benevolent nerves till it was all gone.

There was a strange rumour in Highbury of all the little Perrys being seen with a slice of Mrs. Weston's wedding cake in their hands; but Mr. Woodhouse would never believe it.

## *Chapter 3*

MR. WOODHOUSE was fond of society in his own way. He liked very much to have his friends come and see him; and from various united causes, from his long residence at Hartfield, and his good nature, from his fortune, his house, and his daughter, he could command the visits of his own little circle, in a great measure, as he liked. He had not much intercourse with any families beyond that circle; his horror of late hours, and large dinner parties, made him unfit for any acquaintance but such as would visit him on his own terms. Fortunately for him, Highbury, including Randalls in the same parish, and Donwell Abbey in the parish adjoining, the seat of Mr. Knightley, comprehended many such. Not unfrequently, through Emma's persuasion, he had some of the chosen and the best to dine with him: but evening parties were what he preferred; and, unless he fancied himself at any time unequal to company, there was scarcely an evening in the week in which Emma could not make up a card table for him.

Real, long-standing regard brought the Westons and Mr. Knightley; and by Mr. Elton, a young man living alone without liking it, the privilege of exchanging any vacant evening of his own blank solitude for the elegancies and society of Mr. Woodhouse's drawing room, and the smiles of his lovely daughter, was in no danger of being thrown away.

After these came a second set; among the most come-at-able of whom were Mrs. and Miss Bates, and Mrs. Goddard, three ladies almost always at the service of an invitation from Hartfield, and who were fetched and carried home so often, that Mr. Woodhouse thought it no hardship for either James or the horses. Had it taken place only once a year, it would have been a grievance.

Mrs. Bates, the widow of a former vicar of Highbury, was a very old lady, almost past everything but tea and quadrille[1]. She lived with her single daughter in a very small way, and was considered with all the regard and respect which a harmless old lady, under such untoward circumstances, can excite. Her daughter enjoyed a most uncommon degree of popularity for a woman neither young, handsome, rich, nor married. Miss Bates stood in the very worst predicament in the world for having much of the public favour; and she had no intellectual superiority to make atonement to herself, or frighten those who might hate her into outward respect. She had never boasted either beauty or cleverness. Her youth had passed without distinction, and her middle of life was devoted to the care of a failing mother, and the endeavour to make a small income go as far as possible. And yet she was a happy woman, and a woman whom no one named without good will. It was her own universal good will and contented temper which worked such wonders. She loved everybody, was interested in everybody's happiness, quicksighted to everybody's merits; thought herself a most fortunate creature, and surrounded with blessings in such an excellent mother, and so many good neighbours and friends, and a home that wanted for nothing. The simplicity and cheerfulness of her nature, her contented and grateful spirit, were a recommendation to everybody, and a mine of felicity to herself. She was a great talker upon little matters, which exactly suited Mr. Woodhouse, full of trivial communications and harmless gossip.

Mrs. Goddard was the mistress of a school – not of a seminary, or an establishment, or anything which professed, in long sentences of refined nonsense, to combine liberal acquirements with elegant morality, upon new principles and new

1 A card game.

systems – and where young ladies for enormous pay might be screwed out of health and into vanity – but a real, honest, old fashioned boarding school, where a reasonable quantity of accomplishments were sold at a reasonable price, and where girls might be sent to be out of the way, and scramble themselves into a little education, without any danger of coming back prodigies. Mrs. Goddard's school was in high repute – and very deservedly; for Highbury was reckoned a particularly healthy spot: she had an ample house and garden, gave the children plenty of wholesome food, let them run about a great deal in the summer, and in winter dressed their chilblains with her own hands. It was no wonder that a train of twenty young couple now walked after her to church. She was a plain, motherly kind of woman, who had worked hard in her youth, and now thought herself entitled to the occasional holiday of a tea-visit; and having formerly owed much to Mr. Woodhouse's kindness, felt his particular claim on her to leave her neat parlour, hung round with fancy work, whenever she could, and win or lose a few sixpences by his fireside.

These were the ladies whom Emma found herself very frequently able to collect; and happy was she, for her father's sake, in the power; though, as far as she was herself concerned, it was no remedy for the absence of Mrs. Weston. She was delighted to see her father look comfortable, and very much pleased with herself for contriving things so well; but the quiet prosings of three such women made her feel that every evening so spent was indeed one of the long evenings she had fearfully anticipated.

As she sat one morning, looking forward to exactly such a close of the present day, a note was brought from Mrs. Goddard, requesting, in most respectful terms, to be allowed to bring Miss Smith with her; a most welcome request: for Miss Smith was a girl of seventeen, whom Emma knew very well by sight, and had long felt an interest in, on account of her beauty. A very gracious invitation was returned, and the evening no longer dreaded by the fair mistress of the mansion.

Harriet Smith was the natural[1] daughter of somebody. Somebody had placed her, several years back, at Mrs. Goddard's school, and somebody had lately raised her from the condition of scholar to that of parlour boarder. This was all that was generally known of her history. She had *no* visible friends but what had been acquired at Highbury, and was *now* just returned from a long visit in the country to some young ladies who had been at school there with her.

She was a very pretty girl, and her beauty happened to be of a sort which Emma particularly admired. She was short, plump, and fair, with a fine bloom, blue eyes, light hair, regular features, and a look of great sweetness, and, before the end of the evening, Emma was as much pleased with her manners as her person, and quite determined to continue the acquaintance.

She was not struck by anything remarkably clever in Miss Smith's conversation, but she found her altogether very engaging – not inconveniently shy, not unwilling to talk – and yet so far from pushing, showing so proper and becoming a deference, seeming so pleasantly grateful for being admitted to Hartfield, and so artlessly impressed by the appearance of everything in so superior a style to what she had been used to, that she must have good sense, and deserve encouragement. Encouragement should be given. Those soft blue eyes, and all those natural graces, should not be wasted on the inferior society of Highbury and its connections. The acquaintance she had already formed were unworthy of her. The friends from whom she had just parted, though very good sort of people, must be doing her harm. They were a family of the name of Martin, whom Emma well knew by character, as renting a large farm of Mr. Knightley, and residing in the parish of Donwell – very creditably, she believed she knew Mr. Knightley thought highly of them, but they must be coarse and unpolished, and very unfit to be the intimates of a girl who wanted only a little more knowledge and elegance to be quite perfect. *She* would notice her; she would improve her; she would

1 Illegitimate.

detach her from her bad acquaintance, and introduce her into good society; she would form her opinions and her manners. It would be an interesting, and certainly a very kind undertaking; highly becoming her own situation in life, her leisure, and powers.

She was so busy in admiring those soft blue eyes, in talking and listening, and forming all these schemes in the in-betweens, that the evening flew away at a very unusual rate; and the supper-table, which always closed such parties, and for which she had been used to sit and watch the due time, was all set out and ready, and moved forwards to the fire, before she was aware. With an alacrity beyond the common impulse of a spirit which yet was never indifferent to the credit of doing everything well and attentively, with the real good will of a mind delighted with its own ideas, did she then do all the honours of the meal, and help and recommend the minced chicken and scalloped oysters, with an urgency which she knew would be acceptable to the early hours and civil scruples of their guests.

Upon such occasions poor Mr. Woodhouses feelings were in sad warfare. He loved to have the cloth laid, because it had been the fashion of his youth, but his conviction of suppers being very unwholesome made him rather sorry to see anything put on it; and while his hospitality would have welcomed his visitors to everything, his care for their health made him grieve that they would eat.

Such another small basin of thin gruel as his own was all that he could, with thorough self approbation, recommend; though he might constrain himself, while the ladies were comfortably clearing the nicer things, to say:

"Mrs. Bates, let me propose your venturing on one of these eggs. An egg boiled very soft is not unwholesome. Serle understands boiling an egg better than anybody. I would not recommend an egg boiled by anybody else; but you need not be afraid, they are very small, you see – one of our small eggs will not hurt you. Miss Bates, let Emma help you to a *little* bit of tart

– a *very* little bit. Ours are all apple tarts. You need not be afraid of unwholesome preserves here. I do not advise the custard. Mrs. Goddard, what say you to *half* a glass of wine? A *small* half-glass, put into a tumbler of water? I do not think it could disagree with you."

Emma allowed her father to talk – but supplied her visitors in a much more satisfactory style, and on the present evening had particular pleasure in sending them away happy. The happiness of Miss Smith was quite equal to her intentions. Miss Woodhouse was so great a personage in Highbury, that the prospect of the introduction had given as much panic as pleasure; but the humble, grateful little girl went off with highly gratified feelings, delighted with the affability with which Miss Woodhouse had treated her all the evening, and actually shaken hands with her at last!

# *Chapter 4*

HARRIET SMITH'S intimacy at Hartfield was soon a settled thing. Quick and decided in her ways, Emma lost no time in inviting, encouraging, and telling her to come very often; and as their acquaintance increased, so did their satisfaction in each other. As a walking companion, Emma had very early foreseen how useful she might find her. In that respect Mrs. Weston's loss had been important. Her father never went beyond the shrubbery, where two divisions of the ground sufficed him for his long walk, or his short, as the year varied; and since Mrs. Weston's marriage her exercise had been too much confined. She had ventured once alone to Randalls, but it was not pleasant; and a Harriet Smith, therefore, one whom she could summon at any time to a walk, would be a valuable addition to her privileges. But in every respect, as she saw more of her, she approved her, and was confirmed in all her kind designs.

Harriet certainly was not clever, but she had a sweet, docile, grateful disposition, was totally free from conceit, and only desiring to be guided by any one she looked up to. Her early attachment to herself was very amiable; and her inclination for good company, and power of appreciating what was elegant and clever, showed that there was no want of taste, though strength of understanding must not be expected. Altogether she was quite convinced of Harriet Smith's being exactly the young friend she wanted – exactly the something which her home required. Such a friend as Mrs. Weston was out of the question. Two such could never be granted. Two such she did not want. It was quite a different sort of thing, a sentiment distinct and independent. Mrs. Weston was the object of a regard which had its basis in gratitude and esteem. Harriet would be loved as one to whom she could be useful. For Mrs. Weston there was nothing to be done; for Harriet everything.

Her first attempts at usefulness were in an endeavour to find out who were the parents, but Harriet could not tell. She was ready to tell everything in her power, but on this subject questions were vain. Emma was obliged to fancy what she liked, but she could never believe that in the same situation she should not have discovered the truth. Harriet had no penetration. *She* had been satisfied to hear and believe just what Mrs. Goddard chose to tell her; and looked no farther.

Mrs. Goddard, and the teachers, and the girls and the affairs of the school in general, formed naturally a great part of the conversation – and but for her acquaintance with the Martins of Abbey Mill Farm, it must have been the whole. But the Martins occupied her thoughts a good deal; she had spent two very happy months with them, and now loved to talk of the pleasures of her visit, and describe the many comforts and wonders of the place. Emma encouraged her talkativeness amused by such a picture of another set of beings, and enjoying the youthful simplicity which could speak with so much exultation of Mrs. Martin's having "*two* parlours, two very good parlours, indeed; one of them quite as large as Mrs. Goddard's drawing room; and of her having an upper maid who had lived five-and-twenty years with her; and of their having eight cows, two of them Alderneys, and one a little Welch cow, a very pretty little Welch cow indeed; and of Mrs. Martin's saying as she was so fond of it, it should be called *her* cow; and of their having a very handsome summer-house in their garden, where some day next year they were all to drink tea: a very handsome summer-house, large enough to hold a dozen people."

For some time she was amused, without thinking beyond the immediate cause; but as she came to understand the family better, other feelings arose. She had taken up a wrong idea, fancying it was a mother and daughter, a son and son's wife, who all lived together; but when it appeared that the Mr. Martin, who bore a part in the narrative, and was always mentioned with approbation for his great good nature in doing something or other, was a single man; that there was no young Mrs. Martin, no wife in the case; she did suspect danger to her poor little friend from all this hospitality and kindness, and that, if she were not taken care of, she might be required to sink herself for ever.

With this inspiriting notion, her questions increased in number and meaning; and she particularly led Harriet to talk more of Mr. Martin, and there was evidently no dislike to it. Harriet was very ready to speak of the share he had had in their moonlight walks and merry evening games; and dwelt a good deal upon his being so very good humoured and obliging. He had gone three miles round one day in order to bring her some walnuts, because she had said how fond she was of them, and in everything else he was so very obliging. He had his shepherd's son into the parlour one night on purpose to sing to her. She was very fond of singing. He could sing a little himself. She believed he was very clever, and understood everything. He had a very fine flock, and, while she was with them, he had been bid more for his wool than anybody in the country. She believed everybody spoke well of him. His mother and sisters were very fond of him. Mrs. Martin had told her one day (and there was a blush as she said it,) that it was impossible for anybody to be a better son, and therefore she was sure, whenever he married, he would make a good husband. Not that she *wanted* him to marry. She was in no hurry at all.

"Well done, Mrs. Martin!" thought Emma. "You know what you are about."

"And when she had come away, Mrs. Martin was so very kind as to send Mrs. Goddard a beautiful goose – the finest goose Mrs. Goddard had ever seen. Mrs. Goddard had dressed it on a Sunday, and asked all the three teachers, Miss Nash, and Miss Prince, and Miss Richardson, to sup with her."

"Mr. Martin, I suppose, is not a man of information beyond the line of his own business? He does not read?"

"Oh yes! – that is, no – I do not know – but I believe he has read a good deal – but not what you would think any thing of. He reads the Agricultural Reports, and some other books that lay in one of the window seats, but he reads all *them* to himself. But sometimes of an evening, before we went to cards, he would read something aloud out of the *Elegant Extracts,* very entertaining. And I know he has read the *Vicar of Wakefield.* He never read the *Romance of the Forest*, nor The *Children of the Abbey.* He had never heard of such books before I mentioned them, but he is determined to get them now as soon as ever he can."

The next question was:

"What sort of looking man is Mr. Martin?"

"Oh! not handsome – not at all handsome. I thought him very plain at first, but I do not think him so plain now. One does not, you know, after a time. But did you never see him? He is in Highbury every now and then, and he is sure to ride through every week in his way to Kingston. He has passed you very often."

"That may be, and I may have seen him fifty times, but without having any idea of his name. A young farmer, whether on horseback or on foot, is the very last sort of person to raise my curiosity. The yeomanry are precisely the order of people with whom I feel I can have nothing to do. A degree or two lower, and a creditable appearance might interest me; I might hope to be useful to their families in some way or other. But a farmer can need none of my help, and is, therefore, in one sense, as much above my notice as in every other he is below it."

"To be sure. Oh yes! It is not likely you should ever have observed him; but he knows you very well indeed – I mean by sight."

"I have no doubt of his being a very respectable young man. I know, indeed, that he is so, and, as such, wish him well. What do you imagine his age to be?"

"He was four-and-twenty the 8th of last June, and my birthday is the 23rd – just a fortnight and a day's difference – which is very odd."

"Only four-and-twenty. That is too young to settle. His mother is perfectly right not to be in a hurry. They seem very comfortable as they are, and if she were to take any pains to marry him, she would probably repent it. Six years hence, if he could meet with a good sort of young woman in the same rank as his own, with a little money, it might be very desirable."

"Six years hence! Dear Miss Woodhouse, he would be thirty years old!"

"Well, and that is as early as most men can afford to marry, who are not born to an independence. Mr. Martin, I imagine, has his fortune entirely to make – cannot be at all beforehand with the world. Whatever money he might come into when his father died, whatever his share of the family property, it is, I dare say, all afloat, all employed in his stock, and so forth; and though, with diligence and good luck, he may be rich in time, it is next to impossible that he should have realised any thing yet."

"To be sure, so it is. But they live very comfortably. They have no indoors man, else they do not want for any thing; and Mrs. Martin talks of taking a boy another year."

"I wish you may not get into a scrape, Harriet, whenever he does marry; I mean, as to being acquainted with his wife for though his sisters, from a superior education, are not to be altogether objected to, it does not follow that he might marry anybody at all fit for you to notice. The misfortune of your birth ought to make you particularly careful as to your associates. There can be no doubt of your being a gentleman's daughter, and you must support your claim to that station by everything within your own power, or there will be plenty of people who would take pleasure in degrading you."

"Yes, to be sure, I suppose there are. But while I visit at Hartfield, and you are so kind to me, Miss Woodhouse, I am not afraid of what anybody can do."

"You understand the force of influence pretty well, Harriet; but I would have you so firmly established in good society, as to be independent even of Hartfield and Miss Woodhouse. I want to see you permanently well connected, and to that end it will be advisable to have as few odd acquaintances as may be; and, therefore, I say that if you should still be in this country when Mr. Martin marries, I wish you may not be drawn in by your intimacy with the sisters, to be acquainted with the wife, who will probably be some mere farmer's daughter, without education."

"To be sure. Yes. Not that I think Mr. Martin would ever marry anybody but what had had some education, and been very well brought up. However, I do not mean to set up my opinion against your's – and I am sure I shall not wish for the acquaintance of his wife. I shall always have a great regard for the Miss Martins, especially Elizabeth, and should be very sorry to give them up, for they are quite as well educated as me. But if he marries a very ignorant, vulgar woman, certainly I had better not visit her, if I can help it."

Emma watched her through the fluctuations of this speech, and saw no alarming symptoms of love. The young man had been the first admirer, but she trusted there was no other hold, and that there would be no serious difficulty, on Harriet's side, to oppose any friendly arrangement of her own.

They met Mr. Martin the very next day, as they were walking on the Donwell road. He was on foot, and after looking very respectfully at her, looked with most unfeigned satisfaction at her companion. Emma was not sorry to have such an opportunity of survey; and walking a few yards forward, while they talked together, soon made her quick eye sufficiently acquainted with Mr. Robert Martin. His appearance was very neat, and he looked like a sensible young man, but his person had no other advantage; and when he came to be contrasted with gentlemen, she thought he must lose all the ground he had gained in Harriet's inclination. Harriet was not insensible of manner; she had voluntarily noticed her father's gentleness with admiration as well as wonder. Mr. Martin looked as if he did not know what manner was.

They remained but a few minutes together, as Miss Woodhouse must not be kept waiting; and Harriet then came running to her with a smiling face, and in a flutter of spirits, which Miss Woodhouse hoped very soon to compose.

"Only think of our happening to meet him! How very odd! It was quite a chance, he said, that he had not gone round by Randalls. He did not think we ever walked this road. He thought we walked towards Randalls most days. He has not been able to get the *Romance of the Forest* yet. He was so busy the last time he was at Kingston that he quite forgot it, but he goes again to morrow. So very odd we should happen to meet! Well, Miss Woodhouse, is he like what you expected? What do you think of him? Do you think him so very plain?"

"He is very plain, undoubtedly remarkably plain: but that is nothing compared with his entire want of gentility. I had no right to expect much, and I did not expect much; but I had no idea that he could be so very clownish, so totally without air. I had imagined him, I confess, a degree or two nearer gentility."

"To be sure," said Harriet, in a mortified voice, "he is not so genteel as real gentlemen."

"I think, Harriet, since your acquaintance with us, you have been repeatedly in the company of some such very real gentlemen, that you must yourself be struck with the difference in Mr. Martin. At Hartfield, you have had very good specimens of well-educated, well-bred men. I should be surprised if, after seeing them, you could be in company with Mr. Martin again without perceiving him to be a very inferior creature, and rather wondering at yourself for having ever thought him at all agreeable before. Do not you begin to feel that now? Were not you struck? I am sure you must have been struck by his awkward look and abrupt manner, and the uncouthness of a voice which I heard to be wholly unmodulated as I stood here."

"Certainly, he is not like Mr. Knightley. He has not such a fine air and way of walking as Mr. Knightley. I see the difference plain enough. But Mr. Knightley is so very fine a man!"

"Mr. Knightley's air is so remarkably good that it is not fair to compare Mr. Martin with *him.* You might not see one in a hundred with *gentleman* so plainly written as in Mr. Knightley. But he is not the only gentleman you have been lately used to. What say you to Mr. Weston and Mr. Elton? Compare Mr. Martin with either of *them.* Compare their manner of carrying themselves, of walking, of speaking, of being silent. You must see the difference."

"Oh yes! there is a great difference. But Mr. Weston is almost an old man. Mr. Weston must be between forty and fifty."

"Which makes his good manners the more valuable. The older

a person grows, Harriet, the more important it is that their manners should not be bad; the more glaring and disgusting any loudness, or coarseness, or awkwardness becomes. What is passable in youth is detestable in later age. Mr. Martin is now awkward and abrupt; what will he be at Mr. Weston's time of life?"

"There is no saying, indeed," replied Harriet rather solemnly.

"But there may be pretty good guessing. He will be a completely gross, vulgar farmer, totally inattentive to appearances, and thinking of nothing but profit and loss."

"Will he, indeed? That will be very bad."

"How much his business engrosses him already is very plain from the circumstance of his forgetting to inquire for the book you recommended. He was a great deal too full of the market to think of any thing else – which is just as it should be, for a thriving man. What has he to do with books? And I have no doubt that he will thrive, and be a very rich man in time and his being illiterate and coarse need not disturb *us*."

"I wonder he did not remember the book" was all Harriet's answer, and spoken with a degree of grave displeasure which Emma thought might be safely left to itself. She, therefore, said no more for some time. Her next beginning was: "In one respect, perhaps, Mr. Elton's manners are superior to Mr. Knightley's or Mr. Weston's. They have more gentleness. They might be more safely held up as a pattern. There is an openness, a quickness, almost a bluntness in Mr. Weston, which everybody likes in *him,* because there is so much good humour with it – but that would not do to be copied. Neither would Mr. Knightley's downright, decided, commanding sort of manner, though it suits *him* very well; his figure, and look, and situation in life seem to allow it; but if any young man were to set about copying him, he would not be sufferable. On the contrary, I think a young man might be very safely recommended to take Mr. Elton as a model. Mr. Elton is good humoured, cheerful, obliging, and gentle. He seems to me to be grown particularly gentle of late. I do not know whether he has any design of ingratiating himself with either of us, Harriet, by additional softness, but it strikes me that his manners are softer than they used to be. If he means any thing, it must be to please you. Did not I tell you what he said of you the other day?"

She then repeated some warm personal praise which she had drawn from Mr. Elton, and now did full justice to; and Harriet blushed and smiled, and said she had always thought Mr. Elton very agreeable.

Mr. Elton was the very person fixed on by Emma for driving the young farmer out of Harriet's head. She thought it would be an excellent match; and only too palpably desirable, natural, and probable, for her to have much merit in planning it. She feared it was what everybody else must think of and predict. It was not likely, however, that anybody should have equalled her in the date of the plan, as it had entered her brain during the very first evening of Harriet's coming to Hartfield. The longer she considered it, the greater was her sense of its expediency. Mr. Elton's situation was most suitable, quite the gentleman himself, and without low connections; at the same time, not of any family that could fairly object to the doubtful birth of Harriet. He had a comfortable home for her, and Emma imagined a very sufficient income; for though the vicarage of Highbury was not large, he was known to have some independent property; and she thought very highly of him as a good humoured, well-meaning, respectable young man, without any deficiency of useful understanding or knowledge of the world.

She had already satisfied herself that he thought Harriet a beautiful girl, which she trusted, with such frequent meetings at Hartfield, was foundation enough on his side; and on Harriet's there could be little doubt that the idea of being preferred by him would have all the usual weight and efficacy. And he was really a very pleasing young man, a young man whom any woman not fastidious might like. He was reckoned very handsome; his person much admired in general, though not by her, there being a want of elegance of feature which she could not dispense with: but the girl who could be gratified by a Robert Martin's riding about the country to get walnuts for her might very well be conquered by Mr. Elton's admiration.

## *Chapter 5*

I DO not know what your opinion may be, Mrs. Weston," said Mr. Knightley, "of this great intimacy between Emma and Harriet Smith, but I think it a bad thing."

"A bad thing! Do you really think it a bad thing? why so?"

"I think they will neither of them do the other any good."

"You surprise me! Emma must do Harriet good: and by supplying her with a new object of interest, Harriet may be said to do Emma good. I have been seeing their intimacy with the greatest pleasure. How very differently we feel! Not think they will do each other any good! This will certainly be the beginning of one of our quarrels about Emma, Mr. Knightley."

"Perhaps you think I am come on purpose to quarrel with you, knowing Weston to be out, and that you must still fight your own battle."

"Mr. Weston would undoubtedly support me, if he were here, for he thinks exactly as I do on the subject. We were speaking of it only yesterday, and agreeing how fortunate it was for Emma, that there should be such a girl in Highbury for her to associate with. Mr. Knightley, I shall not allow you to be a fair judge in this case. You are so much used to live alone, that you do not know the value of a companion; and, perhaps no man can be a good judge of the comfort a woman feels in the society of one of her own sex, after being used to it all her life. I can imagine your objection to Harriet Smith. She is not the superior young woman which Emma's friend ought to be. But on the other hand, as Emma wants to see her better informed, it will be an inducement to her to read more herself. They will read together. She means it, I know."

"Emma has been meaning to read more ever since she was twelve years old. I have seen a great many lists of her drawing up at various times of books that she meant to read regularly through – and very good lists they were very well chosen, and very neatly arranged – sometimes alphabetically, and sometimes by some other rule. The list she drew up when only fourteen – I remember thinking it did her judgment so much credit, that I preserved it some time; and I dare say she may have made out a very good list now. But I have done with expecting any course of steady reading from Emma. She will never submit to any thing requiring industry and patience, and a subjection of the fancy to the understanding. Where Miss Taylor failed to stimulate, I may safely affirm that Harriet Smith will do nothing. You never could persuade her to read half so much as you wished. You know you could not."

"I dare say," replied Mrs. Weston, smiling, "that I thought so then; but, since we have parted, I can never remember Emma's omitting to do any thing I wished."

"There is hardly any desiring to refresh such a memory as *that,*" said Mr. Knightley, feelingly; and for a moment or two he had done. "But I," he soon added, "who have had no such charm thrown over my senses, must still see, hear, and remember. Emma is spoiled by being the cleverest of her family. At ten years old, she had the misfortune of being able to answer questions which puzzled her sister at seventeen. She was always quick and assured: Isabella slow and diffident. And ever since she was twelve, Emma has been mistress of the house and of you all. In her mother she lost the only person able to cope with her. She inherits her mother's talents, and must have been under subjection to her."

"I should have been sorry, Mr. Knightley, to be dependent on *your* recommendation, had I quitted Mr. Woodhouse's family and wanted another situation; I do not think you would have spoken a good word for me to anybody. I am sure you always thought me unfit for the office I held."

"Yes," said he, smiling. "You are better placed *here;* very fit for a wife, but not at all for a governess. But you were preparing yourself to be an excellent wife all the time you were at Hartfield. You might not give Emma such a complete education as your powers would seem to promise; but you were receiving a very good education from *her,* on the very material matrimonial point of submitting your own will, and doing as you were bid; and if Weston had asked me to recommend him a wife, I should certainly have named Miss Taylor."

"Thank you. There will be very little merit in making a good wife to such a man as Mr. Weston."

"Why, to own the truth, I am afraid you are rather thrown away, and that with every disposition to bear, there will be nothing to be borne. We will not despair, however. Weston may grow cross from the wantonness of comfort, or his son may plague him."

"I hope not *that.* It is not likely. No, Mr. Knightley, do not foretell vexation from that quarter."

"Not I, indeed. I only name possibilities. I do not pretend to Emma's genius for foretelling and guessing. I hope, with all my heart, the young man may be a Weston in merit, and a Churchill in fortune. But Harriet Smith – I have not half done about Harriet Smith. I think her the very worst sort of companion that Emma could possibly have. She knows nothing herself, and looks upon Emma as knowing everything. She is a flatterer in all her ways; and so much the worse, because undesigned. Her ignorance is hourly flattery. How can Emma imagine she has anything to learn herself, while Harriet is presenting such a delightful inferiority? And as for Harriet, I will venture to say that *she* cannot gain by the acquaintance. Hartfield will only put her out of conceit with all the other places she belongs to. She will grow just refined enough to be uncomfortable with those among whom birth and circumstances have placed her home. I am much mistaken if Emma's doctrines give any strength of mind, or tend at all to make a girl adapt herself rationally to the varieties of her situation in life. They only give a little polish."

"I either depend more upon Emma's good sense than you do, or am more anxious for her present comfort; for I cannot lament the acquaintance. How well she looked last night!"

"Oh! you would rather talk of her person than her mind, would you? Very well; I shall not attempt to deny Emma's being pretty."

"Pretty! say beautiful rather. Can you imagine any thing nearer perfect beauty than Emma altogether – face and figure?"

"I do not know what I could imagine, but I confess that I have seldom seen a face or figure more pleasing to me than hers. But I am a partial old friend."

"Such an eye! – the true hazel eye – and so brilliant! regular features, open countenance, with a complexion! oh! what a bloom of full health, and such a pretty height and size; such a firm and upright figure! There is health, not merely in her bloom, but in her air, her head, her glance. One hears sometimes of a child being 'the picture of health;' now, Emma always gives me the idea of being the complete picture of grown-up health. She is loveliness itself. Mr. Knightley, is not she?"

"I have not a fault to find with her person," he replied. "I think her all you describe. I love to look at her; and I will add this praise, that I do not think her personally vain. Considering how very handsome she is, she appears to be little occupied with it; her vanity lies another way. Mrs. Weston, I am not to be talked out of my dislike of Harriet Smith, or my dread of its doing them both harm."

"And I, Mr. Knightley, am equally stout in my confidence of its not doing them any harm. With all dear Emma's little faults, she is an excellent creature. Where shall we see a better daughter, or a kinder sister, or a truer friend? No, no; she has qualities which may be trusted; she will never lead any one really wrong; she will make no lasting blunder; where Emma errs once, she is in the right a hundred times."

"Very well; I will not plague you any more. Emma shall be an angel, and I will keep my spleen to myself till Christmas brings John and Isabella. John loves Emma with a reasonable and therefore not a blind affection, and Isabella always thinks as he does; except when he is not quite frightened enough about the children. I am sure of having their opinions with me."

"I know that you all love her really too well to be unjust or unkind; but excuse me, Mr. Knightley, if I take the liberty (I consider myself, you know, as having somewhat of the privilege of speech that Emma's mother might have had) the liberty of hinting that I do not think any possible good can arise from Harriet Smith's intimacy being made a matter of much discussion among you. Pray excuse me; but supposing any little inconvenience may be apprehended from the intimacy, it cannot be expected that Emma, accountable to nobody but her father, who perfectly approves the acquaintance, should put an end to it, so long as it is a source of pleasure to herself. It has been so many years my province to give advice, that you cannot be surprised, Mr. Knightley, at this little remains of office."

"Not at all," cried he; "I am much obliged to you for it. It is very good advice, and it shall have a better fate than your advice has often found; for it shall be attended to."

"Mrs. John Knightley is easily alarmed, and might be made unhappy about her sister."

"Be satisfied," said he, "I will not raise any outcry. I will keep my ill humour to myself. I have a very sincere interest in Emma. Isabella does not seem more my sister; has never excited a greater interest; perhaps hardly so great. There is an anxiety, a curiosity in what one feels for Emma. I wonder what will become of her!"

"So do I," said Mrs. Weston gently, "very much."

"She always declares she will never marry, which, of course, means just nothing at all. But I have no idea that she has yet ever seen a man she cared for. It would not be a bad thing for her to be very much in love with a proper object. I should like to see Emma in love, and in some doubt of a return; it would do her good. But there is nobody hereabout to attach her; and she goes so seldom from home."

"There does, indeed, seem as little to tempt her to break her resolution at present," said Mrs. Weston, "as can well be; and while she is so happy at Hartfield, I cannot wish her to be forming any attachment which would be creating such difficulties on poor Mr. Woodhouse's account. I do not recommend matrimony at present to Emma, though I mean no slight to the state, I assure you."

Part of her meaning was to conceal some favourite thoughts of her own and Mr. Weston's on the subject, as much as possible. There were wishes at Randalls respecting Emma's destiny, but it was not desirable to have them suspected; and the quiet transition which Mr. Knightley soon afterwards made to "What does Weston think of the weather; shall we have rain?" – convinced her that he had nothing more to say or surmise about Hartfield.

# Chapter 6

EMMA COULD not feel a doubt of having given Harriet's fancy a proper direction and raised the gratitude of her young vanity to a very good purpose, for she found her decidedly more sensible than before of Mr. Elton's being a remarkably handsome man, with most agreeable manners; and as she had no hesitation in following up the assurance of his admiration by agreeable hints, she was soon pretty confident of creating as much liking on Harriet's side, as there could be any occasion for. She was quite convinced of Mr. Elton's being in the fairest way of falling in love, if not in love already. She had no scruple with regard to him. He talked of Harriet, and praised her so warmly, that she could not suppose anything wanting which a little time would not add. His perception of the striking improvement of Harriet's manner, since her introduction at Hartfield, was not one of the least agreeable proofs of his growing attachment.

"You have given Miss Smith all that she required," said he; "you have made her graceful and easy. She was a beautiful creature when she came to you, but, in my opinion, the attractions you have added are infinitely superior to what she received from nature."

"I am glad you think I have been useful to her; but Harriet only wanted drawing out, and receiving a few, very few hints. She had all the natural grace of sweetness of temper and artlessness in herself. I have done very little."

"If it were admissible to contradict a lady – " said the gallant Mr. Elton.

"I have perhaps given her a little more decision of character – have taught her to think on points which had not fallen in her way before."

"Exactly so; that is what principally strikes me. So much superadded decision of character! Skilful has been the hand!"

"Great has been the pleasure, I am sure. I never met with a disposition more truly amiable."

"I have no doubt of it." And it was spoken with a sort of sighing animation, which had a vast deal of the lover. She was not less pleased another day with the manner in which he seconded a sudden wish of hers, to have Harriet's picture.

"Did you ever have your likeness taken, Harriet?" said she: "did you ever sit for your picture?"

Harriet was on the point of leaving the room, and only stopped to say, with a very interesting naiveté –

"Oh! dear, no – never."

No sooner was she out of sight, than Emma exclaimed:

"What an exquisite possession a good picture of her would be! I would give any money for it. I almost long to attempt her likeness myself. You do not know it I dare say, but two or three years ago I had a great passion for taking likenesses, and attempted several of my friends, and was thought to have a tolerable eye in general. But from one cause or another, I gave it up in disgust. But really, I could almost venture, if Harriet would sit for me. It would be such a delight to have her picture!"

"Let me entreat you," cried Mr. Elton; "it would indeed be a delight! Let me entreat you, Miss Woodhouse, to exercise so charming a talent in favour of your friend. I know what your drawings are. How could you suppose me ignorant? Is not this room rich in specimens of your landscapes and flowers; and has not Mrs. Weston some inimitable figure pieces in her drawing room, at Randalls?"

Yes, good man! thought Emma but what has all that to do with taking likenesses? You know nothing of drawing. Don't pretend to be in raptures about mine. Keep your raptures for Harriet's face. "Well, if you give me such kind encouragement, Mr. Elton, I believe I shall try what I can do. Harriet's features are very delicate, which makes a likeness difficult; and yet there is a peculiarity in the shape of the eye and the lines about the mouth which one ought to catch."

"Exactly so – the shape of the eye and the lines about the mouth – I have not a doubt of your success. Pray, pray attempt it. As you will do it, it will indeed, to use your own words, be an exquisite possession."

"But I am afraid, Mr. Elton, Harriet will not like to sit. She thinks so little of her own beauty. Did not you observe her manner of answering me? How completely it meant, 'why should my picture be drawn?' "

"Oh! yes, I observed it, I assure you. It was not lost on me. But still I cannot imagine she would not be persuaded."

Harriet was soon back again, and the proposal almost immediately made; and she had no scruples which could stand many minutes against the earnest pressing of both the others. Emma wished to go to work directly, and therefore produced the portfolio containing her various attempts at portraits, for not one of them had ever been finished, that they might decide together on the best size for Harriet. Her many beginnings were displayed. Miniatures, half-lengths, whole-lengths, pencil, crayon, and water colours had been all tried in turn. She had always wanted to do everything, and had made more progress both in drawing and music than many might have done with so little labour as she would ever submit to. She played and sang; and drew in almost every style; but steadiness had always been wanting; and in nothing had she approached the degree of excellence which she would have been glad to command, and ought not to have failed of. She was not much deceived as to her own skill either as an artist or a musician, but she was not unwilling to have others deceived, or sorry to know her reputation for accomplishment often higher than it deserved.

There was merit in every drawing – in the least finished, perhaps the most; her style was spirited; but had there been much less, or had there been ten times more, the delight and admiration of her two companions would have been the same. They were both in ecstasies. A likeness pleases everybody; and Miss Woodhouse's performances must be capital.

"No great variety of faces for you," said Emma. "I had only my own family to study from. There is my father – another of my father – but the idea of sitting for his picture made him so nervous, that I could only take him by stealth; neither of them very like therefore. Mrs. Weston again, and again, and again, you see. Dear Mrs. Weston! always my kindest friend on every occasion. She would sit whenever I asked her. There is my sister; and really quite her own little elegant figure! and the face not unlike. I should have made a good likeness of her, if she would have sat longer, but she was in such a hurry to have me draw her four children that she would not be quiet. Then, here come all my attempts at three of those four children – there they are, Henry and John and Bella, from one end of the sheet to the other, and any one of them might do for any one of the rest. She was so eager to have them drawn that I could not refuse; but there is no making children of three or four years old stand still you know; nor can it be very easy to take any likeness of them, beyond the air and complexion, unless they are coarser featured than any of mama's children ever were. Here is my sketch of the fourth, who was a baby. I took him as he was sleeping on the sofa, and it is as strong a likeness of his cockade as you would wish to see. He had nestled down his head most conveniently. That's very like. I am rather proud of little George. The corner of the sofa is very good. Then here is my last," – unclosing a pretty sketch of a gentleman in small size, whole length – my last and my best – my brother, Mr. John Knightley. This did not want much of being finished, when I put it away in a pet, and vowed I would never take another likeness. I could not help being provoked; for after all my pains, and when I had really made a very good likeness of it – (Mrs. Weston and I were quite agreed in thinking it very like)

– only too handsome – too flattering – but that was a fault on the right side – after all this, came poor dear Isabella's cold approbation of "Yes, it was a little like but to be sure it did not do him justice." We had had a great deal of trouble in persuading him to sit at all. It was made a great favour of; and altogether it was more than I could bear; and so I never would finish it, to have it apologised over as an unfavourable likeness, to every morning visitor in Brunswick Square; and, as I said, I did then forswear ever drawing anybody again. But for Harriet's sake, or rather for my own, and as there are no husbands and wives in the case at present, I will break my resolution now."

Mr. Elton seemed very properly struck and delighted by the idea, and was repeating, "No husbands and wives in the case *at present* indeed, as you observe. Exactly so. No husbands and wives," with so interesting a consciousness, that Emma began to consider whether she had not better leave them together at once. But as she wanted to be drawing, the declaration must wait a little longer.

She had soon fixed on the size and sort of portrait. It was to be a whole length in water colours, like Mr. John Knightley's, and was destined, if she could please herself, to hold a very honourable station over the mantelpiece.

The sitting began; and Harriet, smiling and blushing, and afraid of not keeping her attitude and countenance, presented a very sweet mixture of youthful expression to the steady eyes of the artist. But there was no doing any thing, with Mr. Elton fidgeting behind her and watching every touch. She gave him credit for stationing himself where he might gaze and gaze again without offence; but was really obliged to put an end to it, and request him to place himself elsewhere. It then occurred to her to employ him in reading.

"If he would be so good as to read to them, it would be a kindness indeed! It would amuse away the difficulties of her part, and lessen the irksomeness of Miss Smith's."

Mr. Elton was only too happy. Harriet listened, and Emma drew in peace. She must allow him to be still frequently coming to look; any thing less would certainly have been too little in a lover; and he was ready at the smallest intermission of the pencil, to jump up and see the progress, and be charmed. There was no being displeased with such an encourager, for his admiration made him discern a likeness almost before it was possible. She could not respect his eye, but his love and his complaisance were unexceptionable.

The sitting was altogether very satisfactory; she was quite enough pleased with the first day's sketch to wish to go on. There was no want of likeness, she had been fortunate in the attitude, and as she meant to throw in a little improvement to the figure, to give a little more height, and considerably more elegance, she had great confidence of its being in every way a pretty drawing at last, and of its filling its destined place with credit to them both a standing memorial of the beauty of one, the skill of the other, and the friendship of both; with as many other agreeable associations as Mr. Elton's very promising attachment was likely to add.

Harriet was to sit again the next day; and Mr. Elton, just as he ought, entreated for the permission of attending and reading to them again.

"By all means. We shall be most happy to consider you as one of the party."

The same civilities and courtesies, the same success and satisfaction, took place on the morrow, and accompanied the whole progress of the picture, which was rapid and happy. Everybody who saw it was pleased, but Mr. Elton was in continual raptures, and defended it through every criticism.

"Miss Woodhouse has given her friend the only beauty she wanted," observed Mrs. Weston to him not in the least suspecting that she was addressing a lover.

"The expression of the eye is most correct, but Miss Smith has not those eyebrows and eyelashes. It is the fault of her face that she has them not."

"Do you think so?" replied he. "I cannot agree with you. It appears to me a most perfect resemblance in every feature. I never saw such a likeness in my life. We must allow for the effect of shade, you know."

"You have made her too tall, Emma," said Mr. Knightley.

Emma knew that she had, but would not own it; and Mr. Elton warmly added:

"Oh no! – certainly not too tall – not in the least too tall. Consider, she is sitting down which naturally presents a difference – which in short gives exactly the idea – and the proportions must be preserved, you know. Proportions, fore-shortening – oh no! it gives one exactly the idea of such a height as Miss Smith's – exactly so indeed!"

"It is very pretty," said Mr. Woodhouse. "So prettily done! Just as your drawings always are, my dear. I do not know anybody who draws so well as you do. The only thing I do not thoroughly like is, that she seems to be sitting out-of-doors, with only a little shawl over her shoulders and it makes one think she must catch cold."

"But, my dear papa, it is supposed to be summer; a warm day in summer. Look at the tree."

"But it is never safe to sit out-of-doors, my dear."

"You, sir, may say any thing," cried Mr. Elton, "but I must confess that I regard it as a most happy thought, the placing of Miss Smith out of doors; and the tree is touched with such inimitable spirit! Any other situation would have been much less in character. The *naiveté* of Miss Smith's manners – and altogether – oh, it is most admirable! I cannot keep my eyes from it. I never saw such a likeness."

The next thing wanted was to get the picture framed; and

here were a few difficulties. It must be done directly; it must be done in London; the order must go through the hands of some intelligent person whose taste could be depended on; and Isabella, the usual doer of all commissions, must not be applied to, because it was December, and Mr. Woodhouse could not bear the idea of her stirring out of her house in the fogs of December. But no sooner was the distress known to Mr. Elton, than it was removed. His gallantry was always on the alert. "Might he be trusted with the commission, what infinite pleasure should he have in executing it! he could ride to London at any time. It was impossible to say how much he should be gratified by being employed on such an errand."

"He was too good! – she could not endure the thought! – she would not give him such a troublesome office for the world," – brought on the desired repetition of entreaties and assurances, and a very few minutes settled the business.

Mr. Elton was to take the drawing to London, choose the frame, and give the directions; and Emma thought she could so pack it as to ensure its safety without much incommoding him, while he seemed mostly fearful of not being incommoded enough.

"What a precious deposit!" said he with a tender sigh, as he received it.

"This man is almost too gallant to be in love," thought Emma. "I should say so, but that I suppose there may be a hundred different ways of being in love. He is an excellent young man, and will suit Harriet exactly; it will be an 'Exactly so,' as he says himself; but he does sigh and languish, and study for compliments rather more than I could endure as a principal. I come in for a pretty good share as a second. But it is his gratitude on Harriet's account."

# Chapter 7

THE VERY day of Mr. Elton's going to London produced a fresh occasion for Emma's services towards her friend. Harriet had been at Hartfield, as usual, soon after breakfast; and, after a time, had gone home to return again to dinner: she returned, and sooner than had been talked of, and with an agitated, hurried look, announcing something extraordinary to have happened which she was longing to tell. Half a minute brought it all out. She had heard, as soon as she got back to Mrs. Goddard's, that Mr. Martin had been there an hour before, and finding she was not at home, nor particularly expected, had left a little parcel for her from one of his sisters, and gone away; and on opening this parcel, she had actually found, besides the two songs which she had lent Elizabeth to copy, a letter to herself; and this letter was from him – from Mr. Martin – and contained a direct proposal of marriage. "Who could have thought it? She was so surprised she did not know what to do. Yes, quite a proposal of marriage; and a very good letter, at least she thought so. And he wrote as if he really loved her very much – but she did not know – and so, she should come as fast as she could to ask Miss Woodhouse what she should do." Emma was half ashamed of her friend for seeming so pleased and so doubtful.

"Upon my word," she cried, "the young man is determined not to lose anything for want of asking. He will connect himself well if he can."

"Will you read the letter?" cried Harriet. "Pray do. I'd rather you would."

Emma was not sorry to be pressed. She read, and was surprised. The style of the letter was much above her expectation. There were no grammatical errors, but as a composition it would not have disgraced a gentleman; the language, though plain, was strong and unaffected, and the sentiments it conveyed very much to the credit of the writer. It was short, but expressed good sense, warm attachment, liberality, propriety, even delicacy of feeling. She paused over it, while Harriet stood anxiously watching for her opinion, with a "Well, well," and was at last forced to add, "Is it a good letter? or is it too short?"

"Yes, indeed, a very good letter," replied Emma rather slowly "so good a letter, Harriet, that everything considered, I think one of his sisters must have helped him. I can hardly imagine the young man whom I saw talking with you the other day could express himself so well, if left quite to his own powers, and yet it is not the style of a woman; no, certainly, it is too strong and concise; not diffuse enough for a woman. No doubt he is a sensible man, and I suppose may have a natural talent for – thinks strongly and clearly, and when he takes a pen in hand, his thoughts naturally find proper words. It is so with some men. Yes, I understand the sort of mind. Vigorous, decided, with sentiments to a certain point, not coarse. A better written letter, Harriet (returning it,) than I had expected."

"Well," said the still waiting Harriet; "well – and – and what shall I do?"

"What shall you do! In what respect? Do you mean with regard to this letter?"

"Yes."

"But what are you in doubt of? You must answer it of course and speedily."

"Yes. But what shall I say? Dear Miss Woodhouse, do advise me."

"Oh no, no! the letter had much better be all your own. You will express yourself very properly, I am sure. There is no danger of your not being intelligible, which is the first thing. Your meaning must be unequivocal; no doubts or demurs: and such expressions of gratitude and concern for the pain you are inflicting, as propriety requires, will present themselves unbidden to your mind,

I am persuaded. *You* need not be prompted to write with the appearance of sorrow for his disappointment."

"You think I ought to refuse him then," said Harriet, looking down.

"Ought to refuse him! My dear Harriet, what do you mean? Are you in any doubt as to that? I thought – but I beg your pardon, perhaps I have been under a mistake. I certainly have been misunderstanding you, if you feel in doubt as to the *purport* of your answer. I had imagined you were consulting me only as to the wording of it."

Harriet was silent. With a little reserve of manner, Emma continued:

"You mean to return a favourable answer, I collect."

"No, I do not; that is, I do not mean – what shall I do? What would you advise me to do? Pray, dear Miss Woodhouse, tell me what I ought to do."

"I shall not give you any advice, Harriet. I will have nothing to do with it. This is a point which you must settle with your feelings."

"I had no notion that he liked me so very much," said Harriet, contemplating the letter. For a little while Emma persevered in her silence; but beginning to apprehend the bewitching flattery of that letter might be too powerful, she thought it best to say:

"I lay it down as a general rule, Harriet, that if a woman *doubts* as to whether she should accept a man or not, she certainly ought to refuse him. If she can hesitate as to 'Yes,' she ought to say 'No' directly. It is not a state to be safely entered into with doubtful feelings, with half a heart. I thought it my duty as a friend, and older than yourself, to say thus much to you. But do not imagine that I want to influence you."

"Oh! no, I am sure you are a great deal too kind to – but if you would just advise me what I had best do – no, no, I do not mean that – as you say, one's mind ought to be quite made up –

one should not be hesitating – it is a very serious thing. It will be safer to say 'No,' perhaps. Do you think I had better say 'No'?"

"Not for the world," said Emma, smiling graciously, "would I advise you either way. You must be the best judge of your own happiness. If you prefer Mr. Martin to every other person; if you think him the most agreeable man you have ever been in company with, why should you hesitate? You blush, Harriet. Does anybody else occur to you at this moment under such a definition? Harriet, Harriet, do not deceive yourself; do not be run away with by gratitude and compassion. At this moment whom are you thinking of?"

The symptoms were favourable. Instead of answering, Harriet turned away confused, and stood thoughtfully by the fire; and though the letter was still in her hand, it was now mechanically twisted about without regard. Emma waited the result with impatience, but not without strong hopes. At last, with some hesitation, Harriet said:

"Miss Woodhouse, as you will not give me your opinion, I must do as well as I can by myself; and I have now quite determined, and really almost made up my mind to refuse Mr. Martin. Do you think I am right?"

"Perfectly, perfectly right, my dearest Harriet; you are doing just what you ought. While you were at all in suspense I kept my feelings to myself, but now that you are so completely decided I have no hesitation in approving. Dear Harriet, I give myself joy of this. It would have grieved me to lose your acquaintance, which must have been the consequence of your marrying Mr. Martin. While you were in the smallest degree wavering, I said nothing about it, because I would not influence; but it would have been the loss of a friend to me. I could not have visited Mrs. Robert Martin, of Abbey Mill Farm. Now I am secure of you for ever."

Harriet had not surmised her own danger, but the idea of it struck her forcibly.

"You could not have visited me!" she cried, looking aghast. "No, to be sure you could not; but I never thought of that before. That would have been too dreadful! What an escape! Dear Miss Woodhouse, I would not give up the pleasure and honour of being intimate with you for any thing in the world."

"Indeed, Harriet, it would have been a severe pang to lose you; but it must have been. You would have thrown yourself out of all good society. I must have given you up."

"Dear me! How should I ever have borne it! It would have killed me never to come to Hartfield any more!"

"Dear affectionate creature! You would be banished to Abbey Mill Farm! *You* would be confined to the society of the illiterate and vulgar all your life! I wonder how the young man could have the assurance to ask it. He must have a pretty good opinion of himself."

"I do not think he is conceited either, in general," said Harriet, her conscience opposing such censure; "at least, he is very good-natured, and I shall always feel much obliged to him, and have a great regard for – but that is quite a different thing from – and you know, though he may like me, it does not follow that I should – and, certainly I must confess that since my visiting here I have seen people – and if one comes to compare them, person and manners, there is no comparison at all, one is so very handsome and agreeable. However, I do really think Mr. Martin a very amiable young man, and have a great opinion of him; and his being so much attached to me and his writing such a letter but as to leaving you, it is what I would not do upon any consideration."

"Thank you, thank you, my own sweet little friend. We will not be parted. A woman is not to marry a man merely because she is asked, or because he is attached to her, and can write a tolerable letter."

"Oh no; and it is but a short letter too."

Emma felt the bad taste of her friend, but let it pass with a "very true; and it would be a small consolation to her, for the clownish manner which might be offending her every hour of the day, to know that her husband could write a good letter."

"Oh! yes, very. Nobody cares for a letter; the thing is, to be always happy with pleasant companions. I am quite determined to refuse him. But how shall I do? That shall I say?"

Emma assured her there would be no difficulty in the answer, and advised its being written directly, which was agreed to, in the hope of her assistance; and though Emma continued to protest against any assistance being wanted, it was in fact given in the formation of every sentence. The looking over his letter again, in replying to it, had such a softening tendency, that it was particularly necessary to brace her up with a few decisive expressions; and she was so very much concerned at the idea of making him unhappy, and thought so much of what his mother and sisters would think and say, and was so anxious that they should not fancy her ungrateful, that Emma believed if the young man had come in her way at that moment, he would have been accepted after all.

This letter, however, was written, and sealed, and sent. The business was finished, and Harriet safe. She was rather low all the evening, but Emma could allow for her amiable regrets, and sometimes relieved them by speaking of her own affection, sometimes by bringing forward the idea of Mr. Elton.

"I shall never be invited to Abbey Mill again," was said in rather a sorrowful tone.

"Nor, if you were, could I ever bear to part with you, my Harriet. You are a great deal too necessary at Hartfield to be spared to Abbey Mill."

"And I am sure I should never want to go there; for I am never happy but at Hartfield."

Some time afterwards it was, "I think Mrs. Goddard would be very much surprised if she knew what had happened. I am sure Miss Nash would for Miss Nash thinks her own sister very well married, and it is only a linen draper."

"One should be sorry to see greater pride or refinement in the teacher of a school, Harriet. I dare say Miss Nash would envy you such an opportunity as this of being married. Even this conquest would appear valuable in her eyes. As to any thing superior for you, I suppose she is quite in the dark. The attentions of a certain person can hardly be among the tittle-tattle of Highbury yet. Hitherto I fancy you and I are the only people to whom his looks and manners have explained themselves."

Harriet blushed and smiled, and said something about wondering that people should like her so much. The idea of Mr. Elton was certainly cheering; but still, after a time, she was tender hearted again towards the rejected Mr. Martin.

"Now he has got my letter," said she softly. "I wonder what they are all doing – whether his sisters know – if he is unhappy, they will be unhappy too. I hope he will not mind it so very much."

"Let us think of those among our absent friends who are more cheerfully employed," cried Emma. "At this moment, perhaps, Mr. Elton is showing your picture to his mother and sisters, telling how much more beautiful is the original, and after being asked for it five or six times, allowing them to hear your name, your own dear name."

"My picture! But he has left my picture in Bond Street."

"Has he so! Then I know nothing of Mr. Elton. No, my dear little modest Harriet, depend upon it the picture will not be in Bond Street till just before he mounts his horse to morrow. It is his companion all this evening, his solace, his delight. It opens his designs to his family, it introduces you among them, it diffuses through the party those pleasantest feelings of our nature, eager curiosity and warm prepossession. How cheerful, how animated, how suspicious, how busy their imaginations all are!"

Harriet smiled again, and her smiles grew stronger.

# Chapter 8

HARRIET SLEPT at Hartfield that night. For some weeks past she had been spending more than half her time there, and gradually getting to have a bed room appropriated to herself; and Emma judged it best in every respect, safest and kindest, to keep her with them as much as possible just at present. She was obliged to go the next morning for an hour or two to Mrs. Goddard's, but it was then to be settled that she should return to Hartfield, to make a regular visit of some days.

While she was gone, Mr. Knightley called, and sat some time with Mr. Woodhouse and Emma, till Mr. Woodhouse, who had previously made up his mind to walk out, was persuaded by his daughter not to defer it, and was induced by the entreaties of both, though against the scruples of his own civility, to leave Mr. Knightley for that purpose. Mr. Knightley, who had nothing of ceremony about him, was offering by his short, decided answers, an amusing contrast to the protracted apologies and civil hesitations of the other.

"Well, I believe, if you will excuse me, Mr. Knightley, if you will not consider me as doing a very rude thing, I shall take Emma's advice and go out for a quarter of an hour. As the sun is out, I believe I had better take my three turns while I can. I treat you without ceremony, Mr. Knightley. We invalids think we are privileged people."

"My dear sir, do not make a stranger of me."

"I leave an excellent substitute in my daughter. Emma will be happy to entertain you. And therefore I think I will beg your excuse and take my three turns – my winter walk."

"You cannot do better, sir."

"I would ask for the pleasure of your company, Mr. Knightley, but I am a very slow walker, and my pace would be tedious to you; and, besides, you have another long walk before you, to Donwell Abbey."

"Thank you, sir, thank you; I am going this moment myself; and I think the sooner *you* go the better. I will fetch your greatcoat and open the garden door for you."

Mr. Woodhouse at last was off; but Mr. Knightley, instead of being immediately off likewise, sat down again, seemingly inclined for more chat. He began speaking of Harriet, and speaking of her with more voluntary praise than Emma had ever heard before.

"I cannot rate her beauty as you do," said he; "but she is a pretty little creature, and I am inclined to think very well of her disposition. Her character depends upon those she is with; but in good hands she will turn out a valuable woman."

"I am glad you think so; and the good hands, I hope, may not be wanting."

"Come," said he, "you are anxious for a compliment, so I will tell you that you have improved her. You have cured her of her school girl's giggle; she really does you credit."

"Thank you. I should be mortified indeed if I did not believe I had been of some use; but it is not everybody who will bestow praise where they may. *You* do not often overpower me with it."

"You are expecting her again, you say, this morning?"

"Almost every moment. She has been gone longer already than she intended."

"Something has happened to delay her; some visitors perhaps."

"Highbury gossips! Tiresome wretches!"

"Harriet may not consider everybody tiresome that you would."

Emma knew this was too true for contradiction, and therefore said nothing. He presently added, with a smile:

"I do not pretend to fix on times or places, but I must tell you that I have good reason to believe your little friend will soon hear of something to her advantage."

"Indeed! how so? of what sort?"

"A very serious sort, I assure you;" still smiling.

"Very serious! I can think of but one thing – who is in love with her? Who makes you their confidant?"

Emma was more than half in hopes of Mr. Elton's having dropped a hint. Mr. Knightley was a sort of general friend and adviser, and she knew Mr. Elton looked up to him.

"I have reason to think," he replied, "that Harriet Smith will soon have an offer of marriage, and from a most unexceptionable quarter – Robert Martin is the man. Her visit to Abbey Mill, this summer, seems to have done his business. He is desperately in love and means to marry her."

"He is very obliging," said Emma; "but is he sure that Harriet means to marry him?"

"Well, well, means to make her an offer then. Will that do? He came to the Abbey two evenings ago, on purpose to consult me about it. He knows I have a thorough regard for him and all his family, and, I believe, considers me as one of his best friends. He came to ask me whether I thought it would be imprudent in him to settle so early; whether I thought her too young – in short, whether I approved his choice altogether; having some apprehension perhaps of her being considered (especially since *your* making so much of her) as in a line of society above him. I was very much pleased with all that he said. I never hear better sense from any one than Robert Martin. He always speaks to the purpose; open, straightforward, and very well judging. He told me everything; his circumstances and plans, and what they all proposed doing in the event of his marriage. He is an excellent young man, both as son and brother. I had no hesitation in advising him to marry. He proved to me that he could afford it; and that being the case, I was convinced he could not do better. I praised the fair lady too, and altogether sent him away very happy. If he had never esteemed my opinion before, he would have thought highly of me then; and, I dare say, left the house thinking me the best friend and counsellor man ever had. This happened the night before last. Now, as we may fairly suppose, he would not allow much time to pass before he spoke to the lady, and as he does not appear to have spoken yesterday, it is not unlikely that he should be at Mrs. Goddard's to day; and she may be detained by a visitor, without thinking him at all a tiresome wretch."

"Pray, Mr. Knightley," said Emma, who had been smiling to herself through a great part of this speech, "how do you know that Mr. Martin did not speak yesterday?"

"Certainly," replied he, surprised, "I do not absolutely know it; but it may be inferred. Was not she the whole day with you?"

"Come," said she, "I will tell you something, in return for what you have told me. He did speak yesterday – that is, he wrote, and was refused."

This was obliged to be repeated before it could be believed; and Mr. Knightley actually looked red with surprise and displeasure, as he stood up, in tall indignation, and said:

"Then she is a greater simpleton than I ever believed her. What is the foolish girl about?"

"Oh! to be sure," cried Emma, "it is always incomprehensible to a man that a woman should ever refuse an offer of marriage. A man always imagines a woman to be ready for anybody who asks her."

"Nonsense! a man does not imagine any such thing. But what is the meaning of this? Harriet Smith refuses Robert Martin? madness, if it is so; but I hope you are mistaken."

"I saw her answer! – nothing could be clearer."

"You saw her answer! – you wrote her answer too. Emma, this is your doing. You persuaded her to refuse him."

"And if I did, (which, however, I am far from allowing) I should not feel that I had done wrong. Mr. Martin is a very respectable young man, but I cannot admit him to be Harriet's equal; and am rather surprised indeed that he should have ventured to address her. By your account, he does seem to have had some scruples. It is a pity that they were ever got over."

"Not Harriet's equal!" exclaimed Mr. Knightley loudly and warmly; and with calmer asperity, added, a few moments afterwards, "No, he is not her equal indeed, for he is as much her superior in sense as in situation. Emma, your infatuation about that girl blinds you. What are Harriet Smith's claims, either of birth, nature or education, to any connection higher than Robert Martin? She is the natural daughter of nobody knows whom, with probably no settled provision at all, and certainly no respectable relations. She is known only as parlour boarder at a common school. She is not a sensible girl, nor a girl of any information. She has been taught nothing useful, and is too young and too simple to have acquired any thing herself. At her age she can have no experience, and with her little wit, is not very likely ever to have any that can avail her. She is pretty, and she is good tempered, and that is all. My only scruple in advising the match was on his account, as being beneath his deserts, and a bad connection for him. I felt that, as to fortune, in all probability he might do much better; and that as to a rational companion or useful helpmate, he could not do worse. But I could not reason so to a man in love, and was willing to trust to there being no harm in her, to her having that sort of disposition, which, in good hands, like his, might be easily led aright and turn out very well. The advantage of the match I felt to be all on her side; and had not the smallest doubt (nor have I now) that there would be a general cry out upon her extreme good luck. Even *your* satisfaction I made sure of. It crossed my mind immediately that you would not regret your friend's leaving Highbury, for the sake of her being settled so well. I remember saying to myself, 'Even Emma, with all her partiality for Harriet, will think this a good match.'"

"I cannot help wondering at your knowing so little of Emma as to say any such thing. What! think a farmer, (and with all his sense and all his merit Mr. Martin is nothing more,) a good match for my intimate friend! Not regret her leaving Highbury for the sake of marrying a man whom I could never admit as an acquaintance of my own! I wonder you should think it possible for me to have such feelings. I assure you mine are very different. I must think your statement by no means fair. You are not just to Harriet's claims. They would be estimated very differently by others as well as myself; Mr. Martin may be the richest of the two, but he is undoubtedly her inferior as to rank in society. The sphere in which she moves is much above his. It would be a degradation."

"A degradation to illegitimacy and ignorance, to be married to a respectable, intelligent gentleman-farmer!"

"As to the circumstances of her birth, though in a legal sense she may be called Nobody, it will not hold in common sense. She is not to pay for the offence of others, by being held below the level of those with whom she is brought up. There can scarcely be a doubt that her father is a gentleman – and a gentleman of fortune. Her allowance is very liberal; nothing has ever been grudged for her improvement or comfort. That she is a gentleman's daughter, is indubitable to me; that she associates with gentlemen's daughters, no one, I apprehend, will deny. She is superior to Mr. Robert Martin."

"Whoever might be her parents," said Mr. Knightley, "whoever may have had the charge of her, it does not appear to have been any part of their plan to introduce her into what you would call good society. After receiving a very indifferent education she is left in Mrs. Goddard's hands to shift as she can – to move, in short, in Mrs. Goddard's line, to have Mrs. Goddard's acquaintance. Her friends evidently thought this good enough for her; and it *was* good enough. She desired nothing better herself.

Till you chose to turn her into a friend, her mind had no distaste for her own set, nor any ambition beyond it. She was as happy as possible with the Martins in the summer. She had no sense of superiority then. If she has it now, you have given it. You have been no friend to Harriet Smith, Emma. Robert Martin would never have proceeded so far, if he had not felt persuaded of her not being disinclined to him. I know him well. He has too much real feeling to address any woman on the haphazard of selfish passion. And as to conceit, he is the farthest from it of any man I know. Depend upon it he had encouragement."

It was most convenient to Emma not to make a direct reply to this assertion; she chose rather to take up her own line of the subject again.

"You are a very warm friend to Mr. Martin; but, as I said before, are unjust to Harriet. Harriet's claims to marry well are not so contemptible as you represent them. She is not a clever girl, but she has better sense than you are aware of, and does not deserve to have her understanding spoken of so slightingly. Waiving that point, however, and supposing her to be, as you describe her, only pretty and good natured, let me tell you, that in the degree she possesses them, they are not trivial recommendations to the world in general, for she is, in fact, a beautiful girl, and must be thought so by ninety nine people out of an hundred; and till it appears that men are much more philosophic on the subject of beauty than they are generally supposed; till they do fall in love with well informed minds instead of handsome faces, a girl, with such loveliness as Harriet, has a certainty of being admired and sought after, of having the power of choosing from among many, consequently a claim to be nice. Her good nature, too, is not so very slight a claim, comprehending, as it does, real, thorough sweetness of temper and manner, a very humble opinion of herself, and a great readiness to be pleased with other people. I am very much mistaken if your sex in general would not think such beauty, and such temper, the highest claims a woman could possess."

"Upon my word, Emma, to hear you abusing the reason you have, is almost enough to make me think so too. Better be without sense, than misapply it as you do."

"To be sure!" cried she playfully. "I know *that* is the feeling of you all. I know that such a girl as Harriet is exactly what every man delights in – what at once bewitches his senses and satisfies his judgment. Oh! Harriet may pick and choose. Were you, yourself, ever to marry, she is the very woman for you. And is she, at seventeen, just entering into life, just beginning to be known, to be wondered at because she does not accept the first offer she receives? No – pray let her have time to look about her."

"I have always thought it a very foolish intimacy," said Mr. Knightley presently, "though I have kept my thoughts to myself; but I now perceive that it will be a very unfortunate one for Harriet. You will puff her up with such ideas of her own beauty, and of what she has a claim to, that, in a little while, nobody within her reach will be good enough for her. Vanity working on a weak head, produces every sort of mischief. Nothing so easy as for a young lady to raise her expectations too high. Miss Harriet Smith may not find offers of marriage flow in so fast, though she is a very pretty girl. Men of sense, whatever you may choose to say, do not want silly wives. Men of family would not be very fond of connecting themselves with a girl of such obscurity – and most prudent men would be afraid of the inconvenience and disgrace they might be involved in, when the mystery of her parentage came to be revealed. Let her marry Robert Martin, and she is safe, respectable, and happy for ever; but if you encourage her to expect to marry greatly, and teach her to be satisfied with nothing less than a man of consequence and large fortune, she may be a parlour boarder at Mrs. Goddard's all the rest of her life – or, at least, (for Harriet Smith is a girl who will marry somebody or other,) till she grow desperate, and is glad to catch at the old writing-master's son."

"We think so very differently on this point, Mr. Knightley,

that there can be no use in canvassing it. We shall only be making each other more angry. But as to my *letting* her marry Robert Martin, it is impossible; she has refused him, and so decidedly, I think, as must prevent any second application. She must abide by the evil of having refused him, whatever it may be; and as to the refusal itself, I will not pretend to say that I might not influence her a little; but I assure you there was very little for me or for anybody to do. His appearance is so much against him, and his manner so bad, that if she ever were disposed to favour him, she is not now. I can imagine, that before she had seen anybody superior, she might tolerate him. He was the brother of her friends, and he took pains to please her; and altogether, having seen nobody better (that must have been his great assistant) she might not, while she was at Abbey Mill, find him disagreeable. But the case is altered now. She knows now what gentlemen are; and nothing but a gentleman in education and manner has any chance with Harriet."

"Nonsense, errant nonsense, as ever was talked!" cried Mr. Knightley. "Robert Martin's manners have sense, sincerity, and good humour to recommend them; and his mind has more true gentility than Harriet Smith could understand."

Emma made no answer, and tried to look cheerfully unconcerned, but was really feeling uncomfortable and wanting him very much to be gone. She did not repent what she had done; she still thought herself a better judge of such a point of female right and refinement than he could be; but yet she had a sort of habitual respect for his judgment in general, which made her dislike having it so loudly against her; and to have him sitting just opposite to her in angry state, was very disagreeable. Some minutes passed in this unpleasant silence, with only one attempt on Emma's side to talk of the weather, but he made no answer. He was thinking. The result of his thoughts appeared at last in these words.

"Robert Martin has no great loss – if he can but think so; and

I hope it will not be long before he does. Your views for Harriet are best known to yourself; but as you make no secret of your love of match making, it is fair to suppose that views, and plans, and projects you have; and as a friend I shall just hint to you that if Elton is the man, I think it will be all labour in vain."

Emma laughed and disclaimed. He continued:

"Depend upon it, Elton will not do. Elton is a very good sort of man, and a very respectable vicar of Highbury, but not at all likely to make an imprudent match. He knows the value of a good income as well as anybody. Elton may talk sentimentally, but he will act rationally. He is as well acquainted with his own claims, as you can be with Harriet's. He knows that he is a very handsome young man, and a great favourite wherever he goes; and from his general way of talking in unreserved moments, when there are only men present, I am convinced that he does not mean to throw himself away. I have heard him speak with great animation of a large family of young ladies that his sisters are intimate with, who have all twenty thousand pounds apiece."

"I am very much obliged to you," said Emma, laughing again. "If I had set my heart on Mr. Elton's marrying Harriet, it would have been very kind to open my eyes; but at present I only want to keep Harriet to myself. I have done with match-making indeed. I could never hope to equal my own doings at Randalls. I shall leave off while I am well."

"Good morning to you," said he, rising and walking off abruptly. He was very much vexed. He felt the disappointment of the young man, and was mortified to have been the means of promoting it, by the sanction he had given; and the part which he was persuaded Emma had taken in the affair, was provoking him exceedingly.

Emma remained in a state of vexation too; but there was more indistinctness in the causes of her's, than in his. She did not always feel so absolutely satisfied with herself, so entirely convinced that her opinions were right and her adversary's wrong, as Mr. Knightley. He walked off in more complete self-approbation than he left for her. She was not so materially cast down, however, but that a little time and the return of Harriet were very adequate restoratives. Harriet's staying away so long was beginning to make her uneasy. The possibility of the young man's coming to Mrs. Goddard's that morning, and meeting with Harriet and pleading his own cause, gave alarming ideas. The dread of such a failure after all became the prominent uneasiness; and when Harriet appeared, and in very good spirits, and without having any such reason to give for her long absence, she felt a satisfaction which settled her with her own mind, and convinced her, that let Mr. Knightley think or say what he would, she had done nothing which woman's friendship and woman's feelings would not justify.

He had frightened her a little about Mr. Elton; but when she considered that Mr. Knightley could not have observed him as she had done, neither with the interest, nor (she must be allowed to tell herself, in spite of Mr. Knightley's pretensions) with the skill of such an observer on such a question as herself, that he had spoken it hastily and in anger, she was able to believe, that he had rather said what he wished resentfully to be true, than what he knew any thing about. He certainly might have heard Mr. Elton speak with more unreserve than she had ever done, and Mr. Elton might not be of an imprudent, inconsiderate disposition as to money matters; he might naturally be rather attentive than otherwise to them; but then, Mr. Knightley did not make due allowance for the influence of a strong passion at war with all interested motives. Mr. Knightley saw no such passion, and of course thought nothing of its effects; but she saw too much of it to feel a doubt of its overcoming any hesitations that a reasonable prudence might originally suggest; and more than a reasonable, becoming degree of prudence, she was very sure did not belong to Mr. Elton.

Harriet's cheerful look and manner established hers: she came back, not to think of Mr. Martin, but to talk of Mr. Elton. Miss

Nash had been telling her something, which she repeated immediately with great delight. Mr. Perry had been to Mrs. Goddard's to attend a sick child, and Miss Nash had seen him, and he had told Miss Nash, that as he was coming back yesterday from Clayton Park, he had met Mr. Elton, and found to his great surprise, that Mr. Elton was actually on his road to London, and not meaning to return till the morrow, though it was the whist club night, which he had been never known to miss before; and Mr. Perry had remonstrated with him about it, and told him how shabby it was in him, their best player, to absent himself, and tried very much to persuade him to put off his journey only one day; but it would not do; Mr. Elton had been determined to go on, and had said in a very *particular* way indeed, that he was going on business which he would not put off for any inducement in the world; and something about a very enviable commission, and being the bearer of something exceedingly precious. Mr. Perry could not quite understand him, but he was very sure there must be a *lady* in the case, and he told him so; and Mr. Elton only looked very conscious and smiling, and rode off in great spirits. Miss Nash had told her all this, and had talked a great deal more about Mr. Elton; and said, looking so very significantly at her, "that she did not pretend to understand what his business might be, but she only knew that any woman whom Mr. Elton could prefer, she should think the luckiest woman in the world; for, beyond a doubt, Mr. Elton had not his equal for beauty or agreeableness."

# Chapter 9

MR. KNIGHTLEY might quarrel with her, but Emma could not quarrel with herself. He was so much displeased, that it was longer than usual before he came to Hartfield again; and when they did meet, his grave looks showed that she was not forgiven. She was sorry, but could not repent. On the contrary, her plans and proceedings were more and more justified and endeared to her by the general appearances of the next few days.

The Picture, elegantly framed, came safely to hand soon after Mr. Elton's return, and being hung over the mantelpiece of the common sitting room, he got up to look at it, and sighed out his half sentences of admiration just as he ought; and as for Harriet's feelings, they were visibly forming themselves into as strong and steady an attachment as her youth and sort of mind admitted. Emma was soon perfectly satisfied of Mr. Martin's being not otherwise remembered, than as he furnished a contrast with Mr. Elton, of the utmost advantage to the latter.

Her views of improving her little friend's mind, by a great deal of useful reading and conversation, had never yet led to more than a few first chapters, and the intention of going on to morrow. It was much easier to chat than to study; much pleasanter to let her imagination range and work at Harriet's fortune, than to be labouring to enlarge her comprehension or exercise it on sober facts; and the only literary pursuit which engaged Harriet at present, the only mental provision she was making for the evening of life, was the collecting and transcribing all the riddles of every sort that she could meet with, into a thin quarto of hot-pressed paper[1], made up by her friend, and ornamented with ciphers and trophies.

In this age of literature, such collections on a very grand scale are not uncommon. Miss Nash, head-teacher at Mrs. Goddard's, had written out at least three hundred; and Harriet, who had taken the first hint of it from her, hoped, with Miss

1 Self-made and neatly finished volume.

Woodhouse's help, to get a great many more. Emma assisted with her invention, memory and taste; and as Harriet wrote a very pretty hand, it was likely to be an arrangement of the first order, in form as well as quantity.

Mr. Woodhouse was almost as much interested in the business as the girls, and tried very often to recollect something worth their putting in. "So many clever riddles as there used to be when he was young – he wondered he could not remember them! but he hoped he should in time." And it always ended in "Kitty, a fair but frozen maid."

His good friend Perry, too, whom he had spoken to on the subject, did not at present recollect any thing of the riddle kind; but he had desired Perry to be upon the watch, and as he went about so much, something, he thought, might come from that quarter.

It was by no means his daughter's wish that the intellects of Highbury in general should be put under requisition. Mr. Elton was the only one whose assistance she asked. He was invited to contribute any really good enigmas, charades, or conundrums that he might recollect; and she had the pleasure of seeing him most intently at work with his recollections; and at the same time, as she could perceive, most earnestly careful that nothing ungallant, nothing that did not breathe a compliment to the sex should pass his lips. They owed to him their two or three politest puzzles; and the joy and exultation with which at last he recalled, and rather sentimentally recited, that well known charade[1]:

My first doth affliction denote,
    Which my second is destin'd to feel
And my whole is the best antidote
    That affliction to soften and heal,

made her quite sorry to acknowledge that they had transcribed it some pages ago already.

"Why will you not write one yourself for us, Mr. Elton?" said

1 A riddling verse.

she; "that is the only security for its freshness; and nothing could be easier to you."

"Oh no! he had never written, hardly ever, any thing of this kind in his life. The stupidest fellow! He was afraid not even Miss Woodhouse" – he stopped a moment – "or Miss Smith could inspire him."

The very next day however produced some proof of inspiration. He called for a few moments, just to leave a piece of paper on the table containing, as he said, a charade, which a friend of his had addressed to a young lady, the object of his admiration, but which, from his manner, Emma was immediately convinced must be his own.

"I do not offer it for Miss Smith's collection," said he. "Being my friend's, I have no right to expose it in any degree to the public eye, but perhaps you may not dislike looking at it."

The speech was more to Emma than to Harriet, which Emma could understand. There was deep consciousness about him, and he found it easier to meet her eye than her friend's. He was gone the next moment: after another moment's pause:

"Take it," said Emma, smiling, and pushing the paper towards Harriet – "it is for you. Take your own."

But Harriet was in a tremor, and could not touch it; and Emma, never loath to be first, was obliged to examine it herself.

*To Miss –*

CHARADE

My first displays the wealth and pomp of kings,
Lords of the earth! their luxury and ease.
Another view of man, my second brings,
Behold him there, the monarch of the seas!

But ah! united, what reverse we have!
Man's boasted power and freedom, all are flown;

Lord of the earth and sea, he bends a slave,
And woman, lovely woman, reigns alone.

Thy ready wit the word will soon supply,
May its approval beam in that soft eye!

She cast her eye over it, pondered, caught the meaning, read it through again to be quite certain, and quite mistress of the lines, and then passing it to Harriet, sat happily smiling, and saying to herself, while Harriet was puzzling over the paper in all the confusion of hope and dullness, "Very well, Mr. Elton, very well indeed. I have read worse charades. *Courtship* – a very good hint. I give you credit for it. This is feeling your way. This is saying very plainly – 'Pray, Miss Smith, give me leave to pay my addresses to you. Approve my charade and my intentions in the same glance.'

May its approval beam in that soft eye!

Harriet exactly. Soft is the very word for her eye – of all epithets, the justest that could be given.

Thy ready wit the word will soon supply.

Humph – Harriet's ready wit! All the better. A man must be very much in love, indeed, to describe her so. Ah! Mr. Knightley, I wish you had the benefit of this; I think this would convince you. For once in your life you would be obliged to own yourself mistaken. An excellent charade indeed! and very much to the purpose. Things must come to a crisis soon now."

She was obliged to break off from these very pleasant observations, which were otherwise of a sort to run into great length, by the eagerness of Harriet's wondering questions.

"What can it be, Miss Woodhouse? – what can it be? I have not an idea – I cannot guess it in the least. What can it possibly be? Do try to find it out, Miss Woodhouse. Do help me. I never saw any thing so hard. Is it kingdom? I wonder who the friend was – and who could be the young lady. Do you think it is a good one? Can it be woman?

And woman, lovely woman, reigns alone.

Can it be Neptune?

Behold him there, the monarch of the seas!

Or a trident? or a mermaid? or a shark? Oh, no! shark is only one syllable. It must be very clever, or he would not have brought it. Oh! Miss Woodhouse, do you think we shall ever find it out?"

"Mermaids and sharks! Nonsense! My dear Harriet, what are you thinking of? Where would be the use of his bringing us a charade made by a friend upon a mermaid or a shark? Give me the paper and listen.

"For Miss – ," read Miss Smith.

My first displays the wealth and pomp of kings,
Lords of the earth! their luxury and ease.

That is *court.*

Another view of man, my second brings;
Behold him there, the monarch of the seas!

That is *ship* – plain as it can be. Now for the cream.

But ah! united, (*courtship,* you know,) what reverse
we have!
Man's boasted power and freedom, all are flown:
Lord of the earth and sea, he bends a slave,
And woman, lovely woman, reigns alone.

A very proper compliment! and then follows the application, which I think, my dear Harriet, you cannot find much difficulty in comprehending. Read it in comfort to yourself. There can be no doubt of its being written for you and to you."

Harriet could not long resist so delightful a persuasion. She read the concluding lines, and was all flutter and happiness. She could not speak. But she was not wanted to speak. It was enough for her to feel. Emma spoke for her.

"There is so pointed, and so particular a meaning in this compliment," said she, "that I cannot have a doubt as to Mr. Elton's intentions. You are his object – and you will soon receive the completest proof of it. I thought it must be so. I thought I could not be so deceived; but now, it is clear; the state of his mind is as clear and decided, as my wishes on the subject have been ever since I knew you. Yes, Harriet, just so long have I' been wanting the very circumstance to happen what has happened. I could never tell whether an attachment between you and Mr. Elton were most desirable or most natural. Its probability and its eligibility have really so equalled each other! I am very happy. I congratulate you, my dear Harriet, with all my heart. This is an attachment which a woman may well feel pride in creating. This is a connection which offers nothing but good. It will give you everything that you want – consideration, independence, a proper home – it will fix you in the centre of all your real friends, close to Hartfield and to me, and confirm our intimacy for ever. This, Harriet, is an alliance which can never raise a blush in either of us."

"Dear Miss Woodhouse!" and "Dear Miss Woodhouse," was all that Harriet, with many tender embraces could articulate at first; but when they did arrive at something more like conversation, it was sufficiently clear to her friend that she saw, felt, anticipated, and remembered just as she ought. Mr. Elton's superiority had very ample acknowledgment.

"Whatever you say is always right," cried Harriet, "and therefore I suppose, and believe, and hope it must be so; but otherwise I could not have imagined it. It is so much beyond any thing I deserve. Mr. Elton, who might marry anybody! There cannot be two opinions about *him*. He is so very superior. Only think of those sweet verses – To Miss – " Dear me, how clever! Could it really be meant for me?"

"I cannot make a question, or listen to a question about that. It is a certainty. Receive it on my judgment. It is a sort of prologue to the play, a motto to the chapter; and will be soon followed by matter-of-fact prose."

"It is a sort of thing which nobody could have expected. I am sure, a month ago, I had no more idea myself! The strangest things do take place!"

"When Miss Smiths and Mr. Eltons get acquainted – they do indeed – and really it is strange; it is out of the common course that what is so evidently, so palpably desirable – what courts the pre-arrangement of other people, should so immediately shape itself into the proper form. You and Mr. Elton are by situation called together; you belong to one another by every circumstance of your respective homes. Your marrying will be equal to the match at Randalls. There does seem to be a something in the air of Hartfield which gives love exactly the right direction, and sends it into the very channel where it ought to flow.

The course of true love never did run smooth –

A Hartfield edition of Shakespeare would have a long note on that passage."

"That Mr. Elton should really be in love with me – me, of all people, who did not know him, to speak to him, at Michaelmas! And he, the very handsomest man that ever was, and a man that everybody looks up to, quite like Mr. Knightley! His company so sought after, that everybody says he need not eat a single meal by himself if he does not choose it; that he has more invitations than there are days in the week. And so excellent in the Church! Miss Nash has put down all the texts he has ever preached from since he came to Highbury. Dear me! When I look back to the first time I saw him! How little did I think! The two Abbots and I ran into the front room and peeped through the blind when we heard he was going by, and Miss Nash came and scolded us away, and staid to look through herself; however, she called me back presently, and let me look too, which was very good natured. And how beautiful we thought he looked! He was arm in arm with Mr. Cole."

"This is an alliance which, whoever – whatever your friends may be, must be agreeable to them, provided at least they have common sense; and we are not to be addressing our conduct to fools. If they are anxious to see you *happily* married, here is a man whose amiable character gives every assurance of it; if they wish to have you settled in the same country and circle which they have chosen to place you in, here it will be accomplished; and if their only object is that you should, in the common phrase, be *well* married, here is the comfortable fortune, the respectable establishment, the rise in the world which must satisfy them."

"Yes, very true. How nicely you talk; I love to hear you. You understand everything. You and Mr. Elton are one as clever as the other. This charade! If I had studied a twelvemonth, I could never have made any thing like it."

"I thought he meant to try his skill, by his manner of declining it yesterday."

"I do think it is, without exception, the best charade I ever read."

"I never read one more to the purpose, certainly."

"It is as long again as almost all we have had before."

"I do not consider its length as particularly in its favour. Such things in general cannot be too short."

Harriet was too intent on the lines to hear. The most satisfactory comparisons were rising in her mind.

"It is one thing," said she, presently her cheeks in a glow "to have very good sense in a common way, like everybody else, and if there is any thing to say, to sit down and write a letter, and say just what you must, in a short way; and another, to write verses and charades like this."

Emma could not have desired a more spirited rejection of Mr. Martin's prose.

"Such sweet lines!" continued Harriet "these two last! But how shall I ever be able to return the paper, or say I have found it out? Oh! Miss Woodhouse, what can we do about that?"

"Leave it to me. You do nothing. He will be here this evening, I dare say, and then I will give him back, and some nonsense or other will pass between us, and you shall not be committed. Your soft eyes shall choose their own time for beaming. Trust to me."

"Oh! Miss Woodhouse, what a pity that I must not write this beautiful charade into my book! I am sure I have not got one half so good."

"Leave out the two last lines, and there is no reason why you should not write it into your book."

"Oh! but those two lines are – "

"The best of all. Granted; for private enjoyment; and for private enjoyment keep them. They are not at all the less written you know, because you divide them. The couplet does not cease to be, nor does its meaning change. But take it away, and all *appropriation* ceases, and a very pretty gallant charade remains, fit for any collection. Depend upon it, he would not like to have his charade slighted, much better than his passion. A poet in love must be encouraged in both capacities, or neither. Give me the book, I will write it down, and then there can be no possible reflection on you."

Harriet submitted, though her mind could hardly separate the parts, so as to feel quite sure that her friend were not writing down a declaration of love. It seemed too precious an offering for any degree of publicity.

"I shall never let that book go out of my own hands," said she.

"Very well," replied Emma; "a most natural feeling; and the longer it lasts, the better I shall be pleased. But here is my father coming: you will not object to my reading the charade to him. It will be giving him so much pleasure! He loves any thing of the sort, and especially any thing that pays woman a compliment. He has the tenderest spirit of gallantry towards us all! You must let me read it to him."

Harriet looked grave.

"My dear Harriet, you must not refine too much upon this charade. You will betray your feelings improperly, if you are too conscious and too quick, and appear to *affix* more meaning, or even quite all the meaning which may be affixed to it. Do not be overpowered by such a little tribute of admiration. If he had been anxious for secrecy, he would not have left the paper while I was by; but he rather pushed it towards me than towards you. Do not let us be too solemn on the business. He has encouragement enough to proceed, without our sighing out our souls over this charade."

"Oh! no I hope I shall not be ridiculous about it. Do as you please."

Mr. Woodhouse came in, and very soon led to the subject again, by the recurrence of his very frequent inquiry of "Well, my dears, how does your book go on? Have you got any thing fresh?"

"Yes, papa; we have something to read you, something quite fresh. A piece of paper was found on the table this morning (dropped, we suppose, by a fairy) containing a very pretty charade, and we have just copied it in."

She read it to him, just as he liked to have any thing read, slowly and distinctly, and two or three times over, with explanations of every part as she proceeded and he was very much pleased, and, as she had foreseen, especially struck with the complimentary conclusion.

"Aye, that's very just, indeed, that's very properly said. Very true. 'Woman, lovely woman.' It is such a pretty charade, my dear, that I can easily guess what fairy brought it. Nobody could have written so prettily, but you, Emma."

Emma only nodded, and smiled. After a little thinking, and a very tender sigh, he added:

"Ah! it is no difficulty to see who you take after! Your dear mother was so clever at all those things! If I had but her memory! But I can remember nothing; not even that particular riddle which you have heard me mention; I can only recollect the first stanza; and there are several:

Kitty, a fair but frozen maid,
Kindled a flame I yet deplore,
The hoodwink'd boy I called to aid,
Though of his near approach afraid,
So fatal to my suit before.

And that is all that I can recollect of it but it is very clever all the way through. But I think, my dear, you said you had got it."

"Yes, papa, it is written out in our second page. We copied it from the *Elegant Extracts*. It was Garrick's, you know."

"Aye, very true – I wish I could recollect more of it.

Kitty, a fair but frozen maid.

The name makes me think of poor Isabella; for she was very near being christened Catherine after her grandmama. I hope we shall have her here next week. Have you thought, my dear, where you shall put her and what room there will be for the children?"

"Oh! yes she will have her own room, of course; the room she always has; and there is the nursery for the children – just as usual, you know. Why should there be any change?"

"I do not know, my dear but it is so long since she was here! not since last Easter, and then only for a few days. Mr. John Knightley's being a lawyer is very inconvenient. Poor Isabella! she is sadly taken away from us all! and how sorry she will be when she comes, not to see Miss Taylor here"

"She will not be surprised, papa, at least."

"I do not know, my dear. I am sure I was very much surprised when I first heard she was going to be married."

"We must ask Mr. and Mrs. Weston to dine with us, while Isabella is here."

"Yes, my dear, if there is time. But (in a very depressed tone) she is coming for only one week. There will not be time for any thing."

"It is unfortunate that they cannot stay longer but it seems a case of necessity. Mr. John Knightley must be in town again on the 28th, and we ought to be thankful, papa, that we are to have the whole of the time they can give to the country, that two or three days are not to be taken out for the Abbey. Mr. Knightley promises to give up his claim this Christmas though you know it is longer since they were with him, than with us."

"It would be very hard, indeed, my dear, if poor Isabella were to be anywhere but at Hartfield."

Mr. Woodhouse could never allow for Mr. Knightley's claims on his brother, or anybody's claims on Isabella, except his own. He sat musing a little while, and then said:

"But I do not see why poor Isabella should be obliged to go back so soon, though he does. I think, Emma, I shall try and persuade her to stay longer with us. She and the children might stay very well."

"Ah! papa that is what you never have been able to accomplish, and I do not think you ever will. Isabella cannot bear to stay behind her husband."

This was too true for contradiction. Unwelcome as it was, Mr. Woodhouse could only give a submissive sigh; and as Emma saw his spirits affected by the idea of his daughter's attachment to her husband, she immediately led to such a branch of the subject as must raise them.

"Harriet must give us as much of her company as she can while my brother and sister are here. I am sure she will be pleased with the children. We are very proud of the children, are not we, papa? I wonder which she will think the handsomest, Henry or John?"

"Aye, I wonder which she will. Poor little dears, how glad they will be to come. They are very fond of being at Hartfield, Harriet."

"I dare say they are, sir. I am sure I do not know who is not."

"Henry is a fine boy, but John is very like his mama. Henry is the eldest, he was named after me, not after his father. John, the second, is named after his father. Some people are surprised, I believe, that the eldest was not, but Isabella would have him called Henry, which I thought very pretty of her. And he is a very clever boy, indeed. They are all remarkably clever; and they have so many pretty ways. They will come and stand by my chair, and say, 'Grandpapa, can you give me a bit of string?' and once Henry asked me for a knife, but I told him knives were only made for grandpapas. I think their father is too rough with them very often."

"He appears rough to you," said Emma, "because you are so very gentle yourself; but if you could compare him with other papas, you would not think him rough. He wishes his boys to be active and hardy; and if they misbehave, can give them a sharp word now and then; but he is an affectionate father – certainly Mr. John Knightley is an affectionate father. The children are all fond of him."

"And then their uncle comes in, and tosses them up to the ceiling in a very frightful way!"

"But they like it, papa; there is nothing they like so much. It is such enjoyment to them, that if their uncle did not lay down the rule of their taking turns, whichever began would never give way to the other."

"Well, I cannot understand it."

"That is the case with us all, papa. One half of the world cannot understand the pleasures of the other."

Later in the morning, and just as the girls were going to separate in preparation for the regular four o'clock dinner, the hero of this inimitable charade walked in again. Harriet turned away; but Emma could receive him with the usual smile, and her quick eye soon discerned in his the consciousness of having made a push of having thrown a die; and she imagined he had come to see how it might turn up. His ostensible reason, however, was to ask whether Mr. Woodhouse's party could be made up in the evening without him, or whether he should be in the smallest degree necessary at Hartfield. If he were, everything else must give way; but otherwise his friend Cole had been saying so much about his dining with him – had made such a point of it – that he had promised him conditionally to come.

Emma thanked him, but could not allow of his disappointing his friend on their account; her father was sure of his rubber. He re-urged – she re-declined; and he seemed then about to make his bow, when taking the paper from the table, she returned it.

"Oh! here is the charade you were so obliging as to leave with us; thank you for the sight of it. We admired it so much, that I have ventured to write it into Miss Smith's collection. Your friend will not take it amiss I hope. Of course I have not transcribed beyond the first eight lines."

Mr. Elton certainly did not very well know what to say. He looked rather doubtingly – rather confused; said something about "honour," – glanced at Emma and at Harriet, and then seeing the book open on the table, took it up, and examined it very attentively. With the view of passing off an awkward moment, Emma smilingly said:

"You must make my apologies to your friend; but so good a charade must not be confined to one or two. He may be sure of every woman's approbation while he writes with such gallantry."

"I have no hesitation in saying," replied Mr. Elton, though hesitating a good deal while he spoke; "I have no hesitation in saying – at least if my friend feels at all as *I* do – I have not the smallest doubt that, could he see his little effusion honoured as *I* see it, (looking at the book again, and replacing it on the table), he would consider it as the proudest moment of his life."

After this speech he was gone as soon as possible. Emma could not think it too soon; for with all his good and agreeable qualities, there was a sort of parade in his speeches which was very apt to incline her to laugh. She ran away to indulge the inclination, leaving the tender and the sublime of pleasure to Harriet's share.

## Chapter 10

THOUGH NOW the middle of December, there had yet been no weather to prevent the young ladies from tolerably regular exercise; and on the morrow, Emma had a charitable visit to pay to a poor sick family, who lived a little way out of Highbury.

Their road to this detached cottage was down Vicarage Lane, a lane leading at right angles from the broad, though irregular, main street of the place; and, as may be inferred, containing the blessed abode of Mr. Elton. A few inferior dwellings were first to be passed, and then, about a quarter of a mile down the lane rose the Vicarage, an old and not very good house, almost as close to the road as it could be. It had no advantage of situation; but had been very much smartened up by the present proprietor; and, such as it was, there could be no possibility of the two friends passing it without a slackened pace and observing eyes. Emma's remark was:

"There it is. There go you and your riddle book one of these days." Harriet's was:

"Oh, what a sweet house! How very beautiful! There are the yellow curtains that Miss Nash admires so much."

"I do not often walk this way *now*," said Emma, as they proceeded, "but *then* there will be an inducement, and I shall gradually get intimately acquainted with all the hedges, gates, pools and pollards of this part of Highbury."

Harriet, she found, had never in her life been within side the Vicarage, and her curiosity to see it was so extreme, that, considering exteriors and probabilities, Emma could only class it, as a proof of love, with Mr. Elton's seeing ready wit in her.

"I wish we could contrive it," said she; "but I cannot think of any tolerable pretence for going in; no servant that I want to inquire about of his housekeeper – no message from my father."

She pondered, but could think of nothing. After a mutual silence of some minutes, Harriet thus began again:

"I do so wonder, Miss Woodhouse, that you should not be married, or going to be married! – so charming as you are!"

Emma laughed, and replied:

"My being charming, Harriet, is not quite enough to induce me to marry; I must find other people charming – one other person at least. And I am not only, not going to be married, at present, but have very little intention of ever marrying at all."

"Ah! so you say; but I cannot believe it."

"I must see somebody very superior to any one I have seen yet, to be tempted; Mr. Elton, you know, (recollecting herself,) is out of the question: and I do not wish to see any such person. I would rather not be tempted. I cannot really change for the better. If I were to marry, I must expect to repent it."

"Dear me! – it is so odd to hear a woman talk so!"

"I have none of the usual inducements of women to marry. Were I to fall in love, indeed, it would be a different thing! but I never have been in love; it is not my way, or my nature; and I do not think I ever shall. And, without love, I am sure I should be a fool to change such a situation as mine. Fortune I do not want; employment I do not want; consequence I do not want: I believe few married women are half as much mistress of their husband's house as I am of Hartfield; and never, never could I expect to be so truly beloved and important; so always first and always right in any man's eyes as I am in my father's."

"But then, to be an old maid at last, like Miss Bates!"

"That is as formidable an image as you could present, Harriet; and if I thought I should ever be like Miss Bates! so silly, so satisfied, so smiling so prosing so undistinguishing and unfastidious and so apt to tell everything relative to everybody about me, I would marry to morrow. But between us, I am convinced there never can be any likeness, except in being unmarried."

"But still, you will be an old maid! – and that's so dreadful!"

"Never mind, Harriet, I shall not be a poor old maid; and it is poverty only which makes celibacy contemptible to a generous public! A single woman, with a very narrow income, must be a ridiculous, disagreeable old maid! the proper sport of boys and girls, but a single woman, of good fortune, is always respectable, and may be as sensible and pleasant as anybody else. And the distinction is not quite so much against the candour and common sense of the world as appears at first; for a very narrow income has a tendency to contract the mind, and sour the temper. Those who can barely live, and who live perforce in a very small, and generally very inferior, society, may well be illiberal and cross. This does not apply, however, to Miss Bates; she is only too good-natured and too silly to suit me; but, in general, she is very much to the taste of everybody, though single and though poor. Poverty certainly has not contracted her mind; I really believe, if she had only a shilling in the world, she would be very likely to give away sixpence of it; and nobody is afraid of her – that is a great charm."

"Dear me! but what shall you do? how shall you employ yourself when you grow old?"

"If I know myself, Harriet, mine is an active, busy mind, with a great many independent resources; and I do not perceive why I should be more in want of employment at forty or fifty than one-and-twenty. Woman's usual occupations of hand and mind will be as open to me then as they are now; or with no important variation. If I draw less, I shall read more; if I give up music, I shall take to carpet work. And as for objects of interest, objects for the affections, which is in truth the great point of inferiority, the want of which is really the great evil to be avoided in not marrying, I shall be very well off, with all the children of a sister I love so much, to care about. There will be enough of them, in all probability, to supply every sort of sensation that declining life can need. There will be enough for every hope and every fear; and though my attachment to none can equal that of a parent, it suits my ideas of comfort better than what is warmer and blinder. My nephews and nieces! I shall often have a niece with me."

"Do you know Miss Bates's niece? That is, I know you must have seen her a hundred times – but are you acquainted?"

"Oh! yes; we are always forced to be acquainted whenever she comes to Highbury. By the bye, *that* is almost enough to put one out of conceit with a niece. Heaven forbid! at least, that I should ever bore people half so much about all the Knightleys together, as she does about Jane Fairfax. One is sick of the very name of Jane Fairfax. Every letter from her is read forty times over; her compliments to all friends go round and round again; and if she does but send her aunt the pattern of a stomacher[1], or knit a pair of garters for her grandmother, one hears of nothing else for a month. I wish Jane Fairfax very well; but she tires me to death."

1 A colourful and decorative front of an apparel.

They were now approaching the cottage, and all idle topics were superseded. Emma was very compassionate; and the distresses of the poor were as sure of relief from her personal attention and kindness, her counsel and her patience, as from her purse. She understood their ways, could allow for their ignorance and their temptations, had no romantic expectations of extraordinary virtue from those for whom education had done so little; entered into their troubles with ready sympathy, and always gave her assistance with as much intelligence as good will. In the present instance, it was sickness and poverty together which she came to visit; and after remaining there as long as she could give comfort or advice, she quitted the cottage with such an impression of the scene as made her say to Harriet, as they walked away:

"These are the sights, Harriet, to do one good. How trifling they make everything else appear! I feel now as if I could think of nothing but these poor creatures all the rest of the day; and yet, who can say how soon it may all vanish from my mind?"

"Very true," said Harriet. "Poor creatures! one can think of nothing else."

"And really, I do not think the impression will soon be over," said Emma, as she crossed the low hedge, and tottering footstep which ended the narrow, slippery path through the cottage garden, and brought them into the lane again. "I do not think it will," stopping to look once more at all the outward wretchedness of the place, and recall the still greater within.

"Oh! dear, no," said her companion.

They walked on. The lane made a slight bend; and when that bend was passed, Mr. Elton was immediately in sight; and so near as to give Emma time only to say further:

"Ah! Harriet, here comes a very sudden trial of our stability in good thoughts. Well, (smiling,) I hope it may be allowed that if compassion has produced exertion and relief to the sufferers, it has done all that is truly important. If we feel for the wretched, enough to do all we can for them, the rest is empty sympathy, only distressing to ourselves."

Harriet could just answer, "Oh! dear, yes," before the gentleman joined them. The wants and sufferings of the poor family, however, were the first subject on meeting. He had been going to call on them. His visit he would now defer; but they had a very interesting parley about what could be done and should be done. Mr. Elton then turned back to accompany them.

"To fall in with each other on such an errand as this," thought Emma; "to meet in a charitable scheme; this will bring a great increase of love on each side. I should not wonder if it were to bring on the declaration. It must, if I were not here. I wish I were anywhere else."

Anxious to separate herself from them as far as she could, she soon afterwards took possession of a narrow footpath, a little raised on one side of the lane, leaving them together in the main road. But she had not been there two minutes when she found that Harriet's habits of dependence and imitation were bringing her up too, and that, in short, they would both be soon after her. This would not do; she immediately stopped, under pretence of having some alteration to make in the lacing of her half-boot, and stooping down in complete occupation of the footpath, begged them to have the goodness to walk on, and she would follow in half a minute. They did as they were desired; and by the time she judged it reasonable to have done with her boot, she had the comfort of farther delay in her power, being overtaken by a child from the cottage, setting out, according to orders, with her pitcher, to fetch broth from Hartfield. To walk by the side of this child, and talk to and question her, was the most natural thing in the world, or would have been the most natural, had she been acting just then without design; and by this means the others were still able to keep ahead, without any obligation of waiting for her. She gained on them, however, involuntarily: the child's pace was quick, and theirs rather slow; and she was the more concerned at it, from their being evidently in a conversation which interested them. Mr. Elton was speaking with animation, Harriet listening with a very pleased attention; and Emma, having sent the child on, was beginning to think how she might draw back a little more, when they both looked around, and she was obliged to join them.

Mr. Elton was still talking, still engaged in some interesting detail; and Emma experienced some disappointment when she found that he was only giving his fair companion an account of the yesterday's party at his friend Cole's, and that she was come in herself for the Stilton cheese, the north Wiltshire, the butter, the celery, the beet root, and all the dessert.

"This would soon have led to something better, of course," was her consoling reflection; "any thing interests between those who love; and anything will serve as introduction to what is near the heart. If I could but have kept longer away!"

They now walked on together quietly, till within view of the vicarage pales, when a sudden resolution, of at least getting Harriet into the house, made her again find something very much amiss about her boot, and fall behind to arrange it once more. She then broke the lace off short, and dexterously throwing it into a ditch, was presently obliged to entreat them to stop, and acknowledged her inability to put herself to rights so as to be able to walk home in tolerable comfort.

"Part of my lace is gone," said she, "and I do not know how I am to contrive. I really am a most troublesome companion to you both, but I hope I am not often so ill-equipped. Mr. Elton, I must beg leave to stop at your house, and ask your housekeeper for a bit of ribbon or string, or any thing just to keep my boot on."

Mr. Elton looked all happiness at this proposition; and nothing could exceed his alertness and attention in conducting them into his house and endeavouring to make everything appear to advantage. The room they were taken into was the one he chiefly occupied, and looking forwards; behind it was another with which it immediately communicated; the door between them was open, and Emma passed into it with the housekeeper to receive her assistance in the most comfortable manner. She was obliged to leave the door ajar as she found it; but she fully intended that Mr. Elton should close it. It was not closed, however, it still remained ajar; but by engaging the housekeeper in incessant conversation, she hoped to make it practicable for him to choose his own subject in the adjoining room. For ten minutes she could hear nothing but herself. It could be protracted no longer. She was then obliged to be finished, and make her appearance.

The lovers were standing together at one of the windows. It had a most favourable aspect; and, for half a minute, Emma felt the glory of having schemed successfully. But it would not do; he had not come to the point. He had been most agreeable, most delightful; he had told Harriet that he had seen them go by, and had purposely followed them; other little gallantries and allusions had been dropped, but nothing serious.

"Cautious, very cautious," thought Emma; "he advances inch by inch, and will hazard nothing till he believes himself secure."

Still, however, though everything had not been accomplished by her ingenious device, she could not but flatter herself that it had been the occasion of much present enjoyment to both, and must be leading them forward to the great event.

# Chapter 11

MR. ELTON must now be left to himself. It was no longer in Emma's power to superintend his happiness or quicken his measures. The coming of her sister's family was so very near at hand, that first in anticipation, and then in reality, it became henceforth her prime object of interest; and during the ten days of their stay at Hartfield it was not to be expected – she did not herself expect – that any thing beyond occasional, fortuitous assistance could be afforded by her to the lovers. They might advance rapidly if they would, however; they must advance somehow or other whether they would or no. She hardly wished to have more leisure for them. There are people, who the more you do for them, the less they will do for themselves.

Mr. and Mrs. John Knightley, from having been longer than usual absent from Surrey, were exciting of course rather more than the usual interest. Till this year, every long vacation since their marriage had been divided between Hartfield and Donwell Abbey; but all the holidays of this autumn had been given to sea-bathing for the children, and it was therefore many months since they had been seen in a regular way by their Surrey connections, or seen at all by Mr. Woodhouse, who could not be induced to get so far as London, even for poor Isabella's sake; and who consequently was now most nervously and apprehensively happy in forestalling this too short visit.

He thought much of the evils of the journey for her, and not a little of the fatigues of his own horses and coachman who were to bring some of the party the last half of the way; but his alarms were needless; the sixteen miles being happily accomplished, and Mr. and Mrs. John Knightley, their five children, and a competent number of nursery maids, all reaching Hartfield in safety. The bustle and joy of such an arrival, the many to be talked to, welcomed, encouraged, and variously dispersed and disposed of, produced a noise and confusion which his nerves could not have borne under any other cause, nor have endured much longer even for this; but the ways of Hartfield and the feelings of her father were so respected by Mrs. John Knightley, that in spite of maternal solicitude for the immediate enjoyment of her little ones, and for their having instantly all the liberty and attendance, all the eating and drinking, and sleeping and playing, which they could possibly wish for, without the smallest delay, the children were never allowed to be long a disturbance to him, either in themselves or in any restless attendance on them.

Mrs. John Knightley was a pretty, elegant little woman, of gentle, quiet manners, and a disposition remarkably amiable and affectionate; wrapped up in her family; a devoted wife, a doting mother, and so tenderly attached to her father and sister that, but for these higher ties, a warmer love might have seemed impossible. She could never see a fault in any of them. She was not a woman of strong understanding or any quickness; and with this resemblance of her father, she inherited also much of his constitution; was delicate in her own health, over careful of that of her children, had many fears and many nerves, and was as fond of her own Mr. Wingfield in town as her father could be of Mr. Perry. They were alike too, in a general benevolence of temper, and a strong habit of regard for every old acquaintance. Mr. John Knightley was a tall, gentleman like, and very clever man; rising in his profession, domestic, and respectable in his private character; but with reserved manners which prevented his being generally pleasing; and capable of being sometimes out of humour. He was not an ill-tempered man, not so often unreasonably cross as to deserve such a reproach; but his temper was not his great perfection; and, indeed, with such a worshipping wife, it was hardly possible that any natural defects in it should not be increased. The extreme sweetness of her temper must hurt his. He had all the clearness and quickness of mind which she wanted, and he could sometimes act as ungracious, or say a severe thing.

He was not a great favourite with his fair sister-in-law. Nothing wrong in him escaped her. She was quick in feeling the little injuries to Isabella, which Isabella never felt herself. Perhaps she might have passed over more had his manners been flattering to Isabella's sister, but they were only those of a calmly kind brother and friend, without praise and without blindness; but hardly any degree of personal compliment could have made her regardless of that greatest fault of all in her eyes which he sometimes fell into, the want of respectful forbearance towards her father. There he had not always the patience that could have been wished. Mr. Woodhouse's peculiarities and fidgetiness were sometimes provoking him to a rational remonstrance or sharp retort equally ill-bestowed. It did not often happen; for Mr. John Knightley had really a great regard for his father-in-law, and generally a strong sense of what was due to him; but it was too often for Emma's charity, especially as there was all the pain of apprehension frequently to be endured, though the offence came not. The beginning, however, of every visit displayed none but the properest feelings, and this being of necessity so short might be hoped to pass away in unsullied cordiality. They had not been long seated and composed when Mr. Woodhouse, with a melancholy shake of the head and a sigh, called his daughter's attention to the sad change at Hartfield since she had been there last.

"Ah, my dear," said he, "poor Miss Taylor It is a grievous business."

"Oh yes, sir," cried she with ready sympathy, "how you must miss her! And dear Emma, too! What a dreadful loss to you both! I have been so grieved for you. I could not imagine how you could possibly do without her. It is a sad change indeed. But I hope she is pretty well, sir."

"Pretty well, my dear – I hope – pretty well. I do not know but that the place agrees with her tolerably."

Mr. John Knightley here asked Emma quietly whether there were any doubts of the air of Randalls.

"Oh! no none in the least. I never saw Mrs. Weston better

in my life – never looking so well. Papa is only speaking his own regret."

"Very much to the honour of both," was the handsome reply.

"And do you see her, sir, tolerably often?" asked Isabella in the plaintive tone which just suited her father.

Mr. Woodhouse hesitated. "Not near so often, my dear, as I could wish."

"Oh! papa, we have missed seeing them but one entire day since they married. Either in the morning or evening of every day, excepting one, have we seen either Mr. Weston or Mrs. Weston, and generally both, either at Randalls or here and as you may suppose, Isabella, most frequently here. They are very, very kind in their visits. Mr. Weston is really as kind as herself. Papa, if you speak in that melancholy way, you will be giving Isabella a false idea of us all. Everybody must be aware that Miss Taylor must be missed, but everybody ought also to be assured that Mr. and Mrs. Weston do really prevent our missing her by any means to the extent we ourselves anticipated – which is the exact truth."

"Just as it should be," said Mr. John Knightley, "and just as I hoped it was from your letters. Her wish of showing you attention could not be doubted, and his being a disengaged and social man makes it all easy. I have been always telling you, my love, that I had no idea of the change being so very material to Hartfield as you apprehended; and now you have Emma's account, I hope you will be satisfied."

"Why, to be sure," said Mr. Woodhouse – "yes, certainly I cannot deny that Mrs. Weston – poor Mrs. Weston, does come and see us pretty often but then she is always obliged to go away again."

"It would be very hard upon Mr. Weston if she did not, papa. You quite forget poor Mr. Weston."

"I think, indeed," said John Knightley pleasantly, "that Mr. Weston has some little claim. You and I, Emma, will venture to take the part of the poor husband. I, being a husband, and you not being a wife, the claims of the man may very likely strike us with equal force. As for Isabella, she has been married long enough to see the convenience of putting all the Mr. Westons aside as much as she can."

"Me, my love," cried his wife, hearing and understanding only in part. "Are you talking about me? I am sure nobody ought to be, or can be, a greater advocate for matrimony than I am; and if it had not been for the misery of her leaving Hartfield, I should never have thought of Miss Taylor but as the most fortunate woman in the world; and as to slighting Mr. Weston – that excellent Mr. Weston – I think there is nothing he does not deserve. I believe he is one of the very best-tempered men that ever existed. Excepting yourself and your brother, I do not know his equal for temper. I shall never forget his flying Henry's kite for him that very windy day last Easter and ever since his particular kindness last September twelvemonth in writing that note, at twelve o'clock at night, on purpose to assure me that there was no scarlet fever at Cobham, I have been convinced there could not be a more feeling heart nor a better man in existence. If anybody can deserve him, it must be Miss Taylor."

"Where is the young man?" said John Knightley. "Has he been here on this occasion or has he not?"

"He has not been here yet," replied Emma. "There was a strong expectation of his coming soon after the marriage, but it ended in nothing; and I have not heard him mentioned lately."

"But you should tell them of the letter, my dear," said her father. "He wrote a letter to poor Mrs. Weston, to congratulate her, and a very proper, handsome letter it was. She showed it to me. I thought it very well done of him indeed. Whether it was his own idea you know, one cannot tell. He is but young, and his uncle, perhaps – "

"My dear papa, he is three-and-twenty. You forget how time passes."

"Three-and-twenty! is he indeed? Well, I could not have

thought it and he was but two years old when he lost his poor mother! Well, time does fly indeed! and my memory is very bad. However, it was an exceeding good, pretty letter, and gave Mr. and Mrs. Weston a great deal of pleasure. I remember it was written from Weymouth, and dated Sept. 28th and began, 'My dear Madam,' but I forget how it went on; and it was signed 'F. C. Weston Churchill.' I remember that perfectly."

"How very pleasing and proper of him!" cried the good-hearted Mrs. John Knightley. "I have no doubt of his being a most amiable young man. But how sad it is that he should not live at home with his father! There is something so shocking in a child's being taken away from his parents and natural home! I never could comprehend how Mr. Weston could part with him. To give up one's child! I really never could think well of anybody who proposed such a thing to anybody else."

"Nobody ever did think well of the Churchills, I fancy," observed Mr. John Knightley coolly. "But you need not imagine Mr. Weston to have felt what you would feel in giving up Henry or John. Mr. Weston is rather an easy, cheerful-tempered man, than a man of strong feelings; he takes things as he finds them, and makes enjoyment of them somehow or other, depending, I suspect, much more upon what is called *society* for his comforts, that is, upon the power of eating and drinking, and playing whist with his neighbours five times a week, than upon family affection, or any thing that home affords."

Emma could not like what bordered on a reflection on Mr. Weston, and had half a mind to take it up; but she struggled, and let it pass. She would keep the peace if possible; and there was something honourable and valuable in the strong domestic habits, the all-sufficiency of home to himself, whence resulted her brother's disposition to look down on the common rate of social intercourse, and those to whom it was important. It had a high claim to forbearance.

# *Chapter 12*

MR. KNIGHTLEY was to dine with them rather against the inclination of Mr. Woodhouse, who did not like that any one should share with him in Isabella's first day. Emma's sense of right however had decided it; and besides the consideration of what was due to each brother, she had particular pleasure, from the circumstance of the late disagreement between Mr. Knightley and herself, in procuring him the proper invitation.

She hoped they might now become friends again. She thought it was time to make up. Making up indeed would not do. She certainly had not been in the wrong, and *he* would never own that he had. Concession must be out of the question; but it was time to appear to forget that they had ever quarrelled; and she hoped it might rather assist the restoration of friendship, that when he came into the room she had one of the children with her – the youngest, a nice little girl about eight months old, who was now making her first visit to Hartfield, and very happy to be danced about in her aunt's arms. It did assist; for though he began with grave looks and short questions, he was soon led on to talk of them all in the usual way, and to take the child out of her arms with all the unceremoniousness of perfect amity. Emma felt they were friends again; and the conviction giving her at first great satisfaction, and then a little sauciness, she could not help saying, as he was admiring the baby:

"What a comfort it is, that we think alike about our nephews and nieces! As to men and women, our opinions are sometimes very different; but with regard to these children, I observe we never disagree."

"If you were as much guided by nature in your estimate of men and women, and as little under the power of fancy and whim in your dealings with them, as you are where these children are concerned, we might always think alike."

"To be sure – our discordances must always arise from my being in the wrong."

"Yes," said he, smiling" and reason good. I was sixteen years old when you were born."

"A material difference then," she replied" and no doubt you were much my superior in judgment at that period of our lives; but does not the lapse of one-and-twenty years bring our understandings a good deal nearer?"

"Yes a good deal *nearer.*"

"But still, not near enough to give me a chance of being right, if we think differently."

"I have still the advantage of you by sixteen years' experience, and by not being a pretty young woman and a spoiled child. Come, my dear Emma, let us be friends, and say no more about it. Tell your aunt, little Emma, that she ought to set you a better example than to be renewing old grievances, and that if she were not wrong before, she is now."

"That's true," she cried "very true. Little Emma, grow up a better woman than your aunt. Be infinitely cleverer and not half so conceited. Now, Mr. Knightley, a word or two more, and I have done. As far as good intentions went, we were *both* right, and I must say that no effects on my side of the argument have yet proved wrong. I only want to know that Mr. Martin is not very, very bitterly disappointed."

"A man cannot be more so," was his short, full answer.

"Ah! Indeed I am very sorry. Come, shake hands with me."

This had just taken place and with great cordiality, when John Knightley made his appearance, and "How d'ye do, George?" and "John, how are you?" succeeded in the true English style, burying under a calmness that seemed all but indifference, the real attachment which would have led either of them, if requisite, to do everything for the good of the other.

The evening was quiet and conversable, as Mr. Woodhouse

declined cards entirely for the sake of comfortable talk with his dear Isabella, and the little party made two natural divisions; on one side he and his daughter; on the other the two Mr. Knightleys; their subjects totally distinct, or very rarely mixing and Emma only occasionally joining in one or the other.

The brothers talked of their own concerns and pursuits, but principally of those of the elder, whose temper was by much the most communicative, and who was always the greater talker. As a magistrate, he had generally some point of law to consult John about, or, at least, some curious anecdote to give; and as a farmer, as keeping in hand the home farm at Donwell, he had to tell what every field was to bear next year, and to give all such local information as could not fail of being interesting to a brother whose home it had equally been the longest part of his life, and whose attachments were strong. The plan of a drain, the change of a fence, the felling of a tree, and the destination of every acre for wheat, turnips, or spring corn, was entered into with as much equality of interest by John, as his cooler manners rendered possible; and if his willing brother ever left him any thing to inquire about, his inquiries even approached a tone of eagerness.

While they were thus comfortably occupied, Mr. Woodhouse was enjoying a full flow of happy regrets and fearful affection with his daughter.

"My poor dear Isabella," said he, fondly taking her hand, and interrupting, for a few moments, her busy labours for some one of her five children "How long it is, how terribly long since you were here! And how tired you must be after your journey! You must go to bed early, my dear – and I recommend a little gruel to you before you go. You and I will have a nice basin of gruel together. My dear Emma, suppose we all have a little gruel."

Emma could not suppose any such thing, knowing as she did, that both the Mr. Knightleys were as unpersuadable on that article as herself; and two basins only were ordered. After a little more discourse in praise of gruel, with some wondering at its not being taken every evening by everybody, he proceeded to say, with an air of grave reflection:

"It was an awkward business, my dear, your spending the autumn at South End instead of coming here. I never had much opinion of the sea air."

"Mr. Wingfield most strenuously recommended it, sir or we should not have gone. He recommended it for all the children, but particularly for the weakness in little Bella's throat – both sea air and bathing."

"Ah! my dear, but Perry had many doubts about the sea doing her any good; and as to myself, I have been long perfectly convinced, though perhaps I never told you so before, that the sea is very rarely of use to anybody. I am sure it almost killed me once."

"Come, come," cried Emma, feeling this to be an unsafe subject, "I must beg you not to talk of the sea. It makes me envious and miserable; I who have never seen it! South End is prohibited, if you please. My dear Isabella, I have not heard you make one inquiry about Mr. Perry yet; and he never forgets you."

"Oh! good Mr. Perry how is he, sir?"

"Why, pretty well; but not quite well. Poor Perry is bilious, and he has not time to take care of himself – he tells me he has not time to take care of himself which is very sad – but he is always wanted all round the country. I suppose there is not a man in such practice anywhere. But then there is not so clever a man any where."

"And Mrs. Perry and the children, how are they? do the children grow? I have a great regard for Mr. Perry. I hope he will be calling soon. He will be so pleased to see my little ones."

"I hope he will be here to morrow, for I have a question or two to ask him about myself of some consequence. And, my dear, whenever he comes, you had better let him look at little Bella's throat."

"Oh! my dear sir, her throat is so much better that I have hardly any uneasiness about it. Either bathing has been of the greatest service to her, or else it is to be attributed to an excellent embrocation of Mr. Wingfield's, which we have been applying at times ever since August."

"It is not very likely, my dear, that bathing should have been of use to her and if I had known you were wanting an embrocation, I would have spoken to – "

"You seem to me to have forgotten Mrs. and Miss Bates," said Emma, "I have not heard one inquiry after them."

"Oh! the good Bateses I am quite ashamed of myself but you mention them in most of your letters. I hope they are quite well. Good old Mrs. Bates I will call upon her to morrow, and take my children. They are always so pleased to see my children. And that excellent Miss Bates! – such thorough worthy people! How are they, sir?"

"Why, pretty well, my dear, upon the whole. But poor Mrs. Bates had a bad cold about a month ago."

"How sorry I am! But colds were never so prevalent as they have been this autumn. Mr. Wingfield told me that he has never known them more general or heavy except when it has been quite an influenza."

"That has been a good deal the case, my dear; but not to the degree you mention. Perry says that colds have been very general, but not so heavy as he has very often known them in November. Perry does not call it altogether a sickly season."

"No, I do not know that Mr. Wingfield considers it *very* sickly except – "

"Ah! my poor dear child, the truth is, that in London it is always a sickly season. Nobody is healthy in London, nobody can be. It is a dreadful thing to have you forced to live there! – so far off! – and the air so bad!"

"No, indeed *we* are not at all in a bad air. Our part of London is very superior to most others! You must not confound us with London in general, my dear sir. The neighbourhood of Brunswick Square is very different from almost all the rest. We are so very airy! I should be unwilling, I own, to live in any other part of the town; there is hardly any other that I could be satisfied to have my children in: but we are so remarkably airy! Mr. Wingfield thinks the vicinity of Brunswick Square decidedly the most favourable as to air."

"Ah! my dear, it is not like Hartfield. You make the best of it – but after you have been a week at Hartfield, you are all of you different creatures; you do not look like the same. Now I cannot say, that I think you are any of you looking well at present."

"I am sorry to hear you say so, sir; but I assure you, excepting those little nervous head aches and palpitations which I am never entirely free from anywhere, I am quite well myself; and if the children were rather pale before they went to bed, it was only because they were a little more tired than usual, from their journey and the happiness of coming. I hope you will think better of their looks to morrow; for I assure you Mr. Wingfield told me, that he did not believe he had ever sent us off altogether, in such good case. I trust, at least, that you do not think Mr. Knightley looking ill," turning her eyes with affectionate anxiety towards her husband.

"Middling, my dear; I cannot compliment you. I think Mr. John Knightley very far from looking well."

"What is the matter, sir? Did you speak to me?" cried Mr. John Knightley, hearing his own name.

"I am sorry to find, my love, that my father does not think you looking well but I hope it is only from being a little fatigued. I could have wished, however, as you know, that you had seen Mr. Wingfield before you left home."

"My dear Isabella," exclaimed he hastily "pray do not concern yourself about my looks. Be satisfied with doctoring and coddling yourself and the children, and let me look as I choose."

"I did not thoroughly understand what you were telling your brother," cried Emma, "about your friend Mr. Graham's intending to have a bailiff from Scotland, to look after his new estate. What will it answer? Will not the old prejudice be too strong?"

And she talked in this way so long and successfully that, when forced to give her attention again to her father and sister, she had nothing worse to hear than Isabella's kind inquiry after Jane Fairfax; and Jane Fairfax, though no great favourite with her in general, she was at that moment very happy to assist in praising.

"That sweet, amiable Jane Fairfax!" said Mrs. John Knightley. "It is so long since I have seen her, except now and then for a moment accidentally in town! What happiness it must be to her good old grandmother and excellent aunt, when she comes to visit them! I always regret excessively on dear Emma's account that she cannot be more at Highbury; but now their daughter is married, I suppose Colonel and Mrs. Campbell will not be able to part with her at all. She would be such a delightful companion for Emma."

Mr. Woodhouse agreed to it all, but added:

"Our little friend Harriet Smith, however, is just such another pretty kind of young person. You will like Harriet. Emma could not have a better companion than Harriet."

"I am most happy to hear it but only Jane Fairfax one knows to be so very accomplished and superior! and exactly Emma's age."

This topic was discussed very happily, and others succeeded of similar moment, and passed away with similar harmony; but the evening did not close without a little return of agitation. The gruel came and supplied a great deal to be said – much praise and many comments – undoubting decision of its wholesomeness for every constitution, and pretty severe Philippics[1] upon the many houses where it was never met with tolerable; but, unfortunately, among the failures which the daughter had to instance, the most recent, and therefore most prominent, was in her own cook at

1 Curses.

South End, a young woman hired for the time, who never had been able to understand what she meant by a basin of nice smooth gruel, thin, but not too thin. Often as she had wished for and ordered it, she had never been able to get any thing tolerable. Here was a dangerous opening.

"Ah!" said Mr. Woodhouse, shaking his head and fixing his eyes on her with tender concern. The ejaculation in Emma's ear expressed, "Ah! there is no end of the sad consequences of your going to South End. It does not bear talking of." And for a little while she hoped he would not talk of it, and that a silent rumination might suffice to restore him to the relish of his own smooth gruel. After an interval of some minutes, however, he began with:

"I shall always be very sorry that you went to the sea this autumn, instead of coming here."

"But why should you be sorry, sir? I assure you, it did the children a great deal of good."

"And, moreover, if you must go to the sea, it had better not have been to South End. South End is an unhealthy place. Perry was surprised to hear you had fixed upon South End."

"I know there is such an idea with many people, but indeed it is quite a mistake, sir. We all had our health perfectly well there, never found the least inconvenience from the mud; and Mr. Wingfield says it is entirely a mistake to suppose the place unhealthy; and I am sure he may be depended on, for he thoroughly understands the nature of the air, and his own brother and family have been there repeatedly."

"You should have gone to Cromer, my dear, if you went anywhere. Perry was a week at Cromer once, and he holds it to be the best of all the sea bathing places. A fine open sea, he says, and very pure air. And, by what I understand, you might have had lodgings there quite away from the sea – a quarter of a mile off – very comfortable. You should have consulted Perry."

"But, my dear sir, the difference of the journey; only consider how great it would have been. An hundred miles, perhaps, instead of forty."

"Ah! my dear, as Perry says, where health is at stake, nothing else should be considered; and if one is to travel, there is not much to choose between forty miles and an hundred. Better not move at all, better stay in London altogether than travel forty miles to get into a worse air. This is just what Perry said. It seemed to him a very ill judged measure."

Emma's attempts to stop her father had been vain; and when he had reached such a point as this, she could not wonder at her brother-in-law's breaking out.

"Mr. Perry," said he, in a voice of very strong displeasure, "would do as well to keep his opinion till it is asked for. Why does he make it any business of his, to wonder at what I do? – at my taking my family to one part of the coast or another? I may be allowed, I hope, the use of my judgment as well as Mr. Perry. I want his directions no more than his drugs." He paused and growing cooler in a moment, added, with only sarcastic dryness, "If Mr. Perry can tell me how to convey a wife and five children a distance of an hundred and thirty miles with no greater expense or inconvenience than a distance of forty, I should be as willing to prefer Cromer to South End as he could himself."

"True, true," cried Mr. Knightley, with most ready interposition "very true. That's a consideration indeed. But John, as to what I was telling you of my idea of moving the path to Langham, of turning it more to the right that it may not cut through the home meadows, I cannot conceive any difficulty. I should not attempt it, if it were to be the means of inconvenience to the Highbury people, but if you call to mind exactly the present line of the path. . . . The only way of proving it, however, will be to turn to our maps. I shall see you at the Abbey to morrow morning I hope, and then we will look them over, and you shall give me your opinion."

Mr. Woodhouse was rather agitated by such harsh reflections

on his friend Perry, to whom he had, in fact, though unconsciously, been attributing many of his own feelings and expressions; but the soothing attentions of his daughters gradually removed the present evil, and the immediate alertness of one brother, and better recollections of the other, prevented any renewal of it.

# *Chapter 13*

THERE COULD hardly be a happier creature in the world than Mrs. John Knightley, in this short visit to Hartfield, going about every morning among her old acquaintance with her five children, and talking over what she had done every evening with her father and sister. She had nothing to wish otherwise, but that the days did not pass so swiftly. It was a delightful visit; perfect, in being much too short.

In general their evenings were less engaged with friends than their mornings; but one complete dinner engagement, and out of the house too, there was no avoiding, though at Christmas. Mr. Weston would take no denial; they must all dine at Randalls one day; even Mr. Woodhouse was persuaded to think it a possible thing in preference to a division of the party.

How they were all to be conveyed, he would have made a difficulty if he could, but as his son and daughter's carriage and horses were actually at Hartfield, he was not able to make more than a simple question on that head; it hardly amounted to a doubt; nor did it occupy Emma long to convince him that they might in one of the carriages find room for Harriet also.

Harriet, Mr. Elton, and Mr. Knightley, their own especial set, were the only persons invited to meet them; the hours were to be early, as well as the numbers few; Mr. Woodhouse's habits and inclination being consulted in everything.

The evening before this great event (for it was a very great event that Mr. Woodhouse should dine out, on the 24th of December) had been spent by Harriet at Hartfield, and she had gone home so much indisposed with a cold, that, but for her own earnest wish of being nursed by Mrs. Goddard, Emma could not have allowed her to leave the house. Emma called on her the next day, and found her doom already signed with regard to Randalls. She was very feverish and had a bad sore throat: Mrs. Goddard was full of care and affection, Mr. Perry was talked of, and Harriet herself was too ill and low to resist the authority which excluded her from this delightful engagement, though she could not speak of her loss without many tears.

Emma sat with her as long as she could, to attend her in Mrs. Goddard's unavoidable absences, and raise her spirits by representing how much Mr. Elton's would be depressed when he knew her state; and left her at last tolerably comfortable, in the sweet dependence of his having a most comfortless visit, and of their all missing her very much. She had not advanced many yards from Mrs. Goddard's door, when she was met by Mr. Elton himself, evidently coming towards it, and as they walked on slowly together in conversation about the invalid – of whom he, on the rumour of considerable illness, had been going to inquire, that he might carry some report of her to Hartfield – they were overtaken by Mr. John Knightley returning from the daily visit to Donwell, with his two eldest boys, whose healthy, glowing faces showed all the benefit of a country run, and seemed to ensure a quick despatch of the roast mutton and rice pudding they were hastening home for. They joined company and proceeded together. Emma was just describing the nature of her friend's complaint; "a throat very much inflamed, with a great deal of heat about her, a quick, low pulse, etc. and she was sorry to find from Mrs. Goddard that Harriet was liable to very bad sore throats, and had often alarmed her with them." Mr. Elton looked all alarmed on the occasion, as he exclaimed:

"A sore throat! – I hope not infectious. I hope not of a putrid infectious sort. Has Perry seen her? Indeed you should take care of yourself as well as of your friend. Let me entreat you to run no risks. Why does not Perry see her?"

Emma, who was not really at all frightened herself, tranquillised this excess of apprehension by assurances of Mrs. Goddard's experience and care; but as there must still remain a degree of uneasiness which she could not wish to reason away, which she would rather feed and assist than not, she added soon afterwards – as if quite another subject:

"It is so cold, so very cold and looks and feels so very much like snow, that if it were to any other place or with any other party, I should really try not to go out to day and dissuade my father from venturing; but as he has made up his mind, and does not seem to feel the cold himself, I do not like to interfere, as I know it would be so great a disappointment to Mr. and Mrs. Weston. But, upon my word, Mr. Elton, in your case, I should certainly excuse myself. You appear to me a little hoarse already, and when you consider what demand of voice and what fatigues to morrow will bring, I think it would be no more than common prudence to stay at home and take care of yourself to night."

Mr. Elton looked as if he did not very well know what answer to make; which was exactly the case; for though very much gratified by the kind care of such a fair lady, and not liking to resist any advice of her's, he had not really the least inclination to give up the visit; but Emma, too eager and busy in her own previous conceptions and views to hear him impartially, or see him with clear vision, was very well satisfied with his muttering acknowledgment of its being "very cold, certainly very cold," and walked on, rejoicing in having extricated him from Randalls, and secured him the power of sending to inquire after Harriet every hour of the evening.

"You do quite right," said she; "we will make your apologies to Mr. and Mrs. Weston."

But hardly had she so spoken, when she found her brother was civilly offering a seat in his carriage, if the weather were Mr. Elton's only objection, and Mr. Elton actually accepting the offer with much prompt satisfaction. It was a done thing; Mr. Elton was to go, and never had his broad handsome face expressed more pleasure than at this moment; never had his smile been stronger, nor his eyes more exulting than when he next looked at her.

"Well," said she to herself, "this is most strange! After I had got him off so well, to choose to go into company, and leave Harriet ill behind! Most strange indeed! But there is, I believe, in many men, especially single men, such an inclination – such a passion for dining out a dinner engagement is so high in the class of their pleasures, their employments, their dignities, almost their duties, that any thing gives way to it and this must be the case with Mr. Elton; a most valuable, amiable, pleasing young man undoubtedly, and very much in love with Harriet; but still, he cannot refuse an invitation, he must dine out wherever he is asked. What a strange thing love is! he can see ready wit in Harriet, but will not dine alone for her."

Soon afterwards Mr. Elton quitted them, and she could not but do him the justice of feeling that there was a great deal of sentiment in his manner of naming Harriet at parting; in the tone of his voice while assuring her that he should call at Mrs. Goddard's for news of her fair friend, the last thing before he prepared for the happiness of meeting her again, when he hoped to be able to give a better report; and he sighed and smiled himself off in a way that left the balance of approbation much in his favour.

After a few minutes of entire silence between them, John Knightley began with:

"I never in my life saw a man more intent on being agreeable than Mr. Elton. It is downright labour to him where ladies are concerned. With men he can be rational and unaffected, but when he has ladies to please, every feature works."

"Mr. Elton's manners are not perfect," replied Emma; "but where there is a wish to please, one ought to overlook, and one does overlook a great deal. Where a man does his best with only moderate powers, he will have the advantage over negligent superiority. There is such perfect good temper and good will in Mr. Elton as one cannot but value."

"Yes," said Mr. John Knightley presently, with some slyness, "he seems to have a great deal of good will towards *you.*"

"Me!" she replied with a smile of astonishment, "are you imagining me to be Mr. Elton's object?"

"Such an imagination has crossed me, I own, Emma; and if it never occurred to you before, you may as well take it into consideration now."

"Mr. Elton in love with me! What an idea!"

"I do not say it is so; but you will do well to consider whether it is so or not, and to regulate your behaviour accordingly. I think your manners to him encouraging. I speak as a friend, Emma. You had better look about you, and ascertain what you do, and what you mean to do."

"I thank you; but I assure you, you are quite mistaken. Mr. Elton and I are very good friends, and nothing more;" and she walked on, amusing herself in the consideration of the blunders which often arise from a partial knowledge of circumstances, of the mistakes which people of high pretensions to judgment are for ever falling into; and not very well pleased with her brother for imagining her blind and ignorant, and in want of counsel. He said no more.

Mr. Woodhouse had so completely made up his mind to the visit, that in spite of the increasing coldness, he seemed to have no idea of shrinking from it, and set forward at last most punctually with his eldest daughter in his own carriage, with less apparent consciousness of the weather than either of the others; too full of the wonder of his own going, and the pleasure it was to afford at

Randalls to see that it was cold, and too well wrapt up to feel it. The cold, however, was severe; and by the time the second carriage was in motion, a few flakes of snow were finding their way down, and the sky had the appearance of being so overcharged as to want only a milder air to produce a very white world in a very short time.

Emma soon saw that her companion was not in the happiest humour. The preparing and the going abroad in such weather, with the sacrifice of his children after dinner, were evils, were disagreeables at least, which Mr. John Knightley did not by any means like; he anticipated nothing in the visit that could be at all worth the purchase; and the whole of their drive to the vicarage was spent by him in expressing his discontent.

"A man," said he, "must have a very good opinion of himself when he asks people to leave their own fireside, and encounter such a day as this, for the sake of coming to see him. He must think himself a most agreeable fellow; I could not do such a thing. It is the greatest absurdity – actually snowing at this moment! The folly of not allowing people to be comfortable at home and the folly of people's not staying comfortably at home when they can! If we were obliged to go out such an evening as this, by any call of duty or business, what a hardship we should deem it; and here are we, probably with rather thinner clothing than usual, setting forward voluntarily, without excuse, in defiance of the voice of nature, which tells man, in everything given to his view or his feelings, to stay at home himself, and keep all under shelter that he can; here we are setting forward to spend five dull hours in another man's house, with nothing to say or to hear that was not said and heard yesterday, and may not be said and heard again to morrow. Going in dismal weather, to return probably in worse; four horses and four servants taken out for nothing but to convey five idle, shivering creatures into colder rooms and worse company than they might have had at home."

Emma did not find herself equal to give the pleased assent,

which no doubt he was in the habit of receiving, to emulate the "Very true, my love," which must have been usually administered by his travelling companion; but she had resolution enough to refrain from making any answer at all. She could not be complying, she dreaded being quarrelsome; her heroism reached only to silence. She allowed him to talk, and arranged the glasses, and wrapped herself up, without opening her lips.

They arrived, the carriage turned, the step was let down, and Mr. Elton, spruce, black, and smiling, was with them instantly. Emma thought with pleasure of some change of subject. Mr. Elton was all obligation and cheerfulness; he was so very cheerful in his civilities indeed, that she began to think he must have received a different account of Harriet from what had reached her. She had sent while dressing, and the answer had been, "Much the same – not better."

"*My* report from Mrs. Goddard's," said she presently, "was not so pleasant as I had hoped 'Not better' was my answer."

His face lengthened immediately; and his voice was the voice of sentiment as he answered.

"Oh! No – I am grieved to find – I was on the point of telling you that when I called at Mrs. Goddard's door, which I did the very last thing before I returned to dress, I was told that Miss Smith was not better, by no means better, rather worse. Very much grieved and concerned – I had flattered myself that she must be better after such a cordial as I knew had been given her in the morning."

Emma smiled and answered "My visit was of use to the nervous part of her complaint, I hope; but not even I can charm away a sore throat; it is a most severe cold indeed. Mr. Perry has been with her, as you probably heard."

"Yes – I imagined – that is – I did not – "

"He has been used to her in these complaints, and I hope to morrow morning will bring us both a more comfortable report.

But it is impossible not to feel uneasiness. Such a sad loss to our party to day!"

"Dreadful! Exactly so, indeed. She will be missed every moment."

This was very proper; the sigh which accompanied it was really estimable; but it should have lasted longer. Emma was rather in dismay when only half a minute afterwards he began to speak of other things, and in a voice of the greatest alacrity and enjoyment.

"What an excellent device," said he, "the use of a sheep-skin for carriages. How very comfortable they make it; impossible to feel cold with such precautions. The contrivances of modern days indeed have rendered a gentleman's carriage perfectly complete. One is so fenced and guarded from the weather, that not a breath of air can find its way unpermitted. Weather becomes absolutely of no consequence. It is a very cold afternoon – but in this carriage we know nothing of the matter. Ha! snows a little I see."

"Yes," said John Knightley, "and I think we shall have a good deal of it."

"Christmas weather," observed Mr. Elton. "Quite seasonable; and extremely fortunate we may think ourselves that it did not begin yesterday, and prevent this day's party, which it might very possibly have done, for Mr. Woodhouse would hardly have ventured had there been much snow on the ground; but now it is of no consequence. This is quite the season indeed for friendly meetings. At Christmas everybody invites their friends about them, and people think little of even the worst weather. I was snowed up at a friend's house once for a week. Nothing could be pleasanter. I went for only one night, and could not get away till that very day sennight."

Mr. John Knightley looked as if he did not comprehend the pleasure, but said only, coolly:

"I cannot wish to be snowed up a week at Randalls."

At another time Emma might have been amused, but she was

too much astonished now at Mr. Elton's spirits for other feelings. Harriet seemed quite forgotten in the expectation of a pleasant party.

"We are sure of excellent fires," continued he, "and everything in the greatest comfort. Charming people, Mr. and Mrs. Weston; Mrs. Weston indeed is much beyond praise, and he is exactly what one values, so hospitable, and so fond of society; it will be a small party, but where small parties are select, they are perhaps the most agreeable of any. Mr. Weston's dining room does not accommodate more than ten comfortably; and for my part, I would rather, under such circumstances, fall short by two than exceed by two. I think you will agree with me, (turning with a soft air to Emma,) I think I shall certainly have your approbation, though Mr. Knightley perhaps, from being used to the large parties of London, may not quite enter into our feelings."

"I know nothing of the large parties of London, sir – I never dine with anybody."

"Indeed! (in a tone of wonder and pity,) I had no idea that the law had been so great a slavery. Well, sir, the time must come when you will be paid for all this, when you will have little labour and great enjoyment."

"My first enjoyment," replied John Knightley, as they passed through the sweep-gate, "will be to find myself safe at Hartfield again."

# Chapter 14

SOME CHANGE of countenance was necessary for each gentleman as they walked into Mrs. Weston's drawing room; Mr. Elton must compose his joyous looks, and Mr. John Knightley disperse his ill humour. Mr. Elton must smile less, and Mr. John Knightley more, to fit them for the place. Emma might only be as nature prompted, and show herself just as happy as she was. To her it was real enjoyment to be with the Westons. Mr. Weston was a great favourite, and there was not a creature in the world to whom she spoke with such unreserve, as to his wife; not any one, to whom she related with such conviction of being listened to and understood, of being always interesting and always intelligible, the little affairs, arrangements, perplexities, and pleasures of her father and herself. She could tell nothing of Hartfield, in which Mrs. Weston had not a lively concern; and half an hour's uninterrupted communication of all those little matters on which the daily happiness of private life depends, was one of the first gratifications of each.

This was a pleasure which perhaps the whole day's visit might not afford, which certainly did not belong to the present half hour; but the very sight of Mrs. Weston, her smile, her touch, her voice was grateful to Emma, and she determined to think as little as possible of Mr. Elton's oddities, or of any thing else unpleasant, and enjoy all that was enjoyable to the utmost.

The misfortune of Harriet's cold had been pretty well gone through before her arrival. Mr. Woodhouse had been safely seated long enough to give the history of it, besides all the history of his own and Isabella's coming, and of Emma's being to follow, and had indeed just got to the end of his satisfaction that James should come and see his daughter, when the others appeared, and Mrs. Weston, who had been almost wholly engrossed by her attentions to him, was able to turn away and welcome her dear Emma.

Emma's project of forgetting Mr. Elton for a while made her rather sorry to find, when they had all taken their places, that he was close to her. The difficulty was great of driving his strange insensibility towards Harriet, from her mind, while he not only sat at her elbow, but was continually obtruding his happy countenance on her notice, and solicitously addressing her upon every occasion. Instead of forgetting him, his behaviour was such that she could not avoid the internal suggestion of "Can it really be as my brother imagined? can it be possible for this man to be beginning to transfer his affections from Harriet to me? – Absurd and insufferable!" Yet he would be so anxious for her being perfectly warm, would be so interested about her father, and so delighted with Mrs. Weston; and at last would begin admiring her drawings with so much zeal and so little knowledge as seemed terribly like a would be lover, and made it some effort with her to preserve her good manners. For her own sake she could not be rude; and for Harriet's, in the hope that all would yet turn out right, she was even positively civil; but it was an effort; especially as something was going on amongst the others, in the most overpowering period of Mr. Elton's nonsense, which she particularly wished to listen to. She heard enough to know that Mr. Weston was giving some information about his son; she heard the words "my son," and "Frank," and "my son," repeated several times over; and, from a few other half syllables very much suspected that he was announcing an early visit from his son; but before she could quiet Mr. Elton, the subject was so completely past that any reviving question from her would have been awkward.

Now, it so happened that in spite of Emma's resolution of never marrying, there was something in the name, in the idea of Mr. Frank Churchill, which always interested her. She had frequently thought – especially since his father's marriage with Miss Taylor – that if she were to marry, he was the very person to suit her in age, character and condition. He seemed by this connection between the families, quite to belong to her. She could not but suppose it to be a match that everybody who knew them must think of. That Mr. and Mrs. Weston did think of it, she was very strongly persuaded; and though not meaning to be induced by him, or by anybody else, to give up a situation which she believed more replete with good than any she could change it for, she had a great curiosity to see him, a decided intention of finding him pleasant, of being liked by him to a certain degree, and a sort of pleasure in the idea of their being coupled in their friends' imaginations.

With such sensations, Mr. Elton's civilities were dreadfully ill-timed; but she had the comfort of appearing very polite, while feeling very cross and of thinking that the rest of the visit could not possibly pass without bringing forward the same information again, or the substance of it, from the open hearted Mr. Weston. So it proved; for when happily released from Mr. Elton, and seated by Mr. Weston, at dinner, he made use of the very first interval in the cares of hospitality, the very first leisure from the saddle of mutton, to say to her:

"We want only two more to be just the right number. I should like to see two more here, your pretty little friend, Miss Smith, and my son – and then I should say we were quite complete. I believe you did not hear me telling the others in the drawing room that we are expecting Frank. I had a letter from him this morning, and he will be with us within a fortnight."

Emma spoke with a very proper degree of pleasure; and fully assented to his proposition of Mr. Frank Churchill and Miss Smith making their party quite complete.

"He has been wanting to come to us," continued Mr. Weston, "ever since September: every letter has been full of it; but he cannot command his own time. He has those to please who must be pleased, and who (between ourselves) are sometimes to be pleased only by a good many sacrifices. But now I have no doubt of seeing him here about the second week in January."

"What a very great pleasure it will be to you! and Mrs. Weston is so anxious to be acquainted with him, that she must be almost as happy as yourself."

"Yes, she would be, but that she thinks there will be another put off. She does not depend upon his coming so much as I do; but she does not know the parties so well as I do. The case, you see, is – (but this is quite between ourselves: I did not mention a syllable of it in the other room. There are secrets in all families, you know) – The case is, that a party of friends are invited to pay a visit at Enscombe in January; and that Frank's coming depends upon their being put off. If they are not put off, he cannot stir. But I know they will, because it is a family that a certain lady, of some consequence, at Enscombe, has a particular dislike to: and though it is thought necessary to invite them once in two or three years, they always are put off when it comes to the point. I have not the smallest doubt of the issue. I am as confident of seeing Frank here before the middle of January, as I am of being here myself: but your good friend there (nodding towards the upper end of the table) has so few vagaries herself, and has been so little used to them at Hartfield, that she cannot calculate on their effects, as I have been long in the practice of doing."

"I am sorry there should be any thing like doubt in the case," replied Emma; "but am disposed to side with you, Mr. Weston. If you think he will come, I shall think so too; for you know Enscombe."

"Yes – I have some right to that knowledge; though I have never been at the place in my life. She is an odd woman! But I never allow myself to speak ill of her, on Frank's account; for I do believe her to be very fond of him. I used to think she was not capable of being fond of anybody, except herself: but she has always been kind to him (in her way – allowing for little whims and caprices, and expecting everything to be as she likes). And it is no small credit, in my opinion, to him, that he should excite such an affection; for, though I would not say it to anybody else, she has no more heart than a stone to people in general; and the devil of a temper."

Emma liked the subject so well, that she began upon it, to Mrs. Weston, very soon after their moving into the drawing-room: wishing her joy – yet observing, that she knew the first meeting must be rather alarming. Mrs. Weston agreed to it; but added, that she should be very glad to be secure of undergoing the anxiety of a first meeting at the time talked of: "for I cannot depend upon his coming. I cannot be so sanguine as Mr. Weston. I am very much afraid that it will all end in nothing. Mr. Weston, I dare say, has been telling you exactly how the matter stands?"

"Yes it seems to depend upon nothing but the ill humour of Mrs. Churchill, which I imagine to be the most certain thing in the world."

"My Emma!" replied Mrs. Weston, smiling, "what is the certainty of caprice?" Then turning to Isabella, who had not been attending before – "You must know, my dear Mrs. Knightley, that we are by no means so sure of seeing Mr. Frank Churchill, in my opinion, as his father thinks. It depends entirely upon his aunt's spirits and pleasure; in short, upon her temper. To you – to my two daughters – I may venture on the truth. Mrs. Churchill rules at Enscombe, and is a very odd-tempered woman; and his coming now, depends upon her being willing to spare him."

"Oh, Mrs. Churchill; everybody knows Mrs. Churchill," replied Isabella: "and I am sure I never think of that poor young man without the greatest compassion. To be constantly living with an ill-tempered person, must be dreadful. It is what we happily have never known any thing of; but it must be a life of misery. What a blessing, that she never had any children! Poor little creatures, how unhappy she would have made them!"

Emma wished she had been alone with Mrs. Weston. She should then have heard more: Mrs. Weston would speak to her, with a degree of unreserve which she would not hazard with

Isabella; and, she really believed, would scarcely try to conceal any thing relative to the Churchills from her, excepting those views on the young man, of which her own imagination had already given her such instinctive knowledge. But at present there was nothing more to be said. Mr. Woodhouse very soon followed them into the drawing-room. To be sitting long after dinner, was a confinement that he could not endure. Neither wine nor conversation was any thing to him; and gladly did he move to those with whom he was always comfortable.

While he talked to Isabella, however, Emma found an opportunity of saying:

"And so you do not consider this visit from your son as by any means certain. I am sorry for it. The introduction must be unpleasant, whenever it takes place; and the sooner it could be over, the better."

"Yes; and every delay makes one more apprehensive of other delays. Even if this family, the Braithwaites, are put off, I am still afraid that some excuse may be found for disappointing us. I cannot bear to imagine any reluctance on his side; but I am sure there is a great wish on the Churchills' to keep him to themselves. There is jealousy. They are jealous even of his regard for his father. In short, I can feel no dependence on his coming, and I wish Mr. Weston were less sanguine."

"He ought to come," said Emma. "If he could stay only a couple of days, he ought to come; and one can hardly conceive a young man's not having it in his power to do as much as that. A young *woman*, if she fall into bad hands, may be teased, and kept at a distance from those she wants to be with; but one cannot comprehend a young *man's* being under such restraint, as not to be able to spend a week with his father, if he likes it."

"One ought to be at Enscombe, and know the ways of the family, before one decides upon what he can do," replied Mrs. Weston. "One ought to use the same caution, perhaps, in judging of the conduct of any one individual of any one family; but Enscombe, I believe, certainly must not be judged by general rules: *she* is so very unreasonable; and everything gives way to her."

"But she is so fond of the nephew: he is so very great a favourite. Now, according to my idea of Mrs. Churchill, it would be most natural, that while she makes no sacrifice for the comfort of the husband, to whom she owes everything, while she exercises incessant caprice towards him, she should frequently be governed by the nephew, to whom she owes nothing at all."

"My dearest Emma, do not pretend, with your sweet temper, to understand a bad one, or to lay down rules for it: you must let it go its own way. I have no doubt of his having, at times, considerable influence; but it may be perfectly impossible for him to know beforehand *when* it will be."

Emma listened, and then coolly said, "I shall not be satisfied, unless he comes."

"He may have a great deal of influence on some points," continued Mrs. Weston, "and on others, very little: and among those, on which she is beyond his reach, it is but too likely, may be this very circumstance of his coming away from them to visit us."

# Chapter 15

MR. WOODHOUSE was soon ready for his tea; and when he had drank his tea he was quite ready to go home; and it was as much as his three companions could do, to entertain away his notice of the lateness of the hour, before the other gentlemen appeared. Mr. Weston was chatty and convivial, and no friend to early separations of any sort; but at last the drawing room party did receive an augmentation. Mr. Elton, in very good spirits, was one of the first to walk in. Mrs. Weston and Emma were sitting together on a sofa. He joined them immediately, and, with scarcely an invitation, seated himself between them.

Emma, in good spirits too, from the amusement afforded her mind by the expectation of Mr. Frank Churchill, was willing to forget his late improprieties, and be as well satisfied with him as before, and on his making Harriet his very first subject, was ready to listen with most friendly smiles.

He professed himself extremely anxious about her fair friend – her fair, lovely, amiable friend. "Did she know? – had she heard any thing about her, since their being at Randalls? – he felt much anxiety – he must confess that the nature of her complaint alarmed him considerably." And in this style he talked on for some time very properly, not much attending to any answer, but altogether sufficiently awake to the terror of a bad sore throat; and Emma was quite in charity with him.

But at last there seemed a perverse turn; it seemed all at once as if he were more afraid of its being a bad sore throat on her account, than on Harriet's – more anxious that she should escape the infection, than that there should be no infection in the complaint. He began with great earnestness to entreat her to refrain from visiting the sick chamber again, for the present to entreat her to *promise him* not to venture into such hazard till he had seen Mr. Perry and learnt his opinion; and though she tried to laugh it off and bring the subject back into its proper course, there was no putting an end to his extreme solicitude about her. She was vexed. It did appear – there was no concealing it – exactly like the pretence of being in love with her, instead of Harriet; an inconstancy, if real, the most contemptible and abominable! and she had difficulty in behaving with temper. He turned to Mrs. Weston to implore her assistance, "Would not she give him her support? – would not she add her persuasions to his, to induce Miss Woodhouse not to go to Mrs. Goddard's till it were certain that Miss Smith's disorder had no infection? He could not be satisfied without a promise – would not she give him her influence in procuring it?"

"So scrupulous for others," he continued, "and yet so careless for herself! She wanted me to nurse my cold by staying at home to day, and yet will not promise to avoid the danger of catching an ulcerated sore throat herself. Is this fair, Mrs. Weston? Judge between us. Have not I some right to complain? I am sure of your kind support and aid."

Emma saw Mrs. Weston's surprise, and felt that it must be great, at an address which, in words and manner, was assuming to himself the right of first interest in her; and as for herself, she was too much provoked and offended to have the power of directly saying any thing to the purpose. She could only give him a look; but it was such a look as she thought must restore him to his senses, and then left the sofa, removing to a seat by her sister, and giving her all her attention.

She had not time to know how Mr. Elton took the reproof, so rapidly did another subject succeed; for Mr. John Knightley now came into the room from examining the weather, and opened on them all with the information of the ground being covered with snow, and of its still snowing fast, with a strong drifting wind; concluding with these words to Mr. Woodhouse:

"This will prove a spirited beginning of your winter engagements, sir. Something new for your coachman and horses to be making their way through a storm of snow."

Poor Mr. Woodhouse was silent from consternation; but everybody else had something to say; everybody was either surprised or not surprised, and had some question to ask, or some comfort to offer. Mrs. Weston and Emma tried earnestly to cheer him and turn his attention from his son-in-law, who was pursuing his triumph rather unfeelingly.

"I admired your resolution very much, sir," said he, "in venturing out in such weather, for of course you saw there would be snow very soon. Everybody must have seen the snow coming on. I admired your spirit; and I dare say we shall get home very well. Another hour or two's snow can hardly make the road impassable; and we have two carriages; if *one* is blown over in the bleak part of the common field there will be the other at hand. I dare say we shall be all safe at Hartfield before midnight."

Mr. Weston, with triumph of a different sort, was confessing that he had known it to be snowing some time, but had not said a word, lest it should make Mr. Woodhouse uncomfortable, and be an excuse for his hurrying away. As to there being any quantity of snow fallen or likely to fall to impede their return, that was a mere joke; he was afraid they would find no difficulty. He wished the road might be impassable, that he might be able to keep them all at Randalls; and with the utmost good will was sure that accommodation might be found for everybody, calling on his wife to agree with him, that with a little contrivance, everybody might be lodged, which she hardly knew how to do, from the consciousness of there being but two spare rooms in the house.

"What is to be done, my dear Emma? what is to be done?" was Mr. Woodhouse's first exclamation, and all that he could say for some time. To her he looked for comfort; and her assurances of safety, her representation of the excellence of the horses, and of James, and of their having so many friends about them, revived him a little.

His eldest daughter's alarm was equal to his own. The horror of being blocked up at Randalls, while her children were at

Hartfield, was full in her imagination; and fancying the road to be now just passable for adventurous people, but in a state that admitted no delay, she was eager to have it settled, that her father and Emma should remain at Randalls, while she and her husband set forward instantly through all the possible accumulations of drifted snow that might impede them.

"You had better order the carriage directly, my love," said she; "I dare say we shall be able to get along, if we set off directly; and if we do come to any thing very bad, I can get out and walk. I am not at all afraid. I should not mind walking half the way. I could change my shoes, you know, the moment I got home; and it is not the sort of thing that gives me cold."

"Indeed!" replied he. "Then, my dear Isabella, it is the most extraordinary sort of thing in the world, for in general everything does give you cold. Walk home! you are prettily shod for walking home, I dare say. It will be bad enough for the horses."

Isabella turned to Mrs. Weston for her approbation of the plan. Mrs. Weston could only approve. Isabella then went to Emma; but Emma could not so entirely give up the hope of their being all able to get away; and they were still discussing the point, when Mr. Knightley, who had left the room immediately after his brother's first report of the snow, came back again, and told them that he had been out-of-doors to examine, and could answer for there not being the smallest difficulty in their getting home, whenever they liked it, either now or an hour hence. He had gone beyond the sweep – some way along the Highbury road – the snow was nowhere above half an inch deep – in many places hardly enough to whiten the ground; a very few flakes were falling at present, but the clouds were parting, and there was every appearance of its being soon over. He had seen the coachmen, and they both agreed with him in there being nothing to apprehend.

To Isabella, the relief of such tidings was very great, and they were scarcely less acceptable to Emma on her father's account, who was immediately set as much at ease on the subject as his nervous constitution allowed; but the alarm that had been raised could not be appeased so as to admit of any comfort for him while he continued at Randalls. He was satisfied of there being no present danger in returning home, but no assurances could convince him that it was safe to stay; and while the others were variously urging and recommending, Mr. Knightley and Emma settled it in a few brief sentences, thus:

"Your father will not be easy; why do not you go?"

"I am ready, if the others are."

"Shall I ring the bell?"

"Yes, do."

And the bell was rung, and the carriages spoken for. A few minutes more, and Emma hoped to see one troublesome companion deposited in his own house, to get sober and cool, and the other recover his temper and happiness when this visit of hardship were over.

The carriage came; and Mr. Woodhouse, always the first object on such occasions, was carefully attended to his own by Mr. Knightley and Mr. Weston; but not all that either could say could prevent some renewal of alarm at the sight of the snow which had actually fallen, and the discovery of a much darker night than he had been prepared for. "He was afraid they should have a very bad drive. He was afraid poor Isabella would not like it. And there would be poor Emma in the carriage behind. He did not know what they had best do. They must keep as much together as they could;" and James was talked to, and given a charge to go very slow and wait for the other carriage.

Isabella stepped in after her father; John Knightley, forgetting that he did not belong to their party, stepped in after his wife very naturally; so that Emma found, on being escorted and followed into the second carriage by Mr. Elton, that the door was to be lawfully shut on them, and that they were to have a *tête-à-tête* drive. It would not have been the awkwardness of a moment, it would have been rather a pleasure, previous to the suspicions of this very day; she could have talked to him of Harriet, and the three-quarters of a mile would have seemed but one. But now, she would rather it had not happened. She believed he had been drinking too much of Mr. Weston's good wine, and felt sure that he would want to be talking nonsense.

To restrain him as much as might be, by her own manners, she was immediately preparing to speak with exquisite calmness and gravity of the weather and the night; but scarcely had she begun, scarcely had they passed the sweep-gate and joined the other carriage, than she found her subject cut up – her hand seized – her attention demanded, and Mr. Elton actually making violent love to her: availing himself of the precious opportunity, declaring sentiments which must be already well known, hoping – fearing – adoring – ready to die if she refused him; but flattering himself that his ardent attachment and unequalled love and unexampled passion could not fail of having some effect, and in short, very much resolved on being seriously accepted as soon as possible. It really was so. Without scruple – without apology – without much apparent diffidence, Mr. Elton, the lover of Harriet, was professing himself her lover. She tried to stop him; but vainly; he would go on, and say it all. Angry as she was, the thought of the moment made her resolve to restrain herself when she did speak. She felt that half this folly must be drunkenness, and therefore could hope that it might belong only to the passing hour. Accordingly, with a mixture of the serious and the playful, which she hoped would best suit his half-and-half state, she replied:

"I am very much astonished, Mr. Elton. This to *me!* you forget yourself you take me for my friend any message to Miss Smith I shall be happy to deliver; but no more of this to *me,* if you please."

"Miss Smith! message to Miss Smith! What could she possibly mean!" And he repeated her words with such assurance of accent, such boastful pretence of amazement, that she could not help replying with quickness:

"Mr. Elton, this is the most extraordinary conduct! and I can account for it only in one way; you are not yourself, or you could not speak either to me, or of Harriet, in such a manner. Command yourself enough to say no more, and I will endeavour to forget it."

But Mr. Elton had only drunk wine enough to elevate his spirits, not at all to confuse his intellects. He perfectly knew his own meaning; and having warmly protested against her suspicion as most injurious, and slightly touched upon his respect for Miss Smith as her friend, but acknowledging his wonder that Miss Smith should be mentioned at all, he resumed the subject of his own passion, and was very urgent for a favourable answer.

As she thought less of his inebriety, she thought more of his inconstancy and presumption; and with fewer struggles for politeness, replied:

"It is impossible for me to doubt any longer. You have made yourself too clear. Mr. Elton, my astonishment is much beyond any thing I can express. After such behaviour, as I have witnessed during the last month, to Miss Smith – such attentions as I have been in the daily habit of observing – to be addressing me in this manner this is an unsteadiness of character, indeed, which I had not supposed possible! Believe me, sir, I am far, very far, from gratified in being the object of such professions."

"Good Heavens!" cried Mr. Elton, "what can be the meaning of this? Miss Smith! I never thought of Miss Smith in the whole course of my existence, never paid her any attentions, but as your friend: never cared whether she were dead or alive. If she has fancied otherwise, her own wishes have misled her, and I am very sorry extremely sorry But, Miss Smith, indeed! Oh! Miss Woodhouse! who can think of Miss Smith, when Miss Woodhouse is near! No, upon my honour, there is no unsteadiness of character. I have thought only of you. I protest against having paid the smallest attention to any one else. Everything that I have said or done, for many weeks past, has been with the sole view of marking my adoration of yourself. You cannot really, seriously, doubt it. No! (in an accent meant to be insinuating) I am sure you have seen and understood me."

It would be impossible to say what Emma felt, on hearing this which of all her unpleasant sensations was uppermost. She was too completely overpowered to be immediately able to reply: and two moments of silence being ample encouragement for Mr. Elton's sanguine state of mind, he tried to take her hand again, as he joyously exclaimed:

"Charming Miss Woodhouse! allow me to interpret this interesting silence. It confesses that you have long understood me."

"No, sir," cried Emma, "it confesses no such thing. So far from having long understood you, I have been in a most complete error with respect to your views, till this moment. As to myself, I am very sorry that you should have been giving way to any feelings Nothing could be farther from my wishes – your attachment to my friend Harriet – your pursuit of her, (pursuit, it appeared,) gave me great pleasure, and I have been very earnestly wishing you success; but had I supposed that she were not your attraction to Hartfield, I should certainly have thought you judged ill in making your visits so frequent. Am I to believe that you have never sought to recommend yourself particularly to Miss Smith – that you have never thought seriously of her?"

"Never, madam," cried he, affronted in his turn: "never, I assure you. I think seriously of Miss Smith! Miss Smith is a very good sort of girl; and I should be happy to see her respectably settled. I wish her extremely well: and, no doubt, there are men who might not object to – everybody has their level: but as for myself, I am not, I think, quite so much at a loss. I need not so totally despair of an equal alliance, as to be addressing myself to Miss Smith! No, madam, my visits to Hartfield have been for yourself only; and the encouragement I received – "

"Encouragement! I give you encouragement! Sir, you have been entirely mistaken in supposing it. I have seen you only as the admirer of my friend. In no other light could you have been more to me than a common acquaintance. I am exceedingly sorry: but it is well that the mistake ends where it does. Had the same behaviour continued, Miss Smith might have been led into a misconception of your views; not being aware, probably, any more than myself, of the very great inequality which you are so sensible of. But, as it is, the disappointment is single, and, I trust, will not be lasting. I have no thoughts of matrimony at present."

He was too angry to say another word; her manner too decided to invite supplication; and in this state of swelling resentment, and mutually deep mortification, they had to continue together a few minutes longer, for the fears of Mr. Woodhouse had confined them to a foot pace. If there had not been so much anger, there would have been desperate awkwardness; but their straightforward emotions left no room for the little zigzags of embarrassment. Without knowing when the carriage turned into Vicarage Lane, or when it stopped, they found themselves, all at once, at the door of his house; and he was out before another syllable passed. Emma then felt it indispensable to wish him a good night. The compliment was just returned, coldly and proudly; and, under indescribable irritation of spirits, she was then conveyed to Hartfield.

There she was welcomed, with the utmost delight, by her father, who had been trembling for the dangers of a solitary drive from Vicarage Lane – turning a corner which he could never bear to think of – and in strange hands – a mere common coachman – no James; and there it seemed as if her return only were wanted to make everything go well: for Mr. John Knightley, ashamed of his ill humour, was now all kindness and attention; and so particularly solicitous for the comfort of her father, as to seem – if not quite ready to join him in a basin of gruel – perfectly sensible of its being exceedingly wholesome; and the day was concluding in peace and comfort to all their little party, except herself. But her mind had never been in such perturbation; and it needed a very strong effort to appear attentive and cheerful till the usual hour of separating allowed her the relief of quiet reflection.

# Chapter 16

THE HAIR was curled, and the maid sent away, and Emma sat down to think and be miserable. It was a wretched business indeed! Such an overthrow of everything she had been wishing for! Such a development of everything most unwelcome! Such a blow for Harriet! – that was the worst of all. Every part of it brought pain and humiliation, of some sort or other; but, compared with the evil to Harriet, all was light; and she would gladly have submitted to feel yet more mistaken – more in error – more disgraced by misjudgment, than she actually was, could the effects of her blunders have been confined to herself.

"If I had not persuaded Harriet into liking the man, I could have borne any thing. He might have doubled his presumption to me – but poor Harriet!"

How she could have been so deceived! He protested that he had never thought seriously of Harriet – never! She looked back as well as she could; but it was all confusion. She had taken up the idea, she supposed, and made everything bend to it. His manners, however, must have been unmarked, wavering, dubious, or she could not have been so misled.

The picture! How eager he had been about the picture! and the charade! and an hundred other circumstances; how clearly they had seemed to point at Harriet. To be sure, the charade, with its "ready wit" – but then the "soft eyes" – in fact it suited neither;

it was a jumble without taste or truth. Who could have seen through such thick headed nonsense?

Certainly she had often, especially of late, thought his manners to herself unnecessarily gallant; but it had passed as his way, as a mere error of judgment, of knowledge, of taste, as one proof among others that he had not always lived in the best society, that with all the gentleness of his address, true elegance was sometimes wanting; but, till this very day, she had never, for an instant, suspected it to mean any thing but grateful respect to her as Harriet's friend.

To Mr. John Knightley was she indebted for her first idea on the subject, for the first start of its possibility. There was no denying that those brothers had penetration. She remembered what Mr. Knightley had once said to her about Mr. Elton, the caution he had given, the conviction he had professed that Mr. Elton would never marry indiscreetly; and blushed to think how much truer a knowledge of his character had been there shown than any she had reached herself. It was dreadfully mortifying; but Mr. Elton was proving himself, in many respects, the very reverse of what she had meant and believed him – proud, assuming, conceited; very full of his own claims, and little concerned about the feelings of others.

Contrary to the usual course of things, Mr. Elton's wanting to pay his addresses to her had sunk him in her opinion. His professions and his proposals did him no service. She thought nothing of his attachment, and was insulted by his hopes. He wanted to marry well, and having the arrogance to raise his eyes to her, pretended to be in love; but she was perfectly easy as to his not suffering any disappointment that need to be cared for. There had been no real affection either in his language or manners. Sighs and fine words had been given in abundance; but she could hardly devise any set of expressions, or fancy any tone of voice, less allied with real love. She need not trouble herself to pity him. He only wanted to aggrandise and enrich himself; and if Miss

Woodhouse of Hartfield, the heiress of thirty thousand pounds, were not quite so easily obtained as he had fancied, he would soon try for Miss Somebody else with twenty, or with ten.

But that he should talk of encouragement, should consider her as aware of his views, accepting his attentions, meaning (in short), to marry him! – should suppose himself her equal in connection or mind! – look down upon her friend, so well understanding the gradations of rank below him, and be so blind to what rose above, as to fancy himself showing no presumption in addressing her! – It was most provoking.

Perhaps it was not fair to expect him to feel how very much he was her inferior in talent, and all the elegancies of mind. The very want of such equality might prevent his perception of it; but he must know that in fortune and consequence she was greatly his superior. He must know that the Woodhouses had been settled for several generations at Hartfield, the younger branch of a very ancient family and that the Eltons were nobody. The landed property of Hartfield certainly was inconsiderable, being but a sort of notch in the Donwell Abbey estate, to which all the rest of Highbury belonged; but their fortune, from other sources, was such as to make them scarcely secondary to Donwell Abbey itself, in every other kind of consequence; and the Woodhouses had long held a high place in the consideration of the neighbourhood which Mr. Elton had first entered not two years ago, to make his way as he could, without any alliances but in trade, or any thing to recommend him to notice but his situation and his civility. But he had fancied her in love with him; that evidently must have been his dependence; and after raving a little about the seeming incongruity of gentle manners and a conceited head, Emma was obliged in common honesty to stop and admit that her own behaviour to him had been so complaisant and obliging, so full of courtesy and attention, as (supposing her real motive unperceived) might warrant a man of ordinary observation and delicacy, like Mr. Elton, in fancying himself a very decided favourite. If she had so misinterpreted his feelings, *she* had little right to wonder that *he,* with self-interest to blind him, should have mistaken hers.

The first error and the worst lay at her door. It was foolish, it was wrong, to take so active a part in bringing any two people together. It was adventuring too far, assuming too much, making light of what ought to be serious – a trick of what ought to be simple. She was quite concerned and ashamed, and resolved to do such things no more.

"Here have I," said she, "actually talked poor Harriet into being very much attached to this man. She might never have thought of him but for me; and certainly never would have thought of him with hope, if I had not assured her of his attachment, for she is as modest and humble as I used to think him. Oh! that I had been satisfied with persuading her not to accept young Martin. There I was quite right. That was well done of me; but there I should have stopped, and left the rest to time and chance. I was introducing her into good company, and giving her the opportunity of pleasing some one worth having; I ought not to have attempted more. But now, poor girl, her peace is cut up for some time. I have been but half a friend to her; and if she were not to feel this disappointment so very much, I am sure I have not an idea of anybody else who would be at all desirable for her; William Coxe – Oh! no, I could not endure William Coxe – a pert young lawyer."

She stopped to blush and laugh at her own relapse, and then resumed a more serious, more dispiriting cogitation upon what had been, and might be, and must be. The distressing explanation she had to make to Harriet, and all that poor Harriet would be suffering, with the awkwardness of future meetings, the difficulties of continuing or discontinuing the acquaintance, of subduing feelings, concealing resentment, and avoiding éclat, were enough to occupy her in most unmirthful reflections some time longer, and she went to bed at last with nothing settled but the conviction of her having blundered most dreadfully.

To youth and natural cheerfulness like Emma's, though under

temporary gloom at night, the return of day will hardly fail to bring return of spirits. The youth and cheerfulness of morning are in happy analogy, and of powerful operation; and if the distress be not poignant enough to keep the eyes unclosed, they will be sure to open to sensations of softened pain and brighter hope.

Emma got up on the morrow more disposed for comfort than she had gone to bed, more ready to see alleviations of the evil before her, and to depend on getting tolerably out of it.

It was a great consolation that Mr. Elton should not be really in love with her, or so particularly amiable as to make it shocking to disappoint him that Harriet's nature should not be of that superior sort in which the feelings are most acute and retentive and that there could be no necessity for anybody's knowing what had passed except the three principals, and especially for her father's being given a moment's uneasiness about it.

These were very cheering thoughts; and the sight of a great deal of snow on the ground did her further service, for any thing was welcome that might justify their all three being quite asunder at present.

The weather was most favourable for her; though Christmas Day, she could not go to church. Mr. Woodhouse would have been miserable had his daughter attempted it, and she was therefore safe from either exciting or receiving unpleasant and most unsuitable ideas. The ground covered with snow, and the atmosphere in that unsettled state between frost and thaw, which is of all others the most unfriendly for exercise, every morning beginning in rain or snow, and every evening setting in to freeze, she was for many days a most honourable prisoner. No intercourse with Harriet possible but by note; no church for her on Sunday any more than on Christmas Day; and no need to find excuses for Mr. Elton's absenting himself.

It was weather which might fairly confine everybody at home; and though she hoped and believed him to be really taking comfort in some society or other, it was very pleasant to have her father so well satisfied with his being all alone in his own house, too wise to stir out; and to hear him say to Mr. Knightley, whom no weather could keep entirely from them,

"Ah! Mr. Knightley, why do not you stay at home like poor Mr. Elton?"

These days of confinement would have been, but for her private perplexities, remarkably comfortable, as such seclusion exactly suited her brother, whose feelings must always be of great importance to his companions; and he had, besides, so thoroughly cleared off his ill humour at Randalls, that his amiableness never failed him during the rest of his stay at Hartfield. He was always agreeable and obliging, and speaking pleasantly of everybody. But with all the hopes of cheerfulness, and all the present comfort of delay, there was still such an evil hanging over her in the hour of explanation with Harriet, as made it impossible for Emma to be ever perfectly at ease.

# Chapter 17

Mr. and Mrs. John Knightley were not detained long at Hartfield. The weather soon improved enough for those to move who must move; and Mr. Woodhouse having, as usual, tried to persuade his daughter to stay behind with all her children, was obliged to see the whole party set off, and return to his lamentations over the destiny of poor Isabella; which poor Isabella – passing her life with those she doted on, full of their merits, blind to their faults, and always innocently busy, might have been a model of right feminine happiness.

The evening of the very day on which they went brought a

note from Mr. Elton to Mr. Woodhouse, a long, civil, ceremonious note, to say, with Mr. Elton's best compliments: "that he was proposing to leave Highbury the following morning in his way to Bath; where, in compliance with the pressing entreaties of some friends, he had engaged to spend a few weeks, and very much regretted the impossibility he was under, from various circumstances of weather and business, of taking a personal leave of Mr. Woodhouse, of whose friendly civilities he should ever retain a grateful sense and had Mr. Woodhouse any commands, should be happy to attend to them."

Emma was most agreeably surprised. Mr. Elton's absence just at this time was the very thing to be desired. She admired him for contriving it, though not able to give him much credit for the manner in which it was announced. Resentment could not have been more plainly spoken than in a civility to her father, from which she was so pointedly excluded. She had not even a share in his opening compliments. Her name was not mentioned; and there was so striking a change in all this, and such an ill-judged solemnity of leave taking in his graceful acknowledgments, as she thought, at first, could not escape her father's suspicion.

It did, however. Her father was quite taken up with the surprise of so sudden a journey, and his fears that Mr. Elton might never get safely to the end of it, and saw nothing extraordinary in his language. It was a very useful note, for it supplied them with fresh matter for thought and conversation during the rest of their lonely evening. Mr. Woodhouse talked over his alarms, and Emma was in spirits to persuade them away with all her usual promptitude.

She now resolved to keep Harriet no longer in the dark. She had reason to believe her nearly recovered from her cold, and it was desirable that she should have as much time as possible for getting the better of her other complaint before the gentleman's return. She went to Mrs. Goddard's accordingly the very next day, to undergo the necessary penance of communication; and a severe one it was. She had to destroy all the hopes which she had been so industriously feeding to appear in the ungracious character of the one preferred and acknowledge herself grossly mistaken and misjudging in all her ideas on one subject, all her observations, all her convictions, all her prophecies for the last six weeks.

The confession completely renewed her first shame and the sight of Harriet's tears made her think that she should never be in charity with herself again.

Harriet bore the intelligence very well blaming nobody and in everything testifying such an ingenuousness of disposition and lowly opinion of herself, as must appear with particular advantage at that moment to her friend.

Emma was in the humour to value simplicity and modesty to the utmost; and all that was amiable, all that ought to be attaching, seemed on Harriet's side, not her own. Harriet did not consider herself as having any thing to complain of. The affection of such a man as Mr. Elton would have been too great a distinction. She never could have deserved him and nobody but so partial and kind a friend as Miss Woodhouse would have thought it possible.

Her tears fell abundantly but her grief was so truly artless, that no dignity could have made it more respectable in Emma's eyes and she listened to her and tried to console her with all her heart and understanding – really for the time convinced that Harriet was the superior creature of the two and that to resemble her would be more for her own welfare and happiness than all that genius or intelligence could do.

It was rather too late in the day to set about being simple-minded and ignorant; but she left her with every previous resolution confirmed of being humble and discreet, and repressing imagination all the rest of her life. Her second duty now, inferior only to her father's claims, was to promote Harriet's comfort, and endeavour to prove her own affection in some better method than by match-making. She got her to Hartfield, and showed her the most unvarying kindness, striving to occupy and amuse her, and by books and conversation, to drive Mr. Elton from her thoughts.

Time, she knew, must be allowed for this being thoroughly done; and she could suppose herself but an indifferent judge of such matters in general, and very inadequate to sympathise in an attachment to Mr. Elton in particular; but it seemed to her reasonable that at Harriet's age, and with the entire extinction of all hope, such a progress might be made towards a state of composure by the time of Mr. Elton's return, as to allow them all to meet again in the common routine of acquaintance, without any danger of betraying sentiments or increasing them.

Harriet did think him all perfection, and maintained the non-existence of anybody equal to him in person or goodness and did, in truth, prove herself more resolutely in love than Emma had foreseen; but yet it appeared to her so natural, so inevitable to strive against an inclination of that sort *unrequited*, that she could not comprehend its continuing very long in equal force.

If Mr. Elton, on his return, made his own indifference as evident and indubitable as she could not doubt he would anxiously do, she could not imagine Harriet's persisting to place her happiness in the sight or the recollection of him.

Their being fixed, so absolutely fixed, in the same place, was bad for each, for all three. Not one of them had the power of removal, or of effecting any material change of society. They must encounter each other, and make the best of it.

Harriet was farther unfortunate in the tone of her companions at Mrs. Goddard's; Mr. Elton being the adoration of all the teachers and great girls in the school; and it must be at Hartfield only that she could have any chance of hearing him spoken of with cooling moderation or repellent truth. Where the wound had been given, there must the cure be found if anywhere; and Emma felt that, till she saw her in the way of cure, there could be no true peace for herself.

## Chapter 18

MR. FRANK Churchill did not come. When the time proposed drew near, Mrs. Weston's fears were justified in the arrival of a letter of excuse. For the present, he could not be spared, to his "very great mortification and regret; but still he looked forward with the hope of coming to Randalls at no distant period."

Mrs. Weston was exceedingly disappointed – much more disappointed, in fact, than her husband, though her dependence on seeing the young man had been so much more sober: but a sanguine temper, though for ever expecting more good than occurs, does not always pay for its hopes by any proportionate depression. It soon flies over the present failure, and begins to hope again. For half an hour Mr. Weston was surprised and sorry; but then he began to perceive that Frank's coming two or three months later would be a much better plan; better time of the year; better weather; and that he would be able, without any doubt, to stay considerably longer with them than if he had come sooner.

These feelings rapidly restored his comfort, while Mrs. Weston, of a more apprehensive disposition, foresaw nothing but a repetition of excuses and delays; and after all her concern for what her husband was to suffer, suffered a great deal more herself.

Emma was not at this time in a state of spirits to care really about Mr. Frank Churchill's not coming, except as a disappointment at Randalls. The acquaintance at present had no charm for her. She wanted, rather, to be quiet, and out of temptation; but still, as it was desirable that she should appear, in general, like her usual self, she took care to express as much interest in the circumstance, and enter as warmly into Mr. and Mrs. Weston's disappointment, as might naturally belong to their friendship.

She was the first to announce it to Mr. Knightley; and exclaimed quite as much as was necessary, (or, being acting a part, perhaps rather more,) at the conduct of the Churchills, in keeping him away. She then proceeded to say a good deal more than she felt, of the advantage of such an addition to their confined society in Surrey; the pleasure of looking at somebody new; the gala-day to Highbury entire, which the sight of him would have made; and ending with reflections on the Churchills again, found herself directly involved in a disagreement with Mr. Knightley; and, to her great amusement, perceived that she was taking the other side of the question from her real opinion, and making use of Mrs. Weston's arguments against herself.

"The Churchills are very likely in fault," said Mr. Knightley, coolly; "but I dare say he might come if he would."

"I do not know why you should say so. He wishes exceedingly to come; but his uncle and aunt will not spare him."

"I cannot believe that he has not the power of coming, if he made a point of it. It is too unlikely, for me to believe it without proof."

"How odd you are! What has Mr. Frank Churchill done, to make you suppose him such an unnatural creature?"

"I am not supposing him at all an unnatural creature, in suspecting that he may have learnt to be above his connections, and to care very little for any thing but his own pleasure, from living with those who have always set him the example of it. It is a great deal more natural than one could wish, that a young man, brought up by those who are proud, luxurious, and selfish, should be proud, luxurious, and selfish too. If Frank Churchill had wanted to see his father, he would have contrived it between September and January. A man at his age – what is he? three or four-and-twenty – cannot be without the means of doing as much as that. It is impossible."

"That's easily said, and easily felt by you, who have always been your own master. You are the worst judge in the world, Mr. Knightley, of the difficulties of dependence. You do not know what it is to have tempers to manage."

"It is not to be conceived that a man of three or four-and-twenty should not have liberty of mind or limb to that amount. He cannot want money he cannot want leisure. We know, on the contrary, that he has so much of both, that he is glad to get rid of them at the idlest haunts in the kingdom. We hear of him for ever at some watering-place or other. A little while ago, he was at Weymouth. This proves that he can leave the Churchills."

"Yes, sometimes he can."

"And those times are whenever he thinks it worth his while; whenever there is any temptation of pleasure."

"It is very unfair to judge of anybody's conduct, without an intimate knowledge of their situation. Nobody, who has not been in the interior of a family, can say what the difficulties of any individual of that family may be. We ought to be acquainted with Enscombe, and with Mrs. Churchill's temper, before we pretend to decide upon what her nephew can do. He may, at times, be able to do a great deal more than he can at others."

"There is one thing, Emma, which a man can always do, if he chooses, and that is, his duty; not by manoeuvring and finessing, but by vigour and resolution. It is Frank Churchill's duty to pay this attention to his father. He knows it to be so, by his promises and messages; but if he wished to do it, it might be done. A man who felt rightly would say at once, simply and resolutely, to Mrs. Churchill 'Every sacrifice of mere pleasure you will always find me ready to make to your convenience; but I must go and see my father immediately. I know he would be hurt by my failing in such a mark of respect to him on the present occasion. I shall, therefore, set off to morrow.' If he would say so to her at once, in the tone of decision becoming a man, there would be no opposition made to his going."

"No," said Emma, laughing; "but perhaps there might be some made to his coming back again. Such language for a young man entirely dependent, to use! Nobody but you, Mr. Knightley, would imagine it possible. But you have not an idea of what is requisite in situations directly opposite to your own. Mr. Frank Churchill to be making such a speech as that to the uncle and aunt, who have brought him up, and are to provide for him! Standing up in the middle of the room, I suppose, and speaking as loud as he could! How can you imagine such conduct practicable?"

"Depend upon it, Emma, a sensible man would find no difficulty in it. He would feel himself in the right; and the declaration made, of course, as a man of sense would make it, in a proper manner would do him more good, raise him higher, fix his interest stronger with the people he depended on, than all that a line of shifts and expedients can ever do. Respect would be added to affection. They would feel that they could trust him; that the nephew who had done rightly by his father, would do rightly by them; for they know, as well as he does, as well as all the world must know, that he ought to pay this visit to his father; and while meanly exerting their power to delay it, are in their hearts not thinking the better of him for submitting to their whims. Respect for right conduct is felt by everybody. If he would act in this sort of manner, on principle, consistently, regularly, their little minds would bend to his."

"I rather doubt that. You are very fond of bending little minds; but where little minds belong to rich people in authority, I think they have a knack of swelling out, till they are quite as unmanageable as great ones. I can imagine, that if you, as you are, Mr. Knightley, were to be transported and placed all at once in Mr. Frank Churchill's situation, you would be able to say and do just what you have been recommending for him; and it might have a very good effect. The Churchills might not have a word to say in return; but then, you would have no habits of early obedience and long observance to break through. To him who has, it might not be so easy to burst forth at once into perfect independence, and set all their claims on his gratitude and regard at nought. He may have as strong a sense of what would be right, as you can have, without being so equal, under particular circumstances, to act up to it."

"Then it would not be so strong a sense. If it failed to produce equal exertion, it could not be an equal conviction."

"Oh, the difference of situation and habit! I wish you would try to understand what an amiable young man may be likely to feel in directly opposing those, whom as child and boy he has been looking up to all his life."

"Our amiable young man is a very weak young man, if this be the first occasion of his carrying through a resolution to do right against the will of others. It ought to have been a habit with him by this time, of following his duty, instead of consulting expediency. I can allow for the fears of the child, but not of the man. As he became rational, he ought to have roused himself and shaken off all that was unworthy in their authority. He ought to have opposed the first attempt on their side to make him slight his father. Had he begun as he ought, there would have been no difficulty now."

"We shall never agree about him," cried Emma; "but that is nothing extraordinary. I have not the least idea of his being a weak young man: I feel sure that he is not. Mr. Weston would not be blind to folly, though in his own son; but he is very likely to have a more yielding, complying, mild disposition than would suit your notions of man's perfection. I dare say he has; and though it may cut him off from some advantages, it will secure him many others."

"Yes; all the advantages of sitting still when he ought to move, and of leading a life of mere idle pleasure, and fancying himself extremely expert in finding excuses for it. He can sit down and write a fine flourishing letter, full of professions and falsehoods, and persuade himself that he has hit upon the very best method in the world of preserving peace at home and preventing his father's having any right to complain. His letters disgust me."

"Your feelings are singular. They seem to satisfy everybody else."

"I suspect they do not satisfy Mrs. Weston. They hardly can

satisfy a woman of her good sense and quick feelings: standing in a mother's place, but without a mother's affection to blind her. It is on her account that attention to Randalls is doubly due, and she must doubly feel the omission. Had she been a person of consequence herself, he would have come I dare say; and it would not have signified whether he did or no. Can you think your friend behindhand in these sort of considerations? Do you suppose she does not often say all this to herself? No, Emma, your amiable young man can be amiable only in French, not in English. He may be very 'amiable,' have very good manners, and be very agreeable; but he can have no English delicacy towards the feelings of other people – nothing really amiable about him."

"You seem determined to think ill of him."

"Me! not at all," replied Mr. Knightley, rather displeased; "I do not want to think ill of him. I should be as ready to acknowledge his merits as any other man; but I hear of none, except what are merely personal; that he is well-grown and good-looking, with smooth, plausible manners."

"Well, if he have nothing else to recommend him, he will be a treasure at Highbury. We do not often look upon fine young men, well bred and agreeable. We must not be nice and ask for all the virtues into the bargain. Cannot you imagine, Mr. Knightley, what a *sensation* his coming will produce? There will be but one subject throughout the parishes of Donwell and Highbury; but one interest – one object of curiosity; it will be all Mr. Frank Churchill; we shall think and speak of nobody else."

"You will excuse my being so much over powered. If I find him conversable, I shall be glad of his acquaintance; but if he is only a chattering coxcomb, he will not occupy much of my time or thoughts."

"My idea of him is, that he can adapt his conversation to the taste of everybody, and has the power as well as the wish of being universally agreeable. To you, he will talk of farming; to me, of drawing or music; and so on to everybody, having that general information on all subjects which will enable him to follow the lead, or take the lead, just as propriety may require, and to speak extremely well on each; that is my idea of him."

"And mine," said Mr. Knightley warmly, "is, that if he turn out anything like it, he will be the most insufferable fellow breathing! What! at three-and-twenty to be the king of his company – the great man – the practised politician, who is to read everybody's character, and make everybody's talents conduce to the display of his own superiority; to be dispensing his flatteries around, that he may make all appear like fools compared with himself! My dear Emma, your own good sense could not endure such a puppy when it came to the point."

"I will say no more about him," cried Emma – "you turn everything to evil. We are both prejudiced; you against, I for him; and we have no chance of agreeing till he is really here."

"Prejudiced! I am not prejudiced."

"But I am very much, and without being at all ashamed of it. My love for Mr. and Mrs. Weston gives me a decided prejudice in his favour."

"He is a person I never think of from one month's end to another," said Mr. Knightley, with a degree of vexation, which made Emma immediately talk of something else, though she could not comprehend why he should be angry.

To take a dislike to a young man, only because he appeared to be of a different disposition from himself, was unworthy the real liberality of mind which she was always used to acknowledge in him; for with all the high opinion of himself, which she had often laid to his charge, she had never before for a moment supposed it could make him unjust to the merit of another.

# Chapter 19

EMMA AND Harriet had been walking together one morning, and, in Emma's opinion, had been talking enough of Mr. Elton for that day. She could not think that Harriet's solace or her own sins required more; and she was therefore industriously getting rid of the subject as they returned; but it burst out again when she thought she had succeeded, and after speaking some time of what the poor must suffer in winter, and receiving no other answer than a very plaintive – "Mr. Elton is so good to the poor!" she found something else must be done.

They were just approaching the house where lived Mrs. and Miss Bates. She determined to call upon them and seek safety in numbers. There was always sufficient reason for such an attention; Mrs. and Miss Bates loved to be called on, and she knew she was considered by the very few who presumed ever to see imperfection in her, as rather negligent in that respect, and as not contributing what she ought to the stock of their scanty comforts.

She had had many a hint from Mr. Knightley and some from her own heart, as to her deficiency but none were equal to counteract the persuasion of its being very disagreeable – a waste of time – tiresome women – and all the horror of being in danger of falling in with the second rate and third rate of Highbury, who were calling on them for ever, and therefore she seldom went near them. But now she made the sudden resolution of not passing their door without going in observing, as she proposed it to Harriet, that, as well as she could calculate, they were just now quite safe from any letter from Jane Fairfax.

The house belonged to people in business. Mrs. and Miss Bates occupied the drawing-room floor; and there, in the very moderate-sized apartment, which was everything to them, the visitors were most cordially and even gratefully welcomed; the quiet neat old lady, who with her knitting was seated in the warmest corner, wanting even to give up her place to Miss Woodhouse, and her more active, talking daughter, almost ready to overpower them with care and kindness, thanks for their visit, solicitude for their shoes, anxious inquiries after Mr. Woodhouse's health, cheerful communications about her mother's, and sweet-cake from the beaufet[1]: "Mrs.Cole had just been there, just called in for ten minutes, and had been so good as to sit an hour with them, and she had taken a piece of cake and been so kind as to say she liked it very much; and, therefore, she hoped Miss Woodhouse and Miss Smith would do them the favour to eat a piece too."

The mention of the Coles was sure to be followed by that of Mr. Elton. There was intimacy between them, and Mr. Cole had heard from Mr. Elton since his going away. Emma knew what was coming; they must have the letter over again, and settle how long he had been gone, and how much he was engaged in company, and what a favourite he was wherever he went, and how full the Master of the Ceremonies' ball had been; and she went through it very well, with all the interest and all the commendation that could be requisite, and always putting forward to prevent Harriet's being obliged to say a word.

This she had been prepared for when she entered the house; but meant, having once talked him handsomely over, to be no farther incommoded by any troublesome topic, and to wander at large amongst all the Mistresses and Misses of Highbury, and their card-parties. She had not been prepared to have Jane Fairfax succeed Mr. Elton; but he was actually hurried off by Miss Bates, she jumped away from him at last abruptly to the Coles, to usher in a letter from her niece.

"Oh! Yes – Mr. Elton, I understand – certainly as to dancing – Mrs. Cole was telling me that dancing at the rooms at Bath was – Mrs. Cole was so kind as to sit some time with us, talking of Jane; for as soon as she came in, she began inquiring after her, Jane is so very great a favourite there. Whenever she is with us, Mrs. Cole does not know how to show her kindness enough; and

1 A kitchen sideboard.

I must say that Jane deserves it as much as anybody can. And so she began inquiring after her directly, saying, 'I know you cannot have heard from Jane lately, because it is not her time for writing;' and when I immediately said, 'But indeed we have, we had a letter this very morning,' I do not know that I ever saw anybody more surprised. 'Have you, upon your honour?' said she; 'well, that is quite unexpected. Do let me hear what she says.' "

Emma's politeness was at hand directly, to say, with smiling interest:

"Have you heard from Miss Fairfax so lately? I am extremely happy. I hope she is well?"

"Thank you. You are so kind!" replied the happily deceived aunt, while eagerly hunting for the letter. "Oh! here it is. I was sure it could not be far off; but I had put my huswife[1] upon it, you see, without being aware, and so it was quite hid, but I had it in my hand so very lately that I was almost sure it must be on the table. I was reading it to Mrs. Cole, and since she went away, I was reading it again to my mother, for it is such a pleasure to her – a letter from Jane – that she can never hear it often enough; so I knew it could not be far off, and here it is, only just under my huswife – and since you are so kind as to wish to hear what she says; but, first of all, I really must, in justice to Jane, apologise for her writing so short a letter – only two pages you see hardly two and in general she fills the whole paper and crosses half. My mother often wonders that I can make it out so well. She often says, when the letter is first opened, 'Well, Hetty, now I think you will be put to it to make out all that checker-work' – don't you, ma'am? And then I tell her, I am sure she would contrive to make it out herself, if she had nobody to do it for her every word of it – I am sure she would pore over it till she had made out every word. And, indeed, though my mother's eyes are not so good as they were, she can see amazingly well still, thank God! with the help of spectacles. It is such a blessing! My mother's are really very good indeed. Jane often says, when she is here, 'I

1 A small sewing case.

am sure, grandmama, you must have had very strong eyes to see as you do and so much fine work as you have done too! I only wish my eyes may last me as well.' "

All this spoken extremely fast obliged Miss Bates to stop for breath; and Emma said something very civil about the excellence of Miss Fairfax's handwriting.

"You are extremely kind," replied Miss Bates, highly gratified; "you who are such a judge, and write so beautifully yourself. I am sure there is nobody's praise that could give us so much pleasure as Miss Woodhouse's. My mother does not hear; she is a little deaf you know. Ma'am," addressing her, "do you hear what Miss Woodhouse is so obliging to say about Jane's handwriting?"

And Emma had the advantage of hearing her own silly compliment repeated twice over before the good old lady could comprehend it. She was pondering, in the meanwhile, upon the possibility, without seeming very rude, of making her escape from Jane Fairfax's letter, and had almost resolved on hurrying away directly under some slight excuse, when Miss Bates turned to her again and seized her attention.

"My mother's deafness is very trifling you see just nothing at all. By only raising my voice, and saying any thing two or three times over, she is sure to hear; but then she is used to my voice. But it is very remarkable that she should always hear Jane better than she does me. Jane speaks so distinct! However, she will not find her grandmama at all deafer than she was two years ago; which is saying a great deal at my mother's time of life and it really is full two years, you know, since she was here. We never were so long without seeing her before, and as I was telling Mrs. Cole, we shall hardly know how to make enough of her now."

"Are you expecting Miss Fairfax here soon?"

"Oh yes; next week."

"Indeed! that must be a very great pleasure."

"Thank you. You are very kind. Yes, next week. Everybody is so surprised; and everybody says the same obliging things. I am sure she will be as happy to see her friends at Highbury, as they can be to see her. Yes, Friday or Saturday; she cannot say which, because Colonel Campbell will be wanting the carriage himself one of those days. So very good of them to send her the whole way! But they always do, you know. Oh yes, Friday or Saturday next. That is what she writes about. That is the reason of her writing out of rule, as we call it; for, in the common course, we should not have heard from her before next Tuesday or Wednesday."

"Yes, so I imagined. I was afraid there could be little chance of my hearing any thing of Miss Fairfax to day."

"So obliging of you! No, we should not have heard, if it had not been for this particular circumstance, of her being to come here so soon. My mother is so delighted! for she is to be three months with us at least. Three months, she says so, positively, as I am going to have the pleasure of reading to you. The case is, you see, that the Campbells are going to Ireland. Mrs. Dixon has persuaded her father and mother to come over and see her directly. They had not intended to go over till the summer, but she is so impatient to see them again for till she married, last October, she was never away from them so much as a week, which must make it very strange to be in different kingdoms, I was going to say, but however different countries, and so she wrote a very urgent letter to her mother or her father – I declare I do not know which it was, but we shall see presently in Jane's letter – wrote in Mr. Dixon's name as well as her own, to press their coming over directly, and they would give them the meeting in Dublin, and take them back to their country-seat, Baly-craig – a beautiful place, I fancy. Jane has heard a great deal of its beauty; from Mr. Dixon, I mean – I do not know that she ever heard about it from anybody else; but it was very natural, you know, that he should like to speak of his own place while he was paying his addresses

– and as Jane used to be very often walking out with them – for Colonel and Mrs. Campbell were very particular about their daughter's not walking out often with only Mr. Dixon, for which I do not at all blame them; of course she heard everything he might be telling Miss Campbell about his own home in Ireland; and I think she wrote us word that he had shown them some drawings of the place, views that he had taken himself. He is a most amiable, charming young man, I believe. Jane was quite longing to go to Ireland, from his account of things."

At this moment, an ingenious and animating suspicion entering Emma's brain with regard to Jane Fairfax, this charming Mr. Dixon, and the not going to Ireland, she said, with the insidious design of farther discovery:

"You must feel it very fortunate that Miss Fairfax should be allowed to come to you at such a time. Considering the very particular friendship between her and Mrs. Dixon, you could hardly have expected her to be excused from accompanying Colonel and Mrs. Campbell."

"Very true, very true, indeed. The very thing that we have always been rather afraid of; for we should not have liked to have her at such a distance from us, for months together – not able to come if any thing was to happen. But you see, everything turns out for the best. They want her (Mr. and Mrs. Dixon) excessively to come over with Colonel and Mrs. Campbell; quite depend upon it; nothing can be more kind or pressing than their joint invitation, Jane says, as you will hear presently; Mr. Dixon does not seem in the least backward in any attention. He is a most charming young man. Ever since the service he rendered Jane at Weymouth, when they were out in that party on the water, and she, by the sudden whirling round of something or other among the sails, would have been dashed into the sea at once, and actually was all but gone, if he had not, with the greatest presence of mind, caught hold of her habit – (I can never think of it without trembling!) But ever since we had the history of that day, I have been so fond of Mr. Dixon!"

"But, in spite of all her friends' urgency, and her own wish of seeing Ireland, Miss Fairfax prefers devoting the time to you and Mrs. Bates?"

"Yes – entirely her own doing, entirely her own choice; and Colonel and Mrs. Campbell think she does quite right, just what they should recommend; and indeed they particularly wish her to try her native air, as she has not been quite so well as usual lately."

"I am concerned to hear of it. I think they judge wisely. But Mrs. Dixon must be very much disappointed. Mrs. Dixon, I understand, has no remarkable degree of personal beauty; is not, by any means, to be compared with Miss Fairfax."

"Oh! no. You are very obliging to say such things but certainly not. There is no comparison between them. Miss Campbell always was absolutely plain but extremely elegant and amiable."

"Yes, that of course."

"Jane caught a bad cold, poor thing! so long ago as the 7th of November, (as I am going to read to you,) and has never been well since. A long time, is not it, for a cold to hang upon her? She never mentioned it before, because she would not alarm us. Just like her! so considerate! But however, she is so far from well, that her kind friends the Campbells think she had better come home, and try an air that always agrees with her; and they have no doubt that three or four months at Highbury will entirely cure her and it is certainly a great deal better that she should come here, than go to Ireland, if she is unwell. Nobody could nurse her, as we should do."

"It appears to me the most desirable arrangement in the world."

"And so she is to come to us next Friday or Saturday, and the Campbells leave town in their way to Holyhead the Monday following, as you will find from Jane's letter. So sudden! You may guess, dear Miss Woodhouse, what a flurry it has thrown me in! If it was not for the drawback of her illness – but I am afraid we must expect to see her grown thin, and looking very poorly. I must tell you what an unlucky thing happened to me, as to that. I always make a point of reading Jane's letters through to myself first, before I read them aloud to my mother, you know, for fear of there being any thing in them to distress her. Jane desired me to do it, so I always do: and so I began to day with my usual caution; but no sooner did I come to the mention of her being unwell, than I burst out, quite frightened, with 'Bless me! poor Jane is ill!' which my mother, being on the watch, heard distinctly, and was sadly alarmed at. However, when I read on, I found it was not near so bad as I had fancied at first; and I make so light of it now to her, that she does not think much about it. But I cannot imagine how I could be so off my guard. If Jane does not get well soon, we will call in Mr. Perry. The expense shall not be thought of; and though he is so liberal, and so fond of Jane that I dare say he would not mean to charge any thing for attendance, we could not suffer it to be so, you know. He has a wife and family to maintain, and is not to be giving away his time. Well, now I have just given you a hint of what Jane writes about, we will turn to her letter, and I am sure she tells her own story a great deal better than I can tell it for her."

"I am afraid we must be running away," said Emma, glancing at Harriet, and beginning to rise "My father will be expecting us. I had no intention, I thought I had no power of staying more than five minutes, when I first entered the house. I merely called, because I would not pass the door without inquiring after Mrs. Bates; but I have been so pleasantly detained! Now, however, we must wish you and Mrs. Bates good morning."

And not all that could be urged to detain her succeeded. She regained the street happy in this, that though much had been forced on her against her will, though she had in fact heard the whole substance of Jane Fairfax's letter, she had been able to escape the letter itself.

# Chapter 20

JANE FAIRFAX was an orphan, the only child of Mrs. Bates's youngest daughter.

The marriage of Lieut. Fairfax – of the regiment of infantry, and Miss Jane Bates, had had its day of fame and pleasure, hope and interest; but nothing now remained of it, save the melancholy remembrance of him dying in action abroad of his widow sinking under consumption and grief soon afterwards and this girl.

By birth she belonged to Highbury: and when at three years old, on losing her mother, she became the property, the charge, the consolation, the fondling of her grandmother and aunt, there had seemed every probability of her being permanently fixed there; of her being taught only what very limited means could command, and growing up with no advantages of connection or improvement, to be engrafted on what nature had given her in a pleasing person, good understanding, and warm-hearted, well-meaning relations.

But the compassionate feelings of a friend of her father gave a change to her destiny. This was Colonel Campbell, who had very highly regarded Fairfax, as an excellent officer and most deserving young man; and farther, had been indebted to him for such attentions, during a severe camp-fever[1], as he believed had saved his life. These were claims which he did not learn to overlook, though some years passed away from the death of poor Fairfax, before his own return to England put any thing in his power. When he did return, he sought out the child and took notice of her. He was a married man, with only one living child, a girl, about Jane's age: and Jane became their guest, paying them long visits and growing a favourite with all; and before she was nine years old, his daughter's great fondness for her, and his own wish of being a real friend, united to produce an offer from Colonel Campbell of undertaking the whole charge of her education. It was accepted; and from that period Jane had belonged

1 Typhus.

to Colonel Campbell's family, and had lived with them entirely, only visiting her grandmother from time to time.

The plan was that she should be brought up for educating others; the very few hundred pounds which she inherited from her father making independence impossible. To provide for her otherwise was out of Colonel Campbell's power; for though his income, by pay and appointments, was handsome, his fortune was moderate and must be all his daughter's; but, by giving her an education, he hoped to be supplying the means of respectable subsistence hereafter.

Such was Jane Fairfax's history. She had fallen into good hands, known nothing but kindness from the Campbells, and been given an excellent education. Living constantly with right-minded and well-informed people, her heart and understanding had received every advantage of discipline and culture; and Colonel Campbell's residence being in London, every lighter talent had been done full justice to, by the attendance of first-rate masters. Her disposition and abilities were equally worthy of all that friendship could do; and at eighteen or nineteen she was, as far as such an early age can be qualified for the care of children, fully competent to the office of instruction herself; but she was too much beloved to be parted with. Neither father nor mother could promote, and the daughter could not endure it. The evil day was put off. It was easy to decide that she was still too young; and Jane remained with them, sharing, as another daughter, in all the rational pleasures of an elegant society, and a judicious mixture of home and amusement, with only the drawback of the future, the sobering suggestions of her own good understanding – to remind her that all this might soon be over.

The affection of the whole family, the warm attachment of Miss Campbell in particular, was more honourable to each party from the circumstance of Jane's decided superiority both in beauty and acquirements. That nature had given it in feature could not be unseen by the young woman, nor could her higher powers of mind be unfelt by the parents. They continued together with unabated regard however, till the marriage of Miss Campbell, who by that chance, that luck which so often defies anticipation in matrimonial affairs, giving attraction to what is moderate rather than to what is superior, engaged the affections of Mr. Dixon, a young man, rich and agreeable, almost as soon as they were acquainted; and was eligibly and happily settled, while Jane Fairfax had yet her bread to earn.

This event had very lately taken place; too lately for any thing to be yet attempted by her less fortunate friend towards entering on her path of duty; though she had now reached the age which her own judgment had fixed on for beginning. She had long resolved that one-and-twenty should be the period. With the fortitude of a devoted novitiate, she had resolved at one-and-twenty to complete the sacrifice, and retire from all the pleasures of life, of rational intercourse, equal society, peace and hope, to penance and mortification for ever.

The good sense of Colonel and Mrs. Campbell could not oppose such a resolution, though their feelings did. As long as they lived, no exertions would be necessary, their home might be hers for ever; and for their own comfort they would have retained her wholly; but this would be selfishness: what must be at last, had better be soon. Perhaps they began to feel it might have been kinder and wiser to have resisted the temptation of any delay, and spared her from a taste of such enjoyments of ease and leisure as must now be relinquished. Still, however, affection was glad to catch at any reasonable excuse for not hurrying on the wretched moment. She had never been quite well since the time of their daughter's marriage; and till she should have completely recovered her usual strength, they must forbid her engaging in duties, which, so far from being compatible with a weakened frame and varying spirits, seemed, under the most favourable circumstances, to require something more than human perfection of body and mind to be discharged with tolerable comfort.

With regard to her not accompanying them to Ireland, her account to her aunt contained nothing but truth, though there might be some truths not told. It was her own choice to give the time of their absence to Highbury; to spend, perhaps, her last months of perfect liberty with those kind relations to whom she was so very dear: and the Campbells, whatever might be their motive or motives, whether single, or double, or treble, gave the arrangement their ready sanction, and said, that they depended more on a few months spent in her native air, for the recovery of her health, than on any thing else. Certain it was that she was to come; and that Highbury, instead of welcoming that perfect novelty which had been so long promised it – Mr. Frank Churchill – must put up for the present with Jane Fairfax, who could bring only the freshness of a two years' absence.

Emma was sorry; to have to pay civilities to a person she did not like through three long months! to be always doing more than she wished, and less than she ought! Why she did not like Jane Fairfax might be a difficult question to answer; Mr. Knightley had once told her it was because she saw in her the really accomplished young woman, which she wanted to be thought herself; and though the accusation had been eagerly refuted at the time, there were moments of self-examination in which her conscience could not quite acquit her. But "she could never get acquainted with her: she did not know how it was, but there was such coldness and reserve such apparent indifference whether she pleased or not and then, her aunt was such an eternal talker! and she was made such a fuss with by everybody! and it had been always imagined that they were to be so intimate because their ages were the same, everybody had supposed they must be so fond of each other." These were her reasons she had no better.

It was a dislike so little just – every imputed fault was so magnified by fancy, that she never saw Jane Fairfax the first time after any considerable absence, without feeling that she had injured her; and now, when the due visit was paid, on her arrival, after a two years' interval, she was particularly struck with the very appearance and manners, which for those two whole years she had been depreciating. Jane Fairfax was very elegant, remarkably elegant; and she had herself the highest value for elegance. Her height was pretty, just such as almost everybody would think tall, and nobody could think very tall; her figure particularly graceful; her size a most becoming medium, between fat and thin, though a slight appearance of ill health seemed to point out the likeliest evil of the two. Emma could not but feel all this; and then, her face – her features – there was more beauty in them altogether than she had remembered; it was not regular, but it was very pleasing beauty. Her eyes, a deep grey, with dark eye lashes and eyebrows, had never been denied their praise; but the skin, which she had been used to cavil at, as wanting colour, had a clearness and delicacy which really needed no fuller bloom. It was a style of beauty, of which elegance was the reigning character, and as such, she must, in honour, by all her principles, admire it: elegance, which, whether of person or of mind, she saw so little in Highbury. There, not to be vulgar, was distinction, and merit.

In short, she sat, during the first visit, looking at Jane Fairfax with twofold complacency; the sense of pleasure and the sense of rendering justice, and was determining that she would dislike her no longer. When she took in her history, indeed, her situation, as well as her beauty; when she considered what all this elegance was destined to, what she was going to sink from, how she was going to live, it seemed impossible to feel any thing but compassion and respect; especially, if to every well-known particular entitling her to interest, were added the highly probable circumstance of an attachment to Mr. Dixon, which she had so naturally started to herself. In that case, nothing could be more pitiable or more honourable than the sacrifices she had resolved on. Emma was very willing now to acquit her of having seduced Mr. Dixon's actions from his wife, or of any thing mischievous which her imagination had suggested at first. If it were love, it might be simple, single, successless love on her side alone. She might have been unconsciously sucking in the sad poison, while a sharer of his conversation with her friend; and from the best, the purest of motives, might now be denying herself this visit to Ireland, and resolving to divide herself effectually from him and his connections by soon beginning her career of laborious duty.

Upon the whole, Emma left her with such softened, charitable feelings, as made her look around in walking home, and lament that Highbury afforded no young man worthy of giving her independence; nobody that she could wish to scheme about for her.

These were charming feelings but not lasting. Before she had committed herself by any public profession of eternal friendship for Jane Fairfax, or done more towards a recantation of past prejudices and errors, than saying to Mr. Knightley: "She certainly is handsome; she is better than handsome!" Jane had spent an evening at Hartfield with her grandmother and aunt, and everything was relapsing much into its usual state. Former provocations reappeared. The aunt was as tiresome as ever; more tiresome, because anxiety for her health was now added to admiration of her powers; and they had to listen to the description of exactly how little bread and butter she ate for breakfast, and how small a slice of mutton for dinner, as well as to see exhibitions of new caps and new workbags for her mother and herself; and Jane's offences rose again. They had music; Emma was obliged to play; and the thanks and praise which necessarily followed appeared to her an affectation of candour, an air of greatness, meaning only to show off in higher style her own very superior performance. She was, besides, which was the worst of all, so cold, so cautious! There was no getting at her real opinion. Wrapped up in a cloak of politeness, she seemed determined to hazard nothing. She was disgustingly, and suspiciously reserved.

If any thing could be more, where all was most, she was

more reserved on the subject of Weymouth and the Dixons than any thing. She seemed bent on giving no real insight into Mr. Dixon's character, or her own value for his company, or opinion of the suitableness of the match. It was all general approbation and smoothness; nothing delineated or distinguished. It did her no service however. Her caution was thrown away. Emma saw its artifice, and returned to her first surmises. There probably was something more to conceal than her own preference; Mr. Dixon, perhaps, had been very near changing one friend for the other, or been fixed only to Miss Campbell, for the sake of the future twelve thousand pounds.

The like reserve prevailed on other topics. She and Mr. Frank Churchill had been at Weymouth at the same time. It was known that they were a little acquainted; but not a syllable of real information could Emma procure as to what he truly was. "Was he handsome?" "She believed he was reckoned a very fine young man." "Was he agreeable?" "He was generally thought so." "Did he appear a sensible young man; a young man of information?" "At a watering place, or in a common London acquaintance, it was difficult to decide on such points. Manners were all that could be safely judged of, under a much longer knowledge than they yet had of Mr. Churchill. She believed everybody found his manners pleasing." Emma could not forgive her.

# Chapter 21

EMMA COULD not forgive her; but as neither provocation nor resentment were discerned by Mr. Knightley, who had been of the party, and had seen only proper attention and pleasing behaviour on each side, he was expressing the next morning, being at Hartfield again on business with Mr. Woodhouse, his approbation of the whole; not so openly as he might have done had her father been out of the room, but speaking plain enough to be very intelligible to Emma. He had been used to think her unjust to Jane, and had now great pleasure in marking an improvement.

"A very pleasant evening," he began, as soon as Mr. Woodhouse had been talked into what was necessary, told that he understood, and the papers swept away; "particularly pleasant. You and Miss Fairfax gave us some very good music. I do not know a more luxurious state, sir, than sitting at one's ease to be entertained a whole evening by two such young women; sometimes with music and sometimes with conversation. I am sure Miss Fairfax must have found the evening pleasant, Emma. You left nothing undone. I was glad you made her play so much, for having no instrument at her grandmother's, it must have been a real indulgence."

"I am happy you approved," said Emma, smiling; "but I hope I am not often deficient in what is due to guests at Hartfield."

"No, my dear," said her father instantly; "*that* I am sure you are not. There is nobody half so attentive and civil as you are. If any thing, you are too attentive. The muffin last night – if it had been handed round once, I think it would have been enough."

"No," said Mr. Knightley, nearly at the same time; "you are not often deficient; not often deficient either in manner or comprehension. I think you understand me, therefore."

An arch look expressed – "I understand you well enough;" but she said only, "Miss Fairfax is reserved."

"I always told you she was – a little; but you will soon overcome all that part of her reserve which ought to be overcome, all that has its foundation in diffidence. What arises from discretion must be honoured."

"You think her diffident. I do not see it."

"My dear Emma," said he, moving from his chair into one close by her, "you are not going to tell me, I hope, that you had not a pleasant evening."

"Oh! no; I was pleased with my own perseverance in asking questions; and amused to think how little information I obtained."

"I am disappointed," was his only answer.

"I hope everybody had a pleasant evening," said Mr. Woodhouse, in his quiet way. "I had. Once, I felt the fire rather too much; but then I moved back my chair a little, a very little, and it did not disturb me. Miss Bates was very chatty and good-humoured, as she always is, though she speaks rather too quick. However, she is very agreeable, and Mrs. Bates too, in a different way. I like old friends; and Miss Jane Fairfax is a very pretty sort of young lady, a very pretty and a very well-behaved young lady indeed. She must have found the evening agreeable, Mr. Knightley, because she had Emma."

"True, sir; and Emma, because she had Miss Fairfax."

Emma saw his anxiety, and wishing to appease it, at least for the present, said, and with a sincerity which no one could question.

"She is a sort of elegant creature that one cannot keep one's eyes from. I am always watching her to admire; and I do pity her from my heart."

Mr. Knightley looked as if he were more gratified than he cared to express; and before he could make any reply, Mr. Woodhouse, whose thoughts were on the Bates's, said:

"It is a great pity that their circumstances should be so confined! a great pity indeed! and I have often wished – but it is so little one can venture to do – small, trifling presents, of any thing uncommon. Now we have killed a porker, and Emma thinks of sending them a loin or a leg; it is very small and delicate – Hartfield pork is not like any other pork – but still it is pork – and, my dear Emma, unless one could be sure of their making it into steaks, nicely fried, as ours are fried, without the smallest grease, and not roast it, for no stomach can bear roast pork – I think we had better send the leg – don't you think so, my dear?"

"My dear papa, I sent the whole hind-quarter. I knew you would wish it. There will be the leg to be salted, you know, which is so very nice, and the loin to be dressed directly in any manner they like."

"That's right, my dear – very right. I had not thought of it before, but that is the best way. They must not over-salt the leg; and then, if it is not over-salted, and if it is very thoroughly boiled, just as Serle boils ours, and eaten very moderately of, with a boiled turnip, and a little carrot or parsnip, I do not consider it unwholesome."

"Emma," said Mr. Knightley presently, "I have a piece of news for you. You like news – and I heard an article on my way hither that I think will interest you."

"News! Oh! yes, I always like news. What is it? why do you smile so? where did you hear it? at Randalls?"

He had time only to say:

"No, not at Randalls; I have not been near Randalls" – when the door was thrown open, and Miss Bates and Miss Fairfax walked into the room. Full of thanks, and full of news, Miss Bates knew not which to give quickest. Mr. Knightley soon saw that he had lost his moment, and that not another syllable of communication could rest with him.

"Oh! my dear sir, how are you this morning? My dear Miss Woodhouse – I come quite over powered. Such a beautiful hindquarter of pork! You are too bountiful! Have you heard the news? Mr. Elton is going to be married."

Emma had not had time even to think of Mr. Elton, and she was so completely surprised that she could not avoid a little start, and a little blush, at the sound.

"There is my news: I thought it would interest you," said Mr. Knightley, with a smile which implied a conviction of some part of what had passed between them.

"But where could you hear it?" cried Miss Bates. "Where could you possibly hear it, Mr. Knightley? For it is not five minutes since I received Mrs. Cole's note – no, it cannot be more than five – or at least ten – for I had got my bonnet and spencer on, just ready to come out – I was only gone down to speak to Patty again about the pork – Jane was standing in the passage were not you, Jane? for my mother was so afraid that we had not any salting pan large enough. So I said I would go down and see, and Jane said, 'Shall I go down instead? for I think you have a little cold, and Patty has been washing the kitchen.' 'Oh! my dear,' – said I – well, and just then came the note. A Miss Hawkins – that's all I know. A Miss Hawkins of Bath. But, Mr. Knightley, how could you possibly have heard it? for the very moment Mr. Cole told Mrs. Cole of it, she sat down and wrote to me. A Miss Hawkins – "

"I was with Mr. Cole on business an hour and a half ago. He had just read Elton's letter as I was shewn in, and handed it to me directly."

"Well! that is quite – I suppose there never was a piece of news more generally interesting. My dear sir, you really are too bountiful. My mother desires her very best compliments and regards, and a thousand thanks, and says you really quite oppress her."

"We consider our Hartfield pork," replied Mr. Woodhouse – "indeed it certainly is, so very superior to all other pork, that Emma and I cannot have a greater pleasure than – "

"Oh! my dear sir, as my mother says, our friends are only too good to us. If ever there were people who, without having great wealth themselves, had everything they could wish for, I am sure it is us. We may well say that 'our lot is cast in a goodly heritage.' Well, Mr. Knightley, and so you actually saw the letter; well – "

"It was short – merely to announce – but cheerful, exulting, of course." Here was a sly glance at Emma. "He had been so fortunate as to – I forget the precise words – one has no business to remember them. The information was, as you state, that he was going to be married to a Miss Hawkins. By his style, I should imagine it just settled."

"Mr. Elton going to be married!" said Emma, as soon as she could speak. "He will have everybody's wishes for his happiness."

"He is very young to settle," was Mr. Woodhouse's observation. "He had better not be in a hurry. He seemed to me very well off as he was. We were always glad to see him at Hartfield."

"A new neighbour for us all, Miss Woodhouse!" said Miss Bates, joyfully; "my mother is so pleased! she says she cannot bear to have the poor old Vicarage without a mistress. This is great news, indeed. Jane, you have never seen Mr. Elton! no wonder that you have such a curiosity to see him."

Jane's curiosity did not appear of that absorbing nature as wholly to occupy her.

"No I have never seen Mr. Elton," she replied, starting on this appeal; "is he – is he a tall man?"

"Who shall answer that question?" cried Emma. "My father would say 'yes,' Mr. Knightley 'no;' and Miss Bates and I that he is just the happy medium. When you have been here a little longer, Miss Fairfax, you will understand that Mr. Elton is the standard of perfection in Highbury, both in person and mind."

"Very true, Miss Woodhouse, so she will. He is the very best young man But, my dear Jane, if you remember, I told you yesterday he was precisely the height of Mr. Perry. Miss Hawkins, I dare say, an excellent young woman. His extreme attention to my mother – wanting her to sit in the vicarage-pew, that she might hear the better, for my mother is a little deaf, you know – it is not much, but she does not hear quite quick. Jane says that Colonel Campbell is a little deaf. He fancied bathing might be good for it – the warm bath – but she says it did him no lasting benefit. Colonel Campbell, you know, is quite our angel. And Mr. Dixon seems a very charming young man, quite worthy of him. It is such a happiness when good people get together – and they always do. Now, here will be Mr. Elton and Miss Hawkins; and there are the Coles, such very good people; and the Perrys – I suppose there never was a happier or a better couple than Mr. and Mrs. Perry. I say, sir," turning to Mr. Woodhouse, "I think there are few places with such society as Highbury. I always say, we are quite blessed in our neighbours. My dear sir, if there is one thing my mother loves better than another, it is pork – a roast loin of pork – "

"As to who, or what Miss Hawkins is, or how long he has been acquainted with her," said Emma, "nothing I suppose can be known. One feels that it cannot be a very long acquaintance. He has been gone only four weeks."

Nobody had any information to give; and, after a few more wonderings, Emma said:

"You are silent, Miss Fairfax – but I hope you mean to take an interest in this news. You, who have been hearing and seeing so much of late on these subjects, who must have been so deep in the business on Miss Campbell's account – we shall not excuse your being indifferent about Mr. Elton and Miss Hawkins."

"When I have seen Mr. Elton," replied Jane, "I dare say I shall be interested – but I believe it requires *that* with me. And as it is some months since Miss Campbell married, the impression may be a little worn off."

"Yes, he has been gone just four weeks, as you observe, Miss Woodhouse," said Miss Bates, "four weeks yesterday. A Miss Hawkins! Well, I had always rather fancied it would be some young lady hereabouts; not that I ever – Mrs. Cole once whispered to me – but I immediately said, 'No, Mr. Elton is a most worthy young man – but –' In short, I do not think I am particularly quick at those sort of discoveries. I do not pretend to it. What is before me, I see. At the same time, nobody could wonder if Mr. Elton should have aspired – Miss Woodhouse lets me chatter on, so good humouredly. She knows I would not offend for the world. How does Miss Smith do? She seems quite recovered now. Have you heard from Mrs. John Knightley lately? Oh! those dear little children. Jane, do you know I always fancy Mr. Dixon like Mr. John Knightley. I mean in person – tall, and with that sort of look – and not very talkative."

"Quite wrong, my dear aunt; there is no likeness at all."

"Very odd! but one never does form a just idea of anybody beforehand. One takes up a notion, and runs away with it. Mr. Dixon, you say, is not, strictly speaking, handsome?"

"Handsome! Oh! no – far from it – certainly plain. I told you he was plain."

"My dear, you said that Miss Campbell would not allow him to be plain, and that you yourself – "

"Oh! as for me, my judgment is worth nothing. Where I have a regard, I always think a person well looking. But I gave what I believed the general opinion, when I called him plain."

"Well, my dear Jane, I believe we must be running away. The weather does not look well, and grandmama will be uneasy. You are too obliging, my dear Miss Woodhouse; but we really must take leave. This has been a most agreeable piece of news indeed. I shall just go round by Mrs. Cole's; but I shall not stop three minutes: and, Jane, you had better go home directly – I would not have you out in a shower! We think she is the better for

Highbury already. Thank you – we do indeed. I shall not attempt calling on Mrs. Goddard, for I really do not think she cares for any thing but *boiled* pork: when we dress the leg, it will be another thing. Good morning to you, my dear sir. Oh! Mr. Knightley is coming too. Well, that is so very! I am sure if Jane is tired, you will be so kind as to give her your arm. Mr. Elton, and Miss Hawkins! Good morning to you."

Emma, alone with her father, had half her attention wanted by him while he lamented that young people would be in such a hurry to marry – and to marry strangers too – and the other half she could give to her own view of the subject. It was to herself an amusing and a very welcome piece of news, as proving that Mr. Elton could not have suffered long; but she was sorry for Harriet – Harriet must feel it – and all that she could hope was, by giving the first information herself, to save her from hearing it abruptly from others. It was now about the time that she was likely to call. If she were to meet Miss Bates on her way! and upon its beginning to rain, Emma was obliged to expect that the weather would be detaining her at Mrs. Goddard's, and that the intelligence would undoubtedly rush upon her without preparation.

The shower was heavy, but short; and it had not been over five minutes, when in came Harriet, with just the heated, agitated look which hurrying thither with a full heart was likely to give; and the "Oh! Miss Woodhouse, what do you think has happened!" which instantly burst forth, had all the evidence of corresponding perturbation. As the blow was given, Emma felt that she could not now show greater kindness than in listening; and Harriet, unchecked, ran eagerly through what she had to tell. "She had set out from Mrs. Goddard's half an hour ago – she had been afraid it would rain – she had been afraid it would pour down every moment, but she thought she might get to Hartfield first – she had hurried on as fast as possible; but then, as she was passing by the house where a young woman was making up a gown for her, she thought she would just step in and see how it went on;

and though she did not seem to stay half a moment there, soon after she came out it began to rain, and she did not know what to do; so she ran on directly, as fast as she could, and took shelter at Ford's. "Ford's was the principal woollen-draper, linen-draper, and haberdasher's shop united; the shop first in size and fashion in the place." And so, there she had set, without an idea of any thing in the world, full ten minutes, perhaps – when, all of a sudden, who should come in – to be sure it was so very odd! but they always dealt at Ford's – who should come in, but Elizabeth Martin and her brother! Dear Miss Woodhouse! only think. I thought I should have fainted. I did not know what to do. I was sitting near the door – Elizabeth saw me directly; but he did not; he was busy with the umbrella. I am sure she saw me, but she looked away directly, and took no notice; and they both went to quite the farther end of the shop; and I kept sitting near the door! Oh! dear; I was so miserable! I am sure I must have been as white as my gown. I could not go away you know, because of the rain; but I did so wish myself anywhere in the world but there. Oh! dear, Miss Woodhouse well, at last, I fancy, he looked round and saw me; for instead of going on with her buyings, they began whispering to one another. I am sure they were talking of me; and I could not help thinking that he was persuading her to speak to me – (do you think he was, Miss Woodhouse?) – for presently she came forward – came quite up to me, and asked me how I did, and seemed ready to shake hands, if I would. She did not do any of it in the same way that she used; I could see she was altered; but, however, she seemed to try to be very friendly, and we shook hands, and stood talking some time; but I know no more what I said – I was in such a tremble! I remember she said she was sorry we never met now; which I thought almost too kind! Dear, Miss Woodhouse, I was absolutely miserable! By that time, it was beginning to hold up, and I was determined that nothing should stop me from getting away – and then – only think! I found he was coming up towards me too – slowly you know, and as if he did not quite know what to do; and so he came and spoke, and I answered – and I stood for a minute, feeling dreadfully, you know, one can't tell how; and then I took courage, and said it did not rain, and I must go; and so off I set; and I had not got three yards from the door, when he came after me, only to say, if I was going to Hartfield, he thought I had much better go round by Mr. Cole's stables, for I should find the near way quite floated by this rain. Oh! dear, I thought it would have been the death of me! So I said, I was very much obliged to him: you know I could not do less; and then he went back to Elizabeth, and I came round by the stables – I believe I did – but I hardly knew where I was, or any thing about it. Oh! Miss Woodhouse, I would rather have done any thing than have it happen: and yet, you know, there was a sort of satisfaction in seeing him behave so pleasantly and so kindly. And Elizabeth, too. Oh! Miss Woodhouse, do talk to me and make me comfortable again."

Very sincerely did Emma wish to do so; but it was not immediately in her power. She was obliged to stop and think. She was not thoroughly comfortable herself. The young man's conduct, and his sister's, seemed the result of real feeling, and she could not but pity them. As Harriet described it, there had been an interesting mixture of wounded affection and genuine delicacy in their behaviour. But she had believed them to be well-meaning, worthy people before; and what difference did this make in the evils of the connection? It was folly to be disturbed by it. Of course, he must be sorry to lose her – they must be all sorry – ambition, as well as love, had probably been mortified. They might all have hoped to rise by Harriet's acquaintance: and besides, what was the value of Harriet's description? So easily pleased – so little discerning; what signified her praise?

She exerted herself, and did try to make her comfortable, by considering all that had passed as a mere trifle, and quite unworthy of being dwelt on.

"It might be distressing, for the moment," said she; "but you seem to have behaved extremely well; and it is over and may never – can never, as a first meeting – occur again, and therefore you need not think about it."

Harriet said, "very true," and she "would not think about it;" but still she talked of it – still she could talk of nothing else; and Emma, at last, in order to put the Martins out of her head, was obliged to hurry on the news, which she had meant to give with so much tender caution; hardly knowing herself whether to rejoice or be angry, ashamed or only amused, at such a state of mind in poor Harriet – such a conclusion of Mr. Elton's importance with her!

Mr. Elton's rights, however, gradually revived. Though she did not feel the first intelligence as she might have done the day before, or an hour before, its interest soon increased; and before their first conversation was over, she had talked herself into all the sensations of curiosity, wonder and regret, pain and pleasure, as to this fortunate Miss Hawkins, which could conduce to place the Martins under proper subordination in her fancy.

Emma learned to be rather glad that there had been such a meeting. It had been serviceable in deadening the first shock, without retaining any influence to alarm. As Harriet now lived, the Martins could not get at her, without seeking her, where hitherto they had wanted either the courage or the condescension to seek her; for since her refusal of the brother, the sisters never had been at Mrs. Goddard's; and a twelvemonth might pass without their being thrown together again, with any necessity, or even any power of speech.

# *Chapter 22*

HUMAN NATURE is so well disposed towards those who are in interesting situations, that a young person, who either marries or dies, is sure of being kindly spoken of.

A week had not passed since Miss Hawkins's name was first mentioned in Highbury, before she was, by some means or other, discovered to have every recommendation of person and mind; to be handsome, elegant, highly accomplished, and perfectly amiable: and when Mr. Elton himself arrived to triumph in his happy prospects, and circulate the fame of her merits, there was very little more for him to do, than to tell her Christian name, and say whose music she principally played.

Mr. Elton returned, a very happy man. He had gone away rejected and mortified disappointed in a very sanguine hope, after a series of what appeared to him strong encouragement; and not only losing the right lady, but finding himself debased to the level of a very wrong one. He had gone away deeply offended he came back engaged to another and to another as superior, of course, to the first, as under such circumstances what is gained always is to what is lost. He came back gay and self satisfied, eager and busy, caring nothing for Miss Woodhouse, and defying Miss Smith.

The charming Augusta Hawkins, in addition to all the usual advantages of perfect beauty and merit, was in possession of an independent fortune, of so many thousands as would always be called ten; a point of some dignity, as well as some convenience: the story told well; he had not thrown himself away – he had gained a woman of £10,000. or thereabouts; and he had gained her with such delightful rapidity the first hour of introduction had been so very soon followed by distinguishing notice; the history which he had to give Mrs. Cole of the rise and progress of the affair was so glorious the steps so quick, from the accidental rencontre, to the dinner at Mr. Green's, and the party at Mrs. Brown's – smiles and blushes rising in importance – with consciousness and agitation richly scattered the lady had been so easily impressed – so sweetly disposed – had in short, to use a most intelligible phrase, been so very ready to have him, that vanity and prudence were equally contented.

He had caught both substance and shadow both fortune and affection, and was just the happy man he ought to be; talking only of himself and his own concerns – expecting to be congratulated – ready to be laughed at – and, with cordial, fearless smiles, now addressing all the young ladies of the place, to whom, a few weeks ago, he would have been more cautiously gallant.

The wedding was no distant event, as the parties had only themselves to please, and nothing but the necessary preparations to wait for; and when he set out for Bath again, there was a general expectation, which a certain glance of Mrs. Cole's did not seem to contradict, that when he next entered Highbury he would bring his bride.

During his present short stay, Emma had barely seen him; but just enough to feel that the first meeting was over, and to give her the impression of his not being improved by the mixture of pique and pretension, now spread over his air. She was, in fact, beginning very much to wonder that she had ever thought him pleasing at all; and his sight was so inseparably connected with some very disagreeable feelings, that, except in a moral light, as a penance, a lesson, a source of profitable humiliation to her own mind, she would have been thankful to be assured of never seeing him again. She wished him very well; but he gave her pain, and his welfare twenty miles off would administer most satisfaction.

The pain of his continued residence in Highbury, however, must certainly be lessened by his marriage. Many vain solicitudes would be prevented – many awkwardnesses smoothed by it. A *Mrs. Elton* would be an excuse for any change of intercourse; former intimacy might sink without remark. It would be almost beginning their life of civility again.

Of the lady, individually, Emma thought very little. She was good enough for Mr. Elton, no doubt; accomplished enough for Highbury – handsome enough – to look plain, probably, by Harriet's side. As to connection, there Emma was perfectly easy; persuaded, that after all his own vaunted claims and disdain of Harriet, he had done nothing. On that article, truth seemed attainable. *What* she was, must be uncertain; but *who* she was, might be found out; and setting aside the £10,000, it did not appear that she was at all Harriet's superior. She brought no name, no blood, no alliance. Miss Hawkins was the youngest of the two daughters of a Bristol – merchant, of course, he must be called; but, as the whole of the profits of his mercantile life appeared so very moderate, it was not unfair to guess the dignity of his line of trade had been very moderate also. Part of every winter she had been used to spend in Bath; but Bristol was her home, the very heart of Bristol; for though the father and mother had died some years ago, an uncle remained – in the law line nothing more distinctly honourable was hazarded of him, than that he was in the law line; and with him the daughter had lived. Emma guessed him to be the drudge of some attorney, and too stupid to rise. And all the grandeur of the connection seemed dependent on the elder sister, who was *very well married,* to a gentleman in a *great way,* near Bristol, who kept two carriages! That was the wind up of the history; that was the glory of Miss Hawkins.

Could she but have given Harriet her feelings about it all! She had talked her into love; but, alas! she was not so easily to be talked out of it. The charm of an object to occupy the many vacancies of Harriet's mind was not to be talked away. He might be superseded by another; he certainly would indeed; nothing could be clearer; even a Robert Martin would have been sufficient; but nothing else, she feared, would cure her. Harriet was one of those, who, having once begun, would be always in love. And now, poor girl! she was considerably worse from this reappearance of Mr. Elton – She was always having a glimpse of him somewhere or other. Emma saw him only once; but two or three times every day Harriet was sure just to meet with him, or *just* to miss him, *just* to hear his voice, or see his shoulder, *just* to have something occur to preserve him in her fancy, in all the favouring warmth of surprise and conjecture. She was, moreover, perpetually hearing about him; for, excepting when at Hartfield, she was always among those who saw no fault in Mr. Elton, and found nothing so interesting as the discussion of his concerns; and every report, therefore, every guess – all that had already occurred, all that might occur in the arrangement of his affairs, comprehending income, servants, and furniture – was continually in agitation around her. Her regard was receiving strength by invariable praise of him, and her regrets kept alive, and feelings irritated by ceaseless repetitions of Miss Hawkins's happiness, and continual observation of, how much he seemed attached! his air as he walked by the house the very sitting of his hat, being all in proof of how much he was in love!

Had it been allowable entertainment, had there been no pain to her friend, or reproach to herself, in the waverings of Harriet's mind, Emma would have been amused by its variations. Sometimes Mr. Elton predominated, sometimes the Martins; and each was occasionally useful as a check to the other. Mr. Elton's engagement had been the cure of the agitation of meeting Mr. Martin. The unhappiness produced by the knowledge of that engagement had been a little put aside by Elizabeth Martin's calling at Mrs. Goddard's a few days afterwards. Harriet had not been at home; but a note had been prepared and left for her, written in the very style to touch; a small mixture of reproach, with a great deal of kindness; and till Mr. Elton himself appeared, she had been much occupied by it, continually pondering over what could be done in return, and wishing to do more than she dared to confess. But Mr. Elton, in person, had driven away all such cares. While he staid, the Martins were forgotten; and on the very morning of his setting off for Bath again, Emma, to dissipate some of the distress it occasioned, judged it best for her to return Elizabeth Martin's visit.

How that visit was to be acknowledged what would be necessary and what might be safest, had been a point of some doubtful consideration. Absolute neglect of the mother and sisters, when invited to come, would be ingratitude. It must not be: and yet the danger of a renewal of the acquaintance!

After much thinking, she could determine on nothing better, than Harriet's returning the visit; but in a way that, if they had understanding, should convince them that it was to be only a formal acquaintance. She meant to take her in the carriage, leave her at the Abbey Mill, while she drove a little farther, and call for her again so soon, as to allow no time for insidious applications or dangerous recurrences to the past, and give the most decided proof of what degree of intimacy was chosen for the future.

She could think of nothing better; and though there was something in it which her own heart could not approve – something of ingratitude, merely glossed over – it must be done, or what would become of Harriet?

# Chapter 23

SMALL HEART had Harriet for visiting. Only half an hour before her friend called for her at Mrs. Goddard's, her evil stars had led her to the very spot where, at that moment, a trunk, directed to *The Rev. Philip Elton, White Hart, Bath,* was to be seen under the operation of being lifted into the butcher's cart, which was to convey it to where the coaches past; and everything in this world, excepting that trunk and the direction, was consequently a blank.

She went, however; and when they reached the farm, and she was to be put down, at the end of the broad, neat gravel-walk, which led between espalier apple-trees to the front door, the sight of everything which had given her so much pleasure the autumn before, was beginning to revive a little local agitation; and when they parted, Emma observed her to be looking around with a sort of fearful curiosity, which determined her not to allow the visit to exceed the proposed quarter of an hour. She went on herself, to give that portion of time to an old servant who was married, and settled in Donwell.

The quarter of an hour brought her punctually to the white gate again; and Miss Smith receiving her summons, was with her without delay, and unattended by any alarming young man. She came solitarily down the gravel-walk – a Miss Martin just appearing at the door, and parting with her seemingly with ceremonious civility.

Harriet could not very soon give an intelligible account. She was feeling too much; but at last Emma collected from her enough to understand the sort of meeting, and the sort of pain it was creating. She had seen only Mrs. Martin and the two girls. They had received her doubtingly, if not coolly; and nothing beyond the merest commonplace had been talked almost all the time – till just at last, when Mrs. Martin's saying, all of a sudden, that she thought Miss Smith was grown, had brought on a more interesting subject, and a warmer manner. In that very room she had been measured last September, with her two friends. There were the pencilled marks and memorandums on the wainscot by the window. *He* had done it. They all seemed to remember the day, the hour, the party, the occasion – to feel the same consciousness, the same regrets – to be ready to return to the same good understanding; and they were just growing again like themselves, (Harriet, as Emma must suspect, as ready as the best of them to be cordial and happy,) when the carriage reappeared, and all was over. The style of the visit, and the shortness of it, were then felt to be decisive. Fourteen minutes to be given to those with whom she had thankfully passed six weeks not six months ago! Emma could not but picture it all, and feel how justly they might resent, how naturally Harriet must suffer. It was a bad business. She would have given a great deal, or endured a great deal, to have had the Martins in a higher rank of life. They were so deserving, that a *little* higher should have been enough: but as it was, how could she have done otherwise? Impossible! She could not repent. They must be separated; but there was a great deal of pain in the process – so much to herself at this time, that she soon felt the necessity of a little consolation, and resolved on going home by way of Randalls to procure it. Her mind was quite sick of Mr. Elton and the Martins. The refreshment of Randalls was absolutely necessary.

It was a good scheme; but on driving to the door they heard that neither "master nor mistress was at home;" they had both been out some time; the man believed they were gone to Hartfield.

"This is too bad," cried Emma, as they turned away. "And now we shall just miss them; too provoking! I do not know when I have been so disappointed." And she leaned back in the corner, to indulge her murmurs, or to reason them away; probably a little of both – such being the commonest process of a not ill-disposed mind. Presently the carriage stopped; she looked up; it was stopped by Mr. and Mrs. Weston, who were standing to speak to her. There was instant pleasure in the sight of them, and still greater pleasure was conveyed in sound for Mr. Weston immediately accosted her with:

"How d'ye do? how d'ye do? We have been sitting with your father – glad to see him so well. Frank comes to morrow – I had a letter this morning – we see him to morrow by dinner-time to a certainty – he is at Oxford to day, and he comes for a whole fortnight; I knew it would be so. If he had come at Christmas he could not have staid three days; I was always glad he did not come at Christmas; now we are going to have just the right weather for him, fine, dry, settled weather. We shall enjoy him completely; everything has turned out exactly as we could wish."

There was no resisting such news, no possibility of avoiding the influence of such a happy face as Mr. Weston's, confirmed as it all was by the words and the countenance of his wife, fewer and quieter, but not less to the purpose. To know that she thought his coming certain was enough to make Emma consider it so, and sincerely did she rejoice in their joy. It was a most delightful re-animation of exhausted spirits. The worn out past was sunk in the freshness of what was coming; and in the rapidity of half a moment's thought, she hoped Mr. Elton would now be talked of no more.

Mr. Weston gave her the history of the engagements at Enscombe, which allowed his son to answer for having an entire fortnight at his command, as well as the route and the method of his journey; and she listened, and smiled, and congratulated.

"I shall soon bring him over to Hartfield," said he, at the conclusion.

Emma could imagine she saw a touch of the arm at this speech, from his wife.

"We had better move on, Mr. Weston," said she, "we are detaining the girls."

"Well, well, I am ready;" and turning again to Emma, "but you must not be expecting such a *very* fine young man; you have only had *my* account you know; I dare say he is really nothing extraordinary:" though his own sparkling eyes at the moment were speaking a very different conviction.

Emma could look perfectly unconscious and innocent, and answer in a manner that appropriated nothing.

"Think of me to morrow, my dear Emma, about four o'clock," was Mrs. Weston's parting injunction; spoken with some anxiety, and meant only for her.

"Four o'clock! depend upon it he will be here by three," was Mr. Weston's quick amendment; and so ended a most satisfactory meeting. Emma's spirits were mounted quite up to happiness;

everything wore a different air; James and his horses seemed not half so sluggish as before. When she looked at the hedges, she thought the elder at least must soon be coming out; and when she turned round to Harriet, she saw something like a look of spring, a tender smile even there.

"Will Mr. Frank Churchill pass through Bath as well as Oxford?" was a question, however, which did not augur much.

But neither geography nor tranquillity could come all at once, and Emma was now in a humour to resolve that they should both come in time.

The morning of the interesting day arrived, and Mrs. Weston's faithful pupil did not forget either at ten, or eleven, or twelve o'clock, that she was to think of her at four.

"My dear, dear anxious friend," said she, in mental soliloquy, while walking downstairs from her own room, "always over-careful for everybody's comfort but your own; I see you now in all your little fidgets, going again and again into his room, to be sure that all is right." The clock struck twelve as she passed through the hall. " 'Tis twelve; I shall not forget to think of you four hours hence; and by this time to morrow, perhaps, or a little later, I may be thinking of the possibility of their all calling here. I am sure they will bring him soon."

She opened the parlour door, and saw two gentlemen sitting with her father – Mr. Weston and his son. They had been arrived only a few minutes, and Mr. Weston had scarcely finished his explanation of Frank's being a day before his time, and her father was yet in the midst of his very civil welcome and congratulations, when she appeared, to have her share of surprise, introduction, and pleasure.

The Frank Churchill so long talked of, so high in interest, was actually before her he was presented to her, and she did not think too much had been said in his praise; he was a *very* good-looking young man; height, air, address, all were unexceptionable, and his countenance had a great deal of the spirit and liveliness of his father's; he looked quick and sensible. She felt immediately that she should like him; and there was a well-bred ease of manner, and a readiness to talk, which convinced her that he came intending to be acquainted with her, and that acquainted they soon must be.

He had reached Randalls the evening before. She was pleased with the eagerness to arrive which had made him alter his plan, and travel earlier, later, and quicker, that he might gain half a day.

"I told you yesterday," cried Mr. Weston with exultation, "I told you all that he would be here before the time named. I remembered what I used to do myself. One cannot creep upon a journey; one cannot help getting on faster than one has planned; and the pleasure of coming in upon one's friends before the look-out begins, is worth a great deal more than any little exertion it needs."

"It is a great pleasure where one can indulge in it," said the young man, "though there are not many houses that I should presume on so far; but in coming *home* I felt I might do any thing."

The word *home* made his father look on him with fresh complacency. Emma was directly sure that he knew how to make himself agreeable; the conviction was strengthened by what followed. He was very much pleased with Randalls, thought it a most admirably-arranged house, would hardly allow it even to be very small, admired the situation, the walk to Highbury, Highbury itself, Hartfield still more, and professed himself to have always felt the sort of interest in the country which none but one's *own* country gives, and the greatest curiosity to visit it. That he should never have been able to indulge so amiable a feeling before, passed suspiciously through Emma's brain; but still, if it were a falsehood, it was a pleasant one, and pleasantly handled. His manner had no air of study or exaggeration. He did really look and speak as if in a state of no common enjoyment.

Their subjects in general were such as belong to an opening acquaintance. On his side were the inquiries – "Was she a horse-woman? Pleasant rides? Pleasant walks? Had they a large neighbourhood? Highbury, perhaps, afforded society enough? There were several very pretty houses in and about it. Balls – had they balls? Was it a musical society?"

But when satisfied on all these points, and their acquaintance proportionately advanced, he contrived to find an opportunity, while their two fathers were engaged with each other, of introducing his mother-in-law, and speaking of her with so much handsome praise, so much warm admiration, so much gratitude for the happiness she secured to his father, and her very kind reception of himself, as was an additional proof of his knowing how to please – and of his certainly thinking it worth while to try to please her. He did not advance a word of praise beyond what she knew to be thoroughly deserved by Mrs. Weston; but, undoubtedly he could know very little of the matter. He understood what would be welcome; he could be sure of little else. "His father's marriage," he said, "had been the wisest measure, every friend must rejoice in it; and the family from whom he had received such a blessing must be ever considered as having conferred the highest obligation on him."

He got as near as he could to thanking her for Miss Taylor's merits, without seeming quite to forget that in the common course of things it was to be rather supposed that Miss Taylor had formed Miss Woodhouse's character, than Miss Woodhouse Miss Taylor's. And at last, as if resolved to qualify his opinion completely for travelling round to its object, he wound it all up with astonishment at the youth and beauty of her person.

"Elegant, agreeable manners, I was prepared for," said he; "but I confess that, considering everything, I had not expected more than a very tolerably well-looking woman of a certain age; I did not know that I was to find a pretty young woman in Mrs. Weston."

"You cannot see too much perfection in Mrs. Weston for my feelings," said Emma; "were you to guess her to be *eighteen, I* should listen with pleasure; but *she* would be ready to quarrel with you for using such words. Don't let her imagine that you have spoken of her as a pretty young woman."

"I hope I should know better," he replied; "no, depend upon it, (with a gallant bow,) that in addressing Mrs. Weston I should understand whom I might praise without any danger of being thought extravagant in my terms."

Emma wondered whether the same suspicion of what might be expected from their knowing each other, which had taken strong possession of her mind, had ever crossed his; and whether his compliments were to be considered as marks of acquiescence, or proofs of defiance. She must see more of him to understand his ways; at present she only felt they were agreeable.

She had no doubt of what Mr. Weston was often thinking about. His quick eye she detected again and again glancing towards them with a happy expression; and even, when he might have determined not to look, she was confident that he was often listening.

Her own father's perfect exemption from any thought of the kind, the entire deficiency in him of all such sort of penetration or suspicion, was a most comfortable circumstance. Happily he was not farther from approving matrimony than from foreseeing it. Though always objecting to every marriage that was arranged, he never suffered beforehand from the apprehension of any; it seemed as if he could not think so ill of any two persons' understanding as to suppose they meant to marry till it were proved against them. She blessed the favouring blindness. He could now, without the drawback of a single unpleasant surmise, without a glance forward at any possible treachery in his guest, give way to all his natural kind-hearted civility in solicitous inquiries after Mr. Frank Churchill's accommodation on his journey, through the sad evils of sleeping two nights on the road, and express very genuine unmixed anxiety to know that he had certainly escaped catching cold – which, however, he could not allow him to feel quite assured of himself till after another night.

A reasonable visit paid, Mr. Weston began to move. "He must be going. He had business at the Crown about his hay, and a great many errands for Mrs. Weston at Ford's, but he need not hurry anybody else." His son, too well bred to hear the hint, rose immediately also, saying:

"As you are going farther on business, sir, I will take the opportunity of paying a visit, which must be paid some day or other, and therefore may as well be paid now. I have the honour of being acquainted with a neighbour of yours, (turning to Emma,) a lady residing in or near Highbury; a family of the name of Fairfax. I shall have no difficulty, I suppose, in finding the house; though Fairfax, I believe, is not the proper name – I should rather say Barnes, or Bates. Do you know any family of that name?"

"To be sure we do," cried his father; "Mrs. Bates – we passed her house – I saw Miss Bates at the window. True, true, you are acquainted with Miss Fairfax; I remember you knew her at Weymouth, and a fine girl she is. Call upon her, by all means."

"There is no necessity for my calling this morning," said the young man; "another day would do as well; but there was that degree of acquaintance at Weymouth which."

"Oh! go to day, go to day. Do not defer it. What is right to be done cannot be done too soon. And, besides, I must give you a hint, Frank; any want of attention to her *here* should be carefully avoided. You saw her with the Campbells, when she was the equal of everybody she mixed with, but here she is with a poor old grandmother, who has barely enough to live on. If you do not call early it will be a slight."

The son looked convinced.

"I have heard her speak of the acquaintance," said Emma; "she is a very elegant young woman."

He agreed to it, but with so quiet a "Yes," as inclined her almost to doubt his real concurrence; and yet there must be a very distinct sort of elegance for the fashionable world, if Jane

Fairfax could be thought only ordinarily gifted with it.

"If you were never particularly struck by her manners before," said she, "I think you will to day. You will see her to advantage; see her and hear her – no, I am afraid you will not hear her at all, for she has an aunt who never holds her tongue."

"You are acquainted with Miss Jane Fairfax, sir, are you?" said Mr. Woodhouse, always the last to make his way in conversation; "then give me leave to assure you that you will find her a very agreeable young lady. She is staying here on a visit to her grandmama and aunt, very worthy people; I have known them all my life. They will be extremely glad to see you, I am sure; and one of my servants shall go with you to show you the way."

"My dear sir, upon no account in the world; my father can direct me."

"But your father is not going so far; he is only going to the Crown, quite on the other side of the street, and there are a great many houses; you might be very much at a loss, and it is a very dirty walk, unless you keep on the footpath; but my coachman can tell you where you had best cross the street."

Mr. Frank Churchill still declined it, looking as serious as he could, and his father gave his hearty support by calling out, "My good friend, this is quite unnecessary; Frank knows a puddle of water when he sees it, and as to Mrs. Bates's, he may get there from the Crown in a hop, step, and jump."

They were permitted to go alone; and with a cordial nod from one, and a graceful bow from the other, the two gentlemen took leave. Emma remained very well pleased with this beginning of the acquaintance, and could now engage to think of them all at Randalls any hour of the day, with full confidence in their comfort.

## *Chapter 24*

The next morning brought Mr. Frank Churchill again. He came with Mrs. Weston, to whom and to Highbury he seemed to take very cordially. He had been sitting with her, it appeared, most companionably at home, till her usual hour of exercise; and on being desired to choose their walk, immediately fixed on Highbury. "He did not doubt there being very pleasant walks in every direction, but if left to him, he should always choose the same. Highbury, that airy, cheerful, happy-looking Highbury, would be his constant attraction." Highbury, with Mrs. Weston, stood for Hartfield; and she trusted to its bearing the same construction with him. They walked thither directly.

Emma had hardly expected them: for Mr. Weston, who had called in for half a minute, in order to hear that his son was very handsome, knew nothing of their plans; and it was an agreeable surprise to her, therefore, to perceive them walking up to the house together, arm in arm. She was wanting to see him again, and especially to see him in company with Mrs. Weston, upon his behaviour to whom her opinion of him was to depend. If he were deficient there, nothing should make amends for it. But on seeing them together, she became perfectly satisfied. It was not merely in fine words or hyperbolical compliment that he paid his duty; nothing could be more proper or pleasing than his whole manner to her – nothing could more agreeably denote his wish of considering her as a friend and securing her affection. And there was time enough for Emma to form a reasonable judgment, as their visit included all the rest of the morning. They were all three walking about together for an hour or two – first round the shrubberies of Hartfield, and afterwards in Highbury. He was delighted with everything; admired Hartfield sufficiently for Mr. Woodhouse's ear; and when their going farther was resolved on, confessed his wish to be made acquainted with the whole village, and found matter of commendation and interest much oftener than Emma could have supposed.

Some of the objects of his curiosity spoke very amiable feelings. He begged to be shown the house which his father had lived in so long, and which had been the home of his father's father; and on recollecting that an old woman who had nursed him was still living, walked in quest of her cottage from one end of the street to the other; and though in some points of pursuit or observation there was no positive merit, they showed, altogether, a good will towards Highbury in general, which must be very like a merit to those he was with.

Emma watched and decided, that with such feelings as were now shown, it could not be fairly supposed that he had been ever voluntarily absenting himself; that he had not been acting a part, or making a parade of insincere professions; and that Mr. Knightley certainly had not done him justice.

Their first pause was at the Crown Inn, an inconsiderable house, though the principal one of the sort, where a couple of pair of post-horses were kept, more for the convenience of the neighbourhood than from any run on the road; and his companions had not expected to be detained by any interest excited there; but in passing it they gave the history of the large room visibly added; it had been built many years ago for a ball-room, and while the neighbourhood had been in a particularly populous, dancing state, had been occasionally used as such; but such brilliant days had long passed away, and now the highest purpose for which it was ever wanted was to accommodate a whist-club established among the gentlemen and half-gentlemen of the place. He was immediately interested. Its character as a ball-room caught him; and instead of passing on, he stopped for several minutes at the two superior sashed windows which were open, to look in and contemplate its capabilities, and lament that its original purpose should have ceased. He saw no fault in the room, he would acknowledge none which they suggested. No, it was long enough, broad enough, handsome enough. It would hold the very number for comfort. They ought to have balls there at least every fortnight through the winter. Why had not Miss Woodhouse revived the former good old days of the room? She who could do any thing in Highbury! The want of proper families in the place, and the conviction that none beyond the place and its immediate environs could be tempted to attend, were mentioned; but he was not satisfied. He could not be persuaded that so many good looking houses as he saw around him, could not furnish numbers enough for such a meeting; and even when particulars were given and families described, he was still unwilling to admit that the inconvenience of such a mixture would be any thing, or that there would be the smallest difficulty in everybody's returning into their proper place the next morning. He argued like a young man very much bent on dancing; and Emma was rather surprised to see the constitution of the Weston prevail so decidedly against the habits of the Churchills. He seemed to have all the life and spirit, cheerful feelings, and social inclinations of his father, and nothing of the pride or reserve of Enscombe. Of pride, indeed, there was, perhaps, scarcely enough; his indifference to a confusion of rank, bordered too much on inelegance of mind. He could be no judge, however, of the evil he was holding cheap. It was but an effusion of lively spirits.

At last he was persuaded to move on from the front of the Crown; and being now almost facing the house where the Bateses lodged, Emma recollected his intended visit the day before, and asked him if he had paid it.

"Yes, oh! yes" he replied; "I was just going to mention it. A very successful visit: I saw all the three ladies; and felt very much obliged to you for your preparatory hint. If the talking aunt had taken me quite by surprise, it must have been the death of me. As it was, I was only betrayed into paying a most unreasonable visit. Ten minutes would have been all that was necessary, perhaps all that was proper; and I had told my father I should certainly be at home before him but there was no getting away, no pause; and, to my utter astonishment, I found, when he (finding me nowhere else) joined me there at last, that I had been actually sitting with them very nearly three quarters of an hour. The good lady had not given me the possibility of escape before."

"And how did you think Miss Fairfax looking?"

"Ill, very ill – that is, if a young lady can ever be allowed to look ill. But the expression is hardly admissible, Mrs. Weston, is it? Ladies can never look ill. And, seriously, Miss Fairfax is naturally so pale, as almost always to give the appearance of ill health – a most deplorable want of complexion."

Emma would not agree to this, and began a warm defence of Miss Fairfax's complexion. "It was certainly never brilliant, but she would not allow it to have a sickly hue in general; and there was a softness and delicacy in her skin which gave peculiar elegance to the character of her face." He listened with all due deference; acknowledged that he had heard many people say the same – but yet he must confess, that to him nothing could make amends for the want of the fine glow of health. Where features were indifferent, a fine complexion gave beauty to them all; and where they were good, the effect was – fortunately he need not attempt to describe what the effect was.

"Well," said Emma, "there is no disputing about taste. At least you admire her except her complexion."

He shook his head and laughed." I cannot separate Miss Fairfax and her complexion."

"Did you see her often at Weymouth? Were you often in the same society?"

At this moment they were approaching Ford's, and he hastily exclaimed, "Ha! this must be the very shop that everybody attends every day of their lives, as my father informs me. He comes to Highbury himself, he says, six days out of the seven, and has always business at Ford's. If it be not inconvenient to you, pray let us go in, that I may prove myself to belong to the place, to be a true citizen of Highbury. I must buy something at Ford's. It will be taking out my freedom. I dare say they sell gloves."

"Oh! yes, gloves and everything. I do admire your patriotism. You will be adored in Highbury. You were very popular before you came, because you were Mr. Weston's son but lay out half a guinea at Ford's, and your popularity will stand upon your own virtues."

They went in; and while the sleek, well-tied parcels of "Men's Beavers" and "York Tan"[1] were bringing down and displaying on the counter, he said "But I beg your pardon, Miss Woodhouse, you were speaking to me, you were saying something at the very moment of this burst of my *amor patriae*[2]. Do not let me lose it. I assure you the utmost stretch of public fame would not make me amends for the loss of any happiness in private life."

"I merely asked, whether you had known much of Miss Fairfax and her party at Weymouth."

"And now that I understand your question, I must pronounce it to be a very unfair one. It is always the lady's right to decide on the degree of acquaintance. Miss Fairfax must already have given her account. I shall not commit myself by claiming more than she may choose to allow."

"Upon my word! you answer as discreetly as she could do herself. But her account of everything leaves so much to be guessed, she is so very reserved, so very unwilling to give the least information about anybody, that I really think you may say what you like of your acquaintance with her."

"May I, indeed? Then I will speak the truth, and nothing suits me so well. I met her frequently at Weymouth. I had known the Campbells a little in town; and at Weymouth we were very much in the same set. Colonel Campbell is a very agreeable man, and Mrs. Campbell a friendly, warm-hearted woman. I like them all."

"You know Miss Fairfax's situation in life, I conclude; what she is destined to be?"

"Yes – (rather hesitatingly) – I believe I do."

"You get upon delicate subjects, Emma," said Mrs. Weston

1 Types of gloves.
2 Love for the motherland.

smiling; "remember that I am here. Mr. Frank Churchill hardly knows what to say when you speak of Miss Fairfax's situation in life. I will move a little farther off."

"I certainly do forget to think of her," said Emma, "as having ever been any thing but my friend and my dearest friend."

He looked as if he fully understood and honoured such a sentiment.

When the gloves were bought, and they had quitted the shop again – "Did you ever hear the young lady we were speaking of, play?" said Frank Churchill.

"Ever hear her!" repeated Emma. "You forget how much she belongs to Highbury. I have heard her every year of our lives since we both began. She plays charmingly."

"You think so, do you? I wanted the opinion of some one who could really judge. She appeared to me to play well, that is, with considerable taste, but I know nothing of the matter myself. I am excessively fond of music, but without the smallest skill or right of judging of anybody's performance. I have been used to hear her's admired; and I remember one proof of her being thought to play well: a man, a very musical man, and in love with another woman – engaged to her on the point of marriage – would yet never ask that other woman to sit down to the instrument, if the lady in question could sit down instead – never seemed to like to hear one if he could hear the other. That, I thought, in a man of known musical talent, was some proof."

"Proof indeed!" said Emma, highly amused. "Mr. Dixon is very musical, is he? We shall know more about them all, in half an hour, from you, than Miss Fairfax would have vouchsafed in half a year."

"Yes, Mr. Dixon and Miss Campbell were the persons; and I thought it a very strong proof."

"Certainly very strong it was; to own the truth, a great deal stronger than, if I had been Miss Campbell, would have been at all agreeable to me. I could not excuse a man's having more music than love – more ear than eye – a more acute sensibility to fine sounds than to my feelings. How did Miss Campbell appear to like it?"

"It was her very particular friend, you know."

"Poor comfort!" said Emma, laughing. "One would rather have a stranger preferred than one's very particular friend with a stranger it might not recur again but the misery of having a very particular friend always at hand, to do everything better than one does oneself! Poor Mrs. Dixon! Well, I am glad she is gone to settle in Ireland."

"You are right. It was not very flattering to Miss Campbell; but she really did not seem to feel it."

"So much the better or so much the worse: I do not know which. But be it sweetness or be it stupidity in her – quickness of friendship, or dullness of feeling – there was one person, I think, who must have felt it – Miss Fairfax herself. *She* must have felt the improper and dangerous distinction."

"As to that – I do not – "

"Oh! do not imagine that I expect an account of Miss Fairfax's sensations from you, or from anybody else. They are known to no human being, I guess, but herself. But if she continued to play whenever she was asked by Mr. Dixon, one may guess what one chooses."

"There appeared such a perfectly good understanding among them all – " he began rather quickly, but checking himself, added, "however, it is impossible for me to say on what terms they really were – how it might all be behind the scenes. I can only say that there was smoothness outwardly. But you, who have known Miss Fairfax from a child, must be a better judge of her character, and of how she is likely to conduct herself in critical situations, than I can be."

"I have known her from a child, undoubtedly; we have been children and women together; and it is natural to suppose that we should be intimate – that we should have taken to each other whenever she visited her friends. But we never did. I hardly know how it has happened; a little, perhaps, from that wickedness on my side which was prone to take disgust towards a girl so idolized and so cried up as she always was, by her aunt and grandmother, and all their set. And then, her reserve I never could attach myself to any one so completely reserved."

"It is a most repulsive quality, indeed," said he. "Oftentimes very convenient, no doubt, but never pleasing. There is safety in reserve, but no attraction. One cannot love a reserved person."

"Not till the reserve ceases towards oneself; and then the attraction may be the greater. But I must be more in want of a friend, or an agreeable companion, than I have yet been, to take the trouble of conquering anybody's reserve to procure one. Intimacy between Miss Fairfax and me is quite out of the question. I have no reason to think ill of her – not the least – except that such extreme and perpetual cautiousness of word and manner, such a dread of giving a distinct idea about anybody, is apt to suggest suspicions of there being something to conceal."

He perfectly agreed with her: and after walking together so long, and thinking so much alike, Emma felt herself so well acquainted with him, that she could hardly believe it to be only their second meeting. He was not exactly what she had expected; less of the man of the world in some of his notions, less of the spoiled child of fortune, therefore better than she had expected. His ideas seemed more moderate – his feelings warmer. She was particularly struck by his manner of considering Mr. Elton's house, which, as well as the church, he would go and look at, and would not join them in finding much fault with. No, he could not believe it a bad house; not such a house as a man was to be pitied for having. If it were to be shared with the woman he loved, he could not think any man to be pitied for having that house. There must be ample room in it for every real comfort. The man must be a blockhead who wanted more. Mrs. Weston laughed, and said he did not know what he was talking about. Used only to a large house himself, and without ever thinking how many advantages and accommodations were attached to its size, he could be no judge of the privations inevitably belonging to a small one. But Emma, in her own mind, determined that he *did* know what he was talking about, and that he showed a very amiable inclination to settle early in life, and to marry, from worthy motives. He might not be aware of the inroads on domestic peace to be occasioned by no housekeeper's room, or a bad butler's pantry, but no doubt he did perfectly feel that Enscombe could not make him happy, and that whenever he were attached, he would willingly give up much of wealth to be allowed an early establishment.

# *Chapter 25*

EMMA'S VERY good opinion of Frank Churchill was a little shaken the following day, by hearing that he was gone off to London, merely to have his hair cut. A sudden freak seemed to have seized him at breakfast, and he had sent for a chaise and set off, intending to return at dinner, but with no more important view that appeared than having his hair cut. There was certainly no harm in his travelling sixteen miles twice over on such an errand; but there was an air of foppery and nonsense in it which she could not approve. It did not accord with the rationality of plan, the moderation in expense, or even the unselfish warmth of heart, which she had believed herself to discern in him yesterday. Vanity, extravagance, love of change, restlessness of temper, which must be doing something, good or bad; heedlessness as to the pleasure of his father and Mrs. Weston, indifferent as to how his conduct might appear in general; he became liable to all these charges. His father only called him a coxcomb, and thought it a very good story; but that Mrs. Weston did not like it, was clear enough, by her passing it over as quickly as possible, and making no other comment than that "all young people would have their little whims."

With the exception of this little blot, Emma found that his visit hitherto had given her friend only good ideas of him. Mrs. Weston was very ready to say how attentive and pleasant a companion he made himself – how much she saw to like in his disposition altogether. He appeared to have a very open temper – certainly a very cheerful and lively one; she could observe nothing wrong in his notions – a great deal decidedly right; he spoke of his uncle with warm regard – was fond of talking of him said he would be the best man in the world if he were left to himself; and though there was no being attached to the aunt, he acknowledged her kindness with gratitude, and seemed to mean always to speak of her with respect. This was all very promising; and, but for such an unfortunate fancy for having his hair cut, there was nothing to denote him unworthy of the distinguished honour which her imagination had given him; the honour, if not of being really in love with her, of being at least very near it, and saved only by her own indifference – (for still her resolution held of never marrying) – the honour, in short, of being marked out for her by all their joint acquaintance.

Mr. Weston, on his side, added a virtue to the account which must have some weight. He gave her to understand that Frank admired her extremely – thought her very beautiful and very charming; and with so much to be said for him altogether, she found she must not judge him harshly. As Mrs. Weston observed, "all young people would have their little whims."

There was one person among his new acquaintance in Surrey, not so leniently disposed. In general he was judged, throughout the parishes of Donwell and Highbury, with great candour; liberal allowances were made for the little excesses of such a handsome young man – one who smiled so often and bowed so well; but there was one spirit among them not to be softened, from its power of censure, by bows or smiles – Mr. Knightley. The circumstance was told to him at Hartfield; for the moment, he was silent; but Emma heard him almost immediately afterwards say to himself, over a newspaper he held in his hand, "Hum! just the trifling, silly fellow I took him for." She had half a mind to resent; but an instant's observation convinced her that it was really said only to relieve his own feelings, and not meant to provoke; and therefore she let it pass.

Although in one instance the bearers of not good tidings, Mr. and Mrs. Weston's visit this morning was in another respect particularly opportune. Something occurred while they were at Hartfield, to make Emma want their advice; and, which was still more lucky, she wanted exactly the advice they gave.

This was the occurrence – The Coles had been settled some years in Highbury, and were very good sort of people friendly, liberal, and unpretending; but, on the other hand, they were of low origin, in trade, and only moderately genteel. On their first coming into the country, they had lived in proportion to their income, quietly, keeping little company, and that little unexpensively; but the last year or two had brought them a considerable increase of means – the house in town had yielded greater profits, and fortune in general had smiled on them. With their wealth, their views increased; their want of a larger house, their inclination for more company. They added to their house, to their number of servants, to their expenses of every sort; and by this time were, in fortune and style of living, second only to the family at Hartfield. Their love of society, and their new dining room, prepared everybody for their keeping dinner-company; and a few parties, chiefly among the single men, had already taken place. The regular and best families Emma could hardly suppose they would presume to invite – neither Donwell, nor Hartfield, nor Randalls. Nothing should tempt *her* to go, if they did; and she regretted that her father's known habits would be giving her refusal less meaning than she could wish. The Coles were very respectable in their way, but they ought to be taught that it was not for them to arrange the terms on which the superior families would visit them. This lesson, she very much feared, they would receive only from herself; she had little hope of Mr. Knightley, none of Mr. Weston.

But she had made up her mind how to meet this presumption so many weeks before it appeared, that when the insult came at last, it found her very differently affected. Donwell and Randalls had received their invitation, and none had come for her father and herself; and Mrs. Weston's accounting for it with "I suppose they will not take the liberty with you; they know you do not dine out," was not quite sufficient. She felt that she should like to have had the power of refusal; and afterwards, as the idea of the party to be assembled there, consisting precisely of those whose society was dearest to her, occurred again and again, she did not know that she might not have been tempted to accept. Harriet was to be there in the evening, and the Bateses. They had been speaking of it as they walked about Highbury the day before, and Frank Churchill had most earnestly lamented her absence. Might not the evening end in a dance? had been a question of his. The bare possibility of it acted as a farther irritation on her spirits; and her being left in solitary grandeur, even supposing the omission to be intended as a compliment, was but poor comfort.

It was the arrival of this very invitation while the Westons were at Hartfield, which made their presence so acceptable; for though her first remark, on reading it, was that "of course it must be declined," she so very soon proceeded to ask them what they advised her to do, that their advice for her going was most prompt and successful.

She owned that, considering everything, she was not absolutely without inclination for the party. The Coles expressed themselves so properly – there was so much real attention in the manner of it – so much consideration for her father. "They would have solicited the honour earlier, but had been waiting the arrival of a folding-screen from London, which they hoped might keep Mr. Woodhouse from any draught of air, and therefore induce him the more readily to give them the honour of his company. "Upon the whole, she was very persuadable; and it being briefly settled among themselves how it might be done without neglecting his comfort – how certainly Mrs. Goddard, if not Mrs. Bates, might be depended on for bearing him company – Mr. Woodhouse was to be talked into an acquiescence of his daughter's going out to dinner on a day now near at hand, and spending the whole evening away from him. As for *his* going, Emma did not wish him to think it possible, the hours would be too late, and the party too numerous. He was soon pretty well resigned.

"I am not fond of dinner visiting," said he. "I never was. No more is Emma. Late hours do not agree with us. I am sorry Mr. and Mrs. Cole should have done it. I think it would be much better if they would come in one afternoon next summer, and take their tea with us take us in their afternoon walk; which they might do, as our hours are so reasonable, and yet get home without being out in the damp of the evening. The dews of a summer evening are what I would not expose anybody to. However, as they are so very desirous to have dear Emma dine with them, and as you will both be there, and Mr. Knightley too, to take care of her, I cannot wish to prevent it, provided the weather be what it ought, neither damp, nor cold, nor windy." Then turning to Mrs. Weston, with a look of gentle reproach –"Ah! Miss Taylor, if you had not married, you would have staid at home with me."

"Well, sir," cried Mr. Weston, "as I took Miss Taylor away, it is incumbent on me to supply her place, if I can; and I will step to Mrs. Goddard in a moment, if you wish it."

But the idea of any thing to be done in a *moment,* was increasing, not lessening, Mr. Woodhouse's agitation. The ladies knew better how to allay it. Mr. Weston must be quiet, and everything deliberately arranged.

With this treatment, Mr. Woodhouse was soon composed enough for talking as usual. "He should be happy to see Mrs. Goddard. He had a great regard for Mrs. Goddard; and Emma should write a line, and invite her. James could take the note. But first of all, there must be an answer written to Mrs. Cole."

"You will make my excuses, my dear, as civilly as possible. You will say that I am quite an invalid, and go no where, and therefore must decline their obliging invitation; beginning with my *compliments,* of course. But you will do everything right. I need not tell you what is to be done. We must remember to let James know that the carriage will be wanted on Tuesday. I shall have no fears for you with him. We have never been there above once since the new approach was made; but still I have no doubt that James will take you very safely. And when you get there, you must tell him at what time you would have him come for you again; and you had better name an early hour. You will not like staying late. You will get very tired when tea is over."

"But you would not wish me to come away before I am tired, papa?"

"Oh! no, my love; but you will soon be tired. There will be a great many people talking at once. You will not like the noise."

"But, my dear sir," cried Mr. Weston, "if Emma comes away early, it will be breaking up the party."

"And no great harm if it does," said Mr. Woodhouse. "The sooner every party breaks up, the better."

"But you do not consider how it may appear to the Coles. Emma's going away directly after tea might be giving offence. They are good natured people, and think little of their own claims; but still they must feel that anybody's hurrying away is no great compliment; and Miss Woodhouse's doing it would be more thought of than any other person's in the room. You would not wish to disappoint and mortify the Coles, I am sure, sir; friendly, good sort of people as ever lived, and who have been your neighbours these ten years."

"No, upon no account in the world, Mr. Weston; I am much obliged to you for reminding me. I should be extremely sorry to be giving them any pain. I know what worthy people they are. Perry tells me that Mr. Cole never touches malt liquor. You would not think it to look at him, but he is bilious – Mr. Cole is very bilious. No, I would not be the means of giving them any pain. My dear Emma, we must consider this. I am sure, rather than run the risk of hurting Mr. and Mrs. Cole, you would stay a little longer than you might wish. You will not regard being tired. You will be perfectly safe, you know, among your friends."

"Oh yes, papa. I have no fears at all for myself; and I should have no scruples of staying as late as Mrs. Weston, but on your account. I am only afraid of your sitting up for me. I am not afraid of your not being exceedingly comfortable with Mrs. Goddard. She loves piquet[1], you know; but when she is gone home, I am afraid you will be sitting up by yourself, instead of going to bed at your usual time and the idea of that would entirely destroy my comfort. You must promise me not to sit up."

He did, on the condition of some promises on her side: such as that, if she came home cold, she would be sure to warm herself thoroughly; if hungry, that she would take something to eat; that her own maid should sit up for her; and that Serle and the butler should see that everything were safe in the house, as usual.

1 A card game played by two players.

# Chapter 26

FRANK CHURCHILL came back again; and if he kept his father's dinner waiting, it was not known at Hartfield; for Mrs. Weston was too anxious for his being a favourite with Mr. Woodhouse, to betray any imperfection which could be concealed.

He came back, had had his hair cut, and laughed at himself with a very good grace, but without seeming really at all ashamed of what he had done. He had no reason to wish his hair longer, to conceal any confusion of face; no reason to wish the money unspent, to improve his spirits. He was quite as undaunted and as lively as ever; and, after seeing him, Emma thus moralised to herself:

"I do not know whether it ought to be so, but certainly silly things do cease to be silly if they are done by sensible people in an impudent way. Wickedness is always wickedness, but folly is not always folly. It depends upon the character of those who handle it. Mr. Knightley, he is not a trifling, silly young man. If he were, he would have done this differently. He would either have gloried in the achievement, or been ashamed of it. There would have been either the ostentation of a coxcomb, or the evasions of a mind too weak to defend its own vanities. No, I am perfectly sure that he is not trifling or silly."

With Tuesday came the agreeable prospect of seeing him again, and for a longer time than hitherto; of judging of his general manners, and by inference, of the meaning of his manners towards herself; of guessing how soon it might be necessary for her to throw coldness into her air; and of fancying what the observations of all those might be, who were now seeing them together for the first time.

She meant to be very happy, in spite of the scene being laid at Mr. Cole's; and without being able to forget that among the failings of Mr. Elton, even in the days of his favour, none had disturbed her more than his propensity to dine with Mr. Cole.

Her father's comfort was amply secured, Mrs. Bates as well as Mrs. Goddard being able to come; and her last pleasing duty, before she left the house, was to pay her respects to them as they sat together after dinner; and while her father was fondly noticing the beauty of her dress, to make the two ladies all the amends in her power, by helping them to large slices of cake and full glasses of wine, for whatever unwilling self-denial his care of their constitution might have obliged them to practise during the meal. She had provided a plentiful dinner for them; she wished she could know that they had been allowed to eat it.

She followed another carriage to Mr. Cole's door; and was pleased to see that it was Mr. Knightley's; for Mr. Knightley keeping no horses, having little spare money and a great deal of health, activity, and independence, was too apt, in Emma's opinion, to get about as he could, and not use his carriage so often as became the owner of Donwell Abbey. She had an opportunity now of speaking her approbation while warm from her heart, for he stopped to hand her out.

"This is coming as you should do," said she; "like a gentleman. I am quite glad to see you."

He thanked her, observing, "How lucky that we should arrive at the same moment! for, if we had met first in the drawing-room, I doubt whether you would have discerned me to be more of a gentleman than usual. You might not have distinguished how I came, by my look or manner."

"Yes I should, I am sure I should. There is always a look of consciousness or bustle when people come in a way which they know to be beneath them. You think you carry it off very well, I dare say, but with you it is a sort of bravado, an air of affected unconcern; I always observe it whenever I meet you under those circumstances. *Now* you have nothing to try for. You are not afraid of being supposedly ashamed. You are not striving to look taller than anybody else. *Now* I shall really be very happy to walk into the same room with you."

"Nonsensical girl!" was his reply, but not at all in anger.

Emma had as much reason to be satisfied with the rest of the party as with Mr. Knightley. She was received with a cordial respect which could not but please, and given all the consequence she could wish for. When the Westons arrived, the kindest looks of love, the strongest of admiration were for her, from both husband and wife; the son approached her with a cheerful eagerness which marked her as his peculiar object, and at dinner she found him seated by her and, as she firmly believed, not without some dexterity on his side.

The party was rather large, as it included one other family – a proper unobjectionable country family, whom the Coles had the advantage of naming among their acquaintance – and the male part of Mr. Cox's family, the lawyer of Highbury. The less worthy females were to come in the evening, with Miss Bates, Miss Fairfax, and Miss Smith; but already, at dinner, they were too numerous for any subject of conversation to be general; and, while politics and Mr. Elton were talked over, Emma could fairly surrender all her attention to the pleasantness of her neighbour. The first remote sound to which she felt herself obliged to attend, was the name of Jane Fairfax. Mrs. Cole seemed to be relating something of her that was expected to be very interesting. She listened, and found it well worth listening to. That very dear part of Emma, her fancy, received an amusing supply. Mrs. Cole was telling that she had been calling on Miss Bates, and as soon as she entered the room had been struck by the sight of a pianoforte a very elegant looking instrument not a grand, but a large sized square pianoforte; and the substance of the story, the end of all the dialogue which ensued of surprise, and inquiry, and congratulations on her side, and explanations on Miss Bates's, was, that this pianoforte had arrived from Broadwood's the day before, to the great astonishment of both aunt and niece entirely unexpected; that at first, by Miss Bates's account, Jane herself was quite at a loss, quite bewildered to think who could possibly have ordered it but now, they were both perfectly satisfied that it could be from only one quarter; of course it must be from Colonel Campbell.

"One can suppose nothing else," added Mrs. Cole, "and I was only surprised that there could ever have been a doubt. But Jane, it seems, had a letter from them very lately, and not a word was said about it. She knows their ways best; but I should not consider their silence as any reason for their not meaning to make the present. They might choose to surprise her."

Mrs. Cole had many to agree with her; everybody who spoke on the subject was equally convinced that it must come from Colonel Campbell, and equally rejoiced that such a present had been made; and there were enough ready to speak to allow Emma to think her own way, and still listen to Mrs. Cole.

"I declare, I do not know when I have heard any thing that has given me more satisfaction! It always has quite hurt me that Jane Fairfax, who plays so delightfully, should not have an instrument. It seemed quite a shame, especially considering how many houses there are where fine instruments are absolutely thrown away. This is like giving ourselves a slap, to be sure! and it was but yesterday I was telling Mr. Cole, I really was ashamed to look at our new grand pianoforte in the drawing room, while I do not know one note from another, and our little girls, who are but just beginning, perhaps may never make any thing of it; and there is poor Jane Fairfax, who is mistress of music, has not any thing of the nature of an instrument, not even the pitifullest old spinet in the world, to amuse herself with. I was saying this to Mr. Cole but yesterday, and he quite agreed with me; only he is so particularly fond of music that he could not help indulging himself in the purchase, hoping that some of our good neighbours might be so obliging occasionally to put it to a better use than we can; and that really is the reason why the instrument was bought – or else I am sure we ought to be ashamed of it. We are in great hopes that Miss Woodhouse may be prevailed with to try it this evening."

Miss Woodhouse made the proper acquiescence; and finding that nothing more was to be entrapped from any communication of Mrs. Cole's, turned to Frank Churchill.

"Why do you smile?" said she.

"Nay, why do you?"

"Me! I suppose I smile for pleasure at Colonel Campbell's being so rich and so liberal. It is a handsome present."

"Very."

"I rather wonder that it was never made before."

"Perhaps Miss Fairfax has never been staying here so long before."

"Or that he did not give her the use of their own instrument which must now be shut up in London, untouched by anybody."

"That is a grand pianoforte, and he might think it too large for Mrs. Bates's house."

"You may *say* what you choose but your countenance testifies that your *thoughts* on this subject are very much like mine."

"I do not know. I rather believe you are giving me more credit for acuteness than I deserve. I smile because you smile, and shall probably suspect whatever I find you suspect; but at present I do not see what there is to question. If Colonel Campbell is not the person, who can be?"

"What do you say to Mrs. Dixon?"

"Mrs. Dixon! very true indeed. I had not thought of Mrs. Dixon. She must know as well as her father, how acceptable an instrument would be; and perhaps the mode of it, the mystery, the surprise, is more like a young woman's scheme than an elderly man's. It is Mrs. Dixon, I dare say. I told you that your suspicions would guide mine."

"If so, you must extend your suspicions and comprehend Mr. Dixon in them."

"Mr. Dixon. Very well. Yes, I immediately perceive that it

must be the joint present of Mr. and Mrs. Dixon. We were speaking the other day, you know, of his being so warm an admirer of her performance."

"Yes, and what you told me on that head, confirmed an idea which I had entertained before. I do not mean to reflect upon the good intentions of either Mr. Dixon or Miss Fairfax, but I cannot help suspecting either that, after making his proposals to her friend, he had the misfortune to fall in love with her, or that he became conscious of a little attachment on her side. One might guess twenty things without guessing exactly the right; but I am sure there must be a particular cause for her choosing to come to Highbury instead of going with the Campbells to Ireland. Here, she must be leading a life of privation and penance; there it would have been all enjoyment. As to the pretence of trying her native air, I look upon that as a mere excuse. In the summer it might have passed; but what can anybody's native air do for them in the months of January, February, and March? Good fires and carriages would be much more to the purpose in most cases of delicate health, and I dare say in her's. I do not require you to adopt all my suspicions, though you make so noble a profession of doing it, but I honestly tell you what they are."

"And, upon my word, they have an air of great probability. Mr. Dixon's preference of her music to her friend's, I can answer for being very decided."

"And then, he saved her life. Did you ever hear of that? A water party; and by some accident she was falling overboard. He caught her."

"He did. I was there – one of the party."

"Were you really? Well! But you observed nothing of course, for it seems to be a new idea to you. If I had been there, I think I should have made some discoveries."

"I dare say you would; but I, simple I, saw nothing but the fact, that Miss Fairfax was nearly dashed from the vessel and that Mr. Dixon caught her – it was the work of a moment. And though the consequent shock and alarm was very great and much more durable – indeed I believe it was half an hour before any of us were comfortable again – yet that was too general a sensation for any thing of peculiar anxiety to be observable. I do not mean to say, however, that you might not have made discoveries."

The conversation was here interrupted. They were called on to share in the awkwardness of a rather long interval between the courses, and obliged to be as formal and as orderly as the others; but when the table was again safely covered, when every corner dish was placed exactly right, and occupation and ease were generally restored, Emma said:

"The arrival of this pianoforte is decisive with me. I wanted to know a little more, and this tells me quite enough. Depend upon it, we shall soon hear that it is a present from Mr. and Mrs. Dixon."

"And if the Dixons should absolutely deny all knowledge of it we must conclude it to come from the Campbells."

"No, I am sure it is not from the Campbells. Miss Fairfax knows it is not from the Campbells, or they would have been guessed at first. She would not have been puzzled, had she dared fix on them. I may not have convinced you perhaps, but I am perfectly convinced myself that Mr. Dixon is a principal in the business."

"Indeed you injure me if you suppose me unconvinced. Your reasonings carry my judgment along with them entirely. At first, while I supposed you satisfied that Colonel Campbell was the giver, I saw it only as paternal kindness, and thought it the most natural thing in the world. But when you mentioned Mrs. Dixon, I felt how much more probable that it should be the tribute of warm female friendship. And now I can see it in no other light than as an offering of love."

There was no occasion to press the matter farther. The

conviction seemed real; he looked as if he felt it. She said no more – other subjects took their turn; and the rest of the dinner passed away; the dessert succeeded, the children came in, and were talked to and admired amid the usual rate of conversation; a few clever things said, a few downright silly, but by much the larger proportion neither the one nor the other – nothing worse than everyday remarks, dull repetitions, old news, and heavy jokes.

The ladies had not been long in the drawing room, before the other ladies, in their different divisions, arrived. Emma watched the entree of her own particular little friend; and if she could not exult in her dignity and grace, she could not only love the blooming sweetness and the artless manner, but could most heartily rejoice in that light, cheerful, unsentimental disposition which allowed her so many alleviations of pleasure, in the midst of the pangs of disappointed affection. There she sat – and who would have guessed how many tears she had been lately shedding? To be in company, nicely dressed herself and seeing others nicely dressed, to sit and smile and look pretty, and say nothing, was enough for the happiness of the present hour. Jane Fairfax did look and move superior; but Emma suspected she might have been glad to change feelings with Harriet – very glad to have purchased the mortification of having loved – yes, of having loved even Mr. Elton in vain by the surrender of all the dangerous pleasure of knowing herself beloved by the husband of her friend.

In so large a party it was not necessary that Emma should approach her. She did not wish to speak of the pianoforte, she felt too much in the secret herself, to think the appearance of curiosity or interest fair, and therefore purposely kept at a distance; but by the others, the subject was almost immediately introduced, and she saw the blush of consciousness with which congratulations were received, the blush of guilt which accompanied the name of "my excellent friend Colonel Campbell."

Mrs. Weston, kind-hearted and musical, was particularly interested by the circumstance, and Emma could not help being amused at her perseverance in dwelling on the subject; and having so much to ask and to say as to tone, touch, and pedal, totally unsuspicious of that wish of saying as little about it as possible, which she plainly read in the fair heroine's countenance.

They were soon joined by some of the gentlemen; and the very first of the early was Frank Churchill. In he walked, the first and the handsomest; and after paying his compliments *en passant* to Miss Bates and her niece, made his way directly to the opposite side of the circle, where sat Miss Woodhouse; and till he could find a seat by her, would not sit at all. Emma divined what everybody present must be thinking. She was his object, and everybody must perceive it. She introduced him to her friend, Miss Smith, and, at convenient moments afterwards, heard what each thought of the other. "He had never seen so lovely a face, and was delighted with her *naïveté.*" And she – "only to be sure it was paying him too great a compliment, but she did think there were some looks a little like Mr. Elton." Emma restrained her indignation, and only turned from her in silence.

Smiles of intelligence passed between her and the gentleman on first glancing towards Miss Fairfax; but it was most prudent to avoid speech. He told her that he had been impatient to leave the dining-room – hated sitting long – was always the first to move when he could – that his father, Mr. Knightley, Mr. Cox, and Mr. Cole, were left very busy over parish business – that as long as he had staid, however, it had been pleasant enough, as he had found them in general a set of gentlemanlike, sensible men; and spoke so handsomely of Highbury altogether – thought it so abundant in agreeable families – that Emma began to feel she had been used to despise the place rather too much. She questioned him as to the society in Yorkshire the extent of the neighbourhood about Enscombe, and the sort; and could make out from his answers that, as far as Enscombe was concerned, there was very little going on, that their visitings were among a range of great families, none very near; and that even when days were fixed, and invitations accepted, it was an even chance that Mrs. Churchill were not in health and spirits for going; that they made a point of visiting no fresh person; and that, though he had his separate engagements, it was not without difficulty, without considerable address *at times,* that he could get away, or introduce an acquaintance for a night.

She saw that Enscombe could not satisfy, and that Highbury, taken at its best, might reasonably please a young man who had more retirement at home than he liked. His importance at Enscombe was very evident. He did not boast, but it naturally betrayed itself, that he had persuaded his aunt where his uncle could do nothing, and on her laughing and noticing it, he owned that he believed (excepting one or two points) he could *with time* persuade her to any thing. One of those points on which his influence failed, he then mentioned. He had wanted very much to go abroad – had been very eager indeed to be allowed to travel – but she would not hear of it. This had happened the year before. *Now,* he said, he was beginning to have no longer the same wish.

The unpersuadable point, which he did not mention, Emma guessed to be good behaviour to his father.

"I have made a most wretched discovery," said he, after a short pause. "I have been here a week tomorrow – half my time. I never knew days fly so fast. A week tomorrow! And I have hardly begun to enjoy myself. But just got acquainted with Mrs. Weston, and others! I hate the recollection."

"Perhaps you may now begin to regret that you spent one whole day, out of so few, in having your hair cut."

"No," said he, smiling, "that is no subject of regret at all. I have no pleasure in seeing my friends, unless I can believe myself fit to be seen."

The rest of the gentlemen being now in the room, Emma found herself obliged to turn from him for a few minutes, and listen to Mr. Cole. When Mr. Cole had moved away, and her attention could be restored as before, she saw Frank Churchill looking intently across the room at Miss Fairfax, who was sitting exactly opposite.

"What is the matter?" said she.

He started. "Thank you for rousing me," he replied. "I believe I have been very rude; but really Miss Fairfax has done her hair in so odd a way – so very odd a way – that I cannot keep my eyes from her. I never saw any thing so *outré!* Those curls! This must be a fancy of her own. I see nobody else looking like her! I must go and ask her whether it is an Irish fashion. Shall I? Yes, I will – I declare I will and you shall see how she takes it; whether she colours."

He was gone immediately; and Emma soon saw him standing before Miss Fairfax, and talking to her; but as to its effect on the young lady, as he had improvidently placed himself exactly between them, exactly in front of Miss Fairfax, she could absolutely distinguish nothing.

Before he could return to his chair, it was taken by Mrs. Weston.

"This is the luxury of a large party," said she: "one can get near everybody, and say everything. My dear Emma, I am longing to talk to you. I have been making discoveries and forming plans, just like yourself, and I must tell them while the idea is fresh. Do you know how Miss Bates and her niece came here?"

"How? They were invited, were not they?"

"Oh! yes – but how they were conveyed hither? the manner of their coming?"

"They walked, I conclude. How else could they come?"

"Very true. Well, a little while ago it occurred to me how very sad it would be to have Jane Fairfax walking home again, late at night, and cold as the nights are now. And as I looked at her, though I never saw her appear to more advantage, it struck me that she was heated, and would therefore be particularly liable to take cold. Poor girl! I could not bear the idea of it; so, as soon as Mr. Weston came into the room, and I could get at him, I spoke to him about the carriage. You may guess how readily he came into my wishes; and having his approbation, I made my way directly to Miss Bates, to assure her that the carriage would be at her service before it took us home; for I thought it would be making her comfortable at once. Good soul! she was as grateful as possible, you may be sure. 'Nobody was ever so fortunate as herself!' – but with many, many thanks – 'there was no occasion to trouble us, for Mr. Knightley's carriage had brought, and was to take them home again.' I was quite surprised; very glad, I am sure; but really quite surprised. Such a very kind attention – and so thoughtful an attention! the sort of thing that so few men would think of. And, in short, from knowing his usual ways, I am very much inclined to think that it was for their accommodation the carriage was used at all. I do suspect he would not have had a pair of horses for himself, and that it was only as an excuse for assisting them."

"Very likely," said Emma "nothing more likely. I know no man more likely than Mr. Knightley to do the sort of thing – to do any thing really good-natured, useful, considerate, or benevolent. He is not a gallant man, but he is a very humane one; and this, considering Jane Fairfax's ill health, would appear a case of humanity to him; and for an act of unostentatious kindness, there is nobody whom I would fix on more than on Mr. Knightley. I know he had horses to day for we arrived together; and I laughed at him about it, but he said not a word that could betray."

"Well," said Mrs. Weston, smiling, "you give him credit for more simple, disinterested benevolence in this instance than I do; for while Miss Bates was speaking, a suspicion darted into my head, and I have never been able to get it out again. The more I think of it, the more probable it appears. In short, I have made a match between Mr. Knightley and Jane Fairfax. See the consequence of keeping you company! What do you say to it?"

"Mr. Knightley and Jane Fairfax!" exclaimed Emma. "Dear Mrs. Weston, how could you think of such a thing? Mr. Knightley!

Mr. Knightley must not marry! You would not have little Henry cut out from Donwell? Oh! no, no, Henry must have Donwell. I cannot at all consent to Mr. Knightley's marrying; and I am sure it is not at all likely. I am amazed that you should think of such a thing."

"My dear Emma, I have told you what led me to think of it. I do not want the match – I do not want to injure dear little Henry – but the idea has been given me by circumstances; and if Mr. Knightley really wished to marry, you would not have him refrain on Henry's account, a boy of six years old, who knows nothing of the matter?"

"Yes, I would. I could not bear to have Henry supplanted. Mr. Knightley marry! No, I have never had such an idea, and I cannot adopt it now. And Jane Fairfax, too, of all women!"

"Nay, she has always been a first favourite with him, as you very well know."

"But the imprudence of such a match!"

"I am not speaking of its prudence; merely its probability."

"I see no probability in it, unless you have any better foundation than what you mention. His good nature, his humanity, as I tell you, would be quite enough to account for the horses. He has a great regard for the Bateses, you know, independent of Jane Fairfax – and is always glad to show them attention. My dear Mrs. Weston, do not take to match making. You do it very ill. Jane Fairfax mistress of the Abbey! Oh! no, no; every feeling revolts. For his own sake, I would not have him do so mad a thing."

"Imprudent, if you please – but not mad. Excepting inequality of fortune, and perhaps a little disparity of age, I can see nothing unsuitable."

"But Mr. Knightley does not want to marry. I am sure he has not the least idea of it. Do not put it into his head. Why should he marry? He is as happy as possible by himself; with his farm, and his sheep, and his library, and all the parish to manage; and he is extremely fond of his brother's children. He has no occasion to marry, either to fill up his time or his heart."

"My dear Emma, as long as he thinks so, it is so; but if he really loves Jane Fairfax – "

"Nonsense! He does not care about Jane Fairfax. In the way of love, I am sure he does not. He would do any good to her, or her family; but – "

"Well," said Mrs. Weston, laughing, "perhaps the greatest good he could do them, would be to give Jane such a respectable home."

"If it would be good to her, I am sure it would be evil to himself; a very shameful and degrading connection. How would he bear to have Miss Bates belonging to him? To have her haunting the Abbey, and thanking him all day long for his great kindness in marrying Jane? 'So very kind and obliging! But he always had been such a very kind neighbour!' And then fly off, through half a sentence, to her mother's old petticoat. 'Not that it was such a very old petticoat either – for still it would last a great while – and, indeed, she must thankfully say that their petticoats were all very strong.' "

"For shame, Emma! Do not mimic her. You divert me against my conscience. And, upon my word, I do not think Mr. Knightley would be much disturbed by Miss Bates. Little things do not irritate him. She might talk on; and if he wanted to say any thing himself, he would only talk louder, and drown her voice. But the question is not, whether it would be a bad connection for him, but whether he wishes it; and I think he does. I have heard him speak, and so must you, so very highly of Jane Fairfax! The interest he takes in her – his anxiety about her health – his concern that she should have no happier prospect! I have heard him express himself so warmly on those points! Such an admirer of her performance on the pianoforte, and of her voice! I have heard him say that he could listen to her for ever. Oh! and I had almost forgotten one idea that occurred to me – this pianoforte that has been sent here by somebody – though we have all been so well satisfied to consider it a present from the Campbells, may it not be from Mr. Knightley? I cannot help suspecting him. I think he is just the person to do it, even without being in love."

"Then it can be no argument to prove that he is in love. But I do not think it is at all a likely thing for him to do. Mr. Knightley does nothing mysteriously."

"I have heard him lamenting her having no instrument repeatedly; oftener than I should suppose such a circumstance would, in the common course of things, occur to him."

"Very well; and if he had intended to give her one, he would have told her so."

"There might be scruples of delicacy, my dear Emma. I have a very strong notion that it comes from him. I am sure he was particularly silent when Mrs. Cole told us of it at dinner."

"You take up an idea, Mrs. Weston, and run away with it; as you have many a time reproached me with doing. I see no sign of attachment I believe nothing of the pianoforte and proof only shall convince me that Mr. Knightley has any thought of marrying Jane Fairfax."

They combated the point some time longer in the same way; Emma rather gaining ground over the mind of her friend; for Mrs. Weston was the most used of the two to yield; till a little bustle in the room showed them that tea was over, and the instrument in preparation; and at the same moment Mr. Cole approaching to entreat Miss Woodhouse would do them the honour of trying it. Frank Churchill, of whom, in the eagerness of her conversation with Mrs. Weston, she had been seeing nothing, except that he had found a seat by Miss Fairfax, followed Mr. Cole, to add his very pressing entreaties; and as, in every respect, it suited Emma best to lead, she gave a very proper compliance.

She knew the limitations of her own powers too well to attempt more than she could perform with credit; she wanted neither taste nor spirit in the little things which are generally acceptable, and could accompany her own voice well. One accompaniment to her song took her agreeably by surprise a second, slightly but correctly taken by Frank Churchill. Her pardon was duly begged at the close of the song, and everything usual followed. He was accused of having a delightful voice, and a perfect knowledge of music; which was properly denied; and that he knew nothing of the matter, and had no voice at all, roundly asserted. They sang together once more; and Emma would then resign her place to Miss Fairfax, whose performance, both vocal and instrumental, she never could attempt to conceal from herself, was infinitely superior to her own.

With mixed feelings, she seated herself at a little distance from the numbers round the instrument, to listen. Frank Churchill sang again. They had sung together once or twice, it appeared, at Weymouth. But the sight of Mr. Knightley among the most attentive, soon drew away half Emma's mind; and she fell into a train of thinking on the subject of Mrs. Weston's suspicions, to which the sweet sounds of the united voices gave only momentary interruptions. Her objections to Mr. Knightley's marrying did not in the least subside. She could see nothing but evil in it. It would be a great disappointment to Mr. John Knightley; consequently to Isabella. A real injury to the children – a most mortifying change, and material loss to them all; a very great deduction from her father's daily comfort – and, as to herself, she could not at all endure the idea of Jane Fairfax at Donwell Abbey. A Mrs. Knightley for them all to give way to! No – Mr. Knightley must never marry. Little Henry must remain the heir of Donwell.

Presently Mr. Knightley looked back, and came and sat down by her. They talked at first only of the performance. His admiration was certainly very warm; yet she thought, but for Mrs. Weston, it would not have struck her. As a sort of touchstone, however, she began to speak of his kindness in conveying the aunt and niece; and though his answer was in the spirit of cutting the matter short, she believed it to indicate only his disinclination to dwell on any kindness of his own.

"I often feel concern," said she, "that I dare not make our carriage more useful on such occasions. It is not that I am without the wish; but you know how impossible my father would deem it that James should put it to for such a purpose."

"Quite out of the question, quite out of the question," he replied; "but you must often wish it, I am sure." And he smiled with such seeming pleasure at the conviction, that she must proceed another step.

"This present from the Campbells," said she – "this pianoforte is very kindly given."

"Yes," he replied, and without the smallest apparent embarrassment. "But they would have done better had they given her notice of it. Surprises are foolish things. The pleasure is not enhanced, and the inconvenience is often considerable. I should have expected better judgment in Colonel Campbell."

From that moment, Emma could have taken her oath that Mr. Knightley had had no concern in giving the instrument. But whether he were entirely free from peculiar attachment – whether there were no actual preference – remained a little longer doubtful. Towards the end of Jane's second song, her voice grew thick.

"That will do," said he, when it was finished, thinking aloud "you have sung quite enough for one evening – now be quiet."

Another song, however, was soon begged for. "One more; they would not fatigue Miss Fairfax on any account, and would only ask for one more." And Frank Churchill was heard to say, "I think you could manage this without effort; the first part is so very trifling. The strength of the song falls on the second."

Mr. Knightley grew angry.

"That fellow," said he, indignantly, "thinks of nothing but

showing off his own voice. This must not be." And touching Miss Bates, who at that moment passed near "Miss Bates, are you mad, to let your niece sing herself hoarse in this manner? Go, and interfere. They have no mercy on her."

Miss Bates, in her real anxiety for Jane, could hardly stay even to be grateful, before she stepped forward and put an end to all farther singing. Here ceased the concert part of the evening, for Miss Woodhouse and Miss Fairfax were the only young lady performers; but soon (within five minutes) the proposal of dancing – originating nobody exactly knew where – was so effectually promoted by Mr. and Mrs. Cole, that everything was rapidly clearing away, to give proper space. Mrs. Weston, capital in her country-dances, was seated, and beginning an irresistible waltz; and Frank Churchill, coming up with most becoming gallantry to Emma, had secured her hand, and led her up to the top.

While waiting till the other young people could pair themselves off, Emma found time, in spite of the compliments she was receiving on her voice and her taste, to look about, and see what became of Mr. Knightley. This would be a trial. He was no dancer in general. If he were to be very alert in engaging Jane Fairfax now, it might augur something. There was no immediate appearance. No; he was talking to Mrs. Cole – he was looking on unconcerned; Jane was asked by somebody else, and he was still talking to Mrs. Cole.

Emma had no longer an alarm for Henry; his interest was yet safe; and she led off the dance with genuine spirit and enjoyment. Not more than five couple could be mustered; but the rarity and the suddenness of it made it very delightful, and she found herself well matched in a partner. They were a couple worth looking at.

Two dances, unfortunately, were all that could be allowed. It was growing late, and Miss Bates became anxious to get home, on her mother's account. After some attempts, therefore, to be permitted to begin again, they were obliged to thank Mrs. Weston, look sorrowful, and have done.

"Perhaps it is as well," said Frank Churchill, as he attended Emma to her carriage. "I must have asked Miss Fairfax, and her languid dancing would not have agreed with me, after your's."

## *Chapter 27*

EMMA DID not repent her condescension in going to the Coles. The visit afforded her many pleasant recollections the next day; and all that she might be supposed to have lost on the side of dignified seclusion, must be amply repaid in the splendour of popularity. She must have delighted the Coles – worthy people, who deserved to be made happy! And left a name behind her that would not soon die away.

Perfect happiness, even in memory, is not common; and there were two points on which she was not quite easy. She doubted whether she had not transgressed the duty of woman by woman, in betraying her suspicions of Jane Fairfax's feelings to Frank Churchill. It was hardly right; but it had been so strong an idea, that it would escape her, and his submission to all that she told, was a compliment to her penetration, which made it difficult for her to be quite certain that she ought to have held her tongue.

The other circumstance of regret related also to Jane Fairfax; and there she had no doubt. She did unfeignedly and unequivocally regret the inferiority of her own playing and singing. She did most heartily grieve over the idleness of her childhood and sat down and practised vigorously an hour and a half.

She was then interrupted by Harriet's coming in; and if Harriet's praise could have satisfied her, she might soon have been comforted.

"Oh! if I could but play as well as you and Miss Fairfax!"

"Don't class us together, Harriet. My playing is no more like her's, than a lamp is like sunshine."

"Oh! dear I think you play the best of the two. I think you play quite as well as she does. I am sure I had much rather hear you. Everybody last night said how well you played."

"Those who knew any thing about it, must have felt the difference. The truth is, Harriet, that my playing is just good enough to be praised, but Jane Fairfax's is much beyond it."

"Well, I always shall think that you play quite as well as she does, or that if there is any difference nobody would ever find it out. Mr. Cole said how much taste you had; and Mr. Frank Churchill talked a great deal about your taste, and that he valued taste much more than execution."

"Ah! but Jane Fairfax has them both, Harriet."

"Are you sure? I saw she had execution, but I did not know she had any taste. Nobody talked about it. And I hate Italian singing. There is no understanding a word of it. Besides, if she does play so very well, you know, it is no more than she is obliged to do, because she will have to teach. The Coxes were wondering last night whether she would get into any great family. How did you think the Coxes looked?"

"Just as they always do – very vulgar."

"They told me something," said Harriet rather hesitatingly;" but it is nothing of any consequence."

Emma was obliged to ask what they had told her, though fearful of its producing Mr. Elton.

"They told me that Mr. Martin dined with them last Saturday."

"Oh!"

"He came to their father upon some business, and he asked him to stay to dinner."

"Oh!"

"They talked a great deal about him, especially Anne Cox. I do not know what she meant, but she asked me if I thought I should go and stay there again next summer."

"She meant to be impertinently curious, just as such an Anne Cox should be."

"She said he was very agreeable the day he dined there. He sat by her at dinner. Miss Nash thinks either of the Coxes would be very glad to marry him."

"Very likely. I think they are, without exception, the most vulgar girls in Highbury."

Harriet had business at Ford's. Emma thought it most prudent to go with her. Another accidental meeting with the Martins was possible, and in her present state, would be dangerous.

Harriet, tempted by everything and swayed by half a word, was always very long at a purchase; and while she was still hanging over muslins and changing her mind, Emma went to the door for amusement. Much could not be hoped from the traffic of even the busiest part of Highbury; Mr. Perry walking hastily by, Mr. William Cox letting himself in at the office-door, Mr. Cole's carriage horses returning from exercise, or a stray letter-boy on an obstinate mule, were the liveliest objects she could presume to expect; and when her eyes fell only on the butcher with his tray, a tidy old woman travelling homewards from shop with her full basket, two curs quarrelling over a dirty bone, and a string of dawdling children round the baker's little bow-window eyeing the gingerbread, she knew she had no reason to complain, and was amused enough; quite enough still to stand at the door. A mind lively and at ease, can do with seeing nothing, and can see nothing that does not answer.

She looked down the Randalls road. The scene enlarged; two persons appeared; Mrs. Weston and her son-in-law; they were walking into Highbury; to Hartfield of course. They were stopping, however, in the first place at Mrs. Bates's; whose house was a little nearer Randalls than Ford's; and had all but knocked, when

Emma caught their eye. Immediately they crossed the road and came forward to her; and the agreeableness of yesterday's engagement seemed to give fresh pleasure to the present meeting. Mrs. Weston informed her that she was going to call on the Bateses, in order to hear the new instrument.

"For my companion tells me," said she, "that I absolutely promised Miss Bates last night, that I would come this morning. I was not aware of it myself. I did not know that I had fixed a day, but as he says I did, I am going now."

"And while Mrs. Weston pays her visit, I may be allowed, I hope," said Frank Churchill, "to join your party and wait for her at Hartfield if you are going home."

Mrs. Weston was disappointed.

"I thought you meant to go with me. They would be very much pleased."

"Me! I should be quite in the way. But, perhaps I may be equally in the way here. Miss Woodhouse looks as if she did not want me. My aunt always sends me off when she is shopping. She says I fidget her to death; and Miss Woodhouse looks as if she could almost say the same. What am I to do?"

"I am here on no business of my own," said Emma; "I am only waiting for my friend. She will probably have soon done, and then we shall go home. But you had better go with Mrs. Weston and hear the instrument."

"Well if you advise it. But (with a smile) if Colonel Campbell should have employed a careless friend, and if it should prove to have an indifferent tone what shall I say? I shall be no support to Mrs. Weston. She might do very well by herself. A disagreeable truth would be palatable through her lips, but I am the wretchedest being in the world at a civil falsehood."

"I do not believe any such thing," replied Emma. "I am persuaded that you can be as insincere as your neighbours, when it is necessary; but there is no reason to suppose the instrument is indifferent. Quite otherwise indeed, if I understood Miss Fairfax's opinion last night."

"Do come with me," said Mrs. Weston, "if it be not very disagreeable to you. It need not detain us long. We will go to Hartfield afterwards. We will follow them to Hartfield. I really wish you to call with me. It will be felt so great an attention – and I always thought you meant it."

He could say no more; and with the hope of Hartfield to reward him, returned with Mrs. Weston to Mrs. Bates's door. Emma watched them in, and then joined Harriet at the interesting counter, trying, with all the force of her own mind, to convince her that if she wanted plain muslin it was of no use to look at figured; and that a blue ribbon, be it ever so beautiful, would still never match her yellow pattern. At last it was all settled, even to the destination of the parcel.

"Should I send it to Mrs. Goddard's, ma'am?" asked Mrs. Ford. "Yes – no – yes, to Mrs. Goddard's. Only my pattern gown is at Hartfield. No, you shall send it to Hartfield, if you please. But then, Mrs. Goddard will want to see it. And I could take the pattern gown home any day. But I shall want the ribbon directly so it had better go to Hartfield – at least the ribbon. You could make it into two parcels, Mrs. Ford, could not you?"

"It is not worth while, Harriet, to give Mrs. Ford the trouble of two parcels."

"No more it is."

"No trouble in the world, ma'am," said the obliging Mrs. Ford.

"Oh! but indeed I would much rather have it only in one. Then, if you please, you shall send it all to Mrs. Goddard's – I do not know – No, I think, Miss Woodhouse, I may just as well have it sent to Hartfield, and take it home with me at night. What do you advise?"

"That you do not give another half-second to the subject. To Hartfield, if you please, Mrs. Ford."

"Aye, that will be much best," said Harriet, quite satisfied, "I should not at all like to have it sent to Mrs. Goddard's."

Voices approached the shop or rather one voice and two ladies: Mrs. Weston and Miss Bates met them at the door.

"My dear Miss Woodhouse," said the latter, "I am just run across to entreat the favour of you to come and sit down with us a little while, and give us your opinion of our new instrument; you and Miss Smith. How do you do, Miss Smith? Very well I thank you. And I begged Mrs. Weston to come with me, that I might be sure of succeeding."

"I hope Mrs. Bates and Miss Fairfax are – "

"Very well, I am much obliged to you. My mother is delightfully well; and Jane caught no cold last night. How is Mr. Woodhouse? I am so glad to hear such a good account. Mrs. Weston told me you were here. Oh! then, said I, I must run across, I am sure Miss Woodhouse will allow me just to run across and entreat her to come in; my mother will be so very happy to see her and now we are such a nice party, she cannot refuse. 'Aye, pray do,' said Mr. Frank Churchill, 'Miss Woodhouse's opinion of the instrument will be worth having.' But, said I, I shall be more sure of succeeding if one of you will go with me. 'Oh,' said he, 'wait half a minute, till I have finished my job;' For, would you believe it, Miss Woodhouse, there he is, in the most obliging manner in the world, fastening in the rivet of my mother's spectacles. The rivet came out, you know, this morning. So very obliging! For my mother had no use of her spectacles – could not put them on. And, by the bye, everybody ought to have two pair of spectacles; they should indeed. Jane said so. I meant to take them over to John Saunders the first thing I did, but something or other hindered me all the morning; first one thing, then another, there is no saying what, you know. At one time Patty came to say she thought the kitchen chimney wanted sweeping. Oh, said I, Patty do not come with your bad news to me. Here is the rivet of your mistress's spectacles out.

Then the baked apples came home, Mrs. Wallis sent them by her boy; they are extremely civil and obliging to us, the Wallises, always I have heard some people say that Mrs. Wallis can be uncivil and give a very rude answer, but we have never known any thing but the greatest attention from them. And it cannot be for the value of our custom now, for what is our consumption of bread, you know? Only three of us. Besides, dear Jane at present – and she really eats nothing – makes such a shocking breakfast, you would be quite frightened if you saw it. I dare not let my mother know how little she eats so I say one thing and then I say another, and it passes off. But about the middle of the day she gets hungry, and there is nothing she likes so well as these baked apples, and they are extremely wholesome, for I took the opportunity the other day of asking Mr. Perry; I happened to meet him in the street. Not that I had any doubt before I have so often heard Mr. Woodhouse recommend a baked apple. I believe it is the only way that Mr. Woodhouse thinks the fruit thoroughly wholesome. We have apple-dumplings, however, very often. Patty makes an excellent apple-dumpling. Well, Mrs. Weston, you have prevailed, I hope, and these ladies will oblige us."

Emma would be "very happy to wait on Mrs. Bates, etc.," and they did at last move out of the shop, with no farther delay from Miss Bates than –

"How do you do, Mrs. Ford? I beg your pardon. I did not see you before. I hear you have a charming collection of new ribbons from town. Jane came back delighted yesterday. Thank ye, the gloves do very well – only a little too large about the wrist; but Jane is taking them in."

"What was I talking of?" said she, beginning again when they were all in the street.

Emma wondered on what, of all the medley, she would fix.

"I declare I cannot recollect what I was talking of. Oh! my mother's spectacles. So very obliging of Mr. Frank Churchill! 'Oh!' said he, 'I do think I can fasten the rivet; I like a job of this kind excessively.' Which you know showed him to be so very – Indeed I must say that, much as I had heard of him before and much as I had expected, he very far exceeds anything – I do congratulate you, Mrs. Weston, most warmly. He seems everything the fondest parent could – 'Oh!' said he, 'I can fasten the rivet. I like a job of that sort excessively.' I never shall forget his manner. And when I brought out the baked apples from the closet, and hoped our friends would be so very obliging as to take some, 'Oh!' said he directly, 'there is nothing in the way of fruit half so good, and these are the finest-looking home baked apples I ever saw in my life.' That, you know, was so very – And I am sure, by his manner, it was no compliment. Indeed they are very delightful apples, and Mrs. Wallis does them full justice only we do not have them baked more than twice, and Mr. Woodhouse made us promise to have them done three times but Miss Woodhouse will be so good as not to mention it. The apples themselves are the very finest sort for baking, beyond a doubt; all from Donwell – some of Mr. Knightley's most liberal supply. He sends us a sack every year; and certainly there never was such a keeping apple anywhere as one of his trees – I believe there is two of them. My mother says the orchard was always famous in her younger days. But I was really quite shocked the other day for Mr. Knightley called one morning, and Jane was eating these apples, and we talked about them and said how much she enjoyed them, and he asked whether we were not got to the end of our stock. 'I am sure you must be,' said he, 'and I will send you another supply; for I have a great many more than I can ever use. William Larkins let me keep a larger quantity than usual this year. I will send you some more, before they get good for nothing.' So I begged he would not – for really as to ours being gone, I could not absolutely say that we had a great many left – it was but half a dozen indeed; but they should be all kept for Jane; and I could not at all bear that he should be sending us more, so liberal as he had been already; and Jane said the same. And when he was gone, she almost quarrelled with me – no, I should not say quarrelled, for we never had a quarrel in our lives; but she was quite distressed that I had owned the apples were so nearly gone; she wished I had made him believe we had a great many left. Oh, said I, my dear, I did say as much as I could. However, the very same evening William Larkins came over with a large basket of apples, the same sort of apples, a bushel at least, and I was very much obliged, and went down and spoke to William Larkins and said everything, as you may suppose. William Larkins is such an old acquaintance! I am always glad to see him. But, however, I found afterwards from Patty, that William said it was all the apples of *that* sort his master had; he had brought them all – and now his master had not one left to bake or boil. William did not seem to mind it himself, he was so pleased to think his master had sold so many; for William, you know, thinks more of his master's profit than any thing; but Mrs. Hodges, he said, was quite displeased at their being all sent away. She could not bear that her master should not be able to have another apple-tart this spring. He told Patty this, but bid her not mind it, and be sure not to say any thing to us about it, for Mrs. Hodges *would* be cross sometimes, and as long as so many sacks were sold, it did not signify who ate the remainder. And so Patty told me, and I was excessively shocked indeed! I would not have Mr. Knightley know any thing about it for the world! He would be so very – I wanted to keep it from Jane's knowledge; but, unluckily, I had mentioned it before I was aware."

Miss Bates had just done as Patty opened the door; and her visitors walked upstairs without having any regular narration to attend to, pursued only by the sounds of her desultory good will.

"Pray take care, Mrs. Weston, there is a step at the turning. Pray take care, Miss Woodhouse, ours is rather a dark staircase – rather darker and narrower than one could wish. Miss Smith, pray take care. Miss Woodhouse, I am quite concerned, I am sure you hit your foot. Miss Smith, the step at the turning."

# Chapter 28

THE APPEARANCE of the little sitting room as they entered, was tranquillity itself; Mrs. Bates, deprived of her usual employment, slumbering on one side of the fire, Frank Churchill, at a table near her, most deedily occupied about her spectacles, and Jane Fairfax, standing with her back to them, intent on her pianoforte.

Busy as he was, however, the young man was yet able to show a most happy countenance on seeing Emma again.

"This is a pleasure," said he, in rather a low voice, "coming at least ten minutes earlier than I had calculated. You find me trying to be useful; tell me if you think I shall succeed."

"What!" said Mrs. Weston, "have not you finished it yet? you would not earn a very good livelihood as a working silversmith at this rate."

"I have not been working uninterruptedly," he replied, "I have been assisting Miss Fairfax in trying to make her instrument stand steadily, it was not quite firm; an unevenness in the floor, I believe. You see we have been wedging one leg with paper. This was very kind of you to be persuaded to come. I was almost afraid you would be hurrying home."

He contrived that she should be seated by him; and was sufficiently employed in looking out the best baked apple for her, and trying to make her help or advise him in his work, till Jane Fairfax was quite ready to sit down to the pianoforte again. That she was not immediately ready, Emma did suspect to arise from the state of her nerves; she had not yet possessed the instrument long enough to touch it without emotion; she must reason herself into the power of performance; and Emma could not but pity such feelings, whatever their origin, and could not but resolve never to expose them to her neighbour again.

At last Jane began, and though the first bars were feebly given, the powers of the instrument were gradually done full justice to. Mrs. Weston had been delighted before, and was delighted again; Emma joined her in all her praise; and the pianoforte, with every proper discrimination, was pronounced to be altogether of the highest promise.

"Whoever Colonel Campbell might employ," said Frank Churchill, with a smile at Emma, "the person has not chosen ill. I heard a good deal of Colonel Campbell's taste at Weymouth; and the softness of the upper notes I am sure is exactly what he and *all that party* would particularly prize. I dare say, Miss Fairfax, that he either gave his friend very minute directions, or wrote to Broadwood himself. Do not you think so?"

Jane did not look round. She was not obliged to hear. Mrs. Weston had been speaking to her at the same moment.

"It is not fair," said Emma, in a whisper; "mine was a random guess. Do not distress her."

He shook his head with a smile, and looked as if he had very little doubt and very little mercy. Soon afterwards he began again:

"How much your friends in Ireland must be enjoying your pleasure on this occasion, Miss Fairfax. I dare say they often think of you, and wonder which will be the day, the precise day of the instrument's coming to hand. Do you imagine Colonel Campbell knows the business to be going forward just at this time? Do you imagine it to be the consequence of an immediate commission from him, or that he may have sent only a general direction, an order indefinite as to time, to depend upon contingencies and conveniences?"

He paused. She could not but hear; she could not avoid answering:

"Till I have a letter from Colonel Campbell," said she, in a voice of forced calmness, "I can imagine nothing with any confidence. It must be all conjecture."

"Conjecture aye, sometimes one conjectures right, and sometimes one conjectures wrong. I wish I could conjecture how soon I shall make this rivet quite firm. What nonsense one talks, Miss Woodhouse, when hard at work, if one talks at all; your real workmen, I suppose, hold their tongues; but we gentlemen labourers if we get hold of a word – Miss Fairfax said something about conjecturing. There, it is done. I have the pleasure, madam, (to Mrs. Bates,) of restoring your spectacles, healed for the present."

He was very warmly thanked both by mother and daughter; to escape a little from the latter, he went to the pianoforte, and begged Miss Fairfax, who was still sitting at it, to play something more.

"If you are very kind," said he, "it will be one of the waltzes we danced last night; let me live them over again. You did not enjoy them as I did; you appeared tired the whole time. I believe you were glad we danced no longer; but I would have given worlds all the worlds – one ever has to give – for another half hour."

She played.

"What felicity it is to hear a tune again which *has* made one happy! If I mistake not that was danced at Weymouth."

She looked up at him for a moment, coloured deeply, and played something else. He took some music from a chair near the pianoforte, and turning to Emma, said:

"Here is something quite new to me. Do you know it? Cramer. And here are a new set of Irish melodies. That, from such a quarter, one might expect. This was all sent with the instrument. Very thoughtful of Colonel Campbell, was not it? He knew Miss Fairfax could have no music here. I honour that part of the attention particularly; it shows it to have been so thoroughly from the heart. Nothing hastily done; nothing incomplete. True affection only could have prompted it."

Emma wished he would be less pointed, yet could not help being amused; and when on glancing her eye towards Jane Fairfax she caught the remains of a smile, when she saw that with all the deep blush of consciousness, there had been a smile of secret delight, she had less scruple in the amusement, and much less compunction with respect to her. This amiable, upright, perfect Jane Fairfax was apparently cherishing very reprehensible feelings.

He brought all the music to her, and they looked it over together. Emma took the opportunity of whispering:

"You speak too plain. She must understand you."

"I hope she does. I would have her understand me. I am not in the least ashamed of my meaning."

"But really, I am half ashamed, and wish I had never taken up the idea."

"I am very glad you did, and that you communicated it to me. I have now a key to all her odd looks and ways. Leave shame to her. If she does wrong, she ought to feel it."

"She is not entirely without it, I think."

"I do not see much sign of it. She is playing Robin Adair at this moment – *his* favourite."

Shortly afterwards Miss Bates, passing near the window, descried Mr. Knightley on horse back not far off.

"Mr. Knightley I declare! I must speak to him if possible, just to thank him. I will not open the window here; it would give you all cold; but I can go into my mother's room you know. I dare say he will come in when he knows who is here. Quite delightful to have you all meet so! Our little room so honoured!"

She was in the adjoining chamber while she still spoke, and opening the casement there, immediately called Mr. Knightley's attention, and every syllable of their conversation was as distinctly heard by the others, as if it had passed within the same apartment.

"How d'ye do? how d'ye do? Very well, I thank you. So

obliged to you for the carriage last night. We were just in time; my mother just ready for us. Pray come in; do come in. You will find some friends here."

So began Miss Bates; and Mr. Knightley seemed determined to be heard in his turn, for most resolutely and commandingly did he say:

"How is your niece, Miss Bates? I want to inquire after you all, but particularly your niece. How is Miss Fairfax? I hope she caught no cold last night. How is she to day? Tell me how Miss Fairfax is."

And Miss Bates was obliged to give a direct answer before he would hear her in any thing else. The listeners were amused; and Mrs. Weston gave Emma a look of particular meaning. But Emma still shook her head in steady scepticism.

"So obliged to you! so very much obliged to you for the carriage," resumed Miss Bates.

He cut her short with –

"I am going to Kingston. Can I do anything for you?"

"Oh! dear, Kingston – are you? Mrs. Cole was saying the other day she wanted something from Kingston."

"Mrs. Cole has servants to send. Can I do any thing for *you?*"

"No, I thank you. But do come in. Who do you think is here? Miss Woodhouse and Miss Smith; so kind as to call to hear the new pianoforte. Do put up your horse at the Crown, and come in."

"Well," said he, in a deliberating manner, "for five minutes, perhaps."

"And here is Mrs. Weston and Mr. Frank Churchill too! – Quite delightful; so many friends!"

"No, not now, I thank you. I could not stay two minutes. I must get on to Kingston as fast as I can."

"Oh! do come in. They will be so very happy to see you."

"No, no; your room is full enough. I will call another day, and hear the pianoforte."

"Well, I am so sorry! Oh! Mr. Knightley, what a delightful party last night; how extremely pleasant. Did you ever see such dancing? Was not it delightful? Miss Woodhouse and Mr. Frank Churchill; I never saw any thing equal to it."

"Oh! very delightful indeed; I can say nothing less, for I suppose Miss Woodhouse and Mr. Frank Churchill are hearing everything that passes. And (raising his voice still more) I do not see why Miss Fairfax should not be mentioned too. I think Miss Fairfax dances very well; and Mrs. Weston is the very best country-dance player, without exception, in England. Now, if your friends have any gratitude, they will say something pretty loud about you and me in return; but I cannot stay to hear it."

"Oh! Mr. Knightley, one moment more; something of consequence – so shocked! Jane and I are both so shocked about the apples!"

"What is the matter now?"

"To think of your sending us all your store apples. You said you had a great many, and now you have not one left. We really are so shocked! Mrs. Hodges may well be angry. William Larkins mentioned it here. You should not have done it, indeed you should not. Ah! he is off. He never can bear to be thanked. But I thought he would have staid now, and it would have been a pity not to have mentioned – Well, (returning to the room,) I have not been able to succeed. Mr. Knightley cannot stop. He is going to Kingston. He asked me if he could do anything – "

"Yes," said Jane, "we heard his kind offers, we heard everything."

"Oh! yes, my dear, I dare say you might, because you know, the door was open, and the window was open, and Mr. Knightley spoke loud. You must have heard everything to be sure. 'Can I do any thing for you at Kingston?' said he; so I just mentioned – Oh! Miss Woodhouse, must you be going? You seem but just come so very obliging of you."

Emma found it really time to be at home; the visit had already lasted long; and on examining watches, so much of the morning was perceived to be gone, that Mrs. Weston and her companion taking leave also, could allow themselves only to walk with the two young ladies to Hartfield gates, before they set off for Randalls.

## Chapter 29

IT MAY be possible to do without dancing entirely. Instances have been known of young people passing many, many months successively, without being at any ball of any description, and no material injury accrue either to body or mind; but when a beginning is made – when the felicities of rapid motion have once been, though slightly, felt – it must be a very heavy set that does not ask for more.

Frank Churchill had danced once at Highbury, and longed to dance again; and the last half-hour of an evening which Mr. Woodhouse was persuaded to spend with his daughter at Randalls, was passed by the two young people in schemes on the subject. Frank's was the first idea; and his the greatest zeal in pursuing it; for the lady was the best judge of the difficulties, and the most solicitous for accommodation and appearance. But still she had inclination enough for showing people again how delightfully Mr. Frank Churchill and Miss Woodhouse danced – for doing that in which she need not blush to compare herself with Jane Fairfax – and even for simple dancing itself, without any of the wicked aids of vanity – to assist him first in pacing out the room they were in to see what it could be made to hold – and then in taking the dimensions of the other parlour, in the hope of discovering, in spite of all that Mr. Weston could say of their exactly equal size, that it was a little the largest.

His first proposition and request, that the dance begun at Mr. Cole's should be finished there – that the same party should be collected, and the same musician engaged – met with the readiest acquiescence. Mr. Weston entered into the idea with thorough enjoyment, and Mrs. Weston most willingly undertook to play as long as they could wish to dance; and the interesting employment had followed, of reckoning up exactly who there would be, and portioning out the indispensable division of space to every couple.

"You and Miss Smith, and Miss Fairfax, will be three, and the two Miss Coxes five," had been repeated many times over. "And there will be the two Gilberts, young Cox, my father, and myself, besides Mr. Knightley. Yes, that will be quite enough for pleasure. You and Miss Smith, and Miss Fairfax, will be three, and the two Miss Coxes five; and for five couple there will be plenty of room."

But soon it came to be on one side:

"But will there be good room for five couple? I really do not think there will."

On another:

"And after all, five couple are not enough to make it worth while to stand up. Five couple are nothing, when one thinks seriously about it. It will not do to *invite* five couple. It can be allowable only as the thought of the moment."

Somebody said that *Miss* Gilbert was expected at her brother's, and must be invited with the rest. Somebody else believed *Mrs.* Gilbert would have danced the other evening, if she had been asked. A word was put in for a second young Cox; and at last, Mr. Weston naming one family of cousins who must be included, and another of very old acquaintance who could not be left out, it became a certainty that the five couple would be at least ten, and a very interesting speculation in what possible manner they could be disposed of.

The doors of the two rooms were just opposite each other. "Might not they use both rooms, and dance across the passage?" It seemed the best scheme; and yet it was not so good but that many of them wanted a better. Emma said it would be awkward; Mrs. Weston was in distress about the supper; and Mr. Woodhouse opposed it earnestly, on the score of health. It made him so very unhappy, indeed, that it could not be persevered in.

"Oh, no," said he; "it would be the extreme of imprudence. I could not bear it for Emma! Emma is not strong. She would catch a dreadful cold. So would poor little Harriet. So you would all. Mrs. Weston, you would be quite laid up; do not let them talk of such a wild thing. Pray do not let them talk of it. That young man (speaking lower) is very thoughtless. Do not tell his father, but that young man is not quite the thing. He has been opening the doors very often this evening, and keeping them open very inconsiderately. He does not think of the draught. I do not mean to set you against him, but indeed he is not quite the thing!"

Mrs. Weston was sorry for such a charge. She knew the importance of it, and said everything in her power to do it away. Every door was now closed, the passage plan given up, and the first scheme of dancing only in the room they were in resorted to again; and with such good will on Frank Churchill's part, that the space which a quarter of an hour before had been deemed barely sufficient for five couple, was now endeavoured to be made out quite enough for ten.

"We were too magnificent," said he. "We allowed unnecessary room. Ten couple may stand here very well."

Emma demurred. "It would be a crowd a sad crowd; and what could be worse than dancing without space to turn in?"

"Very true," he gravely replied; "it was very bad." But still he went on measuring, and still he ended with:

"I think there will be very tolerable room for ten couple."

"No, no," said she, "you are quite unreasonable. It would be dreadful to be standing so close! Nothing can be farther from pleasure than to be dancing in a crowd, and a crowd in a little room!"

"There is no denying it," he replied. "I agree with you exactly. A crowd in a little room – Miss Woodhouse, you have the art of giving pictures in a few words. Exquisite, quite exquisite! – Still, however, having proceeded so far, one is unwilling to give the matter up. It would be a disappointment to my father – and altogether – I do not know that – I am rather of opinion that ten couple might stand here very well."

Emma perceived that the nature of his gallantry was a little self-willed, and that he would rather oppose than lose the pleasure of dancing with her; but she took the compliment, and forgave the rest. Had she intended ever to marry him, it might have been worth while to pause and consider, and try to understand the value of his preference, and the character of his temper; but for all the purposes of their acquaintance, he was quite amiable enough.

Before the middle of the next day, he was at Hartfield; and he entered the room with such an agreeable smile as certified the continuance of the scheme. It soon appeared that he came to announce an improvement.

"Well, Miss Woodhouse," he almost immediately began, "your inclination for dancing has not been quite frightened away, I hope, by the terrors of my father's little rooms. I bring a new proposal on the subject: a thought of my father's, which waits only your approbation to be acted upon. May I hope for the honour of your hand for the two first dances of this little projected ball, to be given, not at Randalls, but at the Crown Inn?"

"The Crown!"

"Yes; if you and Mr. Woodhouse see no objection, and I trust you cannot, my father hopes his friends will be so kind as to visit him there. Better accommodations, he can promise them, and not a less grateful welcome than at Randalls. It is his own idea. Mrs. Weston sees no objection to it, provided you are satisfied.

This is what we all feel. Oh! you were perfectly right! Ten couple, in either of the Randalls rooms, would have been insufferable – dreadful! I felt how right you were the whole time, but was too anxious for securing *anything* to like to yield. Is not it a good exchange? You consent – I hope you consent?"

"It appears to me a plan that nobody can object to, if Mr. and Mrs. Weston do not. I think it admirable; and, as far as I can answer for myself, shall be most happy – it seems the only improvement that could be. Papa, do you not think it an excellent improvement?"

She was obliged to repeat and explain it, before it was fully comprehended; and then, being quite new, farther representations were necessary to make it acceptable.

"No; he thought it very far from an improvement – a very bad plan – much worse than the other. A room at an inn was always damp and dangerous; never properly aired, or fit to be inhabited. If they must dance, they had better dance at Randalls. He had never been in the room at the Crown in his life – did not know the people who kept it by sight. Oh! no – a very bad plan. They would catch worse colds at the Crown than anywhere."

"I was going to observe, sir," said Frank Churchill, "that one of the great recommendations of this change would be the very little danger of anybody's catching cold – so much less danger at the Crown than at Randalls! Mr. Perry might have reason to regret the alteration, but nobody else could."

"Sir," said Mr. Woodhouse, rather warmly, "you are very much mistaken if you suppose Mr. Perry to be that sort of character. Mr. Perry is extremely concerned when any of us are ill. But I do not understand how the room at the Crown can be safer for you than your father's house."

"From the very circumstance of its being larger, sir. We shall have no occasion to open the windows at all – not once the whole evening; and it is that dreadful habit of opening the windows, letting in cold air upon heated bodies, which (as you well know, sir) does the mischief."

"Open the windows! but surely, Mr. Churchill, nobody would think of opening the windows at Randalls. Nobody could be so imprudent! I never heard of such a thing. Dancing with open windows! I am sure, neither your father nor Mrs. Weston (poor Miss Taylor that was) would suffer it."

"Ah! sir – but a thoughtless young person will sometimes step behind a window-curtain, and throw up a sash, without its being suspected. I have often known it done myself."

"Have you indeed, sir? Bless me! I never could have supposed it. But I live out of the world, and am often astonished at what I hear. However, this does make a difference; and, perhaps, when we come to talk it over – but these sort of things require a good deal of consideration. One cannot resolve upon them in a hurry. If Mr. and Mrs. Weston will be so obliging as to call here one morning, we may talk it over, and see what can be done."

"But, unfortunately, sir, my time is so limited – "

"Oh!" interrupted Emma, "there will be plenty of time for talking everything over. There is no hurry at all. If it can be contrived to be at the Crown, papa, it will be very convenient for the horses. They will be so near their own stable."

"So they will, my dear. That is a great thing. Not that James ever complains; but it is right to spare our horses when we can. If I could be sure of the rooms being thoroughly aired – but is Mrs. Stokes to be trusted? I doubt it. I do not know her, even by sight."

"I can answer for everything of that nature, sir, because it will be under Mrs. Weston's care. Mrs. Weston undertakes to direct the whole."

"There, papa! Now you must be satisfied – our own dear Mrs. Weston, who is carefulness itself. Do not you remember what Mr. Perry said, so many years ago, when I had the measles? 'If *Miss Taylor* undertakes to wrap Miss Emma up, you need not have any fears, sir.' How often have I heard you speak of it as such a compliment to her!"

"Aye, very true. Mr. Perry did say so. I shall never forget it. Poor little Emma! You were very bad with the measles; that is, you would have been very bad, but for Perry's great attention. He came four times a day for a week. He said, from the first, it was a very good sort – which was our great comfort; but the measles are a dreadful complaint. I hope whenever poor Isabella's little ones have the measles, she will send for Perry."

"My father and Mrs. Weston are at the Crown at this moment," said Frank Churchill, "examining the capabilities of the house. I left them there and came on to Hartfield, impatient for your opinion, and hoping you might be persuaded to join them and give your advice on the spot. I was desired to say so from both. It would be the greatest pleasure to them, if you could allow me to attend you there. They can do nothing satisfactorily without you."

Emma was most happy to be called to such a council; and her father, engaging to think it all over while she was gone, the two young people set off together without delay for the Crown. There were Mr. and Mrs. Weston; delighted to see her and receive her approbation, very busy and very happy in their different way; she, in some little distress; and he, finding everything perfect.

"Emma," said she, "this paper is worse than I expected. Look! in places you see it is dreadfully dirty; and the wainscot is more yellow and forlorn than any thing I could have imagined."

"My dear, you are too particular," said her husband. "What does all that signify? You will see nothing of it by candle-light. It will be as clean as Randalls by candle-light. We never see any thing of it on our club-nights."

The ladies here probably exchanged looks which meant, "Men never know when things are dirty or not;" and the gentlemen perhaps thought each to himself, "Women will have their little nonsenses and needless cares."

One perplexity, however, arose, which the gentlemen did not disdain. It regarded a supper-room. At the time of the ballroom's being built, suppers had not been in question; and a small card-room adjoining, was the only addition. What was to be done? This card-room would be wanted as a card-room now; or, if cards were conveniently voted unnecessary by their four selves, still was it not too small for any comfortable supper? Another room of much better size might be secured for the purpose; but it was at the other end of the house, and a long awkward passage must be gone through to get at it. This made a difficulty. Mrs. Weston was afraid of draughts for the young people in that passage; and neither Emma nor the gentlemen could tolerate the prospect of being miserably crowded at supper.

Mrs. Weston proposed having no regular supper; merely sandwiches, &c., set out in the little room; but that was scouted as a wretched suggestion. A private dance, without sitting down to supper, was pronounced an infamous fraud upon the rights of men and women; and Mrs. Weston must not speak of it again. She then took another line of expediency, and looking into the doubtful room, observed:

"I do not think it *is* so very small. We shall not be many, you know."

And Mr. Weston at the same time, walking briskly with long steps through the passage, was calling out:

"You talk a great deal of the length of this passage, my dear. It is a mere nothing after all; and not the least draught from the stairs."

"I wish," said Mrs. Weston, "one could know which arrangement our guests in general would like best. To do what would be most generally pleasing must be our object – if one could but tell what that would be."

"Yes, very true," cried Frank, "very true. You want your neighbours' opinions. I do not wonder at you. If one could ascertain what the chief of them – the Coles, for instance. They are not far off. Shall I call upon them? Or Miss Bates? She is still nearer. And I do not know whether Miss Bates is not as likely to understand the inclinations of the rest of the people as anybody. I think we do want a larger council. Suppose I go and invite Miss Bates to join us?"

"Well – if you please," said Mrs. Weston rather hesitating, "if you think she will be of any use."

"You will get nothing to the purpose from Miss Bates," said Emma. "She will be all delight and gratitude, but she will tell you nothing. She will not even listen to your questions. I see no advantage in consulting Miss Bates."

"But she is so amusing, so extremely amusing! I am very fond of hearing Miss Bates talk. And I need not bring the whole family, you know."

Here Mr. Weston joined them, and on hearing what was proposed, gave it his decided approbation.

"Aye, do, Frank. Go and fetch Miss Bates, and let us end the matter at once. She will enjoy the scheme, I am sure; and I do not know a properer person for showing us how to do away difficulties. Fetch Miss Bates. We are growing a little too nice. She is a standing lesson of how to be happy. But fetch them both. Invite them both."

"Both sir! Can the old lady –?"

"The old lady! No, the young lady, to be sure. I shall think you a great blockhead, Frank, if you bring the aunt without the niece."

"Oh! I beg your pardon, sir. I did not immediately recollect. Undoubtedly if you wish it, I will endeavour to persuade them both." And away he ran.

Long before he reappeared, attending the short, neat, brisk-moving aunt, and her elegant niece – Mrs. Weston, like a sweet-tempered woman and a good wife, had examined the passage again, and found the evils of it much less than she had supposed before – indeed very trifling; and here ended the difficulties of decision. All the rest, in speculation at least, was perfectly smooth. All the minor arrangements of table and chair, lights and music, tea and supper, made themselves; or were left as mere trifles to be settled at any time between Mrs. Weston and Mrs. Stokes. Everybody invited, was certainly to come; Frank had already written to Enscombe to propose staying a few days beyond his fortnight, which could not possibly be refused. And a delightful dance it was to be.

Most cordially, when Miss Bates arrived, did she agree that it must. As a counsellor she was not wanted; but as an approver, (a much safer character,) she was truly welcome. Her approbation, at once general and minute, warm and incessant, could not but please; and for another half-hour they were all walking to and fro, between the different rooms, some suggesting, some attending, and all in happy enjoyment of the future. The party did not break up without Emma's being positively secured for the two first dances by the hero of the evening, nor without her overhearing Mr. Weston whisper to his wife, "He has asked her, my dear. That's right. I knew he would!"

# Chapter 30

ONE THING only was wanting to make the prospect of the ball completely satisfactory to Emma – its being fixed for a day within the granted term of Frank Churchill's stay in Surrey; for, in spite of Mr. Weston's confidence, she could not think it so very impossible that the Churchills might not allow their nephew to remain a day beyond his fortnight. But this was not judged feasible. The preparations must take their time, nothing could be properly ready till the third week were entered on, and for a few days they must be planning, proceeding and hoping in uncertainty at the risk – in her opinion, the great risk – of its being all in vain.

Enscombe however was gracious, gracious – in fact, if not in word. His wish of staying longer evidently did not please; but it was not opposed. All was safe and prosperous; and as the removal of one solicitude generally makes way for another, Emma, being now certain of her ball, began to adopt as the next vexation Mr. Knightley's provoking indifference about it. Either because he did not dance himself, or because the plan had been formed without his being consulted, he seemed resolved that it should not interest him, determined against its exciting any present curiosity, or affording him any future amusement. To her voluntary communications Emma could get no more approving reply, than:

"Very well. If the Westons think it worth while to be at all this trouble for a few hours of noisy entertainment, I have nothing to say against it, but that they shall not choose pleasures for me. Oh! yes, I must be there; I could not refuse; and I will keep as much awake as I can; but I would rather be at home, looking over William Larkins's week's account; much rather, I confess. Pleasure in seeing dancing! not I, indeed – I never look at it – I do not know who does. Fine dancing, I believe, like virtue, must be its own reward. Those who are standing by are usually thinking of something very different."

This Emma felt was aimed at her; and it made her quite angry. It was not in compliment to Jane Fairfax however that he was so indifferent, or so indignant; he was not guided by *her* feelings in reprobating the ball, for *she* enjoyed the thought of it to an extraordinary degree. It made her animated – open-hearted she voluntarily said:

"Oh! Miss Woodhouse, I hope nothing may happen to prevent the ball. What a disappointment it would be! I do look forward to it, I own, with very great pleasure."

It was not to oblige Jane Fairfax therefore that he would have preferred the society of William Larkins. No! – she was more and more convinced that Mrs. Weston was quite mistaken in that surmise. There was a great deal of friendly and of compassionate attachment on his side – but no love.

Alas! there was soon no leisure for quarrelling with Mr. Knightley. Two days of joyful security were immediately followed by the over throw of everything. A letter arrived from Mr. Churchill to urge his nephew's instant return. Mrs. Churchill was unwell far too unwell – to do without him; she had been in a very suffering state (so said her husband) when writing to her nephew two days before, though from her usual unwillingness to give pain, and constant habit of never thinking of herself, she had not mentioned it; but now she was too ill to trifle, and must entreat him to set off for Enscombe without delay.

The substance of this letter was forwarded to Emma, in a note from Mrs. Weston, instantly. As to his going, it was inevitable. He must be gone within a few hours, though without feeling any real alarm for his aunt, to lessen his repugnance. He knew her illnesses; they never occurred but for her own convenience.

Mrs. Weston added, "that he could only allow himself time to hurry to Highbury, after breakfast, and take leave of the few friends there whom he could suppose to feel any interest in him; and that he might be expected at Hartfield very soon."

This wretched note was the finale of Emma's breakfast. When once it had been read, there was no doing any thing, but lament and exclaim. The loss of the ball – the loss of the young man – and all that the young man might be feeling! It was too wretched! Such a delightful evening as it would have been! Everybody so happy! and she and her partner the happiest! "I said it would be so," was the only consolation.

Her father's feelings were quite distinct. He thought principally of Mrs. Churchill's illness, and wanted to know how she was treated; and as for the ball, it was shocking to have dear Emma disappointed; but they would all be safer at home.

Emma was ready for her visitor some time before he appeared; but if this reflected at all upon his impatience, his sorrowful look and total want of spirits when he did come might redeem him. He felt the going away almost too much to speak of it. His dejection was most evident. He sat really lost in thought for the first few minutes; and when rousing himself, it was only to say:

"Of all horrid things, leave-taking is the worst."

"But you will come again," said Emma. "This will not be your only visit to Randalls."

"Ah! – (shaking his head) – the uncertainty of when I may be able to return! I shall try for it with a zeal! It will be the object of all my thoughts and cares! and if my uncle and aunt go to town this spring – but I am afraid – they did not stir last spring – I am afraid it is a custom gone for ever."

"Our poor ball must be quite given up."

"Ah! that ball! why did we wait for anything? – Why not seize the pleasure at once? How often is happiness destroyed by preparation, foolish preparation! You told us it would be so. Oh! Miss Woodhouse, why are you always so right?"

"Indeed, I am very sorry to be right in this instance. I would much rather have been merry than wise."

"If I can come again, we are still to have our ball. My father depends on it. Do not forget your engagement."

Emma looked graciously.

"Such a fortnight as it has been!" he continued; "every day more precious and more delightful than the day before! every day making me less fit to bear any other place. Happy are those, who can remain at Highbury!"

"As you do us such ample justice now," said Emma, laughing, "I will venture to ask, whether you did not come a little doubtfully at first? Do not we rather surpass your expectations? I am sure we do. I am sure you did not much expect to like us. You would not have been so long in coming, if you had had a pleasant idea of Highbury."

He laughed rather consciously; and though denying the sentiment, Emma was convinced that it had been so.

"And you must be off this very morning?"

"Yes; my father is to join me here: we shall walk back together, and I must be off immediately. I am almost afraid that every moment will bring him."

"Not five minutes to spare even for your friends Miss Fairfax and Miss Bates? How unlucky! Miss Bates's powerful, argumentative mind might have strengthened yours."

"Yes – I *have* called there; passing the door, I thought it better. It was a right thing to do. I went in for three minutes, and was detained by Miss Bates's being absent. She was out; and I felt it impossible not to wait till she came in. She is a woman that one may, that one *must* laugh at; but that one would not wish to slight. It was better to pay my visit, then – "

He hesitated, got up, walked to a window.

"In short," said he, "perhaps, Miss Woodhouse – I think you can hardly be quite without suspicion – "

He looked at her, as if wanting to read her thoughts. She hardly knew what to say. It seemed like the forerunner of something absolutely serious, which she did not wish. Forcing herself to speak, therefore, in the hope of putting it by, she calmly said:

"You are quite in the right; it was most natural to pay your visit, then – "

He was silent. She believed he was looking at her; probably reflecting on what she had said, and trying to understand the manner. She heard him sigh. It was natural for him to feel that he had *cause* to sigh. He could not believe her to be encouraging him. A few awkward moments passed, and he sat down again; and in a more determined manner said:

"It was something to feel that all the rest of my time might be given to Hartfield. My regard for Hartfield is most warm – "

He stopped again, rose again, and seemed quite embarrassed. He was more in love with her than Emma had supposed; and who can say how it might have ended, if his father had not made his appearance? Mr. Woodhouse soon followed; and the necessity of exertion made him composed.

A very few minutes more, however, completed the present trial. Mr. Weston, always alert when business was to be done, and as incapable of procrastinating any evil that was inevitable, as of foreseeing any that was doubtful, said, "It was time to go;" and the young man, though he might and did sigh, could not but agree, to take leave.

"I shall hear about you all," said he; that is my chief consolation. I shall hear of everything that is going on among you. I have engaged Mrs. Weston to correspond with me. She has been so kind as to promise it. Oh! the blessing of a female correspondent, when one is really interested in the absent! she will tell me everything. In her letters I shall be at dear Highbury again."

A very friendly shake of the hand, a very earnest "Good bye," closed the speech, and the door had soon shut out Frank Churchill. Short had been the notice – short their meeting; he was gone; and

Emma felt so sorry to part, and foresaw so great a loss to their little society from his absence as to begin to be afraid of being too sorry, and feeling it too much.

It was a sad change. They had been meeting almost every day since his arrival. Certainly his being at Randalls had given great spirit to the last two weeks – indescribable spirit; the idea, the expectation of seeing him which every morning had brought, the assurance of his attentions, his liveliness, his manners! It had been a very happy fortnight, and forlorn must be the sinking from it into the common course of Hartfield days. To complete every other recommendation, he had *almost* told her that he loved her. What strength, or what constancy of affection he might be subject to, was another point; but at present she could not doubt his having a decidedly warm admiration, a conscious preference of herself; and this persuasion, joined to all the rest, made her think that she *must* be a little in love with him, in spite of every previous determination against it.

"I certainly must," said she. "This sensation of listlessness, weariness, stupidity, this disinclination to sit down and employ myself, this feeling of everything's being dull and insipid about the house! I must be in love; I should be the oddest creature in the world if I were not – for a few weeks at least. Well! evil to some is always good to others. I shall have many fellow mourners for the ball, if not for Frank Churchill; but Mr. Knightley will be happy. He may spend the evening with his dear William Larkins now if he likes."

Mr. Knightley, however, showed no triumphant happiness. He could not say that he was sorry on his own account; his very cheerful look would have contradicted him if he had; but he said, and very steadily, that he was sorry for the disappointment of the others, and with considerable kindness added:

"You, Emma, who have so few opportunities of dancing, you are really out of luck; you are very much out of luck!"

It was some days before she saw Jane Fairfax, to judge of

her honest regret in this woeful change; but when they did meet, her composure was odious. She had been particularly unwell, however, suffering from headache to a degree, which made her aunt declare, that had the ball taken place, she did not think Jane could have attended it; and it was charity to impute some of her unbecoming indifference to the languor of ill-health.

## Chapter 31

EMMA CONTINUED to entertain no doubt of her being in love. Her ideas only varied as to the how much. At first, she thought it was a good deal; and afterwards, but little. She had great pleasure in hearing Frank Churchill talked of; and, for his sake, greater pleasure than ever in seeing Mr. and Mrs. Weston; she was very often thinking of him, and quite impatient for a letter, that she might know how he was, how were his spirits, how was his aunt, and what was the chance of his coming to Randalls again this spring. But, on the other hand, she could not admit herself to be unhappy, nor, after the first morning, to be less disposed for employment than usual; she was still busy and cheerful; and, pleasing as he was, she could yet imagine him to have faults; and farther, though thinking of him so much, and, as she sat drawing or working, forming a thousand amusing schemes for the progress and close of their attachment, fancying interesting dialogues, and inventing elegant letters; the conclusion of every imaginary declaration on his side was that she *refused him.* Their affection was always to subside into friendship. Everything tender and charming was to mark their parting; but still they were to part. When she became sensible of this, it struck her that she could not be very much in love; for in spite of her previous and fixed determination never to quit her father, never to marry, a strong attachment certainly must produce more of a struggle than she could foresee in her own feelings.

"I do not find myself making any use of the word *sacrifice,*" said she. "In not one of all my clever replies, my delicate negatives, is there any allusion to making a sacrifice. I do suspect that he is not really necessary to my happiness. So much the better. I certainly will not persuade myself to feel more than I do. I am quite enough in love. I should be sorry to be more."

Upon the whole, she was equally contented with her view of his feelings.

"*He* is undoubtedly very much in love – everything denotes it – very much in love indeed! – and when he comes again, if his affection continue, I must be on my guard not to encourage it. It would be most inexcusable to do otherwise, as my own mind is quite made up. Not that I imagine he can think I have been encouraging him hitherto. No, if he had believed me at all to share his feelings, he would not have been so wretched. Could he have thought himself encouraged, his looks and language at parting would have been different. Still, however, I must be on my guard. This is in the supposition of his attachment continuing what it now is; but I do not know that I expect it will; I do not look upon him to be quite the sort of man – I do not altogether build upon his steadiness or constancy. His feelings are warm, but I can imagine them rather changeable. Every consideration of the subject, in short, makes me thankful that my happiness is not more deeply involved. I shall do very well again after a little while – and then, it will be a good thing over; for they say everybody is in love once in their lives, and I shall have been let off easily."

When his letter to Mrs. Weston arrived, Emma had the perusal of it; and she read it with a degree of pleasure and admiration which made her at first shake her head over her own sensations, and think she had undervalued their strength. It was a long, well written letter, giving the particulars of his journey and of his feelings, expressing all the affection, gratitude, and respect which was natural and honourable, and describing everything exterior and local that could be supposed attractive, with spirit and precision. No suspicious flourishes now of apology or concern; it was the language of real feeling towards Mrs. Weston; and the transition from Highbury to Enscombe, the contrast between the places in some of the first blessings of social life was just enough touched on to show how keenly it was felt, and how much more might have been said but for the restraints of propriety. The charm of her own name was not wanting. *Miss Woodhouse* appeared more than once, and never without a something of pleasing connection, either a compliment to her taste, or a remembrance of what she had said; and in the very last time of its meeting her eye, unadorned as it was by any such broad wreath of gallantry, she yet could discern the effect of her influence and acknowledge the greatest compliment perhaps of all conveyed. Compressed into the very lowest vacant corner were these words – "I had not a spare moment on Tuesday, as you know, for Miss Woodhouse's beautiful little friend. Pray make my excuses and adieus to her." This, Emma could not doubt, was all for herself. Harriet was remembered only from being *her* friend. His information and prospects as to Enscombe were neither worse nor better than had been anticipated; Mrs. Churchill was recovering, and he dared not yet, even in his own imagination, fix a time for coming to Randalls again.

Gratifying, however, and stimulative as was the letter in the material part, its sentiments, she yet found, when it was folded up and returned to Mrs. Weston, that it had not added any lasting warmth – that she could still do without the writer, and that he must learn to do without her. Her intentions were unchanged. Her resolution of refusal only grew more interesting by the addition of a scheme for his subsequent consolation and happiness. His recollection of Harriet, and the words which clothed it – the "beautiful little friend," – suggested to her the idea of Harriet's succeeding her in his affections. Was it impossible? No. Harriet undoubtedly was greatly his inferior in understanding; but he had been very much struck with the loveliness of her face and the warm simplicity of her manner; and all the probabilities of circumstance and connection were in her favour. For Harriet, it would be advantageous and delightful indeed.

"I must not dwell upon it," said she. "I must not think of it. I know the danger of indulging such speculations. But stranger things have happened; and when we cease to care for each other as we do now, it will be the means of confirming us in that sort of true disinterested friendship which I can already look forward to with pleasure."

It was well to have a comfort in store on Harriet's behalf, though it might be wise to let the fancy touch it seldom; for evil in that quarter was at hand. As Frank Churchill's arrival had succeeded Mr. Elton's engagement in the conversation of Highbury, as the latest interest had entirely borne down the first, so now upon Frank Churchill's disappearance, Mr. Elton's concerns were assuming the most irresistible form. His wedding-day was named. He would soon be among them again; Mr. Elton and his bride. There was hardly time to talk over the first letter from Enscombe before "Mr. Elton and his bride" was in everybody's mouth, and Frank Churchill was forgotten. Emma grew sick at the sound. She had had three weeks of happy exemption from Mr. Elton; and Harriet's mind, she had been willing to hope, had been lately gaining strength. With Mr. Weston's ball in view at least, there had been a great deal of insensibility to other things; but it was now too evident that she had not attained such a state of composure as could stand against the actual approach – new carriage, bell-ringing, and all.

Poor Harriet was in a flutter of spirits which required all the reasonings and soothings and attentions of every kind that Emma could give. Emma felt that she could not do too much for her, that Harriet had a right to all her ingenuity and all her patience; but it was heavy work to be for ever convincing without producing any effect, for ever agreed to, without being able to make their opinions the same. Harriet listened submissively, and said: "it was very true it was just as Miss Woodhouse described – it was not worth while to think about them – and she would not think about them any longer" but no change of subject could avail, and the next half hour saw her as anxious and restless about the Eltons as before. At last Emma attacked her on another ground.

"Your allowing yourself to be so occupied and so unhappy about Mr. Elton's marrying, Harriet, is the strongest reproach you can make me. You could not give me a greater reproof for the mistake I fell into. It was all my doing, I know. I have not forgotten it, I assure you. Deceived myself, I did very miserably deceive you and it will be a painful reflection to me for ever. Do not imagine me in danger of forgetting it."

Harriet felt this too much to utter more than a few words of eager exclamation. Emma continued:

"I have not said, exert yourself Harriet for my sake; think less, talk less of Mr. Elton for my sake; because for your own sake rather, I would wish it to be done, for the sake of what is more important than my comfort – a habit of self-command in you, a consideration of what is your duty, an attention to propriety, an endeavour to avoid the suspicions of others, to save your health and credit, and restore your tranquillity. These are the motives which I have been pressing on you. They are very important and sorry I am that you cannot feel them sufficiently to act upon them. My being saved from pain is a very secondary consideration. I want you to save yourself from greater pain. Perhaps I may sometimes have felt that Harriet would not forget what was due – or rather what would be kind by me."

This appeal to her affections did more than all the rest. The idea of wanting gratitude and consideration for Miss Woodhouse, whom she really loved extremely, made her wretched for a while, and when the violence of grief was comforted away, still remained powerful enough to prompt to what was right and support her in it very tolerably.

"You, who have been the best friend I ever had in my life Want gratitude to you! Nobody is equal to you! I care for nobody as I do for you! Oh! Miss Woodhouse, how ungrateful I have been!"

Such expressions, assisted as they were by everything that look and manner could do, made Emma feel that she had never loved Harriet so well, nor valued her affection so highly before.

There is no charm equal to tenderness of heart," said she afterwards to herself. "There is nothing to be compared to it. Warmth and tenderness of heart, with an affectionate, open manner, will beat all the clearness of head in the world, for attraction, I am sure it will. It is tenderness of heart which makes my dear father so generally beloved – which gives Isabella all her popularity. I have it not but I know how to prize and respect it. Harriet is my superior in all the charm and all the felicity it gives. Dear Harriet! I would not change you for the clearest-headed, longest-sighted, best-judging female breathing. Oh! the coldness of a Jane Fairfax! Harriet is worth a hundred such And for a wife – a sensible man's wife – it is invaluable. I mention no names; but happy the man who changes Emma for Harriet!"

# Chapter 32

MRS. ELTON was first seen at church: but though devotion might be interrupted, curiosity could not be satisfied by a bride in a pew, and it must be left for the visits in form which were then to be paid, to settle whether she were very pretty indeed, or only rather pretty, or not pretty at all.

Emma had feelings, less of curiosity than of pride or propriety, to make her resolve on not being the last to pay her respects; and she made a point of Harriet's going with her, that the worst of the business might be gone through as soon as possible.

She could not enter the house again, could not be in the same room to which she had with such vain artifice retreated three months ago, to lace up her boot, without *recollecting.* A thousand vexatious thoughts would recur. Compliments, charades, and horrible blunders; and it was not to be supposed that poor Harriet should not be recollecting too; but she behaved very well, and was only rather pale and silent. The visit was of course short; and there was so much embarrassment and occupation of mind to shorten it, that Emma would not allow herself entirely to form an opinion of the lady, and on no account to give one, beyond the nothing-meaning terms of being "elegantly dressed, and very pleasing."

She did not really like her. She would not be in a hurry to find fault, but she suspected that there was no elegance; ease, but not elegance. She was almost sure that for a young woman, a stranger, a bride, there was too much ease. Her person was rather good; her face not unpretty; but neither feature, nor air, nor voice, nor manner, were elegant. Emma thought at least it would turn out so.

As for Mr. Elton, his manners did not appear – but no, she would not permit a hasty or a witty word from herself about his manners. It was an awkward ceremony at any time to be receiving wedding visits, and a man had need be all grace to acquit himself well through it. The woman was better off; she might have the assistance of fine clothes, and the privilege of bashfulness, but the man had only his own good sense to depend on; and when she considered how peculiarly unlucky poor Mr. Elton was in being in the same room at once with the woman he had just married, the woman he had wanted to marry, and the woman whom he had been expected to marry, she must allow him to have the right to look as little wise, and to be as much affectedly, and as little really easy as could be.

"Well, Miss Woodhouse," said Harriet, when they had quitted the house, and after waiting in vain for her friend to begin; "Well, Miss Woodhouse, (with a gentle sigh,) what do you think of her? Is not she very charming?"

There was a little hesitation in Emma's answer.

"Oh! yes – very – a very pleasing young woman."

"I think her beautiful, quite beautiful."

"Very nicely dressed, indeed; a remarkably elegant gown."

"I am not at all surprised that he should have fallen in love."

"Oh! no there is nothing to surprise one at all. A pretty fortune; and she came in his way."

"I dare say," returned Harriet, sighing again, "I dare say she was very much attached to him."

"Perhaps she might; but it is not every man's fate to marry the woman who loves him best. Miss Hawkins perhaps wanted a home, and thought this the best offer she was likely to have."

"Yes," said Harriet earnestly, "and well she might, nobody could ever have a better. Well, I wish them happy with all my heart. And now, Miss Woodhouse, I do not think I shall mind seeing them again. He is just as superior as ever; but being married, you know, it is quite a different thing. No, indeed, Miss Woodhouse, you need not be afraid; I can sit and admire him now without any great misery. To know that he has not thrown himself away, is such a comfort! She does seem a charming young woman, just what he deserves. Happy creature! He called her 'Augusta.' How delightful!"

When the visit was returned, Emma made up her mind. She could then see more and judge better. From Harriet's happening not to be at Hartfield, and her father's being present to engage Mr. Elton, she had a quarter of an hour of the lady's conversation to herself, and could composedly attend to her; and the quarter of an hour quite convinced her that Mrs. Elton was a vain woman, extremely well satisfied with herself, and thinking much of her own importance; that she meant to shine and be very superior, but with manners which had been formed in a bad school, pert and familiar; that all her notions were drawn from one set of people, and one style of living; that if not foolish she was ignorant, and that her society would certainly do Mr. Elton no good.

Harriet would have been a better match. If not wise or refined herself, she would have connected him with those who were; but Miss Hawkins, it might be fairly supposed from her easy conceit, had been the best of her own set. The rich brother-in-law near Bristol was the pride of the alliance, and his place and his carriages were the pride of him.

The very first subject after being seated was Maple Grove, "My brother Mr. Suckling's seat;" a comparison of Hartfield to Maple Grove. The grounds of Hartfield were small, but neat and pretty; and the house was modern and well-built. Mrs. Elton seemed most favourably impressed by the size of the room, the entrance, and all that she could see or imagine. "Very like Maple Grove indeed! She was quite struck by the likeness! That room was the very shape and size of the morning-room at Maple Grove; her sister's favourite room." Mr. Elton was appealed to. "Was not it astonishingly like? She could really almost fancy herself at Maple Grove."

"And the staircase. You know, as I came in, I observed how very like the staircase was; placed exactly in the same part of the house. I really could not help exclaiming! I assure you, Miss Woodhouse, it is very delightful to me, to be reminded of a place I am so extremely partial to as Maple Grove. I have spent so many happy months there! (with a little sigh of sentiment). A charming place, undoubtedly. Everybody who sees it is struck by its beauty; but to me, it has been quite a home. Whenever you are transplanted, like me, Miss Woodhouse, you will understand how very delightful it is to meet with any thing at all like what one has left behind. I always say this is quite one of the evils of matrimony."

Emma made as slight a reply as she could; but it was fully sufficient for Mrs. Elton, who only wanted to be talking herself.

"So extremely like Maple Grove! And it is not merely the house the grounds, I assure you, as far as I could observe, are strikingly like. The laurels at Maple Grove are in the same profusion as here, and stand very much in the same way – just across the lawn; and I had a glimpse of a fine large tree, with a bench round it, which put me so exactly in mind! My brother and sister will be enchanted with this place. People who have extensive grounds themselves are always pleased with any thing in the same style."

Emma doubted the truth of this sentiment. She had a great idea that people who had extensive grounds themselves cared very little for the extensive grounds of anybody else; but it was not worth while to attack an error so double-dyed, and therefore only said in reply:

"When you have seen more of this country, I am afraid you will think you have over-rated Hartfield. Surrey is full of beauties."

"Oh! yes, I am quite aware of that. It is the garden of England, you know. Surrey is the garden of England."

"Yes; but we must not rest our claims on that distinction. Many counties, I believe, are called the garden of England, as well as Surrey."

"No, I fancy not," replied Mrs. Elton, with a most satisfied smile." I never heard any county but Surrey called so."

Emma was silenced.

"My brother and sister have promised us a visit in the spring, or summer at farthest," continued Mrs. Elton; "and that will be our time for exploring. While they are with us, we shall explore a great deal, I dare say. They will have their barouche-landau[1], of course, which holds four perfectly; and therefore, without saying any thing of *our* carriage, we should be able to explore the different beauties extremely well. They would hardly come in their chaise, I think, at that season of the year. Indeed, when the time draws on, I shall decidedly recommend their bringing the barouche-landau; it will be so very much preferable. When people come into a beautiful country of this sort, you know, Miss Woodhouse, one naturally wishes them to see as much as possible; and Mr. Suckling is extremely fond of exploring. We explored to King's-Weston twice last summer, in that way, most delightfully, just after their first having the barouche-landau. You have many parties of that kind here, I suppose, Miss Woodhouse, every summer?"

"No; not immediately here. We are rather out of distance of the very striking beauties which attract the sort of parties you speak of; and we are a very quiet set of people, I believe; more disposed to stay at home than engage in schemes of pleasure."

"Ah! there is nothing like staying at home for real comfort. Nobody can be more devoted to home than I am. I was quite a proverb for it at Maple Grove. Many a time has Selina said, when she has been going to Bristol, 'I really cannot get this girl to move from the house. I absolutely must go in by myself, though I hate being stuck up in the barouche-landau without a companion; but Augusta, I believe, with her own good will, would never stir beyond the park paling.' Many a time has she said so; and yet I am no advocate for entire seclusion. I think, on the contrary, when people shut themselves up entirely from society, it is a very bad thing; and that it is much more advisable to mix in the world in a proper degree, without living in it either too much or too little. I perfectly understand your situation, however, Miss

1 A carriage with half-open roof-top.

Woodhouse (looking towards Mr. Woodhouse), Your father's state of health must be a great drawback. Why does not he try Bath? Indeed he should. Let me recommend Bath to you. I assure you I have no doubt of its doing Mr. Woodhouse good."

"My father tried it more than once, formerly; but without receiving any benefit; and Mr. Perry, whose name, I dare say, is not unknown to you, does not conceive it would be at all more likely to be useful now."

"Ah! that's a great pity; for I assure you, Miss Woodhouse, where the waters do agree, it is quite wonderful the relief they give. In my Bath life, I have seen such instances of it! And it is so cheerful a place, that it could not fail of being of use to Mr. Woodhouse's spirits, which, I understand, are sometimes much depressed. And as to its recommendations to you, I fancy I need not take much pains to dwell on them. The advantages of Bath to the young are pretty generally understood. It would be a charming introduction for you, who have lived so secluded a life; and I could immediately secure you some of the best society in the place. A line from me would bring you a little host of acquaintance; and my particular friend, Mrs. Partridge, the lady I have always resided with when in Bath, would be most happy to show you any attentions, and would be the very person for you to go into public with."

It was as much as Emma could bear, without being impolite. The idea of her being indebted to Mrs. Elton for what was called an *introduction* – of her going into public under the auspices of a friend of Mrs. Elton's – probably some vulgar, dashing widow, who, with the help of a boarder, just made a shift to live! The dignity of Miss Woodhouse, of Hartfield, was sunk indeed!

She restrained herself, however, from any of the reproofs she could have given, and only thanked Mrs. Elton coolly; "but their going to Bath was quite out of the question; and she was not perfectly convinced that the place might suit her better than her father." And then, to prevent farther outrage and indignation, changed the subject directly.

"I do not ask whether you are musical, Mrs. Elton. Upon these occasions, a lady's character generally precedes her; and Highbury has long known that you are a superior performer."

"Oh! no, indeed; I must protest against any such idea. A superior performer! very far from it, I assure you. Consider from how partial a quarter your information came. I am dotingly fond of music – passionately fond; and my friends say I am not entirely devoid of taste; but as to any thing else, upon my honour my performance is *mediocre* to the last degree. You, Miss Woodhouse, I well know, play delightfully. I assure you it has been the greatest satisfaction, comfort, and delight to me, to hear what a musical society I am got into. I absolutely cannot do without music. It is a necessary of life to me; and having always been used to a very musical society, both at Maple Grove and in Bath, it would have been a most serious sacrifice. I honestly said as much to Mr. E. when he was speaking of my future home, and expressing his fears lest the retirement of it should be disagreeable; and the inferiority of the house too – knowing what I had been accustomed to – of course he was not wholly without apprehension. When he was speaking of it in that way, I honestly said that *the world* I could give up – parties, balls, plays – for I had no fear of retirement. Blessed with so many resources within myself, the world was not necessary to me. I could do very well without it. To those who had no resources it was a different thing; but my resources made me quite independent. And as to smaller-sized rooms than I had been used to, I really could not give it a thought. I hoped I was perfectly equal to any sacrifice of that description. Certainly I had been accustomed to every luxury at Maple Grove; but I did assure him that two carriages were not necessary to my happiness, nor were spacious apartments. 'But,' said I, 'to be quite honest, I do not think I can live without something of a musical society. I condition for nothing else; but without music, life would be a blank to me.' "

"We cannot suppose," said Emma, smiling, "that Mr. Elton would hesitate to assure you of there being a very musical society in Highbury; and I hope you will not find he has outstepped the truth more than may be pardoned, in consideration of the motive."

"No, indeed, I have no doubts at all on that head. I am delighted to find myself in such a circle. I hope we shall have many sweet little concerts together. I think, Miss Woodhouse, you and I must establish a musical club, and have regular weekly meetings at your house, or ours. Will not it be a good plan? If *we* exert ourselves, I think we shall not be long in want of allies. Something of that nature would be particularly desirable for *me,* as an inducement to keep me in practice; for married women, you know – there is a sad story against them, in general. They are but too apt to give up music."

"But you, who are so extremely fond of it – there can be no danger, surely?"

"I should hope not; but really when I look around among my acquaintance, I tremble. Selina has entirely given up music – never touches the instrument though she played sweetly. And the same may be said of Mrs. Jeffereys – Clara Partridge, that was – and of the two Milmans, now Mrs. Bird and Mrs. James Cooper; and of more than I can enumerate. Upon my word it is enough to put one in a fright. I used to be quite angry with Selina; but really I begin now to comprehend that a married woman has many things to call her attention. I believe I was half an hour this morning shut up with my housekeeper."

"But everything of that kind," said Emma, "will soon be in so regular a train – "

"Well," said Mrs. Elton, laughing, "we shall see."

Emma, finding her so determined upon neglecting her music, had nothing more to say; and, after a moment's pause, Mrs. Elton chose another subject.

"We have been calling at Randalls," said she, "and found them both at home; and very pleasant people they seem to be. I like them extremely. Mr. Weston seems an excellent creature – quite a first rate favourite with me already, I assure you. And *she* appears so truly good – there is something so motherly and kind-hearted about her, that it wins upon one directly. She was your governess, I think?"

Emma was almost too much astonished to answer; but Mrs. Elton hardly waited for the affirmative before she went on:

"Having understood as much, I was rather astonished to find her so very lady like! But she is really quite the gentlewoman."

"Mrs. Weston's manners," said Emma, "were always particularly good. Their propriety, simplicity, and elegance, would make them the safest model for any young woman."

"And who do you think came in while we were there?"

Emma was quite at a loss. The tone implied some old acquaintance and how could she possibly guess?

"Knightley!" continued Mrs. Elton; "Knightley himself! Was not it lucky? for, not being within when he called the other day, I had never seen him before; and of course, as so particular a friend of Mr. E.'s, I had a great curiosity. 'My friend Knightley' had been so often mentioned, that I was really impatient to see him; and I must do my *caro sposo*[1] the justice to say that he need not be ashamed of his friend. Knightley is quite the gentleman. I like him very much. Decidedly, I think, a very gentleman like man."

Happily, it was now time to be gone. They were off; and Emma could breathe.

"Insufferable woman!" was her immediate exclamation. "Worse than I had supposed. Absolutely insufferable! Knightley! I could not have believed it. Knightley! – never seen him in her life before, and call him Knightley! and discover that he is a gentleman! A little upstart, vulgar being, with her Mr. E., and her *caro sposo,* and her resources, and all her airs of pert pretension

1 Beloved husband.

and underbred finery. Actually to discover that Mr. Knightley is a gentleman! I doubt whether he will return the compliment, and discover her to be a lady. I could not have believed it! And to propose that she and I should unite to form a musical club! One would fancy we were bosom friends! And Mrs. Weston! Astonished that the person who had brought me up should be a gentle-woman! Worse and worse. I never met with her equal. Much beyond my hopes. Harriet is disgraced by any comparison. Oh! what would Frank Churchill say to her, if he were here? How angry and how diverted he would be! Ah! there I am thinking of him directly. Always the first person to be thought of! How I catch myself out! Frank Churchill comes as regularly into my mind –!"

All this ran so glibly through her thoughts, that by the time her father had arranged himself, after the bustle of the Eltons' departure, and was ready to speak, she was very tolerably capable of attending.

"Well, my dear," he deliberately began, "considering we never saw her before, she seems a very pretty sort of young lady; and I dare say she was very much pleased with you. She speaks a little too quick. A little quickness of voice there is which rather hurts the ear. But I believe I am nice; I do not like strange voices; and nobody speaks like you and poor Miss Taylor. However, she seems a very obliging, pretty-behaved young lady, and no doubt will make him a very good wife. Though I think he had better not have married. I made the best excuses I could for not having been able to wait on him and Mrs. Elton on this happy occasion; I said that I hoped I *should* in the course of the summer. But I ought to have gone before. Not to wait upon a bride is very remiss. Ah! it shows what a sad invalid I am! But I do not like the corner into Vicarage Lane."

"I dare say your apologies were accepted, sir. Mr. Elton knows you."

"Yes: but a young lady – a bride – I ought to have paid my respects to her if possible. It was being very deficient."

"But, my dear papa, you are no friend to matrimony; and therefore why should you be so anxious to pay your respects to a *bride?* It ought to be no recommendation to *you.* It is encouraging people to marry if you make so much of them."

"No, my dear, I never encouraged anybody to marry, but I would always wish to pay every proper attention to a lady – and a bride, especially, is never to be neglected. More is avowedly due to *her.* A bride, you know, my dear, is always the first in company, let the others be who they may."

"Well, papa, if this is not encouragement to marry, I do not know what is. And I should never have expected you to be lending your sanction to such vanity-baits for poor young ladies."

"My dear, you do not understand me. This is a matter of mere common politeness and good-breeding, and has nothing to do with any encouragement to people to marry."

Emma had done. Her father was growing nervous, and could not understand her. Her mind returned to Mrs. Elton's offences, and long, very long, did they occupy her.

# Chapter 33

EMMA WAS not required, by any subsequent discovery, to retract her ill opinion of Mrs. Elton. Her observation had been pretty correct. Such as Mrs. Elton appeared to her on this second interview, such she appeared whenever they met again, self-important, presuming, familiar, ignorant, and ill-bred. She had a little beauty and a little accomplishment, but so little judgment that she thought herself coming with superior knowledge of the world, to enliven and improve a country neighbourhood; and conceived Miss Hawkins to have held such a place in society as Mrs. Elton's consequence only could surpass.

There was no reason to suppose Mr. Elton thought at all differently from his wife. He seemed not merely happy with her, but proud. He had the air of congratulating himself on having brought such a woman to Highbury, as not even Miss Woodhouse could equal; and the greater part of her new acquaintance, disposed to commend, or not in the habit of judging, following the lead of Miss Bates's good will, or taking it for granted that the bride must be as clever and as agreeable as she professed herself, were very well satisfied; so that Mrs. Elton's praise passed from one mouth to another as it ought to do, unimpeded by Miss Woodhouse, who readily continued her first contribution and talked with a good grace of her being "very pleasant and very elegantly dressed."

In one respect Mrs. Elton grew even worse than she had appeared at first. Her feelings altered towards Emma. Offended, probably, by the little encouragement which her proposals of intimacy met with, she drew back in her turn and gradually became much more cold and distant; and though the effect was agreeable, the ill-will which produced it was necessarily increasing Emma's dislike. Her manners, too – and Mr. Elton's – were unpleasant towards Harriet. They were sneering and negligent. Emma hoped it must rapidly work Harriet's cure; but the sensations which could prompt such behaviour sunk them both very much. It was not to be doubted that poor Harriet's attachment had been an offering to conjugal unreserve, and her own share in the story, under a colouring the least favourable to her and the most soothing to him, had in all likelihood been given also. She was, of course, the object of their joint dislike. When they had nothing else to say, it must be always easy to begin abusing Miss Woodhouse; and the enmity which they dared not to show in open disrespect to her, found a broader vent in contemptuous treatment of Harriet.

Mrs. Elton took a great fancy to Jane Fairfax; and from the first. Not merely when a state of warfare with one young lady might be supposed to recommend the other, but from the very first; and she was not satisfied with expressing a natural and reasonable admiration but without solicitation, or plea, or privilege, she must be wanting to assist and befriend her. Before Emma had forfeited her confidence, and about the third time of their meeting, she heard all Mrs. Elton's knight errantry on the subject.

"Jane Fairfax is absolutely charming, Miss Woodhouse. I quite rave about Jane Fairfax. A sweet, interesting creature. So mild and ladylike – and with such talents! I assure you I think she has very extraordinary talents. I do not scruple to say that she plays extremely well. I know enough of music to speak decidedly on that point. Oh! she is absolutely charming! You will laugh at my warmth but, upon my word, I talk of nothing but Jane Fairfax. And her situation is so calculated to affect one! Miss Woodhouse, we must exert ourselves and endeavour to do something for her. We must bring her forward. Such talent as hers must not be suffered to remain unknown. I dare say you have heard those charming lines of the poet:

'Full many a flower is born to blush unseen,
'And waste its fragrance on the desert air.'

We must not allow them to be verified in sweet Jane Fairfax."

"I cannot think there is any danger of it," was Emma's calm

answer: "and when you are better acquainted with Miss Fairfax's situation and understand what her home has been, with Colonel and Mrs. Campbell, I have no idea that you will suppose her talents can be unknown."

"Oh! but dear Miss Woodhouse, she is now in such retirement, such obscurity, so thrown away. Whatever advantages she may have enjoyed with the Campbells are so palpably at an end! And I think she feels it. I am sure she does. She is very timid and silent. One can see that she feels the want of encouragement. I like her the better for it. I must confess it is a recommendation to me. I am a great advocate for timidity – and I am sure one does not often meet with it. But in those who are at all inferior, it is extremely prepossessing. Oh! I assure you, Jane Fairfax is a very delightful character, and interests me more than I can express."

"You appear to feel a great deal but I am not aware how you or any of Miss Fairfax's acquaintance here, any of those who have known her longer than yourself, can show her any other attention than – "

"My dear Miss Woodhouse, a vast deal may be done by those who dare to act. You and I need not be afraid. If we set the example, many will follow it as far as they can; though all have not our situations. *We* have carriages to fetch and convey her home, and *we* live in a style which could not make the addition of Jane Fairfax, at any time, the least inconvenient. I should be extremely displeased if Wright were to send us up such a dinner, as could make me regret having asked *more* than Jane Fairfax to partake of it. I have no idea of that sort of thing. It is not likely that I *should,* considering what I have been used to. My greatest danger, perhaps, in housekeeping, may be quite the other way, in doing too much, and being too careless of expense. Maple Grove will probably be my model more than it ought to be – for we do not at all affect to equal my brother, Mr. Suckling, in income. However, my resolution is taken as to noticing Jane Fairfax. I shall certainly have her very often at my house, shall introduce her wherever I can, shall have musical parties to draw out her talents, and shall be constantly on the watch for an eligible situation. My acquaintance is so very extensive, that I have little doubt of hearing of something to suit her shortly. I shall introduce her, of course, very particularly to my brother and sister when they come to us. I am sure they will like her extremely; and when she gets a little acquainted with them, her fears will completely wear off, for there really is nothing in the manners of either but what is highly conciliating. I shall have her very often indeed while they are with me, and I dare say we shall sometimes find a seat for her in the barouche-landau in some of our exploring parties."

"Poor Jane Fairfax!" thought Emma. "You have not deserved this. You may have done wrong with regard to Mr. Dixon, but this is a punishment beyond what you can have merited! The kindness and protection of Mrs. Elton! – 'Jane Fairfax and Jane Fairfax.' Heavens! Let me not suppose that she dares go about, Emma Woodhouseing me! But upon my honour, there seems no limits to the licentiousness of that woman's tongue!"

Emma had not to listen to such paradings again – to any so exclusively addressed to herself – so disgustingly decorated with a "dear Miss Woodhouse." The change on Mrs. Elton's side soon afterwards appeared, and she was left in peace – neither forced to be the very particular friend of Mrs. Elton, nor, under Mrs. Elton's guidance, the very active patroness of Jane Fairfax, and only sharing with others in a general way, in knowing what was felt, what was meditated, what was done.

She looked on with some amusement. Miss Bates's gratitude for Mrs. Elton's attentions to Jane was in the first style of guileless simplicity and warmth. She was quite one of her worthies – the most amiable, affable, delightful woman – just as accomplished and condescending as Mrs. Elton meant to be considered. Emma's only surprise was that Jane Fairfax should accept those attentions and tolerate Mrs. Elton as she seemed to do. She heard of her walking with the Eltons, sitting with the Eltons, spending a day with the Eltons! This was astonishing! She could not have believed it possible that the taste or the pride of Miss Fairfax could endure such society and friendship as the Vicarage had to offer.

"She is a riddle, quite a riddle!" said she. "To choose to remain here month after month, under privations of every sort! And now to choose the mortification of Mrs. Elton's notice and the penury of her conversation, rather than return to the superior companions who have always loved her with such real, generous affection."

Jane had come to Highbury professedly for three months; the Campbells were gone to Ireland for three months; but now the Campbells had promised their daughter to stay at least till Midsummer, and fresh invitations had arrived for her to join them there. According to Miss Bates – it all came from her – Mrs. Dixon had written most pressingly. Would Jane but go, means were to be found, servants sent, friends contrived – no travelling difficulty allowed to exist; but still she had declined it!

"She must have some motive, more powerful than appears, for refusing this invitation," was Emma's conclusion. "She must be under some sort of penance, inflicted either by the Campbells or herself. There is great fear, great caution, great resolution somewhere. She is *not* to be with the *Dixons*. The decree is issued by somebody. But why must she consent to be with the Eltons? Here is quite a separate puzzle."

Upon her speaking her wonder aloud on that part of the subject, before the few who knew her opinion of Mrs. Elton, Mrs. Weston ventured this apology for Jane.

"We cannot suppose that she has any great enjoyment at the Vicarage, my dear Emma – but it is better than being always at home. Her aunt is a good creature, but, as a constant companion, must be very tiresome. We must consider what Miss Fairfax quits, before we condemn her taste for what she goes to."

"You are right, Mrs. Weston," said Mr. Knightley warmly, "Miss Fairfax is as capable as any of us of forming a just opinion of Mrs. Elton. Could she have chosen with whom to associate, she would not have chosen her. But (with a reproachful smile at Emma) she receives attentions from Mrs. Elton, which nobody else pays her."

Emma felt that Mrs. Weston was giving her a momentary glance; and she was herself struck by his warmth. With a faint blush, she presently replied:

"Such attentions as Mrs. Elton's, I should have imagined, would rather disgust than gratify Miss Fairfax. Mrs. Elton's invitations I should have imagined any thing but inviting."

"I should not wonder," said Mrs. Weston, "if Miss Fairfax were to have been drawn on beyond her own inclination, by her aunt's eagerness in accepting Mrs. Elton's civilities for her. Poor Miss Bates may very likely have committed her niece and hurried her into a greater appearance of intimacy than her own good sense would have dictated, in spite of the very natural wish of a little change."

Both felt rather anxious to hear him speak again; and after a few minutes silence, he said:

"Another thing must be taken into consideration too – Mrs. Elton does not talk to Miss Fairfax as she speaks *of* her. We all know the difference between the pronouns he or she and thou, the plainest spoken amongst us; we all feel the influence of a something beyond common civility in our personal intercourse with each other – a something more early implanted. We cannot give anybody the disagreeable hints that we may have been very full of the hour before. We feel things differently. And besides the operation of this, as a general principle, you may be sure that Miss Fairfax awes Mrs. Elton by her superiority both of mind and manner; and that, face to face, Mrs. Elton treats her with all the respect which she has a claim to. Such a woman as Jane

Fairfax probably never fell in Mrs. Elton's way before – and no degree of vanity can prevent her acknowledging her own comparative littleness in action, if not in consciousness."

"I know how highly you think of Jane Fairfax," said Emma. Little Henry was in her thoughts, and a mixture of alarm and delicacy made her irresolute what else to say.

"Yes," he replied, "anybody may know how highly I think of her."

"And yet," said Emma, beginning hastily and with an arch look, but soon stopping – it was better, however, to know the worst at once – she hurried on – "And yet, perhaps, you may hardly be aware yourself how highly it is. The extent of your admiration may take you by surprise some day or other."

Mr. Knightley was hard at work upon the lower buttons of his thick leather gaiters, and either the exertion of getting them together, or some other cause, brought the colour into his face, as he answered:

"Oh! are you there? But you are miserably behindhand. Mr. Cole gave me a hint of it six weeks ago."

He stopped. Emma felt her foot pressed by Mrs. Weston, and did not herself know what to think. In a moment he went on:

"That will never be, however, I can assure you. Miss Fairfax, I dare say, would not have me if I were to ask her and I am very sure I shall never ask her."

Emma returned her friend's pressure with interest; and was pleased enough to exclaim:

"You are not vain, Mr. Knightley. I will say that for you."

He seemed hardly to hear her; he was thoughtful and in a manner which showed him not pleased, soon afterwards said:

"So you have been settling that I should marry Jane Fairfax?"

"No indeed I have not. You have scolded me too much for match making, for me to presume to take such a liberty with you. What I said just now, meant nothing. One says those sort of things, of course, without any idea of a serious meaning. Oh! no, upon my word I have not the smallest wish for your marrying Jane Fairfax or Jane anybody. You would not come in and sit with us in this comfortable way, if you were married."

Mr. Knightley was thoughtful again. The result of his reverie was, "No, Emma, I do not think the extent of my admiration for her will ever take me by surprise. I never had a thought of her in that way, I assure you."

And soon afterwards, "Jane Fairfax is a very charming young woman – but not even Jane Fairfax is perfect. She has a fault. She has not the open temper which a man would wish for in a wife."

Emma could not but rejoice to hear that she had a fault.

"Well," said she, "and you soon silenced Mr. Cole, I suppose?"

"Yes, very soon. He gave me a quiet hint; I told him he was mistaken; he asked my pardon and said no more. Cole does not want to be wiser or wittier than his neighbours."

"In that respect how unlike dear Mrs. Elton, who wants to be wiser and wittier than all the world! I wonder how she speaks of the Coles – what she calls them! How can she find any appellation for them, deep enough in familiar vulgarity? She calls you, Knightley what can she do for Mr. Cole? And so I am not to be surprised that Jane Fairfax accepts her civilities and consents to be with her. Mrs. Weston, your argument weighs most with me. I can much more readily enter into the temptation of getting away from Miss Bates, than I can believe in the triumph of Miss Fairfax's mind over Mrs. Elton. I have no faith in Mrs. Elton's acknowledging herself the inferior in thought, word, or deed; or in her being under any restraint beyond her own scanty rule of good breeding. I cannot imagine that she will not be continually insulting her visitor with praise, encouragement, and offers of service; that she will not be continually detailing her magnificent intentions, from the procuring her a permanent situation to the including her in those delightful exploring parties which are to take place in the barouche-landau."

"Jane Fairfax has feeling," said Mr. Knightley "I do not accuse her of want of feeling. Her sensibilities, I suspect, are strong and her temper excellent in its power of forbearance, patience, self-control; but it wants openness. She is reserved, more reserved, I think, than she used to be: and I love an open temper. No till Cole alluded to my supposed attachment, it had never entered my head. I saw Jane Fairfax and conversed with her, with admiration and pleasure always, but with no thought beyond."

"Well, Mrs. Weston," said Emma triumphantly when he left them, "what do you say now to Mr. Knightley's marrying Jane Fairfax?"

"Why, really, dear Emma, I say that he is so very much occupied by the idea of not being in love with her, that I should not wonder if it were to end in his being so at last. Do not beat me."

## *Chapter 34*

EVERYBODY IN and about Highbury who had ever visited Mr. Elton, was disposed to pay him attention on his marriage. Dinner parties and evening parties were made for him and his lady; and invitations flowed in so fast that she had soon the pleasure of apprehending they were never to have a disengaged day.

"I see how it is," said she. "I see what a life I am to lead among you. Upon my word we shall be absolutely dissipated. We really seem quite the fashion. If this is living in the country, it is nothing very formidable. From Monday next to Saturday, I assure you we have not a disengaged day! A woman with fewer resources than I have, need not have been at a loss."

No invitation came amiss to her. Her Bath habits made evening parties perfectly natural to her, and Maple Grove had given her a taste for dinners. She was a little shocked at the want of two drawing-rooms, at the poor attempt at rout-cakes, and there being no ice in the Highbury card-parties. Mrs. Bates, Mrs. Perry, Mrs. Goddard and others, were a good deal behind hand in knowledge of the world, but *she* would soon show them how everything ought to be arranged. In the course of the spring she must return their civilities by one very superior party in which her card-tables should be set out with their separate candles and unbroken packs in the true style and more waiters engaged for the evening than their own establishment could furnish, to carry round the refreshments at exactly the proper hour, and in the proper order.

Emma, in the meanwhile, could not be satisfied without a dinner at Hartfield for the Eltons. They must not do less than others, or she should be exposed to odious suspicions, and imagined capable of pitiful resentment. A dinner there must be. After Emma had talked about it for ten minutes, Mr. Woodhouse felt no unwillingness, and only made the usual stipulation of not sitting at the bottom of the table himself, with the usual regular difficulty of deciding who should do it for him.

The persons to be invited, required little thought. Besides the Eltons, it must be the Westons and Mr. Knightley; so far it was all of course and it was hardly less inevitable that poor little Harriet must be asked to make the eighth: but this invitation was not given with equal satisfaction, and on many accounts Emma was particularly pleased by Harriet's begging to be allowed to decline it. "She would rather not be in *his* company more than she could help. She was not yet quite able to see him and his charming happy wife together, without feeling uncomfortable. If Miss Woodhouse would not be displeased, she would rather stay at home." It was precisely what Emma would have wished, had she deemed it possible enough for wishing. She was delighted with the fortitude of her little friend – for fortitude she knew it was in her to give up being in company and stay at home; and she could now invite the very person whom she really wanted to make the eighth, Jane Fairfax. Since her last conversation with Mrs. Weston and Mr. Knightley, she was more conscience-stricken about Jane Fairfax than she had often been. Mr. Knightley's words dwelt with her. He had said that Jane Fairfax received attentions from Mrs. Elton which nobody else paid her.

"This is very true," said she, "at least as far as relates to me, which was all that was meant and it is very shameful. Of the same age and always knowing her I ought to have been more her friend. She will never like me now. I have neglected her too long. But I will show her greater attention than I have done."

Every invitation was successful. They were all disengaged and all happy. The preparatory interest of this dinner, however, was not yet over. A circumstance rather unlucky occurred. The two eldest little Knightleys were engaged to pay their grandpapa and aunt a visit of some weeks in the spring, and their papa now proposed bringing them, and staying one whole day at Hartfield – which one day would be the very day of this party. His professional engagements did not allow of his being put off, but both father and daughter were disturbed by its happening so. Mr. Woodhouse considered eight persons at dinner together as the utmost that his nerves could bear – and here would be a ninth and Emma apprehended that it would be a ninth – very much out of humour at not being able to come even to Hartfield for forty-eight hours without falling in with a dinner party.

She comforted her father better than she could comfort herself, by representing that though he certainly would make them nine, yet he always said so little, that the increase of noise would be very immaterial. She thought it in reality a sad exchange for herself, to have him with his grave looks and reluctant conversation opposed to her instead of his brother.

The event was more favourable to Mr. Woodhouse than to Emma. John Knightley came; but Mr. Weston was unexpectedly summoned to town and must be absent on the very day. He might be able to join them in the evening, but certainly not to dinner. Mr. Woodhouse was quite at ease; and seeing him so, with the arrival of the little boys and the philosophic composure of her brother on hearing his fate, removed the chief of even Emma's vexation.

The day came, the party were punctually assembled, and Mr. John Knightley seemed early to devote himself to the business of being agreeable. Instead of drawing his brother off to a window while they waited for dinner, he was talking to Miss Fairfax. Mrs. Elton, as elegant as lace and pearls could make her, he looked at in silence – wanting only to observe enough for Isabella's information – but Miss Fairfax was an old acquaintance and a quiet girl, and he could talk to her. He had met her before breakfast as he was returning from a walk with his little boys, when it had been just beginning to rain. It was natural to have some civil hopes on the subject, and he said:

"I hope you did not venture far, Miss Fairfax, this morning, or I am sure you must have been wet. *We* scarcely got home in time. I hope you turned directly."

"I went only to the post office," said she, "and reached home before the rain was much. It is my daily errand. I always fetch the letters when I am here. It saves trouble, and is a something to get me out. A walk before breakfast does me good."

"Not a walk in the rain, I should imagine."

"No, but it did not absolutely rain when I set out."

Mr. John Knightley smiled, and replied:

"That is to say, you chose to have your walk, for you were not six yards from your own door when I had the pleasure of meeting you; and Henry and John had seen more drops than they could count long before. The post office has a great charm at one period of our lives. When you have lived to my age, you will begin to think letters are never worth going through the rain for."

There was a little blush, and then this answer:

"I must not hope to be ever situated as you are, in the midst of every dearest connection, and therefore I cannot expect that simply growing older should make me indifferent about letters."

"Indifferent! Oh! no – I never conceived you could become indifferent. Letters are no matter of indifference; they are generally a very positive curse."

"You are speaking of letters of business; mine are letters of friendship."

"I have often thought them the worst of the two," replied he coolly. "Business, you know, may bring money, but friendship hardly ever does."

"Ah! you are not serious now. I know Mr. John Knightley too well – I am very sure he understands the value of friendship as well as anybody. I can easily believe that letters are very little to you, much less than to me, but it is not your being ten years older than myself which makes the difference, it is not age, but situation. You have everybody dearest to you always at hand, I, probably, never shall again; and therefore till I have outlived all my affections, a post office, I think, must always have power to draw me out, in worse weather than to day."

"When I talked of your being altered by time, by the progress of years," said John Knightley, "I meant to imply the change of situation which time usually brings. I consider one as including the other. Time will generally lessen the interest of every attachment not within the daily circle – but that is not the change I had in view for you. As an old friend, you will allow me to hope, Miss Fairfax, that ten years hence you may have as many concentrated objects as I have."

It was kindly said, and very far from giving offence. A pleasant "thank you" seemed meant to laugh it off, but a blush, a quivering lip, a tear in the eye, showed that it was felt beyond a laugh. Her attention was now claimed by Mr. Woodhouse, who being, according to his custom on such occasions, making the circle of his guests, and paying his particular compliments to the ladies, was ending with her – and with all his mildest urbanity, said:

"I am very sorry to hear, Miss Fairfax, of your being out this morning in the rain. Young ladies should take care of themselves. Young ladies are delicate plants. They should take care of their health and their complexion. My dear, did you change your stockings?"

"Yes, sir, I did indeed; and I am very much obliged by your kind solicitude about me."

"My dear Miss Fairfax, young ladies are very sure to be cared for. I hope your good grand mama and aunt are well. They are some of my very old friends. I wish my health allowed me to be a better neighbour. You do us a great deal of honour to day, I am sure. My daughter and I are both highly sensible of your goodness, and have the greatest satisfaction in seeing you at Hartfield."

The kind-hearted, polite old man might then sit down and feel that he had done his duty, and made every fair lady welcome and easy.

By this time, the walk in the rain had reached Mrs. Elton, and her remonstrances now opened upon Jane.

"My dear Jane, what is this I hear? Going to the post office in the rain! This must not be, I assure you. You sad girl, how could you do such a thing? It is a sign I was not there to take care of you."

Jane very patiently assured her that she had not caught any cold.

"Oh! do not tell *me*. You really are a very sad girl, and do not know how to take care of yourself. To the post office indeed! Mrs. Weston, did you ever hear the like? You and I must positively exert our authority."

"My advice," said Mrs. Weston kindly and persuasively, "I certainly do feel tempted to give. Miss Fairfax, you must not run such risks. Liable as you have been to severe colds, indeed you ought to be particularly careful, especially at this time of the year.

The spring I always think requires more than common care. Better wait an hour or two, or even half a day for your letters, than run the risk of bringing on your cough again. Now do not you feel that you had? Yes, I am sure you are much too reasonable. You look as if you would not do such a thing again."

"Oh! she *shall not* do such a thing again," – eagerly rejoined Mrs. Elton. "We will not allow her to do such a thing again:" and nodding significantly – "there must be some arrangement made, there must indeed. I shall speak to Mr. E. The man who fetches our letters every morning (one of our men, I forget his name) shall inquire for yours too and bring them to you. That will obviate all difficulties you know; and from us I really think, my dear Jane, you can have no scruple to accept such an accommodation."

"You are extremely kind," said Jane; "but I cannot give up my early walk. I am advised to be out-of-doors as much as I can, I must walk somewhere, and the post office is an object; and upon my word, I have scarcely ever had a bad morning before."

"My dear Jane, say no more about it. The thing is determined, that is (laughing affectedly) as far as I can presume to determine any thing without the concurrence of my lord and master. You know, Mrs. Weston, you and I must be cautious how we express ourselves. But I do flatter myself, my dear Jane, that my influence is not entirely worn out. If I meet with no insuperable difficulties therefore, consider that point as settled."

"Excuse me," said Jane earnestly, "I cannot by any means consent to such an arrangement, so needlessly troublesome to your servant. If the errand were not a pleasure to me, it could be done, as it always is when I am not here, by my grandmama's – "

"Oh! my dear; but so much as Patty has to do! And it is a kindness to employ our men."

Jane looked as if she did not mean to be conquered; but instead of answering, she began speaking again to Mr. John Knightley.

"The post office is a wonderful establishment!" said she.

"The regularity and despatch of it! If one thinks of all that it has to do, and all that it does so well, it is really astonishing!"

"It is certainly very well regulated."

"So seldom that any negligence or blunder appears! So seldom that a letter, among the thousands that are constantly passing about the kingdom, is even carried wrong – and not one in a million, I suppose, actually lost! And when one considers the variety of hands, and of bad hands too, that are to be deciphered, it increases the wonder."

"The clerks grow expert from habit. They must begin with some quickness of sight and hand, and exercise improves them. If you want any farther explanation," continued he, smiling, "they are paid for it. That is the key to a great deal of capacity. The public pays and must be served well."

The varieties of handwriting were farther talked of, and the usual observations made.

"I have heard it asserted," said John Knightley, "that the same sort of handwriting often prevails in a family; and where the same master teaches, it is natural enough. But for that reason, I should imagine the likeness must be chiefly confined to the females, for boys have very little teaching after an early age, and scramble into any hand they can get. Isabella and Emma, I think, do write very much alike. I have not always known their writing apart."

"Yes," said his brother hesitatingly, "there is a likeness. I know what you mean – but Emma's hand is the strongest."

"Isabella and Emma both write beautifully," said Mr. Woodhouse; "and always did. And so does poor Mrs. Weston" with half a sigh and half a smile at her.

"I never saw any gentleman's handwriting" – Emma began, looking also at Mrs. Weston; but stopped, on perceiving that Mrs. Weston was attending to some one else – and the pause gave her time to reflect, "Now, how am I going to introduce him? Am I unequal to speaking his name at once before all these people? Is it necessary for me to use any roundabout phrase? Your Yorkshire friend – your correspondent in Yorkshire; that would be the way, I suppose, if I were very bad. No, I can pronounce his name without the smallest distress. I certainly get better and better. Now for it."

Mrs. Weston was disengaged and Emma began again – "Mr. Frank Churchill writes one of the best gentleman's hands I ever saw."

"I do not admire it," said Mr. Knightley. "It is too small – wants strength. It is like a woman's writing."

This was not submitted to by either lady. They vindicated him against the base aspersion. "No, it by no means wanted strength – it was not a large hand, but very clear and certainly strong. Had not Mrs. Weston any letter about her to produce?" No, she had heard from him very lately, but having answered the letter, had put it away.

"If we were in the other room," said Emma – "if I had my writing desk, I am sure I could produce a specimen. I have a note of his. Do not you remember, Mrs. Weston, employing him to write for you one day?"

"He chose to say he was employed."

"Well, well, I have that note; and can show it after dinner to convince Mr. Knightley."

"Oh! when a gallant young man, like Mr. Frank Churchill," said Mr. Knightley dryly, "writes to a fair lady like Miss Woodhouse, he will, of course, put forth his best."

Dinner was on table. Mrs. Elton, before she could be spoken to, was ready; and before Mr. Woodhouse had reached her with his request to be allowed to hand her into the dining-parlour, was saying:

"Must I go first? I really am ashamed of always leading the way."

Jane's solicitude about fetching her own letters had not

escaped Emma. She had heard and seen it all; and felt some curiosity to know whether the wet walk of this morning had produced any. She suspected that it *had;* that it would not have been so resolutely encountered but in full expectation of hearing from some one very dear, and that it had not been in vain. She thought there was an air of greater happiness than usual – a glow both of complexion and spirits.

She could have made an inquiry or two, as to the expedition and the expense of the Irish mails; it was at her tongue's end – but she abstained. She was quite determined not to utter a word that should hurt Jane Fairfax's feelings; and they followed the other ladies out of the room, arm-in-arm, with an appearance of good will highly becoming to the beauty and grace of each.

## *Chapter 35*

WHEN THE ladies returned to the drawing-room after dinner, Emma found it hardly possible to prevent their making two distinct parties; with so much perseverance in judging and behaving ill did Mrs. Elton engross Jane Fairfax and slight herself. She and Mrs. Weston were obliged to be almost always either talking together or silent together. Mrs. Elton left them no choice. If Jane repressed her for a little time, she soon began again; and though much that passed between them was in a half whisper, especially on Mrs. Elton's side, there was no avoiding a knowledge of their principal subjects: The post office – catching cold – fetching letters – and friendship, were long under discussion; and to them succeeded one, which must be at least equally unpleasant to Jane – inquiries whether she had yet heard of any situation likely to suit her, and professions of Mrs. Elton's meditated activity.

"Here is April come!" said she, "I get quite anxious about you. June will soon be here."

"But I have never fixed on June or any other month – merely looked forward to the summer in general."

"But have you really heard of nothing?"

"I have not even made any inquiry; I do not wish to make any yet."

"Oh! my dear, we cannot begin too early; you are not aware of the difficulty of procuring exactly the desirable thing."

"I not aware!" said Jane, shaking her head; "dear Mrs. Elton, who can have thought of it as I have done?"

"But you have not seen so much of the world as I have. You do not know how many candidates there always are for the first situations. I saw a vast deal of that in the neighbourhood round Maple Grove. A cousin of Mr. Suckling, Mrs. Bragge, had such an infinity of applications; everybody was anxious to be in her family, for she moves in the first circle. Wax-candles in the schoolroom! You may imagine how desirable! Of all houses in the kingdom Mrs. Bragge's is the one I would most wish to see you in."

"Colonel and Mrs. Campbell are to be in town again by midsummer," said Jane. "I must spend some time with them; I am sure they will want it; afterwards I may probably be glad to dispose of myself. But I would not wish you to take the trouble of making any inquiries at present."

"Trouble! aye, I know your scruples. You are afraid of giving me trouble; but I assure you, my dear Jane, the Campbells can hardly be more interested about you than I am. I shall write to Mrs. Partridge in a day or two, and shall give her a strict charge to be on the look out for any thing eligible."

"Thank you, but I would rather you did not mention the subject to her; till the time draws nearer, I do not wish to be giving anybody trouble."

"But, my dear child, the time *is* drawing near; here is April, and June, or say even July, is very near, with such business to accomplish before us. Your inexperience really amuses me! A situation such as you deserve, and your friends would require for you, is no everyday occurrence, is not obtained at a moment's notice; indeed, indeed, we must begin inquiring directly."

"Excuse me, ma'am, but this is by no means my intention; I make no inquiry myself, and should be sorry to have any made by my friends. When I am quite determined as to the time, I am not at all afraid of being long unemployed. There are places in town, offices, where inquiry would soon produce something – Offices for the sale not quite of human flesh but of human intellect."

"Oh! my dear, human flesh! You quite shock me; if you mean a fling at the slave trade, I assure you Mr. Suckling was always rather a friend to the abolition."

"I did not mean – I was not thinking of the slave trade," replied Jane; "governess-trade, I assure you, was all that I had in view; widely different certainly as to the guilt of those who carry it on; but as to the greater misery of the victims, I do not know where it lies. But I only mean to say that there are advertising offices, and that by applying to them I should have no doubt of very soon meeting with something that would do."

"Something that would do!" repeated Mrs. Elton. "Aye, *that* may suit your humble ideas of yourself; I know what a modest creature you are; but it will not satisfy your friends to have you taking up with any thing that may offer, any inferior, commonplace situation, in a family not moving in a certain circle, or able to command the elegancies of life."

"You are very obliging; but as to all that, I am very indifferent; it would be no object to me to be with the rich; my mortifications, I think, would only be the greater; I should suffer more from comparison. A gentleman's family is all that I should condition for."

"I know you, I know you; you would take up with any thing; but I shall be a little more nice, and I am sure the good Campbells will be quite on my side; with your superior talents, you have a right to move in the first circle. Your musical knowledge alone would entitle you to name your own terms, have as many rooms as you like, and mix in the family as much as you chose; that is – I do not know – if you knew the harp, you might do all that, I am very sure; but you sing as well as play; yes, I really believe you might, even without the harp, stipulate for what you chose; and you must and shall be delightfully, honourably and comfortably settled before the Campbells or I have any rest."

"You may well class the delight, the honour, and the comfort of such a situation together," said Jane, "they are pretty sure to be equal; however, I am very serious in not wishing any thing to be attempted at present for me. I am exceedingly obliged to you, Mrs. Elton, I am obliged to anybody who feels for me, but I am quite serious in wishing nothing to be done till the summer. For two or three months longer I shall remain where I am, and as I am."

"And I am quite serious too, I assure you," replied Mrs. Elton gaily, "in resolving to be always on the watch, and employing my friends to watch also, that nothing really unexceptionable may pass us."

In this style she ran on; never thoroughly stopped by any thing till Mr. Woodhouse came into the room; her vanity had then a change of object, and Emma heard her saying in the same half whisper to Jane:

"Here comes this dear old beau of mine, I protest! Only think of his gallantry in coming away before the other men! what a dear creature he is; I assure you I like him excessively. I admire all that quaint, old-fashioned politeness; it is much more to my taste than modern ease; modern ease often disgusts me. But this good old Mr. Woodhouse, I wish you had heard his gallant speeches to me at dinner. Oh! I assure you I began to think my *caro sposo* would be absolutely jealous. I fancy I am rather a favourite; he took notice of my gown. How do you like it? Selina's choice – handsome, I think, but I do not know whether it is not over-trimmed; I have the greatest dislike to the idea of being over-trimmed quite a horror of finery. I must put on a few ornaments *now,* because it is expected of me. A bride, you know, must appear like a bride, but my natural taste is all for simplicity; a simple style of dress – is so infinitely preferable to finery. But I am quite in the minority, I believe; few people seem to value simplicity of dress, show and finery are everything. I have some notion of putting such a trimming as this to my white and silver poplin. Do you think it will look well?"

The whole party were but just reassembled in the drawing room when Mr. Weston made his appearance among them. He had returned to a late dinner, and walked to Hartfield as soon as it was over. He had been too much expected by the best judges, for surprise – but there was great joy. Mr. Woodhouse was almost as glad to see him now, as he would have been sorry to see him before. John Knightley only was in mute astonishment. That a man who might have spent his evening quietly at home after a day of business in London, should set off again, and walk half a mile to another man's house, for the sake of being in mixed company till bed time, of finishing his day in the efforts of civility and the noise of numbers, was a circumstance to strike him deeply. A man who had been in motion since eight o'clock in the morning, and might now have been still – who had been long talking, and might have been silent – who had been in more than one crowd, and might have been alone! Such a man, to quit the tranquillity and independence of his own fireside, and on the evening of a cold sleety April day rush out again into the world! Could he by a touch of his finger have instantly taken back his wife, there would have been a motive; but his coming would probably prolong rather than break up the party. John Knightley looked at him with amazement, then shrugged his shoulders, and said, "I could not have believed it even of him."

Mr. Weston meanwhile, perfectly unsuspicious of the indignation he was exciting, happy and cheerful as usual, and with all the right of being principal talker, which a day spent anywhere from home confers, was making himself agreeable among the rest; and having satisfied the inquiries of his wife as to his dinner, convincing her that none of all her careful directions to the servants had been forgotten, and spread abroad what public news he had heard, was proceeding to a family communication, which, though principally addressed to Mrs. Weston, he had not the smallest doubt of being highly interesting to everybody in the room. He gave her a letter – it was from Frank, and to herself; he had met with it in his way, and had taken the liberty of opening it.

"Read it, read it," said he – "it will give you pleasure; only a few lines – will not take you long; read it to Emma."

The two ladies looked over it together; and he sat smiling and talking to them the whole time, in a voice a little subdued, but very audible to everybody.

"Well, he is coming, you see; good news, I think. Well, what do you say to it? I always told you he would be here again soon, did not I? Anne, my dear, did not I always tell you so, and you would not believe me? In town next week, you see – at the latest, I dare say; for *she* is as impatient as the black gentleman[1] when anything is to be done; most likely they will be there to morrow or Saturday. As to her illness, all nothing of course. But it is an excellent thing to have Frank among us again, so near as town. They will stay a good while when they do come, and he will be half his time with us. This is precisely what I wanted. Well, pretty good news, is not it? Have you finished it? Has Emma read it all? Put it up, put it up; we will have a good talk about it some other time, but it will not do now. I shall only just mention the circumstance to the others in a common way."

Mrs. Weston was most comfortably pleased on the occasion. Her looks and words had nothing to restrain them. She was happy, she knew *she* was happy, and knew she ought to be happy. Her

1 Euphemistic reference to the devil.

congratulations were warm and open; but Emma could not speak so fluently. She was a little occupied in weighing her own feelings, and trying to understand the degree of her agitation, which she rather thought was considerable.

Mr. Weston, however, too eager to be very observant, too communicative to want others to talk, was very well satisfied with what she did say, and soon moved away to make the rest of his friends happy by a partial communication of what the whole room must have overheard already.

It was well that he took everybody's joy for granted, or he might not have thought either Mr. Woodhouse or Mr. Knightley particularly delighted. They were the first entitled, after Mrs. Weston and Emma, to be made happy; from them he would have proceeded to Miss Fairfax, but she was so deep in conversation with John Knightley, that it would have been too positive an interruption; and finding himself close to Mrs. Elton, and her attention disengaged, he necessarily began on the subject with her.

# *Chapter 36*

I HOPE I shall soon have the pleasure of introducing my son to you," said Mr. Weston.

Mrs. Elton, very willing to suppose a particular compliment intended her by such a hope, smiled most graciously.

"You have heard of a certain Frank Churchill, I presume," he continued "and know him to be my son, though he does not bear my name."

"Oh! yes, and I shall be very happy in his acquaintance. I am sure Mr. Elton will lose no time in calling on him; and we shall both have great pleasure in seeing him at the Vicarage."

"You are very obliging. Frank will be extremely happy, I am sure. He is to be in town next week, if not sooner. We have notice of it in a letter to day. I met the letters in my way this morning, and seeing my son's hand, presumed to open it though it was not directed to me – it was to Mrs. Weston. She is his principal correspondent, I assure you. I hardly ever get a letter."

"And so you absolutely opened what was directed to her! Oh! Mr. Weston (laughing affectedly) I must protest against that. A most dangerous precedent indeed! I beg you will not let your neighbours follow your example. Upon my word, if this is what I am to expect, we married women must begin to exert ourselves! Oh! Mr. Weston, I could not have believed it of you!"

"Aye, we men are sad fellows. You must take care of yourself, Mrs. Elton. This letter tells us – it is a short letter written in a hurry, merely to give us notice – it tells us that they are all coming up to town directly, on Mrs. Churchill's account she has not been well the whole winter, and thinks Enscombe too cold for her so they are all to move southward without loss of time."

"Indeed! from Yorkshire, I think. Enscombe is in Yorkshire?"

"Yes, they are about one hundred and ninety miles from London, a considerable journey."

"Yes, upon my word, very considerable. Sixty-five miles farther than from Maple Grove to London. But what is distance, Mr. Weston, to people of large fortune? You would be amazed to hear how my brother, Mr. Suckling, sometimes flies about. You will hardly believe me but twice in one week he and Mr. Bragge went to London and back again with four horses."

"The evil of the distance from Enscombe," said Mr. Weston, "is, that Mrs. Churchill, *as we understand,* has not been able to leave the sofa for a week together. In Frank's last letter she complained, he said, of being too weak to get into her conservatory without having both his arm and his uncle's! This, you know.

speaks a great degree of weakness but now she is so impatient to be in town, that she means to sleep only two nights on the road – so Frank writes word. Certainly, delicate ladies have very extraordinary constitutions, Mrs. Elton. You must grant me that."

"No, indeed, I shall grant you nothing. I Always take the part of my own sex. I do indeed. I give you notice You will find me a formidable antagonist on that point. I always stand up for women and I assure you, if you knew how Selina feels with respect to sleeping at an inn, you would not wonder at Mrs. Churchill's making incredible exertions to avoid it. Selina says it is quite horror to her and I believe I have caught a little of her nicety. She always travels with her own sheets; an excellent precaution. Does Mrs. Churchill do the same?"

"Depend upon it, Mrs. Churchill does everything that any other fine lady ever did. Mrs. Churchill will not be second to any lady in the land for – "

Mrs. Elton eagerly interposed with:

"Oh! Mr. Weston, do not mistake me. Selina is no fine lady, I assure you. Do not run away with such an idea."

"Is not she? Then she is no rule for Mrs. Churchill, who is as thorough a fine lady as anybody ever beheld."

Mrs. Elton began to think she had been wrong in disclaiming so warmly. It was by no means her object to have it believed that her sister was not a fine lady; perhaps there was want of spirit in the pretence of it; and she was considering in what way she had best retract, when Mr. Weston went on.

"Mrs. Churchill is not much in my good graces, as you may suspect but this is quite between ourselves. She is very fond of Frank, and therefore I would not speak ill of her. Besides, she is out of health now; but *that* indeed, by her own account, she has always been. I would not say so to everybody, Mrs. Elton, but I have not much faith in Mrs. Churchill's illness."

"If she is really ill, why not go to Bath, Mr. Weston? –To Bath, or to Clifton?"

"She has taken it into her head that Enscombe is too cold for her. The fact is, I suppose, that she is tired of Enscombe. She has now been a longer time stationary there, than she ever was before, and she begins to want change. It is a retired place. A fine place, but very retired."

"Aye like Maple Grove, I dare say. Nothing can stand more retired from the road than Maple Grove. Such an immense plantation all round it! You seem shut out from everything – in the most complete retirement. And Mrs. Churchill probably has not health or spirits like Selina to enjoy that sort of seclusion. Or, perhaps she may not have resources enough in herself to be qualified for a country life. I always say a woman cannot have too many resources and I feel very thankful that I have so many myself as to be quite independent of society."

"Frank was here in February for a fortnight."

"So I remember to have heard. He will find an *addition* to the society of Highbury when he comes again; that is, if I may presume to call myself an addition. But perhaps he may never have heard of there being such a creature in the world."

This was too loud a call for a compliment to be passed by, and Mr. Weston, with a very good grace, immediately exclaimed:

"My dear madam! Nobody but yourself could imagine such a thing possible. Not heard of you! I believe Mrs. Weston's letters lately have been full of very little else than Mrs. Elton."

He had done his duty and could return to his son.

"When Frank left us," continued he, "it was quite uncertain when we might see him again, which makes this day's news doubly welcome. It has been completely unexpected. That is, I always had a strong persuasion he would be here again soon, I was sure something favourable would turn up – but nobody believed me. He and Mrs. Weston were both dreadfully desponding. 'How could he contrive to come? And how could it be supposed that his uncle and aunt would spare him again?' and so forth I always felt that something would happen in our favour; and so it has, you see. I have observed, Mrs. Elton, in the course of my life, that if things are going untowardly one month, they are sure to mend the next."

"Very true, Mr. Weston, perfectly true. It is just what I used to say to a certain gentleman in company in the days of courtship, when, because things did not go quite right – did not proceed with all the rapidity which suited his feelings – he was apt to be in despair, and exclaim that he was sure at this rate it would be *May* before Hymen's saffron robe[1] would be put on for us. Oh! the pains I have been at to dispel those gloomy ideas and give him cheerfuller views! The carriage – we had disappointments about the carriage; one morning, I remember, he came to me quite in despair."

She was stopped by a slight fit of coughing, and Mr. Weston instantly seized the opportunity of going on.

"You were mentioning May. May is the very month which Mrs. Churchill is ordered, or has ordered herself, to spend in some warmer place than Enscombe – in short, to spend in London; so that we have the agreeable prospect of frequent visits from Frank the whole spring – precisely the season of the year which one should have chosen for it; days almost at the longest; weather genial and pleasant, always inviting one out, and never too hot for exercise. When he was here before, we made the best of it; but there was a good deal of wet, damp, cheerless weather; there always is in February, you know, and we could not do half that we intended. Now will be the time. This will be complete enjoyment; and I do not know, Mrs. Elton, whether the uncertainty of our meetings, the sort of constant expectation there will be of his coming in to day or to morrow, and at any hour, may not be more friendly to happiness than having him actually in the house. I think it is so. I think it is the state of mind which gives most spirit and delight. I hope you will be pleased with my son; but you must not expect a prodigy. He is generally thought a fine

1 Saffron gown of the God of Matrimony.

young man, but do not expect a prodigy. Mrs. Weston's partiality for him is very great, and, as you may suppose, most gratifying to me. She thinks nobody equal to him."

"And I assure you, Mr. Weston, I have very little doubt that my opinion will be decidedly in his favour. I have heard so much in praise of Mr. Frank Churchill. At the same time it is fair to observe, that I am one of those who always judge for themselves, and are by no means implicitly guided by others. I give you notice that as I find your son, so I shall judge of him. I am no flatterer."

Mr. Weston was musing.

"I hope," said he presently, "I have not been severe upon poor Mrs. Churchill. If she is ill I should be sorry to do her injustice; but there are some traits in her character which make it difficult for me to speak of her with the forbearance I could wish. You cannot be ignorant, Mrs. Elton, of my connection with the family, nor of the treatment I have met with; and, between ourselves, the whole blame of it is to be laid to her. She was the instigator. Frank's mother would never have been slighted as she was but for her. Mr. Churchill has pride; but his pride is nothing to his wife's: his is a quiet, indolent, gentleman-like sort of pride that would harm nobody, and only make himself a little helpless and tiresome; but her pride is arrogance and insolence! And what inclines one less to bear, she has no fair pretence of family or blood. She was nobody when he married her, barely the daughter of a gentleman; but ever since her being turned into a Churchill she has out-Churchill'd them all in high and mighty claims: but in herself, I assure you, she is an upstart."

"Only think! well, that must be infinitely provoking! I have quite a horror of upstarts. Maple Grove has given me a thorough disgust to people of that sort; for there is a family in that neighbourhood who are such an annoyance to my brother and sister from the airs they give themselves! Your description of Mrs. Churchill made me think of them directly. People of the name of Tupman, very lately settled there, and encumbered with many low connections, but giving themselves immense airs, and expecting to be on a footing with the old-established families. A year and a half is the very utmost that they can have lived at West Hall; and how they got their fortune nobody knows. They came from Birmingham, which is not a place to promise much, you know, Mr. Weston. One has not great hopes from Birmingham. I always say there is something direful in the sound: but nothing more is positively known of the Tupmans, though a good many things I assure you are suspected; and yet by their manners they evidently think themselves equal even to my brother, Mr. Suckling, who happens to be one of their nearest neighbours. It is infinitely too bad. Mr. Suckling, who has been eleven years a resident at Maple Grove, and whose father had it before him – I believe, at least – I am almost sure that old Mr. Suckling had completed the purchase before his death."

They were interrupted. Tea was carried around, and Mr. Weston, having said all that he wanted, soon took the opportunity of walking away.

After tea, Mr. and Mrs. Weston, and Mr. Elton sat down with Mr. Woodhouse to cards. The remaining five were left to their own powers, and Emma doubted their getting on very well; for Mr. Knightley seemed little disposed for conversation; Mrs. Elton was wanting notice, which nobody had inclination to pay, and she was herself in a worry of spirits which would have made her prefer being silent.

Mr. John Knightley proved more talkative than his brother. He was to leave them early the next day; and he soon began with:

"Well, Emma, I do not believe I have any thing more to say about the boys; but you have your sister's letter, and everything is down at full length there we may be sure. My charge would be much more concise than her's, and probably not much in the same spirit; all that I have to recommend being comprised in – do not spoil them, and do not physic them."

"I rather hope to satisfy you both," said Emma, "for I shall do all in my power to make them happy, which will be enough for Isabella; and happiness must preclude false indulgence and physic."

"And if you find them troublesome, you must send them home again."

"That is very likely. You think so, do not you?"

"I hope I am aware that they may be too noisy for your father or even may be some encumbrance to you, if your visiting engagements continue to increase as much as they have done lately."

"Increase!"

"Certainly; you must be sensible that the last half-year has made a great difference in your way of life."

"Difference! No indeed I am not."

"There can be no doubt of your being much more engaged with company than you used to be. Witness this very time. Here am I come down for only one day, and you are engaged with a dinner-party! When did it happen before, or any thing like it? Your neighbourhood is increasing, and you mix more with it. A little while ago, every letter to Isabella brought an account of fresh gaieties; dinners at Mr. Cole's, or balls at the Crown. The difference which Randalls, Randalls alone makes in your goings on, is very great."

"Yes," said his brother quickly, "it is Randalls that does it all."

"Very well and as Randalls, I suppose, is not likely to have less influence than heretofore, it strikes me as a possible thing, Emma, that Henry and John may be sometimes in the way. And if they are, I only beg you to send them home."

"No," cried Mr. Knightley, "that need not be the consequence. Let them be sent to Donwell. I shall certainly be at leisure."

"Upon my word," exclaimed Emma, "you amuse me! I should like to know how many of all my numerous engagements take place without your being of the party; and why I am to be supposed in danger of wanting leisure to attend to the little boys. These amazing engagements of mine – what have they been? Dining once with the Coles and having a ball talked of, which never took place. I can understand you – (nodding at Mr. John Knightley) – your good fortune in meeting with so many of your friends at once here, delights you too much to pass unnoticed. But you, (turning to Mr. Knightley,) who know how very, very seldom I am ever two hours from Hartfield – why you should foresee such a series of dissipation for me, I cannot imagine. And as to my dear little boys, I must say, that if Aunt Emma has not time for them, I do not think they would fare much better with Uncle Knightley, who is absent from home about five hours where she is absent one – and who, when he is at home, is either reading to himself or settling his accounts."

Mr. Knightley seemed to be trying not to smile; and succeeded without difficulty, upon Mrs. Elton's beginning to talk to him.

## Chapter 37

A VERY little quiet reflection was enough to satisfy Emma as to the nature of her agitation on hearing this news of Frank Churchill. She was soon convinced that it was not for herself she was feeling at all apprehensive or embarrassed; it was for him. Her own attachment had really subsided into a mere nothing – it was not worth thinking of; but if he, who had undoubtedly been always so much the most in love of the two, were to be returning with the same warmth of sentiment which he had taken away, it would be very distressing. If a separation of two months should not have cooled him, there were dangers and evils before her; caution for him and for herself would be necessary. She did not mean to have her own affections entangled again, and it would be incumbent on her to avoid any encouragement of his.

She wished she might be able to keep him from an absolute declaration. That would be so very painful a conclusion of their present acquaintance! and yet, she could not help rather anticipating something decisive. She felt as if the spring would not pass without bringing a crisis, an event, a something to alter her present composed and tranquil state.

It was not very long, though rather longer than Mr. Weston had foreseen, before she had the power of forming some opinion of Frank Churchill's feelings. The Enscombe family were not in town quite so soon as had been imagined, but he was at Highbury very soon afterwards. He rode down for a couple of hours; he could not yet do more; but as he came from Randalls immediately to Hartfield, she could then exercise all her quick observation, and speedily determine how he was influenced, and how she must act. They met with the utmost friendliness. There could be no doubt of his great pleasure in seeing her. But she had an almost instant doubt of his caring for her as he had done, of his feeling the same tenderness in the same degree. She watched him well. It was a clear thing he was less in love than he had been. Absence, with the conviction probably of her indifference, had produced this very natural and very desirable effect.

He was in high spirits; as ready to talk and laugh as ever, and seemed delighted to speak of his former visit, and recur to old stories: and he was not without agitation. It was not in his calmness that she read his comparative difference. He was not calm; his spirits were evidently fluttered; there was restlessness about him. Lively as he was, it seemed a liveliness that did not satisfy himself; but what decided her belief on the subject, was his staying only a quarter of an hour, and hurrying away to make other calls in Highbury. "He had seen a group of old acquaintance in the street as he passed – he had not stopped, he would not stop for more than a word – but he had the vanity to think they would be disappointed if he did not call, and much as he wished to stay longer at Hartfield, he must hurry off." She had no doubt as to his being less in love but neither his agitated spirits, nor his hurrying away, seemed like a perfect cure; and she was rather inclined to think it implied a dread of her returning power, and a discreet resolution of not trusting himself with her long.

This was the only visit from Frank Churchill in the course of ten days. He was often hoping, intending to come but was always prevented. His aunt could not bear to have him leave her. Such was his own account at Randall's. If he were quite sincere, if he really tried to come, it was to be inferred that Mrs. Churchill's removal to London had been of no service to the wilful or nervous part of her disorder. That she was really ill was very certain; he had declared himself convinced of it, at Randalls. Though much might be fancy, he could not doubt, when he looked back, that she was in a weaker state of health than she had been half a year ago. He did not believe it to proceed from any thing that care and medicine might not remove, or at least that she might not have many years of existence before her; but he could not be prevailed on, by all his father's doubts, to say that her complaints were merely imaginary, or that she was as strong as ever.

It soon appeared that London was not the place for her. She could not endure its noise. Her nerves were under continual irritation and suffering; and by the ten days' end, her nephew's letter to Randalls communicated a change of plan. They were going to remove immediately to Richmond. Mrs. Churchill had been recommended to the medical skill of an eminent person there, and had otherwise a fancy for the place. A ready-furnished house in a favourite spot was engaged, and much benefit expected from the change.

Emma heard that Frank wrote in the highest spirits of this arrangement, and seemed most fully to appreciate the blessing of having two months before him of such near neighbourhood to many dear friends for the house was taken for May and June. She was told that now he wrote with the greatest confidence of being often with them, almost as often as he could even wish.

Emma saw how Mr. Weston understood these joyous

prospects. He was considering her as the source of all the happiness they offered. She hoped it was not so. Two months must bring it to the proof.

Mr. Weston's own happiness was indisputable. He was quite delighted. It was the very circumstance he could have wished for. Now, it would be really having Frank in their neighbourhood. What were nine miles to a young man? An hour's ride. He would be always coming over. The difference in that respect of Richmond and London was enough to make the whole difference of seeing him always and seeing him never. Sixteen miles – nay, eighteen – it must be full eighteen to Manchester street – was a serious obstacle. Were he ever able to get away, the day would be spent in coming and returning. There was no comfort in having him in London; he might as well be at Enscombe; but Richmond was the very distance for easy intercourse. Better than nearer!

One good thing was immediately brought to a certainty by this removal – the ball at the Crown. It had not been forgotten before, but it had been soon acknowledged vain to attempt to fix a day. Now, however, it was absolutely to be; every preparation was resumed, and very soon after the Churchills had removed to Richmond, a few lines from Frank, to say that his aunt felt already much better for the change, and that he had no doubt of being able to join them for twenty-four hours at any given time, induced them to name as early a day as possible.

Mr. Weston's ball was to be a real thing. A very few to morrows stood between the young people of Highbury and happiness.

Mr. Woodhouse was resigned. The time of year lightened the evil to him. May was better for everything than February. Mrs. Bates was engaged to spend the evening at Hartfield, James had due notice, and he sanguinely hoped that neither dear little Henry nor dear little John would have any thing the matter with them, while dear Emma were gone.

# Chapter 38

NO MISFORTUNE occurred, again to prevent the ball. The day approached, the day arrived; and after a morning of some anxious watching, Frank Churchill, in all the certainty of his own self, reached Randalls before dinner, and everything was safe.

No second meeting had there yet been between him and Emma. The room at the Crown was to witness it; but it would be better than a common meeting in a crowd. Mr. Weston had been so very earnest in his entreaties for her arriving there as soon as possible after themselves, for the purpose of taking her opinion as to the propriety and comfort of the rooms before any other persons came, that she could not refuse him, and must therefore spend some quiet interval in the young man's company. She was to convey Harriet, and they drove to the Crown in good time, the Randalls party just sufficiently before them.

Frank Churchill seemed to have been on the watch; and though he did not say much, his eyes declared that he meant to have a delightful evening. They all walked about together, to see that everything was as it should be; and within a few minutes were joined by the contents of another carriage, which Emma could not hear the sound of at first, without great surprise. "So unreasonably early!" she was going to exclaim; but she presently found that it was a family of old friends, who were coming, like herself, by particular desire, to help Mr. Weston's judgment; and they were so very closely followed by another carriage of cousins, who had been entreated to come early with the same distinguishing earnestness, on the same errand, that it seemed as if half the company might soon be collected together for the purpose of preparatory inspection.

Emma perceived that her taste was not the only taste on which Mr. Weston depended, and felt, that to be the favourite and intimate of a man who had so many intimates and confidantes, was not the very first distinction in the scale of vanity. She liked his open manners, but a little less of open-heartedness would have made him a higher character. General benevolence, but not general friendship, made a man what he ought to be. She could fancy such a man.

The whole party walked about, and looked, and praised again; and then, having nothing else to do, formed a sort of half-circle round the fire, to observe in their various modes, till other subjects were started, that, though *May,* a fire in the evening was still very pleasant.

Emma found that it was not Mr. Weston's fault that the number of privy councillors was not yet larger. They had stopped at Mrs. Bates's door to offer the use of their carriage, but the aunt and niece were to be brought by the Eltons.

Frank was standing by her, but not steadily; there was a restlessness, which showed a mind not at ease. He was looking about, he was going to the door, he was watching for the sound of other carriages – impatient to begin, or afraid of being always near her.

Mrs. Elton was spoken of. "I think she must be here soon," said he. "I have a great curiosity to see Mrs. Elton, I have heard so much of her. It cannot be long, I think, before she comes."

A carriage was heard. He was on the move immediately; but coming back, said:

"I am forgetting that I am not acquainted with her. I have never seen either Mr. or Mrs. Elton. I have no business to put myself forward."

Mr. and Mrs. Elton appeared; and all the smiles and the proprieties passed.

"But Miss Bates and Miss Fairfax!" said Mr. Weston, looking about. "We thought you were to bring them."

The mistake had been slight. The carriage was sent for them

now. Emma longed to know what Frank's first opinion of Mrs. Elton might be; how he was affected by the studied elegance of her dress, and her smiles of graciousness. He was immediately qualifying himself to form an opinion, by giving her very proper attention, after the introduction had passed.

In a few minutes the carriage returned. Somebody talked of rain. "I will see that there are umbrellas, sir," said Frank to his father: "Miss Bates must not be forgotten:" and away he went. Mr. Weston was following; but Mrs. Elton detained him, to gratify him by her opinion of his son; and so briskly did she begin, that the young man himself, though by no means moving slowly, could hardly be out of hearing.

"A very fine young man indeed, Mr. Weston. You know I candidly told you I should form my own opinion; and I am happy to say that I am extremely pleased with him. You may believe me. I never compliment. I think him a very handsome young man, and his manners are precisely what I like and approve – so truly the gentleman, without the least conceit or puppyism. You must know I have a vast dislike to puppies – quite a horror of them. They were never tolerated at Maple Grove. Neither Mr. Suckling nor me had ever any patience with them; and we sometimes used to say very cutting things! Selina, who is mild almost to a fault, bore with them much better."

While she talked of his son, Mr. Weston's attention was chained; but when she got to Maple Grove, he could recollect that there were ladies just arriving to be attended to, and with happy smiles must hurry away.

Mrs. Elton turned to Mrs. Weston. "I have no doubt of its being our carriage with Miss Bates and Jane. Our coachman and horses are so extremely expeditious! I believe we drive faster than anybody. What a pleasure it is to send one's carriage for a friend! I understand you were so kind as to offer, but another time it will be quite unnecessary. You may be very sure I shall always take care of *them.*"

Miss Bates and Miss Fairfax, escorted by the two gentlemen, walked into the room; and Mrs. Elton seemed to think it as much her duty as Mrs. Weston's to receive them. Her gestures and movements might be understood by any one who looked on like Emma; but her words, everybody's words, were soon lost under the incessant flow of Miss Bates, who came in talking, and had not finished her speech under many minutes after her being admitted into the circle at the fire. As the door opened she was heard:

"So very obliging of you! No rain at all. Nothing to signify. I do not care for myself. Quite thick shoes. And Jane declares – Well! (as soon as she was within the door) Well! This is brilliant indeed! This is admirable! Excellently contrived, upon my word. Nothing wanting. Could not have imagined it. So well lighted up! Jane, Jane, look! did you ever see anything –? Oh! Mr. Weston, you must really have had Aladdin's lamp. Good Mrs. Stokes would not know her own room again. I saw her as I came in; she was standing at the entrance. 'Oh! Mrs. Stokes,' said I – but I had not time for more." She was now met by Mrs. Weston. "Very well, I thank you, ma'am. I hope you are quite well. Very happy to hear it. So afraid you might have a headache! seeing you pass by so often, and knowing how much trouble you must have. Delighted to hear it indeed. Ah! dear Mrs. Elton, so obliged to you for the carriage! excellent time. Jane and I quite ready. Did not keep the horses a moment. Most comfortable carriage. Oh! and I am sure our thanks are due to you, Mrs. Weston, on that score. Mrs. Elton had most kindly sent Jane a note, or we should have been. But two such offers in one day! Never were such neighbours. I said to my mother, 'Upon my word, ma'am –' Thank you, my mother is remarkably well. Gone to Mr. Woodhouse's. I made her take her shawl – for the evenings are not warm – her large new shawl, Mrs. Dixon's wedding present. So kind of her to think of my mother! Bought at Weymouth, you know Mr. Dixon's choice. There were three others, Jane says, which they hesitated about some time. Colonel Campbell rather preferred an olive. My dear Jane, are you sure you did not wet your feet? It was but a drop or two, but I am so afraid: but Mr. Frank Churchill was so extremely – and there was a mat to step upon I shall never forget his extreme politeness. – Oh! Mr. Frank Churchill, I must tell you my mother's spectacles have never been in fault since; the rivet never came out again. My mother often talks of your good nature. Does not she, Jane? Do we not often talk of Mr. Frank Churchill? Ah! here's Miss Woodhouse. Dear Miss Woodhouse, how do you do? Very well I thank you, quite well. This is meeting quite in fairy land! Such a transformation! Must not compliment, I know (eyeing Emma most complacently) – that would be rude but upon my word, Miss Woodhouse, you do look – how do you like Jane's hair? You are a judge. She did it all herself. Quite wonderful how she does her hair! No hairdresser from London I think could – Ah! Dr. Hughes I declare – and Mrs. Hughes. Must go and speak to Dr. and Mrs. Hughes for a moment. How do you do? How do you do? Very well, I thank you. This is delightful, is not it? Where's dear Mr. Richard? Oh! there he is. Don't disturb him. Much better employed talking to the young ladies. How do you do, Mr. Richard? I saw you the other day as you rode through the town Mrs. Otway, I protest! and good Mr. Otway, and Miss Otway and Miss Caroline. Such a host of friends! and Mr. George and Mr. Arthur! How do you do? How do you all do? Quite well, I am much obliged to you. Never better. Don't I hear another carriage? Who can this be? very likely the worthy Coles. Upon my word, this is charming to be standing about among such friends! And such a noble fire! I am quite roasted. No coffee, I thank you, for I, never take coffee. A little tea if you please, sir, by-and-bye, no hurry Oh! here it comes. Everything so good!"

Frank Churchill returned to his station by Emma; and as soon as Miss Bates was quiet, she found herself necessarily overhearing the discourse of Mrs. Elton and Miss Fairfax, who were standing a little way behind her. He was thoughtful. Whether he were overhearing too, she could not determine. After a good many compliments to Jane on her dress and look – compliments very quietly and properly taken – Mrs. Elton was evidently wanting to be complimented herself – and it was, "How do you like my gown? How do you like my trimming? How has Wright done my hair?" with many other relative questions, all answered with patient politeness. Mrs. Elton then said:

"Nobody can think less of dress in general than I do but upon such an occasion as this, when everybody's eyes are so much upon me, and in compliment to the Westons who I have no doubt are giving this ball chiefly to do me honour I would not wish to be inferior to others. And I see very few pearls in the room except mine. So Frank Churchill is a capital dancer, I understand. We shall see if our styles suit. A fine young man certainly is Frank Churchill. I like him very well."

At this moment Frank began talking so vigorously, that Emma could not but imagine he had overheard his own praises, and did not want to hear more; and the voices of the ladies were drowned for a while, till another suspension brought Mrs. Elton's tones again distinctly forward. Mr. Elton had just joined them, and his wife was exclaiming:

"Oh! you have found us out at last, have you, in our seclusion? I was this moment telling Jane, I thought you would begin to be impatient for tidings of us."

"Jane!" repeated Frank Churchill, with a look of surprise and displeasure. "That is easy but Miss Fairfax does not disapprove it, I suppose."

"How do you like Mrs. Elton?" said Emma in a whisper.

"Not at all."

"You are ungrateful."

"Ungrateful! What do you mean?" Then changing from a frown to a smile "No, do not tell me – I do not want to know what you mean. Where is my father? When are we to begin dancing?"

Emma could hardly understand him; he seemed in an odd humour. He walked off to find his father, but was quickly back again with both Mr. and Mrs. Weston. He had met with them in a little perplexity, which must be laid before Emma. It had just occurred to Mrs. Weston that Mrs. Elton must be asked to begin the ball; that she would expect it; which interfered with all their wishes of giving Emma that distinction. Emma heard the sad truth with fortitude.

"And what are we to do for a proper partner for her?" said Mr. Weston. "She will think Frank ought to ask her."

Frank turned instantly to Emma, to claim her former promise; and boasted himself an engaged man, which his father looked his most perfect approbation of – and it then appeared that Mrs. Weston was wanting *him* to dance with Mrs. Elton himself, and that their business was to help to persuade him into it, which was done pretty soon. Mr. Weston and Mrs. Elton led the way, Mr. Frank Churchill and Miss Woodhouse followed. Emma must submit to stand second to Mrs. Elton, though she had always considered the ball as peculiarly for her. It was almost enough to make her think of marrying.

Mrs. Elton had undoubtedly the advantage, at this time, in vanity completely gratified; for though she had intended to begin with Frank Churchill, she could not lose by the change. Mr. Weston might be his son's superior. In spite of this little rub, however, Emma was smiling with enjoyment, delighted to see the respectable length of the set as it was forming, and to feel that she had so many hours of unusual festivity before her. She was more disturbed by Mr. Knightley's not dancing than by any thing else. There he was, among the standers-by, where he ought not to be; he ought to be dancing, not classing himself with the husbands, and fathers, and whist players, who were pretending to feel an interest in the dance till their rubbers were made up, – so young as he looked!

He could not have appeared to greater advantage perhaps anywhere, than where he had placed himself. His tall, firm, upright figure, among the bulky forms and stooping shoulders of the elderly men, was such as Emma felt must draw everybody's eyes; and, excepting her own partner, there was not one among the whole row of young men who could be compared with him. He moved a few steps nearer, and those few steps were enough to prove in how gentlemanlike a manner, with what natural grace, he must have danced, would he but take the trouble. Whenever she caught his eye, she forced him to smile; but in general he was looking grave. She wished he could love a ball-room better, and could like Frank Churchill better. He seemed often observing her. She must not flatter herself that he thought of her dancing, but if he were criticising her behaviour, she did not feel afraid. There was nothing like flirtation between her and her partner. They seemed more like cheerful, easy friends, than lovers. That Frank Churchill thought less of her than he had done, was indubitable.

The ball proceeded pleasantly. The anxious cares, the incessant attentions of Mrs. Weston, were not thrown away. Everybody seemed happy; and the praise of being a delightful ball, which is seldom bestowed till after a ball has ceased to be, was repeatedly given in the very beginning of the existence of this. Of very important, very recordable events, it was not more productive than such meetings usually are. There was one, however, which Emma thought something of. The two last dances before supper were begun, and Harriet had no partner; the only young lady sitting down; and so equal had been hitherto the number of dancers, that how there could be any one disengaged was the wonder! But Emma's wonder lessened soon afterwards, on seeing Mr. Elton sauntering about. He would not ask Harriet to dance if it were possible to be avoided: she was sure he would not – and she was expecting him every moment to escape into the card-room.

Escape, however, was not his plan. He came to the part of the room where the sitters-by were collected, spoke to some, and walked about in front of them, as if to show his liberty, and his resolution of maintaining it. He did not omit being sometimes directly before Miss Smith, or speaking to those who were close to her. – Emma saw it. She was not yet dancing; she was working her way up from the bottom, and had therefore leisure to look around, and by only turning her head a little she saw it all. When she was half way up the set, the whole group were exactly behind her, and she would no longer allow her eyes to watch; but Mr. Elton was so near, that she heard every syllable of a dialogue which just then took place between him and Mrs. Weston; and she perceived that his wife, who was standing immediately above her, was not only listening also, but even encouraging him by significant glances. The kind hearted, gentle Mrs. Weston had left her seat to join him and say, "Do you not dance, Mr. Elton?" to which his prompt reply was, "Most readily, Mrs. Weston, if you will dance with me."

"Me! oh! no – I would get you a better partner than myself. I am no dancer."

"If Mrs. Gilbert wishes to dance," said he, "I shall have great pleasure, I am sure for, though beginning to feel myself rather an old married man, and that my dancing days are over, it would give me very great pleasure at any time to stand up with an old friend like Mrs. Gilbert."

"Mrs. Gilbert does not mean to dance, but there is a young lady disengaged whom I should be very glad to see dancing – Miss Smith."

"Miss Smith! – oh! – I had not observed. You are extremely obliging – and if I were not an old married man – but my dancing days are over, Mrs. Weston. You will excuse me. Any thing else I should be most happy to do, at your command – but my dancing days are over."

Mrs. Weston said no more; and Emma could imagine with what surprise and mortification she must be returning to her seat.

This was Mr. Elton! the amiable, obliging, gentle Mr. Elton. She looked around for a moment; he had joined Mr. Knightley at a little distance, and was arranging himself for settled conversation, while smiles of high glee passed between him and his wife.

She would not look again. Her heart was in a glow, and she feared her face might be as hot.

In another moment a happier sight caught her; Mr. Knightley leading Harriet to the set! Never had she been more surprised, seldom more delighted, than at that instant. She was all pleasure and gratitude, both for Harriet and herself, and longed to be thanking him; and though too distant for speech, her countenance said much, as soon as she could catch his eye again.

His dancing proved to be just what she had believed it, extremely good; and Harriet would have seemed almost too lucky, if it had not been for the cruel state of things before, and for the very complete enjoyment and very high sense of the distinction which her happy features announced. It was not thrown away on her, she bounded higher than ever, flew farther down the middle, and was in a continual course of smiles.

Mr. Elton had retreated into the card room, looking (Emma trusted) very foolish. She did not think he was quite so hardened as his wife, though growing very like her; *she* spoke some of her feelings, by observing audibly to her partner:

"Knightley has taken pity on poor little Miss Smith! Very good-natured, I declare."

Supper was announced. The move began; and Miss Bates might be heard from that moment, without interruption, till her being seated at the table and taking up her spoon.

"Jane, Jane, my dear Jane, where are you? Here is your tippet. Mrs. Weston begs you to put on your tippet. She says she is afraid there will be draughts in the passage, though everything has been done – One door nailed up – Quantities of matting – My dear Jane, indeed you must. Mr. Churchill, oh! you are too obliging! How well you put it on – so gratified! Excellent dancing indeed! Yes, my dear, I ran home, as I said I should, to help grandmama to bed, and got back again, and nobody missed me. I set off without saying a word, just as I told you. Grandmama was quite well, had a charming evening with Mr. Woodhouse, a vast deal of chat, and backgammon. Tea was made downstairs, biscuits and baked apples and wine before she came away: amazing luck in some of her throws: and she inquired a great deal about you, how you were amused, and who were your partners. 'Oh!' said I, 'I shall not forestall Jane; I left her dancing with Mr. George Otway; she will love to tell you all about it herself to morrow: her first partner was Mr. Elton, I do not know who will ask her next, perhaps Mr. William Cox.' My dear sir, you are too obliging. Is there nobody you would not rather? I am not helpless. Sir, you are most kind. Upon my word, Jane on one arm, and me on the other! Stop, stop, let us stand a little back, Mrs. Elton is going; dear Mrs. Elton, how elegant she looks! Beautiful lace! Now we all follow in her train. Quite the queen of the evening! Well, here we are at the passage. Two steps, Jane, take care of the two steps. Oh! no, there is but one. Well, I was persuaded there were two. How very odd! I was convinced there were two, and there is but one. I never saw any thing equal to the comfort and style Candles everywhere. I was telling you of your grandmama, Jane – There was a little disappointment. The baked apples and biscuits, excellent in their way, you know; but there was a delicate fricassee of sweetbread and some asparagus brought in at first, and good Mr. Woodhouse, not thinking the asparagus quite boiled enough, sent it all out again. Now there is nothing grandmama loves better than sweetbread and asparagus – so she was rather disappointed, but we agreed we would not speak of it to anybody, for fear of its getting round to dear Miss Woodhouse, who would be so very much concerned! Well, this is brilliant! I am all amazement! – could not have supposed anything! Such elegance and profusion! I have seen nothing like it since – Well, where shall we sit? where shall we sit? Anywhere.

so that Jane is not in a draught. Where *I* sit is of no consequence. Oh! do you recommend this side? Well, I am sure, Mr. Churchill – only it seems too good – but just as you please. What you direct in this house cannot be wrong. Dear Jane, how shall we ever recollect half the dishes for grandmama? Soup too! Bless me! I should not be helped so soon, but it smells most excellent, and I cannot help beginning."

Emma had no opportunity of speaking to Mr. Knightley till after supper; but, when they were all in the ball-room again, her eyes invited him irresistibly to come to her and be thanked. He was warm in his reprobation of Mr. Elton's conduct; it had been unpardonable rudeness; and Mrs. Elton's looks also received the due share of censure.

"They aimed at wounding more than Harriet," said he. "Emma, why is it that they are your enemies?"

He looked with smiling penetration; and, on receiving no answer, added, "*She* ought not to be angry with you, I suspect, whatever he may be. To that surmise, you say nothing, of course; but confess, Emma, that you did want him to marry Harriet."

"I did," replied Emma, "and they cannot forgive me."

He shook his head; but there was a smile of indulgence with it, and he only said:

"I shall not scold you. I leave you to your own reflections."

"Can you trust me with such flatterers? Does my vain spirit ever tell me I am wrong?"

"Not your vain spirit, but your serious spirit. If one leads you wrong, I am sure the other tells you of it."

"I do own myself to have been completely mistaken in Mr. Elton. There is a littleness about him which you discovered, and which I did not: and I was fully convinced of his being in love with Harriet. It was through a series of strange blunders!"

"And, in return for your acknowledging so much, I will do

you the justice to say, that you would have chosen for him better than he has chosen for himself. Harriet Smith has some first rate qualities, which Mrs. Elton is totally without. An unpretending, single-minded, artless girl – infinitely to be preferred by any man of sense and taste to such a woman as Mrs. Elton. I found Harriet more conversable than I expected."

Emma was extremely gratified. They were interrupted by the bustle of Mr. Weston calling on everybody to begin dancing again.

"Come Miss Woodhouse, Miss Otway, Miss Fairfax, what are you all doing? Come Emma, set your companions the example. Everybody is lazy! Everybody is asleep!"

"I am ready," said Emma, "whenever I am wanted."

"Whom are you going to dance with?" asked Mr. Knightley.

She hesitated a moment, and then replied, "With you, if you will ask me."

"Will you?" said he, offering his hand.

"Indeed I will. You have shown that you can dance, and you know we are not really so much brother and sister as to make it at all improper."

"Brother and sister! – no, indeed."

## Chapter 39

THIS LITTLE explanation with Mr. Knightley gave Emma considerable pleasure. It was one of the agreeable recollections of the ball, which she walked about the lawn the next morning to enjoy. She was extremely glad that they had come to so good an understanding respecting the Eltons, and that their opinions of both husband and wife were so much alike; and his praise of Harriet, his concession in her favour, was peculiarly gratifying. The impertinence of the Eltons, which for a few minutes had threatened to ruin the rest of her evening, had been the occasion of some of its highest satisfactions; and she looked forward to another happy result – the cure of Harriet's infatuation. From Harriet's manner of speaking of the circumstance before they quitted the ball-room, she had strong hopes. It seemed as if her eyes were suddenly opened, and she were enabled to see that Mr. Elton was not the superior creature she had believed him. The fever was over, and Emma could harbour little fear of the pulse being quickened again by injurious courtesy. She depended on the evil feelings of the Eltons for supplying all the discipline of pointed neglect that could be farther requisite. Harriet rational, Frank Churchill not too much in love, and Mr. Knightley not wanting to quarrel with her, how very happy a summer must be before her!

She was not to see Frank Churchill this morning. He had told her that he could not allow himself the pleasure of stopping at Hartfield, as he was to be at home by the middle of the day. She did not regret it.

Having arranged all these matters, looked them through, and put them all to rights, she was just turning to the house with spirits freshened up for the demands of the two little boys, as well as of their grandpapa, when the great iron sweep-gate opened, and two persons entered whom she had never less expected to see together – Frank Churchill, with Harriet leaning on his arm – actually Harriet! A moment sufficed to convince her that something extraordinary had happened. Harriet looked white and frightened, and he was trying to cheer her. The iron gates and the front door were not twenty yards asunder; they were all three soon in the hall, and Harriet immediately sinking into a chair fainted away.

A young lady who faints, must be recovered; questions must be answered, and surprises be explained. Such events are very interesting, but the suspense of them cannot last long. A few minutes made Emma acquainted with the whole.

Miss Smith, and Miss Bickerton, another parlour boarder at Mrs. Goddard's, who had been also at the ball, had walked out together, and taken a road, the Richmond road – which, though apparently public enough for safety, had led them into alarm. About half a mile beyond Highbury, making a sudden turn, and deeply shaded by elms on each side, it became for a considerable stretch very retired; and when the young ladies had advanced some way into it, they had suddenly perceived at a small distance before them, on a broader patch of greensward by the side, a party of gypsies. A child on the watch, came towards them to beg; and Miss Bickerton, excessively frightened, gave a great scream, and calling on Harriet to follow her, ran up a steep bank, cleared a slight hedge at the top, and made the best of her way by a short cut back to Highbury. But poor Harriet could not follow. She had suffered very much from cramp after dancing, and her first attempt to mount the bank brought on such a return of it as made her absolutely powerless and in this state, and exceedingly terrified, she had been obliged to remain.

How the trampers might have behaved, had the young ladies been more courageous, must be doubtful; but such an invitation for attack could not be resisted; and Harriet was soon assailed by half a dozen children, headed by a stout woman and a great boy, all clamorous, and impertinent in look, though not absolutely in word. More and more frightened, she immediately promised them money, and taking out her purse, gave them a shilling, and begged them not to want more, or to use her ill. She was then able to walk, though but slowly, and was moving away – but her terror and her purse were too tempting, and she was followed, or rather surrounded, by the whole gang, demanding more.

In this state Frank Churchill had found her, she trembling and conditioning, they loud and insolent. By a most fortunate chance his leaving Highbury had been delayed so as to bring him to her assistance at this critical moment. The pleasantness of the morning had induced him to walk forward, and leave his horses to meet him by another road, a mile or two beyond Highbury and happening to have borrowed a pair of scissors the night before of Miss Bates, and to have forgotten to restore them, he had been obliged to stop at her door, and go in for a few minutes: he was therefore later than he had intended; and being on foot, was unseen by the whole party till almost close to them. The terror which the woman and boy had been creating in Harriet was then their own portion. He had left them completely frightened; and Harriet eagerly clinging to him, and hardly able to speak, had just strength enough to reach Hartfield, before her spirits were quite overcome. It was his idea to bring her to Hartfield: he had thought of no other place.

This was the amount of the whole story – of his communication and of Harriet's as soon as she had recovered her senses and speech. He dared not stay longer than to see her well; these several delays left him not another minute to lose; and Emma engaging to give assurance of her safety to Mrs. Goddard, and notice of there being such a set of people in the neighbourhood to Mr. Knightley, he set off, with all the grateful blessings that she could utter for her friend and herself.

Such an adventure as this – a fine young man and a lovely young woman thrown together in such a way – could hardly fail of suggesting certain ideas to the coldest heart and the steadiest brain. So Emma thought, at least. Could a linguist, could a grammarian, could even a mathematician have seen what she did, have witnessed their appearance together, and heard their history of it, without feeling that circumstances had been at work to make them peculiarly interesting to each other? How much more must an imaginist, like herself, be on fire with speculation and foresight! especially with such a groundwork of anticipation as her mind had already made.

It was a very extraordinary thing! Nothing of the sort had ever occurred before to any young ladies in the place, within her memory; no rencontre, no alarm of the kind; and now it had happened to the very person, and at the very hour, when the other very person was chancing to pass by to rescue her! It certainly was very extraordinary! And knowing, as she did, the favourable state of mind of each at this period, it struck her the more. He was wishing to get the better of his attachment to herself, she just recovering from her mania for Mr. Elton. It seemed as if everything united to promise the most interesting consequences. It was not possible that the occurrence should not be strongly recommending each to the other.

In the few minutes' conversation which she had yet had with him, while Harriet had been partially insensible, he had spoken of her terror, her *naïveté,* her fervour as she seized and clung to his arm, with a sensibility amused and delighted; and just at last, after Harriet's own account had been given, he had expressed his indignation at the abominable folly of Miss Bickerton in the warmest terms. Everything was to take its natural course, however, neither impelled nor assisted. She would not stir a step, nor drop a hint. No, she had had enough of interference. There could be no harm in a scheme, a mere passive scheme. It was no more than a wish. Beyond it she would on no account proceed.

Emma's first resolution was to keep her father from the knowledge of what had passed, aware of the anxiety and alarm it would occasion: but she soon felt that concealment must be impossible. Within half an hour it was known all over Highbury. It was the very event to engage those who talk most – the young and the low; and all the youth and servants in the place were soon in the happiness of frightful news. The last night's ball seemed lost in the gypsies. Poor Mr. Woodhouse trembled as he sat, and, as Emma had foreseen, would scarcely be satisfied without their promising never to go beyond the shrubbery again. It was some comfort to him that many inquiries after himself and Miss Woodhouse (for his neighbours knew that he loved to be inquired after), as well as Miss Smith, were coming in during the rest of the day; and he had the pleasure of returning for answer, that they were all very indifferent which, though not exactly true, for she was perfectly well, and Harriet not much otherwise, Emma would not interfere with. She had an unhappy state of health in general for the child of such a man, for she hardly knew what indisposition was; and if he did not invent illnesses for her, she could make no figure in a message.

The gypsies did not wait for the operations of justice; they took themselves off in a hurry. The young ladies of Highbury might have walked again in safety before their panic began, and the whole history dwindled soon into a matter of little importance but to Emma and her nephews: in her imagination it maintained its ground, and Henry and John were still asking every day for the story of Harriet and the gypsies, and still tenaciously setting her right if she varied in the slightest particular from the original recital.

# Chapter 40

A VERY few days had passed after this adventure, when Harriet came one morning to Emma with a small parcel in her hand, and after sitting down and hesitating, thus began:

"Miss Woodhouse – if you are at leisure, I have something that I should like to tell you, a sort of confession to make – and then, you know, it will be over."

Emma was a good deal surprised; but begged her to speak. There was a seriousness in Harriet's manner which prepared her, quite as much as her words, for something more than ordinary.

"It is my duty, and I am sure it is my wish," she continued, "to have no reserves with you on this subject. As I am happily quite an altered creature in *one respect,* it is very fit that you should have the satisfaction of knowing it. I do not want to say more than is necessary I am too much ashamed of having given way as I have done, and I dare say you understand me."

"Yes," said Emma, "I hope I do."

"How I could so long a time be fancying myself!" cried Harriet, warmly. "It seems like madness! I can see nothing at all extraordinary in him now. I do not care whether I meet him or not, except that of the two I had rather not see him, and indeed I would go any distance round to avoid him, but I do not envy his wife in the least; I neither admire her nor envy her, as I have done: she is very charming, I dare say, and all that, but I think her very ill tempered and disagreeable, I shall never forget her look the other night! However, I assure you, Miss Woodhouse, I wish her no evil. No, let them be ever so happy together, it will not give me another moment's pang: and to convince you that I have been speaking truth, I am now going to destroy – what I ought to have destroyed long ago – what I ought never to have kept I know that very well (blushing as she spoke). However, now I will destroy it all and it is my particular wish to do it in your presence, that you may see how rational I am grown. Cannot you guess what this parcel holds?" said she, with a conscious look.

"Not the least in the world. Did he ever give you any thing?"

"No – I cannot call them gifts; but they are things that I have valued very much."

She held the parcel towards her, and Emma read the words *Most precious treasures* on the top. Her curiosity was greatly excited. Harriet unfolded the parcel, and she looked on with impatience. Within abundance of silver paper was a pretty little Tunbridgeware[1] box, which Harriet opened: it was well lined with the softest cotton; but, excepting the cotton, Emma saw only a small piece of court plaster[2].

"Now," said Harriet, "you *must* recollect."

"No, indeed I do not."

"Dear me! I should not have thought it possible you could forget what passed in this very room about court plaster, one of the very last times we ever met in it! It was but a very few days before I had my sore throat – just before Mr. and Mrs. John Knightley came I think the very evening. Do not you remember his cutting his finger with your new penknife, and your recommending court-plaster? But, as you had none about you, and knew I had, you desired me to supply him; and so I took mine out and cut him a piece; but it was a great deal too large, and he cut it smaller, and kept playing some time with what was left, before he gave it back to me. And so then, in my nonsense, I could not help making a treasure of it so I put it by never to be used, and looked at it now and then as a great treat."

"My dearest Harriet!" cried Emma, putting her hand before her face, and jumping up, "you make me more ashamed of myself than I can bear. Remember it? Aye, I remember it all now; all, except your saving this relic I knew nothing of that till this moment – but the cutting the finger, and my recommending court plaster, and saying I had none about me! Oh! my sins, my sins! – And I

1 Finely crafted wooden curios.
2 Plaster used for sticking (the beauty spots).

had plenty all the while in my pocket! One of my senseless tricks! I deserve to be under a continual blush all the rest of my life. Well (sitting down again) go on what else?"

"And had you really some at hand yourself? I am sure I never suspected it, you did it so naturally."

"And so you actually put this piece of court-plaster by for his sake!" said Emma, recovering from her state of shame and feeling divided between wonder and amusement. And secretly she added to herself, "Lord bless me! when should I ever have thought of putting by in cotton a piece of court plaster that Frank Churchill had been pulling about! I never was equal to this."

"Here," resumed Harriet, turning to her box again, "here is something still more valuable – I mean that *has been* more valuable – because this is what did really once belong to him, which the court plaster never did."

Emma was quite eager to see this superior treasure. It was the end of an old pencil, the part without any lead.

"This was really his," said Harriet. "Do not you remember one morning? – no, I dare say you do not. But one morning – I forget exactly the day – but perhaps it was the Tuesday or Wednesday before *that evening,* he wanted to make a memorandum in his pocket book; it was about spruce beer. Mr. Knightley had been telling him something about brewing spruce-beer, and he wanted to put it down; but when he took out his pencil, there was so little lead that he soon cut it all away, and it would not do, so you lent him another, and this was left upon the table as good for nothing. But I kept my eye on it; and, as soon as I dared, caught it up, and never parted with it again from that moment."

"I do remember it," cried Emma; "I perfectly remember it. Talking about spruce beer. Oh! yes Mr. Knightley and I both saying we liked it, and Mr. Elton's seeming resolved to learn to like it too. I perfectly remember it. Stop; Mr. Knightley was standing just here, was not he? I have an idea he was standing just here."

"Ah! I do not know. I cannot recollect. It is very odd, but I cannot recollect. Mr. Elton was sitting here, I remember, much about where I am now."

"Well, go on."

"Oh! that's all. I have nothing more to show you, or to say except that I am now going to throw them both behind the fire, and I wish you to see me do it."

"My poor dear Harriet! and have you actually found happiness in treasuring up these things?"

"Yes, simpleton as I was! but I am quite ashamed of it now, and wish I could forget as easily as I can burn them. It was very wrong of me, you know, to keep any remembrances, after he was married. I knew it was – but had not resolution enough to part with them."

"But, Harriet, is it necessary to burn the court-plaster? I have not a word to say for the bit of old pencil, but the court plaster might be useful."

"I shall be happier to burn it," replied Harriet. "It has a disagreeable look to me. I must get rid of everything. There it goes, and there is an end, thank Heaven! of Mr. Elton."

"And when," thought Emma, "will there be a beginning of Mr. Churchill?"

She had soon afterwards reason to believe that the beginning was already made, and could not but hope that the gipsy, though she had *told* no fortune, might be proved to have made Harriet's. About a fortnight after the alarm, they came to a sufficient explanation, and quite undesignedly. Emma was not thinking of it at the moment, which made the information she received more valuable. She merely said, in the course of some trivial chat, "Well, Harriet, whenever you marry I would advise you to do so and so" – and thought no more of it, till after a minute's silence she heard Harriet say in a very serious tone, "I shall never marry."

Emma then looked up, and immediately saw how it was; and

after a moment's debate, as to whether it should pass unnoticed or not, replied:

"Never marry! This is a new resolution."

"It is one that I shall never change, however."

After another short hesitation, "I hope it does not proceed from – I hope it is not in compliment to Mr. Elton?"

"Mr. Elton indeed!" cried Harriet indignantly. "Oh! no" – and Emma could just catch the words, "so superior to Mr. Elton!"

She then took a longer time for consideration. Should she proceed no farther? Should she let it pass, and seem to suspect nothing? Perhaps Harriet might think her cold or angry if she did; or perhaps if she were totally silent, it might only drive Harriet into asking her to hear too much; and against any thing like such an unreserve as had been, such an open and frequent discussion of hopes and chances, she was perfectly resolved. She believed it would be wiser for her to say and know at once, all that she meant to say and know. Plain dealing was always best. She had previously determined how far she would proceed, on any application of the sort; and it would be safer for both, to have the judicious law of her own brain laid down with speed. She was decided, and thus spoke:

"Harriet, I will not affect to be in doubt of your meaning. Your resolution, or rather your expectation of never marrying, results from an idea that the person whom you might prefer, would be too greatly your superior in situation to think of you. Is not it so?"

"Oh! Miss Woodhouse, believe me I have not the presumption to suppose – Indeed I am not so mad. But it is a pleasure to me to admire him at a distance and to think of his infinite superiority to all the rest of the world, with the gratitude, wonder, and veneration, which are so proper, in me especially."

"I am not at all surprised at you, Harriet. The service he rendered you was enough to warm your heart."

"Service! oh! it was such an inexpressible obligation! The very recollection of it, and all that I felt at the time when I saw him coming – his noble look and my wretchedness before. Such a change! In one moment such a change! From perfect misery to perfect happiness!"

"It is very natural. It is natural, and it is honourable. Yes, honourable, I think, to choose so well and so gratefully. But that it will be a fortunate preference is more that I can promise. I do not advise you to give way to it, Harriet. I do not by any means engage for its being returned. Consider what you are about. Perhaps it will be wisest in you to check your feelings while you can: at any rate do not let them carry you far, unless you are persuaded of his liking you. Be observant of him. Let his behaviour be the guide of your sensations. I give you this caution now, because I shall never speak to you again on the subject. I am determined against all interference. Henceforward I know nothing of the matter. Let no name ever pass our lips. We were very wrong before; we will be cautious now. He is your superior, no doubt, and there do seem objections and obstacles of a very serious nature; but yet, Harriet, more wonderful things have taken place, there have been matches of greater disparity. But take care of yourself. I would not have you too sanguine; though, however it may end, be assured your raising your thoughts to *him,* is a mark of good taste which I shall always know how to value."

Harriet kissed her hand in silent and submissive gratitude. Emma was very decided in thinking such an attachment no bad thing for her friend. Its tendency would be to raise and refine her mind – and it must be saving her from the danger of degradation.

# *Chapter 41*

IN THIS state of schemes, and hopes, and connivance, June opened upon Hartfield. To Highbury in general it brought no material change. The Eltons were still talking of a visit from the Sucklings, and of the use to be made of their barouche-landau; and Jane Fairfax was still at her grandmother's; and as the return of the Campbells from Ireland was again delayed, and August, instead of Midsummer, fixed for it, she was likely to remain there full two months longer, provided at least she were able to defeat Mrs. Elton's activity in her service, and save herself from being hurried into a delightful situation against her will.

Mr. Knightley, who, for some reason best known to himself, had certainly taken an early dislike to Frank Churchill, was only growing to dislike him more. He began to suspect him of some double dealing in his pursuit of Emma. That Emma was his object appeared indisputable. Everything declared it; his own attentions, his father's hints, his mother-in-law's guarded silence; it was all in unison; words, conduct, discretion, and indiscretion, told the same story. But while so many were devoting him to Emma, and Emma herself making him over to Harriet, Mr. Knightley began to suspect him of some inclination to trifle with Jane Fairfax. He could not understand it; but there were symptoms of intelligence between them – he thought so at least – symptoms of admiration on his side, which, having once observed, he could not persuade himself to think entirely void of meaning, however he might wish to escape any of Emma's errors of imagination. *She* was not present when the suspicion first arose. He was dining with the Randalls family, and Jane, at the Eltons'; and he had seen a look, more than a single look, at Miss Fairfax, which, from the admirer of Miss Woodhouse, seemed somewhat out of place. When he was again in their company, he could not help remembering what he had seen; nor could he avoid observations which, unless it were like Cowper and his fire at twilight:

"Myself creating what I saw,"

brought him yet stronger suspicion of there being a something of private liking, of private understanding even, between Frank Churchill and Jane.

He had walked up one day after dinner, as he very often did, to spend his evening at Hartfield. Emma and Harriet were going to walk; he joined them; and, on returning, they fell in with a larger party, who, like themselves, judged it wisest to take their exercise early, as the weather threatened rain; Mr. and Mrs. Weston and their son, Miss Bates and her niece, who had accidentally met. They all united; and, on reaching Hartfield gates, Emma, who knew it was exactly the sort of visiting that would be welcome to her father, pressed them all to go in and drink tea with him. The Randalls party agreed to it immediately; and after a pretty long speech from Miss Bates, which few persons listened to, she also found it possible to accept dear Miss Woodhouse's most obliging invitation.

As they were turning into the grounds, Mr. Perry passed by on horseback. The gentlemen spoke of his horse.

"By the bye," said Frank Churchill to Mrs. Weston presently, "what became of Mr. Perry's plan of setting up his carriage?"

Mrs. Weston looked surprised, and said, "I did not know that he ever had any such plan."

"Nay, I had it from you. You wrote to me about it three months ago."

"Me! impossible!"

"Indeed you did. I remember it perfectly. You mentioned it as what was certainly to be very soon. Mrs. Perry had told somebody, and was extremely happy about it. It was owing to *her* persuasion, as she thought his being out in bad weather did him a great deal of harm. You must remember it now?"

"Upon my word I never heard of it till this moment."

"Never! really, never! Bless me! how could it be? Then I must have dreamt it – but I was completely persuaded – Miss Smith, you walk as if you were tired. You will not be sorry to find yourself at home."

"What is this? What is this?" cried Mr. Weston, "about Perry and a carriage? Is Perry going to set up his carriage, Frank? I am glad he can afford it. You had it from himself, had you?"

"No, sir," replied his son, laughing, "I seem to have had it from nobody. Very odd! I really was persuaded of Mrs. Weston's having mentioned it in one of her letters to Enscombe, many weeks ago, with all these particulars but as she declares she never heard a syllable of it before, of course it must have been a dream. I am a great dreamer. I dream of everybody at Highbury when I am away and when I have gone through my particular friends, then I begin dreaming of Mr. and Mrs. Perry."

"It is odd though," observed his father, "that you should have had such a regular connected dream about people whom it was not very likely you should be thinking of at Enscombe. Perry's setting up his carriage! and his wife's persuading him to it, out of care for his health – just what will happen, I have no doubt, some time or other; only a little premature. What an air of probability sometimes runs through a dream! And at others, what a heap of absurdities it is! Well, Frank, your dream certainly shows that Highbury is in your thoughts when you are absent. Emma, you are a great dreamer, I think?"

Emma was out of hearing. She had hurried on before her guests to prepare her father for their appearance, and was beyond the reach of Mr. Weston's hint.

"Why, to own the truth," cried Miss Bates, who had been trying in vain to be heard the last two minutes, "if I must speak on this subject, there is no denying that Mr. Frank Churchill might have – I do not mean to say that he did not dream it – I am sure I have sometimes the oddest dreams in the world – but if I am questioned about it, I must acknowledge that there was such an idea last spring; for Mrs. Perry herself mentioned it to my mother, and the Coles knew of it as well as ourselves – but it was quite a secret, known to nobody else, and only thought of about three days. Mrs. Perry was very anxious that he should have a carriage, and came to my mother in great spirits one morning because she thought she had prevailed. Jane, don't you remember grandmama's telling us of it when we got home? I forget where we had been walking to – very likely to Randalls; yes, I think it was to Randalls. Mrs. Perry was always particularly fond of my mother – indeed I do not know who is not – and she had mentioned it to her in confidence; she had no objection to her telling us, of course, but it was not to go beyond: and, from that day to this, I never mentioned it to a soul that I know of. At the same time, I will not positively answer for my having never dropped a hint, because I know I do sometimes pop out a thing before I am aware. I am a talker, you know; I am rather a talker; and now and then I have let a thing escape me which I should not. I am not like Jane; I wish I were. I will answer for it *she* never betrayed the least thing in the world. Where is she? Oh! just behind. Perfectly remember Mrs. Perry's coming. Extraordinary dream, indeed!"

They were entering the hall. Mr. Knightley's eyes had preceded Miss Bates's in a glance at Jane. From Frank Churchill's face, where he thought he saw confusion suppressed or laughed away, he had involuntarily turned to hers; but she was indeed behind, and too busy with her shawl. Mr. Weston had walked in. The two other gentlemen waited at the door to let her pass. Mr. Knightley suspected in Frank Churchill the determination of catching her eye – he seemed watching her intently – in vain, however, if it were so Jane passed between them into the hall, and looked at neither.

There was no time for farther remark or explanation. The

dream must be borne with, and Mr. Knightley must take his seat with the rest round the large modern circular table which Emma had introduced at Hartfield, and which none but Emma could have had power to place there and persuade her father to use, instead of the small sized Pembroke, on which two of his daily meals had, for forty years been crowded. Tea passed pleasantly, and nobody seemed in a hurry to move.

"Miss Woodhouse," said Frank Churchill, after examining a table behind him, which he could reach as he sat, "have your nephews taken away their alphabets – their box of letters? It used to stand here. Where is it? This is a sort of dull-looking evening, that ought to be treated rather as winter than summer. We had great amusement with those letters one morning. I want to puzzle you again."

Emma was pleased with the thought; and producing the box, the table was quickly scattered over with alphabets, which no one seemed so much disposed to employ as their two selves. They were rapidly forming words for each other, or for anybody else who would be puzzled. The quietness of the game made it particularly eligible for Mr. Woodhouse, who had often been distressed by the more animated sort, which Mr. Weston had occasionally introduced, and who now sat happily occupied in lamenting, with tender melancholy, over the departure of the "poor little boys," or in fondly pointing out, as he took up any stray letter near him, how beautifully Emma had written it.

Frank Churchill placed a word before Miss Fairfax. She gave a slight glance round the table, and applied herself to it. Frank was next to Emma, Jane opposite to them and Mr. Knightley so placed as to see them all; and it was his object to see as much as he could, with as little apparent observation. The word was discovered, and with a faint smile pushed away. If meant to be immediately mixed with the others, and buried from sight, she should have looked on the table instead of looking just across, for it was not mixed; and Harriet, eager after every fresh word, and finding out none, directly took it up, and fell to work. She was sitting by Mr. Knightley, and turned to him for help. The word was *blunder;* and as Harriet exultingly proclaimed it, there was a blush on Jane's cheek which gave it a meaning not otherwise ostensible. Mr. Knightley connected it with the dream; but how it could all be, was beyond his comprehension. How the delicacy, the discretion of his favourite could have been so lain asleep! He feared there must be some decided involvement. Disingenuousness and double-dealing seemed to meet him at every turn. These letters were but the vehicle for gallantry and trick. It was a child's play, chosen to conceal a deeper game on Frank Churchill's part.

With great indignation did he continue to observe him; with great alarm and distrust, to observe also his two blinded companions. He saw a short word prepared for Emma, and given to her with a look sly and demure. He saw that Emma had soon made it out, and found it highly entertaining, though it was something which she judged it proper to appear to censure; for she said, "Nonsense! for shame!" He heard Frank Churchill next say, with a glance towards Jane, "I will give it to her – shall I?" and as clearly heard Emma opposing it with eager laughing warmth. "No, no, you must not; you shall not, indeed."

It was done however. This gallant young man, who seemed to love without feeling, and to recommend himself without complaisance, directly handed over the word to Miss Fairfax, and with a particular degree of sedate civility entreated her to study it. Mr. Knightley's excessive curiosity to know what this word might be, made him seize every possible moment for darting his eye towards it, and it was not long before he saw it to be *Dixon.* Jane Fairfax's perception seemed to accompany his; her comprehension was certainly more equal to the covert meaning, the superior intelligence, of those five letters so arranged. She was evidently displeased; looked up, and seeing herself watched, blushed more deeply than he had ever perceived her, and saying only, "I did not know that proper names were allowed," pushed away the letters with even an angry spirit, and looked resolved to be engaged by no other word that could be offered. Her face was averted from those who had made the attack, and turned towards her aunt.

"Aye, very true, my dear," cried the latter, though Jane had not spoken a word "I was just going to say the same thing. It is time for us to be going indeed. The evening is closing in, and grandmama will be looking for us. My dear sir, you are too obliging. We really must wish you good night."

Jane's alertness in moving, proved her as ready as her aunt had preconceived. She was immediately up, and wanting to quit the table; but so many were also moving, that she could not get away; and Mr. Knightley thought he saw another collection of letters anxiously pushed towards her, and resolutely swept away by her unexamined. She was afterwards looking for her shawl – Frank Churchill was looking also it was growing dusk, and the room was in confusion; and how they parted, Mr. Knightley could not tell.

He remained at Hartfield after all the rest, his thoughts full of what he had seen; so full, that when the candles came to assist his observations, he must – yes, he certainly must, as a friend – an anxious friend – give Emma some hint, ask her some question. He could not see her in a situation of such danger, without trying to preserve her. It was his duty.

"Pray, Emma," said he, "may I ask in what lay the great amusement, the poignant sting of the last word given to you and Miss Fairfax? I saw the word, and am curious to know how it could be so very entertaining to the one, and so very distressing to the other."

Emma was extremely confused. She could not endure to give him the true explanation; for though her suspicions were by no means removed, she was really ashamed of having ever imparted them.

"Oh!" she cried in evident embarrassment, "it all meant nothing; a mere joke among ourselves."

"The joke," he replied gravely, "seemed confined to you and Mr. Churchill."

He had hoped she would speak again, but she did not. She would rather busy herself about any thing than speak. He sat a little while in doubt. A variety of evils crossed his mind. Interference – fruitless interference. Emma's confusion, and the acknowledged intimacy, seemed to declare her affection engaged. Yet he would speak. He owed it to her, to risk any thing that might be involved in an unwelcome interference, rather than her welfare; to encounter any thing, rather than the remembrance of neglect in such a cause.

"My dear Emma," said he at last, with earnest kindness, "do you think you perfectly understand the degree of acquaintance between the gentleman and lady we have been speaking of?"

"Between Mr. Frank Churchill and Miss Fairfax? Oh! yes, perfectly. Why do you make a doubt of it?"

"Have you never at any time had reason to think that he admired her, or that she admired him?"

"Never, never!" she cried with a most open eagerness "Never, for the twentieth part of a moment, did such an idea occur to me. And how could it possibly come into your head?"

"I have lately imagined that I saw symptoms of attachment between them certain expressive looks, which I did not believe meant to be public."

"Oh! you amuse me excessively. I am delighted to find that you can vouchsafe to let your imagination wander, but it will not do – very sorry to check you in your first essay, but indeed it will not do. There is no admiration between them, I do assure you; and the appearances which have caught you, have arisen from some peculiar circumstances feelings rather of a totally different nature, it is impossible exactly to explain – there is a good deal of nonsense in it – but the part which is capable of being communicated, which is sense, is, that they are as far from any attachment or admiration for one another, as any two beings in the world can be. That is, I *presume* it to be so on her side, and I can *answer* for its being so on his. I will answer for the gentleman's indifference."

She spoke with a confidence which staggered, with a satisfaction which silenced, Mr. Knightley. She was in gay spirits, and would have prolonged the conversation, wanting to hear the particulars of his suspicions, every look described, and all the wheres and hows of a circumstance which highly entertained her: but his gaiety did not meet hers. He found he could not be useful, and his feelings were too much irritated for talking. That he might not be irritated into an absolute fever, by the fire which Mr. Woodhouse's tender habits required almost every evening throughout the year, he soon afterwards took a hasty leave, and walked home to the coolness and solitude of Donwell Abbey.

## Chapter 42

AFTER BEING long fed with hopes of a speedy visit from Mr. and Mrs. Suckling, the Highbury world were obliged to endure the mortification of hearing that they could not possibly come till the autumn. No such importation of novelties could enrich their intellectual stores at present. In the daily interchange of news, they must be again restricted to the other topics with which for a while the Sucklings' coming had been united, such as the last accounts of Mrs. Churchill, whose health seemed every day to supply a different report, and the situation of Mrs. Weston, whose happiness it was to be hoped might eventually be as much increased by the arrival of a child, as that of all her neighbours was by the approach of it.

Mrs. Elton was very much disappointed. It was the delay of a great deal of pleasure and parade. Her introductions and recommendations must all wait, and every projected party be still only talked of. So she thought at first; but a little consideration convinced her that everything need not be put off. Why should not they explore to Box Hill though the Sucklings did not come? They could go there again with them in the autumn. It was settled that they should go to Box Hill. That there was to be such a party had been long generally known: it had even given the idea of another. Emma had never been to Box Hill; she wished to see what everybody found so well worth seeing, and she and Mr. Weston had agreed to choose some fine morning and drive thither. Two or three more of the chosen only were to be admitted to join them, and it was to be done in a quiet, unpretending, elegant way, infinitely superior to the bustle and preparation, the regular eating and drinking, and picnic parade of the Eltons and the Sucklings.

This was so very well understood between them, that Emma could not but feel some surprise, and a little displeasure, on hearing from Mr. Weston that he had been proposing to Mrs. Elton, as her brother and sister had failed her, that the two parties should unite, and go together; and that as Mrs. Elton had very readily acceded to it, so it was to be, if she had no objection. Now, as her objection was nothing but her very great dislike of Mrs. Elton, of which Mr. Weston must already be perfectly aware, it was not worth bringing forward again: it could not be done without a reproof to him, which would be giving pain to his wife; and she found herself therefore obliged to consent to an arrangement which she would have done a great deal to avoid; an arrangement which would probably expose her even to the degradation of being said to be of Mrs. Elton's party! Every feeling was offended; and the forbearance of her outward submission left a heavy arrear due of secret severity in her reflections on the unmanageable goodwill of Mr. Weston's temper.

"I am glad you approve of what I have done," said he very

comfortably. "But I thought you would. Such schemes as these are nothing without numbers. One cannot have too large a party. A large party secures its own amusement. And she is a good-natured woman after all. One could not leave her out."

Emma denied none of it aloud, and agreed to none of it in private.

It was now the middle of June, and the weather fine; and Mrs. Elton was growing impatient to name the day, and settle with Mr. Weston as to pigeon-pies and cold lamb, when a lame carriage-horse threw everything into sad uncertainty. It might be weeks, it might be only a few days, before the horse were useable; but no preparations could be ventured on, and it was all melancholy stagnation. Mrs. Elton's resources were inadequate to such an attack.

"Is not this most vexations, Knightley?" she cried. "And such weather for exploring! These delays and disappointments are quite odious. What are we to do? The year will wear away at this rate, and nothing done. Before this time last year I assure you we had had a delightful exploring party from Maple Grove to Kings Weston."

"You had better explore to Donwell," replied Mr. Knightley. "That may be done without horses. Come, and eat my strawberries. They are ripening fast."

If Mr. Knightley did not begin seriously, he was obliged to proceed so, for his proposal was caught at with delight; and the "Oh! I should like it of all things," was not plainer in words than manner. Donwell was famous for its strawberry-beds, which seemed a plea for the invitation: but no plea was necessary; cabbage-beds would have been enough to tempt the lady, who only wanted to be going somewhere. She promised him again and again to come – much oftener than he doubted – and was extremely gratified by such a proof of intimacy, such a distinguishing compliment as she chose to consider it.

"You may depend upon me," said she. "I certainly will come. Name your day, and I will come. You will allow me to bring Jane Fairfax?"

"I cannot name a day," said he, "till I have spoken to some others whom I would wish to meet you."

"Oh! leave all that to me. Only give me a *carte blanche.* I am Lady Patroness, you know. It is my party. I will bring friends with me."

"I hope you will bring Elton," said he: "but I will not trouble you to give any other invitations."

"Oh! now you are looking very sly; but consider – you need not be afraid of delegating power to *me.* I am no young lady on her preferment. Married women, you know, may be safely authorised. It is my party. Leave it all to me. I will invite your guests."

"No," he calmly replied, "there is but one married woman in the world whom I can ever allow to invite what guests she pleases to Donwell, and that one is – "

"Mrs. Weston, I suppose," interrupted Mrs. Elton, rather mortified.

"No – Mrs. Knightley; and till she is in being, I will manage such matters myself."

"Ah! you are an odd creature!" she cried, satisfied to have no one preferred to herself. "You are a humourist, and may say what you like. Quite a humourist. Well, I shall bring Jane with me – Jane and her aunt. The rest I leave to you. I have no objections at all to meeting the Hartfield family. Don't scruple. I know you are attached to them."

"You certainly will meet them if I can prevail; and I shall call on Miss Bates on my way home."

"That's quite unnecessary; I see Jane every day; but as you like. It is to be a morning scheme, you know, Knightley; quite a simple thing. I shall wear a large bonnet, and bring one of my little baskets hanging on my arm. Here – probably this basket with pink ribbon. Nothing can be more simple, you see. And Jane will have such another. There is to be no form or parade – a sort of gipsy party. We are to walk about your gardens, and gather the strawberries ourselves, and sit under trees; and whatever else you may like to provide, it is to be all out of doors a table spread in the shade, you know. Everything as natural and simple as possible. Is not that your idea?"

"Not quite. My idea of the simple and the natural will be to have the table spread in the dining room. The nature and the simplicity of gentlemen and ladies, with their servants and furniture, I think is best observed by meals within doors. When you are tired of eating strawberries in the garden, there shall be cold meat in the house."

"Well – as you please; only don't have a great set-out. And, by the bye, can I, or my housekeeper be of any use to you with our opinion? Pray be sincere, Knightley. If you wish me to talk to Mrs. Hodges, or to inspect anything – "

"I have not the least wish for it, I thank you."

"Well – but if any difficulties should arise, my housekeeper is extremely clever."

"I will answer for it, that mine thinks herself full as clever, and would spurn anybody's assistance."

"I wish we had a donkey. The thing would be for us all to come on donkeys, Jane, Miss Bates, and me and my *caro sposo* walking by. I really must talk to him about purchasing a donkey. In a country life I conceive it to be a sort of necessary; for, let a woman have ever so many resources, it is not possible for her to be always shut up at home; and very long walks, you know – in summer there is dust, and in winter there is dirt."

"You will not find either, between Donwell and Highbury. Donwell Lane is never dusty, and now it is perfectly dry. Come on a donkey, however, if you prefer it. You can borrow Mrs. Cole's. I would wish everything to be as much to your taste as possible."

"That I am sure you would. Indeed I do you justice, my good friend. Under that peculiar sort of dry, blunt manner, I know you have the warmest heart. As I tell Mr. E., you are a thorough humourist. Yes, believe me, Knightley; I am fully sensible of your attention to me in the whole of this scheme. You have hit upon the very thing to please me."

Mr. Knightley had another reason for avoiding a table in the shade. He wished to persuade Mr. Woodhouse, as well as Emma, to join the party; and he knew that to have any of them sitting down out of doors to eat would inevitably make him ill. Mr. Woodhouse must not, under the specious pretence of a morning drive, and an hour or two spent at Donwell, be tempted away to his misery.

He was invited on good faith. No lurking horrors were to upbraid him for his easy credulity. He did consent. He had not been at Donwell for two years. "Some very fine morning, he, and Emma, and Harriet, could go very well; and he could sit still with Mrs. Weston, while the dear girls walked about the gardens. He did not suppose they could be damp now, in the middle of the day. He should like to see the old house again exceedingly, and should be very happy to meet Mr. and Mrs. Elton, and any other of his neighbours. He could not see any objection at all to his, and Emma's, and Harriet's going there some very fine morning. He thought it very well done of Mr. Knightley to invite them very kind and sensible much cleverer than dining out. He was not fond of dining out."

Mr. Knightley was fortunate in everybody's most ready concurrence. The invitation was everywhere so well received, that it seemed as if, like Mrs. Elton, they were all taking the scheme as a particular compliment to themselves. Emma and Harriet professed very high expectations of pleasure from it; and Mr. Weston, unasked, promised to get Frank over to join them, if possible; a proof of approbation and gratitude which could have been dispensed with. Mr. Knightley was then obliged to say that he should be glad to see him; and Mr. Weston engaged to lose no time in writing, and spare no arguments to induce him to come.

In the meanwhile the lame horse recovered so fast, that the party to Box Hill was again under happy consideration; and at last Donwell was settled for one day, and Box Hill for the next, the weather appearing exactly right.

Under a bright mid-day sun, at almost Midsummer, Mr. Woodhouse was safely conveyed in his carriage, with one window down, to partake of this al fresco party; and in one of the most comfortable rooms in the Abbey, especially prepared for him by a fire all the morning, he was happily placed, quite at his ease, ready to talk with pleasure of what had been achieved, and advise everybody to come and sit down, and not to heat themselves. Mrs. Weston, who seemed to have walked there on purpose to be tired, and sit all the time with him, remained, when all the others were invited or persuaded out, his patient listener and sympathiser.

It was so long since Emma had been at the Abbey, that as soon as she was satisfied of her father's comfort, she was glad to leave him, and look around her; eager to refresh and correct her memory with more particular observation, more exact understanding of a house and grounds which must ever be so interesting to her and all her family.

She felt all the honest pride and complacency which her alliance with the present and future proprietor could fairly warrant, as she viewed the respectable size and style of the building, its suitable, becoming, characteristic situation, low and sheltered its ample gardens stretching down to meadows washed by a stream, of which the Abbey, with all the old neglect of prospect, had scarcely a sight – and its abundance of timber in rows and avenues, which neither fashion nor extravagance had rooted up. The house was larger than Hartfield, and totally unlike it, covering a good deal of ground, rambling and irregular, with many comfortable, and one or two handsome rooms. It was just what it ought to be, and it looked what it was and Emma felt an increasing respect for it, as the residence of a family of such true gentility, untainted in blood and understanding. Some faults of temper John Knightley had; but Isabella had connected herself unexceptionably. She had given them neither men, nor names, nor places, that could raise a blush. These were pleasant feelings, and she walked about and indulged them till it was necessary to do as the others did, and collect round the strawberry-beds. The whole party were assembled, excepting Frank Churchill, who was expected every moment from Richmond; and Mrs. Elton, in all her apparatus of happiness, her large bonnet and her basket, was very ready to lead the way in gathering, accepting, or talking strawberries, and only strawberries, could now be thought or spoken of. "The best fruit in England – everybody's favourite – always wholesome. These the finest beds and finest sorts. Delightful to gather for oneself – the only way of really enjoying them. Morning decidedly the best time – never tired – every sort good – hautboy infinitely superior – no comparison – the others hardly eatable – hautboys very scarce – Chili preferred – white wood finest flavour of all – price of strawberries in London – abundance about Bristol – Maple Grove – cultivation – beds when to be renewed – gardeners thinking exactly different – no general rule – gardeners never to be put out of their way – delicious fruit – only too rich to be eaten much of – inferior to cherries – currants more refreshing – only objection to gathering strawberries the stooping – glaring sun – tired to death – could bear it no longer – must go and sit in the shade."

Such, for half an hour, was the conversation interrupted only once by Mrs. Weston, who came out, in her solicitude after her son-in-law, to inquire if he were come and she was a little uneasy. She had some fears of his horse.

Seats tolerably in the shade were found; and now Emma was obliged to overhear what Mrs. Elton and Jane Fairfax were talking of. A situation, a most desirable situation, was in question. Mrs. Elton had received notice of it that morning, and was in raptures.

It was not with Mrs. Suckling, it was not with Mrs. Bragge, but in felicity and splendour it fell short only of them: it was with a cousin of Mrs. Bragge, an acquaintance of Mrs. Suckling, a lady known at Maple Grove. Delightful, charming, superior, first circles, spheres, lines, ranks, everything and Mrs. Elton was wild to have the offer closed with immediately. On her side, all was warmth, energy, and triumph and she positively refused to take her friend's negative, though Miss Fairfax continued to assure her that she would not at present engage in anything – repeating the same motives which she had been heard to urge before. Still Mrs. Elton insisted on being authorised to write an acquiescence by the morrow's post. How Jane could bear it at all, was astonishing to Emma. She did look vexed, she did speak pointedly – and at last, with a decision of action unusual to her, proposed a removal. "Should not they walk? Would not Mr. Knightley show them the gardens – all the gardens? She wished to see the whole extent." The pertinacity of her friend seemed more than she could bear.

It was hot; and after walking some time over the gardens in a scattered, dispersed way, scarcely any three together, they insensibly followed one another to the delicious shade of a broad short avenue of limes, which stretching beyond the garden at an equal distance from the river, seemed the finish of the pleasure grounds. It led to nothing; nothing but a view at the end over a low stone wall with high pillars, which seemed intended, in their erection, to give the appearance of an approach to the house, which never had been there. Disputable, however, as might be the taste of such a termination, it was in itself a charming walk, and the view which closed it extremely pretty. The considerable slope, at nearly the foot of which the Abbey stood, gradually acquired a steeper form beyond its grounds; and at half a mile distant was a bank of considerable abruptness and grandeur, well clothed with wood; and at the bottom of this bank, favourably placed and sheltered, rose the Abbey Mill Farm, with meadows in front, and the river making a close and handsome curve around it.

It was a sweet view – sweet to the eye and the mind. English verdure, English culture, English comfort, seen under a sun bright, without being oppressive.

In this walk Emma and Mr. Weston found all the others assembled; and towards this view she immediately perceived Mr. Knightley and Harriet distinct from the rest, quietly leading the way. Mr. Knightley and Harriet! It was an odd *tête-à-tête;* but she was glad to see it. There had been a time when he would have scorned her as a companion, and turned from her with little ceremony. Now they seemed in pleasant conversation. There had been a time also when Emma would have been sorry to see Harriet in a spot so favourable for the Abbey Mill Farm; but now she feared it not. It might be safely viewed with all its appendages of prosperity and beauty, its rich pastures, spreading flocks, orchard in blossom, and light column of smoke ascending. She joined them at the wall, and found them more engaged in talking than in looking around. He was giving Harriet information as to modes of agriculture, etc. and Emma received a smile which seemed to say, "These are my own concerns. I have a right to talk on such subjects, without being suspected of introducing Robert Martin." She did not suspect him. It was too old a story. Robert Martin had probably ceased to think of Harriet. They took a few turns together along the walk. The shade was most refreshing, and Emma found it the pleasantest part of the day.

The next remove was to the house; they must all go in and eat; and they were all seated and busy, and still Frank Churchill did not come. Mrs. Weston looked, and looked in vain. His father would not own himself uneasy, and laughed at her fears; but she could not be cured of wishing that he would part with his black mare. He had expressed himself as to coming, with more than common certainty. "His aunt was so much better, that he had not a doubt of getting over to them." Mrs. Churchill's state, however, as many were ready to remind her, was liable to such sudden variation as might disappoint her nephew in the most reasonable dependence and Mrs. Weston was at last persuaded to believe, or to say, that it must be by some attack of Mrs. Churchill that he was prevented coming. Emma looked at Harriet while the point was under consideration; she behaved very well, and betrayed no emotion.

The cold repast was over, and the party were to go out once more to see what had not yet been seen, the old Abbey fish-ponds; perhaps get as far as the clover, which was to be begun cutting on the morrow, or, at any rate, have the pleasure of being hot, and growing cool again. Mr. Woodhouse, who had already taken his little round in the highest part of the gardens, where no damps from the river were imagined even by him, stirred no more; and his daughter resolved to remain with him, that Mrs. Weston might be persuaded away by her husband to the exercise and variety which her spirits seemed to need.

Mr. Knightley had done all in his power for Mr. Woodhouse's entertainment. Books of engravings, drawers of medals, cameos, corals, shells, and every other family collection within his cabinets, had been prepared for his old friend, to while away the morning; and the kindness had perfectly answered. Mr. Woodhouse had been exceedingly well amused. Mrs. Weston had been showing them all to him, and now he would show them all to Emma; fortunate in having no other resemblance to a child, than in a total want of taste for what he saw, for he was slow, constant, and methodical. Before this second looking over was begun, however, Emma walked into the hall for the sake of a few moments' free observation of the entrance and ground-plot of the house and was hardly there, when Jane Fairfax appeared, coming quickly in from the garden, and with a look of escape. Little expecting to meet Miss Woodhouse so soon, there was a start at first; but Miss Woodhouse was the very person she was in quest of.

"Will you be so kind," said she, "when I am missed, as to say that I am gone home? I am going this moment. My aunt is not aware how late it is, nor how long we have been absent but I am sure we shall be wanted, and I am determined to go directly. I have said nothing about it to anybody. It would only be giving trouble and distress. Some are gone to the ponds, and some to the lime-walk. Till they all come in I shall not be missed; and when they do, will you have the goodness to say that I am gone?"

"Certainly, if you wish it; but you are not going to walk to Highbury alone?"

"Yes what should hurt me? I walk fast. I shall be at home in twenty minutes."

"But it is too far, indeed it is, to be walking quite alone. Let my father's servant go with you. Let me order the carriage. It can be round in five minutes."

"Thank you, thank you – but on no account – I would rather walk. And for *me* to be afraid of walking alone! I, who may so soon have to guard others!"

She spoke with great agitation; and Emma very feelingly replied, "That can be no reason for your being exposed to danger now. I must order the carriage. The heat even would be danger. You are fatigued already."

"I am," she answered "I am fatigued; but it is not the sort of fatigue – quick walking will refresh me. Miss Woodhouse, we all know at times what it is to be wearied in spirits. Mine, I confess, are exhausted. The greatest kindness you can show me, will be to let me have my own way, and only say that I am gone when it is necessary."

Emma had not another word to oppose. She saw it all; and entering into her feelings, promoted her quitting the house immediately, and watched her safely off with the zeal of a friend. Her parting look was grateful and her parting words, "Oh! Miss Woodhouse, the comfort of being sometimes alone!" seemed to burst from an overcharged heart, and to describe somewhat of the continual endurance to be practised by her, even towards some of those who loved her best.

"Such a home, indeed! such an aunt!" said Emma, as she turned back into the hall again. "I do pity you. And the more sensibility you betray of their just horrors, the more I shall like you."

Jane had not been gone a quarter of an hour, and they had only accomplished some views of St. Mark's Place, Venice, when Frank Churchill entered the room. Emma had not been thinking of him, she had forgotten to think of him but she was very glad to see him. Mrs. Weston would be at ease. The black mare was blameless; *they* were right who had named Mrs. Churchill as the cause. He had been detained by a temporary increase of illness in her; a nervous seizure, which had lasted some hours and he had quite given up every thought of coming, till very late; and had he known how hot a ride he should have, and how late, with all his hurry, he must be, he believed he should not have come at all. The heat was excessive; he had never suffered any thing like it – almost wished he had staid at home – nothing killed him like heat – he could bear any degree of cold, etc., but heat was intolerable and he sat down, at the greatest possible distance from the slight remains of Mr. Woodhouse's fire, looking very deplorable.

"You will soon be cooler, if you sit still," said Emma.

"As soon as I am cooler I shall go back again. I could very well be spared but such a point had been made of my coming! You will all be going soon I suppose; the whole party breaking up. I met *one* as I came – madness in such weather! – absolute madness!"

Emma listened, and looked, and soon perceived that Frank Churchill's state might be best defined by the expressive phrase of being out of humour. Some people were always cross when they were hot. Such might be his constitution; and as she knew that eating and drinking were often the cure of such incidental complaints, she recommended his taking some refreshment; he would find abundance of everything in the dining-room; and she humanely pointed out the door.

"No he should not eat. He was not hungry; it would only

make him hotter." In two minutes, however, he relented in his own favour; and muttering something about spruce beer, walked off. Emma returned all her attention to her father, saying in secret –

"I am glad I have done being in love with him. I should not like a man who is so soon discomposed by a hot morning. Harriet's sweet easy temper will not mind it."

He was gone long enough to have had a very comfortable meal, and came back all the better – grown quite cool and, with good manners, like himself able to draw a chair close to them, take an interest in their employment; and regret, in a reasonable way, that he should be so late. He was not in his best spirits, but seemed trying to improve them; and, at last, made himself talk nonsense very agreeably. They were looking over views in Switzerland.

"As soon as my aunt gets well, I shall go abroad," said he. "I shall never be easy till I have seen some of these places. You will have my sketches, some time or other, to look at – or my tour to read – or my poem. I shall do something to expose myself."

"That may be – but not by sketches in Switzerland. You will never go to Switzerland. Your uncle and aunt will never allow you to leave England."

"They may be induced to go too. A warm climate may be prescribed for her. I have more than half an expectation of our all going abroad. I assure you I have. I feel a strong persuasion, this morning, that I shall soon be abroad. I ought to travel. I am tired of doing nothing. I want a change. I am serious, Miss Woodhouse, whatever your penetrating eyes may fancy – I am sick of England and would leave it to morrow, if I could."

"You are sick of prosperity and indulgence. Cannot you invent a few hardships for yourself, and be contented to stay?"

"*I* sick of prosperity and indulgence! You are quite mistaken. I do not look upon myself as either prosperous or indulged. I am thwarted in everything material. I do not consider myself at all a fortunate person."

"You are not quite so miserable, though, as when you first came. Go and eat and drink a little more, and you will do very well. Another slice of cold meat, another draught of Madeira and water, will make you nearly on a par with the rest of us."

"No – I shall not stir. I shall sit by you. You are my best cure."

"We are going to Box Hill to morrow; you will join us. It is not Switzerland, but it will be something for a young man so much in want of a change. You will stay, and go with us?"

"No, certainly not; I shall go home in the cool of the evening."

"But you may come again in the cool of to morrow morning."

"No – It will not be worth while. If I come, I shall be cross."

"Then pray stay at Richmond."

"But if I do, I shall be crosser still. I can never bear to think of you all there without me."

"These are difficulties which you must settle for yourself. Choose your own degree of crossness. I shall press you no more."

The rest of the party were now returning, and all were soon collected. With some there was great joy at the sight of Frank Churchill; others took it very composedly; but there was a very general distress and disturbance on Miss Fairfax's disappearance being explained. That it was time for everybody to go, concluded the subject; and with a short final arrangement for the next day's scheme, they parted. Frank Churchill's little inclination to exclude himself increased so much, that his last words to Emma were –

"Well; if you wish me to stay and join the party, I will."

She smiled her acceptance; and nothing less than a summons from Richmond was to take him back before the following evening.

# Chapter 43

THEY HAD a very fine day for Box Hill; and all the other outward circumstances of arrangement, accommodation, and punctuality, were in favour of a pleasant party. Mr. Weston directed the whole, officiating safely between Hartfield and the Vicarage, and everybody was in good time. Emma and Harriet went together; Miss Bates and her niece, with the Eltons; the gentlemen on horseback. Mrs. Weston remained with Mr. Woodhouse. Nothing was wanting but to be happy when they got there. Seven miles were travelled in expectation of enjoyment, and everybody had a burst of admiration on first arriving; but in the general amount of the day there was deficiency. There was a languor, a want of spirits, a want of union, which could not be got over. They separated too much into parties. The Eltons walked together; Mr. Knightley took charge of Miss Bates and Jane; and Emma and Harriet belonged to Frank Churchill. And Mr. Weston tried, in vain, to make them harmonise better. It seemed at first an accidental division, but it never materially varied. Mr. and Mrs. Elton, indeed, showed no unwillingness to mix, and be as agreeable as they could; but during the two whole hours that were spent on the hill, there seemed a principle of separation, between the other parties, too strong for any fine prospects, or any cold collation, or any cheerful Mr. Weston, to remove.

At first it was downright dullness to Emma. She had never seen Frank Churchill so silent and stupid. He said nothing worth hearing – looked without seeing – admired without intelligence – listened without knowing what she said. While he was so dull, it was no wonder that Harriet should be dull likewise; and they were both insufferable.

When they all sat down it was better; to her taste a great deal better – for Frank Churchill grew talkative and gay, making her his first object. Every distinguishing attention that could be paid, was paid to her. To amuse her, and be agreeable in her eyes, seemed all that he cared for – and Emma, glad to be enlivened, not sorry to be flattered, was gay and easy too, and gave him all the friendly encouragement, the admission to be gallant, which she had ever given in the first and most animating period of their acquaintance; but which now, in her own estimation, meant nothing, though in the judgment of most people looking on it must have had such an appearance as no English word but flirtation could very well describe. "Mr. Frank Churchill and Miss Woodhouse flirted together excessively." They were laying themselves open to that very phrase – and to having it sent off in a letter to Maple Grove by one lady, to Ireland by another. Not that Emma was gay and thoughtless from any real felicity; it was rather because she felt less happy than she had expected. She laughed because she was disappointed; and though she liked him for his attentions, and thought them all, whether in friendship, admiration, or playfulness, extremely judicious, they were not winning back her heart. She still intended him for her friend.

"How much I am obliged to you," said he, "for telling me to come to day! If it had not been for you, I should certainly have lost all the happiness of this party. I had quite determined to go away again."

"Yes, you were very cross; and I do not know what about, except that you were too late for the best strawberries. I was a kinder friend than you deserved. But you were humble. You begged hard to be commanded to come."

"Don't say I was cross. I was fatigued. The heat overcame me."

"It is hotter to day."

"Not to my feelings. I am perfectly comfortable to day."

"You are comfortable because you are under command."

"Your command? Yes."

"Perhaps I intended you to say so, but I meant self-command. You had, somehow or other, broken bounds yesterday. and run away from your own management; but to day you are got back again – and as I cannot be always with you, it is best to believe your temper under your own command rather than mine."

"It comes to the same thing. I can have no self-command without a motive. You order me, whether you speak or not. And you can be always with me. You are always with me."

"Dating from three o'clock yesterday. My perpetual influence could not begin earlier, or you would not have been so much out of humour before."

"Three o'clock yesterday! That is your date. I thought I had seen you first in February."

"Your gallantry is really unanswerable. But (lowering her voice) nobody speaks except ourselves, and it is rather too much to be talking nonsense for the entertainment of seven silent people."

"I say nothing of which I am ashamed," replied he, with lively impudence. "I saw you first in February. Let everybody on the Hill hear me if they can. Let my accents swell to Mickleham on one side, and Dorking on the other. I saw you first in February." And then whispering "Our companions are excessively stupid. What shall we do to rouse them? Any nonsense will serve. They *shall* talk. Ladies and gentlemen, I am ordered by Miss Woodhouse (who, wherever she is, presides) to say, that she desires to know what you are all thinking of?"

Some laughed, and answered good-humouredly. Miss Bates said a great deal; Mrs. Elton swelled at the idea of Miss Woodhouse's presiding; Mr. Knightley's answer was the most distinct.

"Is Miss Woodhouse sure that she would like to hear what we are all thinking of?"

"Oh, no, no!" cried Emma, laughing as carelessly as she could – "Upon no account in the world. It is the very last thing I would stand the brunt of just now. Let me hear any thing rather than what you are all thinking of. I will not say quite all. There are one or two, perhaps, (glancing at Mr. Weston and Harriet,) whose thoughts I might not be afraid of knowing."

"It is a sort of thing," cried Mrs. Elton emphatically, "which *I* should not have thought myself privileged to inquire into. Though, perhaps, as the *Chaperon* of the party – *I* never was in any circle – exploring parties – young ladies – married women – "

Her mutterings were chiefly to her husband; and he murmured, in reply –

"Very true, my love, very true. Exactly so, indeed – quite unheard of – but some ladies say any thing. Better pass it off as a joke. Everybody knows what is due to you."

"It will not do," whispered Frank to Emma; "they are most of them affronted. I will attack them with more address. Ladies and gentlemen I am ordered by Miss Woodhouse to say, that she waives her right of knowing exactly what you may all be thinking of, and only requires something very entertaining from each of you, in a general way. Here are seven of you, besides myself, (who, she is pleased to say, am very entertaining already,) and she only demands from each of you either one thing very clever, be it prose or verse, original or repeated or two things moderately clever or three things very dull indeed, and she engages to laugh heartily at them all."

"Oh! very well," exclaimed Miss Bates, "then I need not be uneasy. 'Three things very dull indeed.' That will just do for me, you know. I shall be sure to say three dull things as soon as ever I open my mouth, shan't I? (looking round with the most good humoured dependence on everybody's assent) Do not you all think I shall?"

Emma could not resist.

"Ah! ma'am, but there may be a difficulty. Pardon me but you will be limited as to number – only three at once."

Miss Bates, deceived by the mock ceremony of her manner, did not immediately catch her meaning; but, when it burst on her, it could not anger, though a slight blush showed that it could pain her.

"Ah! Well – to be sure. Yes, I see what she means, (turning to Mr. Knightley,) and I will try to hold my tongue. I must make myself very disagreeable, or she would not have said such a thing to an old friend."

"I like your plan," cried Mr. Weston. "Agreed, agreed. I will do my best. I am making a conundrum. How will a conundrum reckon?"

"Low, I am afraid, sir, very low," answered his son; "but we shall be indulgent especially to any one who leads the way."

"No, no," said Emma, "it will not reckon low. A conundrum of Mr. Weston's shall clear him and his next neighbour. Come, sir, pray let me hear it."

"I doubt its being very clever myself," said Mr. Weston. "It is too much a matter of fact, but here it is. What two letters of the alphabet are there, that express perfection?"

"What two letters – express perfection! I am sure I do not know."

"Ah! you will never guess. You, (to Emma), I am certain, will never guess. I will tell you. M and A: Emma. Do you understand?"

Understanding and gratification came together. It might be a very indifferent piece of wit, but Emma found a great deal to laugh at and enjoy in it and so did Frank and Harriet. It did not seem to touch the rest of the party equally; some looked very stupid about it, and Mr. Knightley gravely said:

"This explains the sort of clever thing that is wanted, and Mr. Weston has done very well for himself; but he must have knocked up everybody else. *Perfection* should not have come quite so soon."

"Oh! for myself, I protest I must be excused," said Mrs. Elton; "I really cannot attempt – I am not at all fond of the sort of thing. I had an acrostic once sent to me upon my own name, which I was not at all pleased with. I knew who it came from. An abominable puppy! You know who I mean (nodding to her husband). These kind of things are very well at Christmas, when one is sitting round the fire; but quite out of place, in my opinion, when one is exploring about the country in summer. Miss Woodhouse must excuse me. I am not one of those who have witty things at everybody's service. I do not pretend to be a wit. I have a great deal of vivacity in my own way, but I really must be allowed to judge when to speak and when to hold my tongue. Pass us, if you please, Mr. Churchill. Pass Mr. E., Knightley, Jane, and myself. We have nothing clever to say – not one of us.

"Yes, yes, pray pass me," added her husband, with a sort of sneering consciousness; "I have nothing to say that can entertain Miss Woodhouse, or any other young lady. An old married man – quite good for nothing. Shall we walk, Augusta?"

"With all my heart. I am really tired of exploring so long on one spot. Come, Jane, take my other arm."

Jane declined it, however, and the husband and wife walked off. "Happy couple!" said Frank Churchill, as soon as they were out of hearing: "How well they suit one another! Very lucky – marrying as they did, upon an acquaintance formed only in a public place! They only knew each other, I think, a few weeks in Bath! Peculiarly lucky! for as to any real knowledge of a person's disposition that Bath, or any public place, can give – it is all nothing; there can be no knowledge. It is only by seeing women in their own homes, among their own set, just as they always are, that you can form any just judgment. Short of that, it is all guess and luck – and will generally be ill luck. How many a man has committed himself on a short acquaintance, and rued it all the rest of his life!"

Miss Fairfax, who had seldom spoken before, except among her own confederates, spoke now.

"Such things do occur, undoubtedly." She was stopped by a

cough. Frank Churchill turned towards her to listen.

"You were speaking," said he, gravely. She recovered her voice.

"I was only going to observe, that though such unfortunate circumstances do sometimes occur both to men and women, I cannot imagine them to be very frequent. A hasty and imprudent attachment may arise – but there is generally time to recover from it afterwards. I would be understood to mean, that it can be only weak, irresolute characters, (whose happiness must be always at the mercy of chance,) who will suffer an unfortunate acquaintance to be an inconvenience, an oppression for ever."

He made no answer; merely looked, and bowed in submission; and soon afterwards said, in a lively tone:

"Well, I have so little confidence in my own judgment, that whenever I marry, I hope some body will choose my wife for me. Will you? (turning to Emma.) Will you choose a wife for me? – I am sure I should like anybody fixed on by you. You provide for the family, you know, (with a smile at his father). Find some body for me. I am in no hurry. Adopt her, educate her."

"And make her like myself."

"By all means, if you can."

"Very well. I undertake the commission. You shall have a charming wife."

"She must be very lively, and have hazel eyes. I care for nothing else. I shall go abroad for a couple of years – and when I return, I shall come to you for my wife. Remember."

Emma was in no danger of forgetting. It was a commission to touch every favourite feeling. Would not Harriet be the very creature described? Hazel eyes excepted, two years more might make her all that he wished. He might even have Harriet in his thoughts at the moment; who could say? Referring the education to her seemed to imply it.

"Now, ma'am," said Jane to her aunt, "shall we join Mrs. Elton?"

"If you please, my dear. With all my heart. I am quite ready. I was ready to have gone with her, but this will do just as well. We shall soon overtake her. There she is – no, that's somebody else. That's one of the ladies in the Irish car party, not at all like her. Well, I declare – "

They walked off, followed in half a minute by Mr. Knightley. Mr. Weston, his son, Emma, and Harriet, only remained; and the young man's spirits now rose to a pitch almost unpleasant. Even Emma grew tired at last of flattery and merriment, and wished herself rather walking quietly about with any of the others, or sitting almost alone, and quite unattended to, in tranquil observation of the beautiful views beneath her. The appearance of the servants looking out for them to give notice of the carriages was a joyful sight; and even the bustle of collecting and preparing to depart, and the solicitude of Mrs. Elton to have her carriage first, were gladly endured, in the prospect of the quiet drive home which was to close the very questionable enjoyments of this day of pleasure. Such another scheme, composed of so many ill-assorted people, she hoped never to be betrayed into again.

While waiting for the carriage, she found Mr. Knightley by her side. He looked around, as if to see that no one were near, and then said:

"Emma, I must once more speak to you as I have been used to do: a privilege rather endured than allowed, perhaps, but I must still use it. I cannot see you acting wrong, without a remonstrance. How could you be so unfeeling to Miss Bates? How could you be so insolent in your wit to a woman of her character, age, and situation? Emma, I had not thought it possible."

Emma recollected, blushed, was sorry, but tried to laugh it off.

"Nay, how could I help saying what I did? Nobody could have helped it. It was not so very bad. I dare say she did not understand me."

"I assure you she did. She felt your full meaning. She has

talked of it since. I wish you could have heard how she talked of it – with what candour and generosity. I wish you could have heard her honouring your forbearance, in being able to pay her such attentions, as she was for ever receiving from yourself and your father, when her society must be so irksome."

"Oh!" cried Emma, "I know there is not a better creature in the world: but you must allow, that what is good and what is ridiculous are most unfortunately blended in her."

"They are blended," said he, "I acknowledge; and, were she prosperous, I could allow much for the occasional prevalence of the ridiculous over the good. Were she a woman of fortune, I would leave every harmless absurdity to take its chance, I would not quarrel with you for any liberties of manner. Were she your equal in situation – but, Emma, consider how far this is from being the case. She is poor; she has sunk from the comforts she was born to; and, if she live to old age, must probably sink more. Her situation should secure your compassion. It was badly done, indeed! You, whom she had known from an infant, whom she had seen grow up from a period when her notice was an honour – to have you now, in thoughtless spirits, and the pride of the moment, laugh at her, humble her – and before her niece, too – and before others, many of whom (certainly *some,*) would be entirely guided by your treatment of her. This is not pleasant to you, Emma – and it is very far from pleasant to me; but I must, I will – I tell you truths while I can; satisfied with proving myself your friend by very faithful counsel, and trusting that you will some time or other do me greater justice than you can do now."

While they talked, they were advancing towards the carriage; it was ready; and, before she could speak again, he had handed her in. He had misinterpreted the feelings which had kept her face averted, and her tongue motionless. They were combined only of anger against herself, mortification, and deep concern. She had not been able to speak; and, on entering the carriage, sunk back for a moment overcome then reproaching herself for having taken no leave, making no acknowledgment, parting in apparent sullenness, she looked out with voice and hand eager to show a difference; but it was just too late. He had turned away, and the horses were in motion. She continued to look back, but in vain; and soon, with what appeared unusual speed, they were half way down the hill, and everything left far behind. She was vexed beyond what could have been expressed – almost beyond what she could conceal. Never had she felt so agitated, mortified, grieved, at any circumstance in her life. She was most forcibly struck. The truth of this representation there was no denying. She felt it at her heart. How could she have been so brutal, so cruel to Miss Bates! How could she have exposed herself to such ill opinion in any one she valued! And how suffer him to leave her without saying one word of gratitude, of concurrence, of common kindness!

Time did not compose her. As she reflected more, she seemed but to feel it more. She never had been so depressed. Happily it was not necessary to speak. There was only Harriet, who seemed not in spirits herself, fagged, and very willing to be silent; and Emma felt the tears running down her cheeks almost all the way home, without being at any trouble to check them, extraordinary as they were.

# Chapter 44

THE WRETCHEDNESS of a scheme to Box Hill was in Emma's thoughts all the evening. How it might be considered by the rest of the party, she could not tell. They, in their different homes, and their different ways, might be looking back on it with pleasure; but in her view it was a morning more completely misspent, more totally bare of rational satisfaction at the time, and more to be abhorred in recollection, than any she had ever passed. A whole evening of back gammon with her father, was felicity to it. *There*, indeed, lay real pleasure, for there she was giving up the sweetest hours of the twenty-four to his comfort; and feeling that, unmerited as might be the degree of his fond affection and confiding esteem, she could not, in her general conduct, be open to any severe reproach. As a daughter, she hoped she was not without a heart. She hoped no one could have said to her, "How could you be so unfeeling to your father? – I must, I will tell you truths while I can." Miss Bates should never again – no never! If attention, in future, could do away the past, she might hope to be forgiven. She had been often remiss, her conscience told her so; remiss, perhaps, more in thought than fact; scornful, ungracious. But it should be so no more. In the warmth of true contrition, she would call upon her the very next morning, and it should be the beginning, on her side, of a regular, equal, kindly intercourse.

She was just as determined when the morrow came, and went early, that nothing might prevent her. It was not unlikely, she thought, that she might see Mr. Knightley on her way; or, perhaps, he might come in while she were paying her visit. She had no objection. She would not be ashamed of the appearance of the penitence, so justly and truly hers. Her eyes were towards Donwell as she walked, but she saw him not.

"The ladies were all at home." She had never rejoiced at the sound before, nor ever before entered the passage, nor walked up the stairs, with any wish of giving pleasure, but in conferring obligation, or of deriving it, except in subsequent ridicule.

There was a bustle on her approach; a good deal of moving and talking. She heard Miss Bates's voice, something was to be done in a hurry; the maid looked frightened and awkward; hoped she would be pleased to wait a moment, and then ushered her in too soon. The aunt and niece seemed both escaping into the adjoining room. Jane she had a distinct glimpse of, looking extremely ill; and, before the door had shut them out, she heard Miss Bates saying, "Well, my dear, I shall *say* you are laid down upon the bed, and I am sure you are ill enough."

Poor old Mrs. Bates, civil and humble as usual, looked as if she did not quite understand what was going on.

"I am afraid Jane is not very well," said she, "but I do not know; they *tell* me she is well. I dare say my daughter will be here presently, Miss Woodhouse. I hope you find a chair. I wish Hetty had not gone. I am very little able – have you a chair, ma'am? Do you sit where you like? I am sure she will be here presently."

Emma seriously hoped she would. She had a moment's fear of Miss Bates keeping away from her. But Miss Bates soon came – "Very happy and obliged" – but Emma's conscience told her that there was not the same cheerful volubility as before – less ease of look and manner. A very friendly inquiry after Miss Fairfax, she hoped, might lead the way to a return of old feelings. The touch seemed immediate.

"Ah! Miss Woodhouse, how kind you are! I suppose you have heard – and are come to give us joy. This does not seem much like joy, indeed, in me (twinkling away a tear or two) but it will be very trying for us to part with her, after having had her so long, and she has a dreadful headache just now, writing all the morning: such long letters, you know, to be written to Colonel Campbell, and Mrs. Dixon. 'My dear,' said I, 'you will blind yourself' for tears were in her eyes perpetually. One cannot wonder, one cannot wonder. It is a great change; and though she is amazingly fortunate – such a situation, I suppose, as no young woman before ever met with on first going out do not think us ungrateful, Miss Woodhouse, for such surprising good fortune (again dispersing her tears) – but, poor dear soul! if you were to see what a headache she has. When one is in great pain, you know one cannot feel any blessing quite as it may deserve. She is as low as possible. To look at her, nobody would think how delighted and happy she is to have secured such a situation. You will excuse her not coming to you she is not able she is gone into her own room I want her to lie down upon the bed. 'My dear,' said I, 'I shall say you are laid down upon the bed:' but, however, she is not; she is walking about the room. But, now that she has written her letters, she says she shall soon be well. She will be extremely sorry to miss seeing you, Miss Woodhouse, but your kindness will excuse her. You were kept waiting at the door I was quite ashamed but somehow there was a little bustle for it so happened that we had not heard the knock, and till you were on the stairs, we did not know anybody was coming. 'It is only Mrs. Cole,' said I, 'depend upon it. Nobody else would come so early.' – 'Well,' said she, 'it must be borne some time or other, and it may as well be now.' But then Patty came in, and said it was you. 'Oh!' said I, 'it is Miss Woodhouse: I am sure you will like to see her' – 'I can see nobody,' said she; and up she got, and would go away; and that was what made us keep you waiting and extremely sorry and ashamed we were. 'If you must go, my dear,' said I, 'you must, and I will say you are laid down upon the bed." '

Emma was most sincerely interested. Her heart had been long growing kinder towards Jane; and this picture of her present sufferings acted as a cure of every former ungenerous suspicion, and left her nothing but pity; and the remembrance of the less just and less gentle sensations of the past, obliged her to admit that Jane might very naturally resolve on seeing Mrs. Cole or any other steady friend, when she might not bear to see herself. She spoke as she felt, with earnest regret and solicitude – sincerely wishing that the circumstances which she collected from Miss Bates to be now actually determined on, might be as much for Miss Fairfax's advantage and comfort as possible.

"It must be a severe trial to them all. She had understood it was to be delayed till Colonel Campbell's return."

"So very kind!" replied Miss Bates. "But you are always kind."

There was no bearing such an "always;" and to break through her dreadful gratitude, Emma made the direct inquiry of.

"Where may I ask? is Miss Fairfax going?"

"To a Mrs. Smallridge – charming woman – most superior – to have the charge of her three little girls – delightful children. Impossible that any situation could be more replete with comfort; if we except, perhaps, Mrs. Suckling's own family, and Mrs. Bragge's; but Mrs. Smallridge is intimate with both, and in the very same neighbourhood – lives only four miles from Maple Grove. Jane will be only four miles from Maple Grove."

"Mrs. Elton, I suppose, has been the person to whom Miss Fairfax owes – "

"Yes, our good Mrs. Elton. The most indefatigable, true friend. She would not take a denial. She would not let Jane say, 'No;' for when Jane first heard of it, (it was the day before yesterday, the very morning we were at Donwell,) when Jane first heard of it, she was quite decided against accepting the offer, and for the reasons you mention; exactly as you say, she had made up her mind to close with nothing till Colonel Campbell's return, and nothing should induce her to enter into any engagement at present – and so she told Mrs. Elton over and over again – and I am sure I had no more idea that she would change her mind! – but that good Mrs. Elton, whose judgment never fails her, saw farther than I did. It is not everybody that would have stood out in such a kind way as she did, and refuse to take Jane's answer; but she positively declared she would not write any such denial yesterday, as Jane wished her; she would wait – and, sure enough, yesterday evening it was all settled that Jane should go. Quite a surprise to me! I had not the least idea! Jane took Mrs. Elton aside, and told her at once, that upon thinking over the advantages of Mrs. Smallridge's situation, she had come to the resolution of accepting it. I did not know a word of it till it was all settled."

"You spent the evening with Mrs. Elton?"

"Yes, all of us; Mrs. Elton would have us come. It was settled so, upon the hill, while we were walking about with Mr. Knightley. 'You *must all* spend your evening with us,' said she – 'I positively must have you *all* come.' "

"Mr. Knightley was there too, was he?"

"No, not Mr. Knightley; he declined it from the first; and though I thought he would come, because Mrs. Elton declared she would not let him off, he did not; but my mother, and Jane, and I, were all there, and a very agreeable evening we had. Such kind friends, you know, Miss Woodhouse, one must always find agreeable, though everybody seemed rather fagged after the morning's party. Even pleasure, you know, is fatiguing – and I cannot say that any of them seemed very much to have enjoyed it. However, I shall always think it a very pleasant party, and feel extremely obliged to the kind friends who included me in it."

"Miss Fairfax, I suppose, though you were not aware of it, had been making up her mind the whole day?"

"I dare say she had."

"Whenever the time may come, it must be unwelcome to her and all her friends – but I hope her engagement will have every alleviation that is possible – I mean, as to the character and manners of the family."

"Thank you, dear Miss Woodhouse. Yes, indeed, there is everything in the world that can make her happy in it. Except the

Sucklings and Bragges, there is not such another nursery establishment, so liberal and elegant, in all Mrs. Elton's acquaintance. Mrs. Smallridge, a most delightful woman! – A style of living almost equal to Maple Grove – and as to the children, except the little Sucklings and little Bragges, there are not such elegant sweet children anywhere. Jane will be treated with such regard and kindness! It will be nothing but pleasure – a life of pleasure. And her salary! I really cannot venture to name her salary to you, Miss Woodhouse. Even you, used as you are to great sums, would hardly believe that so much could be given to a young person like Jane."

"Ah! madam," cried Emma, "if other children are at all like what I remember to have been myself, I should think five times the amount of what I have ever yet heard named as a salary on such occasions, dearly earned."

"You are so noble in your ideas!"

"And when is Miss Fairfax to leave you?"

"Very soon, very soon, indeed; that's the worst of it. Within a fortnight. Mrs. Smallridge is in a great hurry. My poor mother does not know how to bear it. So then, I try to put it out of her thoughts, and say, Come ma'am, do not let us think about it any more."

"Her friends must all be sorry to lose her; and will not Colonel and Mrs. Campbell be sorry to find that she has engaged herself before their return?"

"Yes; Jane says she is sure they will; but yet, this is such a situation as she cannot feel herself justified in declining. I was so astonished when she first told me what she had been saying to Mrs. Elton, and when Mrs. Elton at the same moment came congratulating me upon it! It was before tea – stay – no, it could not be before tea, because we were just going to cards – and yet it was before tea, because I remember thinking – Oh! no, now I recollect, now I have it; something happened before tea, but not that. Mr. Elton was called out of the room before tea, old John Abdy's son wanted to speak with him. Poor old John – I have a great regard for him; he was clerk to my poor father twenty-seven years; and now, poor old man, he is bed ridden, and very poorly with the rheumatic gout in his joints – I must go and see him to day; and so will Jane, I am sure, if she gets out at all. And poor John's son came to talk to Mr. Elton about relief from the parish; he is very well-to-do himself, you know, being head man at the Crown – ostler, and everything of that sort – but still he cannot keep his father without some help; and so, when Mr. Elton came back, he told us what John ostler had been telling him, and then it came out about the chaise having been sent to Randalls to take Mr. Frank Churchill to Richmond. That was what happened before tea. It was after tea that Jane spoke to Mrs. Elton."

Miss Bates would hardly give Emma time to say how perfectly new this circumstance was to her; but as without supposing it possible that she could be ignorant of any of the particulars of Mr. Frank Churchill's going, she proceeded to give them all, it was of no consequence.

What Mr. Elton had learned from the ostler on the subject, being the accumulation of the ostler's own knowledge, and the knowledge of the servants at Randalls, was, that a messenger had come over from Richmond soon after the return of the party from Box Hill – which messenger, however, had been no more than was expected; and that Mr. Churchill had sent his nephew a few lines, containing, upon the whole, a tolerable account of Mrs. Churchill, and only wishing him not to delay coming back beyond the next morning early; but that Mr. Frank Churchill having resolved to go home directly, without waiting at all, and his horse seeming to have got a cold, Tom had been sent off immediately for the Crown chaise, and the ostler had stood out and seen it pass by, the boy going a good pace, and driving very steady.

There was nothing in all this either to astonish or interest, and it caught Emma's attention only as it united with the subject which already engaged her mind. The contrast between Mrs. Churchill's importance in the world, and Jane Fairfax's, struck her; one was everything, the other nothing – and she sat musing on the difference of woman's destiny, and quite unconscious on what her eyes were fixed, till roused by Miss Bates's saying:

"Aye, I see what you are thinking of, the pianoforte. What is to become of that? Very true. Poor dear Jane was talking of it just now. 'You must go,' said she. 'You and I must part. You will have no business here. Let it stay, however,' said she; 'give it house-room till Colonel Campbell comes back. I shall talk about it to him; he will settle for me; he will help me out of all my difficulties.' And to this day, I do believe, she knows not whether it was his present or his daughter's."

Now Emma was obliged to think of the pianoforte; and the remembrance of all her former fanciful and unfair conjectures was so little pleasing, that she soon allowed herself to believe her visit had been long enough; and, with a repetition of everything that she could venture to say of the good wishes which she really felt, took leave.

## *Chapter 45*

EMMA'S PENSIVE meditations, as she walked home, were not interrupted; but on entering the parlour, she found those who must rouse her. Mr. Knightley and Harriet had arrived during her absence, and were sitting with her father. Mr. Knightley immediately got up, and in a manner decidedly graver than usual, said:

"I would not go away without seeing you, but I have no time to spare, and therefore must now be gone directly. I am going to London, to spend a few days with John and Isabella. Have you any thing to send or say, besides the 'love,' which nobody carries?"

"Nothing at all. But is not this a sudden scheme?"

"Yes – rather – I have been thinking of it some little time."

Emma was sure he had not forgiven her; he looked unlike himself. Time, however, she thought, would tell him that they ought to be friends again. While he stood, as if meaning to go, but not going – her father began his inquiries.

"Well, my dear, and did you get there safely? – And how did you find my worthy old friend and her daughter? – I dare say they must have been very much obliged to you for coming. Dear Emma has been to call on Mrs. and Miss Bates, Mr. Knightley, as I told you before. She is always so attentive to them!"

Emma's colour was heightened by this unjust praise; and with a smile, and shake of the head, which spoke much, she looked at Mr. Knightley. It seemed as if there were an instantaneous impression in her favour, as if his eyes received the truth from her's, and all that had passed of good in her feelings were at once caught and honoured. He looked at her with a glow of regard. She was warmly gratified – and in another moment still more so, by a little movement of more than common friendliness on his part. He took her hand; whether she had not herself made the first motion, she could not say – she might, perhaps, have rather offered it but he took her hand, pressed it, and certainly was on the point of carrying it to his lips when, from some fancy or other, he suddenly let it go. Why he should feel such a scruple, why he should change his mind when it was all but done, she could not perceive. He would have judged better, she thought, if he had not stopped. The intention, however, was indubitable; and whether it was that his manners had in general so little gallantry, or however else it happened, but she thought nothing became him more. It was with him, of so simple, yet so dignified a nature. She could not but recall the attempt with great satisfaction. It spoke such perfect amity. He left them immediately afterwards –

gone in a moment. He always moved with the alertness of a mind which could neither be undecided nor dilatory, but now he seemed more sudden than usual in his disappearance.

Emma could not regret her having gone to Miss Bates, but she wished she had left her ten minutes earlier; it would have been a great pleasure to talk over Jane Fairfax's situation with Mr. Knightley. Neither would she regret that he should be going to Brunswick Square, for she knew how much his visit would be enjoyed – but it might have happened at a better time – and to have had longer notice of it, would have been pleasanter. They parted thorough friends, however; she could not be deceived as to the meaning of his countenance, and his unfinished gallantry; it was all done to assure her that she had fully recovered his good opinion. He had been sitting with them half an hour, she found. It was a pity that she had not come back earlier!

In the hope of diverting her father's thoughts from the disagreeableness of Mr. Knightley's going to London; and going so suddenly; and going on horseback, which she knew would be all very bad; Emma communicated her news of Jane Fairfax, and her dependence on the effect was justified; it supplied a very useful check – interested, without disturbing him. He had long made up his mind to Jane Fairfax's going out as governess, and could talk of it cheerfully, but Mr. Knightley's going to London had been an unexpected blow.

"I am very glad, indeed, my dear, to hear she is to be so comfortably settled. Mrs. Elton is very good-natured and agreeable, and I dare say her acquaintance are just what they ought to be. I hope it is a dry situation, and that her health will be taken good care of. It ought to be a first object, as I am sure poor Miss Taylor's always was with me. You know, my dear, she is going to be to this new lady what Miss Taylor was to us. And I hope she will be better off in one respect, and not be induced to go away after it has been her home so long."

The following day brought news from Richmond to throw

everything else into the background. An express arrived at Randalls to announce the death of Mrs. Churchill! Though her nephew had had no particular reason to hasten back on her account, she had not lived above six-and-thirty hours after his return. A sudden seizure of a different nature from any thing foreboded by her general state, had carried her off after a short struggle. The great Mrs. Churchill was no more.

It was felt as such things must be felt. Everybody had a degree of gravity and sorrow; tenderness towards the departed, solicitude for the surviving friends; and, in a reasonable time, curiosity to know where she would be buried. Goldsmith tells us, that when lovely woman stoops to folly, she has nothing to do but to die; and when she stoops to be disagreeable, it is equally to be recommended as a clearer of ill-fame. Mrs. Churchill, after being disliked at least twenty-five years, was now spoken of with compassionate allowances. In one point she was fully justified. She had never been admitted before to be seriously ill. The event acquitted her of all the fancifulness, and all the selfishness of imaginary complaints.

"Poor Mrs. Churchill! no doubt she had been suffering a great deal: more than anybody had ever supposed – and continual pain would try the temper. It was a sad event – a great shock – with all her faults, what would Mr. Churchill do without her? Mr. Churchill's loss would be dreadful indeed. Mr. Churchill would never get over it." Even Mr. Weston shook his head, and looked solemn, and said, "Ah! poor woman, who would have thought it!" and resolved, that his mourning should be as handsome as possible; and his wife sat sighing and moralising over her broad hems with a commiseration and good sense, true and steady. How it would affect Frank was among the earliest thoughts of both. It was also a very early speculation with Emma. The character of Mrs. Churchill, the grief of her husband – her mind glanced over them both with awe and compassion – and then rested with lightened feelings on how Frank might be affected by the event, how benefited, how freed. She saw in a moment all the possible good. Now, an attachment to Harriet Smith would have nothing to encounter. Mr. Churchill, independent of his wife, was feared by nobody; an easy, guidable man, to be persuaded into any thing by his nephew. All that remained to be wished was, that the nephew should form the attachment, as, with all her goodwill in the cause, Emma could feel no certainty of its being already formed.

Harriet behaved extremely well on the occasion – with great self-command. What ever she might feel of brighter hope, she betrayed nothing. Emma was gratified, to observe such a proof in her of strengthened character, and refrained from any allusion that might endanger its maintenance. They spoke, therefore, of Mrs. Churchill's death with mutual forbearance.

Short letters from Frank were received at Randalls, communicating all that was immediately important of their state and plans. Mr. Churchill was better than could be expected; and their first removal, on the departure of the funeral for Yorkshire, was to be to the house of a very old friend in Windsor, to whom Mr. Churchill had been promising a visit the last ten years. At present, there was nothing to be done for Harriet; good wishes for the future were all that could yet be possible on Emma's side.

It was a more pressing concern to show attention to Jane Fairfax, whose prospects were closing, while Harriet's opened, and whose engagements now allowed of no delay in any one at Highbury, who wished to show her kindness and with Emma it was grown into a first wish. She had scarcely a stronger regret than for her past coldness; and the person, whom she had been so many months neglecting, was now the very one on whom she would have lavished every distinction of regard or sympathy. She wanted to be of use to her; wanted to show a value for her society, and testify respect and consideration. She resolved to prevail on her to spend a day at Hartfield. A note was written to urge it. The invitation was refused, and by a verbal message.

"Miss Fairfax was not well enough to write;" and when Mr. Perry called at Hartfield, the same morning, it appeared that she was so much indisposed as to have been visited, though against her own consent, by himself, and that she was suffering under severe headaches, and a nervous fever to a degree, which made him doubt the possibility of her going to Mrs. Smallridge's at the time proposed. Her health seemed for the moment completely deranged – appetite quite gone and though there were no absolutely alarming symptoms, nothing touching the pulmonary complaint, which was the standing apprehension of the family, Mr. Perry was uneasy about her. He thought she had undertaken more than she was equal to, and that she felt it so herself, though she would not own it. Her spirits seemed overcome. Her present home, he could not but observe, was unfavourable to a nervous disorder; – confined always to one room; he could have wished it otherwise and her good aunt, though his very old friend, he must acknowledge to be not the best companion for an invalid of that description. Her care and attention could not be questioned; they were, in fact, only too great. He very much feared that Miss Fairfax derived more evil than good from them. Emma listened with the warmest concern; grieved for her more and more, and looked around eager to discover some way of being useful. To take her – be it only an hour or two – from her aunt, to give her change of air and scene, and quiet rational conversation, even for an hour or two, might do her good; and the following morning she wrote again to say, in the most feeling language she could command, that she would call for her in the carriage at any hour that Jane would name – mentioning that she had Mr. Perry's decided opinion, in favour of such exercise for his patient. The answer was only in this short note:

"Miss Fairfax's compliments and thanks, but is quite unequal to any exercise."

Emma felt that her own note had deserved something better; but it was impossible to quarrel with words, whose tremulous inequality showed indisposition so plainly, and she thought only of how she might best counteract this unwillingness to be seen or assisted. In spite of the answer, therefore, she ordered the carriage, and drove to Mrs. Bates's, in the hope that Jane would be induced to join her – but it would not do; Miss Bates came to the carriage door, all gratitude, and agreeing with her most earnestly in thinking an airing might be of the greatest service – and everything that message could do was tried – but all in vain. Miss Bates was obliged to return without success; Jane was quite unpersuadable; the mere proposal of going out seemed to make her worse. Emma wished she could have seen her, and tried her own powers; but, almost before she could hint the wish, Miss Bates made it appear that she had promised her niece on no account to let Miss Woodhouse in. "Indeed, the truth was, that poor dear Jane could not bear to see anybody – anybody at all – Mrs. Elton, indeed, could not be denied – and Mrs. Cole had made such a point – and Mrs. Perry had said so much – but, except them, Jane would really see nobody."

Emma did not want to be classed with the Mrs. Eltons, the Mrs. Perrys, and the Mrs. Coles, who would force themselves anywhere; neither could she feel any right of preference herself – she submitted, therefore, and only questioned Miss Bates farther as to her niece's appetite and diet, which she longed to be able to assist. On that subject poor Miss Bates was very unhappy, and very communicative; Jane would hardly eat any thing: Mr. Perry recommended nourishing food; but everything they could command (and never had anybody such good neighbours) was distasteful.

Emma, on reaching home, called the housekeeper directly, to an examination of her stores; and some arrowroot of very superior quality was speedily despatched to Miss Bates with a most friendly note. In half an hour the arrowroot was returned, with a thousand thanks from Miss Bates, but "dear Jane would not be satisfied without its being sent back; it was a thing she could not take –

and, moreover, she insisted on her saying, that she was not at all in want of anything."

When Emma afterwards heard that Jane Fairfax had been seen wandering about the meadows, at some distance from Highbury, on the afternoon of the very day on which she had, under the plea of being unequal to any exercise, so peremptorily refused to go out with her in the carriage, she could have no doubt – putting everything together – that Jane was resolved to receive no kindness from her. She was sorry, very sorry. Her heart was grieved for a state which seemed but the more pitiable from this sort of irritation of spirits, inconsistency of action, and inequality of powers; and it mortified her that she was given so little credit for proper feeling, or esteemed so little worthy as a friend: but she had the consolation of knowing that her intentions were good, and of being able to say to herself, that could Mr. Knightley have been privy to all her attempts of assisting Jane Fairfax, could he even have seen into her heart, he would not, on this occasion, have found any thing to reprove.

# Chapter 46

ONE MORNING, about ten days after Mrs. Churchill's decease, Emma was called downstairs to Mr. Weston, who "could not stay five minutes, and wanted particularly to speak with her." He met her at the parlour door, and hardly asking her how she did, in the natural key of his voice, sunk it immediately, to say, unheard by her father:

"Can you come to Randalls at any time this morning? Do, if it be possible. Mrs. Weston wants to see you. She must see you."

"Is she unwell?"

"No, no, not at all only a little agitated. She would have ordered the carriage, and come to you, but she must see you *alone,* and that you know (nodding towards her father) Humph! Can you come?"

"Certainly. This moment, if you please. It is impossible to refuse what you ask in such a way. But what can be the matter? Is she really not ill?"

"Depend upon me but ask no more questions. You will know it all in time. The most unaccountable business! But hush, hush!"

To guess what all this meant, was impossible even for Emma. Something really important seemed announced by his looks; but, as her friend was well, she endeavoured not to be uneasy, and settling it with her father, that she would take her walk now, she and Mr. Weston were soon out of the house together and on their way at a quick pace for Randalls.

"Now," said Emma, when they were fairly beyond the sweep gates – "now Mr. Weston, do let me know what has happened."

"No, no," he gravely replied. "Don't ask me. I promised my wife to leave it all to her. She will break it to you better than I can. Do not be impatient, Emma; it will all come out too soon."

"Break it to me," cried Emma, standing still with terror. "Good God! Mr. Weston, tell me at once. Something has happened in Brunswick Square. I know it has. Tell me, I charge you tell me this moment what it is."

"No, indeed you are mistaken."

"Mr. Weston do not trifle with me. Consider how many of my dearest friends are now in Brunswick Square. Which of them is it? I charge you by all that is sacred, not to attempt concealment."

"Upon my word, Emma – "

"Your word! why not your honour! why not say upon your honour, that it has nothing to do with any of them? Good Heavens!

What can be *broke* to me, that does not relate to one of that family?"

"Upon my honour," said he very seriously, "it does not. It is not in the smallest degree connected with any human being of the name of Knightley."

Emma's courage returned, and she walked on.

"I was wrong," he continued, "in talking of its being *broke* to you. I should not have used the expression. In fact, it does not concern you it concerns only myself, that is, we hope. Humph! In short, my dear Emma, there is no occasion to be so uneasy about it. I don't say that it is not a disagreeable business – but things might be much worse. If we walk fast, we shall soon be at Randalls."

Emma found that she must wait; and now it required little effort. She asked no more questions therefore, merely employed her own fancy, and that soon pointed out to her the probability of its being some money concern – something just come to light, of a disagreeable nature in the circumstances of the family, something which the late event at Richmond had brought forward. Her fancy was very active. Half a dozen natural children, perhaps and poor Frank cut off! This, though very undesirable, would be no matter of agony to her. It inspired little more than an animating curiosity.

"Who is that gentleman on horseback?" said she, as they proceeded speaking more to assist Mr. Weston in keeping his secret, than with any other view.

"I do not know. One of the Otways – not Frank; it is not Frank, I assure you. You will not see him. He is half-way to Windsor by this time."

"Has your son been with you, then?"

"Oh! yes did not you know? Well, well, never mind."

For a moment he was silent; and then added, in a tone much more guarded and demure:

"Yes, Frank came over this morning, just to ask us how we did."

They hurried on, and were speedily at Randalls. "Well, my dear," said he, as they entered the room "I have brought her, and now I hope you will soon be better. I shall leave you together. There is no use in delay. I shall not be far off, if you want me." And Emma distinctly heard him add, in a lower tone, before he quitted the room – "I have been as good as my word. She has not the least idea."

Mrs. Weston was looking so ill, and had an air of so much perturbation, that Emma's uneasiness increased; and the moment they were alone, she eagerly said:

"What is it my dear friend? Something of a very unpleasant nature, I find, has occurred; do let me know directly what it is. I have been walking all this way in complete suspense. We both abhor suspense. Do not let mine continue longer. It will do you good to speak of your distress, whatever it may be."

"Have you indeed no idea?" said Mrs. Weston in a trembling voice. "Cannot you, my dear Emma – cannot you form a guess as to what you are to hear?"

"So far as that it relates to Mr. Frank Churchill, I do guess."

"You are right. It does relate to him, and I will tell you directly;" (resuming her work, and seeming resolved against looking up.) "He has been here this very morning, on a most extraordinary errand. It is impossible to express our surprise. He came to speak to his father on a subject – to announce an attachment – "

She stopped to breathe. Emma thought first of herself, and then of Harriet.

"More than an attachment, indeed," resumed Mrs. Weston; "an engagement – a positive engagement. What will you say, Emma – what will anybody say – when it is known that Frank Churchill and Miss Fairfax are engaged; nay, that they have been long engaged!"

Emma even jumped with surprise; and, horror struck, exclaimed:

"Jane Fairfax! Good God! You are not serious? You do not mean it?"

"You may well be amazed," returned Mrs. Weston, still averting her eyes, and talking on with eagerness, that Emma might have time to recover – "You may well be amazed. But it is even so. There has been a solemn engagement between them ever since October – formed at Weymouth, and kept a secret from everybody. Not a creature knowing it but themselves – neither the Campbells, nor her family, nor his. It is so wonderful, that though perfectly convinced of the fact, it is yet almost incredible to myself. I can hardly believe it. I thought I knew him."

Emma scarcely heard what was said. Her mind was divided between two ideas her own former conversations with him about Miss Fairfax; and poor Harriet; and for some time she could only exclaim, and require confirmation, repeated confirmation.

"Well," said she at last, trying to recover herself; "this is a circumstance which I must think of at least half a day, before I can at all comprehend it. What! – engaged to her all the winter – before either of them came to Highbury?"

"Engaged since October – secretly engaged. It has hurt me, Emma, very much. It has hurt his father equally. *Some part* of his conduct we cannot excuse."

Emma pondered a moment, and then replied, "I will not pretend not to understand you; and to give you all the relief in my power, be assured that no such effect has followed his attentions to me, as you are apprehensive of."

Mrs. Weston looked up, afraid to believe; but Emma's countenance was as steady as her words.

"That you may have less difficulty in believing this boast, of my present perfect indifference," she continued, "I will farther tell you, that there was a period in the early part of our acquaintance, when I did like him – when I was very much disposed to be attached – to him nay, was attached and how it came to cease, is perhaps the wonder. Fortunately, however, it did cease. I have really for some time past – for at least these three months – cared nothing about him. You may believe me, Mrs. Weston. This is the simple truth."

Mrs. Weston kissed her with tears of joy; and when she could find utterance, assured her, that this protestation had done her more good than any thing else in the world could do.

"Mr. Weston will be almost as much relieved as myself," said she. "On this point we have been wretched. It was our darling wish that you might be attached to each other and we were persuaded that it was so. Imagine what we have been feeling on your account."

"I have escaped; and that I should escape, may be a matter of grateful wonder to you and myself. But this does not acquit him, Mrs. Weston; and I must say, that I think him greatly to blame. What right had he to come among us with affection and faith engaged, and with manners so very disengaged? What right had he to endeavour to please, as he certainly did to distinguish any one young woman with persevering attention, as he certainly did – while he really belonged to another? How could he tell what mischief he might be doing? How could he tell that he might not be making me in love with him? very wrong, very wrong indeed."

"From something that he said, my dear Emma, I rather imagine – "

"And how could *she* bear such behaviour! Composure with a witness! to look on, while repeated attentions were offering to another woman, before her face, and not resent it. That is a degree of placidity, which I can neither comprehend nor respect."

"There were misunderstandings between them, Emma; he said so expressly. He had not time to enter into much explanation. He was here only a quarter of an hour, and in a state of agitation which did not allow the full use even of the time he could stay –

but that there had been misunderstandings he decidedly said. The present crisis, indeed, seemed to be brought on by them; and those misunderstandings might very possibly arise from the impropriety of his conduct."

"Impropriety! Oh! Mrs. Weston it is too calm a censure. Much, much beyond impropriety! It has sunk him – I cannot say how it has sunk him in my opinion. So unlike what a man should be! None of that upright integrity, that strict adherence to truth and principle, that disdain of trick and littleness, which a man should display in every transaction of his life."

"Nay, dear Emma, now I must take his part; for though he has been wrong in this instance, I have known him long enough to answer for his having many, very many, good qualities; and – "

"Good God!" cried Emma, not attending to her. "Mrs. Smallridge, too! Jane actually on the point of going as governess! What could he mean by such horrible indelicacy? To suffer her to engage herself – to suffer her even to think of such a measure!"

"He knew nothing about it, Emma. On this article I can fully acquit him. It was a private resolution of hers, not communicated to him or at least not communicated in a way to carry conviction. Till yesterday, I know he said he was in the dark as to her plans. They burst on him, I do not know how, but by some letter or message – and it was the discovery of what she was doing, of this very project of hers, which determined him to come forward at once, own it all to his uncle, throw himself on his kindness, and, in short, put an end to the miserable state of concealment that had been carrying on so long."

Emma began to listen better.

"I am to hear from him soon," continued Mrs. Weston. "He told me at parting, that he should soon write; and he spoke in a manner which seemed to promise me many particulars that could not be given now. Let us wait, therefore, for this letter. It may bring many extenuations. It may make many things intelligible and excusable which now are not to be understood. Don't let us be severe, don't let us be in a hurry to condemn him. Let us have patience. I must love him; and now that I am satisfied on one point, the one material point, I am sincerely anxious for its all turning out well, and ready to hope that it may. They must both have suffered a great deal under such a system of secrecy and concealment."

"*His* sufferings," replied Emma dryly, "do not appear to have done him much harm. Well, and how did Mr. Churchill take it?"

"Most favourably for his nephew – gave his consent with scarcely a difficulty. Conceive what the events of a week have done in that family! While poor Mrs. Churchill lived, I suppose there could not have been a hope, a chance, a possibility; but scarcely are her remains at rest in the family vault, than her husband is persuaded to act exactly opposite to what she would have required. What a blessing it is, when undue influence does not survive the grave! He gave his consent with very little persuasion."

"Ah!" thought Emma, "he would have done as much for Harriet."

"This was settled last night, and Frank was off with the light this morning. He stopped at Highbury, at the Bates's, I fancy, some time and then came on hither; but was in such a hurry to get back to his uncle, to whom he is just now more necessary than ever, that, as I tell you, he could stay with us but a quarter of an hour. He was very much agitated – very much indeed – to a degree that made him appear quite a different creature from any thing I had ever seen him before. In addition to all the rest, there had been the shock of finding her so very unwell, which he had had no previous suspicion of and there was every appearance of his having been feeling a great deal."

"And do you really believe the affair to have been carrying on with such perfect secrecy? The Campbells, the Dixons – did none of them know of the engagement?"

Emma could not speak the name of Dixon without a little blush.

"None; not one. He positively said that it had been known to no being in the world but their two selves."

"Well," said Emma, "I suppose we shall gradually grow reconciled to the idea, and I wish them very happy. But I shall always think it a very abominable sort of proceeding. What has it been but a system of hypocrisy and deceit, espionage, and treachery? To come among us with professions of openness and simplicity; and such a league in secret to judge us all! Here have we been, the whole winter and spring, completely duped, fancying ourselves all on an equal footing of truth and honour, with two people in the midst of us who may have been carrying around, comparing and sitting in judgment on sentiments and words that were never meant for both to hear. They must take the consequence, if they have heard each other spoken of in a way not perfectly agreeable!"

"I am quite easy on that head," replied Mrs. Weston. "I am very sure that I never said any thing of either to the other, which both might not have heard."

"You are in luck. Your only blunder was confined to my ear, when you imagined a certain friend of ours in love with the lady."

"True. But as I have always had a thoroughly good opinion of Miss Fairfax, I never could, under any blunder, have spoken ill of her; and as to speaking ill of him, there I must have been safe."

At this moment Mr. Weston appeared at a little distance from the window, evidently on the watch. His wife gave him a look which invited him in; and, while he was coming around, added:

"Now, dearest Emma, let me intreat you to say and look everything that may set his heart at ease, and incline him to be satisfied with the match. Let us make the best of it – and, indeed, almost everything may be fairly said in her favour. It is not a connection to gratify; but if Mr. Churchill does not feel that, why should we? and it may be a very fortunate circumstance for him – for Frank, I mean – that he should have attached himself to a girl of such steadiness of character and good judgment as I have always given her credit for and still am disposed to give her credit for, in spite of this one great deviation from the strict rule of right. And how much may be said in her situation for even that error!"

"Much, indeed!" cried Emma feelingly. "If a woman can ever be excused for thinking only of herself, it is in a situation like Jane Fairfax's. Of such, one may almost say, that 'the world is not their's, nor the world's law.'"

She met Mr. Weston on his entrance, with a smiling countenance, exclaiming:

"A very pretty trick you have been playing me, upon my word! This was a device, I suppose, to sport with my curiosity, and exercise my talent of guessing. But you really frightened me. I thought you had lost half your property, at least. And here, instead of its being a matter of condolence, it turns out to be one of congratulation. I congratulate you, Mr. Weston, with all my heart, on the prospect of having one of the most lovely and accomplished young women in England for your daughter."

A glance or two between him and his wife, convinced him that all was as right as this speech proclaimed; and its happy effect on his spirits was immediate. His air and voice recovered their usual briskness: he shook her heartily and gratefully by the hand, and entered on the subject in a manner to prove, that he now only wanted time and persuasion to think the engagement no very bad thing. His companions suggested only what could palliate imprudence, or smooth objections; and by the time they had talked it all over together, and he had talked it all over again with Emma, in their walk back to Hartfield, he was become perfectly reconciled, and not far from thinking it the very best thing that Frank could possibly have done.

# *Chapter 47*

HARRIET, POOR Harriet!" – Those were the words; in them lay the tormenting ideas which Emma could not get rid of, and which constituted the real misery of the business to her. Frank Churchill had behaved very ill by herself – very ill in many ways – but it was not so much *his* behaviour as her *own,* which made her so angry with him. It was the scrape which he had drawn her into on Harriet's account, that gave the deepest hue to his offence. Poor Harriet! to be a second time the dupe of her misconceptions and flattery. Mr. Knightley had spoken prophetically, when he once said, "Emma, you have been no friend to Harriet Smith." She was afraid she had done her nothing but disservice. It was true that she had not to charge herself, in this instance as in the former, with being the sole and original author of the mischief; with having suggested such feelings as might otherwise never have entered Harriet's imagination; for Harriet had acknowledged her admiration and preference of Frank Churchill before she had ever given her a hint on the subject; but she felt completely guilty of having encouraged what she might have repressed. She might have prevented the indulgence and increase of such sentiments. Her influence would have been enough. And now she was very conscious that she ought to have prevented them. She felt that she had been risking her friend's happiness on most insufficient grounds. Common sense would have directed her to tell Harriet, that she must not allow herself to think of him, and that there were five hundred chances to one against his ever caring for her. "But, with common sense," she added, "I am afraid I have had little to do."

She was extremely angry with herself. If she could not have been angry with Frank Churchill too, it would have been dreadful. As for Jane Fairfax, she might at least relieve her feelings from any present solicitude on her account. Harriet would be anxiety enough; she need no longer be unhappy about Jane, whose troubles and whose ill health having, of course, the same origin, must be equally under cure. Her days of insignificance and evil were over. She would soon be well, and happy, and prosperous. Emma could now imagine why her own attentions had been slighted. This discovery laid many smaller matters open. No doubt it had been from jealousy. In Jane's eyes she had been a rival; and well might any thing she could offer of assistance or regard be repulsed. An airing in the Hartfield carriage would have been the rack, and arrowroot from the Hartfield storeroom must have been poison. She understood it all; and as far as her mind could disengage itself from the injustice and selfishness of angry feelings, she acknowledged that Jane Fairfax would have neither elevation nor happiness beyond her desert. But poor Harriet was such an engrossing charge! There was little sympathy to be spared for anybody else. Emma was sadly fearful that this second disappointment would be more severe than the first. Considering the very superior claims of the object, it ought; and judging by its apparently stronger effect on Harriet's mind, producing reserve and self command, it would. She must communicate the painful truth, however, and as soon as possible. An injunction of secrecy had been among Mr. Weston's parting words. "For the present, the whole affair was to be completely a secret. Mr. Churchill had made a point of it, as a token of respect to the wife he had so very recently lost; and everybody admitted it to be no more than due decorum." Emma had promised; but still Harriet must be excepted. It was her superior duty.

In spite of her vexation, she could not help feeling it almost ridiculous, that she should have the very same distressing and delicate office to perform by Harriet, which Mrs. Weston had just gone through by herself. The intelligence, which had been so anxiously announced to her, she was now to be anxiously announcing to another. Her heart beat quick on hearing Harriet's footstep and voice; so, she supposed, had poor Mrs. Weston felt when she was approaching Randalls. Could the event of the disclosure bear an equal resemblance! But of that, unfortunately, there could be no chance.

"Well, Miss Woodhouse!" cried Harriet, coming eagerly into the room "is not this the oddest news that ever was?"

"What news do you mean?" replied Emma, unable to guess, by look or voice, whether Harriet could indeed have received any hint.

"About Jane Fairfax. Did you ever hear any thing so strange? Oh! – you need not be afraid of owning it to me, for Mr. Weston has told me himself. I met him just now. He told me it was to be a great secret; and, therefore, I should not think of mentioning it to anybody but you, but he said you knew it."

"What did Mr. Weston tell you?" said Emma, still perplexed.

"Oh! he told me all about it; that Jane Fairfax and Mr. Frank Churchill are to be married, and that they have been privately engaged to one another this long while. How very odd!"

It was, indeed, so odd; Harriet's behaviour was so extremely odd, that Emma did not know how to understand it. Her character appeared absolutely changed. She seemed to propose showing no agitation, or disappointment, or peculiar concern in the discovery. Emma looked at her, quite unable to speak.

"Had you any idea," cried Harriet, "of his being in love with her? You, perhaps, might. You (blushing as she spoke) who can see into everybody's heart; but nobody else – "

"Upon my word," said Emma, "I begin to doubt my having any such talent. Can you seriously ask me, Harriet, whether I imagined him attached to another woman at the very time that I was – tacitly if not openly – encouraging you to give way to your own feelings? I never had the slightest suspicion, till within the last hour, of Mr. Frank Churchill's having the least regard for Jane Fairfax. You may be very sure that if I had, I should have cautioned you accordingly."

"Me!" cried Harriet, colouring, and astonished. "Why should

you caution me? You do not think I care about Mr. Frank Churchill."

"I am delighted to hear you speak so stoutly on the subject," replied Emma, smiling; "but you do not mean to deny that there was a time – and not very distant either – when you gave me reason to understand that you did care about him?"

"Him! – never, never. Dear Miss Woodhouse, how could you so mistake me?" turning away distressed.

"Harriet!" cried Emma, after a moment's pause "What do you mean? – Good Heavens! what do you mean? – Mistake you! – Am I to suppose then?"

She could not speak another word. Her voice was lost; and she sat down, waiting in great terror till Harriet should answer.

Harriet, who was standing at some distance, and with face turned from her, did not immediately say any thing; and when she did speak, it was in a voice nearly as agitated as Emma's.

"I should not have thought it possible," she began, "that you could have misunderstood me! I know we agreed never to name him – but considering how infinitely superior he is to everybody else, I should not have thought it possible that I could be supposed to mean any other person. Mr. Frank Churchill, indeed! I do not know who would ever look at him in the company of the other. I hope I have a better taste than to think of Mr. Frank Churchill, who is like nobody by his side. And that you should have been so mistaken, is amazing! – I am sure, but for believing that you entirely approved and meant to encourage me in my attachment, I should have considered it at first too great a presumption almost, to dare to think of him. At first, if you had not told me that more wonderful things had happened; that there had been matches of greater disparity (those were your very words); I should not have dared to give way to – I should not have thought it possible But if *you,* who had been always acquainted with him – "

"Harriet!" cried Emma, collecting herself resolutely "Let us understand each other now, without the possibility of farther mistake. Are you speaking of – Mr. Knightley?"

"To be sure I am. I never could have an idea of anybody else and so I thought you knew. When we talked about him, it was as clear as possible."

"Not quite," returned Emma, with forced calmness, "for all that you then said, appeared to me to relate to a different person. I could almost assert that you had *named* Mr. Frank Churchill. I am sure the service Mr. Frank Churchill had rendered you, in protecting you from the gypsies, was spoken of."

"Oh! Miss Woodhouse, how you do forget!"

"My dear Harriet, I perfectly remember the substance of what I said on the occasion. I told you that I did not wonder at your attachment; that considering the service he had rendered you, it was extremely natural: and you agreed to it, expressing yourself very warmly as to your sense of that service, and mentioning even what your sensations had been in seeing him come forward to your rescue. The impression of it is strong on my memory."

"Oh, dear," cried Harriet, "now I recollect what you mean; but I was thinking of something very different at the time. It was not the gypsies – it was not Mr. Frank Churchill that I meant. No! (with some elevation) I was thinking of a much more precious circumstance – of Mr. Knightley's coming and asking me to dance, when Mr. Elton would not stand up with me; and when there was no other partner in the room. That was the kind action; that was the noble benevolence and generosity; that was the service which made me begin to feel how superior he was to every other being upon earth."

"Good God!" cried Emma, "this has been a most unfortunate – most deplorable mistake! What is to be done?"

"You would not have encouraged me, then, if you had understood me? At least, however, I cannot be worse off than I should have been, if the other had been the person; and now – it *is* possible – "

She paused a few moments. Emma could not speak.

"I do not wonder, Miss Woodhouse," she resumed, "that you should feel a great difference between the two, as to me or as to anybody. You must think one five hundred million times more above me than the other. But I hope, Miss Woodhouse, that supposing – that if – strange as it may appear – But you know they were your own words, that *more* wonderful things had happened, matches of *greater* disparity had taken place than between Mr. Frank Churchill and me; and, therefore, it seems as if such a thing even as this, may have occurred before – and if I should be so fortunate, beyond expression, as to – if Mr. Knightley should really – if *he* does not mind the disparity, I hope, dear Miss Woodhouse, you will not set yourself against it, and try to put difficulties in the way. But you are too good for that, I am sure."

Harriet was standing at one of the windows. Emma turned round to look at her in consternation, and hastily said:

"Have you any idea of Mr. Knightley's returning your affection?"

"Yes," replied Harriet modestly, but not fearfully: "I must say that I have."

Emma's eyes were instantly withdrawn; and she sat silently meditating, in a fixed attitude, for a few minutes. A few minutes were sufficient for making her acquainted with her own heart. A mind like hers, once opening to suspicion, made rapid progress. She touched she admitted she acknowledged the whole truth. Why was it so much worse that Harriet should be in love with Mr. Knightley, than with Frank Churchill? Why was the evil so dreadfully increased by Harriet's having some hope of a return? It darted through her, with the speed of an arrow, that Mr. Knightley must marry no one but herself!

Her own conduct, as well as her own heart, was before her in the same few minutes. She saw it all with a clearness which had never blessed her before. How improperly had she been acting by Harriet! How inconsiderate, how indelicate, how irrational, how unfeeling had been her conduct! What blindness, what madness, had led her on! It struck her with dreadful force, and she was ready to give it every bad name in the world. Some portion of respect for herself, however, in spite of all these demerits some concern for her own appearance, and a strong sense of justice by Harriet (there would be no need of *compassion* to the girl who believed herself loved by Mr. Knightley – but justice required that she should not be made unhappy by any coldness now,) gave Emma the resolution to sit and endure farther with calmness, with even apparent kindness. For her own advantage indeed, it was fit that the utmost extent of Harriet's hopes should be enquired into; and Harriet had done nothing to forfeit the regard and interest which had been so voluntarily formed and maintained or to deserve to be slighted by the person, whose counsels had never led her right. Rousing from reflection, therefore, and subduing her emotion, she turned to Harriet again, and, in a more inviting accent, renewed the conversation; for as to the subject which had first introduced it, the wonderful story of Jane Fairfax, that was quite sunk and lost. Neither of them thought but of Mr. Knightley and themselves.

Harriet, who had been standing in no unhappy reverie, was yet very glad to be called from it, by the now encouraging manner of such a judge, and such a friend as Miss Woodhouse, and only wanted invitation, to give the history of her hopes with great, though trembling delight. Emma's tremblings as she asked, and as she listened, were better concealed than Harriet's, but they were not less. Her voice was not unsteady; but her mind was in all the perturbation that such a development of self, such a burst of threatening evil, such a confusion of sudden and perplexing emotions, must create. She listened with much inward suffering, but with great outward patience, to Harriet's detail. Methodical, or well arranged, or very well delivered, it could not be expected to be; but it contained, when separated from all the feebleness and tautology of the narration, a substance to sink her spirit especially with the corroborating circumstances, which her own memory brought in favour of Mr. Knightley's most improved opinion of Harriet.

Harriet had been conscious of a difference in his behaviour ever since those two decisive dances. Emma knew that he had, on that occasion, found her much superior to his expectation. From that evening, or at least from the time of Miss Woodhouse's encouraging her to think of him, Harriet had begun to be sensible of his talking to her much more than he had been used to do, and of his having indeed quite a different manner towards her; a manner of kindness and sweetness! Latterly she had been more and more aware of it. When they had been all walking together, he had so often come and walked by her, and talked so very delightfully! He seemed to want to be acquainted with her. Emma knew it to have been very much the case. She had often observed the change, to almost the same extent. Harriet repeated expressions of approbation and praise from him – and Emma felt them to be in the closest agreement with what she had known of his opinion of Harriet. He praised her for being without art or affectation, for having simple, honest, generous, feelings. She knew that he saw such recommendations in Harriet; he had dwelt on them to her more than once. Much that lived in Harriet's memory, many little particulars of the notice she had received from him, a look, a speech, a removal from one chair to another, a compliment implied, a preference inferred, had been unnoticed, because unsuspected, by Emma. Circumstances that might swell to half an hour's relation, and contained multiplied proofs to her who had seen them, had passed undiscerned by her who now heard them; but the two latest occurrences to be mentioned – the two of strongest promise to Harriet – were not without some degree of witness from Emma herself. The first, was his walking with her apart from the others, in the lime-walk at Donwell, where they had been walking some time before Emma came, and he had taken pains (as she was convinced) to draw her from the rest to himself and at first, he had talked to her in a more particular way than he had ever done before – in a very particular way indeed! (Harriet could not recall it without a blush.) He seemed to be almost asking her, whether her affections were engaged. But as soon as she (Miss Woodhouse) appeared likely to join them, he changed the subject, and began talking about farming: The second, was his having sat talking with her nearly half an hour before Emma came back from her visit, the very last morning of his being at Hartfield – though, when he first came in, he had said that he could not stay five minutes – and his having told her, during their conversation, that though he must go to London, it was very much against his inclination that he left home at all, which was much more (as Emma felt) than he had acknowledged to her. The superior degree of confidence towards Harriet, which this one article marked, gave her severe pain.

On the subject of the first of the two circumstances, she did, after a little reflection, venture the following question. "Might he not? – Is not it possible, that when enquiring, as you thought, into the state of your affections, he might be alluding to Mr. Martin – he might have Mr. Martin's interest in view? But Harriet rejected the suspicion with spirit.

"Mr. Martin! No indeed! – There was not a hint of Mr. Martin. I hope I know better now, than to care for Mr. Martin, or to be suspected of it."

When Harriet had closed her evidence, she appealed to her dear Miss Woodhouse, to say whether she had not good ground for hope.

"I never should have presumed to think of it at first," said she, "but for you. You told me to observe him carefully, and let his behaviour be the rule of mine – and so I have. But now I seem to feel that I may deserve him; and that if he does choose me, it will not be any thing so very wonderful."

The bitter feelings occasioned by this speech, the many bitter feelings, made the utmost exertion necessary on Emma's side, to enable her to say on reply:

"Harriet, I will only venture to declare, that Mr. Knightley is the last man in the world, who would intentionally give any woman the idea of his feeling for her more than he really does."

Harriet seemed ready to worship her friend for a sentence so satisfactory; and Emma was only saved from raptures and fondness, which at that moment would have been dreadful penance, by the sound of her father's footsteps. He was coming through the hall. Harriet was too much agitated to encounter him. "She could not compose herself – Mr. Woodhouse would be alarmed – she had better go;" with most ready encouragement from her friend, therefore, she passed off through another door – and the moment she was gone, this was the spontaneous burst of Emma's feelings: "Oh God! that I had never seen her!"

The rest of the day, the following night, were hardly enough for her thoughts. She was bewildered amidst the confusion of all that had rushed on her within the last few hours. Every moment had brought a fresh surprise; and every surprise must be matter of humiliation to her. How to understand it all! How to understand the deceptions she had been thus practising on herself, and living under! The blunders, the blindness of her own head and heart! she sat still, she walked about, she tried her own room, she tried the shrubbery – in every place, every posture, she perceived that she had acted most weakly; that she had been imposed on by others in a most mortifying degree; that she had been imposing on herself in a degree yet more mortifying; that she was wretched, and should probably find this day but the beginning of wretchedness.

To understand, thoroughly understand her own heart, was the first endeavour. To that point went every leisure moment which her father's claims on her allowed, and every moment of involuntary absence of mind.

How long had Mr. Knightley been so dear to her, as every

feeling declared him now to be? When had his influence, such influence begun? When had he succeeded to that place in her affection, which Frank Churchill had once, for a short period, occupied? – She looked back; she compared the two – compared them, as they had always stood in her estimation, from the time of the latter's becoming known to her – and as they must at any time have been compared by her, had it – oh! had it, by any blessed felicity, occurred to her, to institute the comparison. She saw that there never had been a time when she did not consider Mr. Knightley as infinitely the superior, or when his regard for her had not been infinitely the most dear. She saw, that in persuading herself, in fancying, in acting to the contrary, she had been entirely under a delusion, totally ignorant of her own heart – and, in short, that she had never really cared for Frank Churchill at all!

This was the conclusion of the first series of reflection. This was the knowledge of herself, on the first question of inquiry, which she reached; and without being long in reaching it. She was most sorrowfully indignant; ashamed of every sensation but the one revealed to her – her affection for Mr. Knightley. Every other part of her mind was disgusting.

With insufferable vanity had she believed herself in the secret of everybody's feelings; with unpardonable arrogance proposed to arrange everybody's destiny. She was proved to have been universally mistaken; and she had not quite done nothing – for she had done mischief. She had brought evil on Harriet, on herself, and she too much feared, on Mr. Knightley. Were this most unequal of all connections to take place, on her must rest all the reproach of having given it a beginning; for his attachment, she must believe to be produced only by a consciousness of Harriet's; and even were this not the case, he would never have known Harriet at all but for her folly.

Mr. Knightley and Harriet Smith! It was a union to distance every wonder of the kind. The attachment of Frank Churchill and Jane Fairfax became commonplace, threadbare, stale in the comparison, exciting no surprise, presenting no disparity, affording nothing to be said or thought. Mr. Knightley and Harriet Smith! Such an elevation on her side! Such a debasement on his! It was horrible to Emma to think how it must sink him in the general opinion, to foresee the smiles, the sneers, the merriment it would prompt at his expense; the mortification and disdain of his brother, the thousand inconveniences to himself. Could it be? No; it was impossible. And yet it was far, very far, from impossible. Was it a new circumstance for a man of first-rate abilities to be captivated by very inferior powers? Was it new for one, perhaps too busy to seek, to be the prize of a girl who would seek him? Was it new for any thing in this world to be unequal, inconsistent, incongruous – or for chance and circumstance (as second causes) to direct the human fate?

Oh! had she never brought Harriet forward! Had she left her where she ought, and where he had told her she ought! Had she not, with a folly which no tongue could express, prevented her marrying the unexceptionable young man who would have made her happy and respectable in the line of life to which she ought to belong all would have been safe; none of this dreadful sequel would have been.

How Harriet could ever have had the presumption to raise her thoughts to Mr. Knightley! How she could dare to fancy herself the chosen of such a man till actually assured of it! But Harriet was less humble, had fewer scruples than formerly. Her inferiority, whether of mind or situation, seemed little felt. She had seemed more sensible of Mr. Elton's being to stoop in marrying her, than she now seemed of Mr. Knightley's. Alas! was not that her own doing too? Who had been at pains to give Harriet notions of self-consequence but herself? Who but herself had taught her, that she was to elevate herself if possible, and that her claims were great to a high worldly establishment? If Harriet, from being humble, were grown vain, it was her doing too.

# *Chapter 48*

TILL NOW that she was threatened with its loss, Emma had never known how much of her happiness depended on being *first* with Mr. Knightley, first in interest and affection. Satisfied that it was so, and feeling it her due, she had enjoyed it without reflection; and only in the dread of being supplanted, found how inexpressibly important it had been. Long, very long, she felt she had been first; for, having no female connections of his own, there had been only Isabella whose claims could be compared with hers, and she had always known exactly how far he loved and esteemed Isabella. She had herself been first with him for many years past. She had not deserved it; she had often been negligent or perverse, slighting his advice, or even wilfully opposing him, insensible of half his merits, and quarrelling with him because he would not acknowledge her false and insolent estimate of her own – but still, from family attachment and habit, and thorough excellence of mind, he had loved her, and watched over her from a girl, with an endeavour to improve her, and an anxiety for her doing right, which no other creature had at all shared. In spite of all her faults, she knew she was dear to him; might she not say, very dear? When the suggestions of hope, however, which must follow here, presented themselves, she could not presume to indulge them. Harriet Smith might think herself not unworthy of being peculiarly, exclusively, passionately loved by Mr. Knightley. *She* could not. She could not flatter herself with any idea of blindness in his attachment to *her*. She had received a very recent proof of its impartiality. How shocked had he been by her behaviour to Miss Bates! How directly, how strongly had he expressed himself to her on the subject! Not too strongly for the offence – but far, far too strongly to issue from any feeling softer than upright justice and clear-sighted goodwill. She had no hope, nothing to deserve the name of hope, that he could have that sort of affection for herself which was now in question; but there was a hope (at times a slight one, at times much stronger,) that Harriet might have deceived herself, and be overrating his regard for *her*. Wish it she must, for his sake – be the consequence nothing to herself, but his remaining single all his life. Could she be secure of that, indeed, of his never marrying at all, she believed she should be perfectly satisfied. Let him but continue the same Mr. Knightley to her and her father, the same Mr. Knightley to all the world; let Donwell and Hartfield lose none of their precious intercourse of friendship and confidence, and her peace would be fully secured. Marriage, in fact, would not do for her. It would be incompatible with what she owed to her father, and with what she felt for him. Nothing should separate her from her father. She would not marry, even if she were asked by Mr. Knightley.

It must be her ardent wish that Harriet might be disappointed; and she hoped, that when able to see them together again, she might at least be able to ascertain what the chances for it were. She should see them henceforward with the closest observance; and wretchedly as she had hitherto misunderstood even those she was watching, she did not know how to admit that she could be blinded here. He was expected back every day. The power of observation would be soon given frightfully soon it appeared when her thoughts were in one course. In the meanwhile, she resolved against seeing Harriet. It would do neither of them good, it would do the subject no good, to be talking of it farther. She was resolved not to be convinced, as long as she could doubt, and yet had no authority for opposing Harriet's confidence. To talk would be only to irritate. She wrote to her, therefore, kindly, but decisively, to beg that she would not, at present, come to Hartfield; acknowledging it to be her conviction, that all farther confidential discussion of *one* topic had better be avoided; and hoping, that if a few days were allowed to pass before they met again, except in the company of others – she objected only to a *tête-à-tête* – they might be able to act as if they had forgotten the conversation of yesterday. Harriet submitted, and approved, and was grateful.

This point was just arranged, when a visitor arrived to tear Emma's thoughts a little from the one subject which had engrossed them, sleeping or waking, the last twenty-four hours – Mrs. Weston, who had been calling on her daughter-in-law elect, and took Hartfield in her way home, almost as much in duty to Emma as in pleasure to herself, to relate all the particulars of so interesting an interview.

Mr. Weston had accompanied her to Mrs. Bates's, and gone through his share of this essential attention most handsomely; but she having then induced Miss Fairfax to join her in an airing, was now returned with much more to say, and much more to say with satisfaction, than a quarter of an hour spent in Mrs. Bates's parlour, with all the encumbrance of awkward feelings, could have afforded.

A little curiosity Emma had; and she made the most of it while her friend related. Mrs. Weston had set off to pay the visit in a good deal of agitation herself; and in the first place had wished not to go at all at present, to be allowed merely to write to Miss Fairfax instead, and to defer this ceremonious call till a little time had passed, and Mr. Churchill could be reconciled to the engagement's becoming known; as, considering everything, she thought such a visit could not be paid without leading to reports: but Mr. Weston had thought differently; he was extremely anxious to show his approbation to Miss Fairfax and her family, and did not conceive that any suspicion could be excited by it; or if it were, that it would be of any consequence; for "such things," he observed, "always got about." Emma smiled, and felt that Mr. Weston had very good reason for saying so. They had gone, in short – and very great had been the evident distress and confusion of the lady. She had hardly been able to speak a word, and every look and action had shown how deeply she was suffering from consciousness. The quiet, heart felt satisfaction of the old lady, and the rapturous delight of her daughter who proved even too joyous to talk as usual, had been a gratifying, yet almost an affecting, scene. They were both so truly respectable in their happiness, so disinterested in every sensation; thought so much of Jane; so much of everybody, and so little of themselves, that every kindly feeling was at work for them. Miss Fairfax's recent illness had offered a fair plea for Mrs. Weston to invite her to an airing; she had drawn back and declined at first, but, on being pressed had yielded; and, in the course of their drive, Mrs. Weston had, by gentle encouragement, overcome so much of her embarrassment, as to bring her to converse on the important subject. Apologies for her seemingly ungracious silence in their first reception, and the warmest expressions of the gratitude she was always feeling towards herself and Mr. Weston, must necessarily open the cause; but when these effusions were put by, they had talked a good deal of the present and of the future state of the engagement. Mrs. Weston was convinced that such conversation must be the greatest relief to her companion, pent up within her own mind as everything had so long been, and was very much pleased with all that she had said on the subject.

"On the misery of what she had suffered, during the concealment of so many months," continued Mrs. Weston, "she was energetic. This was one of her expressions. 'I will not say, that since I entered into the engagement I have not had some happy moments; but I can say, that I have never known the blessing of one tranquil hour:' – and the quivering lip, Emma, which uttered it, was an attestation that I felt at my heart."

"Poor girl!" said Emma. "She thinks herself wrong, then, for having consented to a private engagement?"

"Wrong! No one, I believe, can blame her more than she is disposed to blame herself. 'The consequence,' said she, 'has been a state of perpetual suffering to me; and so it ought. But after all the punishment that misconduct can bring, it is still not less misconduct. Pain is no expiation. I never can be blameless. I have been acting contrary to all my sense of right; and the fortunate turn that everything has taken, and the kindness I am now receiving, is what my conscience tells me ought not to be.' 'Do not imagine, madam,' she continued, 'that I was taught wrong. Do not let any reflection fall on the principles or the care of the friends who brought me up. The error has been all my own; and I do assure you that, with all the excuse that present circumstances may appear to give, I shall yet dread making the story known to Colonel Campbell.' "

"Poor girl!" said Emma again. "She loves him then excessively, I suppose. It must have been from attachment only, that she could be led to form the engagement. Her affection must have overpowered her judgment."

"Yes, I have no doubt of her being extremely attached to him."

"I am afraid," returned Emma, sighing, "that I must often have contributed to make her unhappy."

"On your side, my love, it was very innocently done. But she probably had something of that in her thoughts, when alluding to the misunderstandings which he had given us hints of before. One natural consequence of the evil she had involved herself in," she said, "was that of making her *unreasonable*. The consciousness of having done amiss, had exposed her to a thousand inquietudes, and made her captious and irritable to a degree that must have been – that had been – hard for him to bear. 'I did not make the allowances,' said she, 'which I ought to have done, for his temper and spirits – his delightful spirits and that gaiety, that playfulness of disposition, which, under any other circumstances, would, I am sure, have been as constantly bewitching to me, as they were at first.' She then began to speak of you, and of the great kindness you had shown her during her illness; and with a blush which showed me how it was all connected, desired me, whenever I had an opportunity, to thank you – I could not thank you too much – for every wish and every endeavour to do her good. She was sensible that you had never received any proper acknowledgment from herself."

"If I did not know her to be happy now," said Emma, seriously, "which, in spite of every little drawback from her scrupulous conscience, she must be, I could not bear these thanks; for, oh! Mrs. Weston, if there were an account drawn up of the evil and the good I have done Miss Fairfax! – Well (checking herself, and trying to be more lively), this is all to be forgotten. You are very kind to bring me these interesting particulars. They show her to the greatest advantage. I am sure she is very good I hope she will be very happy. It is fit that the fortune should be on his side, for I think the merit will be all on hers."

Such a conclusion could not pass unanswered by Mrs. Weston. She thought well of Frank in almost every respect; and, what was more, she loved him very much, and her defence was, therefore, earnest. She talked with a great deal of reason, and at least equal affection but she had too much to urge for Emma's attention; it was soon gone to Brunswick Square or to Donwell; she forgot to attempt to listen; and when Mrs. Weston ended with, "We have not yet had the letter we are so anxious for, you know, but I hope it will soon come," she was obliged to pause before she answered, and at last obliged to answer at random, before she could at all recollect what letter it was which they were so anxious for.

"Are you well, my Emma?" was Mrs. Weston's parting question.

"Oh! perfectly. I am always well, you know. Be sure to give me intelligence of the letter as soon as possible."

Mrs. Weston's communications furnished Emma with more food for unpleasant reflection, by increasing her esteem and compassion, and her sense of past injustice towards Miss Fairfax. She bitterly regretted not having sought a closer acquaintance with her, and blushed for the envious feelings which had certainly been, in some measure, the cause. Had she followed Mr. Knightley's known wishes, in paying that attention to Miss Fairfax, which was every way her due; had she tried to know her better; had she done her part towards intimacy; had she endeavoured to find a friend there instead of in Harriet Smith; she must, in all probability, have been spared from every pain which pressed on her now. Birth, abilities, and education, had been equally marking one as an associate for her, to be received with gratitude; and the other – what was she? Supposing even that they had never become intimate friends; that she had never been admitted into Miss Fairfax's confidence on this important matter – which was most probable – still, in knowing her as she ought, and as she might, she must have been preserved from the abominable suspicions of an improper attachment to Mr. Dixon, which she had not only so foolishly fashioned and harboured herself, but had so unpardonably imparted; an idea which she greatly feared had been made a subject of material distress to the delicacy of Jane's feelings, by the levity or carelessness of Frank Churchill's. Of all the sources of evil surrounding the former, since her coming to Highbury, she was persuaded that she must herself have been the worst. She must have been a perpetual enemy. They never could have been all three together, without her having stabbed Jane Fairfax's peace in a thousand instances; and on Box Hill, perhaps, it had been the agony of a mind that would bear no more.

The evening of this day was very long, and melancholy, at Hartfield. The weather added what it could of gloom. A cold stormy rain set in, and nothing of July appeared but in the trees and shrubs, which the wind was despoiling, and the length of the day, which only made such cruel sights the longer visible.

The weather affected Mr. Woodhouse, and he could only be kept tolerably comfortable by almost ceaseless attention on his daughter's side, and by exertions which had never cost her half so much before. It reminded her of their first forlorn *tête-à-tête,* on the evening of Mrs. Weston's wedding-day; but Mr. Knightley had walked in then, soon after tea, and dissipated every melancholy fancy. Alas! such delightful proofs of Hartfield's attraction, as those sort of visits conveyed, might shortly be over. The picture which she had then drawn of the privations of the approaching winter, had proved erroneous; no friends had deserted them, no pleasures had been lost. But her present forebodings she feared would experience no similar contradiction. The prospect before her now, was threatening to a degree that could not be entirely dispelled – that might not be even partially brightened. If all took place that might take place among the circle of her friends, Hartfield must be comparatively deserted; and she left to cheer her father with the spirits only of ruined happiness.

The child to be born at Randalls must be a tie there even dearer than herself; and Mrs. Weston's heart and time would be occupied by it. They should lose her; and, probably, in great measure, her husband also. Frank Churchill would return among them no more; and Miss Fairfax, it was reasonable to suppose, would soon cease to belong to Highbury. They would be married, and settled either at or near Enscombe. All that were good would be withdrawn; and if to these losses, the loss of Donwell were to be added, what would remain of cheerful or of rational society within their reach? Mr. Knightley to be no longer coming there for his evening comfort! No longer walking in at all hours, as if ever willing to change his own home for their's! How was it to be endured? And if he were to be lost to them for Harriet's sake; if he were to be thought of hereafter, as finding in Harriet's society all that he wanted; if Harriet were to be the chosen, the first, the dearest, the friend, the wife to whom he looked for all the best blessings of existence; what could be increasing Emma's wretchedness but the reflection never far distant from her mind, that it had been all her own work?

When it came to such a pitch as this, she was not able to refrain from a start, or a heavy sigh, or even from walking about the room for a few seconds and the only source whence any thing like consolation or composure could be drawn, was in the resolution of her own better conduct, and the hope that, however inferior in spirit and gaiety might be the following and every future winter of her life to the past, it would yet find her more rational, more acquainted with herself, and leave her less to regret when it were gone.

# Chapter 49

THE WEATHER continued much the same all the following morning; and the same loneliness, and the same melancholy, seemed to reign at Hartfield but in the afternoon it cleared; the wind changed into a softer quarter; the clouds were carried off; the sun appeared; it was summer again. With all the eagerness which such a transition gives, Emma resolved to be out of doors as soon as possible. Never had the exquisite sight, smell, sensation of nature, tranquil, warm, and brilliant after a storm, been more attractive to her. She longed for the serenity they might gradually introduce; and on Mr. Perry's coming in soon after dinner, with a disengaged hour to give her father, she lost no time ill hurrying into the shrubbery. There, with spirits freshened, and thoughts a little relieved, she had taken a few turns, when she saw Mr. Knightley passing through the garden door, and coming towards her. It was the first intimation of his being returned from London. She had been thinking of him the moment before, as unquestionably sixteen miles distant. There was time only for the quickest arrangement of mind. She must be composed and calm. In half a minute they were together. The "How-d'ye-do's" were quiet and constrained on each side. She asked after their mutual friends; they were all well. When had he left them? Only that morning. He must have had a wet ride. – Yes! – He meant to walk with her, she found. "He had just looked into the dining-room, and as he was not wanted there, preferred being out-of-doors." She thought he neither looked nor spoke cheerfully; and the first possible cause for it, suggested by her fears, was, that he had perhaps been communicating his plans to his brother, and was pained by the manner in which they had been received.

They walked together. He was silent. She thought he was often looking at her, and trying for a fuller view of her face than it suited her to give. And this belief produced another dread. Perhaps he wanted to speak to her, of his attachment to Harriet; he might be watching for encouragement to begin. She did not, could not, feel equal to lead the way to any such subject. He must do it all himself. Yet she could not bear this silence. With him it was most unnatural. She considered resolved and, trying to smile, began:

"You have some news to hear, now you are come back, that will rather surprise you."

"Have I?" said he quietly, and looking at her; "of what nature?"

"Oh! the best nature in the world – a wedding."

After waiting a moment, as if to be sure she intended to say no more, he replied:

"If you mean Miss Fairfax and Frank Churchill, I have heard that already."

"How is it possible?" cried Emma, turning her glowing cheeks towards him; for, while she spoke, it occurred to her that he might have called at Mrs. Goddard's on his way.

"I had a few lines on parish business from Mr. Weston this morning, and at the end of them he gave me a brief account of what had happened."

Emma was quite relieved, and could presently say, with a little more composure:

"*You* probably have been less surprised than any of us, for you have had your suspicions. I have not forgotten that you once tried to give me a caution. I wish I had attended to it – but (with a sinking voice and a heavy sigh) I seem to have been doomed to blindness."

For a moment or two nothing was said, and she was unsuspicious of having excited any particular interest, till she found her arm drawn within his, and pressed against his heart, and heard him thus saying, in a tone of great sensibility, speaking low:

"Time, my dearest Emma, time will heal the wound. Your own excellent sense your exertions for your father's sake I know you will not allow yourself – " Her arm was pressed again, as he added, in a more broken and subdued accent, "The feelings of the warmest friendship – indignation – abominable scoundrel!" And in a louder, steadier tone, he concluded with, "He will soon be gone. They will soon be in Yorkshire. I am sorry for her. She deserves a better fate."

Emma understood him; and as soon as she could recover from the flutter of pleasure, excited by such tender consideration, replied:

"You are very kind but you are mistaken and I must set you right. I am not in want of that sort of compassion. My blindness to what was going on, led me to act by them in a way that I must always be ashamed of, and I was very foolishly tempted to say and do many things which may well lay me open to unpleasant conjectures, but I have no other reason to regret that I was not in the secret earlier."

"Emma!" cried he, looking eagerly at her, "are you, indeed?" – but checking himself – "No, no, I understand you – forgive me I am pleased that you can say even so much. He is no object of regret, indeed! and it will not be very long, I hope, before that becomes the acknowledgment of more than your reason. Fortunate that your affections were not farther entangled! I could never, I confess, from your manners, assure myself as to the degree of what you felt – I could only be certain that there was a preference – and a preference which I never believed him to deserve. He is a disgrace to the name of man. And is he to be rewarded with that sweet young woman? Jane, Jane, you will be a miserable creature."

"Mr. Knightley," said Emma, trying to be lively, but really confused – "I am in a very extraordinary situation. I cannot let you continue in your error; and yet, perhaps, since my manners gave such an impression, I have as much reason to be ashamed of confessing that I never have been at all attached to the person we are speaking of, as it might be natural for a woman to feel in confessing exactly the reverse. But I never have."

He listened in perfect silence. She wished him to speak, but he would not. She supposed she must say more before she were entitled to his clemency; but it was a hard case to be obliged still to lower herself in his opinion. She went on, however.

"I have very little to say for my own conduct. I was tempted by his attentions, and allowed myself to appear pleased. An old story, probably – a common case – and no more than has happened to hundreds of my sex before; and yet it may not be the more excusable in one who sets up as I do for Understanding. Many circumstances assisted the temptation. He was the son of Mr. Weston – he was continually here – I always found him very pleasant – and, in short, for (with a sigh) let me swell out the causes ever so ingeniously, they all centre in this at last – my vanity was flattered, and I allowed his attentions. Latterly, however – for some time, indeed – I have had no idea of their meaning any thing. I thought them a habit, a trick, nothing that called for seriousness on my side. He has imposed on me, but he has not injured me. I have never been attached to him. And now I can tolerably comprehend his behaviour. He never wished to attach me. It was merely a blind to conceal his real situation with another. It was his object to blind all about him; and no one, I am sure, could be more effectually blinded than myself – except that I was *not* blinded – that it was my good fortune – that, in short, I was somehow or other safe from him."

She had hoped for an answer here – for a few words to say that her conduct was at least intelligible; but he was silent; and, as far as she could judge, deep in thought. At last, and tolerably in his usual tone, he said:

"I have never had a high opinion of Frank Churchill. I can suppose, however, that I may have underrated him. My acquaintance with him has been but trifling. And even if I have not underrated him hitherto, he may yet turn out well. With such a woman he has a chance. I have no motive for wishing him ill –

and for her sake, whose happiness will be involved in his good character and conduct, I shall certainly wish him well."

"I have no doubt of their being happy together," said Emma; "I believe them to be very mutually and very sincerely attached."

"He is a most fortunate man!" returned Mr. Knightley, with energy. "So early in life – at thrcc-and-twenty – a period when, if a man chooses a wife, he generally chooses ill. At three-and-twenty to have drawn such a prize! What years of felicity that man, in all human calculation, has before him! Assured of the love of such a woman – the disinterested love – for Jane Fairfax's character vouches for her disinterestedness; everything in his favour – equality of situation – I mean, as far as regards society, and all the habits and manners that are important; equality in every point but one – and that one, since the purity of her heart is not to be doubted, such as must increase his felicity, for it will be his to bestow the only advantages she wants. A man would always wish to give a woman a better home than the one he takes her from; and he who can do it, where there is no doubt of her regard, must, I think, be the happiest of mortals. Frank Churchill is, indeed, the favourite of fortune. Everything turns out for his good. He meets with a young woman at a watering-place, gains her affection, cannot even weary her by negligent treatment – and had he and all his family sought round the world for a perfect wife for him, they could not have found her superior. His aunt is in the way. His aunt dies. He has only to speak. His friends are eager to promote his happiness. He had used everybody ill – and they are all delighted to forgive him. He is a fortunate man indeed!"

"You speak as if you envied him."

"And I do envy him, Emma. In one respect he is the object of my envy."

Emma could say no more. They seemed to be within half a sentence of Harriet, and her immediate feeling was to avert the subject, if possible. She made her plan; she would speak of something totally different – the children in Brunswick Square; and she only waited for breath to begin, when Mr. Knightley startled her, by saying:

"You will not ask me what is the point of envy. You are determined, I see, to have no curiosity. You are wise – but I cannot be wise. Emma, I must tell you what you will not ask, though I may wish it unsaid the next moment."

"Oh! then, don't speak it, don't speak it," she eagerly cried. "Take a little time, consider, do not commit yourself."

"Thank you," said he, in an accent of deep mortification, and not another syllable followed.

Emma could not bear to give him pain. He was wishing to confide in her – perhaps to consult her; cost her what it would, she would listen. She might assist his resolution, or reconcile him to it; she might give just praise to Harriet, or, by representing to him his own independence, relieve him from that state of indecision, which must be more intolerable than any alternative to such a mind as his. They had reached the house.

"You are going in, I suppose?" said he.

"No," replied Emma quite confirmed by the depressed manner in which he still spoke "I should like to take another turn. Mr. Perry is not gone." And, after proceeding a few steps, she added – "I stopped you ungraciously, just now, Mr. Knightley, and, I am afraid, gave you pain. But if you have any wish to speak openly to me as a friend, or to ask my opinion of any thing that you may have in contemplation – as a friend, indeed, you may command me. I will hear whatever you like. I will tell you exactly what I think."

"As a friend!" repeated Mr. Knightley. "Emma, that I fear is a word – no, I have no wish Stay, yes, why should I hesitate? I have gone too far already for concealment. Emma, I accept your offer, extraordinary as it may seem, I accept it, and refer myself to you as a friend. Tell me, then, have I no chance of ever succeeding?"

He stopped in his earnestness to look the question, and the expression of his eyes overpowered her.

"My dearest Emma," said he, "for dearest you will always be, whatever the event of this hour's conversation, my dearest, most beloved Emma – tell me at once. Say 'No,' if it is to be said." She could really say nothing. "You are silent," he cried, with great animation; "absolutely silent! at present I ask no more."

Emma was almost ready to sink under the agitation of this moment. The dread of being awakened from the happiest dream, was perhaps the most prominent feeling.

"I cannot make speeches, Emma:" he soon resumed; and in a tone of such sincere, decided, intelligible tenderness as was tolerably convincing. "If I loved you less, I might be able to talk about it more. But you know what I am. You hear nothing but truth from me. I have blamed you, and lectured you, and you have borne it as no other woman in England would have borne it. Bear with the truths I would tell you now, dearest Emma, as well as you have borne with them. The manner, perhaps, may have as little to recommend them. God knows, I have been a very indifferent lover. But you understand me. Yes, you see, you understand my feelings – and will return them if you can. At present, I ask only to hear – once to hear your voice."

While he spoke, Emma's mind was most busy, and, with all the wonderful velocity of thought, had been able – and yet without losing a word – to catch and comprehend the exact truth of the whole; to see that Harriet's hopes had been entirely groundless, a mistake, a delusion, as complete a delusion as any of her own – that Harriet was nothing; that she was everything herself; that what she had been saying relative to Harriet had been all taken as the language of her own feelings; and that her agitation, her doubts, her reluctance, her discouragement, had been all received as discouragement from herself. And not only was there time for these convictions, with all their glow of attendant happiness; there was time also to rejoice that Harriet's secret had not escaped her, and to resolve that it need not, and should not. It was all the service she could now render her poor friend; for as to any of that heroism of sentiment which might have prompted her to entreat him to transfer his affection from herself to Harriet, as infinitely the most worthy of the two – or even the more simple sublimity of resolving to refuse him at once and for ever, without vouchsafing any motive, because he could not marry them both – Emma had it not. She felt for Harriet, with pain and with contrition; but no flight of generosity run mad, opposing all that could be probable or reasonable, entered her brain. She had led her friend astray, and it would be a reproach to her for ever; but her judgment was as strong as her feelings, and as strong as it had ever been before, in reprobating any such alliance for him, as most unequal and degrading. Her way was clear, though not quite smooth. She spoke then, on being so entreated. What did she say? Just what she ought, of course. A lady always does. She said enough to show there need not be despair – and to invite him to say more himself. He *had* despaired at one period; he had received such an injunction to caution and silence, as for the time crushed every hope; she had begun by refusing to hear him. The change had perhaps been somewhat sudden; her proposal of taking another turn, her renewing the conversation which she had just put an end to, might be a little extraordinary! She felt its inconsistency; but Mr. Knightley was so obliging as to put up with it, and seek no farther explanation.

Seldom, very seldom, does complete truth belong to any human disclosure; seldom can it happen that something is not a little disguised, or a little mistaken; but where, as in this case, though the conduct is mistaken, the feelings are not, it may not be very material. Mr. Knightley could not impute to Emma a more relenting heart than she possessed, or a heart more disposed to accept of his.

He had, in fact, been wholly unsuspicious of his own influence. He had followed her into the shrubbery with no idea of trying it. He had come, in his anxiety to see how she bore Frank Churchill's engagement, with no selfish view, no view at all, but of endeavouring, if she allowed him an opening, to soothe or to counsel her. The rest had been the work of the moment, the immediate effect of what he heard, on his feelings. The delightful assurance of her total indifference towards Frank Churchill, of her having a heart completely disengaged from him, had given birth to the hope, that, in time, he might gain her affection himself; but it had been no present hope he had only, in the momentary conquest of eagerness over judgment, aspired to be told that she did not forbid his attempt to attach her. The superior hopes which gradually opened were so much the more enchanting. The affection, which he had been asking to be allowed to create, if he could, was already his! Within half an hour, he had passed from a thoroughly distressed state of mind, to something so like perfect happiness, that it could bear no other name.

Her change was equal. This one half hour had given to each the same precious certainty of being beloved, had cleared from each the same degree of ignorance, jealousy, or distrust. On his side, there had been a long-standing jealousy, old as the arrival, or even the expectation, of Frank Churchill. He had been in love with Emma, and jealous of Frank Churchill, from about the same period, one sentiment having probably enlightened him as to the other. It was his jealousy of Frank Churchill that had taken him from the country. The Box Hill party had decided him on going away. He would save himself from witnessing again such permitted, encouraged attentions. He had gone to learn to be indifferent. But he had gone to a wrong place. There was too much domestic happiness in his brother's house; woman wore too amiable a form in it; Isabella was too much like Emma – differing only in those striking inferiorities, which always brought the other in brilliancy before him, for much to have been done, even had his time been longer. He had stayed on, however, vigorously, day after day – till this very morning's post had conveyed the history of Jane Fairfax. Then, with the gladness which must be felt, nay, which he did not scruple to feel, having never believed Frank Churchill to be at all deserving Emma, was there so much fond solicitude, so much keen anxiety for her, that he could stay no longer. He had ridden home through the rain; and had walked up directly after dinner, to see how this sweetest and best of all creatures, faultless in spite of all her faults, bore the discovery.

He had found her agitated and low. Frank Churchill was a villain. He heard her declare that she had never loved him. Frank Churchill's character was not desperate. She was his own Emma, by hand and word, when they returned into the house; and if he could have thought of Frank Churchill then, he might have deemed him a very good sort of fellow.

# *Chapter 50*

WHAT TOTALLY different feelings did Emma take back into the house from what she had brought out! She had then been only daring to hope for a little respite of suffering; she was now in an exquisite flutter of happiness – and such happiness moreover as she believed must still be greater when the flutter should have passed away.

They sat down to tea – the same party round the same table – how often it had been collected! and how often had her eyes fallen on the same shrubs in the lawn, and observed the same beautiful effect of the western sun! But never in such a state of spirits, never in any thing like it; and it was with difficulty that she could summon enough of her usual self to be the attentive lady of the house, or even the attentive daughter.

Poor Mr. Woodhouse little suspected what was plotting against him in the breast of that man whom he was so cordially welcoming, and so anxiously hoping might not have taken cold from his ride. Could he have seen the heart, he would have cared very little for the lungs; but without the most distant imagination of the impending evil, without the slightest perception of any thing extraordinary in the looks or ways of either, he repeated to them very comfortably all the articles of news he had received from Mr. Perry, and talked on with much self-contentment, totally unsuspicious of what they could have told him in return.

As long as Mr. Knightley remained with them, Emma's fever continued; but when he was gone, she began to be a little tranquillised and subdued and in the course of the sleepless night, which was the tax for such an evening, she found one or two such very serious points to consider, as made her feel, that even her happiness must have some alloy. Her father – and Harriet. She could not be alone without feeling the full weight of their separate claims; and how to guard the comfort of both to the utmost, was the question. With respect to her father, it was a question soon answered. She hardly knew yet what Mr. Knightley would ask; but a very short parley with her own heart produced the most solemn resolution of never quitting her father. She even wept over the idea of it, as a sin of thought. While he lived, it must be only an engagement; but she flattered herself, that if divested of the danger of drawing her away, it might become an increase of comfort to him. How to do her best by Harriet, was of more difficult decision; how to spare her from any unnecessary pain; how to make her any possible atonement; how to appear least her enemy? On these subjects, her perplexity and distress were very great – and her mind had to pass again and again through every bitter reproach and sorrowful regret that had ever surrounded it. She could only resolve at last, that she would still avoid a meeting with her, and communicate all that need be told by letter; that it would be inexpressibly desirable to have her removed just now for a time from Highbury, and – indulging in one scheme more – nearly resolved, that it might be practicable to get an invitation for her to Brunswick Square. Isabella had been pleased with Harriet; and a few weeks spent in London must give her some amusement. She did not think it in Harriet's nature to escape being benefited by novelty and variety, by the streets, the shops, and the children. At any rate, it would be a proof of attention and kindness in herself, from whom everything was due; a separation for the present; an averting of the evil day, when they must all be together again.

She rose early, and wrote her letter to Harriet; an employment which left her so very serious, so nearly sad, that Mr. Knightley, in walking up to Hartfield to breakfast, did not arrive at all too soon; and half an hour stolen afterwards to go over the same ground again with him, literally and figuratively, was quite necessary to reinstate her in a proper share of the happiness of the evening before.

He had not left her long – by no means long enough for her to have the slightest inclination for thinking of anybody else – when a letter was brought to her from Randalls – a very thick letter; she guessed what it must contain, and deprecated the necessity of reading it. She was now in perfect charity with Frank Churchill; she wanted no explanations, she wanted only to have her thoughts to herself – and as for understanding any thing he wrote, she was sure she was incapable of it. It must be waded through, however. She opened the packet; it was too surely so; a note from Mrs. Weston to herself, ushered in the letter from Frank to Mrs. Weston:

> "I have the greatest pleasure, my dear Emma, in forwarding to you the enclosed. I know what thorough justice you will do it, and have scarcely a doubt of its happy effect. I think we shall never materially disagree about the writer again; but I will not delay you by a long preface. We are quite well. This letter has been the cure

of all the little nervousness I have been feeling lately. I did not quite like your looks on Tuesday, but it was an ungenial morning; and though you will never own being affected by weather, I think everybody feels a north-east wind. I felt for your dear father very much in the storm of Tuesday afternoon and yesterday morning, but had the comfort of hearing last night, by Mr. Perry, that it had not made him ill. – Yours ever,

A. W.

[To Mrs. Weston.]

Windsor – *July.*

MY DEAR MADAM – "If I made myself intelligible yesterday, this letter will be expected; but expected or not, I know it will be read with candour and indulgence. You are all goodness, and I believe there will be need of even all your goodness to allow for some parts of my past conduct. But I have been forgiven by one who had still more to resent. My courage rises while I write. It is very difficult for the prosperous to be humble. I have already met with such success in two applications for pardon, that I may be in danger of thinking myself too sure of yours, and of those among your friends who have had any ground of offence. You must all endeavour to comprehend the exact nature of my situation when I first arrived at Randalls; you must consider me as having a secret which was to be kept at all hazards. This was the fact. My right to place myself in a situation requiring such concealment, is another question. I shall not discuss it here. For my temptation to *think* it a right, I refer every caviller to a brick house, sashed windows below, and casements above, in Highbury. I dared not address her openly; my difficulties in the then state of Enscombe must be too well known to require definition; and I was fortunate enough to prevail, before we parted at Weymouth, and to induce the most upright female mind in the creation to stoop in charity to a secret engagement. Had she refused, I should have gone mad. But you will be ready to say, what was your hope in doing this? What did you look forward to? To anything, everything – to time, chance, circumstance, slow effects, sudden bursts, perseverance and weariness, health and sickness. Every possibility of good was before me, and the first of blessings secured, in obtaining her promises of faith and correspondence. If you need farther explanation, I have the honour, my dear madam, of being your husband's son, and the advantage of inheriting a disposition to hope for good, which no inheritance of houses or lands can ever equal the value of. See me, then, under these circumstances, arriving on my first visit to Randalls; and here I am conscious of wrong, for that visit might have been sooner paid. You will look back and see that I did not come till Miss Fairfax was in Highbury; and as you were the person slighted, you will forgive me instantly; but I must work on my father's compassion, by reminding him, that so long as I absented myself from his house, so long I lost the blessing of knowing you. My behaviour, during the very happy fortnight which I spent with you, did not, I hope, lay me open to reprehension, excepting on one point. And now I come to the principal, the only important part of my conduct while belonging to you, which excites my own anxiety, or requires very solicitous explanation. With the greatest respect, and the warmest friendship, do I mention Miss Woodhouse; my father perhaps will think I ought to add, with the deepest humiliation. A few words which dropped from him yesterday spoke his opinion, and some censure I acknowledge myself liable to. My behaviour to Miss Woodhouse indicated, I believe, more than it ought. In order to assist a concealment so essential to me, I was led on to make more than an allowable use of the sort of intimacy into which we were immediately thrown. I cannot deny that Miss Woodhouse was my ostensible object – but I am sure you will believe the declaration, that had I not been convinced of her indifference, I would not have been induced by any selfish views to go on. Amiable and delightful as Miss Woodhouse is, she never gave me the idea of a young woman likely to be attached; and that she was perfectly free from any tendency to being attached to me, was as much my conviction as my wish. She received my attentions with an easy, friendly, good-humoured playfulness, which exactly suited me. We seemed to understand each other. From our relative situation, those attentions were her due, and were felt to be so. Whether Miss Woodhouse began really to understand me before the expiration of that fortnight, I cannot say; when I called to take leave of her, I remember that I was within a moment of confessing the truth, and I then fancied she was not without suspicion; but I have no doubt of her having since detected me – at least in some degree. She may not have surmised the whole, but her quickness must have penetrated a part. I cannot doubt it. You will find, whenever the subject becomes freed from its present restraints, that it did not take her wholly by surprise. She frequently gave me hints of it. I remember her telling me at the ball, that I owed Mrs. Elton gratitude for her attentions to Miss Fairfax. I hope this history of my conduct towards her will be admitted by you and my father as great extenuation of what you saw amiss. While you considered me as having sinned against Emma Woodhouse, I could deserve nothing from either. Acquit me here, and procure for me, when it is allowable, the acquittal and good wishes of that said Emma Woodhouse, whom I regard with so much brotherly affection, as to long to have her as deeply and as happily in love as myself. Whatever strange things I said or did during that fortnight, you have now a key to. My heart was in Highbury, and my business was to get my body thither as often as might be, and with the least suspicion. If you remember any queernesses, set them all to the right account. Of the pianoforte so much talked of, I feel it only necessary to say, that its being ordered was absolutely unknown to Miss F – , who would never have allowed me to send it, had any choice been given her. The delicacy of her mind throughout the whole engagement, my dear madam, is much beyond my power of doing justice to. You will soon, I earnestly hope, know her thoroughly yourself. No description can describe her. She must tell you herself what she is yet not by word, for never was there a human creature who would so designedly suppress her own merit. Since I began this letter, which will be longer than I foresaw, I have heard from her. She gives a good account of her own health; but as she never complains, I dare not depend. I want to have your opinion of her looks. I know you will soon call on her; she is living in dread of the visit. Perhaps it is paid already. Let me hear from you without delay; I am impatient for a thousand particulars. Remember how few minutes I was at Randalls, and in how bewildered, how mad a state: and I am not much better yet; still insane either from happiness or misery. When I think of the kindness and favour I have met with, of her excellence and patience, and my uncle's generosity, I am mad with joy: but when I recollect all the uneasiness I occasioned her, and how little I deserve to be forgiven, I am mad with anger. If I could but see her again! But I must not propose it yet. My uncle has been too good for me to encroach. I must still add to this long letter. You have not heard all that you ought to hear. I could not give any connected detail yesterday; but the suddenness, and, in one light, the unseasonableness with which the affair burst out, needs explanation; for though the event of the 26th ult., as you will conclude, immediately opened to me the happiest prospects, I should not have presumed on such early measures, but from the very particular circumstances, which left me not an hour to lose. I should myself have shrunk from any thing so hasty, and she would have felt every scruple of mine with multiplied strength and refinement. But I had no choice. The hasty engagement she had entered into with that woman – here, my dear madam, I was obliged to leave off abruptly, to recollect and compose myself. I have been walking over the country, and am now, I hope, rational enough to make the rest of my letter what it ought to be. It is, in fact, a most mortifying retrospect for me. I behaved shamefully. And here I can admit, that my manners to Miss W., in being unpleasant to Miss F., were highly blameable. *She* disapproved them, which ought to have been enough. My plea of concealing the truth she did not think sufficient. She was displeased; I thought unreasonably so: I thought her, on a thousand occasions, unnecessarily scrupulous and cautious: I thought her even cold. But she was always right. If I had followed her judgment, and subdued my spirits to the level of what she deemed proper, I should have escaped the greatest unhappiness I have ever known. We quarrelled. Do you remember the morning spent at Donwell? *There* every little dissatisfaction that had occurred before came to a crisis. I was late; I met her walking home by herself, and wanted to walk with her, but she would not suffer it. She absolutely refused to allow me, which I then thought most unreasonable. Now, however, I see nothing in it but a very natural and consistent degree of discretion. While I, to blind the world to our engagement, was behaving one hour with objectionable particularity to another woman, was she to be consenting the next to a proposal which might have made every previous caution useless? Had we been met walking together between Donwell and Highbury, the truth must have been suspected. I was mad enough, however, to resent. I doubted her affection. I doubted it more the next day on Box Hill; when, provoked by such conduct on my side, such shameful, insolent neglect of her, and such apparent devotion to Miss W., as it would have been impossible for any woman of sense to endure, she spoke her resentment in a form of words perfectly intelligible to me. In short, my dear madam, it was a quarrel blameless on her side, abominable on mine; and I returned the same evening to Richmond, though I might have staid with you till the next morning, merely because I would be as angry with her as possible. Even then, I was not such a fool as not to mean to be reconciled in time; but I was the injured person – injured by her coldness – and I went away determined that she should make the first advances. I shall always congratulate myself that you were not of the Box Hill party. Had you witnessed my behaviour there, I can hardly suppose you would ever have thought well of me again. Its effect upon her appears in the immediate resolution it produced: as soon as she found I was really gone from Randalls, she closed with the offer of that officious Mrs. Elton; the whole system of whose treatment of her, by the bye, has ever filled me with indignation and hatred. I must not quarrel with a spirit of forbearance which has been so richly extended towards myself; but, otherwise, I should loudly protest against the share of it which that woman has known. "Jane," indeed! You will observe that I have not yet indulged myself in calling her by that name, even to you. Think, then, what I must have endured in hearing it bandied between the Eltons with all the vulgarity of needless repetition, and all the insolence of imaginary superiority. Have patience with me, I shall soon have done. She closed with this offer, resolving to break with me entirely, and wrote the next day to tell me that we never were to meet again. *She felt the engagement to be a source of repentance and misery to each: she dissolved it.* This letter reached me on the very morning of my poor aunt's death. I answered it within an hour; but from the confusion of my mind, and the multiplicity of business falling on me at once, my answer, instead of being sent with all the many other letters of that day, was locked up in my writing-desk; and I, trusting that I had written enough, though but a few lines, to satisfy her, remained without any uneasiness. I was rather disappointed that I did not hear from her again speedily; but I made excuses for her, and was too busy, and may I add? Too cheerful in my views to be captious. We removed to Windsor; and two days afterwards I received a parcel from her – my own letters all returned! and a few lines at the same time by the post, stating her extreme surprise at not having had the smallest reply to her last; and adding, that as silence on such a point could not be misconstrued, and as it must be equally desirable to both to have every subordinate arrangement concluded as soon as possible, she now sent me, by a safe conveyance, all my letters, and requested, that if I could not directly command hers, so as to send them to Highbury within a week, I would forward them after that period to her at — , in short, the full direction to Mr. Smallridge's, near Bristol, stared me in the face. I knew the name, the place, I knew all about it, and instantly saw what she had been doing. It was perfectly accordant with that resolution of character which I knew her to possess; and the secrecy she had maintained, as to any such design in her former letter, was equally descriptive of its anxious delicacy. For the world would not she have seemed to threaten me. Imagine the shock; imagine how, till I had actually detected my own blunder, I raved at the blunders of the post. What was to be done? One thing only. I must speak to my uncle. Without his sanction I could not hope to be listened to again. I spoke; circumstances were in my favour; the late event had softened away his pride, and he was, earlier than I could have anticipated, wholly reconciled and complying; and could say at last, poor man! with a deep sigh, that he wished I might find as much happiness in the marriage state as he had done. I felt that it would be of a different sort. Are you disposed to pity me for what I must have suffered in opening the cause to him, for my suspense while all was at stake? No; do not pity me till I reached Highbury, and saw how ill I had made her. Do not pity me till I saw her wan, sick looks. I reached Highbury at the time of day when, from my knowledge of their late breakfast-hour, I was certain of a good chance of finding her alone. I was not disappointed; and at last I was not disappointed either in the object of my journey. A great deal of very reasonable, very just displeasure I had to persuade away. But it is done; we are reconciled, dearer, much dearer, than ever, and no moment's uneasiness can ever occur between us again. Now, my dear madam, I will release you; but I could not conclude before. A thousand and a thousand thanks for all the kindness you have ever shown me, and ten thousand for the attentions your heart will dictate towards her. If you think me in a way to be happier than I deserve, I am quite of your opinion. Miss W. calls me the child of good fortune. I hope she is right. In one respect, my good fortune is undoubted, that of being able to subscribe myself.

Your obliged and affectionate Son,

F. C. WESTON CHURCHILL.

# Chapter 51

THIS LETTER must make its way to Emma's feelings. She was obliged, in spite of her previous determination to the contrary, to do it all the justice that Mrs. Weston foretold. As soon as she came to her own name, it was irresistible; every line relating to herself was interesting, and almost every line agreeable; and when this charm ceased, the subject could still maintain itself, by the natural return of her former regard for the writer, and the very strong attraction which any picture of love must have for her at that moment. She never stopped till she had gone through the whole; and though it was impossible not to feel that he had been wrong, yet he had been less wrong than she had supposed and he had suffered, and was very sorry and he was so grateful to Mrs. Weston, and so much in love with Miss Fairfax, and she was so happy herself, that there was no being severe; and could he have entered the room, she must have shaken hands with him as heartily as ever.

She thought so well of the letter, that when Mr. Knightley came again, she desired him to read it. She was sure of Mrs. Weston's wishing it to be communicated; especially to one, who, like Mr. Knightley, had seen so much to blame in his conduct.

"I shall be very glad to look it over," said he; "but it seems long. I will take it home with me at night."

But that would not do. Mr. Weston was to call in the evening, and she must return it by him.

"I would rather be talking to you," he replied; "but as it seems a matter of justice, it shall be done."

He began – stopping, however, almost directly to say, "Had I been offered the sight of one of this gentleman's letters to his mother-in-law a few months ago, Emma, it would not have been taken with such indifference."

He proceeded a little farther, reading to himself; and then, with a smile, observed, "Humph! a fine complimentary opening: But it is his way. One man's style must not be the rule of another's. We will not be severe."

"It will be natural for me," he added shortly afterwards, "to speak my opinion aloud as I read. By doing it, I shall feel that I am near you. It will not be so great a loss of time: but if you dislike it – "

"Not at all. I should wish it."

Mr. Knightley returned to his reading with greater alacrity.

"He trifles here," said he, "as to the temptation. He knows he is wrong, and has nothing rational to urge. Bad. He ought not to have formed the engagement. 'His father's disposition' – he is unjust, however, to his father. Mr. Weston's sanguine temper was a blessing on all his upright and honourable exertions; but Mr. Weston earned every present comfort before he endeavoured to gain it. Very true; he did not come till Miss Fairfax was here."

"And I have not forgotten," said Emma, "how sure you were that he might have come sooner if he would. You pass it over very handsomely but you were perfectly right."

"I was not quite impartial in my judgment, Emma: but yet, I think had *you* not been in the case I should still have distrusted him."

When he came to Miss Woodhouse, he was obliged to read the whole of it aloud – all that related to her – with a smile; a look; a shake of the head; a word or two of assent, or disapprobation; or merely of love, as the subject required; concluding, however, seriously, and, after steady reflection, thus:

"Very bad – though it might have been worse. Playing a most dangerous game. Too much indebted to the event for his acquittal. No judge of his own manners by you. Always deceived in fact by his own wishes, and regardless of little besides his own convenience. Fancying you to have fathomed his secret. Natural enough! his own mind full of intrigue, that he should suspect it in others. Mystery; finesse – how they pervert the understanding! My Emma, does not everything serve to prove more and more the beauty of truth and sincerity in all our dealings with each other?"

Emma agreed to it, and with a blush of sensibility on Harriet's account, which she could not give any sincere explanation of.

"You had better go on," said she.

He did so, but very soon stopped again to say, "the pianoforte! Ah! That was the act of a very, very young man, one too young to consider whether the inconvenience of it might not very much exceed the pleasure. A boyish scheme, indeed! I cannot comprehend a man's wishing to give a woman any proof of affection which he knows she would rather dispense with; and he did know that she would have prevented the instrument's coming if she could."

After this, he made some progress without any pause. Frank Churchill's confession of having behaved shamefully was the first thing to call for more than a word in passing.

"I perfectly agree with you, sir," was then his remark. "You did behave very shamefully. You never wrote a truer line." And having gone through what immediately followed of the basis of their disagreement, and his persisting to act in direct opposition to Jane Fairfax's sense of right, he made a fuller pause to say, "This is very bad. He had induced her to place herself, for his sake, in a situation of extreme difficulty and uneasiness, and it should have been his first object to prevent her from suffering unnecessarily. She must have had much more to contend with, in carrying on the correspondence, than he could. He should have respected even unreasonable scruples, had there been such; but hers were all reasonable. We must look to her one fault, and remember that she had done a wrong thing in consenting to the engagement, to bear that she should have been in such a state of punishment."

Emma knew that he was now getting to the Box Hill party, and grew uncomfortable. Her own behaviour had been so very improper! She was deeply ashamed, and a little afraid of his next look. It was all read, however, steadily, attentively, and without the smallest remark; and, excepting one momentary glance at her, instantly withdrawn, in the fear of giving pain no remembrance of Box Hill seemed to exist.

"There is no saying much for the delicacy of our good friends, the Eltons," was his next observation. "His feelings are natural. What! actually resolve to break with him entirely! She felt the engagement to be a source of repentance and misery to each she dissolved it. What a view this gives of her sense of his behaviour! Well, he must be a most extraordinary – "

"Nay, nay, read on. You will find how very much he suffers."

"I hope he does," replied Mr. Knightley coolly, and resuming the letter. " 'Smallridge!' What does this mean? What is all this?"

"She had engaged to go as governess to Mrs. Smallridge's children – a dear friend of Mrs. Elton's – a neighbour of Maple Grove; and, by the bye, I wonder how Mrs. Elton bears the disappointment?"

"Say nothing, my dear Emma, while you oblige me to read – not even of Mrs. Elton. Only one page more. I shall soon have done. What a letter the man writes!"

"I wish you would read it with a kinder spirit towards him."

"Well, there *is* feeling here. He does seem to have suffered in finding her ill. Certainly, I can have no doubt of his being fond of her. 'Dearer, much dearer than ever.' I hope he may long continue to feel all the value of such a reconciliation. He is a very liberal thanker, with his thousands and tens of thousands. 'Happier than I deserve.' Come, he knows himself there. 'Miss Woodhouse calls me the child of good fortune.' Those were Miss Woodhouse's words, were they? And a fine ending – and there is the letter. The child of good fortune! That was your name for him, was it?"

"You do not appear so well satisfied with his letter as I am; but still you must, at least I hope you must, think the better of him for it. I hope it does him some service with you."

"Yes, certainly it does. He has had great faults – faults of inconsideration and thoughtlessness; and I am very much of his opinion in thinking him likely to be happier than he deserves: but still as he is, beyond a doubt, really attached to Miss Fairfax, and will soon, it may be hoped, have the advantage of being constantly with her, I am very ready to believe his character will improve, and acquire from hers the steadiness and delicacy of principle that it wants. And now, let me talk to you of something else. I have another person's interest at present so much at heart, that I cannot think any longer about Frank Churchill. Ever since I left you this morning, Emma, my mind has been hard at work on one subject."

The subject followed; it was in plain, unaffected, gentlemanlike English, such as Mr. Knightley used even to the woman he was in love with, how to be able to ask her to marry him, without attacking the happiness of her father. Emma's answer was ready at the first word. "While her dear father lived, any change of condition must be impossible for her. She could never quit him." Part only of this answer, however, was admitted. The impossibility of her quitting her father, Mr. Knightley felt as strongly as herself; but the inadmissibility of any other change, he could not agree to. He had been thinking it over most deeply, most intently; he had at first hoped to induce Mr. Woodhouse to remove with her to Donwell; he had wanted to believe it feasible, but his knowledge of Mr. Woodhouse would not suffer him to deceive himself long; and now he confessed his persuasion, that such a transplantation would be a risk of her father's comfort, perhaps even of his life, which must not be hazarded. Mr. Woodhouse taken from Hartfield! No, he felt that it ought not to be attempted. But the plan which had arisen on the sacrifice of this, he trusted his dearest Emma would not find in any respect objectionable; it was, that he should be received at Hartfield; that so long as her father's happiness – in other words his life – required Hartfield to continue her home, it should be his likewise.

Of their all removing to Donwell, Emma had already had her own passing thoughts. Like him, she had tried the scheme and rejected it; but such an alternative as this had not occurred to her. She was sensible of all the affection it evinced. She felt that, in quitting Donwell, he must be sacrificing a great deal of independence of hours and habits; that in living constantly with her father, and in no house of his own, there would be much, very much, to be borne with. She promised to think of it, and advised him to think of it more; but he was fully convinced, that no reflection could alter his wishes or his opinion on the subject. He had given it, he could assure her, very long and calm consideration; he had been walking away from William Larkins the whole morning, to have his thoughts to himself.

"Ah! there is one difficulty unprovided for," cried Emma. "I am sure William Larkins will not like it. You must get his consent before you ask mine."

She promised, however, to think of it; and pretty nearly promised, moreover, to think of it, with the intention of finding it a very good scheme.

It is remarkable, that Emma, in the many, very many, points of view in which she was now beginning to consider Donwell Abbey, was never struck with any sense of injury to her nephew Henry, whose rights as heir expectant had formerly been so tenaciously regarded. Think she must of the possible difference to the poor little boy; and yet she only gave herself a saucy conscious smile about it, and found amusement in detecting the real cause of that violent dislike of Mr. Knightley's marrying Jane Fairfax, or anybody else, which at the time she had wholly imputed to the amiable solicitude of the sister and the aunt.

This proposal of his, this plan of marrying and continuing at

Hartfield – the more she contemplated it, the more pleasing it became. His evils seemed to lessen, her own advantages to increase, their mutual good to outweigh every drawback. Such a companion for herself in the periods of anxiety and cheerlessness before her! Such a partner in all those duties and cares to which time must be giving increase of melancholy!

She would have been too happy but for poor Harriet; but every blessing of her own seemed to involve and advance the sufferings of her friend, who must now be even excluded from Hartfield. The delightful family party which Emma was securing for herself, poor Harriet must, in mere charitable caution, be kept at a distance from. She would be a loser in every way. Emma could not deplore her future absence as any deduction from her own enjoyment. In such a party, Harriet would be rather a dead weight than otherwise; but for the poor girl herself, it seemed a peculiarly cruel necessity that was to be placing her in such a state of unmerited punishment.

In time, of course, Mr. Knightley would be forgotten, that is, supplanted; but this could not be expected to happen very early. Mr. Knightley himself would be doing nothing to assist the cure; not like Mr. Elton. Mr. Knightley, always so kind, so feeling, so truly considerate for everybody, would never deserve to be less worshipped than now; and it really was too much to hope even of Harriet, that she could be in love with more than *three* men in one year.

## Chapter 52

It was a very great relief to Emma to find Harriet as desirous as herself to avoid a meeting. Their intercourse was painful enough by letter. How much worse, had they been obliged to meet!

Harriet expressed herself very much as might be supposed, without reproaches, or apparent sense of ill usage; and yet Emma fancied there was a something of resentment, a something bordering on it in her style, which increased the desirableness of their being separate. It might be only her own consciousness; but it seemed as if an angel only could have been quite without resentment under such a stroke.

She had no difficulty in procuring Isabella's invitation; and she was fortunate in having a sufficient reason for asking it, without resorting to invention. There was a tooth amiss. Harriet really wished, and had wished some time, to consult a dentist. Mrs. John Knightley was delighted to be of use; any thing of ill health was a recommendation to her and though not so fond of a dentist as of a Mr. Wingfield, she was quite eager to have Harriet under her care. When it was thus settled on her sister's side, Emma proposed it to her friend, and found her very persuadable. Harriet was to go; she was invited for at least a fortnight; she was to be conveyed in Mr. Woodhouse's carriage. It was all arranged, it was all completed, and Harriet was safe in Brunswick Square.

Now Emma could, indeed, enjoy Mr. Knightley's visits; now she could talk, and she could listen with true happiness, unchecked by that sense of injustice, of guilt, of something most painful, which had haunted her when remembering how disappointed a heart was near her, how much might at that moment, and at a little distance, be enduring by the feelings which she had led astray herself.

The difference of Harriet at Mrs. Goddard's, or in London, made perhaps an unreasonable difference in Emma's sensations; but she could not think of her in London without objects of curiosity and employment, which must be averting the past, and carrying her out of herself.

She would not allow any other anxiety to succeed directly to the place in her mind which Harriet had occupied. There was a communication before her, one which *she* only could be competent to make – the confession of her engagement to her father; but she would have nothing to do with it at present. She had resolved to defer the disclosure till Mrs. Weston were safe and well. No additional agitation should be thrown at this period among those she loved – and the evil should not act on herself by anticipation before the appointed time. A fortnight, at least, of leisure and peace of mind, to crown every warmer, but more agitating, delight, should be hers.

She soon resolved, equally as a duty and a pleasure, to employ half an hour of this holiday of spirits in calling on Miss Fairfax. She ought to go – and she was longing to see her; the resemblance of their present situations increasing every other motive of goodwill. It would be a *secret* satisfaction; but the consciousness of a similarity of prospect would certainly add to the interest with which she should attend to any thing Jane might communicate.

She went – she had driven once unsuccessfully to the door, but had not been into the house since the morning after Box Hill, when poor Jane had been in such distress as had filled her with compassion, though all the worst of her sufferings had been unsuspected. The fear of being still unwelcome, determined her, though assured of their being at home, to wait in the passage, and send up her name. She heard Patty announcing it; but no such bustle succeeded as poor Miss Bates had before made so happily intelligible. No; she heard nothing but the instant reply of, "Beg her to walk up;" and a moment afterwards she was met on the stairs by Jane herself, coming eagerly forward, as if no other reception of her were felt sufficient. Emma had never seen her look so well, so lovely, so engaging. There was consciousness, animation, and warmth; there was everything which her countenance or manner could ever have wanted. She came forward with an offered hand; and said, in a low, but very feeling tone:

"This is most kind, indeed! Miss Woodhouse, it is impossible for me to express – I hope you will believe – Excuse me for being so entirely without words."

Emma was gratified, and would soon have shown no want of words, if the sound of Mrs. Elton's voice from the sitting-room had not checked her, and made it expedient to compress all her friendly and all her congratulatory sensations into a very, very earnest shake of the hand.

Mrs. Bates and Mrs. Elton were together. Miss Bates was out, which accounted for the previous tranquillity. Emma could have wished Mrs. Elton elsewhere; but she was in a humour to have patience with everybody; and as Mrs. Elton met her with unusual graciousness, she hoped the rencontre would do them no harm.

She soon believed herself to penetrate Mrs. Elton's thoughts, and understand why she was, like herself, in happy spirits; it was being in Miss Fairfax's confidence, and fancying herself acquainted with what was still a secret to other people. Emma saw symptoms of it immediately in the expression of her face; and while paying her own compliments to Mrs. Bates, and appearing to attend to the good old lady's replies, she saw her with a sort of anxious parade of mystery fold up a letter which she had apparently been reading aloud to Miss Fairfax, and return it into the purple and gold reticule by her side, saying, with significant nods:

"We can finish this some other time, you know. You and I shall not want opportunities. And, in fact, you have heard all the essential already. I only wanted to prove to you that Mrs. S. admits our apology, and is not offended. You see how delightfully she writes. Oh! she is a sweet creature! You would have doted on her, had you gone. But not a word more. Let us be discreet –

quite on our good behaviour. Hush! You remember those lines – I forget the poem at this moment:

> For when a lady's in the case,
> You know all other things give place.

Now I say, my dear, in our case, for *lady,* read – mum! a word to the wise. I am in a fine flow of spirits, ain't I? But I want to set your heart at ease as to Mrs. S. My representation, you see, has quite appeased her."

And again, on Emma's merely turning her head to look at Mrs. Bates's knitting, she added, in a half whisper:

"I mentioned no *names,* you will observe. Oh! no; cautious as a minister of state. I managed it extremely well."

Emma could not doubt. It was a palpable display, repeated on every possible occasion. When they had all talked a little while in harmony of the weather and Mrs. Weston, she found herself abruptly addressed with:

"Do not you think, Miss Woodhouse, our saucy little friend here is charmingly recovered? Do not you think her cure does Perry the highest credit? (here was a side glance of great meaning at Jane.) Upon my word, Perry has restored her in a wonderful short time! Oh! if you had seen her, as I did, when she was at the worst!" And when Mrs. Bates was saying something to Emma, whispered farther, "We do not say a word of any *assistance* that Perry might have; not a word of a certain young physician from Windsor. Oh! no; Perry shall have all the credit."

"I have scarcely had the pleasure of seeing you, Miss Woodhouse," she shortly afterwards began, "since the party to Box Hill. Very pleasant party. But yet I think there was something wanting. Things did not seem – that is, there seemed a little cloud upon the spirits of some. So it appeared to me at least, but I might be mistaken. However, I think it answered so far as to tempt one to go again. What say you both to our collecting the same party, and exploring to Box Hill again, while the fine weather lasts? It must be the same party, you know – quite the same party, not one exception."

Soon after this Miss Bates came in, and Emma could not help being diverted by the perplexity of her first answer to herself, resulting, she supposed, from doubt of what might be said, and impatience to say everything.

"Thank you, dear Miss Woodhouse, you are all kindness. It is impossible to say – Yes, indeed, I quite understand – dearest Jane's prospects – that is, I do not mean. But she is charmingly recovered. How is Mr. Woodhouse? I am so glad. Quite out of my power. Such a happy little circle as you find us here. Yes, indeed. Charming young man! That is so very friendly; I mean good Mr. Perry! Such attention to Jane!" And from her great, her more than commonly thankful delight towards Mrs. Elton for being there, Emma guessed that there had been a little show of resentment towards Jane, from the vicarage quarter, which was now graciously overcome. After a few whispers, indeed, which placed it beyond a guess, Mrs. Elton, speaking louder, said:

"Yes, here I am, my good friend; and here I have been so long, that anywhere else I should think it necessary to apologise; but, the truth is, that I am waiting for my lord and master. He promised to join me here, and pay his respects to you."

"What! are we to have the pleasure of a call from Mr. Elton? That will be a favour indeed! for I know gentlemen do not like morning visits, and Mr. Elton's time is so engaged."

"Upon my word it is, Miss Bates. He really is engaged from morning to night. There is no end of people's coming to him, on some pretence or other. The magistrates, and overseers, and churchwardens, are always wanting his opinion. They seem not able to do any thing without him. 'Upon my word, Mr. E.,' I often say, 'rather you than I. I do not know what would become of my crayons and my instrument, if I had half so many applicants.' Bad enough as it is, for I absolutely neglect them both to an unpardonable degree. I believe I have not played a bar this fortnight. However, he is coming, I assure you: yes, indeed, on purpose to wait on you all." And putting up her hand to screen her words from Emma "A congratulatory visit, you know. Oh! yes, quite indispensable."

Miss Bates looked about her, so happily!

"He promised to come to me as soon as he could disengage himself from Knightley; but he and Knightley are shut up together in deep consultation. Mr. E. is Knightley's right hand."

Emma would not have smiled for the world, and only said, "Is Mr. Elton gone on foot to Donwell? He will have a hot walk."

"Oh! no, it is a meeting at the Crown – a regular meeting. Weston and Cole will be there too; but one is apt to speak only of those who lead. I fancy Mr. E. and Knightley have everything their own way."

"Have not you mistaken the day?" said Emma. "I am almost certain that the meeting at the Crown is not till to morrow. Mr. Knightley was at Hartfield yesterday, and spoke of it as for Saturday."

"Oh! no, the meeting is certainly to day," was the abrupt answer, which denoted the impossibility of any blunder on Mrs. Elton's side. "I do believe," she continued, "this is the most troublesome parish that ever was. We never heard of such things at Maple Grove."

"Your parish there was small," said Jane.

"Upon my word, my dear, I do not know, for I never heard the subject talked of."

"But it is proved by the smallness of the school, which I have heard you speak of, as under the patronage of your sister and Mrs. Bragge; the only school, and not more than five-and-twenty children."

"Ah! you clever creature, that's very true. What a thinking brain you have! I say, Jane, what a perfect character you and I should make, if we could be shaken together. My liveliness and your solidity would produce perfection. Not that I presume to insinuate, however, that *some* people may not think *you* perfection already. But hush – not a word, if you please."

It seemed an unnecessary caution; Jane was wanting to give her words, not to Mrs. Elton, but to Miss Woodhouse, as the latter plainly saw. The wish of distinguishing her, as far as civility permitted, was very evident, though it could not often proceed beyond a look.

Mr. Elton made his appearance. His lady greeted him with some of her sparkling vivacity.

"Very pretty, sir, upon my word; to send me on here, to be an encumbrance to my friends, so long before you vouchsafe to come! But you knew what a dutiful creature you had to deal with. You knew I should not stir till my lord and master appeared. Here have I been sitting this hour, giving these young ladies a sample of true conjugal obedience for who can say, you know, how soon it may be wanted?"

Mr. Elton was so hot and tired, that all this wit seemed thrown away. His civilities to the other ladies must be paid; but his subsequent object was to lament over himself for the heat he was suffering, and the walk he had had for nothing.

"When I got to Donwell," said he, "Knightley could not be found. Very odd! very unaccountable! after the note I sent him this morning, and the message he returned, that he should certainly be at home till one."

"Donwell!" cried his wife. "My dear Mr. E., you have not been to Donwell! You mean the Crown; you come from the meeting at the Crown."

"No, no, that's to morrow; and I particularly wanted to see Knightley to day on that very account. Such a dreadful broiling morning! I went over the fields too (speaking in a tone of great ill usage,) which made it so much the worse. And then not to find him at home! I assure you I am not at all pleased. And no apology left, no message for me. The housekeeper declared she knew nothing of my being expected. Very extraordinary! And nobody knew at all which way he was gone. Perhaps to Hartfield, perhaps to the Abbey Mill, perhaps into his woods. Miss Woodhouse, this is not like our friend Knightley! Can you explain it?"

Emma amused herself by protesting that it was very extraordinary, indeed, and that she had not a syllable to say for him.

"I cannot imagine," said Mrs. Elton, (feeling the indignity as a wife ought to do,) "I cannot imagine how he could do such a thing by you, of all people in the world! The very last person whom one should expect to be forgotten! My dear Mr. E., he must have left a message for you, I am sure he must. Not even Knightley could be so very eccentric; and his servants forgot it. Depend upon it, that was the case: and very likely to happen with the Donwell servants, who are all, I have often observed, extremely awkward and remiss. I am sure I would not have such a creature as his Harry stand at our sideboard for any consideration. And as for Mrs. Hodges, Wright holds her very cheap indeed. She promised Wright a receipt[1], and never sent it."

"I met William Larkins," continued Mr. Elton, "as I got near the house, and he told me I should not find his master at home, but I did not believe him. William seemed rather out of humour. He did not know what was come to his master lately, he said, but he could hardly ever get the speech of him. I have nothing to do with William's wants, but it really is of very great importance that I should see Knightley to day; and it becomes a matter, therefore, of very serious inconvenience that I should have had this hot walk to no purpose."

Emma felt that she could not do better than go home directly. In all probability she was at this very time waited for there; and Mr. Knightley might be preserved from sinking deeper in aggression towards Mr. Elton, if not towards William Larkins.

She was pleased, on taking leave, to find Miss Fairfax

1 A recipe.

determined to attend her out of the room, to go with her even downstairs; it gave her an opportunity which she immediately made use of, to say:

"It is as well, perhaps, that I have not had the possibility. Had you not been surrounded by other friends, I might have been tempted to introduce a subject, to ask questions, to speak more openly than might have been strictly correct. I feel that I should certainly have been impertinent."

"Oh!" cried Jane, with a blush and hesitation which Emma thought infinitely more becoming to her than all the elegance of all her usual composure – "there would have been no danger. The danger would have been of my wearying you. You could not have gratified me more than by expressing an interest – Indeed, Miss Woodhouse, (speaking more collectedly,) with the consciousness which I have of misconduct – very great misconduct – it is particularly consoling to me to know that those of my friends, whose good opinion is most worth preserving, are not disgusted to such a degree as to – I have no time for half that I could wish to say. I long to make apologies, excuses, to urge something for myself. I feel it so very due. But, unfortunately – in short, if your compassion does not stand my friend – "

"Oh! you are too scrupulous, indeed you are," cried Emma warmly, and taking her hand. "You owe me no apologies; and everybody to whom you might be supposed to owe them, is so perfectly satisfied, so delighted even – "

"You are very kind, but I know what my manners were to you. So cold and artificial! I had always a part to act. It was a life of deceit! I know that I must have disgusted you."

"Pray say no more. I feel that all the apologies should be on my side. Let us forgive each other at once. We must do whatever is to be done quickest, and I think our feelings will lose no time there. I hope you have pleasant accounts from Windsor?"

"Very."

"And the next news, I suppose, will be, that we are to lose you just as I begin to know you."

"Oh! as to all that, of course nothing can be thought of yet. I am here till claimed by Colonel and Mrs. Campbell."

"Nothing can be actually settled yet, perhaps," replied Emma, smiling – "but, excuse me, it must be thought of."

The smile was returned as Jane answered:

"You are very right; it has been thought of. And I will own to you, (I am sure it will be safe), that so far as our living with Mr. Churchill at Enscombe, it is settled. There must be three months, at least, of deep mourning; but when they are over, I imagine there will be nothing more to wait for."

"Thank you, thank you. This is just what I wanted to be assured of. Oh! if you knew how much I love everything that is decided and open! Good bye, good bye."

# *Chapter 53*

MRS. WESTON'S friends were all made happy by her safety; and if the satisfaction of her well-doing could be increased to Emma, it was by knowing her to be the mother of a little girl. She had been decided in wishing for a Miss Weston. She would not acknowledge that it was with any view of making a match for her, hereafter, with either of Isabella's sons; but she was convinced that a daughter would suit both father and mother best. It would be a great comfort to Mr. Weston, as he grew older – and even Mr. Weston might be growing older ten years hence – to have his fireside enlivened by the sports and the nonsense, the freaks and the fancies of a child never banished from home; and Mrs. Weston

– no one could doubt that a daughter would be most to her; and it would be quite a pity that any one who so well knew how to teach, should not have their powers in exercise again.

"She has had the advantage, you know, of practising on me," she continued – "like La Baronne d'Almane on La Comtesse d'Ostalis, in Madame de Genlis's *Adelaide and Theodore,* and we shall now see her own little Adelaide educated on a more perfect plan."

"That is," replied Mr. Knightley, "she will indulge her even more than she did you, and believe that she does not indulge her at all. It will be the only difference."

"Poor child!" cried Emma; "at that rate, what will become of her?"

"Nothing very bad. The fate of thousands. She will be disagreeable in infancy, and correct herself as she grows older. I am losing all my bitterness against spoilt children, my dearest Emma. I, who am owing all my happiness to *you,* would not it be horrible ingratitude in me to be severe on them?"

Emma laughed, and replied: "But I had the assistance of all your endeavours to counteract the indulgence of other people. I doubt whether my own sense would have corrected me without it."

"Do you? I have no doubt. Nature gave you understanding: Miss Taylor gave you principles. You must have done well. My interference was quite as likely to do harm as good. It was very natural for you to say, what right has he to lecture me? And I am afraid very natural for you to feel that it was done in a disagreeable manner. I do not believe I did you any good. The good was all to myself, by making you an object of the tenderest affection to me. I could not think about you so much without doting on you, faults and all; and by dint of fancying so many errors, have been in love with you ever since you were thirteen at least."

"I am sure you were of use to me," cried Emma. "I was very often influenced rightly by you – oftener than I would own at the time. I am very sure you did me good. And if poor little Anna Weston is to be spoiled, it will be the greatest humanity in you to do as much for her as you have done for me, except falling in love with her when she is thirteen."

"How often, when you were a girl, have you said to me, with one of your saucy looks 'Mr. Knightley, I am going to do so-and-so; papa says I may, or I have Miss Taylor's leave' – something which, you knew, I did not approve. In such cases my interference was giving you two bad feelings instead of one."

"What an amiable creature I was! No wonder you should hold my speeches in such affectionate remembrance."

" 'Mr. Knightley.' You always called me, 'Mr. Knightley;' and, from habit, it has not so very formal a sound. And yet it is formal. I want you to call me something else, but I do not know what."

"I remember once calling you 'George,' in one of my amiable fits, about ten years ago. I did it because I thought it would offend you; but, as you made no objection, I never did it again."

"And cannot you call me 'George' now?"

"Impossible! I never can call you any thing but 'Mr. Knightley.' I will not promise even to equal the elegant terseness of Mrs. Elton, by calling you Mr. K. But I will promise," she added presently, laughing and blushing." I will promise to call you once by your Christian name. I do not say when, but perhaps you may guess where; in the building in which N. takes M. for better, for worse."

Emma grieved that she could not be more openly just to one important service which his better sense would have rendered her, to the advice which would have saved her from the worst of all her womanly follies – her wilful intimacy with Harriet Smith; but it was too tender a subject. She could not enter on it. Harriet was very seldom mentioned between them. This, on his side, might merely proceed from her not being thought of; but Emma was rather inclined to attribute it to delicacy, and a suspicion, from some appearances, that their friendship were declining. She was aware herself, that, parting under any other circumstances, they certainly should have corresponded more, and that her intelligence would not have rested, as it now almost wholly did, on Isabella's letters. He might observe that it was so. The pain of being obliged to practise concealment towards him, was very little inferior to the pain of having made Harriet unhappy.

Isabella sent quite as good an account of her visitor as could be expected; on her first arrival she had thought her out of spirits, which appeared perfectly natural, as there was a dentist to be consulted; but, since that business had been over, she did not appear to find Harriet different from what she had known her before. Isabella, to be sure, was no very quick observer; yet if Harriet had not been equal to playing with the children, it would not have escaped her. Emma's comforts and hopes were most agreeably carried on, by Harriet's being to stay longer; her fortnight was likely to be a month at least. Mr. and Mrs. John Knightley were to come down in August, and she was invited to remain till they could bring her back.

"John does not even mention your friend," said Mr. Knightley. "Here is his answer, if you like to see it."

It was the answer to the communication of his intended marriage. Emma accepted it with a very eager hand, with an impatience all alive to know what he would say about it, and not at all checked by hearing that her friend was unmentioned.

"John enters like a brother into my happiness," continued Mr. Knightley, "but he is no complimenter; and though I well know him to have, likewise, a most brotherly affection for you, he is so far from making flourishes, that any other young woman might think him rather cool in her praise. But I am not afraid of your seeing what he writes."

"He writes like a sensible man," replied Emma, when she had read the letter. "I honour his sincerity. It is very plain that he considers the good fortune of the engagement as all on my side, but that he is not without hope of my growing, in time, as worthy of your affection, as you think me already. Had he said any thing to bear a different construction, I should not have believed him."

"My Emma, he means no such thing. He only means – "

"He and I should differ very little in our estimation of the two" – interrupted she, with a sort of serious smile – "much less, perhaps, than he is aware of, if we could enter without ceremony or reserve on the subject."

"Emma, my dear Emma – "

"Oh!" she cried with more thorough gaiety, "if you fancy your brother does not do me justice, only wait till my dear father is in the secret, and hear his opinion. Depend upon it, he will be much farther from doing you justice. He will think all the happiness, all the advantage, on your side of the question; all the merit on mine. I wish I may not sink into 'poor Emma' with him at once. His tender compassion towards oppressed worth can go no farther."

"Ah!" he cried, "I wish your father might be half as easily convinced as John will be, of our having every right that equal worth can give, to be happy together. I am amused by one part of John's letter – did you notice it? – where he says, that my information did not take him wholly by surprise, that he was rather in expectation of hearing something of the kind."

"If I understand your brother, he only means so far as your having some thoughts of marrying. He had no idea of me. He seems perfectly unprepared for that."

"Yes, yes – but I am amused that he should have seen so far into my feelings. What has he been judging by? I am not conscious of any difference in my spirits or conversation that could prepare him at this time for my marrying any more than at another. But it was so, I suppose. I dare say there was a difference when I was staying with them the other day. I believe I did not play with the children quite so much as usual. I remember one evening the poor boys saying, 'Uncle seems always tired now.' "

The time was coming when the news must spread farther, and other persons' reception of it tried. As soon as Mrs. Weston was sufficiently recovered to admit Mr. Woodhouse's visits, Emma having it in view that her gentle reasonings should be employed in the cause, resolved first to announce it at home, and then at Randalls. But how to break it to her father at last! She had bound herself to do it, in such an hour of Mr. Knightley's absence, or when it came to the point her heart would have failed her, and she must have put it off; but Mr. Knightley was to come at such a time, and follow up the beginning she was to make. She was forced to speak, and to speak cheerfully too. She must not make it a more decided subject of misery to him, by a melancholy tone herself. She must not appear to think it a misfortune. With all the spirits she could command, she prepared him first for something strange, and then, in a few words, said, that if his consent and approbation could be obtained – which, she trusted, would be attended with no difficulty, since it was a plan to promote the happiness of all – she and Mr. Knightley meant to marry; by which means Hartfield would receive the constant addition of that person's company whom she knew he loved, next to his daughters and Mrs. Weston, best in the world.

Poor man! it was at first a considerable shock to him, and he tried earnestly to dissuade her from it. She was reminded, more than once, of having always said she would never marry, and assured that it would be a great deal better for her to remain single; and told of poor Isabella, and poor Miss Taylor. But it would not do. Emma hung about him affectionately, and smiled, and said it must be so; and that he must not class her with Isabella and Mrs. Weston, whose marriages taking them from Hartfield, had, indeed, made a melancholy change: but she was not going from Hartfield; she should be always there; she was introducing no change in their numbers or their comforts but for the better; and she was very sure that he would be a great deal the happier for having Mr. Knightley always at hand, when he were once got used to the idea. Did he not love Mr. Knightley very much? He would not deny that he did, she was sure. Whom did he ever want to consult on business but Mr. Knightley? Who was so useful to him, who so ready to write his letters, who so glad to assist him? Who so cheerful, so attentive, so attached to him? Would not he like to have him always on the spot? Yes. That was all very true. Mr. Knightley could not be there too often; he should be glad to see him every day; but they did see him every day as it was. Why could not they go on as they had done?

Mr. Woodhouse could not be soon reconciled; but the worst was overcome, the idea was given; time and continual repetition must do the rest. To Emma's entreaties and assurances succeeded Mr. Knightley's, whose fond praise of her gave the subject even a kind of welcome; and he was soon used to be talked to by each, on every fair occasion. They had all the assistance which Isabella could give, by letters of the strongest approbation; and Mrs. Weston was ready, on the first meeting, to consider the subject in the most serviceable light first, as a settled, and, secondly, as a good one – well aware of the nearly equal importance of the two recommendations to Mr. Woodhouse's mind. It was agreed upon, as what was to be; and everybody by whom he was used to be guided assuring him that it would be for his happiness; and having some feelings himself which almost admitted it, he began to think that some time or other – in another year or two, perhaps it might not be so very bad if the marriage did take place.

Mrs. Weston was acting no part, feigning no feelings in all that she said to him in favour of the event. She had been extremely surprised, never more so, than when Emma first opened the affair to her; but she saw in it only increase of happiness to all, and had no scruple in urging him to the utmost. She had such a regard for Mr. Knightley, as to think he deserved even her dearest Emma; and it was in every respect so proper, suitable, and unexceptionable a connection, and in one respect, one point of the highest importance, so peculiarly eligible, so singularly fortunate, that now it seemed as if Emma could not safely have attached herself to any other creature, and that she had herself been the stupidest of beings in not having thought of it, and wished it long ago. How very few of those men in a rank of life to address Emma would have renounced their own home for Hartfield! And who but Mr. Knightley could know and bear with Mr. Woodhouse, so as to make such an arrangement desirable! The difficulty of disposing of poor Mr. Woodhouse had been always felt in her husband's plans and her own, for a marriage between Frank and Emma. How to settle the claims of Enscombe and Hartfield had been a continual impediment – less acknowledged by Mr. Weston than by herself – but even he had never been able to finish the subject better than by saying: "Those matters will take care of themselves; the young people will find a way." But here there was nothing to be shifted off in a wild speculation on the future. It was all right, all open, all equal. No sacrifice on any side worth the name. It was a union of the highest promise of felicity in itself, and without one real, rational difficulty to oppose or delay it.

Mrs. Weston, with her baby on her knee, indulging in such reflections as these, was one of the happiest women in the world. If any thing could increase her delight, it was perceiving that the baby would soon have outgrown its first set of caps.

The news was universally a surprise wherever it spread; and Mr. Weston had his five minutes share of it; but five minutes were enough to familiarise the idea to his quickness of mind. He saw the advantages of the match, and rejoiced in them with all the constancy of his wife; but the wonder of it was very soon nothing; and by the end of an hour he was not far from believing that he had always foreseen it.

"It is to be a secret, I conclude," said he. "These matters are always a secret, till it is found out that everybody knows them. Only let me be told when I may speak out. I wonder whether Jane has any suspicion."

He went to Highbury the next morning, and satisfied himself on that point. He told her the news. Was not she like a daughter, his eldest daughter? He must tell her; and Miss Bates being present, it passed, of course, to Mrs. Cole, Mrs. Perry, and Mrs. Elton, immediately afterwards. It was no more than the principals were prepared for; they had calculated from the time of its being known at Randalls, how soon it would be over Highbury; and were thinking of themselves, as the evening wonder in many a family circle, with great sagacity.

In general, it was a very well approved match. Some might think him, and others might think her, the most in luck. One set might recommend their all removing to Donwell, and leaving Hartfield for the John Knightleys; and another might predict disagreements among their servants; but yet, upon the whole, there was no serious objection raised, except in one habitation – the Vicarage. There, the surprise was not softened by any satisfaction. Mr. Elton cared little about it, compared with his wife; he only hoped "the young lady's pride would now be contented;" and supposed "she had always meant to catch Knightley if she could;" and, on the point of living at Hartfield, could daringly exclaim, "Rather he than I!" But Mrs. Elton was very much discomposed indeed. "Poor Knightley! poor fellow! Sad business for him. She was extremely concerned; for, though very eccentric, he had a thousand good qualities. How could he be so taken in? Did not think him at all in love – not in the least. Poor Knightley! There would be an end of all pleasant intercourse with him. How happy he had been to come and dine with them whenever they asked him! But that would be all over now. Poor fellow! No more exploring parties to Donwell made for *her.* Oh! no; there would be a Mrs. Knightley to throw cold water on everything. Extremely disagreeable! But she was not at all sorry that she had abused the housekeeper the other day. – Shocking plan, living together. It would never do. She knew a family near Maple Grove who had tried it, and been obliged to separate before the end of the first quarter.

# Chapter 54

TIME PASSED on. A few more to morrows, and the party from London would be arriving. It was an alarming change; and Emma was thinking of it one morning, as what must bring a great deal to agitate and grieve her, when Mr. Knightley came in, and distressing thoughts were put by. After the first chat of pleasure he was silent; and then, in a graver tone, began with:

"I have something to tell you, Emma; some news."

"Good or bad?" said she, quickly, looking up in his face.

"I do not know which it ought to be called."

"Oh! good I am sure. I see it in your countenance. You are trying not to smile."

"I am afraid," said he, composing his features, "I am very much afraid, my dear Emma, that you will not smile when you hear it."

"Indeed! but why so? I can hardly imagine that any thing which pleases or amuses you, should not please and amuse me too."

"There is one subject," he replied, "I hope but one, on which we do not think alike." He paused a moment, again smiling, with his eyes fixed on her face. "Does nothing occur to you? Do not you recollect? Harriet Smith."

Her cheeks flushed at the name, and she felt afraid of something, though she knew not what.

"Have you heard from her yourself this morning?" cried he. "You have, I believe, and know the whole."

"No, I have not; I know nothing; pray tell me."

"You are prepared for the worst, I see and very bad it is. Harriet Smith marries Robert Martin."

Emma gave a start, which did not seem like being prepared and her eyes, in eager gaze, said, "No, this is impossible!" but her lips were closed.

"It is so, indeed," continued Mr. Knightley; "I have it from Robert Martin himself. He left me not half an hour ago."

She was still looking at him with the most speaking amazement.

"You like it, my Emma, as little as I feared – I wish our opinions were the same. But in time they will. Time, you may be sure, will make one or the other of us think differently; and, in the meanwhile, we need not talk much on the subject."

"You mistake me, you quite mistake me," she replied, exerting herself. "It is not that such a circumstance would now make me unhappy, but I cannot believe it. It seems an impossibility! You cannot mean to say, that Harriet Smith has accepted Robert Martin. You cannot mean that he has even proposed to her again – yet. You only mean, that he intends it."

"I mean that he has done it," answered Mr. Knightley, with smiling but determined decision, "and been accepted."

"Good God!" she cried. "Well!" Then having recourse to her work-basket, in excuse for leaning down her face, and concealing all the exquisite feelings of delight and entertainment which she knew she must be expressing, she added, "Well, now tell me everything; make this intelligible to me. How, where, when? Let me know it all. I never was more surprised – but it does not make me unhappy, I assure you. How – how has it been possible?"

"It is a very simple story. He went to town on business three days ago, and I got him to take charge of some papers which I was wanting to send to John. He delivered these papers to John, at his chambers, and was asked by him to join their party the same evening to Astley's. They were going to take the two eldest boys to Astley's. The party was to be our brother and sister, Henry, John – and Miss Smith. My friend Robert could not resist. They called for him in their way; were all extremely amused; and my brother asked him to dine with them the next day which he did and in the course of that visit (as I understand) he found an opportunity of speaking to Harriet; and certainly did not speak in vain. She made him, by her acceptance, as happy even as he is deserving. He came down by yesterday's coach, and was with me this morning immediately after breakfast, to report his proceedings, first on my affairs, and then on his own. This is all that I can relate of the how, where, and when. Your friend Harriet will make a much longer history when you see her. She will give you all the minute particulars, which only woman's language can make interesting. In our communications we deal only in the great. However, I must say, that Robert Martin's heart seemed for *him,* and to *me,* very overflowing; and that he did mention, without its being much to the purpose, that on quitting their box at Astley's, my brother took charge of Mrs. John Knightley and little John, and he followed with Miss Smith and Henry; and that at one time they were in such a crowd, as to make Miss Smith rather uneasy."

He stopped. Emma dared not attempt any immediate reply. To speak, she was sure would be to betray a most unreasonable degree of happiness. She must wait a moment, or he would think her mad. Her silence disturbed him; and after observing her a little while, he added:

"Emma, my love, you said that this circumstance would not now make you unhappy; but I am afraid it gives you more pain than you expected. His situation is an evil but you must consider it as what satisfies your friend; and I will answer for your thinking better and better of him as you know him more. His good sense and good principles would delight you. As far as the man is concerned, you could not wish your friend in better hands. His rank in society I would alter if I could, which is saying a great deal I assure you, Emma. You laugh at me about William Larkins; but I could quite as ill spare Robert Martin."

He wanted her to look up and smile; and having now brought herself not to smile too broadly she did cheerfully answering:

"You need not be at any pains to reconcile me to the match. I think Harriet is doing extremely well. *Her* connections may be worse than *his.* In respectability of character, there can be no doubt that they are. I have been silent from surprise merely – excessive surprise. You cannot imagine how suddenly it has come on me! how peculiarly unprepared I was! For I had reason to believe her very lately more determined against him, much more, than she was before."

"You ought to know your friend best," replied Mr. Knightley; "but I should say she was a good-tempered, soft-hearted girl, not likely to be very, very determined against any young man who told her he loved her."

Emma could not help laughing as she answered, "Upon my word, I believe you know her quite as well as I do. But, Mr. Knightley, are you perfectly sure that she has absolutely and downright *accepted* him. I could suppose she might in time but can she already? Did not you misunderstand him? You were both talking of other things; of business, shows of cattle, or new drills and might not you, in the confusion of so many subjects, mistake him? It was not Harriet's hand that he was certain of – it was the dimensions of some famous ox."

The contrast between the countenance and air of Mr. Knightley and Robert Martin was, at this moment, so strong to Emma's feelings, and so strong was the recollection of all that had so recently passed on Harriet's side, so fresh the sound of those words, spoken with such emphasis, "No, I hope I know better than to think of Robert Martin," that she was really expecting the intelligence to prove, in some measure, premature. It could not be otherwise.

"Do you dare say this?" cried Mr. Knightley. "Do you dare to suppose me so great a blockhead, as not to know what a man is talking of? What do you deserve?"

"Oh! I always deserve the best treatment, because I never put up with any other; and, therefore, you must give me a plain, direct answer. Are you quite sure that you understand the terms on which Mr. Martin and Harriet now are?"

"I am quite sure," he replied, speaking very distinctly, "that he told me she had accepted him; and that there was no obscurity, nothing doubtful, in the words he used; and I think I can give you a proof that it must be so. He asked my opinion as to what he was now to do. He knew of no one but Mrs. Goddard to whom he could apply for information of her relations or friends. Could I mention any thing more fit to be done, than to go to Mrs. Goddard? I assured him that I could not. Then, he said, he would endeavour to see her in the course of this day."

"I am perfectly satisfied," replied Emma, with the brightest smiles, "and most sincerely wish them happy."

"You are materially changed since we talked on this subject before."

"I hope so – for at that time I was a fool."

"And I am changed also; for I am now very willing to grant you all Harriet's good qualities. I have taken some pains for your sake, and for Robert Martin's sake, (whom I have always had reason to believe as much in love with her as ever,) to get acquainted with her. I have often talked to her a good deal. You must have seen that I did. Sometimes, indeed, I have thought you were half suspecting me of pleading poor Martin's cause, which was never the case; but, from all my observations, I am convinced of her being an artless, amiable girl, with very good notions, very seriously good principles, and placing her happiness in the affections and utility of domestic life. Much of this, I have no doubt, she may thank you for."

"Me!" cried Emma, shaking her head. "Ah! poor Harriet!"

She checked herself, however, and submitted quietly to a little more praise than she deserved.

Their conversation was soon afterwards closed by the entrance of her father. She was not sorry. She wanted to be alone. Her mind was in a state of flutter and wonder, which made it impossible for her to be collected. She was in dancing, singing, exclaiming spirits;

and till she had moved about, and talked to herself, and laughed and reflected, she could be fit for nothing rational.

Her father's business was to announce James's being gone out to put the horses to, preparatory to their now daily drive to Randalls; and she had, therefore, an immediate excuse for disappearing.

The joy, the gratitude, the exquisite delight of her sensations may be imagined. The sole grievance and alloy thus removed in the prospect of Harriet's welfare, she was really in danger of becoming too happy for security. What had she to wish for? Nothing, but to grow more worthy of him, whose intentions and judgment had been ever so superior to her own. Nothing, but that the lessons of her past folly might teach her humility and circumspection in future.

Serious she was, very serious in her thankfulness, and in her resolutions; and yet there was no preventing a laugh, sometimes in the very midst of them. She must laugh at such a close – Such an end of the doleful disappointment of five weeks back – Such a heart – such a Harriet!

Now there would be pleasure in her returning. Everything would be a pleasure. It would be a great pleasure to know Robert Martin.

High in the rank of her most serious and heartfelt felicities, was the reflection that all necessity of concealment from Mr. Knightley would soon be over. The disguise, equivocation, mystery, so hateful to her to practise, might soon be over. She could now look forward to giving him that full and perfect confidence which her disposition was most ready to welcome as a duty.

In the gayest and happiest spirits she set forward with her father; not always listening, but always agreeing to what he said; and, whether in speech or silence, conniving at the comfortable persuasion of his being obliged to go to Randalls every day, or poor Mrs. Weston would be disappointed.

They arrived. Mrs. Weston was alone in the drawing-room: but hardly had they been told of the baby, and Mr. Woodhouse received the thanks for coming, which he asked for, when a glimpse was caught through the blind, of two figures passing near the window.

"It is Frank and Miss Fairfax," said Mrs. Weston. "I was just going to tell you of our agreeable surprise in seeing him arrive this morning. He stays till to morrow, and Miss Fairfax has been persuaded to spend the day with us. They are coming in, I hope."

In half a minute they were in the room. Emma was extremely glad to see him but there was a degree of confusion – a number of embarrassing recollections on each side. They met readily and smiling, but with a consciousness which at first allowed little to be said; and having all sat down again, there was for some time such a blank in the circle, that Emma began to doubt whether the wish now indulged, which she had long felt, of seeing Frank Churchill once more, and of seeing him with Jane, would yield its proportion of pleasure. When Mr. Weston joined the party, however, and when the baby was fetched, there was no longer a want of subject or animation or of courage and opportunity for Frank Churchill to draw near her and say:

"I have to thank you, Miss Woodhouse, for a very kind forgiving message in one of Mrs. Weston's letters. I hope time has not made you less willing to pardon. I hope you do not retract what you then said."

"No, indeed," cried Emma, most happy to begin, "not in the least. I am particularly glad to see and shake hands with you and to give you joy in person."

He thanked her with all his heart, and continued some time to speak with serious feeling of his gratitude and happiness.

"Is not she looking well?" said he, turning his eyes towards Jane. "Better than she ever used to do? You see how my father and Mrs. Weston dote upon her."

But his spirits were soon rising again, and with laughing eyes, after mentioning the expected return of the Campbells, he named the name of Dixon. Emma blushed, and forbade its being pronounced in her hearing.

"I can never think of it," she cried, "without extreme shame."

"The shame," he answered, "is all mine, or ought to be. But is it possible that you had no suspicion? I mean of late. Early, I know, you had none."

"I never had the smallest, I assure you."

"That appears quite wonderful. I was once very near – and I wish I had it would have been better. But though I was always doing wrong things, they were very *bad* wrong things, and such as did me no service. It would have been a much better transgression had I broken the bond of secrecy and told you everything."

"It is not now worth a regret," said Emma.

"I have some hope," resumed he, "of my uncle's being persuaded to pay a visit at Randalls; he wants to be introduced to her. When the Campbells are returned, we shall meet them in London, and continue there, I trust, till we may carry her northward. But now, I am at such a distance from her – is not it hard, Miss Woodhouse? Till this morning, we have not once met since the day of reconciliation. Don't you pity me?"

Emma spoke her pity so very kindly, that with a sudden accession of gay thought, he cried:

"Ah! by the bye," then sinking his voice, and looking demure for the moment "I hope Mr. Knightley is well?" He paused. She coloured and laughed. "I know you saw my letter, and think you may remember my wish in your favour. Let me return your congratulations. I assure you that I have heard the news with the warmest interest and satisfaction. He is a man whom I cannot presume to praise."

Emma was delighted, and only wanted him to go on in the

same style; but his mind was the next moment in his own concerns and with his own Jane, and his next words were:

"Did you ever see such a skin? Such smoothness! such delicacy! And yet without being actually fair. One cannot call her fair. It is a most uncommon complexion, with her dark eyelashes and hair – a most distinguishing complexion! So peculiarly the lady in it. Just colour enough for beauty."

"I have always admired her complexion," replied Emma, archly; "but do not I remember the time when you found fault with her for being so pale? When we first began to talk of her. – Have you quite forgotten?"

"Oh! no what an impudent dog I was! How could I dare – "

But he laughed so heartily at the recollection, that Emma could not help saying:

"I do suspect that in the midst of your perplexities at that time, you had very great amusement in tricking us all. I am sure you had. I am sure it was a consolation to you."

"Oh! no, no, no how can you suspect me of such a thing? I was the most miserable wretch!"

"Not quite so miserable as to be insensible to mirth. I am sure it was a source of high entertainment to you, to feel that you were taking us all in. Perhaps I am the readier to suspect, because, to tell you the truth, I think it might have been some amusement to myself in the same situation. I think there is a little likeness between us."

He bowed.

"If not in our dispositions," she presently added, with a look of true sensibility, "there is a likeness in our destiny; the destiny which bids fair to connect us with two characters so much superior to our own."

"True, true," he answered, warmly. "No, not true on your side. You can have no superior, but most true on mine. She is a complete angel. Look at her. Is not she an angel in every gesture? Observe the turn of her throat. Observe her eyes, as she is looking up at my father. You will be glad to hear (inclining his head, and whispering seriously) that my uncle means to give her all my aunt's jewels. They are to be new set. I am resolved to have some in an ornament for the head. Will not it be beautiful in her dark hair?"

"Very beautiful, indeed," replied Emma; and she spoke so kindly, that he gratefully burst out:

"How delighted I am to see you again! and to see you in such excellent looks! I would not have missed this meeting for the world. I should certainly have called at Hartfield, had you failed to come."

The others had been talking of the child, Mrs. Weston giving an account of a little alarm she had been under, the evening before, from the infant's appearing not quite well. She believed she had been foolish, but it had alarmed her, and she had been within half a minute of sending for Mr. Perry. Perhaps she ought to be ashamed, but Mr. Weston had been almost as uneasy as herself. In ten minutes, however, the child had been perfectly well again. This was her history; and particularly interesting it was to Mr. Woodhouse, who commended her very much for thinking of sending for Perry, and only regretted that she had not done it. "She should always send for Perry, if the child appeared in the slightest degree disordered, were it only for a moment. She could not be too soon alarmed, nor send for Perry too often. It was a pity, perhaps, that he had not come last night; for, though the child seemed well now – very well considering – it would probably have been better if Perry had seen it."

Frank Churchill caught the name.

"Perry!" said he to Emma, and trying, as he spoke, to catch Miss Fairfax's eye. "My friend Mr. Perry! What are they saying about Mr. Perry? Has he been here this morning? And how does he travel now? Has he set up his carriage?"

Emma soon recollected, and understood him; and while she joined in the laugh, it was evident from Jane's countenance that she too was really hearing him, though trying to seem deaf.

"Such an extraordinary dream of mine!" he cried. "I can never think of it without laughing. She hears us, she hears us, Miss Woodhouse. I see it in her cheek, her smile, her vain attempt to frown. Look at her. Do not you see that, at this instant, the very passage of her own letter, which sent me the report, is passing under her eye that the whole blunder is spread before her that she can attend to nothing else, though pretending to listen to the others?"

Jane was forced to smile completely, for a moment; and the smile partly remained as she turned towards him, and said in a conscious, low, yet steady voice:

"How you can bear such recollections, is astonishing to me! They *will* sometimes obtrude but how you can *court* them!"

He had a great deal to say in return, and very entertainingly; but Emma's feelings were chiefly with Jane, in the argument; and on leaving Randalls, and falling naturally into a comparison of the two men, she felt, that pleased as she had been to see Frank Churchill, and really regarding him as she did with friendship, she had never been more sensible of Mr. Knightley's high superiority of character. The happiness of this most happy day, received its completion, in the animated contemplation of his worth which this comparison produced.

# Chapter 55

IF EMMA had still, at intervals, an anxious feeling for Harriet, a momentary doubt of its being possible for her to be really cured of her attachment to Mr. Knightley, and really able to accept another man from unbiased inclination, it was not long that she had to suffer from the recurrence of any such uncertainty. A very few days brought the party from London, and she had no sooner an opportunity of being one hour alone with Harriet, than she became perfectly satisfied unaccountable as it was! that Robert Martin had thoroughly supplanted Mr. Knightley, and was now forming all her views of happiness.

Harriet was a little distressed – did look a little foolish at first: but having once owned that she had been presumptuous and silly, and self-deceived, before, her pain and confusion seemed to die away with the words, and leave her without a care for the past, and with the fullest exultation in the present and future; for, as to her friend's approbation, Emma had instantly removed every fear of that nature, by meeting her with the most unqualified congratulations. Harriet was most happy to give every particular of the evening at Astley's, and the dinner the next day; she could dwell on it all with the utmost delight. But what did such particulars explain? The fact was, as Emma could now acknowledge, that Harriet had always liked Robert Martin; and that his continuing to love her had been irresistible. Beyond this, it must ever be unintelligible to Emma.

The event, however, was most joyful; and every day was giving her fresh reason for thinking so. Harriet's parentage became known. She proved to be the daughter of a tradesman, rich enough to afford her the comfortable maintenance which had ever been hers, and decent enough to have always wished for concealment. Such was the blood of gentility which Emma had formerly been so ready to vouch for! It was likely to be as untainted, perhaps, as the blood of many a gentleman: but what a connection had she been preparing for Mr. Knightley or for the Churchills or even for Mr. Elton! The stain of illegitimacy, unbleached by nobility or wealth, would have been a stain indeed.

No objection was raised on the father's side; the young man was treated liberally; it was all as it should be: and as Emma became acquainted with Robert Martin, who was now introduced at Hartfield, she fully acknowledged in him all the appearance of sense and worth which could bid fairest for her little friend. She had no doubt of Harriet's happiness with any good-tempered man; but with him, and in the home he offered, there would be the hope of more, of security, stability, and improvement. She would be placed in the midst of those who loved her, and who had better sense than herself; retired enough for safety, and occupied enough for cheerfulness. She would be never led into temptation, nor left for it to find her out. She would be respectable and happy; and Emma admitted her to be the luckiest creature in the world, to have created so steady and persevering an affection in such a man; or, if not quite the luckiest, to yield only to herself.

Harriet, necessarily drawn away by her engagements with the Martins, was less and less at Hartfield; which was not to be regretted. The intimacy between her and Emma must sink; their friendship must change into a calmer sort of goodwill; and, fortunately, what ought to be, and must be, seemed already beginning, and in the most gradual, natural manner.

Before the end of September, Emma attended Harriet to church, and saw her hand bestowed on Robert Martin with so complete a satisfaction, as no remembrances, even connected with Mr. Elton as he stood before them, could impair. Perhaps, indeed, at that time she scarcely saw Mr. Elton, but as the clergyman whose blessing at the altar might next fall on herself. Robert Martin and Harriet Smith, the latest couple engaged of the three, were the first to be married.

Jane Fairfax had already quitted Highbury, and was restored

to the comforts of her beloved home with the Campbells. The Mr. Churchills were also in town; and they were only waiting for November.

The intermediate month was the one fixed on, as far as they dared, by Emma and Mr. Knightley. They had determined that their marriage ought to be concluded while John and Isabella were still at Hartfield, to allow them the fortnight's absence in a tour to the sea-side, which was the plan. John and Isabella, and every other friend, were agreed in approving it. But Mr. Woodhouse – how was Mr. Woodhouse to be induced to consent? He, who had never yet alluded to their marriage but as a distant event.

When first sounded on the subject, he was so miserable, that they were almost hopeless. A second allusion, indeed, gave less pain. He began to think it was to be, and that he could not prevent it – a very promising step of the mind on its way to resignation. Still, however, he was not happy. Nay, he appeared so much otherwise, that his daughter's courage failed. She could not bear to see him suffering, to know him fancying himself neglected; and though her understanding almost acquiesced in the assurance of both the Mr. Knightleys, that when once the event were over, his distress would be soon over too, she hesitated – she could not proceed.

In this state of suspense they were befriended, not by any sudden illumination of Mr. Woodhouse's mind, or any wonderful change of his nervous system, but by the operation of the same system in another way. Mrs. Weston's poultry-house was robbed one night of all her turkeys – evidently by the ingenuity of man. Other poultry – yards in the neighbourhood also suffered. Pilfering was *house-breaking* to Mr. Woodhouse's fears. He was very uneasy; and but for the sense of his son-in-law's protection, would have been under wretched alarm every night of his life. The strength, resolution, and presence of mind of the Mr. Knightleys, commanded his fullest dependence. While either of them protected him and his, Hartfield was safe. But Mr. John Knightley must be in London again by the end of the first week in November.

The result of this distress was, that, with a much more voluntary, cheerful consent than his daughter had ever presumed to hope for at the moment, she was able to fix her wedding-day and Mr. Elton was called on, within a month from the marriage of Mr. and Mrs. Robert Martin, to join the hands of Mr. Knightley and Miss Woodhouse.

The wedding was very much like other weddings, where the parties have no taste for finery or parade; and Mrs. Elton, from the particulars detailed by her husband, thought it all extremely shabby, and very inferior to her own. "Very little white satin, very few lace veils; a most pitiful business! Selina would stare when she heard of it." But, in spite of these deficiencies, the wishes, the hopes, the confidence, the predictions of the small band of true friends who witnessed the ceremony, were fully answered in the perfect happiness of the union.

**THE END**

# PRIDE
# &
# PREJUDICE

# Chapter 1

It is a truth universally acknowledged, that a single man in possession of a good fortune, must be in want of a wife.

However little known the feelings or views of such a man may be on his first entering a neighbourhood, this truth is so well fixed in the minds of the surrounding families, that he is considered as the rightful property of some one or other of their daughters.

"My dear Mr. Bennet," said his lady to him one day, "have you heard that Netherfield Park is let at last?"

Mr. Bennet replied that he had not.

"But it is," returned she; "for Mrs. Long has just been here, and she told me all about it.

Mr. Bennet made no answer.

"Do you not want to know who has taken it?" cried his wife impatiently.

"*You* want to tell me, and I have no objection to hearing it."

This was invitation enough.

"Why, my dear, you must know, Mrs. Long says that Netherfield is taken by a young man of large fortune from the north of England; that he came down on Monday in a chaise and four to see the place, and was so much delighted with it that he agreed with Mr. Morris immediately; that he is to take possession before Michaelmas, and some of his servants are to be in the house by the end of next week."

"What is his name?"

"Bingley."

"Is he married or single?"

"Oh! single, my dear, to be sure! A single man of large fortune;

four or five thousand a year. What a fine thing for our girls!"

"How so? how can it affect them?"

"My dear Mr. Bennet," replied his wife, "how can you be so tiresome! You must know that I am thinking of his marrying one of them."

"Is that his design in settling here?"

"Design! nonsense, how can you talk so! But it is very likely that he *may* fall in love with one of them, and therefore you must visit him as soon as he comes."

"I see no occasion for that. You and the girls may go, or you may send them by themselves, which perhaps will be still better, for as you are as handsome as any of them, Mr. Bingley might like you the best of the party."

"My dear, you flatter me. I certainly *have* had my share of beauty, but I do not pretend to be anything extraordinary now. When a woman has five grown-up daughters, she ought to give over thinking of her own beauty."

"In such cases, a woman has not often much beauty to think of."

"But, my dear, you must indeed go and see Mr. Bingley when he comes into the neighbourhood."

"It is more than I engage for, I assure you."

"But consider your daughters. Only think what an establishment it would be for one of them. Sir William and Lady Lucas are determined to go, merely on that account, for in general you know they visit no newcomers. Indeed you must go, for it will be impossible for *us* to visit him, if you do not."

"You are over-scrupulous surely. I dare say Mr. Bingley will be very glad to see you; and I will send a few lines by you to assure him of my hearty consent to his marrying whichever he chooses of the girls; though I must throw in a good word for my little Lizzy."

"I desire you will do no such thing. Lizzy is not a bit better than the others; and I am sure she is not half so handsome as Jane, nor half so good-humoured as Lydia. But you are always giving *her* the preference."

"They have none of them much to recommend them," replied he; "they are all silly and ignorant like other girls; but Lizzy has something more of quickness than her sisters."

"Mr. Bennet, how can you abuse your own children in such a way? You take delight in vexing me. You have no compassion on my poor nerves."

"You mistake me, my dear. I have a high respect for your nerves. They are my old friends. I have heard you mention them with consideration these twenty years at least."

"Ah! you do not know what I suffer."

"But I hope you will get over it, and live to see many young men of four thousand a year come into the neighborhood."

"It will be no use to us, if twenty such should come since you will not visit them."

"Depend upon it, my dear, that when there are twenty, I will visit them all."

Mr. Bennet was so odd a mixture of quick parts, sarcastic humour, reserve, and caprice, that the experience of three and twenty years had been insufficient to make his wife understand his character. *Her* mind was less difficult to develop. She was a woman of mean understanding, little information, and uncertain temper. When she was discontented she fancied herself nervous. The business of her life was to get her daughters married; its solace was visiting and news.

# Chapter 2

MR. BENNET was among the earliest of those who waited on Mr. Bingley. He had always intended to visit him, though to the last always assuring his wife that he should not go; and till the evening after the visit was paid, she had no knowledge of it. It was then disclosed in the following manner. Observing his second daughter employed in trimming a hat, he suddenly addressed her with,

"I hope Mr. Bingley will like it Lizzy."

"We are not in a way to know *what* Mr. Bingley likes," said her mother resentfully, "since we are not to visit."

"But you forget, mamma," said Elizabeth, "that we shall meet him at the assemblies, and that Mrs. Long has promised to introduce him."

"I do not believe Mrs. Long will do any such thing. She has two nieces of her own. She is a selfish, hypocritical woman, and I have no opinion of her."

"No more have I," said Mr. Bennet; "and I am glad to find that you do not depend on her serving you."

Mrs. Bennet deigned not to make any reply; but unable to contain herself, began scolding one of her daughters.

"Don't keep coughing so, Kitty, for heavens's sake! Have a little compassion on my nerves. You tear them to pieces."

"Kitty has no discretion in her coughs," said her father; "she times them ill."

"I do not cough for my own amusement," replied Kitty fretfully.

"When is your next ball to be, Lizzy?"

"Tomorrow fortnight."

"Aye, so it is," cried her mother, "and Mrs. Long does not

come back till the day before; so, it will be impossible for her to introduce him, for she will not know him herself."

"Then, my dear, you may have the advantage of your friend, and introduce Mr. Bingley to *her*."

"Impossible, Mr. Bennet, impossible, when I am not acquainted with him myself; how can you be so teasing?"

"I honour your circumspection. A fortnight's acquaintance is certainly very little. One cannot know what a man really is by the end of a fortnight. But if *we* do not venture, somebody else will; and after all, Mrs. Long and her nieces must stand their chance; and therefore, as she will think it an act of kindness, if you decline the office, I will take it on myself."

The girls stared at their father. Mrs. Bennet said only, "Nonsense, nonsense!"

"What can be the meaning of that emphatic exclamation?" cried he. "Do you consider the forms of introduction, and the stress that is laid on them, as nonsense? I cannot quite agree with you *there*. What say you, Mary? for you are a young lady of deep reflection I know, and read great books, and make extracts."

Mary wished to say something very sensible, but knew not how.

"While Mary is adjusting her ideas," he continued, "let us return to Mr. Bingley."

"I am sick of Mr. Bingley," cried his wife.

"I am sorry to hear *that*; but why did you not tell me that so before? If I had known as much this morning, I certainly would not have called on him. It is very unlucky; but as I have actually paid the visit, we cannot escape the acquaintance now."

The astonishment of the ladies was just what he wished; that of Mrs. Bennet perhaps surpassing the rest; though when the first tumult of joy was over, she began to declare that it was what she had expected all the while.

"How good it was in you, my dear Mr. Bennet! But I knew I should persuade you at last. I was sure you loved your girls too well to neglect such an acquaintance. Well, how pleased I am! and it is such a good joke, too, that you should have gone this morning, and never said a word about it till now."

"Now, Kitty, you may cough as much as you choose," said Mr. Bennet; and, as he spoke, he left the room, fatigued with the raptures of his wife.

"What an excellent father you have, girls!" said she, when the door was shut. "I do not know how you will ever make him amends for his kindness; or me either, for that matter. At our time of life, it is not so pleasant I can tell you, to be making new acquaintance every day; but for your sakes, we would do anything. Lydia, my love, though you *are* the youngest, I dare say Mr. Bingley will dance with you at the next ball."

"Oh!" said Lydia stoutly, "I am not afraid; for though I *am* the youngest, I'm the tallest."

The rest of the evening was spent in conjecturing how soon he would return Mr. Bennet's visit, and determining when they should ask him to dinner.

# Chapter 3

NOT ALL that Mrs. Bennet, however, with the assistance of her five daughters, could ask on the subject was sufficient to draw from her husband any satisfactory description of Mr. Bingley. They attacked him in various ways; with barefaced questions, ingenious suppositions, and distant surmises; but he eluded the skill of them all; and they were at last obliged to accept the second-hand intelligence of their neighbour Lady Lucas. Her report was highly favourable. Sir William had been delighted with him. He was quite young, wonderfully handsome, extremely agreeable, and to crown the whole, he meant to be at the next assembly with a large party. Nothing could be more delightful! To be fond of dancing was a certain step towards falling in love; and very lively hopes of Mr. Bingley's heart were entertained.

"If I can but see one of my daughters happily settled at Netherfield," said Mrs. Bennet to her husband, "and all the others equally well married, I shall have nothing to wish for."

In a few days Mr. Bingley returned Mr. Bennet's visit, and sat about ten minutes with him in his library. He had entertained hopes of being admitted to a sight of the young ladies, of whose beauty he had heard much; but he saw only the father. The ladies were somewhat more fortunate, for they had the advantage of ascertaining from an upper window, that he wore a blue coat and rode a black horse.

An invitation to dinner was soon afterwards dispatched; and already had Mrs. Bennet planned the courses that were to do credit to her housekeeping, when an answer arrived which deferred it all. Mr. Bingley was obliged to be in town the following day, and consequently unable to accept the honour of their invitation, &c. Mrs. Bennet was quite disconcerted. She could not imagine what business he could have in town so soon after his arrival in Hertfordshire; and she began to fear that he might be always flying about from one place to another, and never settled at Netherfield as he ought to be. Lady Lucas quieted her fears a little by starting the idea of his being gone to London only to get a large party for the ball; and a report soon followed that Mr. Bingley was to bring twelve ladies and seven gentlemen with him to the assembly. The girls grieved over such a number of ladies, but were comforted the day before the ball by hearing, that instead of twelve, he brought only six with him from London, his five sisters and a cousin. And when the party entered the assembly room, it consisted of only five altogether: Mr. Bingley, his two sisters, the husband of the eldest, and another young man.

Mr. Bingley was good looking and gentlemanlike; he had a pleasant countenance, and easy, unaffected manners. His sisters were fine women, with an air of decided fashion. His brother-in-law, Mr. Hurst, merely looked the gentleman; but his friend Mr. Darcy soon drew the attention of the room by his fine, tall person, handsome features, noble mien, and the report which was in general circulation within five minutes after his entrance, of his having ten thousand a year. The gentlemen pronounced him to be a fine figure of a man, the ladies declared he was much handsomer than Mr. Bingley, and he was looked at with great admiration for about half the evening, till his manners gave a disgust which turned the tide of his popularity; for he was discovered to be proud, to be above his company, and above being pleased; and not all his large estate in Derbyshire could then save him from having a most forbidding, disagreeable countenance, and being unworthy to be compared with his friend.

Mr. Bingley had soon made himself acquainted with all the principal people in the room; he was lively and unreserved, danced every dance, was angry that the ball closed so early, and talked of giving one himself at Netherfield. Such amiable qualities must speak for themselves. What a contrast between him and his friend! Mr. Darcy danced only once with Mrs. Hurst and once with Miss Bingley, declined being introduced to any other lady, and spent the rest of the evening in walking about the room, speaking occasionally to one of his own party. His character was decided. He was the proudest, most disagreeable man in the world, and everybody hoped that he would never come there again. Amongst the most violent against him was Mrs. Bennet, whose dislike of his general behaviour, was sharpened into particular resentment, by his having slighted one of her daughters.

Elizabeth Bennet had been obliged, by the scarcity of

gentlemen, to sit down for two dances; and during part of that time, Mr. Darcy had been standing near enough for her to overhear a conversation between him and Mr. Bingley, who came from the dance for a few minutes, to press his friend to join it.

"Come, Darcy," said he, "I must have you dance. I hate to see you standing about by yourself in this stupid manner. You had much better dance."

"I certainly shall not. You know how I detest it, unless I am particularly acquainted with my partner. At such an assembly as this, it would be insupportable. Your sisters are engaged, and there is not another woman in the room, whom it would not be a punishment to me to stand up with."

"I would not be so fastidious as you are," cried Bingley, "for a kingdom! Upon my honour, I never met with so many pleasant girls in my life, as I have this evening; and there are several of them you see uncommonly pretty."

"*You* are dancing with the only handsome girl in the room," said Mr. Darcy, looking at the eldest Miss Bennet.

"Oh! she is the most beautiful creature I ever beheld! But there is one of her sisters sitting down just behind you, who is very pretty, and I dare say, very agreeable. Do let me ask my partner to introduce you."

"Which do you mean?" and turning round, he looked for a moment at Elizabeth, till catching her eye, he withdrew his own and coldly said, "She is tolerable; but not handsome enough to tempt *me*; I am in no humour at present to give consequence to young ladies who are slighted by other men. You had better return to your partner and enjoy her smiles, for you are wasting your time with me."

Mr. Bingley followed his advice. Mr. Darcy walked off; and Elizabeth remained with no very cordial feelings towards him. She told the story however with great spirit among her friends; for she had a lively, playful disposition, which delighted in anything ridiculous.

The evening altogether passed off pleasantly to the whole family. Mrs. Bennet had seen her eldest daughter much admired by the Netherfield party. Mr. Bingley had danced with her twice, and she had been distinguished by his sisters. Jane was as much gratified by this, as her mother could be, though in a quieter way. Elizabeth felt Jane's pleasure. Mary had heard herself mentioned to Miss Bingley as the most accomplished girl in the neighbourhood; and Catherine and Lydia had been fortunate enough to be never without partners, which was all that they had yet learnt to care for at a ball. They returned therefore in good spirits to Longbourn, the village where they lived, and of which they were the principal inhabitants. They found Mr. Bennet still up. With a book he was regardless of time; and on the present occasion he had a good deal of curiosity as to the event of an evening which had raised such splendid expectations. He had rather hoped that his wife's views on the stranger would be disappointed; but he soon found that he had a very different story to hear.

"Oh! my dear Mr. Bennet," as she entered the room, "we have had a most delightful evening, a most excellent ball. I wish you had been there. Jane was so admired, nothing could be like it. Everybody said how well she looked; and Mr. Bingley thought her quite beautiful, and danced with her twice. Only think of *that* my dear; he actually danced with her twice; and she was the only creature in the room that he asked a second time. First of all, he asked Miss Lucas. I was so vexed to see him stand up with her; but, however, he did not admire her at all; indeed, nobody can, you know; and he seemed quite struck with Jane as she was going down the dance. So, he enquired who she was, and got introduced, and asked her for the two next. Then, the two third he danced with Miss King, and the two fourth with Maria Lucas, and the two fifth with Jane again, and the two sixth with Lizzy, and the Boulanger – '

"If he had had any compassion for *me*," cried her husband impatiently, "he would not have danced half so much! For God's sake, say no more of his partners. Oh! that he had sprained his ankle in the first dance!"

"Oh! my dear," continued Mrs. Bennet, "I am quite delighted with him. He is so excessively handsome! and his sisters are charming women. I never in my life saw anything more elegant than their dresses. I dare say the lace upon Mrs. Hurst's gown – "

Here she was interrupted again. Mr. Bennet protested against any description of finery. She was therefore obliged to seek another branch of the subject, and related, with much bitterness of spirit and some exaggeration, the shocking rudeness of Mr. Darcy.

"But I can assure you," she added, "that Lizzy does not lose much by not suiting *his* fancy; for he is a most disagreeable, horrid man, not at all worth pleasing. So high and so conceited that there was no enduring him! He walked here, and he walked there, fancying himself so very great! Not handsome enough to dance with! I wish you had been there, my dear, to have given him one of your setdowns. I quite detest the man."

## Chapter 4

WHEN JANE and Elizabeth were alone, the former, who had been cautious in her praise of Mr. Bingley before, expressed to her sister how very much she admired him.

"He is just what a young man ought to be," said she, "sensible, good-humoured, lively; and I never saw such happy manners! –

so much ease, with such perfect good breeding!"

"He is also handsome," replied Elizabeth, "which a young man ought likewise to be, if he possibly can. His character is thereby complete."

"I was very much flattered by his asking me to dance a second time. I did not expect such a compliment."

"Did you not? *I* did for you. But that is one great difference between us. Compliments always take *you* by surprise, and *me* never. What could be more natural than his asking you again? He could not help seeing that you were about five times as pretty as every other woman in the room. No thanks to his gallantry for that. Well, he certainly is very agreeable, and I give you leave to like him. You have liked many a stupider person."

"Dear Lizzy!"

"Oh! you are a great deal too apt you know, to like people in general. You never see a fault in anybody. All the world are good and agreeable in your eyes. I never heard you speak ill of a human being in my life."

"I would not wish to be hasty in censuring anyone; but I always speak what I think."

"I know you do; and it is *that* which makes the wonder. With *your* good sense, to be so honestly blind to the follies and nonsense of others! Affectation of candour is common enough; – one meets with it everywhere. But to be candid without ostentation or design – to take the good of everybody's character and make it still better, and say nothing of the bad – belongs to you alone. And so, you like this man's sisters too, do you? Their manners are not equal to his."

"Certainly not, at first. But they are very pleasing women when you converse with them. Miss Bingley is to live with her brother, and keep his house; and I am much mistaken if we shall not find a very charming neighbour in her."

Elizabeth listened in silence, but was not convinced; their behaviour at the assembly had not been calculated to please in general; and with more quickness of observation and less pliancy of temper than her sister, and with a judgement too unassailed by any attention to herself, she was very little disposed to approve them. They were in fact very fine ladies; not deficient in good humour when they were pleased, nor in the power of being agreeable when they chose it; but proud and conceited. They were rather handsome, had been educated in one of the first private seminaries in town, had a fortune of twenty thousand pounds, were in the habit of spending more than they ought, and of associating with people of rank; and were therefore in every respect entitled to think well of themselves, and meanly of others. They were of a respectable family in the north of England; a circumstance more deeply impressed on their memories than that their brother's fortune and their own had been acquired by trade.

Mr. Bingley inherited property to the amount of nearly an hundred thousand pounds from his father, who had intended to purchase an estate, but did not live to do it. – Mr. Bingley intended it likewise, and sometimes made choice of his county; but as he was now provided with a good house and the liberty of a manor, it was doubtful to many of those who best knew the easiness of his temper, whether he might not spend the remainder of his days at Netherfield, and leave the next generation to purchase.

His sisters were very anxious for his having an estate of his own; but though he was now established only as tenant, Miss Bingley was by no means unwilling to preside at his table, nor was Mrs. Hurst, who had married a man of more fashion than fortune, less disposed to consider his house as her home when it suited her. Mr. Bingley had not been of age two years, when he was tempted by an accidental recommendation to look at Netherfield House. He did look at it and into it for half an hour, was pleased with the situation and the principal rooms, satisfied with what the owner said in its praise, and took it immediately.

Between him and Darcy there was a very steady friendship, in spite of a great opposition of character. – Bingley was endeared to Darcy by the easiness, openness, ductility of his temper, though no disposition could offer a greater contrast to his own, and though with his own he never appeared dissatisfied. On the strength of Darcy's regard Bingley had the firmest reliance, and of his judgement the highest opinion. In understanding Darcy was the superior. Bingley was by no means deficient, but Darcy was clever. He was at the same time haughty, reserved, and fastidious, and his manners, though well bred, were not inviting. In that respect his friend had greatly the advantage. Bingley was sure of being liked wherever he appeared, Darcy was continually giving offence.

The manner in which they spoke of the Meryton assembly was sufficiently characteristic. Bingley had never met with pleasanter people or prettier girls in his life; everybody had been most kind and attentive to him, there had been no formality, no stiffness, he had soon felt acquainted with all the room; and as to Miss Bennet, he could not conceive an angel more beautiful. Darcy, on the contrary, had seen a collection of people in whom there was little beauty and no fashion, for none of whom he had felt the smallest interest, and from none received either attention or pleasure. Miss Bennet he acknowledged to be pretty, but she smiled too much.

Mrs. Hurst and her sister allowed it to be so – but still they admired her and liked her, and pronounced her to be a sweet girl, and one whom they should not object to know more of. Miss Bennet was therefore established as a sweet girl, and their brother felt authorised by such commendation to think of her as he chose.

# Chapter 5

WITHIN A short walk of Longbourn lived a family with whom the Bennets were particularly intimate. Sir William Lucas had been formerly in trade in Meryton, where he had made a tolerable fortune and risen to the honour of knighthood by an address to the King, during his mayoralty. The distinction had perhaps been felt too strongly. It had given him a disgust to his business and to his residence in a small market town; and quitting them both, he had removed with his family to a house about a mile from Meryton, denominated from that period Lucas Lodge, where he could think with pleasure of his own importance, and unshackled by business, occupy himself solely in being civil to all the world. For though elated by his rank, it did not render him supercilious; on the contrary, he was all attention to everybody. By nature inoffensive, friendly and obliging, his presentation at St. James's had made him courteous.

Lady Lucas was a very good kind of woman, not too clever to be a valuable neighbour to Mrs. Bennet. – They had several children. The eldest of them, a sensible, intelligent young woman, about twenty-seven, was Elizabeth's intimate friend.

That the Miss Lucases and the Miss Bennets should meet to talk over a ball was absolutely necessary; and the morning after the assembly brought the former to Longbourn to hear and to communicate.

"*You* began the evening well, Charlotte," said Mrs. Bennet with civil self-command to Miss Lucas. "*You* were Mr. Bingley's first choice."

"Yes; – but he seemed to like his second better."

"Oh! – you mean Jane, I suppose – because he danced with her twice. To be sure that *did* seem as if he admired her – indeed I rather believe he *did* – I heard something about it – but I hardly know what – something about Mr. Robinson."

"Perhaps you mean what I overheard between him and Mr. Robinson; did I not mention it to you? Mr. Robinson's asking him how he liked our Meryton assemblies, and whether he did not think there were a great many pretty women in the room, and *which* he thought the prettiest? and his answering immediately to the last question – Oh! the eldest Miss Bennet beyond a doubt, there cannot be two opinions on that point."

"Upon my word! – Well, that is very decided indeed – that does seem as if – but however, it may all come to nothing you know."

"*My* overhearings were more to the purpose than *yours*, Eliza," said Charlotte. "Mr. Darcy is not so well worth listening to as his friend, is he? – Poor Eliza! – to be only just *tolerable*."

"I beg you would not put it into Lizzy's head to be vexed by his ill-treatment; for he is such a disagreeable man that it would be quite a misfortune to be liked by him. Mrs. Long told me last night that he sat close to her for half-an-hour without once opening his lips."

"Are you quite sure, Ma'am? – is not there a little mistake?" said Jane. "I certainly saw Mr. Darcy speaking to her."

"Aye – because she asked him at last how he liked Netherfield, and he could not help answering her; – but she said he seemed very angry at being spoken to."

"Miss Bingley told me," said Jane, "that he never speaks much unless among his intimate acquaintance. With *them* he is remarkably agreeable."

"I do not believe a word of it, my dear. If he had been so very agreeable he would have talked to Mrs. Long. But I can guess how it was; everybody says that he is ate up with pride, and I dare say he had heard somehow that Mrs. Long does not keep a carriage, and had come to the ball in a hack chaise."

"I do not mind his not talking to Mrs. Long," said Miss Lucas, "but I wish he had danced with Eliza."

"Another time, Lizzy," said her mother, "I would not dance with *him*, if I were you."

"I believe, Ma'am, I may safely promise you *never* to dance with him."

"His pride," said Miss Lucas, "does not offend *me* so much as pride often does, because there is an excuse for it. One cannot wonder that so very fine a young man, with family, fortune, everything in his favour, should think highly of himself. If I may so express it, he has a *right* to be proud."

"That is very true," replied Elizabeth, "and I could easily forgive *his* pride, if he had not mortified *mine*."

"Pride," observed Mary, who piqued herself upon the solidity of her reflections, "is a very common failing, I believe. By all that I have ever read, I am convinced that it is very common indeed, that human nature is particularly prone to it, and that there are very few of us who do not cherish a feeling of self-complacency on the score of some quality or other, real or imaginary. Vanity and pride are different things, though the words are often used synonymously. A person may be proud without being vain. Pride relates more to our opinion of ourselves, vanity to what we would have others think of us."

"If I were as rich as Mr. Darcy," cried a young Lucas who came with his sisters, "I should not care how proud I was. I would keep a pack of foxhounds, and drink a bottle of wine every day."

"Then you would drink a great deal more than you ought," said Mrs. Bennet; "and if I were to see you at it I should take away your bottle directly."

The boy protested that she should not; she continued to declare that she would, and the argument ended only with the visit.

# Chapter 6

THE LADIES of Longbourn soon waited on those of Netherfield. The visit was returned in due form. Miss Bennet's pleasing manners grew on the good will of Mrs. Hurst and Miss Bingley; and though the mother was found to be intolerable and the younger sisters not worth speaking to, a wish of being better acquainted with *them,* was expressed towards the two eldest. By Jane, this attention was received with the greatest pleasure; but Elizabeth still saw superciliousness in their treatment of everybody, hardly excepting even her sister, and could not like them; though their kindness to Jane, such as it was, had a value as arising in all probability from the influence of their brother's admiration. It was generally evident whenever they met, that he *did* admire her; and to *her* it was equally evident that Jane was yielding to the preference which she had begun to entertain for him from the first, and was in a way to be very much in love; but she considered with pleasure that it was not likely to be discovered by the world in general, since Jane united with great strength of feeling, a composure of temper and a uniform cheerfulness of manner, which would guard her from the suspicions of the impertinent. She mentioned this to her friend Miss Lucas.

"It may perhaps be pleasant," replied Charlotte, "to be able to impose on the public in such a case; but it is sometimes a disadvantage to be so very guarded. If a woman conceals her affection with the same skill from the object of it, she may lose the opportunity of fixing him; and it will then be but poor consolation to believe the world equally in the dark. There is so much of gratitude or vanity in almost every attachment, that it is not safe to leave any to itself. We can all *begin* freely – a slight preference is natural enough; but there are very few of us who have heart enough to be really in love without encouragement. In nine cases out of ten, a woman had better show *more* affection than she feels. Bingley likes your sister undoubtedly; but he may never do more than like her, if she does not help him on."

"But she does help him on, as much as her nature will allow. If *I* can perceive her regard for him, he must be a simpleton indeed not to discover it too."

"Remember, Eliza, that he does not know Jane's disposition as you do."

"But if a woman is partial to a man, and does not endeavour to conceal it, he must find it out."

"Perhaps he must, if he sees enough of her. But though Bingley and Jane meet tolerably often, it is never for many hours together; and as they always see each other in large mixed parties, it is impossible that every moment should be employed in conversing together. Jane should therefore make the most of every half hour in which she can command his attention. When she is secure of him, there will be leisure for falling in love as much as she chooses."

"Your plan is a good one," replied Elizabeth, "where nothing is in question but the desire of being well married; and if I were determined to get a rich husband, or any husband, I dare say I should adopt it. But these are not Jane's feelings; she is not acting by design. As yet, she cannot even be certain of the degree of her own regard, nor of its reasonableness. She has known him only a fortnight. She danced four dances with him at Meryton; she saw him one morning at his own house, and has since dined in company with him four times. This is not quite enough to make her understand his character."

"Not as you represent it. Had she merely *dined* with him, she might only have discovered whether he had a good appetite; but you must remember that four evenings have been also spent together – and four evenings may do a great deal."

"Yes; these four evenings have enabled them to ascertain that they both like Vingt-un better than Commerce; but with respect to any other leading characteristic, I do not imagine that much has been unfolded."

"Well," said Charlotte, "I wish Jane success with all my heart; and if she were married to him tomorrow, I should think she had as good a chance of happiness, as if she were to be studying his character for a twelvemonth. Happiness in marriage is entirely a matter of chance. If the dispositions of the parties are ever so well known to each other, or ever so similar beforehand, it does not advance their felicity in the least. They always continue to grow sufficiently unlike afterwards to have their share of vexation; and it is better to know as little as possible of the defects of the person with whom you are to pass your life."

"You make me laugh, Charlotte; but it is not sound. You know it is not sound, and that you would never act in this way yourself."

Occupied in observing Mr. Bingley's attentions to her sister, Elizabeth was far from suspecting that she was herself becoming an object of some interest in the eyes of his friend. Mr. Darcy had at first scarcely allowed her to be pretty; he had looked at her without admiration at the ball; and when they next met, he looked at her only to criticise. But no sooner had he made it clear to himself and his friends that she had hardly a good feature in her face, than he began to find it was rendered uncommonly intelligent by the beautiful expression of her dark eyes. To this discovery succeeded some others equally mortifying. Though he had detected with a critical eye more than one failure of perfect symmetry in her form, he was forced to acknowledge her figure to be light and pleasing; and in spite of his asserting that her manners were not those of the fashionable world, he was caught by their easy playfulness. Of this she was perfectly unaware; – to her he was only the man who made himself agreeable nowhere, and who had not thought her handsome enough to dance with.

He began to wish to know more of her, and as a step towards conversing with her himself, attended to her conversation with others. His doing so drew her notice. It was at Sir William Lucas's, where a large party were assembled.

"What does Mr. Darcy mean," said she to Charlotte, "by listening to my conversation with Colonel Forster?"

"That is a question which Mr. Darcy only can answer."

"But if he does it any more I shall certainly let him know that I see what he is about. He has a very satirical eye, and if I do not begin by being impertinent myself, I shall soon grow afraid of him."

On his approaching them soon afterwards, though without seeming to have any intention of speaking, Miss Lucas defied her friend to mention such a subject to him; which immediately provoking Elizabeth to do it, she turned to him and said,

"Did you not think, Mr. Darcy, that I expressed myself uncommonly well just now, when I was teasing Colonel Forster to give us a ball at Meryton?"

"With great energy; – but it is a subject which always makes a lady energetic."

"You are severe on us."

"It will be *her* turn soon to be teased," said Miss Lucas. "I am going to open the instrument, Eliza, and you know what follows."

"You are a very strange creature by way of a friend! – always wanting me to play and sing before anybody and everybody! – If my vanity had taken a musical turn, you would have been invaluable, but as it is, I would really rather not sit down before those who must be in the habit of hearing the very best performers." On Miss Lucas's persevering, however, she added, "Very well, if it must be so, it must." And gravely glancing at Mr. Darcy, "There is a fine old saying, which everybody here is of course familiar with – 'Keep your breath to cool your porridge' – and I shall keep mine to swell my song."

Her performance was pleasing, though by no means capital. After a song or two, and before she could reply to the entreaties of several that she would sing again, she was eagerly succeeded at the instrument by her sister Mary, who having, in consequence of being the only plain one in the family, worked hard for knowledge and accomplishments, was always impatient for display.

Mary had neither genius nor taste; and though vanity had given her application, it had given her likewise a pedantic air and conceited manner, which would have injured a higher degree of excellence than she had reached. Elizabeth, easy and unaffected, had been listened to with much more pleasure, though not playing half so well; and Mary, at the end of a long concerto, was glad to purchase praise and gratitude by Scotch and Irish airs, at the request of her younger sisters, who with some of the Lucases and two or three officers joined eagerly in dancing at one end of the room.

Mr. Darcy stood near them in silent indignation at such a mode of passing the evening, to the exclusion of all conversation, and was too much engrossed by his own thoughts to perceive that Sir William Lucas was his neighbour, till Sir William thus began.

"What a charming amusement for young people this is, Mr. Darcy! – There is nothing like dancing after all. – I consider it as one of the first refinements of polished society."

"Certainly, Sir; – and it has the advantage also of being in vogue amongst the less polished societies of the world. – Every savage can dance."

Sir William only smiled. "Your friend performs delightfully;" he continued after a pause, on seeing Bingley join the group; – "and I doubt not that you are an adept in the science yourself, Mr. Darcy."

"You saw me dance at Meryton, I believe, Sir."

"Yes, indeed, and received no inconsiderable pleasure from the sight. Do you often dance at St. James's?"

"Never, sir."

"Do you not think it would be a proper compliment to the place?"

"It is a compliment which I never pay to any place if I can avoid it."

"You have a house in town, I conclude?"

Mr. Darcy bowed.

"I had once some thoughts of fixing in town myself – for I am fond of superior society; but I did not feel quite certain that the air of London would agree with Lady Lucas."

He paused in hopes of an answer; but his companion was not disposed to make any; and Elizabeth at that instant moving towards them, he was struck with the notion of doing a very gallant thing, and called out to her:

"My dear Miss Eliza, why are you not dancing? – Mr. Darcy, you must allow me to present this young lady to you as a very desirable partner. – You cannot refuse to dance, I am sure, when so much beauty is before you." And taking her hand, he would have given it to Mr. Darcy, who, though extremely surprised, was not unwilling to receive it, when she instantly drew back, and said with some discomposure to Sir William,

"Indeed, Sir, I have not the least intention of dancing. – I entreat you not to suppose that I moved this way in order to beg for a partner."

Mr. Darcy with grave propriety requested to be allowed the honour of her hand, but in vain. Elizabeth was determined; nor did Sir William at all shake her purpose by his attempt at persuasion.

"You excel so much in the dance, Miss Eliza, that it is cruel to deny me the happiness of seeing you; and though this gentleman dislikes the amusement in general, he can have no objection, I am sure, to oblige us for one halfhour."

"Mr. Darcy is all politeness," said Elizabeth, smiling.

"He is indeed – but considering the inducement, my dear Miss Eliza, we cannot wonder at his complaisance; for who would object to such a partner?"

Elizabeth looked archly, and turned away. Her resistance had not injured her with the gentleman, and he was thinking of her with some complacency, when thus accosted by Miss Bingley,

"I can guess the subject of your reverie."

"I should imagine not."

"You are considering how insupportable it would be to pass many evenings in this manner – in such society; and indeed I am quite of your opinion. I was never more annoyed! The insipidity, and yet the noise; the nothingness and yet the self-importance of all these people! – What would I give to hear your strictures on them!"

"Your conjecture is totally wrong, I assure you. My mind was more agreeably engaged. I have been meditating on the very great pleasure which a pair of fine eyes in the face of a pretty woman can bestow."

Miss Bingley immediately fixed her eyes on his face, and desired he would tell her what lady had the credit of inspiring such reflections. Mr. Darcy replied with great intrepidity,

"Miss Elizabeth Bennet."

"Miss Elizabeth Bennet!" repeated Miss Bingley. "I am all astonishment. How long has she been such a favourite? – and pray when am I to wish you joy?"

"That is exactly the question which I expected you to ask. A lady's imagination is very rapid; it jumps from admiration to love, from love to matrimony in a moment. I knew you would be wishing me joy."

"Nay, if you are so serious about it, I shall consider the matter as absolutely settled. You will be having a charming mother-in-law, indeed, and of course she will be always at Pemberley with you."

He listened to her with perfect indifference, while she chose to entertain herself in this manner, and as his composure convinced her that all was safe, her wit flowed long.

# *Chapter 7*

MR. BENNET's property consisted almost entirely in an estate of two thousand a year, which, unfortunately for his daughters, was entailed in default of heirs male, on a distant relation; and their mother's fortune, though ample for her situation in life, could but ill supply the deficiency of his. Her father had been an attorney in Meryton, and had left her four thousand pounds.

She had a sister married to a Mr. Philips, who had been a clerk to their father, and succeeded him in the business, and a brother settled in London in a respectable line of trade.

The village of Longbourn was only one mile from Meryton; a most convenient distance for the young ladies, who were usually tempted thither three or four times a week, to pay their duty to their aunt and to a milliner's shop just over the way. The two youngest of the family, Catherine and Lydia, were particularly frequent in these attentions; their minds were more vacant than their sisters', and when nothing better offered, a walk to Meryton was necessary to amuse their morning hours and furnish conversation for the evening; and however bare of news the country in general might be, they always contrived to learn some from their aunt. At present, indeed, they were well supplied both with news and happiness by the recent arrival of a militia regiment in the neighbourhood; it was to remain the whole winter, and Meryton was the headquarters.

Their visits to Mrs. Philips were now productive of the most interesting intelligence. Every day added something to their knowledge of the officers' names and connections. Their lodgings were not long a secret, and at length they began to know the officers themselves. Mr. Philips visited them all, and this opened to his nieces a store of felicity unknown before. They could talk of nothing but officers; and Mr. Bingley's large fortune, the mention of which gave animation to their mother, was worthless in their eyes when opposed to the regimentals of an ensign.

After listening one morning to their effusions on this subject, Mr. Bennet coolly observed,

"From all that I can collect by your manner of talking, you must be two of the silliest girls in the country. I have suspected it some time, but I am now convinced."

Catherine was disconcerted, and made no answer; but Lydia, with perfect indifference, continued to express her admiration of Captain Carter, and her hope of seeing him in the course of the day, as he was going the next morning to London.

"I am astonished, my dear," said Mrs. Bennet, "that you should be so ready to think your own children silly. If I wished to think slightingly of anybody's children, it should not be of my own however."

"If my children are silly I must hope to be always sensible of it."

"Yes – but as it happens, they are all of them very clever."

"This is the only point, I flatter myself, on which we do not agree. I had hoped that our sentiments coincided in every particular, but I must so far differ from you as to think our two youngest daughters uncommonly foolish."

"My dear Mr. Bennet, you must not expect such girls to have the sense of their father and mother. – When they get to our age I dare say they will not think about officers any more than we do. I remember the time when I liked a red coat myself very well – and indeed so I do still at my heart; and if a smart young colonel, with five or six thousand a year, should want one of my girls, I shall not say nay to him; and I thought Colonel Forster looked very becoming the other night at Sir William's in his regimentals."

"Mamma," cried Lydia, "my aunt says that Colonel Forster and Captain Carter do not go so often to Miss Watson's as they did when they first came; she sees them now very often standing in Clarke's library."

Mrs. Bennet was prevented replying by the entrance of the footman with a note for Miss Bennet; it came from Netherfield, and the servant waited for an answer. Mrs. Bennet's eyes sparkled with pleasure, and she was eagerly calling out, while her daughter read,

"Well, Jane, who is it from? what is it about? what does he say? Well, Jane, make haste and tell us; make haste, my love."

"It is from Miss Bingley," said Jane, and then read it aloud.

'My dear Friend,

"If you are not so compassionate as to dine today with Louisa and me, we shall be in danger of hating each other for the rest of our lives, for a whole day's tete-a-tete between two women can never end without a quarrel. Come as soon as you can on the receipt of this. My brother and the gentlemen are to dine with the officers. Yours ever,

Caroline Bingley.'

"With the officers!" cried Lydia. "I wonder my aunt did not tell us of *that*."

"Dining out," said Mrs. Bennet, "that is very unlucky."

"Can I have the carriage?" said Jane.

"No, my dear, you had better go on horseback, because it seems likely to rain; and then you must stay all night."

"That would be a good scheme," said Elizabeth, "if you were sure that they would not offer to send her home."

"Oh! but the gentlemen will have Mr. Bingley's chaise to go to Meryton, and the Hursts have no horses to theirs."

"I had much rather go in the coach."

"But, my dear, your father cannot spare the horses, I am sure. They are wanted in the farm, Mr. Bennet, are they not?

"They are wanted in the farm much oftener than I can get them."

"But if you have got them today," said Elizabeth, "my mother's purpose will be answered."

She did at last extort from her father an acknowledgment that the horses were engaged. Jane was therefore obliged to go on horseback, and her mother attended her to the door with many cheerful prognostics of a bad day. Her hopes were answered; Jane had not been gone long before it rained hard. Her sisters were uneasy for her, but her mother was delighted. The rain continued the whole evening without intermission; Jane certainly could not come back.

"This was a lucky idea of mine, indeed!" said Mrs. Bennet, more than once, as if the credit of making it rain were all her own. Till the next morning, however, she was not aware of all the felicity of her contrivance. Breakfast was scarcely over when a servant from Netherfield brought the following note for Elizabeth:

MY DEAREST LIZZY,

I find myself very unwell this morning, which, I suppose,

is to be imputed to my getting wet through yesterday. My kind friends will not hear of my returning home till I am better. They insist also on my seeing Mr. Jones – therefore do not be alarmed if you should hear of his having been to me – and excepting a sore-throat and headache there is not much the matter with me.

Yours, &c.

"Well, my dear," said Mr. Bennet, when Elizabeth had read the note aloud, "if your daughter should have a dangerous fit of illness, if she should die, it would be a comfort to know that it was all in pursuit of Mr. Bingley, and under your orders."

"Oh! I am not at all afraid of her dying. People do not die of little trifling colds. She will be taken good care of. As long as she stays there, it is all very well. I would go and see her, if I could have the carriage."

Elizabeth, feeling really anxious, was determined to go to her, though the carriage was not to be had; and as she was no horse-woman, walking was her only alternative. She declared her resolution.

"How can you be so silly," cried her mother, "as to think of such a thing, in all this dirt! You will not be fit to be seen when you get there."

"I shall be very fit to see Jane – which is all I want."

"Is this a hint to me, Lizzy," said her father, "to send for the horses?"

"No, indeed. I do not wish to avoid the walk. The distance is nothing, when one has a motive; only three miles. I shall be back by dinner."

"I admire the activity of your benevolence," observed Mary, "but every impulse of feeling should be guided by reason; and, in my opinion, exertion should always be in proportion to what is required."

"We will go as far as Meryton with you," said Catherine and Lydia. Elizabeth accepted their company, and the three young ladies set off together.

"If we make haste," said Lydia, as they walked along, "perhaps we may see something of Captain Carter before he goes."

In Meryton they parted; the two youngest repaired to the lodgings of one of the officers' wives, and Elizabeth continued her walk alone, crossing field after field at a quick pace, jumping over stiles and springing over puddles with impatient activity, and finding herself at last within view of the house, with weary ankles, dirty stockings, and a face glowing with the warmth of exercise.

She was shown into the breakfast-parlour, where all but Jane were assembled, and where her appearance created a great deal of surprise. That she should have walked three miles so early in the day, in such dirty weather, and by herself, was almost incredible to Mrs. Hurst and Miss Bingley; and Elizabeth was convinced that they held her in contempt for it. She was received, however, very politely by them; and in their brother's manners there was something better than politeness; there was good humour and kindness. – Mr. Darcy said very little, and Mr. Hurst nothing at all. The former was divided between admiration of the brilliancy which exercise had given to her complexion, and doubt as to the occasion's justifying her coming so far alone. The latter was thinking only of his breakfast.

Her enquiries after her sister were not very favourably answered. Miss Bennet had slept ill, and though up, was very feverish, and not well enough to leave her room. Elizabeth was glad to be taken to her immediately; and Jane, who had only been withheld by the fear of giving alarm or inconvenience, from expressing in her note how much she longed for such a visit, was delighted at her entrance. She was not equal, however, to much conversation, and when Miss Bingley left them together, could attempt little beside expressions of gratitude for the extraordinary kindness she was treated with. Elizabeth silently attended her.

When breakfast was over, they were joined by the sisters; and Elizabeth began to like them herself, when she saw how much affection and solicitude they showed for Jane. The apothecary came, and having examined his patient, said, as might be supposed, that she had caught a violent cold, and that they must endeavour to get the better of it; advised her to return to bed, and promised her some draughts. The advice was followed readily, for the feverish symptoms increased, and her head ached acutely. Elizabeth did not quit her room for a moment, nor were the other ladies often absent; the gentlemen being out, they had in fact nothing to do elsewhere.

When the clock struck three, Elizabeth felt that she must go; and very unwillingly said so. Miss Bingley offered her the carriage, and she only wanted a little pressing to accept it, when Jane testified such concern in parting with her, that Miss Bingley was obliged to convert the offer of the chaise into an invitation to remain at Netherfield for the present. Elizabeth most thankfully consented, and a servant was dispatched to Longbourn to acquaint the family with her stay, and bring back a supply of clothes.

## *Chapter 8*

At five O'clock the two ladies retired to dress, and at half past six Elizabeth was summoned to dinner. To the civil enquiries which then poured in, and amongst which she had the pleasure of distinguishing the much superior solicitude of Mr. Bingley's, she could not make a very favourable answer. Jane was by no means better. The sisters, on hearing this, repeated three or four times how much they were grieved, how shocking it was to have a bad cold, and how excessively they disliked being ill themselves; and then thought no more of the matter: and their indifference towards Jane when not immediately before them, restored Elizabeth to the enjoyment of all her original dislike.

Their brother, indeed, was the only one of the party whom she could regard with any complacency. His anxiety for Jane was evident, and his attentions to herself most pleasing, and they prevented her feeling herself so much an intruder as she believed she was considered by the others. She had very little notice from any but him. Miss Bingley was engrossed by Mr. Darcy, her sister scarcely less so; and as for Mr. Hurst, by whom Elizabeth sat, he was an indolent man, who lived only to eat, drink, and play at cards; who when he found her prefer a plain dish to a ragout, had nothing to say to her.

When dinner was over, she returned directly to Jane, and Miss Bingley began abusing her as soon as she was out of the room. Her manners were pronounced to be very bad indeed, a mixture of pride and impertinence; she had no conversation, no style, no taste, no beauty. Mrs. Hurst thought the same, and added,

"She has nothing, in short, to recommend her, but being an excellent walker. I shall never forget her appearance this morning. She really looked almost wild."

"She did indeed, Louisa. I could hardly keep my countenance. Very nonsensical to come at all! Why must *she* be scampering about the country, because her sister had a cold? Her hair so untidy, so blowsy!"

"Yes, and her petticoat; I hope you saw her petticoat, six inches deep in mud, I am absolutely certain; and the gown which had been let down to hide it, not doing its office."

"Your picture may be very exact, Louisa," said Bingley; "but this was all lost upon me. I thought Miss Elizabeth Bennet looked remarkably well, when she came into the room this morning. Her dirty petticoat quite escaped my notice."

"*You* observed it, Mr. Darcy, I am sure," said Miss Bingley; "and I am inclined to think that you would not wish to see *your sister* make such an exhibition."

"Certainly not."

"To walk three miles, or four miles, or five miles, or whatever it is, above her ankles in dirt, and alone, quite alone! what could she mean by it? It seems to me to show an abominable sort of conceited independence, a most country town indifference to decorum."

"It shows an affection for her sister that is very pleasing," said Bingley.

"I am afraid, Mr. Darcy," observed Miss Bingley, in a half whisper, "that this adventure has rather affected your admiration of her fine eyes."

"Not at all," he replied; "they were brightened by the exercise." – A short pause followed this speech, and Mrs. Hurst began again.

"I have an excessive regard for Jane Bennet, she is really a very sweet girl, and I wish with all my heart she were well settled. But with such a father and mother, and such low connections, I am afraid there is no chance of it."

"I think I have heard you say, that their uncle is an attorney in Meryton."

"Yes; and they have another, who lives somewhere near Cheapside."

"That is capital," added her sister, and they both laughed heartily.

"If they had uncles enough to fill *all* Cheapside," cried Bingley, "it would not make them one jot less agreeable."

"But it must very materially lessen their chance of marrying men of any consideration in the world," replied Darcy.

To this speech Bingley made no answer; but his sisters gave it their hearty assent, and indulged their mirth for some time at the expense of their dear friend's vulgar relations.

With a renewal of tenderness, however, they returned to her room on leaving the dining-parlour, and sat with her till summoned to coffee. She was still very poorly, and Elizabeth would not quit her at all, till late in the evening, when she had the comfort of seeing her asleep, and when it appeared to her rather right than pleasant that she should go downstairs herself. On entering the drawing-room she found the whole party at loo, and was immediately invited to join them; but suspecting them to be playing high she declined it, and making her sister the excuse, said she would amuse herself for the short time she could stay below with a book. Mr. Hurst looked at her with astonishment.

"Do you prefer reading to cards?" said he; "that is rather singular."

"Miss Eliza Bennet," said Miss Bingley, "despises cards. She is a great reader, and has no pleasure in anything else."

"I deserve neither such praise nor such censure," cried Elizabeth; "I am *not* a great reader, and I have pleasure in many things."

"In nursing your sister I am sure you have pleasure," said Bingley; "and I hope it will soon be increased by seeing her quite well."

Elizabeth thanked him from her heart, and then walked towards a table where a few books were lying. He immediately offered to fetch her others; all that his library afforded.

"And I wish my collection were larger for your benefit and my own credit, but I am an idle fellow, and though I have not many, I have more than I ever looked into."

Elizabeth assured him that she could suit herself perfectly with those in the room.

"I am astonished," said Miss Bingley, "that my father should have left so small a collection of books. – What a delightful library you have at Pemberley, Mr. Darcy!"

"It ought to be good," he replied, "it has been the work of many generations."

"And then you have added so much to it yourself, you are always buying books."

"I cannot comprehend the neglect of a family library in such days as these."

"Neglect! I am sure you neglect nothing that can add to the beauties of that noble place. Charles, when you build *your* house, I wish it may be half as delightful as Pemberley."

"I wish it may."

"But I would really advise you to make your purchase in that neighbourhood, and take Pemberley for a kind of model. There is not a finer county in England than Derbyshire."

"With all my heart; I will buy Pemberley itself if Darcy will sell it."

"I am talking of possibilities, Charles."

"Upon my word, Caroline, I should think it more possible to get Pemberley by purchase than by imitation."

Elizabeth was so much caught with what passed, as to leave her very little attention for her book; and soon laying it wholly aside, she drew near the card-table, and stationed herself between Mr. Bingley and his eldest sister to observe the game."

"Is Miss Darcy much grown since the spring?" said Miss Bingley; "will she be as tall as I am?"

"I think she will. She is now about Miss Elizabeth Bennet's height, or rather taller."

"How I long to see her again! I never met anybody who

delighted me so much. Such a countenance, such manners! and so extremely accomplished for her age! Her performance on the piano-forte is exquisite."

"It is amazing to me," said Bingley, "how young ladies can have patience to be so very accomplished, as they all are."

"All young ladies accomplished! My dear Charles, what do you mean?"

"Yes, all of them, I think. They all paint tables, cover screens, and net purses. I scarcely know anyone who cannot do all this, and I am sure I never heard a young lady spoken of for the first time, without being informed that she was very accomplished."

"Your list of the common extent of accomplishments," said Darcy, "has too much truth. The word is applied to many a woman who deserves it not otherwise than by netting a purse, or covering a screen. But I am very far from agreeing with you in your estimation of ladies in general. I cannot boast of knowing more than half a dozen, in the whole range of my acquaintance, that are really accomplished."

"Nor I, I am sure," said Miss Bingley.

"Then," observed Elizabeth, "you must comprehend a great deal in your idea of an accomplished woman."

"Yes, I do comprehend a great deal in it."

"Oh! certainly," cried his faithful assistant, "no one can be really esteemed accomplished, who does not greatly surpass what is usually met with. A woman must have a thorough knowledge of music, singing, drawing, dancing, and the modern languages, to deserve the word; and besides all this, she must possess a certain something in her air and manner of walking, the tone of her voice, her address and expressions, or the word will be but half deserved."

"All this she must possess," added Darcy, "and to all this she must yet add something more substantial, in the improvement of her mind by extensive reading."

"I am no longer surprised at your knowing *only* six accomplished women. I rather wonder now at your knowing *any*."

"Are you so severe upon your own sex, as to doubt the possibility of all this?"

"*I* never saw such a woman. *I* never saw such capacity, and taste, and application, and elegance, as you describe, united."

Mrs. Hurst and Miss Bingley both cried out against the injustice of her implied doubt, and were both protesting that they knew many women who answered this description, when Mr. Hurst called them to order, with bitter complaints of their inattention to what was going forward. As all conversation was thereby at an end, Elizabeth soon afterwards left the room.

"Eliza Bennet," said Miss Bingley, when the door was closed on her, "is one of those young ladies who seek to recommend themselves to the other sex, by undervaluing their own; and with many men, I dare say, it succeeds. But, in my opinion, it is a paltry device, a very mean art."

"Undoubtedly," replied Darcy, to whom this remark was chiefly addressed, "there is meanness in *all* the arts which ladies sometimes condescend to employ for captivation. Whatever bears affinity to cunning is despicable."

Miss Bingley was not so entirely satisfied with this reply as to continue the subject.

Elizabeth joined them again only to say that her sister was worse, and that she could not leave her. Bingley urged Mr. Jones's being sent for immediately; while his sisters, convinced that no country advice could be of any service, recommended an express to town for one of the most eminent physicians. This, she would not hear of; but she was not so unwilling to comply with their brother's proposal; and it was settled that Mr. Jones should be sent for early in the morning, if Miss Bennet were not decidedly better. Bingley was quite uncomfortable; his sisters declared that they were miserable: They solaced their wretchedness, however, by duets after supper, while he could find no better relief to his feelings than by giving his housekeeper directions that every possible attention might be paid to the sick lady and her sister.

# Chapter 9

ELIZABETH PASSED the chief of the night in her sister's room, and in the morning had the pleasure of being able to send a tolerable answer to the enquiries which she very early received from Mr. Bingley by a housemaid, and some time aftrwards from the two elegant ladies who waited on his sisters. In site of this amendment, however, she requested to have a note sent to Longbourn, desiring her mother to visit Jane, and form her own judgement of her situation. The note was immediately dispatched, and its contents as quickly complied with. Mrs. Bennet, accompanied by her two youngest girls, reached Netherfield soon after the family breakfast.

Had she found Jane in any apparent danger, Mrs. Bennet would have been very miserable; but being satisfied on seeing her that her illness was not alarming, she had no wish of her recovering immediately, as her restoration to health would probably remove her from Netherfield. She would not listen therefore to her daughter's proposal of being carried home; neither did the apothecary, who arrived about the same time, think it at all advisable. After sitting a little while with Jane, on Miss Bingley's appearance and invitation, the mother and three daughters all attended her into the breakfast-parlour. Bingley met them with hopes that Mrs. Bennet had not found Miss Bennet worse than she expected.

"Indeed I have, Sir," was her answer. "She is a great deal too ill to be moved. Mr. Jones says we must not think of moving her. We must trespass a little longer on your kindness."

"Removed!" cried Bingley. "It must not be thought of. My sister, I am sure, will not hear of her removal."

"You may depend upon it, Madam," said Miss Bingley, with cold civility, "that Miss Bennet shall receive every possible attention while she remains with us."

Mrs. Bennet was profuse in her acknowledgements.

"I am sure," she added, "if it was not for such good friends I do not know what would become of her, for she is very ill indeed, and suffers a vast deal, though with the greatest patience in the world, which is always the way with her, for she has, without exception, the sweetest temper I ever met with. I often tell my other girls they are nothing to *her*. You have a sweet room here, Mr. Bingley, and a charming prospect over that gravel walk. I do not know a place in the country that is equal to Netherfield. You will not think of quitting it in a hurry I hope, though you have but a short lease."

"Whatever I do is done in a hurry," replied he; "and therefore if I should resolve to quit Netherfield, I should probably be off in five minutes. At present, however, I consider myself as quite fixed here."

"That is exactly what I should have supposed of you," said Elizabeth.

"You begin to comprehend me, do you?" cried he, turning towards her.

"Oh! yes – I understand you perfectly."

"I wish I might take this for a compliment; but to be so easily seen through I am afraid is pitiful."

"That is as it happens. It does not necessarily follow that a deep, intricate character is more or less estimable than such a one as yours."

"Lizzy," cried her mother, "remember where you are, and do not run on in the wild manner that you are suffered to do at home."

"I did not know before," continued Bingley immediately, "that you were a studier of character. It must be an amusing study."

"Yes, but intricate characters are the *most* amusing. They have at least that advantage."

"The country," said Darcy, "can in general supply but few subjects for such a study. In a country neighbourhood you move in a very confined and unvarying society."

"But people themselves alter so much, that there is something new to be observed in them for ever."

"Yes, indeed," cried Mrs. Bennet, offended by his manner of mentioning a country neighbourhood. "I assure you there is quite as much of *that* going on in the country as in town."

Everybody was surprised; and Darcy, after looking at her for a moment, turned silently away. Mrs. Bennet, who fancied she had gained a complete victory over him, continued her triumph.

"I cannot see that London has any great advantage over the country for my part, except the shops and public places. The country is a vast deal pleasanter, is it not, Mr. Bingley?"

"When I am in the country," he replied, "I never wish to leave it; and when I am in town it is pretty much the same. They have each their advantages, and I can be equally happy in either."

"Aye – that is because you have the right disposition. But that gentleman," looking at Darcy, "seemed to think the country was nothing at all."

"Indeed, Mamma, you are mistaken," said Elizabeth, blushing for her mother. "You quite mistook Mr. Darcy. He only meant that there were not such a variety of people to be met with in the country as in town, which you must acknowledge to be true."

"Certainly, my dear, nobody said there were; but as to not

meeting with many people in this neighbourhood, I believe there are few neighbourhoods larger. I know we dine with four and twenty families."

Nothing but concern for Elizabeth could enable Bingley to keep his countenance. His sister was less delicate, and directed her eye towards Mr. Darcy with a very expressive smile. Elizabeth, for the sake of saying something that might turn her mother's thoughts, now asked her if Charlotte Lucas had been at Longbourn since *her* coming away.

"Yes, she called yesterday with her father. What an agreeable man Sir William is, Mr. Bingley – is not he? so much the man of fashion! so genteel and so easy! – He has always something to say to everybody. – *That* is my idea of good breeding; and those persons who fancy themselves very important, and never open their mouths, quite mistake the matter."

"Did Charlotte dine with you?"

"No, she would go home. I fancy she was wanted about the mince pies. For my part, Mr. Bingley, *I* always keep servants that can do their own work; *my* daughters are brought up differently. But everybody is to judge for themselves, and the Lucases are very good sort of girls, I assure you. It is a pity they are not handsome! Not that *I* think Charlotte so *very* plain – but then she is our particular friend."

"She seems a very pleasant young woman." said Bingley.

"Oh! dear, yes; – but you must own she is very plain. Lady Lucas herself has often said so, and envied me Jane's beauty. I do not like to boast of my own child, but to be sure, Jane – one does not often see anybody better looking. It is what everybody says. I do not trust my own partiality. When she was only fifteen, there was a gentleman at my brother Gardiner's in town, so much in love with her, that my sister-in-law was sure he would make her an offer before we came away. But however he did not. Perhaps he thought her too young. However, he wrote some verses on her, and very pretty they were."

"And so ended his affection," said Elizabeth impatiently. "There has been many a one, I fancy, overcome in the same way. I wonder who first discovered the efficacy of poetry in driving away love!"

"I have been used to consider poetry as the *food* of love," said Darcy.

"Of a fine, stout, healthy love it may. Everything nourishes what is strong already. But if it be only a slight, thin sort of inclination, I am convinced that one good sonnet will starve it entirely away."

Darcy only smiled; and the general pause which ensued made Elizabeth tremble lest her mother should be exposing herself again. She longed to speak, but could think of nothing to say; and after a short silence Mrs. Bennet began repeating her thanks to Mr. Bingley for his kindness to Jane, with an apology for troubling him also with Lizzy. Mr. Bingley was unaffectedly civil in his answer, and forced his younger sister to be civil also, and say what the occasion required. She performed her part indeed without much graciousness, but Mrs. Bennet was satisfied, and soon afterwards ordered her carriage. Upon this signal, the youngest of her daughters put herself forward. The two girls had been whispering to each other during the whole visit, and the result of it was, that the youngest should tax Mr. Bingley with having promised on his first coming into the country to give a ball at Netherfield.

Lydia was a stout, well-grown girl of fifteen, with a fine complexion and good-humoured countenance; a favourite with her mother, whose affection had brought her into public at an early age. She had high animal spirits, and a sort of natural self-consequence, which the attentions of the officers, to whom her uncle's good dinners and her own easy manners recommended her, had increased into assurance. She was very equal therefore to address Mr. Bingley on the subject of the ball, and abruptly reminded him of his promise; adding, that it would be the most shameful thing in the world if he did not keep it. His answer to this sudden attack was delightful to her mother's ear.

"I am perfectly ready, I assure you, to keep my engagement; and when your sister is recovered, you shall if you please name the very day of the ball. But you would not wish to be dancing while she is ill."

Lydia declared herself satisfied. "Oh! yes – it would be much better to wait till Jane was well, and by that time most likely Captain Carter would be at Meryton again. And when you have given *your* ball," she added, "I shall insist on their giving one also. I shall tell Colonel Forster it will be quite a shame if he does not."

Mrs. Bennet and her daughters then departed, and Elizabeth returned instantly to Jane, leaving her own and her relations' behaviour to the remarks of the two ladies and Mr. Darcy; the latter of whom, however, could not be prevailed on to join in their censure of *her*, in spite of all Miss Bingley's witticisms on *fine eyes*.

## *Chapter 10*

THE DAY passed much as the day before had done. Mrs. Hurst and Miss Bingley had spent some hours of the morning with the invalid, who continued, though slowly, to mend; and in the evening Elizabeth joined their party in the drawing-room. The loo table, however, did not appear. Mr. Darcy was writing, and Miss Bingley, seated near him, was watching the progress of his letter, and repeatedly calling off his attention by messages to his sister. Mr. Hurst and Mr. Bingley were at piquet, and Mrs. Hurst was observing their game.

Elizabeth took up some needlework, and was sufficiently amused in attending to what passed between Darcy and his companion. The perpetual commendations of the lady either on his hand-writing, or on the evenness of his lines, or on the length of his letter, with the perfect unconcern with which her praises were received, formed a curious dialogue, and was exactly in unison with her opinion of each.

"How delighted Miss Darcy will be to receive such a letter!"

He made no answer.

"You write uncommonly fast."

"You are mistaken. I write rather slowly."

"How many letters you must have occasion to write in the course of a year! Letters of business too! How odious I should think them!"

"It is fortunate, then, that they fall to my lot instead of to yours."

"Pray tell your sister that I long to see her."

"I have already told her so once, by your desire."

"I am afraid you do not like your pen. Let me mend it for you. I mend pens remarkably well."

"Thank you – but I always mend my own."

"How can you contrive to write so even?"

He was silent.

"Tell your sister I am delighted to hear of her improvement on the harp, and pray let her know that I am quite in raptures with her beautiful little design for a table, and I think it infinitely superior to Miss Grantley's."

"Will you give me leave to defer your raptures till I write

again? – At present I have not room to do them justice."

"Oh! it is of no consequence. I shall see her in January. But do you always write such charming long letters to her, Mr. Darcy?"

"They are generally long; but whether always charming, it is not for me to determine."

"It is a rule with me, that a person who can write a long letter, with ease, cannot write ill."

"That will not do for a compliment to Darcy, Caroline," cried her brother, – "because he does *not* write with ease. He studies too much for words of four syllables. – Do not you, Darcy?"

"My style of writing is very different from yours."

"Oh!" cried Miss Bingley, "Charles writes in the most careless way imaginable. He leaves out half his words, and blots the rest."

"My ideas flow so rapidly that I have not time to express them – by which means my letters sometimes convey no ideas at all to my correspondents."

"Your humility, Mr. Bingley," said Elizabeth, "must disarm reproof."

"Nothing is more deceitful," said Darcy, "than the appearance of humility. It is often only carelessness of opinion, and sometimes an indirect boast."

"And which of the two do you call *my* little recent piece of modesty?"

"The indirect boast; – for you are really proud of your defects in writing, because you consider them as proceeding from a rapidity of thought and carelessness of execution, which if not estimable, you think at least highly interesting. The power of doing anything with quickness is always much prized by the possessor, and often without any attention to the imperfection of the performance. When you told Mrs. Bennet this morning that if you ever resolved on quitting Netherfield you should be gone in five minutes, you meant it to be a sort of panegyric, of compliment to yourself – and yet what is there so very laudable in a precipitance which must leave very necessary business undone, and can be of no real advantage to yourself or anyone else?"

"Nay," cried Bingley, "this is too much, to remember at night all the foolish things that were said in the morning. And yet, upon my honour, I believed what I said of myself to be true, and I believe it at this moment. At least, therefore, I did not assume the character of needless precipitance merely to show off before the ladies."

"I dare say you believed it; but I am by no means convinced that you would be gone with such celerity. Your conduct would be quite as dependent on chance as that of any man I know; and if, as you were mounting your horse, a friend were to say, 'Bingley, you had better stay till next week,' you would probably do it, you would probably not go – and, at another word, might stay a month."

"You have only proved by this," cried Elizabeth, "that Mr. Bingley did not do justice to his own disposition. You have shown him off now much more than he did himself."

"I am exceedingly gratified," said Bingley, "by your converting what my friend says into a compliment on the sweetness of my temper. But I am afraid you are giving it a turn which that gentleman did by no means intend; for he would certainly think the better of me, if under such a circumstance I were to give a flat denial, and ride off as fast as I could."

"Would Mr. Darcy then consider the rashness of your original intention as atoned for by your obstinacy in adhering to it?"

"Upon my word, I cannot exactly explain the matter, Darcy must speak for himself."

"You expect me to account for opinions which you choose to call mine, but which I have never acknowledged. Allowing the case, however, to stand according to your representation, you must remember, Miss Bennet, that the friend who is supposed to desire his return to the house, and the delay of his plan, has merely desired it, asked it without offering one argument in favour of its propriety."

"To yield readily – easily – to the *persuasion* of a friend is no merit with you."

"To yield without conviction is no compliment to the understanding of either."

"You appear to me, Mr. Darcy, to allow nothing for the influence of friendship and affection. A regard for the requester would often make one readily yield to a request, without waiting for arguments to reason one into it. I am not particularly speaking of such a case as you have supposed about Mr. Bingley. We may as well wait, perhaps, till the circumstance occurs, before we discuss the discretion of his behaviour thereupon. But in general and ordinary cases between friend and friend, where one of them is desired by the other to change a resolution of no very great moment, should you think ill of that person for complying with the desire, without waiting to be argued into it?"

"Will it not be advisable, before we proceed on this subject, to arrange with rather more precision the degree of importance which is to appertain to this request, as well as the degree of intimacy subsisting between the parties?"

"By all means," cried Bingley; "let us hear all the particulars, not forgetting their comparative height and size; for that will have more weight in the argument, Miss Bennet, than you may be aware of. I assure you that if Darcy were not such a great tall fellow, in comparison with myself, I should not pay him half so much deference. I declare I do not know a more awful object than Darcy, on particular occasions, and in particular places; at his own house especially, and of a Sunday evening when he has nothing to do."

Mr. Darcy smiled; but Elizabeth thought she could perceive that he was rather offended; and therefore checked her laugh.

Miss Bingley warmly resented the indignity he had received, in an expostulation with her brother for talking such nonsense.

"I see your design, Bingley," said his friend. – "You dislike an argument, and want to silence this."

"Perhaps I do. Arguments are too much like disputes. If you and Miss Bennet will defer yours till I am out of the room, I shall be very thankful; and then you may say whatever you like of me."

"What you ask," said Elizabeth, "is no sacrifice on my side; and Mr. Darcy had much better finish his letter."

Mr. Darcy took her advice, and did finish his letter.

When that business was over, he applied to Miss Bingley and Elizabeth for an indulgence of some music. Miss Bingley moved with some alacrity to the piano-forte; and after a polite request that Elizabeth would lead the way, which the other as politely and more earnestly negatived, she seated herself.

Mrs. Hurst sang with her sister, and while they were thus employed Elizabeth could not help observing as she turned over some music books that lay on the instrument, how frequently Mr. Darcy's eyes were fixed on her. She hardly knew how to suppose that she could be an object of admiration to so great a man; and yet that he should look at her because he disliked her, was still more strange. She could only imagine however at last, that she drew his notice because there was something about her more wrong and reprehensible, according to his ideas of right, than in any other person present. The supposition did not pain her. She liked him too little to care for his approbation.

After playing some Italian songs, Miss Bingley varied the charm by a lively Scotch air; and soon afterwards Mr. Darcy, drawing near Elizabeth, said to her –

"Do you not feel a great inclination, Miss Bennet, to seize such an opportunity of dancing a reel?"

She smiled, but made no answer. He repeated the question, with some surprise at her silence.

"Oh!" said she, "I heard you before, but I could not immediately determine what to say in reply. You wanted me, I know, to say "Yes," that you might have the pleasure of despising my taste; but I always delight in overthrowing those kind of schemes, and cheating a person of their premeditated contempt. I have therefore, made up my mind to tell you, that I do not want to dance a reel at all – and now despise me if you dare."

"Indeed I do not dare."

Elizabeth, having rather expected to affront him, was amazed at his gallantry; but there was a mixture of sweetness and archness in her manner which made it difficult for her to affront anybody; and Darcy had never been so bewitched by any woman as he was by her. He really believed, that were it not for the inferiority of her connections, he should be in some danger.

Miss Bingley saw, or suspected enough to be jealous; and her great anxiety for the recovery of her dear friend Jane, received some assistance from her desire of getting rid of Elizabeth.

She often tried to provoke Darcy into disliking her guest, by talking of their supposed marriage, and planning his happiness in such an alliance.

"I hope," said she, as they were walking together in the shrubbery the next day, "you will give your mother-in-law a few hints, when this desirable event takes place, as to the advantage of holding her tongue; and if you can compass it, do cure the younger girls of running after the officers. – And, if I may mention so delicate a subject, endeavour to check that little something, bordering on conceit and impertinence, which your lady possesses."

"Have you anything else to propose for my domestic felicity?"

"Oh! yes. – Do let the portraits of your uncle and aunt Philips get placed in the gallery at Pemberley. Put them next to your great uncle the judge. They are in the same profession, you know; only in different lines. As for your Elizabeth's picture, you must not attempt to have it taken, for what painter could do justice to those beautiful eyes?"

"It would not be easy, indeed, to catch their expression, but their colour and shape, and the eye-lashes, so remarkably fine, might be copied."

At that moment they were met from another walk, by Mrs. Hurst and Elizabeth herself.

"I did not know that you intended to walk," said Miss Bingley, in some confusion, lest they had been overheard.

"You used us abominably ill," answered Mrs. Hurst, "in running away without telling us that you were coming out."

Then taking the disengaged arm of Mr. Darcy, she left Elizabeth to walk by herself. The path just admitted three. Mr. Darcy felt their rudeness and immediately said, –

"This walk is not wide enough for our party. We had better go into the avenue."

But Elizabeth, who had not the least inclination to remain with them, laughingly answered,

"No, no; stay where you are. – You are charmingly group'd, and appear to uncommon advantage. The picturesque would be spoilt by admitting a fourth. Good bye."

She then ran gaily off, rejoicing as she rambled about, in the hope of being at home again in a day or two. Jane was already so much recovered as to intend leaving her room for a couple of hours that evening.

# Chapter 11

WHEN THE ladies removed after dinner, Elizabeth ran up to her sister, and seeing her well guarded from cold, attended her into the drawing-room; where she was welcomed by her two friends with many professions of pleasure; and Elizabeth had never seen them so agreeable as they were during the hour which passed before the gentlemen appeared. Their powers of conversation were considerable. They could describe an entertainment with accuracy, relate an anecdote with humour, and laugh at their acquaintance with spirit.

But when the gentlemen entered, Jane was no longer the first object. Miss Bingley's eyes were instantly turned towards Darcy, and she had something to say to him before he had advanced many steps. He addressed himself directly to Miss Bennet, with a polite congratulation; Mr. Hurst also made her a slight bow, and said he was "very glad"; but diffuseness and warmth remained for Bingley's salutation. He was full of joy and attention. The first half-hour was spent in piling up the fire, lest she should suffer from the change of room; and she removed at his desire to the other side of the fire-place, that she might be farther from the door. He then sat down by her, and talked scarcely to anyone else. Elizabeth, at work in the opposite corner, saw it all with great delight.

When tea was over, Mr. Hurst reminded his sister-in-law of the card-table – but in vain. She had obtained private intelligence that Mr. Darcy did not wish for cards; and Mr. Hurst soon found even his open petition rejected. She assured him that no one intended to play, and the silence of the whole party on the subject, seemed to justify her. Mr. Hurst had therefore nothing to do, but to stretch himself on one of the sofas and go to sleep. Darcy took up a book; Miss Bingley did the same; and Mrs. Hurst, principally occupied in playing with her bracelets and rings, joined now and then in her brother's conversation with Miss Bennet.

Miss Bingley's attention was quite as much engaged in watching Mr. Darcy's progress through *his* book, as in reading her own; and she was perpetually either making some enquiry, or looking at his page. She could not win him, however, to any conversation; he merely answered her question, and read on. At length, quite exhausted by the attempt to be amused with her own book, which she had only chosen because it was the second volume of his, she gave a great yawn and said, "How pleasant it is to spend an evening in this way! I declare after all there is no enjoyment like reading! How much sooner one tires of anything than of a book! – When I have a house of my own, I shall be miserable if I have not an excellent library."

No one made any reply. She then yawned again, threw aside her book, and cast her eyes round the room in quest of some amusement; when hearing her brother mentioning a ball to Miss Bennet, she turned suddenly towards him and said.

"By the bye, Charles, are you really serious in meditating a dance at Netherfield? – I would advise you, before you determine on it, to consult the wishes of the present party; I am much mistaken if there are not some among us to whom a ball would be rather a punishment than a pleasure."

"If you mean Darcy," cried her brother, "he may go to bed, if he chooses, before it begins – but as for the ball, it is quite a settled thing; and as soon as Nicholls has made white soup enough I shall send round my cards."

"I should like balls infinitely better," she replied, "if they were carried on in a different manner; but there is something insufferably tedious in the usual process of such a meeting. It would surely be much more rational if conversation instead of dancing made the order of the day."

"Much more rational, my dear Caroline, I dare say, but it would not be near so much like a ball."

Miss Bingley made no answer, and soon afterwards got up and walked about the room. Her figure was elegant, and she walked well; – but Darcy, at whom it was all aimed, was still inflexibly studious. In the desperation of her feelings she resolved on one effort more; and, turning to Elizabeth, said,

"Miss Eliza Bennet, let me persuade you to follow my example, and take a turn about the room. – I assure you it is very refreshing after sitting so long in one attitude."

Elizabeth was surprised, but agreed to it immediately. Miss Bingley succeeded no less in the real object of her civility; Mr. Darcy looked up. He was as much awake to the novelty of attention in that quarter as Elizabeth herself could be, and unconsciously closed his book. He was directly invited to join their party, but he declined it, observing, that he could imagine but two motives for their choosing to walk up and down the room together, with either of which motives his joining them would interfere. "What could he mean? she was dying to know what could be his meaning?"– and asked Elizabeth whether she could at all understand him?

"Not at all," was her answer; "but depend upon it, he means to be severe on us, and our surest way of disappointing him, will be to ask nothing about it."

Miss Bingley, however, was incapable of disappointing Mr. Darcy in anything, and persevered therefore in requiring an explanation of his two motives.

"I have not the smallest objection to explaining them," said he, as soon as she allowed him to speak. "You either choose this method of passing the evening because you are in each other's confidence and have secret affairs to discuss, or because you are conscious that your figures appear to the greatest advantage in walking; – if the first, I should be completely in your way; – and if the second, I can admire you much better as I sit by the fire."

"Oh! shocking!" cried Miss Bingley. "I never heard anything so abominable. How shall we punish him for such a speech?"

"Nothing so easy, if you have but the inclination," said Elizabeth. "We can all plague and punish one another. Tease him – laugh at him. – Intimate as you are, you must know how it is to be done."

"But upon my honour I do *not*. I do assure you that my intimacy has not yet taught me *that*. Tease calmness of temper and presence of mind! No, no – I feel he may defy us there. And as to laughter, we will not expose ourselves, if you please, by attempting to laugh without a subject. Mr. Darcy may hug himself."

"Mr. Darcy is not to be laughed at!" cried Elizabeth. "That is an uncommon advantage, and uncommon I hope it will continue, for it would be a great loss to *me* to have many such acquaintance. I dearly love a laugh."

"Miss Bingley," said he, "has given me credit for more than can be. The wisest and the best of men, nay, the wisest and best of their actions, may be rendered ridiculous by a person whose first object in life is a joke."

"Certainly," replied Elizabeth – "there are such people, but I hope I am not one of *them*. I hope I never ridicule what is wise or good. Follies and nonsense, whims and inconsistencies *do* divert me, I own, and I laugh at them whenever I can. – But these, I suppose, are precisely what you are without."

"Perhaps that is not possible for anyone. But it has been the study of my life to avoid those weaknesses which often expose a strong understanding to ridicule."

"Such as vanity and pride."

"Yes, vanity is a weakness indeed. But pride – where there is a real superiority of mind, pride will be always under good regulation."

Elizabeth turned away to hide a smile.

"Your examination of Mr. Darcy is over, I presume," said Miss Bingley; "and pray what is the result?"

"I am perfectly convinced by it that Mr. Darcy has no defect. He owns it himself without disguise."

"No," – said Darcy, "I have made no such pretension. I have faults enough, but they are not, I hope, of understanding. My temper I dare not vouch for. – It is I believe too little yielding – certainly too little for the convenience of the world. I cannot forget the follies and vices of others so soon as I ought, nor their offences against myself. My feelings are not puffed about with every attempt to move them. My temper would perhaps be called resentful. – My good opinion once lost is lost for ever."

"*That* is a failing indeed!" – cried Elizabeth. "Implacable resentment *is* a shade in a character. But you have chosen your fault well. – I really cannot *laugh* at it. You are safe from me."

"There is, I believe, in every disposition a tendency to some particular evil, a natural defect, which not even the best education can overcome."

"And *your* defect is a propensity to hate everybody."

"And yours, "he replied with a smile, "is wilfully to misunderstand them."

"Do let us have a little music," – cried Miss Bingley, tired of a conversation in which she had no share. – "Louisa, you will not mind my waking Mr. Hurst."

Her sister made not the smallest objection, and the pianoforte was opened, and Darcy, after a few moments' recollection, was not sorry for it. He began to feel the danger of paying Elizabeth too much attention.

# *Chapter 12*

In consequence of an agreement between the sisters, Elizabeth wrote the next morning to her mother, to beg that the carriage might be sent for them in the course of the day. But Mrs. Bennet, who had calculated on her daughters remaining at Netherfield till the following Tuesday, which would exactly finish Jane's week, could not bring herself to receive them with pleasure before. Her answer, therefore, was not propitious, at least not to Elizabeth's wishes, for she was impatient to get home. Mrs. Bennet sent them word that they could not possibly have the carriage before Tuesday; and in her postscript it was added, that if Mr. Bingley and his sister pressed them to stay longer, she could spare them very well. – Against staying longer, however, Elizabeth was positively resolved – nor did she much expect it would be asked; and fearful, on the contrary, as being considered as intruding themselves needlessly long, she urged Jane to borrow Mr. Bingley's carriage immediately, and at length it was settled that their original design of leaving Netherfield that morning should be mentioned, and the request made.

The communication excited many professions of concern; and enough was said of wishing them to stay at least till the following day to work on Jane; and till the morrow, their going was deferred. Miss Bingley was then sorry that she had proposed the delay, for her jealousy and dislike of one sister much exceeded her affection for the other.

The master of the house heard with real sorrow that they were to go so soon, and repeatedly tried to persuade Miss Bennet that it would not be safe for her – that she was not enough recovered; but Jane was firm where she felt herself to be right.

To Mr. Darcy it was welcome intelligence – Elizabeth had been at Netherfield long enough. She attracted him more than he liked – and Miss Bingley was uncivil to *her*, and more teasing than usual to himself. He wisely resolved to be particularly careful that no sign of admiration should *now* escape him, nothing that could elevate her with the hope of influencing his felicity; sensible that if such an idea had been suggested, his behaviour during the last day must have material weight in confirming or crushing it. Steady to his purpose, he scarcely spoke ten words to her through the whole of Saturday, and though they were at one time left by themselves for half an hour, he adhered most conscientiously to his book, and would not even look at her.

On Sunday, after morning service, the separation, so agreeable to almost all, took place. Miss Bingley's civility to Elizabeth increased at last very rapidly, as well as her affection for Jane; and when they parted, after assuring the latter of the pleasure it would always give her to see her either at Longbourn or Netherfield, and embracing her most tenderly, she even shook hands with the former. – Elizabeth took leave of the whole party in the liveliest of spirits.

They were not welcomed home very cordially by their mother. Mrs. Bennet wondered at their coming, and thought them very wrong to give so much trouble, and was sure Jane would have caught cold again. – But their father, though very laconic in his expressions of pleasure, was really glad to see them; he had felt their importance in the family circle. The evening conversation, when they were all assembled, had lost much of its animation, and almost all its sense, by the absence of Jane and Elizabeth.

They found Mary, as usual, deep in the study of thorough bass and human nature; and had some new extracts to admire, and some new observations of thread-bare morality to listen to. Catherine and Lydia had information for them of a different sort. Much had been done, and much had been said in the regiment since the preceding Wednesday; several of the officers had dined lately with their uncle, a private had been flogged, and it had actually been hinted that Colonel Forster was going to be married.

# Chapter 13

"I HOPE, my dear," said Mr. Bennet to his wife, as they were at breakfast the next morning, "that you have ordered a good dinner today, because I have reason to expect an addition to our family party."

"Who do you mean, my dear? I know of nobody that is coming, I am sure, unless Charlotte Lucas should happen to call in, and I hope *my* dinners are good enough for her. I do not believe she often sees such at home."

"The person of whom I speak, is a gentleman, and a stranger." Mrs. Bennet's eyes sparkled. – "A gentleman and a stranger! It is Mr. Bingley I am sure! Why Jane – you never dropped a word of this; you sly thing! Well, I am sure I shall be extremely glad to see Mr. Bingley. – But – good lord! how unlucky! there is not a bit of fish to be got today. Lydia, my love, ring the bell. I must speak to Hill, this moment."

"It is *not* Mr. Bingley," said her husband; "it is a person whom I never saw in the whole course of my life."

This roused a general astonishment; and he had the pleasure of being eagerly questioned by his wife and five daughters at once.

After amusing himself some time with their curiosity, he thus explained. "About a month ago I received this letter, and about a fortnight ago I answered it, for I thought it a case of some delicacy, and requiring early attention. It is from my cousin, Mr. Collins, who, when I am dead, may turn you all out of this house as soon as he pleases."

"Oh! my dear," cried his wife, "I cannot bear to hear that mentioned. Pray do not talk of that odious man. I do think it is the hardest thing in the world, that your estate should be entailed away from your own children; and I am sure if I had been you,

I should have tried long ago to do something or other about it."

Jane and Elizabeth attempted to explain to her the nature of an entail. They had often attempted it before, but it was a subject on which Mrs. Bennet was beyond the reach of reason; and she continued to rail bitterly against the cruelty of settling an estate away from a family of five daughters, in favour of a man whom nobody cared anything about.

"It certainly is a most iniquitous affair," said Mr. Bennet, "and nothing can clear Mr. Collins from the guilt of inheriting Longbourn. But if you will listen to his letter, you may perhaps be a little softened by his manner of expressing himself."

"No, that I am sure I shall not; and I think it was very impertinent of him to write to you at all, and very hypocritical. I hate such false friends. Why could not he keep on quarrelling with you, as his father did before him?"

"Why, indeed, he does seem to have had some filial scruples on that head, as you will hear."

" '*Hunsford, near Westerham, Kent, 15th October.*

" 'DEAR SIR,

The disagreement subsisting between yourself and my late honoured father, always gave me much uneasiness, and since I have had the misfortune to lose him, I have frequently wished to heal the breach; but for some time I was kept back by my own doubts, fearing lest it might seem disrespectful to his memory for me to be on good terms with anyone, with whom it had always pleased him to be at variance.' There, Mrs. Bennet. 'My mind however is now made up on the subject, for having received ordination at Easter, I have been so fortunate as to be distinguished by the patronage of the Right Honourable Lady Catherine de Bourgh, widow of Sir Lewis de Bourgh, whose bounty and beneficence has preferred me to the valuable rectory of this parish, where it shall be my earnest endeavour to demean myself with grateful respect towards her ladyship, and be ever ready to perform those rites and ceremonies which are instituted by the Church of England. As a clergyman, moreover, I feel it my duty to promote and establish the blessing of peace in all families within the reach of my influence; and on these grounds I flatter myself that my present overtures of good-will are highly commendable, and that the circumstance of my being next in the entail of Longbourn estate, will be kindly overlooked on your side, and not lead you to reject the offered olive-branch. I cannot be otherwise than concerned at being the means of injuring your amiable daughters, and beg leave to apologise for it, as well as to assure you of my readiness to make them every possible amends, – but of this hereafter. If you should have no objection to receive me into your house, I propose myself the satisfaction of waiting on you and your family, Monday, November 18th, by four o'clock, and shall probably trespass on your hospitality till the Saturday se'night following, which I can do without any inconvenience, as Lady Catherine is far from objecting to my occasional absence on a Sunday, provided that some other clergyman is engaged to do the duty of the day. I remain, dear sir, with respectful compliments to your lady and daughters, your well-wisher and friend,

WILLIAM COLLINS.'

"At four o'clock, therefore, we may expect this peace-making gentleman," said Mr. Bennet, as he folded up the letter. "He seems to be a most conscientious and polite young man, upon my word; and I doubt not will prove a valuable acquaintance, especially if Lady Catherine should be so indulgent as to let him come to us again."

"There is some sense in what he says about the girls however; and if he is disposed to make them any amends, I shall not be the person to discourage him."

"Though it is difficult," said Jane, "to guess in what way he can mean to make us the atonement he thinks our due, the wish is certainly to his credit."

Elizabeth was chiefly struck with his extraordinary deference for Lady Catherine, and his kind intention of christening, marrying, and burying his parishioners whenever it were required.

"He must be an oddity, I think," said she. "I cannot make him out. – There is something very pompous in his style. – And what can he mean by apologizing for being next in the entail? – We cannot suppose he would help it, if he could. – Can he be a sensible man, sir?"

"No, my dear; I think not. I have great hopes of finding him quite the reverse. There is a mixture of servility and self-importance in his letter, which promises well. I am impatient to see him."

"In point of composition," said Mary, "his letter does not seem defective. The idea of the olive branch perhaps is not wholly new, yet I think it is well expressed."

To Catherine and Lydia, neither the letter nor its writer were in any degree interesting. It was next to impossible that their cousin should come in a scarlet coat, and it was now some weeks since they had received pleasure from the society of a man in any other colour. As for their mother, Mr. Collins's letter had done away much of her ill-will, and she was preparing to see him with a degree of composure, which astonished her husband and daughters.

Mr. Collins was punctual to his time, and was received with great politeness by the whole family. Mr. Bennet indeed said little; but the ladies were ready enough to talk, and Mr. Collins seemed neither in need of encouragement, nor inclined to be silent himself.

He was a tall, heavy-looking young man of five and twenty. His air was grave and stately, and his manners were very formal. He had not been long seated before he complimented Mrs. Bennet on having so fine a family of daughters; said he had heard much of their beauty, but that, in this instance, fame had fallen short of the truth; and added, that he did not doubt her seeing them all in due time well disposed of in marriage. This gallantry was not much to the taste of some of his hearers, but Mrs. Bennet, who quarrelled with no compliments, answered most readily.

"You are very kind, sir, I am sure; and I wish with all my heart it may prove so; for else they will be destitute enough. Things are settled so oddly."

"You allude perhaps to the entail of this estate."

"Ah! sir, I do indeed. It is a grievous affair to my poor girls, you must confess. Not that I mean to find fault with *you*, for such things I know are all chance in this world. There is no knowing how estates will go when once they come to be entailed."

"I am very sensible madam, of the hardship to my fair cousins, – and could say much on the subject but that I am cautious of appearing forward and precipitate. But I can assure the young ladies that I come prepared to admire them. At present I will not say more, but perhaps when we are better acquainted –"

He was interrupted by a summons to dinner; and the girls smiled on each other. They were not the only objects of Mr. Collin's admiration. The hall, the dining-room, and all its furniture were examined and praised; and his commendation of everything would have touched Mrs. Bennet's heart, but for the mortifying supposition of his viewing it all as his own future property. The dinner too in its turn was highly admired; and he begged to know to which of his fair cousins, the excellence of its cookery was owing. But here he was set right by Mrs. Bennet, who assured him with some asperity that they were very well able to keep a good cook, and that her daughters had nothing to do in the kitchen. He begged pardon for having displeased her. In a softened tone she declared herself not at all offended; but he continued to apologise for about a quarter of an hour.

# Chapter 14

DURING DINNER, Mr. Bennet scarcely spoke at all; but when the servants were withdrawn, he thought it time to have some conversation with his guest, and therefore started a subject in which he expected him to shine, by observing that he seemed very fortunate in his patroness. Lady Catherine de Bourgh's attention to his wishes, and consideration for his comfort, appeared very remarkable. Mr. Bennet could not have chosen better. Mr. Collins was eloquent in her praise. The subject elevated him to more than usual solemnity of manner, and with a most important aspect he protested that he had never in his life witnessed such behaviour in a person of rank – such affability and condescension, as he had himself experienced from Lady Catherine. She had been graciously pleased to approve of both the discourses, which he had already had the honour of preaching before her. She had also asked him twice to dine at Rosings, and had sent for him only the Saturday before, to make up her pool of quadrille in the evening. Lady Catherine was reckoned proud by many people he knew, but *he* had never seen anything but affability in her. She had always spoken to him as she would to any other gentleman; she made not the smallest objection to his joining in the society of the neighbourhood, nor to his leaving his parish occasionally for a week or two, to visit his relations. She had even condescended to advise him to marry as soon as he could, provided he chose with discretion; and had once paid him a visit in his humble parsonage; where she had perfectly approved all the alterations he had been making, and had even vouchsafed to suggest some herself – some shelves in the closets upstairs."

"That is all very proper and civil, I am sure," said Mrs. Bennet, "and I dare say she is a very agreeable woman. It is a pity that great ladies in general are not more like her. Does she live near you, sir?"

"The garden in which stands my humble abode, is separated only by a lane from Rosings Park, her ladyship's residence."

"I think you said she was a widow, sir? has she any family?"

"She has one only daughter, the heiress of Rosings, and of very extensive property."

"Ah!" said Mrs. Bennet, shaking her head, "then she is better off than many girls. And what sort of young lady is she? is she handsome?"

"She is a most charming young lady indeed. Lady Catherine herself says that in point of true beauty, Miss de Bourgh is far superior to the handsomest of her sex, because there is that in her features which marks the young woman of distinguished birth. She is unfortunately of a sickly constitution, which has prevented her making that progress in many accomplishments, which she could not otherwise have failed of; as I am informed by the lady who superintended her education, and who still resides with them. But she is perfectly amiable, and often condescends to drive by my humble abode in her little phaeton and ponies."

"Has she been presented? I do not remember her name among the ladies at court."

"Her indifferent state of health unhappily prevents her being in town; and by that means, as I told Lady Catherine myself one day, has deprived the British court of its brightest ornament. Her ladyship seemed pleased with the idea; and you may imagine that I am happy on every occasion to offer those little delicate compliments which are always acceptable to ladies. I have more than once observed to Lady Catherine, that her charming daughter seemed born to be a duchess, and that the most elevated rank, instead of giving her consequence, would be adorned by her. – These are the kind of little things which please her ladyship, and it is a sort of attention which I conceive myself peculiarly bound to pay."

"You judge very properly," said Mr. Bennet, "and it is happy for you that you possess the talent of flattering with delicacy. May I ask whether these pleasing attentions proceed from the impulse of the moment, or are the result of previous study?"

"They arise chiefly from what is passing at the time, and though I sometimes amuse myself with suggesting and arranging such little elegant compliments as may be adapted to ordinary occasions, I always wish to give them as unstudied an air as possible."

Mr. Bennet's expectations were fully answered. His cousin was as absurd as he had hoped, and he listened to him with the keenest enjoyment, maintaining at the same time the most resolute composure of countenance, and except in an occasional glance at Elizabeth, requiring no partner in his pleasure.

By tea-time however the dose had been enough, and Mr. Bennet was glad to take his guest into the drawing-room again, and when tea was over, glad to invite him to read aloud to the ladies. Mr. Collins readily assented, and a book was produced; but on beholding it, (for everything announced it to be from a circulating library), he started back, and begging pardon, protested that he never read novels. – Kitty stared at him, and Lydia exclaimed. – Other books were produced, and after some deliberation he chose Fordyce's Sermons. Lydia gaped as he opened the volume, and before he had, with very monotonous solemnity, read three pages, she interrupted him with,

"Do you know, mamma, that my uncle Philips talks of turning away Richard, and if he does, Colonel Forster will hire him. My aunt told me so herself on Saturday. I shall walk to Meryton to-morrow to hear more about it, and to ask when Mr. Denny comes back from town."

Lydia was bid by her two eldest sisters to hold her tongue; but Mr. Collins, much offended, laid aside his book, and said,

"I have often observed how little young ladies are interested by books of a serious stamp, though written solely for their benefit. It amazes me, I confess; – for certainly, there can be nothing so advantageous to them as instruction. But I will no longer importune my young cousin."

Then turning to Mr. Bennet, he offered himself as his antagonist at backgammon. Mr. Bennet accepted the challenge, observing that he acted very wisely in leaving the girls to their own trifling amusements. Mrs. Bennet and her daughters apologised most civilly for Lydia's interruption, and promised that it should not occur again, if he would resume his book; but Mr. Collins, after assuring them that he bore his young cousin no ill-will, and should never resent her behaviour as any affront, seated himself at another table with Mr. Bennet, and prepared for backgammon.

## *Chapter 15*

MR. COLLINS was not a sensible man, and the deficiency of nature had been but little assisted by education or society; the greatest part of his life having been spent under the guidance of an illiterate and miserly father; and though he belonged to one of the universities, he had merely kept the necessary terms, without forming at it any useful acquaintance. The subjection in which his father had brought him up, had given him originally great humility of manner, but it was now a good deal counteracted by the self-conceit of a weak head, living in retirement, and the consequential feelings of early and unexpected prosperity. A fortunate chance had recommended him to Lady Catherine de Bourgh when the living of Hunsford was vacant; and the respect which he felt for her high rank, and his veneration for her as his patroness, mingling with a very good opinion of himself, of his authority as a clergyman, and his rights as rector, made him altogether a mixture of pride and obsequiousness, self-importance and humility.

Having now a good house and a very sufficient income, he intended to marry; and in seeking a reconciliation with the Longbourn family he had a wife in view, as he meant to choose one of the daughters, if he found them as handsome and amiable as they were represented by common report. This was his plan off amends – of atonement – for inheriting their father's estate; and he thought it an excellent one, full of eligibility and suitableness, and excessively generous and disinterested on his own part.

His plan did not vary on seeing them. – Miss Bennet's lovely face confirmed his views, and established all his strictest notions of what was due to seniority; and for the first evening *she* was his settled choice. The next morning, however, made an alteration; for in a quarter of an hour's tete-a-tete with Mrs. Bennet before breakfast, a conversation beginning with his parsonage-house, and leading naturally to the avowal of his hopes, that a mistress for it might be found at Longbourn, produced from her, amid very complaisant smiles and general encouragement, a caution against the very Jane he had fixed on. – "As to her *younger* daughters she could not take upon her to say – she could not positively answer – but she did not *know* of any prepossession;– her *eldest* daughter, she must just mention – she felt it incumbent on her to hint, was likely to be very soon engaged."

Mr. Collins had only to change from Jane to Elizabeth – and it was soon done – done while Mrs. Bennet was stirring the fire. Elizabeth, equally next to Jane in birth and beauty, succeeded her of course.

Mrs. Bennet treasured up the hint, and trusted that she might soon have two daughters married; and the man whom she could not bear to speak of the day before, was now high in her good graces.

Lydia's intention of walking to Meryton was not forgotten; every sister except Mary agreed to go with her; and Mr. Collins was to attend them, at the request of Mr. Bennet, who was most anxious to get rid of him, and have his library to himself; for thither Mr. Collins had followed him after breakfast; and there he would continue, nominally engaged with one of the largest folios in the collection, but really talking to Mr. Bennet, with little cessation, of his house and garden at Hunsford. Such doings discomposed Mr. Bennet exceedingly. In his library he had been always sure of leisure and tranquillity; and though prepared, as he told Elizabeth, to meet with folly and conceit in every other room in the house, he was used to be free from them there; his civility, therefore, was most prompt in inviting Mr. Collins to join his daughters in their walk; and Mr. Collins, being in fact much better fitted for a walker than a reader, was extremely well pleased to close his large book, and go.

In pompous nothings on his side, and civil assents on that of his cousins, their time passed till they entered Meryton. The attention of the younger ones was then no longer to be gained by *him*. Their eyes were immediately wandering up in the street in quest of the officers, and nothing less than a very smart bonnet indeed, or a really new muslin in a shop window, could recall them.

But the attention of every lady was soon caught by a young

man, whom they had never seen before, of most gentlemanlike appearance, walking with an officer on the other side of the way. The officer was the very Mr. Denny, concerning whose return from London Lydia came to enquire, and he bowed as they passed. All were struck with the stranger's air, all wondered who he could be; and Kitty and Lydia, determined if possible to find out, led the way across the street, under pretence of wanting something in an opposite shop, and fortunately had just gained the pavement when the two gentlemen turning back had reached the same spot. Mr. Denny addressed them directly, and entreated permission to introduce his friend, Mr. Wickham, who had returned with him the day before from town, and he was happy to say had accepted a commission in their corps. This was exactly as it should be; for the young man wanted only regimentals to make him completely charming. His appearance was greatly in his favour; he had all the best part of beauty, a fine countenance, a good figure, and very pleasing address. The introduction was followed up on his side by a happy readiness of conversation – a readiness at the same time perfectly correct and unassuming; and the whole party were still standing and talking together very agreeably, when the sound of horses drew their notice, and Darcy and Bingley were seen riding down the street. On distinguishing the ladies of the group, the two gentlemen came directly towards them, and began the usual civilities. Bingley was the principal spokesman, and Miss Bennet the principal object. He was then, he said, on his way to Longbourn on purpose to enquire after her. Mr. Darcy corroborated it with a bow, and was beginning to determine not to fix his eyes on Elizabeth, when they were suddenly arrested by the sight of the stranger, and Elizabeth happening to see the countenance of both as they looked at each other, was all astonishment at the effect of the meeting. Both changed colour, one looked white, the other red. Mr. Wickham, after a few moments, touched his hat – a salutation which Mr. Darcy just deigned to return. What could be the meaning of it? – It was impossible to imagine; it was impossible not to long to know.

In another minute Mr. Bingley, but without seeming to have noticed what passed, took leave and rode on with his friend.

Mr. Denny and Mr. Wickham walked with the young ladies to the door of Mr. Philip's house, and then made their bows, in spite of Miss Lydia's pressing entreaties that they would come in, and even in spite of Mrs. Philips' throwing up the parlour window, and loudly seconding the invitation.

Mrs. Philips was always glad to see her nieces; and the two eldest, from their recent absence, were particularly welcome, and she was eagerly expressing her surprise at their sudden return home, which, as their own carriage had not fetched them, she should have known nothing about, if she had not happened to see Mr. Jones's shop boy in the street, who had told her that they were not to send any more draughts to Netherfield because the Miss Bennets were come away, when her civility was claimed towards Mr. Collins by Jane's introduction of him. She received him with her very best politeness, which he returned with as much more, apologizing for his intrusion, without any previous acquaintance with her, which he could not help flattering himself however might be justified by his relationship to the young ladies who introduced him to her notice. Mrs. Philips was quite awed by such an excess of good breeding; but her contemplation of one stranger was soon put to an end to by exclamations and inquiries about the other, of whom, however, she could only tell her nieces what they already knew, that Mr. Denny had brought him from London, and that he was to have a lieutenant's commission in the —shire. She had been watching him the last hour, she said, as he walked up and down the street, and had Mr. Wickham appeared Kitty and Lydia would certainly have continued the occupation, but unluckily no one passed the windows now except a few of the officers, who in comparison with the stranger, were become "stupid, disagreeable fellows." Some of them were to dine with the Philipses the next day, and their aunt promised to make her husband call on Mr. Wickham, and give him an invitation also, if the family from Longbourn would come in the evening. This was agreed to, and Mrs. Philips protested that they would have a nice comfortable noisy game of lottery tickets, and a little bit of hot supper afterwards. The prospect of such delights was very cheering, and they parted in mutual good spirits. Mr. Collins repeated his apologies in quitting the room, and was assured with unwearying civility that they were perfectly needless.

As they walked home, Elizabeth related to Jane what she had seen pass between the two gentlemen; but though Jane would have defended either or both, had they appeared to be wrong, she could no more explain such behaviour than her sister.

Mr. Collins on his return highly gratified Mrs. Bennet by admiring Mrs. Philips's manners and politeness. He protested that except Lady Catherine and her daughter, he had never seen a more elegant woman; for she had not only received him with the utmost civility, but had even pointedly included him in her invitation for the next evening, although utterly unknown to her before. Something, he supposed might be attributed to his connection with them, but yet he had never met with so much attention in the whole course of his life.

## *Chapter 16*

As no objection was made to the young people's engagement with their aunt, and all Mr. Collins's scruples of leaving Mr. and Mrs. Bennet for a single evening during his visit were most steadily resisted, the coach conveyed him and his five cousins at a suitable hour to Meryton; and the girls had the pleasure of hearing, as they entered the drawing-room, that Mr. Wickham had accepted their uncle's invitation, and was then in the house.

When this information was given, and they had all taken their seats, Mr. Collins was at leisure to look around him and admire, and he was so much struck with the size and furniture of the apartment, that he declared he might almost have supposed himself in the small summer breakfast-parlour at Rosings; a comparison that did not at first convey much gratification; but when Mrs. Philips understood from him what Rosings was, and who was its proprietor, when she had listened to the description of only one of Lady Catherine's drawing-rooms, and found that the chimney-piece alone had cost eight hundred pounds, she felt all the force of the compliment, and would hardly have resented a comparison with the housekeeper's room.

In describing to her all the grandeur of Lady Catherine and her mansion, with occasional digressions in praise of his own humble abode, and the improvements it was receiving, he was happily employed until the gentlemen joined them; and he found in Mrs. Philips a very attentive listener, whose opinion of his consequence increased with what she heard, and who was resolving to retail it all among her neighbours as soon as she could. To the girls, who could not listen to their cousin, and who had nothing to do but to wish for an instrument, and examine their own indifferent imitations of china on the mantelpiece, the interval of waiting appeared very long. It was over at last however. The gentlemen did approach; and when Mr. Wickham walked into the room, Elizabeth felt that she had neither been seeing him before, nor thinking of him since, with the smallest degree of unreasonable admiration. The officers of the —shire were in general a very creditable, gentlemanlike set, and the best of them were of the present party; but Mr. Wickham was as far beyond them all in person, countenance, air, and walk, as *they* were superior to the broad-faced stuffy uncle Philips, breathing port wine, who followed them into the room.

Mr. Wickham was the happy man towards whom almost every female eye was turned, and Elizabeth was the happy woman by whom he finally seated himself; and the agreeable manner in which he immediately fell into conversation, though it was only on its being a wet night, and on the probability of a rainy season, made her feel that the commonest, dullest, most thread-bare topic might be rendered interesting by the skill of the speaker.

With such rivals for the notice of the fair, as Mr. Wickham and the officers, Mr. Collins seemed likely to sink into insignificance; to the young ladies he certainly was nothing; but he had still at intervals a kind listener in Mrs. Philips, and was, by her watchfulness, most abundantly supplied with coffee and muffin.

When the card-tables were placed, he had an opportunity of obliging her in return, by sitting down to whist.

"I know little of the game, at present," said he, "but I shall be glad to improve myself, for in my situation in life –" Mrs. Phillips was very thankful for his compliance, but could not wait for his reason.

Mr. Wickham did not play at whist, and with ready delight was he received at the other table between Elizabeth and Lydia. At first there seemed danger of Lydia's engrossing him entirely, for she was a most determined talker; but being likewise extremely fond of lottery tickets, she soon grew too much interested in the game, too eager in making bets and exclaiming after prizes, to have attention for anyone in particular. Allowing for the common demands of the game, Mr. Wickham was therefore at leisure to talk to Elizabeth, and she was very willing to hear him, though what she chiefly wished to hear she could not hope to be told, the history of his acquaintance with Mr. Darcy. She dared not even mention that gentleman. Her curiosity however was unexpectedly relieved. Mr. Wickham began the subject himself.

He enquired how far Netherfield was from Meryton; and, after receiving her answer, asked in an hesitating manner how long Mr. Darcy had been staying there.

"About a month," said Elizabeth; and then, unwilling to let the subject drop, added, "He is a man of very large property in Derbyshire, I understand."

"Yes," replied Mr. Wickham; – "his estate there is a noble one. A clear ten thousand per annum. You could not have met with a person more capable of giving you certain information on that head than myself, – for I have been connected with his family in a particular manner from my infancy."

Elizabeth could not but look surprised.

"You may well be surprised, Miss Bennet, at such an assertion, after seeing, as you probably might, the very cold manner of our meeting yesterday. – Are you much acquainted with Mr. Darcy?"

"As much as I ever wish to be," cried Elizabeth warmly. – "I have spent four days in the same house with him, and I think him very disagreeable."

"I have no right to give *my* opinion," said Wickham, "as to his being agreeable or otherwise. I am not qualified to form one. I have known him too long and too well to be a fair judge. It is impossible for *me* to be impartial. But I believe your opinion of him would in general astonish – and perhaps you would not express it quite so strongly anywhere else. – Here you are in your own family."

"Upon my word, I say no more *here* than I might say in any house in the neighbourhood, except Netherfield. He is not at all liked in Hertfordshire. Everybody is disgusted with his pride. You will not find him more favourably spoken of by any one."

"I cannot pretend to be sorry," said Wickham, after a short interruption, "that he or that any man should not be estimated beyond their deserts; but with *him* I believe it does not often happen. The world is blinded by his fortune and consequence, or frightened by his high and imposing manners, and sees him only as he chooses to be seen."

"I should take him, even on *my* slight acquaintance, to be an ill-tempered man." Wickham only shook his head.

"I wonder," said he, at the next opportunity of speaking, "whether he is likely to be in this country much longer."

"I do not at all know; but I *heard* nothing of his going away when I was at Netherfield. I hope your plans in favour of the —shire will not be affected by his being in the neighbourhood."

"Oh! no – it is not for *me* to be driven away by Mr. Darcy. If *he* wishes to avoid seeing *me*, he must go. We are not on friendly terms, and it always gives me pain to meet him, but I have no reason for avoiding *him* but what I might proclaim to all the world, a sense of very great ill-usage, and most painful regrets at his being what he is. His father, Miss Bennet, the late Mr. Darcy, was one of the best men that ever breathed, and the truest friend I ever had; and I can never be in company with this Mr. Darcy without being grieved to the soul by a thousand tender recollections. His behaviour to myself has been scandalous; but I verily believe I could forgive him anything and everything, rather than his disappointing the hopes and disgracing the memory of his father."

Elizabeth found the interest of the subject increase, and listened with all her heart; but the delicacy of it prevented farther enquiry.

Mr. Wickham began to speak on more general topics, Meryton, the neighbourhood, the society, appearing highly pleased with all that he had yet seen, and speaking of the latter especially, with gentle but very intelligible gallantry.

"It was the prospect of constant society, and good society," he added, "which was my chief inducement to enter the —shire. I knew it to be a most respectable, agreeable corps, and my friend Denny tempted me farther by his account of their present quarters, and the very great attentions and excellent acquaintance Meryton had procured them. Society, I own, is necessary to me.

I have been a disappointed man, and my spirits will not bear solitude. I *must* have employment and society. A military life is not what I was intended for, but circumstances have now made it eligible. The church *ought* to have been my profession – I was brought up for the church, and I should at this time have been in possession of a most valuable living, had it pleased the gentleman we were speaking of just now."

"Indeed!"

"Yes – the late Mr. Darcy bequeathed me the next presentation of the best living in his gift. He was my godfather, and excessively attached to me. I cannot do justice to his kindness. He meant to provide for me amply, and thought he had done it; but when the living fell, it was given elsewhere."

"Good heavenss!" cried Elizabeth; "but how could *that* be? – How could his will be disregarded? – Why did not you seek legal redress?"

"There was just such an informality in the terms of the bequest as to give me no hope from law. A man of honour could not have doubted the intention, but Mr. Darcy chose to doubt it – or to treat it as merely conditional recommendation, and to assert that I had forfeited all claim to it by extravagance, imprudence, in short anything or nothing. Certain it is, that the living became vacant two years ago, exactly as I was of an age to hold it, and that it was given to another man; and no less certain is it, that I cannot accuse myself of having really done anything to deserve to lose it. I have a warm, unguarded temper, and I may perhaps have sometimes spoken my opinion *of* him, and *to* him, too freely. I can recall nothing worse. But the fact is, that we are very different sort of men, and that he hates me."

"This is quite shocking! – He deserves to be publicly disgraced."

"Some time or other he *will* be – but it shall not be by *me*. Till I can forget his father, I can never defy or expose *him*."

Elizabeth honoured him for such feelings, and thought him handsomer than ever as he expressed them.

"But what," said she, after a pause, "can have been his motive? – what can have induced him to behave so cruelly?"

"A thorough, determined dislike of me – a dislike which I cannot but attribute in some measure to jealousy. Had the late Mr. Darcy liked me less, his son might have borne with me better; but his father's uncommon attachment to me, irritated him I believe very early in life. He had not a temper to bear the sort of competition in which we stood – the sort of preference which was often given to me."

"I had not thought Mr. Darcy so bad as this – though I have never liked him, I had not thought so very ill of him.– I had supposed him to be despising his fellow-creatures in general, but did not suspect him of descending to such malicious revenge, such injustice, such inhumanity as this."

After a few minutes' reflection, however, she continued, "I *do* remember his boasting one day, at Netherfield, of the implacability of his resentments, of his having an unforgiving temper. His disposition must be dreadful."

"I will not trust myself on the subject," replied Wickham; "*I* can hardly be just to him."

Elizabeth was again deep in thought, and after a time exclaimed, "To treat in such a manner, the godson, the friend, the favourite of his father!" – She could have added, "A young man too, like *you*, whose very countenance may vouch for your being amiable" – but she contented herself with, "And one, too, who had probably been his own companion from childhood, connected together, as I think you said, in the closest manner!"

"We were born in the same parish, within the same park, the greatest part of our youth was passed together; inmates of the same house, sharing the same amusements, objects of the same parental care. *My* father began life in the profession which your uncle Mr. Philips, appears to do so much credit to – but he gave up everything to be of use to the late Mr. Darcy, and devoted all his time to the care of the Pemberley property. He was most highly esteemed by Mr. Darcy, a most intimate, confidential friend. Mr. Darcy often acknowledged himself to be under the greatest obligations to my father's active superintendence, and when immediately before my father's death, Mr. Darcy gave him a voluntary promise of providing for me, I am convinced that he felt it to be as much a debt of gratitude to *him*, as of affection to myself."

"How strange!" cried Elizabeth. "How abominable! – I wonder that the very pride of this Mr. Darcy has not made him just to you! – If from no better motive, that he should not have been too proud to be dishonest – for dishonesty I must call it."

"It *is* wonderful," – replied Wickham, – "for almost all his actions may be traced to pride; – and pride had often been his best friend. It has connected him nearer with virtue than with any other feeling. But we are none of us consistent; and in his behaviour to me, there were stronger impulses even than pride."

"Can such abominable pride as his, have ever done him good?"

"Yes. It has often led him to be liberal and generous, – to give his money freely, to display hospitality, to assist his tenants, and relieve the poor. Family pride, and *filial* pride, for he is very proud of what his father was, have done this. Not to appear to disgrace his family, to degenerate from the popular qualities, or lose the influence of the Pemberley House, is a powerful motive. He has also *brotherly* pride, which with *some* brotherly affection, makes him a very kind and careful guardian of his sister; and you will hear him generally cried up as the most attentive and best of brothers."

"What sort of a girl is Miss Darcy?"

He shook his head. – "I wish I could call her amiable. It gives me pain to speak ill of a Darcy. But she is too much like her brother – very, very proud. – As a child, she was affectionate and pleasing, and extremely fond of me; and I have devoted hours and hours to her amusement. But she is nothing to me now. She is a handsome girl, about fifteen or sixteen, and I understand highly accomplished. Since her father's death, her home has been London, where a lady lives with her, and superintends her education."

After many pauses and many trials of other subjects, Elizabeth could not help reverting once more to the first, and saying,

"I am astonished at his intimacy with Mr. Bingley! How can Mr. Bingley, who seems good humour itself, and is, I really believe, truly amiable, be in friendship with such a man? How can they suit each other? – Do you know Mr. Bingley?"

"Not at all."

"He is a sweet-tempered, amiable, charming man. He cannot know what Mr. Darcy is."

"Probably not; – but Mr. Darcy can please where he chooses. He does not want abilities. He can be a conversible companion if he thinks it worth his while. Among those who are at all his equals in consequence, he is a very different man from what he is to the less prosperous. His pride never deserts him; but with the rich, he is liberal-minded, just, sincere, rational, honourable, and perhaps agreeable, – allowing something for fortune and figure."

The whist party soon afterwards breaking up, the players gathered round the other table, and Mr. Collins took his station between his cousin Elizabeth and Mrs. Philips. – The usual inquiries as to his success was made by the latter. It had not been very great; he had lost every point; but when Mrs. Philips began to express her concern thereupon, he assured her with much earnest gravity that it was not of the least importance, that he considered the money as a mere trifle, and begged she would not make herself uneasy.

I know very well, madam," said he, "that when persons sit

down to a card-table, they must take their chance of these things, – and happily I am not in such circumstances as to make five shillings any object. There are undoubtedly many who could not say the same, but thanks to Lady Catherine de Bourgh, I am removed far beyond the necessity of regarding little matters."

Mr. Wickham's attention was caught; and after observing Mr. Collins for a few moments, he asked Elizabeth in a low voice whether her relations were very intimately acquainted with the family of de Bourgh.

"Lady Catherine de Bourgh," she replied, "has very lately given him a living. I hardly know how Mr. Collins was first introduced to her notice, but he certainly has not known her long."

"You know of course that Lady Catherine de Bourgh and Lady Anne Darcy were sisters; consequently that she is aunt to the present Mr. Darcy."

"No, indeed, I did not. – I knew nothing at all of Lady Catherine's connections. I never heard of her existence till the day before yesterday."

"Her daughter, Miss de Bourgh, will have a very large fortune, and it is believed that she and her cousin will unite the two estates."

This information made Elizabeth smile, as she thought of poor Miss Bingley. Vain indeed must be all her attentions, vain and useless her affection for his sister and her praise of himself, if he were already self-destined to another.

"Mr. Collins," said she, "speaks highly both of Lady Catherine and her daughter; but from some particulars that he has related of her ladyship, I suspect his gratitude misleads him, and that in spite of her being his patroness, she is an arrogant, conceited woman."

"I believe her to be both in a great degree," replied Wickham; "I have not seen her for many years, but I very well remember that I never liked her, and that her manners were dictatorial and insolent. She has the reputation of being remarkably sensible and clever; but I rather believe she derives part of her abilities from her rank and fortune, part from her authoritative manner, and the rest from the pride of her nephew, who chooses that everyone connected with him should have an understanding of the first class."

Elizabeth allowed that he had given a very rational account of it, and they continued talking together with mutual satisfaction till supper put an end to cards; and gave the rest of the ladies their share of Mr. Wickham's attentions. There could be no conversation in the noise of Mrs. Philips's supper party, but his manners recommended him to everybody. Whatever he said, was said well; and whatever he did, done gracefully. Elizabeth went away with her head full of him. She could think of nothing but of Mr. Wickham, and of what he had told her, all the way home; but there was not time for her even to mention his name as they went, for neither Lydia nor Mr. Collins were once silent. Lydia talked incessantly of lottery tickets, of the fish she had lost and the fish she had won, and Mr. Collins, in describing the civility of Mr. and Mrs. Philips, protesting that he did not in the least regard his losses at whist, enumerating all the dishes at supper, and repeatedly fearing that he crowded his cousins, had more to say than he could well manage before the carriage stopped at Longbourn House.

## *Chapter 17*

ELIZABETH RELATED to Jane the next day, what had passed between Mr. Wickham and herself. Jane listened with astonishment and concern; – she knew not how to believe that Mr. Darcy could be so unworthy of Mr. Bingley's regard; and yet, it was not in her nature to question the veracity of a young man of such amiable appearance as Wickham. – The possibility of his having really endured such unkindness, was enough to interest all her tender feelings; and nothing therefore remained to be done, but to think well of them both, to defend the conduct of each, and throw into the account of accident or mistake, whatever could not be otherwise explained.

"They have both," said she, "been deceived, I dare say, in some way or other, of which we can form no idea. Interested people have perhaps misrepresented each to the other. It is, in short, impossible for us to conjecture the causes or circumstances which may have alienated them, without actual blame on either side."

"Very true, indeed; – and now, my dear Jane, what have you got to say on behalf of the interested people who have probably been concerned in the business? – Do clear *them* too, or we shall be obliged to think ill of somebody"

"Laugh as much as you choose, but you will not laugh me out of my opinion. My dearest Lizzy, do but consider in what a disgraceful light it places Mr. Darcy, to be treating his father's favourite in such a manner, – one, whom his father had promised to provide for. – It is impossible. No man of common humanity, no man who had any value for his character, could be capable of it. Can his most intimate friends be so excessively deceived by him? oh! no."

"I can much more easily believe Mr. Bingley's being imposed on, than that Mr. Wickham should invent such a history of himself as he gave me last night; names, facts, everything mentioned without ceremony. – If it be not so, let Mr. Darcy contradict it. Besides, there was truth in his looks."

"It is difficult indeed – it is distressing. – One does not know what to think."

"I beg your pardon; – one knows exactly what to think."

But Jane could think with certainty on only one point – that

Mr. Bingley, if he *had been* imposed on, would have much to suffer when the affair became public.

The two young ladies were summoned from the shrubbery where this conversation passed, by the arrival of some of the very persons of whom they had been speaking; Mr. Bingley and his sisters came to give their personal invitation for the long-expected ball at Netherfield, which was fixed for the following Tuesday. The two ladies were delighted to see their dear friend again, called it an age since they had met, and repeatedly asked what she had been doing with herself since their separation. To the rest of the family they paid little attention; avoiding Mrs. Bennet as much as possible, saying not much to Elizabeth, and nothing at all to the others. They were soon gone again, rising from their seats with an activity which took their brother by surprise, and hurrying off as if eager to escape from Mrs. Bennet's civilities.

The prospect of the Netherfield ball was extremely agreeable to every female of the family. Mrs. Bennet chose to consider it as given in compliment to her eldest daughter, and was particularly flattered by receiving the invitation from Mr. Bingley himself, instead of a ceremonious card. Jane pictured to herself a happy evening in the society of her two friends, and the attentions of their brother; and Elizabeth thought with pleasure of dancing a great deal with Mr. Wickham, and of seeing a confirmation of everything in Mr. Darcy's look and behaviour. The happiness anticipated by Catherine and Lydia depended less on any single event, or any particular person, for though they each, like Elizabeth, meant to dance half the evening with Mr. Wickham, he was by no means the only partner who could satisfy them, and a ball was at any rate, a ball. And even Mary could assure her family that she had no disinclination for it.

"While I can have my mornings to myself," said she, "it is enough – I think it is no sacrifice to join occasionally in evening engagements. Society has claims on us all; and I profess myself one of those who consider intervals of recreation and amusement as desirable for everybody."

Elizabeth's spirits were so high on the occasion, that though she did not often speak unnecessarily to Mr. Collins, she could not help asking him whether he intended to accept Mr. Bingley's invitation, and if he did, whether he would think it proper to join in the evening's amusement; and she was rather surprised to find that he entertained no scruple whatever on that head, and was very far from dreading a rebuke either from the Archbishop, or Lady Catherine de Bourgh, by venturing to dance.

"I am by no means of the opinion, I assure you," said he, "that a ball of this kind, given by a young man of character, to respectable people, can have any evil tendency; and I am so far from objecting to dancing myself that I shall hope to be honoured with the hands of all my fair cousins in the course of the evening, and I take this opportunity of soliciting yours, Miss Elizabeth, for the two first dances especially, – a preference which I trust my cousin Jane will attribute to the right cause, and not to any disrespect for her."

Elizabeth felt herself completely taken in. She had fully proposed being engaged by Mr. Wickham for those very dances: – and to have Mr. Collins instead! her liveliness had been never worse timed. There was no help for it however. Mr. Wickham's happiness and her own was per force delayed a little longer, and Mr. Collins's proposal accepted with as good a grace as she could. She was not the better pleased with his gallantry, from the idea it suggested of something more. – It now first struck her, that *she* was selected from among her sisters as worthy of being mistress of Hunsford Parsonage, and of assisting to form a quadrille table at Rosings, in the absence of more eligible visitors. The idea soon reached to conviction, as she observed his increasing civilities toward herself, and heard his frequent attempt at a compliment on her wit and vivacity; and though more astonished than gratified herself, by this effect of her charms, it was not long before her mother gave her to understand that the probability of their marriage was extremely agreeable to *her*. Elizabeth however did not choose to take the hint, being well aware that a serious dispute must be the consequence of any reply. Mr. Collins might never make the offer, and till he did, it was useless to quarrel about him.

If there had not been a Netherfield ball to prepare for and talk of, the younger Miss Bennets would have been in a pitiable state at this time, for from the day of the invitation, to the day of the ball, there was such a succession of rain as prevented their walking to Meryton once. No aunt, no officers, no news could be sought after; – the very shoe-roses for Netherfield were got by proxy. Even Elizabeth might have found some trial of her patience in weather, which totally suspended the improvement of her acquaintance with Mr. Wickham; and nothing less than a dance on Tuesday, could have made such a Friday, Saturday, Sunday, and Monday, endurable to Kitty and Lydia.

# *Chapter 18*

TILL ELIZABETH entered the drawing-room at Netherfield and looked in vain for Mr. Wickham among the cluster of red coats there assembled, a doubt of his being present had never occurred to her. The certainty of meeting him had not been checked by any of those recollections that might not unreasonably have alarmed her. She had dressed with more than usual care, and prepared in the highest spirits for the conquest of all that remained unsubdued of his heart, trusting that it was not more than might be won in the course of the evening. But in an instant arose the dreadful suspicion of his being purposely omitted for Mr. Darcy's pleasure in the Bingleys' invitation to the officers; and though this was not exactly the case, the absolute fact of his absence was pronounced by his friend Mr. Denny, to whom Lydia eagerly applied, and who told them that Wickham had been obliged to go to town on business the day before, and was not yet returned; adding, with a significant smile,

"I do not imagine his business would have called him away just now, if he had not wished to avoid a certain gentleman here."

This part of his intelligence, though unheard by Lydia, was caught by Elizabeth, and as it assured her that Darcy was not less answerable for Wickham's absence than if her first surmise had been just, every feeling of displeasure against the former was so sharpened by immediate disappointment, that she could hardly reply with tolerable civility to the polite inquiries which he directly afterwards approached to make. – Attention, forbearance, patience with Darcy, was injury to Wickham. She was resolved against any sort of conversation with him, and turned away with a degree of ill humour which she could not wholly surmount even in speaking to Mr. Bingley, whose blind partiality provoked her.

But Elizabeth was not formed for ill-humour; and though every prospect of her own was destroyed for the evening, it could not dwell long on her spirits; and having told all her griefs to Charlotte Lucas, whom she had not seen for a week, she was soon able to make a voluntary transition to the oddities of her cousin, and to point him out to her particular notice. The two first dances, however, brought a return of distress; they were dances of mortification. Mr. Collins, awkward and solemn, apologising instead of attending, and often moving wrong without being aware of it, gave her all the shame and misery which a disagreeable partner for a couple of dances can give. The moment of her release from him was ecstasy.

She danced next with an officer, and had the refreshment of talking of Wickham, and of hearing that he was universally liked. When those dances were over she returned to Charlotte Lucas, and was in conversation with her, when she found herself suddenly addressed by Mr. Darcy, who took her so much by surprise in his application for her hand, that, without knowing what she did, she accepted him. He walked away again immediately, and she was left to fret over her own want of presence of mind; Charlotte tried to console her.

"I dare say you will find him very agreeable."

"Heavens forbid! – *That* would be the greatest misfortune of all! – To find a man agreeable whom one is determined to hate! – Do not wish me such an evil."

When the dancing recommenced, however, and Darcy approached to claim her hand, Charlotte could not help cautioning her in a whisper not to be a simpleton and allow her fancy for Wickham to make her appear unpleasant in the eyes of a man ten times his consequence. Elizabeth made no answer, and took her place in the set, amazed at the dignity to which she was arrived in being allowed to stand opposite to Mr. Darcy, and reading in her neighbours' looks their equal amazement in beholding it. They stood for some time without speaking a word; and she began to imagine that their silence was to last through the two dances, and at first was resolved not to break it; till suddenly fancying that it would be the greater punishment to her partner to oblige him to talk, she made some slight observation on the dance. He replied, and was again silent. After a pause of some minutes she addressed him a second time with

"It is *your* turn to say something now, Mr. Darcy. – *I* talked about the dance, and *you* ought to make some sort of remark on the size of the room, or the number of couples."

He smiled, and assured her that whatever she wished him to say should be said.

"Very well. – That reply will do for the present. – Perhaps by and by I may observe that private balls are much pleasanter than public ones. – But *now* we may be silent."

"Do you talk by rule then, while you are dancing?"

"Sometimes. One must speak a little, you know. It would look odd to be entirely silent for half an hour together, and yet for the advantage of *some*, conversation ought to be so arranged as that they may have the trouble of saying as little as possible."

"Are you consulting your own feelings in the present case, or do you imagine that you are gratifying mine?"

"Both," replied Elizabeth archly; "for I have always seen a great similarity in the turn of our minds. – We are each of an unsocial, taciturn disposition, unwilling to speak, unless we expect to say something that will amaze the whole room, and be handed down to posterity with all the éclat of a proverb."

"This is no very striking resemblance of your own character, I am sure," said he. "How near it may be to *mine*, I cannot pretend to say. – *You* think it a faithful portrait undoubtedly."

"I must not decide on my own performance."

He made no answer, and they were again silent till they had gone down the dance, when he asked her if she and her sisters did not very often walk to Meryton. She answered in the affirmative, and, unable to resist the temptation, added, "When you met us there the other day, we had just been forming a new acquaintance."

The effect was immediate. A deeper shade of hauteur overspread his features, but he said not a word, and Elizabeth, though blaming herself for her own weakness, could not go on. At length Darcy spoke, and in a constrained manner said,

"Mr. Wickham is blessed with such happy manners as may ensure his *making* friends – whether he may be equally capable of *retaining* them, is less certain."

"He has been so unlucky as to lose *your* friendship," replied Elizabeth with emphasis, "and in a manner which he is likely to suffer from all his life."

Darcy made no answer, and seemed desirous of changing the subject. At that moment Sir William Lucas appeared close to them, meaning to pass through the set to the other side of the room; but on perceiving Mr. Darcy he stopped with a bow of superior courtesy to compliment him on his dancing and his partner.

"I have been most highly gratified indeed, my dear Sir. Such very superior dancing is not often seen. It is evident that you belong to the first circles. Allow me to say, however, that your fair partner does not disgrace you, and that I must hope to have this pleasure often repeated, especially when a certain desirable event, my dear Eliza (glancing at her sister and Bingley,) shall take place. What congratulations will then flow in! I appeal to Mr. Darcy: – but let me not interrupt you, Sir. – You will not thank me for detaining you from the bewitching converse of that young lady, whose bright eyes are also upbraiding me."

The latter part of this address was scarcely heard by Darcy; but Sir William's allusion to his friend seemed to strike him forcibly, and his eyes were directed with a very serious expression towards Bingley and Jane, who were dancing together. Recovering himself, however, shortly, he turned to his partner, and said,

"Sir William's interruption has made me forget what we were talking of."

"I do not think we were speaking at all. Sir William could not have interrupted any two people in the room who had less to say for themselves. – We have tried two or three subjects already without success, and what we are to talk of next I cannot imagine."

"What do you think of books?" said he, smiling.

"Books – Oh! no. – I am sure we never read the same, or not with the same feelings."

"I am sorry you think so; but if that be the case, there can at least be no want of subject. – We may compare our different opinions."

"No – I cannot talk of books in a ball-room; my head is always full of something else."

"The *present* always occupies you in such scenes – does it?" said he, with a look of doubt.

"Yes, always," she replied, without knowing what she said, for her thoughts had wandered far from the subject, as soon afterwards appeared by her suddenly exclaiming, "I remember hearing you once say, Mr. Darcy, that you hardly ever forgave, that your resentment once created was unappeasable. You are very cautious, I suppose, as to its *being created*."

"I am," said he, with a firm voice.

"And never allow yourself to be blinded by prejudice?"

"I hope not."

"It is particularly incumbent on those who never change their opinion, to be secure of judging properly at first."

"May I ask to what these questions tend?"

"Merely to the illustration of *your* character," said she, endeavouring to shake off her gravity. "I am trying to make it out."

"And what is your success?"

She shook her head. "I do not get on at all. I hear such different accounts of you as puzzle me exceedingly."

"I can readily believe," answered he gravely, "that report may vary greatly with respect to me; and I could wish, Miss Bennet, that you were not to sketch my character at the present moment, as there is reason to fear that the performance would reflect no credit on either."

"But if I do not take your likeness now, I may never have another opportunity."

"I would by no means suspend any pleasure of yours," he coldly replied. She said no more, and they went down the other dance and parted in silence; and on each side dissatisfied, though not to an equal degree, for in Darcy's breast there was a tolerable powerful feeling towards her, which soon procured her pardon, and directed all his anger against another.

They had not long separated when Miss Bingley came towards her, and with an expression of civil disdain accosted her,

"So, Miss Eliza, I hear you are quite delighted with George Wickham! – Your sister has been talking to me about him, and asking me a thousand questions; and I find that the young man forgot to tell you, among his other communications, that he was the son of old Wickham, the late Mr. Darcy's steward. Let me recommend you, however, as a friend, not to give implicit confidence to all his assertions; for as to Mr. Darcy's using him ill, it is perfectly false; for, on the contrary, he has been always remarkably kind to him, though George Wickham has treated Mr. Darcy in a most infamous manner. I do not know the particulars, but I know very well that Mr. Darcy is not in the least to blame, that he cannot bear to hear George Wickham mentioned, and that though my brother thought he could not well avoid including him in his invitation to the officers, he was excessively glad to find that he had taken himself out of the way. His coming into the country at all, is a most insolent thing indeed, and I wonder how he could presume to do it. I pity you, Miss Eliza, for this discovery of your favourite's guilt; but really considering his descent, one could not expect much better."

"His guilt and his descent appear by your account to be the same," said Elizabeth angrily; "for I have heard you accuse him of nothing worse than of being the son of Mr. Darcy's steward, and of *that*, I can assure you, he informed me himself."

"I beg your pardon," replied Miss Bingley, turning away with a sneer. "Excuse my interference. – It was kindly meant."

"Insolent girl!" said Elizabeth to herself. – "You are much mistaken if you expect to influence me by such a paltry attack as this. I see nothing in it but your own wilful ignorance and the malice of Mr. Darcy." She then sought her eldest sister, who had undertaken to make inquiries on the same subject of Bingley.

Jane met her with a smile of such sweet complacency, a glow of such happy expression, as sufficiently marked how well she was satisfied with the occurrences of the evening. – Elizabeth instantly read her feelings, and at that moment solicitude for Wickham, resentment against his enemies, and everything else gave way before the hope of Jane's being in the fairest way for happiness.

"I want to know," said she, with a countenance no less smiling than her sister's, "what you have learnt about Mr. Wickham. But perhaps you have been too pleasantly engaged to think of any third person; in which case you may be sure of my pardon."

"No," replied Jane, "I have not forgotten him; but I have nothing satisfactory to tell you. Mr. Bingley does not know the whole of his history, and is quite ignorant of the circumstances which have principally offended Mr. Darcy; but he will vouch for the good conduct, the probity and honour of his friend, and is perfectly convinced that Mr. Wickham has deserved much less attention from Mr. Darcy than he has received; and I am sorry to say that by his account as well as his sister's, Mr. Wickham is by no means a respectable young man. I am afraid he has been very imprudent, and has deserved to lose Mr. Darcy's regard."

"Mr. Bingley does not know Mr. Wickham himself?"

"No; he never saw him till the other morning at Meryton."

"This account then is what he has received from Mr. Darcy. I am perfectly satisfied. But what does he say of the living?"

"He does not exactly recollect the circumstances, though he has heard them from Mr. Darcy more than once, but he believes that it was left to him *conditionally* only."

"I have not a doubt of Mr. Bingley's sincerity," said Elizabeth warmly; "but you must excuse my not being convinced by assurances only. Mr. Bingley's defence of his friend was a very able one I dare say, but since he is unacquainted with several parts of the story, and has learnt the rest from that friend himself,

I shall venture still to think of both gentlemen as I did before."

She then changed the discourse to one more gratifying to each, and on which there could be no difference of sentiment. Elizabeth listened with delight to the happy, though modest hopes which Jane entertained of Mr. Bingley's regard, and said all in her power to heighten her confidence in it. On their being joined by Mr. Bingley himself, Elizabeth withdrew to Miss Lucas; to whose enquiry after the pleasantness of her last partner she had scarcely replied, before Mr. Collins came up to them and told her with great exultation that he had just been so fortunate as to make a most important discovery.

"I have found out," said he, "by a singular accident, that there is now in the room a near relation of my patroness. I happened to overhear the gentleman himself mentioning to the young lady who does the honours of the house the names of his cousin Miss de Bourgh, and of her mother Lady Catherine. How wonderfully these sort of things occur! Who would have thought of my meeting with – perhaps – a nephew of Lady Catherine de Bourgh in this assembly! – I am most thankful that the discovery is made in time for me to pay my respects to him, which I am now going to do, and trust he will excuse my not having done it before. My total ignorance of the connection must plead my apology."

"You are not going to introduce yourself to Mr. Darcy?"

"Indeed I am. I shall entreat his pardon for not having done it earlier. I believe him to be Lady Catherine's *nephew*. It will be in my power to assure him that her ladyship was quite well yesterday se'nnight."

Elizabeth tried hard to dissuade him from such a scheme; assuring him that Mr. Darcy would consider his addressing him without introduction as an impertinent freedom, rather than a compliment to his aunt; that it was not in the least necessary there should be any notice on either side, and that if it were, it must belong to Mr. Darcy, the superior in consequence, to begin the acquaintance. – Mr. Collins listened to her with the determined air of following his own inclination, and when she ceased speaking, replied thus,

"My dear Miss Elizabeth, I have the highest opinion in the world in your excellent judgement in all matters within the scope of your understanding, but permit me to say that there must be a wide difference between the established forms of ceremony amongst the laity, and those which regulate the clergy; for give me leave to observe that I consider the clerical office as equal in point of dignity with the highest rank in the kingdom – provided that a proper humility of behaviour is at the same time maintained. You must therefore allow me to follow the dictates of my conscience on this occasion, which leads me to perform what I look on as a point of duty. Pardon me for neglecting to profit by your advice, which on every other subject shall be my constant guide, though in the case before us I consider myself more fitted by education and habitual study to decide on what is right than a young lady like yourself." And with a low bow he left her to attack Mr. Darcy, whose reception of his advances she eagerly watched, and whose astonishment at being so addressed was very evident. Her cousin prefaced his speech with a solemn bow, and though she could not hear a word of it, she felt as if hearing it all, and saw in the motion of his lips the words "apology," "Hunsford," and "Lady Catherine de Bourgh." – It vexed her to see him expose himself to such a man. Mr. Darcy was eyeing him with unrestrained wonder, and when at last Mr. Collins allowed him time to speak, replied with an air of distant civility. Mr. Collins, however, was not discouraged from speaking again, and Mr. Darcy's contempt seemed abundantly increasing with the length of his second speech, and at the end of it he only made him a slight bow, and moved another way. Mr. Collins then returned to Elizabeth.

"I have no reason, I assure you," said he, "to be dissatisfied with my reception. Mr. Darcy seemed much pleased with the attention. He answered me with the utmost civility, and even paid me the compliment of saying, that he was so well convinced of Lady Catherine's discernment as to be certain she could never bestow a favour unworthily. It was really a very handsome thought. Upon the whole, I am much pleased with him."

As Elizabeth had no longer any interest of her own to pursue, she turned her attention almost entirely on her sister and Mr. Bingley, and the train of agreeable reflections which her observations gave birth to, made her perhaps almost as happy as Jane. She saw her in idea settled in that very house in all the felicity which a marriage of true affection could bestow; and she felt capable under such circumstances, of endeavouring even to like Bingley's two sisters. Her mother's thoughts she plainly saw were bent the same way, and she determined not to venture near her, lest she might hear too much. When they sat down to supper, therefore, she considered it a most unlucky perverseness which placed them within one of each other; and deeply was she vexed to find that her mother was talking to that one person (Lady Lucas) freely, openly, and of nothing else but her expectation that Jane would soon be married to Mr. Bingley. – It was an animating subject, and Mrs. Bennet seemed incapable of fatigue while enumerating the advantages of the match. His being such a charming young man, and so rich, and living but three miles from them, were the first points of self-gratulation; and then it was such a comfort to think how fond the two sisters were of Jane, and to be certain that they must desire the connection as much as she could do. It was, moreover, such a promising thing for her younger daughters, as Jane's marrying so greatly must throw them in the way of other rich men; and lastly, it was so pleasant at her time of life to be able to consign her single daughters to the care of their sister, that she might not be obliged to go into company more than she liked. It was necessary to make this circumstance a matter of pleasure, because on such occasions it is the etiquette; but no one was less likely than Mrs. Bennet to find comfort in staying home at any period of her life. She concluded with many good wishes that Lady Lucas might soon be equally fortunate, though evidently and triumphantly believing there was no chance of it.

In vain did Elizabeth endeavour to check the rapidity of her mother's words, or persuade her to describe her felicity in a less audible whisper; for to her inexpressible vexation, she could perceive that the chief of it was overheard by Mr. Darcy, who sat opposite to them. Her mother only scolded her for being nonsensical.

"What is Mr. Darcy to me, pray, that I should be afraid of him? I am sure we owe him no such particular civility as to be obliged to say nothing *he* may not like to hear."

"For heavens's sake, madam, speak lower. – What advantage can it be to you to offend Mr. Darcy? – You will never recommend yourself to his friend by so doing!"

Nothing that she could say, however, had any influence. Her mother would talk of her views in the same intelligible tone. Elizabeth blushed and blushed again with shame and vexation. She could not help frequently glancing her eye at Mr. Darcy, though every glance convinced her of what she dreaded; for though he was not always looking at her mother, she was convinced that his attention was invariably fixed by her. The expression of his face changed gradually from indignant contempt to a composed and steady gravity.

At length however Mrs. Bennet had no more to say; and Lady Lucas, who had been long yawning at the repetition of delights which she saw no likelihood of sharing, was left to the comforts of cold ham and chicken. Elizabeth now began to revive. But not long was the interval of tranquillity; for when supper was over, singing was talked of, and she had the mortification of seeing Mary, after very little entreaty, preparing to oblige the company. By many significant looks and silent entreaties, did she endeavour to prevent such a proof of complaisance, – but in vain; Mary would not understand them; such an opportunity of exhibiting was delightful to her, and she began her song. Elizabeth's eyes were fixed on her with most painful sensations; and she watched her progress through the several stanzas with an impatience which was very ill rewarded at their close; for Mary, on receiving amongst the thanks of the table, the hint of a hope that she might be prevailed on to favour them again, after the pause of half a minute began another. Mary's powers were by no means fitted for such a display; her voice was weak, and her manner affected. – Elizabeth was in agonies. She looked at Jane, to see how she bore it; but Jane was very composedly talking to Bingley. She looked at his two sisters, and saw them making signs of derision at each other, and at Darcy, who continued however impenetrably grave. She looked at her father to entreat his interference, lest Mary should be singing all night. He took the hint, and when Mary had finished her second song, said aloud,

"That will do extremely well, child. You have delighted us long enough. Let the other young ladies have time to exhibit."

Mary, though pretending not to hear, was somewhat disconcerted; and Elizabeth sorry for her, and sorry for her father's speech, was afraid her anxiety had done no good. – Others of the party were now applied to.

"If I," said Mr. Collins, "were so fortunate as to be able to sing, I should have great pleasure, I am sure, in obliging the company with an air; for I consider music as a very innocent diversion, and perfectly compatible with the profession of a clergyman. – I do not mean however to assert that we can be justified in devoting too much of our time to music, for there are certainly other things to be attended to. The rector of a parish has much to do. – In the first place, he must make such an agreement for tithes as may be beneficial to himself and not offensive to his patron. He must write his own sermons; and the time that remains will not be too much for his parish duties, and the care and improvement of his dwelling, which he cannot be excused from making as comfortable as possible. And I do not think it of light importance that he should have attentive and conciliatory manners towards everybody, especially towards those to whom he owes his preferment. I cannot acquit him of that duty; nor could I think well of the man who should omit an occasion of testifying his respect towards anybody connected with the family." And with a bow to Mr. Darcy, he concluded his speech, which had been spoken so loud as to be heard by half the room. – Many stared. – Many smiled; but no one looked more amused than Mr. Bennet himself, while his wife seriously commended Mr. Collins for having spoken so sensibly, and observed in a half-whisper to Lady Lucas, that he was a remarkably clever, good kind of young man.

To Elizabeth it appeared, that had her family made an agreement to expose themselves as much as they could during the evening, it would have been impossible for them to play their parts with more spirit, or finer success; and happy did she think it for Bingley and her sister that some of the exhibition had escaped his notice, and that his feelings were not of a sort to be much distressed by the folly which he must have witnessed. That his two sisters and Mr. Darcy, however, should have such an opportunity of ridiculing her relations was bad enough, and she could not determine whether the silent contempt of the gentleman, or the insolent smiles of the ladies, were more intolerable.

The rest of the evening brought her little amusement. She was teased by Mr. Collins, who continued most perseveringly by her side, and though he could not prevail with her to dance with him again, put it out of her power to dance with others. In vain did she entreat him to stand up with somebody else, and offer to introduce him to any young lady in the room. He assured her that as to dancing, he was perfectly indifferent to it; that his chief object was by delicate attentions to recommend himself to her, and that he should therefore make a point of remaining close to her the whole evening. There was no arguing upon such a project. She owed her greatest relief to her friend Miss Lucas, who often joined them, and good-naturedly engaged Mr. Collins's conversation to herself.

She was at least free from the offence of Mr. Darcy's farther notice; though often standing within a very short distance of her, quite disengaged, he never came near enough to speak. She felt it to be the probable consequence of her allusions to Mr. Wickham, and rejoiced in it.

The Longbourn party were the last of all the company to depart; and, by a manœuvre of Mrs. Bennet had to wait for their carriages a quarter of an hour after everybody else was gone, which gave them time to see how heartily they were wished away by some of the family. Mrs. Hurst and her sister scarcely opened their mouths except to complain of fatigue, and were evidently impatient to have the house to themselves. They repulsed every attempt of Mrs. Bennet at conversation, and by so doing, threw a languor over the whole party, which was very little relieved by the long speeches of Mr. Collins, who was complimenting Mr. Bingley and his sisters on the elegance of their entertainment, and the hospitality and politeness which had marked their behaviour to their guests. Darcy said nothing at all. Mr. Bennet, in equal silence, was enjoying the scene. Mr. Bingley and Jane were standing together, a little detached from the rest, and talked only to each other. Elizabeth preserved as steady a silence as either Mrs. Hurst or Miss Bingley; and even Lydia was too much fatigued to utter more than the occasional exclamation of "Lord, how tired I am!" accompanied by a violent yawn.

When at length they arose to take leave, Mrs. Bennet was most pressingly civil in her hope of seeing the whole family soon at Longbourn; and addressed herself particularly to Mr. Bingley, to assure him how happy he would make them, by eating a family dinner with them at any time, without the ceremony of a formal invitation. Bingley was all grateful pleasure, and he readily engaged for taking the earliest opportunity of waiting on her, after his return from London, whither he was obliged to go the next day for a short time.

Mrs. Bennet was perfectly satisfied; and quitted the house under the delightful persuasion that, allowing for the necessary preparations of settlements, new carriages and wedding clothes, she should undoubtedly see her daughter settled at Netherfield, in the course of three or four months. Of having another daughter married to Mr. Collins, she thought with equal certainty, and with considerable, though not equal, pleasure. Elizabeth was the least dear to her of all her children; and though the man and the match were quite good enough for *her*, the worth of each was eclipsed by Mr. Bingley and Netherfield.

# Chapter 19

THE NEXT day opened a new scene at Longbourn. Mr. Collins made his declaration in form. Having resolved to do it without loss of time, as his leave of absence extended only to the following Saturday, and having no feelings of diffidence to make it distressing to himself even at the moment, he set about it in a very orderly manner, with all the observances which he supposed a regular part of the business. On finding Mrs. Bennet, Elizabeth, and one of the younger girls together, soon after breakfast, he addressed the mother in these words,

"May I hope, Madam, for your interest with your fair daughter Elizabeth, when I solicit for the honour of a private audience with her in the course of this morning?"

Before Elizabeth had time for anything but a blush of surprise, Mrs. Bennet instantly answered,

"Oh dear! – Yes – certainly. – I am sure Lizzy will be very happy – I am sure she can have no objection. – Come, Kitty, I want you upstairs." And gathering her work together, she was hastening away, when Elizabeth called out,

"Dear Ma'am, do not go. – I beg you will not go. – Mr. Collins must excuse me. – He can have nothing to say to me that anybody need not hear. I am going away myself."

"No, no, nonsense, Lizzy. – I desire you will stay where you are." – And upon Elizabeth's seeming really, with vexed and embarrassed looks, about to escape, she added, "Lizzy, I *insist* upon your staying and hearing Mr. Collins."

Elizabeth would not oppose such an injunction – and a moment's consideration making her also sensible that it would be wisest to get it over as soon and as quietly as possible, she sat down again, and tried to conceal by incessant employment the feelings which were divided between distress and diversion. Mrs. Bennet and Kitty walked off, and as soon as they were gone Mr. Collins began.

"Believe me, my dear Miss Elizabeth, that your modesty, so far from doing you any disservice, rather adds to your other perfections. You would have been less amiable in my eyes had there *not* been this little unwillingness; but allow me to assure you that I have your respected mother's permission for this address. You can hardly doubt the purport of my discourse, however your natural delicacy may lead you to dissemble; my attentions have been too marked to be mistaken. Almost as soon as I entered the house I singled you out as the companion of my future life. But before I am run away with by my feelings on this subject, perhaps it will be advisable for me to state my reasons for marrying – and moreover for coming into Hertfordshire with the design of selecting a wife, as I certainly did."

The idea of Mr. Collins, with all his solemn composure, being run away with by his feelings, made Elizabeth so near laughing that she could not use the short pause he allowed in any attempt to stop him farther, and he continued:

"My reasons for marrying are, first, that I think it a right thing for every clergyman in easy circumstances (like myself) to set the example of matrimony in his parish. Secondly, that I am convinced that it will add very greatly to my happiness; and thirdly – which perhaps I ought to have mentioned earlier, that it is the particular advice and recommendation of the very noble lady whom I have the honour of calling patroness. Twice has she condescended to give me her opinion (unasked too!) on this subject; and it was but the very Saturday night before I left Hunsford – between our pools at quadrille, while Mrs. Jenkinson was arranging Miss de Bourgh's foot-stool, that she said, 'Mr. Collins, you must marry. A clergyman like you must marry. – Choose properly, choose a gentlewoman for *my* sake; and for your *own*, let her be an active, useful sort of person, not brought up high, but able to make a small income go a good way. This is my advice. Find such a woman as soon as you can, bring her to Hunsford, and I will visit her.' Allow me, by the way, to observe, my fair cousin, that I do not reckon the notice and kindness of Lady Catherine de Bourgh as among the least of the advantages in my power to offer. You will find her manners beyond anything I can describe; and your wit and vivacity I think must be acceptable to her, especially when tempered with the silence and respect which her rank will inevitably excite. Thus much for my general intention in favour of matrimony; it remains to be told why my views were directed towards Longbourn instead of my own neighbourhood, where I assure you there are many amiable young women. But the fact is, that being, as I am, to inherit this estate after the death of your honoured father, (who, however, may live many years longer,) I could not satisfy myself without resolving to choose a wife from among his daughters, that the loss to them might be as little as possible, when the melancholy event takes place – which, however, as I have already said, may not be for several years. This has been my motive, my fair cousin, and I flatter myself it will not sink me in your esteem. And now nothing remains for me but to assure you in the most animated language of the violence of my affection. To fortune I am perfectly indifferent, and shall make no demand of that nature on your father, since I am well aware that it could not be complied with; and that one thousand pounds in the 4 per cents. which will not be yours till after your mother's decease, is all that you may ever be entitled to. On that head, therefore, I shall be uniformly silent; and you may assure yourself that no ungenerous reproach shall ever pass my lips when we are married."

It was absolutely necessary to interrupt him now.

"You are too hasty, Sir," she cried. "You forget that I have made no answer. Let me do it without farther loss of time. Accept my thanks for the compliment you are paying me. I am very sensible of the honour of your proposals, but it is impossible for me to do otherwise than to decline them."

"I am not now to learn," replied Mr. Collins, with a formal wave of the hand, "that it is usual with young ladies to reject the addresses of the man whom they secretly mean to accept, when he first applies for their favour; and that sometimes the refusal is repeated a second or even a third time. I am therefore by no means discouraged by what you have just said, and shall hope to lead you to the altar ere long."

"Upon my word, Sir," cried Elizabeth, "your hope is rather an extraordinary one after my declaration. I do assure you that I am not one of those young ladies (if such young ladies there are) who are so daring as to risk their happiness on the chance of being asked a second time. I am perfectly serious in my refusal. – You could not make *me* happy, and I am convinced that I am the last woman in the world who would make *you* so. – Nay, were your friend Lady Catherine to know me, I am persuaded she would find me in every respect ill qualified for the situation."

"Were it certain that Lady Catherine would think so," said Mr. Collins very gravely – "but I cannot imagine that her ladyship would at all disapprove of you. And you may be certain that when I have the honour of seeing her again I shall speak in the highest terms of your modesty, economy, and other amiable qualifications."

"Indeed, Mr. Collins, all praise of me will be unnecessary. You must give me leave to judge for myself, and pay me the compliment of believing what I say. I wish you very happy and very rich, and by refusing your hand, do all in my power to prevent your being otherwise. In making me the offer, you must have satisfied the delicacy of your feelings with regard to my family, and may take possession of Longbourn estate whenever it falls, without any self-reproach. This matter may be considered, therefore, as finally settled." And rising as she thus spoke, she would have quitted the room, had not Mr. Collins thus addressed her:

"When I do myself the honour of speaking to you next on the subject I shall hope to receive a more favourable answer than you have now given me; though I am far from accusing you of cruelty at present, because I know it to be the established custom of your sex to reject a man on the first application, and perhaps you have even now said as much to encourage my suit as would be consistent with the true delicacy of the female character."

"Really, Mr. Collins," cried Elizabeth with some warmth, "you puzzle me exceedingly. If what I have hitherto said can appear to you in the form of encouragement, I know not how to express my refusal in such a way as may convince you of its being one."

"You must give me leave to flatter myself, my dear cousin, that your refusal of my addresses is merely words of course. My reasons for believing it are briefly these: – It does not appear to me that my hand is unworthy of your acceptance, or that the establishment I can offer would be any other than highly desirable.

My situation in life, my connections with the family of de Bourgh, and my relationship to your own, are circumstances highly in my favour; and you should take it into farther consideration, that in spite of your manifold attractions, it is by no means certain that another offer of marriage may ever be made you. Your portion is unhappily so small that it will in all likelihood undo the effects of your loveliness and amiable qualifications. As I must therefore conclude that you are not serious in your rejection of me, I shall choose to attribute it to your wish of increasing my love by suspense, according to the usual practice of elegant females."

"I do assure you, Sir, that I have no pretension whatever to that kind of elegance which consists in tormenting a respectable man. I would rather be paid the compliment of being believed sincere. I thank you again and again for the honour you have done me in your proposals, but to accept them is absolutely impossible. My feelings in every respect forbid it. Can I speak plainer? Do not consider me now as an elegant female intending to plague you, but as a rational creature speaking the truth from her heart."

"You are uniformly charming!" cried he, with an air of awkward gallantry; "and I am persuaded that when sanctioned by the express authority of both your excellent parents, my proposals will not fail of being acceptable."

To such perseverance in wilful self-deception Elizabeth would make no reply, and immediately and in silence withdrew; determined, that if he persisted in considering her repeated refusals as flattering encouragement, to apply to her father, whose negative might be uttered in such a manner as must be decisive, and whose behaviour at least could not be mistaken for the affectation and coquetry of an elegant female.

# *Chapter 20*

Mr. Collins was not left long to the silent contemplation of his successful love; for Mrs. Bennet, having dawdled about in the vestibule to watch for the end of the conference, no sooner saw Elizabeth open the door and with quick step pass her towards the staircase, than she entered the breakfast-room, and congratulated both him and herself in warm terms on the happy prospect or their nearer connection. Mr. Collins received and returned these felicitations with equal pleasure, and then proceeded to relate the particulars of their interview, with the result of which he trusted he had every reason to be satisfied, since the refusal which his cousin had steadfastly given him would naturally flow from her bashful modesty and the genuine delicacy of her character.

This information, however, startled Mrs. Bennet; – she would have been glad to be equally satisfied that her daughter had meant to encourage him by protesting against his proposals, but she dared not to believe it, and could not help saying so.

"But depend upon it, Mr. Collins," she added, "that Lizzy shall be brought to reason. I will speak to her about it myself directly. She is a very headstrong foolish girl, and does not know her own interest; but I will *make* her know it."

"Pardon me for interrupting you, Madam," cried Mr. Collins; "but if she is really headstrong and foolish, I know not whether she would altogether be a very desirable wife to a man in my situation, who naturally looks for happiness in the marriage state. If therefore she actually persists in rejecting my suit, perhaps it were better not to force her into accepting me, because if liable to such defects of temper, she could not contribute much to my felicity."

"Sir, you quite misunderstand me," said Mrs. Bennet, alarmed.

"Lizzy is only headstrong in such matters as these. In everything else she is as good-natured a girl as ever lived. I will go directly to Mr. Bennet, and we shall very soon settle it with her, I am sure."

She would not give him time to reply, but hurrying instantly to her husband, called out as she entered the library,

"Oh! Mr. Bennet, you are wanted immediately; we are all in an uproar. You must come and make Lizzy marry Mr. Collins, for she vows she will not have him, and if you do not make haste he will change his mind and not have *her*."

Mr. Bennet raised his eyes from his book as she entered, and fixed them on her face with a calm unconcern which was not in the least altered by her communication.

"I have not the pleasure of understanding you," said he, when she had finished her speech. "Of what are you talking?"

"Of Mr. Collins and Lizzy. Lizzy declares she will not have Mr. Collins, and Mr. Collins begins to say that he will not have Lizzy."

"And what am I to do on the occasion? – It seems an hopeless business."

"Speak to Lizzy about it yourself. Tell her that you insist upon her marrying him."

"Let her be called down. She shall hear my opinion."

Mrs. Bennet rang the bell, and Miss Elizabeth was summoned to the library.

"Come here, child," cried her father as she appeared. "I have sent for you on an affair of importance. I understand that Mr. Collins has made you an offer of marriage. Is it true?" Elizabeth replied that it was. "Very well – and this offer of marriage you have refused?"

"I have, Sir."

"Very well. We now come to the point. Your mother insists upon your accepting it. Is not it so, Mrs. Bennet?"

"Yes, or I will never see her again."

"An unhappy alternative is before you, Elizabeth. From this day you must be a stranger to one of your parents. – Your mother will never see you again if you do *not* marry Mr. Collins, and I will never see you again if you *do*."

Elizabeth could not but smile at such a conclusion of such a beginning; but Mrs. Bennet, who had persuaded herself that her husband regarded the affair as she wished, was excessively disappointed.

"What do you mean, Mr. Bennet, by talking this way? You promised me to *insist* upon her marrying him."

"My dear," replied her husband, "I have two small favours to request. First, that you will allow me the free use of my understanding on the present occasion; and secondly, of my room. I shall be glad to have the library to myself as soon as may be."

Not yet, however, in spite of her disappointment in her husband, did Mrs. Bennet give up the point. She talked to Elizabeth again and again; coaxed and threatened her by turns. She endeavoured to secure Jane in her interest; but Jane with all possible mildness declined interfering; – and Elizabeth sometimes with real earnestness and sometimes with playful gaiety replied to her attacks. Though her manner varied however, her determination never did.

Mr. Collins, meanwhile, was meditating in solitude on what had passed. He thought too well of himself to comprehend on what motive his cousin could refuse him; and though his pride was hurt, he suffered in no other way. His regard for her was quite imaginary; and the possibility of her deserving her mother's reproach prevented his feeling any regret.

While the family were in this confusion, Charlotte Lucas came to spend the day with them. She was met in the vestibule by Lydia, who, flying to her, cried in a half whisper, "I am glad you are come, for there is such fun here! – What do you think has happened this morning? – Mr. Collins has made an offer to Lizzy, and she will not have him."

Charlotte had hardly time to answer, before they were joined by Kitty, who came to tell the same news, and no sooner had they entered the breakfast-room, where Mrs. Bennet was alone, than she likewise began on the subject, calling on Miss Lucas for her compassion, and entreating her to persuade her friend Lizzy to comply with the wishes of all her family. "Pray do, my dear Miss Lucas," she added in a melancholy tone, "for nobody is on my side, nobody takes part with me, I am cruelly used, nobody feels for my poor nerves."

Charlotte's reply was spared by the entrance of Jane and Elizabeth.

"Aye, there she comes," continued Mrs. Bennet, "looking as unconcerned as may be, and caring no more for us than if we were at York, provided she can have her own way. – But I tell you what, Miss Lizzy, if you take it into your head to go on refusing every offer of marriage in this way, you will never get a husband at all – and I am sure I do not know who is to maintain you when your father is dead. – *I* shall not be able to keep you – and so I warn you. – I have done with you from this very day. – I told you in the library, you know, that I should never speak to you again, and you will find me as good as my word. I have no pleasure in talking to undutiful children. – Not that I have much pleasure indeed in talking to anybody. People who suffer as I do from nervous complaints can have no great inclination for talking. Nobody can tell what I suffer! – But it is always so. Those who do not complain are never pitied."

Her daughters listened in silence to this effusion, sensible that any attempt to reason with or soothe her would only increase the irritation. She talked on, therefore, without interruption from any of them till they were joined by Mr. Collins, who entered with an air more stately than usual, and on perceiving whom, she said to the girls,

"Now, I do insist upon it, that you, all of you, hold your tongues, and let Mr. Collins and me have a little conversation together."

Elizabeth passed quietly out of the room, Jane and Kitty followed, but Lydia stood her ground, determined to hear all she could; and Charlotte, detained first by the civility of Mr. Collins, whose inquiries after herself and all her family were very minute, and then by a little curiosity, satisfied herself with walking to the window and pretending not to hear. In a doleful voice Mrs. Bennet thus began the projected conversation –

"Oh! Mr. Collins!"

"My dear Madam," replied he, "let us be for ever silent on this point. Far be it from me," he presently continued in a voice that marked his displeasure, "to resent the behaviour of your daughter. Resignation to inevitable evils is the duty of us all; the peculiar duty of a young man who has been so fortunate as I have been in early preferment; and I trust I am resigned. Perhaps not the less so from feeling a doubt of my positive happiness had my fair cousin honoured me with her hand; for I have often observed that resignation is never so perfect as when the blessing denied begins to lose somewhat of its value in our estimation. You will not, I hope, consider me as showing any disrespect to your family, my dear Madam, by thus withdrawing my pretensions to your daughter's favour, without having paid yourself and Mr. Bennet the compliment of requesting you to interpose your authority on my behalf. My conduct may I fear be objectionable in having accepted my dismission from your daughter's lips instead of your own. But we are all liable to error. I have certainly meant well through the whole affair. My object has been to secure an amiable companion for myself, with due consideration for the advantage of all your family, and if my *manner* has been at all reprehensible, I here beg leave to apologise."

# Chapter 21

THE DISCUSSION of Mr. Collins's offer was now nearly at an end, and Elizabeth had only to suffer from the uncomfortable feelings necessarily attending it, and occasionally from some peevish allusion of her mother. As for the gentleman himself, *his* feelings were chiefly expressed, not by embarrassment or dejection, or by trying to avoid her, but by stiffness of manner and resentful silence. He scarcely ever spoke to her, and the assiduous attentions which he had been so sensible of himself, were transferred for the rest of the day to Miss Lucas, whose civility in listening to him was a seasonable relief to them all, and especially to her friend.

The morrow produced no abatement of Mrs. Bennet's ill humour or ill health. Mr. Collins was also in the same state of angry pride. Elizabeth had hoped that his resentment might shorten his visit, but his plan did not appear in the least affected by it. He was always to have gone on Saturday, and to Saturday he still meant to stay.

After breakfast, the girls walked to Meryton to enquire if Mr. Wickham were returned, and to lament over his absence from the Netherfield ball. He joined them on their entering the town and attended them to their aunt's, where his regret and vexation, and the concern of everybody was well talked over. – To Elizabeth, however, he voluntarily acknowledged that the necessity of his absence *had* been self-imposed.

"I found," said he, "as the time drew near, that I had better not meet Mr. Darcy; – that to be in the same room, the same party with him for so many hours together, might be more than I could bear, and that scenes might arise unpleasant to more than myself."

She highly approved his forbearance, and they had leisure for a full discussion of it, and for all the commendation which they civilly bestowed on each other, as Wickham and another officer walked back with them to Longbourn, and during the walk, he particularly attended to her. His accompanying them was a double advantage; she felt all the compliment it offered to herself, and it was most acceptable as an occasion of introducing him to her father and mother.

Soon after their return, a letter was delivered to Miss Bennet; it came from Netherfield, and was opened immediately. The envelope contained a sheet of elegant, little, hot pressed paper, well covered with a lady's fair, flowing hand; and Elizabeth saw her sister's countenance change as she read it, and saw her dwelling intently on some particular passages. Jane recollected herself soon, and putting the letter away, tried to join with her usual cheerfulness in the general conversation; but Elizabeth felt an anxiety on the subject which drew off her attention even from Wickham; and no sooner had he and his companion taken leave, than a glance from Jane invited her to follow her upstairs. When they had gained their own room, Jane taking out her letter, said,

"This is from Caroline Bingley; what it contains, has surprised me a good deal. The whole party have left Netherfield by this time, and are on their way to town; and without any intention of coming back again. You shall hear what she says."

She then read the first sentence aloud, which comprised the information of their having just resolved to follow their brother to town directly, and of their meaning to dine that day in Grosvenor

Street, where Mr. Hurst had a house. The next was in these words. "I do not pretend to regret anything I shall leave in Hertfordshire, except your society, my dearest friend; but we will hope at some future period, to enjoy many returns of the delightful intercourse we have known, and in the meanwhile may lessen the pain of separation by a very frequent and most unreserved correspondence. I depend on you for that." To these highflown expressions, Elizabeth listened with all the insensibility of distrust; and though the suddenness of their removal surprised her, she saw nothing in it really to lament; it was not to be supposed that their absence from Netherfield would prevent Mr. Bingley's being there; and as to the loss of their society, she was persuaded that Jane must soon cease to regard it, in the enjoyment of his.

"It is unlucky," said she, after a short pause, "that you should not be able to see your friends before they leave the country. But may we not hope that the period of future happiness to which Miss Bingley looks forward, may arrive earlier than she is aware, and that the delightful intercourse you have known as friends, will be renewed with yet greater satisfaction as sisters? – Mr. Bingley will not be detained in London by them."

"Caroline decidedly says that none of the party will return into Hertfordshire this winter. I will read it to you –

"When my brother left us yesterday, he imagined that the business which took him to London, might be concluded in three or four days, but as we are certain it cannot be so, and at the same time convinced that when Charles gets to town, he will be in no hurry to leave it again, we have determined on following him thither, that he may not be obliged to spend his vacant hours in a comfortless hotel. Many of my acquaintance are already there for the winter; I wish that I could hear that you, my dearest friend, had any intention of making one in the crowd, but of that I despair. I sincerely hope your Christmas in Hertfordshire may abound in the gaieties which that season generally brings, and that your beaux will be so numerous as to prevent your feeling the loss of the three, of whom we shall deprive you."

"It is evident by this," added Jane, "that he comes back no more this winter."

"It is only evident that Miss Bingley does not mean he *should*."

"Why will you think so? It must be his own doing. – He is his own maser. But you do not know *all*. I *will* read you the passage which prticularly hurts me. I will have no reserves from *you*."

"Mr. Darcy is impatient to see his sister, and to confess the truth, *we* are scarcely less eager to meet her again. I really do not think Georgiana Darcy has her equal for beauty, elegance, and accomplishments; and the affection she inspires in Louisa and myself, is heightened into something still more interesting, from the hope we dare to entertain of her being hereafter our sister. I do not know whether I ever before mentioned to you my feelings on this subject, but I will not leave the country without confiding them, and I trust you will not esteem them unreasonable. My brother admires her greatly already, he will have frequent opportunity now of seeing her on the most intimate footing, her relations all wish the connection as much as his own, and a sister's partiality is not misleading me, I think, when I call Charles most capable of engaging any woman's heart. With all these circumstances to favour an attachment and nothing to prevent it, am I wrong, my dearest Jane, in indulging the hope of an event which will secure the happiness of so many?"

"What do you think of *this* sentence, my dear Lizzy?" – said Jane as she finished it. "Is it not clear enough? – Does it not expressly declare that Caroline neither expects nor wishes me to be her sister; that she is perfectly convinced of her brother's indifference, and that if she suspects the nature of my feelings for him, she means (most kindly!) to put me on my guard? Can there be any other opinion on the subject?"

"Yes, there can; for mine is totally different. – Will you hear it?"

"Most willingly."

"You shall have it in a few words. Miss Bingley sees that her brother is in love with you, and wants him to marry Miss Darcy. She follows him to town in the hope of keeping him there, and tries to persuade you that he does not care about you."

Jane shook her head.

"Indeed, Jane, you ought to believe me. – No one who has ever seen you together, can doubt his affection. Miss Bingley, I am sure, cannot. She is not such a simpleton. Could she have seen half as much love in Mr. Darcy for herself, she would have ordered her wedding clothes. But the case is this. We are not rich enough, or grand enough for them; and she is the more anxious to get Miss Darcy for her brother, from the notion that when there has been *one* intermarriage, she may have less trouble in achieving a second; in which there is certainly some ingenuity, and I dare say it would succeed, if Miss de Bourgh were out of the way. But, my dearest Jane, you cannot seriously imagine that because Miss Bingley tells you her brother greatly admires Miss Darcy, he is in the smallest degree less sensible of *your* merit than when he took leave of you on Tuesday, or that it will be in her power to persuade him that instead of being in love with you, he is very much in love with her friend."

"If we thought alike of Miss Bingley," replied Jane, "your representation of all this, might make me quite easy. But I know the foundation is unjust. Caroline is incapable of wilfully deceiving anyone; and all that I can hope in this case is, that she is deceiving herself."

"That is right. – You could not have started a more happy idea, since you will not take comfort in mine. Believe her to be deceived, by all means. You have now done your duty by her, and must fret no longer."

"But, my dear sister, can I be happy, even supposing the best, in accepting a man whose sisters and friends are all wishing him to marry elsewhere?"

"You must decide for yourself," said Elizabeth; "and if upon mature deliberation, you find that the misery of disobliging his two sisters is more than equivalent to the happiness of being his wife, I advise you by all means to refuse him."

"How can you talk so?" – said Jane faintly smiling, – "You must know that though I should be exceedingly grieved at their disapprobation, I could not hesitate."

"I did not think you would; – and that being the case, I cannot consider your situation with much compassion."

"But if he returns no more this winter, my choice will never be required. A thousand things may arise in six months!"

The idea of his returning no more Elizabeth treated with the utmost contempt. It appeared to her merely the suggestion of Caroline's interested wishes, and she could not for a moment suppose that those wishes, however openly or artfully spoken, could influence a young man so totally independent of everyone.

She represented to her sister as forcibly as possible what she felt on the subject, and had soon the pleasure of seeing its happy effect. Jane's temper was not desponding, and she was gradually led to hope, though the diffidence of affection sometimes overcame the hope, that Bingley would return to Netherfield and answer every wish of her heart.

They agreed that Mrs. Bennet should only hear of the departure of the family, without being alarmed on the score of the gentleman's conduct; but even this partial communication gave her a great deal of concern, and she bewailed it as exceedingly unlucky that the ladies should happen to go away, just as they were all getting so intimate together. After lamenting it however at some length, she had the consolation of thinking that Mr. Bingley would be soon down again and soon dining at Longbourn, and the conclusion of all was the comfortable declaration that, though he had been invited only to a family dinner, she would take care to have two full courses.

## Chapter 22

The Bennets were engaged to dine with the Lucases, and again during the chief of the day, was Miss Lucas so kind as to listen to Mr. Collins. Elizabeth took an opportunity of thanking her. "It keeps him in good humour," said she, "and I am more obliged to you than I can express." Charlotte assured her friend of her satisfaction in being useful, and that it amply repaid her for the little sacrifice of her time. This was very amiable, but Charlotte's kindness extended farther than Elizabeth had any conception of; – its object was nothing less, than to secure her from any return of Mr. Collins's addresses, by engaging them towards herself. Such was Miss Lucas's scheme; and appearances were so favourable that when they parted at night, she would have felt almost secure of success if he had not been to leave Hertfordshire so very soon. But here, she did injustice to the fire and independence of his character, for it led him to escape out of Longbourn House the next morning with admirable slyness, and hasten to Lucas Lodge to throw himself at her feet. He was anxious to avoid the notice of his cousins, from a conviction that if they saw him depart, they could not fail to conjecture his design, and he was not willing to have the attempt known till its success could be known likewise; for though feeling almost secure, and with reason, for Charlotte had been tolerably encouraging, he was comparatively diffident since the adventure of Wednesday. His reception however was of the most flattering kind. Miss Lucas perceived him from an upper window as he walked towards the house, and instantly set out to meet him accidentally in the lane. But little had she dared to hope that so much love and eloquence awaited her there.

In as short a time as Mr. Collins's long speeches would allow, everything was settled between them to the satisfaction of both; and as they entered the house, he earnestly entreated her to name the day that was to make him the happiest of men; and though such a solicitation must be waived for the present, the lady felt no inclination to trifle with his happiness. The stupidity with which he was favoured by nature, must guard his courtship from any charm that could make a woman wish for its continuance; and Miss Lucas, who accepted him solely from the pure and disinterested desire of an establishment, cared not how soon that establishment were gained.

Sir William and Lady Lucas were speedily applied to for their consent; and it was bestowed with a most joyful alacrity. Mr. Collins's present circumstances made it a most eligible match for their daughter, to whom they could give little fortune; and his prospects of future wealth were exceedingly fair. Lady Lucas began directly to calculate with more interest than the matter had ever excited before, how many years longer Mr. Bennet was likely to live; and Sir William gave it as his decided opinion, that whenever Mr. Collins should be in possession of the Longbourn estate, it would be highly expedient that both he and his wife should make their appearance at St. James's. The whole family in short were properly overjoyed on the occasion. The younger girls formed hopes of *coming out* a year or two sooner than they might otherwise have done; and the boys were relieved from their apprehension of Charlotte's dying an old maid. Charlotte herself was tolerably composed. She had gained her point, and had time to consider of it. Her reflections were in general satisfactory. Mr. Collins to be sure was neither sensible nor agreeable; his society was irksome, and his attachment to her must be imaginary. But still he would be her husband. – Without thinking highly either of men or matrimony, marriage had always been her object; it was the only honourable provision for well-educated young women of small fortune, and however uncertain of giving happiness, must be their pleasantest preservative from want. This preservative she had now obtained; and at the age of twenty-seven, without having ever been handsome, she felt all the good luck of it. The least agreeable circumstance in the business, was the surprise it must occasion to Elizabeth Bennet, whose friendship she valued beyond that of any other person. Elizabeth would wonder, and probably would blame her; and though her resolution was not to be shaken, her feelings must be hurt by such a disapprobation. She resolved to give her the information herself, and therefore charged Mr. Collins when he returned to Longbourn to dinner, to drop no hint of what had passed before any of the family. A promise of secrecy was of course very dutifully given, but it could not be kept without difficulty; for the curiosity excited by his long absence, burst forth in such very direct questions on his return, as required some ingenuity to evade, and he was at the same time exercising great self-denial, for he was longing to publish his prosperous love.

As he was to begin his journey too early on the morrow to see any of the family, the ceremony of leave-taking was performed when the ladies moved for the night; and Mrs. Bennet with great politeness and cordiality said how happy they should be to see him at Longbourn again, whenever his other engagements might allow him to visit them.

"My dear madam," he replied, "this invitation is particularly gratifying, because it is what I have been hoping to receive; and you may be very certain that I shall avail myself of it as soon as possible."

They were all astonished; and Mr. Bennet, who could by no means wish for so speedy a return, immediately said,

"But is there not danger of Lady Catherine's disapprobation here, my good sir? – You had better neglect your relations, than run the risk of offending your patroness."

"My dear sir," replied Mr. Collins, "I am particularly obliged to you for this friendly caution, and you may depend upon my not taking so material a step without her ladyship's concurrence."

"You cannot be too much upon your guard. Risk anything rather than her displeasure; and if you find it likely to be raised by your coming to us again, which I should think exceedingly probable, stay quietly at home, and be satisfied that *we* shall take no offence."

"Believe me, my dear sir, my gratitude is warmly excited by such affectionate attention; and depend upon it, you will speedily receive from me a letter of thanks for this, as well as for every other mark of your regard during my stay in Hertfordshire. As for my fair cousins, though my absence may not be long enough to render it necessary, I shall now take the liberty of wishing them health and happiness, not excepting my cousin Elizabeth."

With proper civilities the ladies then withdrew; all of them equally surprised to find that he meditated a quick return. Mrs. Bennet wished to understand by it that he thought of paying his addresses to one of her younger girls, and Mary might have been prevailed on to accept him. She rated his abilities much higher than any of the others; there was a solidity in his reflections which often struck her, and though by no means so clever as herself, she thought that if encouraged to read and improve himself by such an example as hers, he might become a very agreeable companion. But on the following morning, every hope of this kind was done away. Miss Lucas called soon after breakfast, and in a private conference with Elizabeth related the event of the day before.

The possibility of Mr. Collins's fancying himself in love with her friend had once occurred to Elizabeth within the last day or two; but that Charlotte could encourage him, seemed almost as far from possibility as that she could encourage him herself, and her astonishment was consequently so great as to overcome at first the bounds of decorum, and she could not help crying out:

"Engaged to Mr. Collins! my dear Charlotte, – impossible!"

The steady countenance which Miss Lucas had commanded in telling her story, gave way to a momentary confusion here on receiving so direct a reproach; though, as it was no more than she expected, she soon regained her composure, and calmly replied,

"Why should you be surprised, my dear Eliza? – Do you think it incredible that Mr. Collins should be able to procure any woman's good opinion, because he was not so happy as to succeed with you?"

But Elizabeth had now recollected herself, and making a strong effort for it, was able to assure her with tolerable firmness that the prospect of their relationship was highly grateful to her, and that she wished her all imaginable happiness.

"I see what you are feeling," replied Charlotte, – "you must be surprised, very much surprised, – so lately as Mr. Collins was wishing to marry you. But when you have had time to think it over, I hope you will be satisfied with what I have done. I am not romantic you know. I never was. I ask only a comfortable home; and considering Mr. Collins's character, connections, and situation in life, I am convinced that my chance of happiness with him is as fair, as most people can boast on entering the marriage state."

Elizabeth quietly answered "Undoubtedly;" – and after an awkward pause, they returned to the rest of the family. Charlotte did not stay much longer, and Elizabeth was then left to reflect on what she had heard. It was a long time before she became at all reconciled to the idea of so unsuitable a match. The strangeness of Mr. Collins's making two offers of marriage within three days, was nothing in comparison of his being now accepted. She had always felt that Charlotte's opinion of matrimony was not exactly like her own, but she could not have supposed it possible that when called into action, she would have sacrificed every better feeling to worldly advantage. Charlotte the wife of Mr. Collins was a most humiliating picture! – And to the pang of a friend disgracing herself and sunk in her esteem, was added the distressing conviction that it was impossible for that friend to be tolerably happy in the lot she had chosen.

## *Chapter 23*

ELIZABETH WAS sitting with her mother and sisters, reflecting on what she had heard, and doubting whether she was authorised to mention it, when Sir William Lucas himself appeared, sent by his daughter to announce her engagement to the family. With many compliments to them, and much self-gratulation on the prospect of a connection between the houses, he unfolded the matter, – to an audience not merely wondering, but incredulous; for Mrs. Bennet, with more perseverance than politeness, protested he must be entirely mistaken, and Lydia, always unguarded and often uncivil, boisterously exclaimed,

"Good Lord! Sir William, how can you tell such a story? – Do you not know that Mr. Collins wants to marry Lizzy?"

Nothing less than the complaisance of a courtier could have borne without anger such treatment; but Sir William's good breeding carried him through it all; and though he begged leave to be positive as to the truth of his information, he listened to all their impertinence with the most forbearing courtesy.

Elizabeth, feeling it incumbent on her to relieve him from so unpleasant a situation, now put herself forward to confirm his account, by mentioning her prior knowledge of it from Charlotte herself; and endeavoured to put a stop to the exclamations of her mother and sisters, by the earnestness of her congratulations to Sir William, in which she was readily joined by Jane, and by making a variety of remarks on the happiness that might be expected from the match, the excellent character of Mr. Collins, and the convenient distance of Hunsford from London.

Mrs. Bennet was in fact too much overpowered to say a great deal while Sir William remained; but no sooner had he left them than her feelings found a rapid vent. In the first place, she persisted in disbelieving the whole of the matter; secondly, she was very sure that Mr. Collins had been taken in; thirdly, she trusted that they would never be happy together; and fourthly, that the match might be broken off. Two inferences, however, were plainly deduced from the whole; one, that Elizabeth was the real cause of all the mischief; and the other, that she herself had been barbarously used by them all; and on these two points she principally dwelt during the rest of the day. Nothing could console and nothing could appease her. – Nor did that day wear out her resentment. A week elapsed before she could see Elizabeth without scolding her, a month passed away before she could speak to Sir William or Lady Lucas without being rude, and many months were gone before she could at all forgive her daughter.

Mr. Bennet's emotions were much more tranquil on the occasion, and such as he did experience he pronounced to be of a most agreeable sort; for it gratified him, he said, to discover that Charlotte Lucas, whom he had been used to think tolerably sensible, was as foolish as his wife, and more foolish than his daughter!

Jane confessed herself a little surprised at the match; but she said less of her astonishment than of her earnest desire for their happiness; nor could Elizabeth persuade her to consider it as improbable. Kitty and Lydia were far from envying Miss Lucas, for Mr. Collins was only a clergyman; and it affected them in no other way than as piece of news to spread at Meryton.

Lady Lucas could not be insensible of triumph on being able to retort on Mrs. Bennet the comfort of having a daughter well married; and she called at Longbourn rather oftener than usual to say how happy she was, though Mrs. Bennet's sour looks and ill-natured remarks might have been enough to drive happiness away.

Between Elizabeth and Charlotte there was a restraint which kept them mutually silent on the subject; and Elizabeth felt persuaded that no real confidence could ever subsist between them again. Her disappointment in Charlotte made her turn with fonder regard to her sister, of whose rectitude and delicacy she was sure her opinion could never be shaken, and for whose happiness she grew daily more anxious, as Bingley had now been gone a week, and nothing was heard of his return.

Jane had sent Caroline an early answer to her letter, and was counting the days till she might reasonably hope to hear again. The promised letter of thanks from Mr. Collins arrived on Tuesday, addressed to their father, and written with all the solemnity of gratitude which a twelvemonth's abode in the family might have prompted. After discharging his conscience on that head, he proceeded to inform them, with many rapturous expressions, of his happiness in having obtained the affection of their amiable neighbour, Miss Lucas, and then explained that it was merely with the view of enjoying her society that he had been so ready to close with their kind wish of seeing him again at Longbourn, whither he hoped to be able to return on Monday fortnight; for Lady Catherine, he added, so heartily approved his marriage, that she wished it to take place as soon as possible, which he trusted would be an unanswerable argument with his amiable Charlotte to name an early day for making him the happiest of men.

Mr. Collins's return into Hertfordshire was no longer a matter of pleasure to Mrs. Bennet. On the contrary she was as much disposed to complain of it as her husband. – It was very strange that he should come to Longbourn instead of to Lucas Lodge; it was also very inconvenient and exceedingly troublesome. – She hated having visitors in the house while her health was so indifferent, and lovers were of all people the most disagreeable. Such were the gentle murmurs of Mrs. Bennet, and they gave way only to the greater distress of Mr. Bingley's continued absence.

Neither Jane nor Elizabeth were comfortable on this subject. Day after day passed away without bringing any other tidings of him than the report which shortly prevailed in Meryton of his coming no more to Netherfield the whole winter; a report which highly incensed Mrs. Bennet, and which she never failed to contradict as a most scandalous falsehood.

Even Elizabeth began to fear – not that Bingley was indifferent – but that his sisters would be successful in keeping him away. Unwilling as she was to admit an idea so destructive of Jane's happiness, and so dishonourable to the stability of her lover, she could not prevent its frequently recurring. The united efforts of his two unfeeling sisters and of his overpowering friend, assisted by the attractions of Miss Darcy and the amusements of London, might be too much, she feared, for the strength of his attachment.

As for Jane, *her* anxiety under this suspense was, of course, more painful than Elizabeth's; but whatever she felt she was desirous of concealing, and between herself and Elizabeth, therefore, the subject was never alluded to. But as no such delicacy restrained her mother, an hour seldom passed in which she did not talk of Bingley, express her impatience for his arrival, or even require Jane to confess that if he did not come back, she should think herself very ill used. It needed all Jane's steady mildness to bear these attacks with tolerable tranquillity.

Mr. Collins returned most punctually on the Monday fortnight, but his reception at Longbourn was not quite so gracious as it had been on his first introduction. He was too happy, however, to need much attention; and luckily for the others, the business of love-making relieved them from a great deal of his company. The chief of every day was spent by him at Lucas Lodge, and he sometimes returned to Longbourn only in time to make an apology for his absence before the family went to bed.

Mrs. Bennet was really in a most pitiable state. The very mention of anything concerning the match threw her into an agony of ill-humour, and wherever she went she was sure of hearing it talked of. The sight of Miss Lucas was odious to her. As her successor in that house, she regarded her with jealous abhorrence. Whenever Charlotte came to see them she concluded her to be anticipating the hour of possession; and whenever she spoke in a low voice to Mr. Collins, was convinced that they were talking of the Longbourn estate, and resolving to turn herself and her daughters out of the house, as soon as Mr. Bennet were dead. She complained bitterly of all this to her husband.

"Indeed, Mr. Bennet," said she, "it is very hard to think that Charlotte Lucas should ever be mistress of this house, that *I* should be forced to make way for *her*, and live to see her take my place in it!"

"My dear, do not give way to such gloomy thoughts. Let us hope for better things. Let us flatter ourselves that *I* may be the survivor."

This was not very consoling to Mrs. Bennet, and, therefore, instead of making any answer, she went on as before,

"I cannot bear to think that they should have all this estate. If it was not for the entail I should not mind it."

"What should not you mind?"

"I should not mind anything at all."

"Let us be thankful that you are preserved from a state of

such insensibility."

"I never can be thankful, Mr. Bennet, for anything about the entail. How anyone could have the conscience to entail away an estate from one's own daughters I cannot understand; and all for the sake of Mr. Collins too! – Why should *he* have it more than anybody else?"

"I leave it to yourself to determine," said Mr. Bennet.

# *Chapter 24*

MISS BINGLEY's letter arrived, and put an end to doubt. The very first sentence conveyed the assurance of their being all settled in London for the winter, and concluded with her brother's regret at not having had time to pay his respects to his friends in Hertfordshire before he left the country.

Hope was over, entirely over; and when Jane could attend to the rest of the letter, she found little, except the professed affection of the writer, that could give her any comfort. Miss Darcy's praise occupied the chief of it. Her many attractions were again dwelt on, and Caroline boasted joyfully of their increasing intimacy, and ventured to predict the accomplishment of the wishes which had been unfolded in her former letter. She wrote also with great pleasure of her brother's being an inmate of Mr. Darcy's house, and mentioned with raptures, some plans of the latter with regard to new furniture.

Elizabeth, to whom Jane very soon communicated the chief of all this, heard it in silent indignation. Her heart was divided between concern for her sister, and resentment against all the others. To Caroline's assertion of her brother's being partial to

Miss Darcy she paid no credit. That he was really fond of Jane, she doubted no more than she had ever done; and much as she had always been disposed to like him, she could not think without anger, hardly without contempt, on that easiness of temper, that want of proper resolution which now made him the slave of his designing friends, and led him to sacrifice his own happiness to the caprice of their inclinations. Had his own happiness, however, been the only sacrifice, he might have been allowed to sport with it in whatever manner he thought best; but her sister's was involved in it, as she thought he must be sensible himself. It was a subject, in short, on which reflection would be long indulged, and must be unavailing. She could think of nothing else, and yet whether Bingley's regard had really died away, or were suppressed by his friends' interference; whether he had been aware of Jane's attachment, or whether it had escaped his observation; whichever were the case, though her opinion of him must be materially affected by the difference, her sister's situation remained the same, her peace equally wounded.

A day or two passed before Jane had courage to speak of her feelings to Elizabeth; but at last on Mrs. Bennet's leaving them together, after a longer irritation than usual about Netherfield and its master, she could not help saying.

"Oh! that my dear mother had more command over herself; she can have no idea of the pain she gives me by her continual reflections on him. But I will not repine. It cannot last long. He will be forgot, and we shall all be as we were before."

Elizabeth looked at her sister with incredulous solicitude, but said nothing.

"You doubt me," cried Jane, slightly colouring; "indeed you have no reason. He may live in my memory as the most amiable man of my acquaintance, but that is all. I have nothing either to hope or fear, and nothing to reproach him with. Thank God! I have not *that* pain. A little time therefore. – I shall certainly try to get the better."

With a stronger voice she soon added, "I have this comfort immediately, that it has not been more than an error of fancy on my side, and that it has done no harm to anyone but myself."

"My dear Jane!" exclaimed Elizabeth, "you are too good. Your sweetness and disinterestedness are really angelic; I do not know what to say to you. I feel as if I had never done you justice, or loved you as you deserve."

Miss Bennet eagerly disclaimed all extraordinary merit, and threw back the praise on her sister's warm affection.

"Nay," said Elizabeth, "this is not fair. *You* wish to think all the world respectable, and are hurt if I speak ill of anybody. *I* only want to think *you* perfect, and you set yourself against it. Do not be afraid of my running into any excess, of my encroaching on your privilege of universal good will. You need not. There are few people whom I really love, and still fewer of whom I think well. The more I see of the world, the more am I dissatisfied with it; and every day confirms my belief of the inconsistency of all human characters, and of the little dependence that can be placed on the appearance of either merit or sense. I have met with two instances lately; one I will not mention; the other is Charlotte's marriage. It is unaccountable! in every view it is unaccountable!"

"My dear Lizzy, do not give way to such feelings as these. They will ruin your happiness. You do not make allowance enough for difference of situation and temper. Consider Mr. Collins's respectability, and Charlotte's prudent, steady character. Remember that she is one of a large family; that as to fortune, it is a most eligible match; and be ready to believe, for everybody's sake, that she may feel something like regard and esteem for our cousin."

"To oblige you, I would try to believe almost anything, but no one else could be benefited by such a belief as this; for were

I persuaded that Charlotte had any regard for him, I should only think worse of her understanding, than I now do of her heart. My dear Jane, Mr. Collins is a conceited, pompous, narrow-minded, silly man; you know he is, as well as I do; and you must feel, as well as I do, that the woman who marries him, cannot have a proper way of thinking. You shall not defend her, though it is Charlotte Lucas. You shall not, for the sake of one individual, change the meaning of principle and integrity, nor endeavour to persuade yourself or me, that selfishness is prudence, and insensibility of danger, security for happiness."

"I must think your language too strong in speaking of both," replied Jane; "and I hope you will be convinced of it, by seeing them happy together. But enough of this. You alluded to something else. You mentioned *two* instances. I cannot misunderstand you, but I entreat you, dear Lizzy, not to pain me by thinking *that person* to blame, and saying your opinion of him is sunk. We must not be so ready to fancy ourselves intentionally injured. We must not expect a lively young man to be always so guarded and circumspect. It is very often nothing but our own vanity that deceives us. Women fancy admiration means more than it does."

"And men take care that they should."

"If it is designedly done, they cannot be justified; but I have no idea of there being so much design in the world as some persons imagine.

"I am far from attributing any part of Mr. Bingley's conduct to design," said Elizabeth; "but without scheming to do wrong, or to make others unhappy, there may be error, and there may be misery. Thoughtlessness, want of attention to other people's feelings, and want of resolution, will do the business."

"And do you impute it to either of those?"

"Yes; to the last. But if I go on, I shall displease you by saying what I think of persons you esteem. Stop me whilst you can."

"You persist, then, in supposing his sisters influence him."

Yes, in conjunction with his friend."

"I cannot believe it. Why should they try to influence him? They can only wish his happiness, and if he is attached to me, no other woman can secure it."

"Your first position is false. They may wish many things besides his happiness; they may wish his increase of wealth and consequence; they may wish him to marry a girl who has all the importance of money, great connections, and pride."

"Beyond a doubt, they *do* wish him to choose Miss Darcy," replied Jane; "but this may be from better feelings than you are supposing. They have known her much longer than they have known me; no wonder if they love her better. But, whatever may be their own wishes, it is very unlikely they should have opposed their brother's. What sister would think herself at liberty to do it, unless there were something very objectionable? If they believed him attached to me, they would not try to part us; if he were so, they could not succeed. By supposing such an affection, you make everybody acting unnaturally and wrong, and me most unhappy. Do not distress me by the idea. I am not ashamed of having been mistaken – or, at least, it is slight, it is nothing in comparison of what I should feel in thinking ill of him or his sisters. Let me take it in the best light, in the light in which it may be understood."

Elizabeth could not oppose such a wish; and from this time Mr. Bingley's name was scarcely ever mentioned between them."

Mrs. Bennet still continued to wonder and repine at his returning no more, and though a day seldom passed in which Elizabeth did not account for it clearly, there seemed little chance of her ever considering it with less perplexity. Her daughter endeavoured to convince her of what she did not believe herself, that his attentions to Jane had been merely the effect of a common and transient liking, which ceased when he saw her no more; but though the probability of the statement was admitted at the time, she had the same story to repeat every day. Mrs. Bennet's best comfort was, that Mr. Bingley must be down again in the summer.

Mr. Bennet treated the matter differently. "So, Lizzy," said he one day, "your sister is crossed in love I find. I congratulate her. Next to being married, a girl likes to be crossed in love a little now and then. It is something to think of, and it gives her a sort of distinction among her companions. When is your turn to come? You will hardly bear to be long outdone by Jane. Now is your time. Here are officers enough in Meryton to disappoint all the young ladies in the country. Let Wickham be *your* man. He is a pleasant fellow, and would jilt you creditably."

"Thank you, Sir, but a less agreeable man would satisfy me. We must not all expect Jane's good fortune."

"True," said Mr. Bennet, "but it is a comfort to think that, whatever of that kind may befall you, you have an affectionate mother who will make the most of it."

Mr. Wickham's society was of material service in dispelling the gloom, which the late perverse occurrences had thrown on many of the Longbourn family. They saw him often, and to his other recommendations was now added that of general unreserve. The whole of what Elizabeth had already heard, his claims on Mr. Darcy, and all that he had suffered from him, was now openly acknowledged and publicly canvassed; and everybody was pleased to think how much they had always disliked Mr. Darcy before they had known anything of the matter.

Miss Bennet was the only creature who could suppose there might be any extenuating circumstances in the case, unknown to the society of Hertfordshire; her mild and steady candour always pleaded for allowances, and urged the possibility of mistakes – but by everybody else Mr. Darcy was condemned as the worst of men.

# Chapter 25

AFTER A week spent in professions of love and schemes of felicity, Mr. Collins was called from his amiable Charlotte by the arrival of Saturday. The pain of separation, however, might be alleviated on his side, by preparations for the reception of his bride, as he had reason to hope, that shortly after his next return into Hertfordshire, the day would be fixed that was to make him the happiest of men. He took leave of his relations at Longbourn with as much solemnity as before; wished his fair cousins health and happiness again, and promised their father another letter of thanks.

On the following Monday, Mrs. Bennet had the pleasure of receiving her brother and his wife, who came as usual to spend the Christmas at Longbourn. Mr. Gardiner was a sensible, gentlemanlike man, greatly superior to his sister as well by nature as education. The Netherfield ladies would have had difficulty in believing that a man who lived by trade, and within view of his own warehouses, could have been so well bred and agreeable. Mrs. Gardiner, who was several years younger than Mrs. Bennet and Mrs. Philips, was an amiable, intelligent, elegant woman, and a great favourite with all her Longbourn nieces. Between the two eldest and herself especially, there subsisted a very particular regard. They had frequently been staying with her in town.

The first part of Mrs. Gardiner's business on her arrival, was to distribute her presents and describe the newest fashions. When this was done, she had a less active part to play. It became her turn to listen, Mrs. Bennet had many grievances to relate, and much to complain of. They had all been very ill-used since she last saw her sister. Two of her girls had been on the point of marriage, and after all there was nothing in it.

"I do not blame Jane," she continued, "for Jane would have got Mr. Bingley, if she could. But Lizzy! Oh, sister! it is very hard to think that she might have been Mr. Collins's wife by this time, had it not been for her own perverseness. He made her an offer in this very room, and she refused him. The consequence of it is, that Lady Lucas will have a daughter married before I have, and that the Longbourn estate is just as much entailed as ever. The Lucases are very artful people indeed, sister. They are all for what they can get. I am sorry to say it of them, but so it is. It makes me very nervous and poorly, to be thwarted so in my own family, and to have neighbours who think of themselves before anybody else. However, your coming just at this time is the greatest of comforts, and I am very glad to hear what you tell us, of long sleeves."

Mrs. Gardiner, to whom the chief of this news had been given before, in the course of Jane and Elizabeth's correspondence with her, made her sister a slight answer, and in compassion to her nieces turned the conversation.

When alone with Elizabeth afterwards, she spoke more on the subject. "It seems likely to have been a desirable match for Jane," said she. "I am sorry it went off. But these things happen so often! A young man, such as you describe Mr. Bingley, so easily falls in love with a pretty girl for a few weeks, and when accident separates them, so easily forgets her, that these sort of inconsistencies are very frequent."

"An excellent consolation in its way," said Elizabeth, "but it will not do for *us*. We do not suffer by *accident*. It does not often happen that the interference of friends will persuade a young man of independent fortune to think no more of a girl, whom he was violently in love with only a few days before."

"But that expression of 'violently in love' is so hackneyed, so doubtful, so indefinite, that it gives me very little idea. It is as often applied to feelings which arise from an half-hour's acquaintance, as to a real, strong attachment. Pray, how *violent* was Mr. Bingley's love?"

"I never saw a more promising inclination. He was growing quite inattentive to other people, and wholly engrossed by her. Every time they met, it was more decided and remarkable. At his own ball he offended two or three young ladies, by not asking them to dance, and I spoke to him twice myself, without receiving an answer. Could there be finer symptoms? Is not general incivility the very essence of love?"

"Oh, yes! – of that kind of love which I suppose him to have felt. Poor Jane! I am sorry for her, because, with her disposition, she may not get over it immediately. It had better have happened to *you*, Lizzy; you would have laughed yourself out of it sooner. But do you think she would be prevailed on to go back with us? Change of scene might be of service – and perhaps a little relief from home, may be as useful as anything."

Elizabeth was exceedingly pleased with this proposal, and felt persuaded of her sister's ready acquiescence.

"I hope," added Mrs. Gardiner, "that no consideration with regard to this young man will influence her. We live in so different a part of town, all our connections are so different, and, as you well know, we go out so little, that it is very improbable that they should meet at all, unless he really comes to see her."

"And *that* is quite impossible; for he is now in the custody of his friend, and Mr. Darcy would no more suffer him to call on Jane in such a part of London! My dear aunt, how could you think of it? Mr. Darcy may perhaps have *heard* of such a place as Gracechurch Street, but he would hardly think a month's ablution enough to cleanse him from its impurities, were he once to enter it; and depend upon it, Mr. Bingley never stirs without him."

"So much the better. I hope they will not meet at all. But does Jane not correspond with the sister? *She* will not be able to help calling."

"She will drop the acquaintance entirely."

But in spite of the certainty in which Elizabeth affected to place this point, as well as the still more interesting one of Bingley's being withheld from seeing Jane, she felt a solicitude on the subject which convinced her, on examination, that she did not consider it entirely hopeless. It was possible, and sometimes she thought it probable, that his affection might be re-animated, and the influence of his friends successfully combated by the more natural influence of Jane's attractions.

Miss Bennet accepted her aunt's invitation with pleasure; and the Bingleys were no otherwise in her thoughts at the same time, than as she hoped that, by Caroline's not living in the same house with her brother, she might occasionally spend a morning with her, without any danger of seeing him.

The Gardiners stayed a week at Longbourn; and what with the Philipses, the Lucases, and the officers, there was not a day without its engagement. Mrs. Bennet had so carefully provided for the entertainment of her brother and sister, that they did not once sit down to a family dinner. When the engagement was for home, some of the officers always made part of it, of which officers Mr. Wickham was sure to be one; and on these occasions, Mrs. Gardiner, rendered suspicious by Elizabeth's warm commendation of him, narrowly observed them both. Without supposing them, from what she saw, to be very seriously in love, their preference of each other was plain enough to make her a little uneasy; and she resolved to speak to Elizabeth on the subject before she left Hertfordshire, and represent to her the imprudence of encouraging such an attachment.

To Mrs. Gardiner, Wickham had one means of affording pleasure, unconnected with his general powers. About ten or a dozen years ago, before her marriage, she had spent a considerable time in that very part of Derbyshire, to which he belonged. They had, therefore, many acquaintance in common; and, though Wickham had been little there since the death of Darcy's father, five years before, it was yet in his power to give her fresher intelligence of her former friends, than she had been in the way of procuring.

Mrs. Gardiner had seen Pemberly, and known the late Mr. Darcy by character perfectly well. Here consequently was an inexhaustible subject of discourse. In comparing her recollection of Pemberly, with the minute description which Wickham could give, and in bestowing her tribute of praise on the character of its late possessor, she was delighting both him and herself. On being made acquainted with the present Mr. Darcy's treatment of him, she tried to remember something of that gentleman's reputed disposition when quite a lad, which might agree with it, and was confident at last, that she recollected having heard Mr. Fitzwilliam Darcy formerly spoken of as a very proud, ill-natured boy.

## *Chapter 26*

Mrs. Gardiner's caution to Elizabeth was punctually and kindly given on the first favourable opportunity of speaking to her alone; after honestly telling her what she thought, she thus went on:

"You are too sensible a girl, Lizzy, to fall in love merely because you are warned against it; and, therefore, I am not afraid of speaking openly. Seriously, I would have you be on your guard. Do not involve yourself, or endeavour to involve him in an affection which the want of fortune would make so very imprudent. I have nothing to say against *him*; he is a most interesting young man; and if he had the fortune he ought to have, I should think you could not do better. But as it is – you must not let your fancy run away with you. You have sense, and we all expect you to use it. Your father would depend on *your* resolution and good conduct, I am sure. You must not disappoint your father."

"My dear aunt, this is being serious indeed."

"Yes, and I hope to engage you to be serious likewise."

"Well, then, you need not be under any alarm. I will take care of myself, and of Mr. Wickham too. He shall not be in love with me, if I can prevent it."

"Elizabeth, you are not serious now."

"I beg your pardon. I will try again. At present I am not in love with Mr. Wickham; no, I certainly am not. But he is, beyond all comparison, the most agreeable man I ever saw – and if he becomes really attached to me – I believe it will be better that he should not. I see the imprudence of it. – Oh! *that* abominable Mr. Darcy! – My father's opinion of me does me the greatest honour; and I should be miserable to forfeit it. My father, however, is partial to Mr. Wickham. In short, my dear aunt, I should be very sorry to be the means of making any of you unhappy; but since we see every day that where there is affection, young people are seldom withheld by immediate want of fortune, from entering into engagements with each other, how can I promise to be wiser than so many of my fellow creatures if I am tempted, or how am I even to know that it would be wisdom to resist? All that I can promise you, therefore, is not to be in a hurry. I will not be in a hurry to believe myself his first object. When I am in company with him, I will not be wishing. In short, I will do my best."

"Perhaps it will be as well if you discourage his coming here so very often. At least, you should not *remind* your mother of inviting him."

"As I did the other day," said Elizabeth, with a conscious smile; "very true, it will be wise in me to refrain from *that*. But do not imagine that he is always here so often. It is on your account that he has been so frequently invited this week. You know my mother's ideas as to the necessity of constant company for her friends. But really, and upon my honour, I will try to do what I think to be the wisest; and now, I hope you are satisfied."

Her aunt assured her that she was; and Elizabeth having thanked her for the kindness of her hints, they parted; a wonderful instance of advice being given on such a point, without being resented.

Mr. Collins returned into Hertfordshire soon after it had been quitted by the Gardiners and Jane; but as he took up his abode with the Lucases, his arrival was no great inconvenience to Mrs. Bennet. His marriage was now fast approaching, and she was at length so far resigned as to think it inevitable, and even repeatedly to say in an ill-natured tone that she '*wished* they might be happy.' Thursday was to be the wedding day, and on Wednesday Miss Lucas paid her farewell visit; and when she rose to take leave, Elizabeth, ashamed of her mother's ungracious and reluctant good wishes, and sincerely affected herself, accompanied her out of the room. As they went downstairs together, Charlotte said,

"I shall depend on hearing from you very often, Eliza."

"*That* you certainly shall."

"And I have another favour to ask. Will you come and see me?"

"We shall often meet, I hope, in Hertfordshire."

"I am not likely to leave Kent for some time. Promise me, therefore, to come to Hunsford."

Elizabeth could not refuse, though she foresaw little pleasure in the visit.

"My father and Maria are coming to me in March," added Charlotte, "and I hope you will consent to be of the party. Indeed, Eliza, you will be as welcome as either of them."

The wedding took place; the bride and bridegroom set off for Kent from the church door, and everybody had as much to say or to hear on the subject as usual. Elizabeth soon heard from her friend; and their correspondence was as regular and frequent as it had ever been; that it should be equally unreserved was impossible. Elizabeth could never address her without feeling that all the comfort of intimacy was over, and, though determined not to slacken as correspondent, it was for the sake of what had been, rather than what was. Charlotte's first letters were received with a good deal of eagerness; there could not but be curiosity to know how she would speak of her new home, how she would like Lady Catherine, and how happy she would dare pronounce herself to be; though, when the letters were read, Elizabeth felt that Charlotte expressed herself on every point exactly as she might have foreseen. She wrote cheerfully, seemed surrounded with comforts, and mentioned nothing which she could not praise. The house, furniture, neighbourhood, and roads, were all to her taste, and Lady Catherine's behaviour was most friendly and obliging. It was Mr. Collins's picture of Hunsford and Rosings rationally softened; and Elizabeth perceived that she must wait for her own visit there, to know the rest.

Jane had already written a few lines to her sister to announce their safe arrival in London; and when she wrote again, Elizabeth hoped it would be in her power to say something of the Bingleys.

Her impatience for this second letter was as well rewarded as impatience generally is. Jane had been a week in town, without either seeing or hearing from Caroline. She accounted for it, however, by supposing that her last letter to her friend from Longbourn, had by some accident been lost.

"My aunt," she continued, "is going tomorrow into that part of the town, and I shall take the opportunity of calling in Grosvenor Street."

She wrote again when the visit was paid, and she had seen Miss Bingley. "I did not think Caroline in spirits," were her words, "but she was very glad to see me, and reproached me for giving her no notice of my coming to London. I was right, therefore;

my last letter had never reached her. I enquired after their brother, of course. He was well, but so much engaged with Mr. Darcy that they scarcely ever saw him. I found that Miss Darcy was expected to dinner. I wish I could see her. My visit was not long, as Caroline and Mrs. Hurst were going out. I dare say I shall soon see them here."

Elizabeth shook her head over this letter. It convinced her, that accident only could discover to Mr. Bingley her sister's being in town.

Four weeks passed away, and Jane saw nothing of him. She endeavoured to persuade herself that she did not regret it; but she could no longer be blind to Miss Bingley's inattention. After waiting at home every morning for a fortnight, and inventing every evening a fresh excuse for her, the visitor did at last appear; but the shortness of her stay, and yet more, the alteration of her manner, would allow Jane to deceive herself no longer. The letter which she wrote on this occasion to her sister, will prove what she felt.

> My dearest Lizzy will, I am sure, be incapable of triumphing in her better judgement, at my expense, when I confess myself to have been entirely deceived in Miss Bingley's regard for me. But, my dear sister, though the event has proved you right, do not think me obstinate if I still assert, that, considering what her behaviour was, my confidence was as natural as your suspicion. I do not at all comprehend her reason for wishing to be intimate with me, but if the same circumstances were to happen again, I am sure I should be deceived again. Caroline did not return my visit till yesterday; and not a note, not a line, did I receive in the meantime. When she did come, it was very evident that she had no pleasure in it; she made a slight, formal, apology, for not calling before, said not a word of wishing to see me again, and was in every respect so altered a creature, that when she went away, I was perfectly resolved to continue the acquaintance no longer. I pity, though I cannot help blaming

her. She was very wrong in singling me out as she did; I can safely say that every advance to intimacy began on her side. But I pity her, because she must feel that she has been acting wrong, and because I am very sure that anxiety for her brother is the cause of it. I need not explain myself farther; and though *we* know this anxiety to be quite needless, yet if she feels it, it will easily account for her behaviour to me; and so deservedly dear as he is to his sister, whatever anxiety she may feel on his behalf is natural and amiable. I cannot but wonder, however, at her having any such fears now, because, if he had at all cared about me, we must have met, long, long ago. He knows of my being in town, I am certain, from something she said herself; and yet it should seem by her manner of talking, as if she wanted to persuade herself that he is really partial to Miss Darcy. I cannot understand it. If I were not afraid of judging harshly, I should be almost tempted to say, that there is a strong appearance of duplicity in all this. But I will endeavour to banish every painful thought, and think only of what will make me happy, your affection, and the invariable kindness of my dear uncle and aunt. Let me hear from you very soon. Miss Bingley said something of his never returning to Netherfield again, of giving up the house, but not with any certainty. We had better not mention it. I am extremely glad that you have such pleasant accounts from our friends at Hunsford. Pray go to see them, with Sir William and Maria. I am sure you will be very comfortable there.

Yours, &c.

This letter gave Elizabeth some pain; but her spirits returned as she considered that Jane would no longer be duped, by the sister at least. All expectation from the brother was now absolutely over. She would not even wish for a renewal of his attentions. His character sunk on every review of it; and as punishment for him, as well as possible advantage to Jane, she seriously hoped he might really soon marry Mr. Darcy's sister, as, by Wickham's account, she would make him abundantly regret what he had thrown away.

Mrs. Gardiner about this time reminded Elizabeth of her promise concerning that gentleman, and required information; and Elizabeth had such to send as might rather give contentment to her aunt than to herself. His apparent partiality had subsided, his attentions were over, he was the admirer of someone else. Elizabeth was watchful enough to see it all, but she could see it and write of it without material pain. Her heart had been but slightly touched, and her vanity was satisfied with believing that *she* would have been his only choice, had fortune permitted it. The sudden acquisition of ten thousand pounds was the most remarkable charm of the young lady, to whom he was now rendering himself agreeable; but Elizabeth, less clear-sighted perhaps in his case than in Charlotte's, did not quarrel with him for his wish of independence. Nothing, on the contrary, could be more natural; and while able to suppose that it cost him a few struggles to relinquish her, she was ready to allow it a wise and desirable measure for both, and could very sincerely wish him happy.

All this was acknowledged to Mrs. Gardiner; and after relating the circumstances, she thus went on:– "I am now convinced, my dear aunt, that I have never been much in love; for had I really experienced that pure and elevating passion, I should at present detest his very name, and wish him all manner of evil. But my feelings are not only cordial towards *him*; they are even impartial towards Miss King. I cannot find out that I hate her at all, or that I am in the least unwilling to think her a very good sort of girl. There can be no love in all this. My watchfulness has been effectual; and though I should certainly be a more interesting object to all my acquaintance, were I distractedly in love with him, I cannot say that I regret my comparative insignificance. Importance may sometimes be purchased too dearly. Kitty and

Lydia take his defection much more to heart than I do. They are young in the ways of the world, and not yet open to the mortifying conviction that handsome young men must have something to live on, as well as the plain."

## *Chapter 27*

WITH NO greater events than these in the Longbourn family, and otherwise diversified by little beyond the walks to Meryton, sometimes dirty and sometimes cold, did January and February pass away. March was to take Elizabeth to Hunsford. She had not at first thought very seriously of going thither; but Charlotte, she soon found, was depending on the plan, and she gradually learned to consider it herself with greater pleasure as well as greater certainty. Absence had increased her desire of seeing Charlotte again, and weakened her disgust of Mr. Collins. There was novelty in the scheme, and as, with such a mother and such uncompanionable sisters, home could not be faultless, a little change was not unwelcome for its own sake. The journey would moreover give her a peep at Jane; and, in short, as the time drew near, she would have been very sorry for any delay. Everything, however, went on smoothly, and was finally settled according to Charlotte's first sketch. She was to accompany Sir William and his second daughter. The improvement of spending a night in London was added in time, and the plan became perfect as plan could be.

The only pain was in leaving her father, who would certainly miss her, and who, when it came to the point, so little liked her going, that he told her to write to him, and almost promised to answer her letter.

The farewell between herself and Mr. Wickham was perfectly friendly; on his side even more. His present pursuit could not make him forget that Elizabeth had been the first to excite and to deserve his attention, the first to listen and to pity, the first to be admired; and in his manner of bidding her adieu, wishing her every enjoyment, reminding her of what she was to expect in Lady Catherine de Bourgh, and trusting their opinion of her – their opinion of everybody – would always coincide, there was a solicitude, an interest which she felt must ever attach her to him with a most sincere regard; and she parted from him convinced, that whether married or single, he must always be her model of the amiable and pleasing.

Her fellow-travellers the next day, were not of a kind to make her think him less agreeable. Sir William Lucas, and his daughter Maria, a good-humoured girl, but as empty-headed as himself, had nothing to say that could be worth hearing, and were listened to with about as much delight as the rattle of the chaise. Elizabeth loved absurdities, but she had known Sir William's too long. He could tell her nothing new of the wonders of his presentation and knighthood; and his civilities were worn out like his information.

It was a journey of only twenty-four miles, and they began it so early as to be in Gracechurch Street by noon. As they drove to Mr. Gardiner's door, Jane was at a drawing-room window watching their arrival; when they entered the passage she was there to welcome them, and Elizabeth, looking earnestly in her face, was pleased to see it healthful and lovely as ever. On the stairs were a troop of little boys and girls, whose eagerness for their cousin's appearance would not allow them to wait in the drawing-room, and whose shyness, as they had not seen her for a twelvemonth, prevented their coming lower. All was joy and kindness. The day passed most pleasantly away; the morning in bustle and shopping, and the evening at one of the theatres.

Elizabeth then contrived to sit by her aunt. Their first subject was her sister; and she was more grieved than astonished to hear, in reply to her minute enquiries, that though Jane always struggled to support her spirits, there were periods of dejection. It was reasonable, however, to hope, that they would not continue long. Mrs. Gardiner gave her the particulars also of Miss Bingley's visit in Gracechurch Street, and repeated conversations occurring at different times between Jane and herself, which proved that the former had, from her heart, given up the acquaintance.

Mrs. Gardiner then rallied her niece on Wickham's desertion, and complimented her on bearing it so well.

"But my dear Elizabeth," she added, "what sort of girl is Miss King? I should be sorry to think our friend mercenary."

"Pray, my dear aunt, what is the difference in matrimonial affairs, between the mercenary and the prudent motive? Where does discretion end, and avarice begin? Last Christmas you were afraid of his marrying me, because it would be imprudent; and now, because he is trying to get a girl with only ten thousand pounds, you want to find out that he is mercenary."

"If you will only tell me what sort of girl Miss King is, I shall know what to think."

"She is a very good kind of girl, I believe. I know no harm of her."

"But he paid her not the smallest attention, till her grandfather's death made her mistress of this fortune."

"No – what should he? If it was not allowable for him to gain *my* affections because I had no money, what occasion could there be for making love to a girl whom he did not care about, and who was equally poor?"

"But there seems indelicacy in directing his attentions towards her, so soon after this event."

"A man in distressed circumstances has not time for all those elegant decorums which other people may observe. If *she* does not object to it, why should *we*?"

"*Her* not objecting, does not justify *him*. It only shows her being deficient in something herself – sense or feeling."

"Well," cried Elizabeth, "have it as you choose. *He* shall be mercenary, and *she* shall be foolish."

"No, Lizzy, that is what I do *not* choose. I should be sorry, you know, to think ill of a young man who has lived so long in Derbyshire."

"Oh! if that is all, I have a very poor opinion of young men who live in Derbyshire; and their intimate friends who live in Hertfordshire are not much better. I am sick of them all. Thank Heaven! I am going tomorrow where I shall find a man who has not one agreeable quality, who has neither manner nor sense to recommend him. Stupid men are the only ones worth knowing, after all."

"Take care, Lizzy; that speech savours strongly of disappointment."

Before they were separated by the conclusion of the play, she had the unexpected happiness of an invitation to accompany her uncle and aunt in a tour of pleasure which they proposed taking in the summer.

"We have not quite determined how far it shall carry us," said Mrs. Gardiner, "but perhaps to the Lakes."

No scheme could have been more agreeable to Elizabeth, and her acceptance of the invitation was most ready and grateful. "My dear, dear aunt," she rapturously cried, "what delight! what felicity! You give me fresh life and vigour. Adieu to disappointment and spleen. What are men to rocks and mountains? Oh! what hours of transport we shall spend! And when we *do* return, it shall not be like other travellers, without being able to give one accurate idea of anything. We *will* know where we have gone – we *will* recollect what we have seen. Lakes, mountains, and rivers, shall not be jumbled together in our imaginations; nor, when we attempt to describe any particular scene, will we begin quarrelling about its relative situation. Let *our* first effusions be less insupportable than those of the generality of travellers."

# Chapter 28

EVERY OBJECT in the next day's journey was new and interesting to Elizabeth; and her spirits were in a state of enjoyment; for she had seen her sister looking so well as to banish all fear for her health, and the prospect of her northern tour was a constant source of delight.

When they left the high road for the lane to Hunsford, every eye was in search of the Parsonage, and every turning expected to bring it in view. The paling of Rosings Park was their boundary on one side. Elizabeth smiled at the recollection of all that she had heard of its inhabitants.

At length the Parsonage was discernible. The garden sloping to the road, the house standing in it, the green pales and the laurel hedge, everything declared they were arriving. Mr. Collins and Charlotte appeared at the door, and the carriage stopped at the small gate, which led by a short gravel walk to the house, amidst the nods and smiles of the whole party. In a moment they were all out of the chaise, rejoicing at the sight of each other. Mrs. Collins welcomed her friend with the liveliest pleasure, and Elizabeth was more and more satisfied with coming, when she found herself so affectionately received. She saw instantly that her cousin's manners were not altered by his marriage; his formal civility was just what it had been, and he detained her some minutes at the gate to hear and satisfy his enquiries after all her family. They were then, with no other delay than his pointing out the neatness of the entrance, taken into the house; and as soon as they were in the parlour, he welcomed them a second time with ostentatious formality to his humble abode, and punctually repeated all his wife's offers of refreshment.

Elizabeth was prepared to see him in his glory; and he could not help fancying that in displaying the good proportion of the room, its aspect and its furniture, he addressed himself particularly to her, as if wishing to make her feel what she had lost in refusing him. But though everything seemed neat and comfortable, she was not able to gratify him by any sigh of repentance; and rather looked with wonder at her friend that she could have so cheerful an air, with such a companion. When Mr. Collins said anything of which his wife might reasonably be ashamed, which certainly was not unseldom, she involuntarily turned her eye on Charlotte. Once or twice she could discern a faint blush; but in general Charlotte wisely did not hear. After sitting long enough to admire every article of furniture in the room, from the sideboard to the fender, to give an account of their journey and of all that had happened in London, Mr. Collins invited them to take a stroll in the garden, which was large and well laid out, and to the cultivation of which he attended himself. To work in his garden was one of his most respectable pleasures; and Elizabeth admired the command of countenance with which Charlotte talked of the healthfulness of the exercise, and owned she encouraged it as much as possible. Here, leading the way through every walk and cross walk, and scarcely allowing them an interval to utter the praises he asked for, every view was pointed out with a minuteness which left beauty entirely behind. He could number the fields in every direction, and could tell how many tress there were in the most distant clump. But of all the views which his garden, or which the country, or the kingdom could boast, none were to be compared with the prospect of Rosings, afforded by an opening in the trees that bordered the park nearly opposite the front of his house. It was a handsome modern building, well situated on rising ground.

From his garden, Mr. Collins would have led them round his two meadows, but the ladies not having shoes to encounter the remains of a white frost, turned back; and while Sir William accompanied him, Charlotte took her sister and friend over the house, extremely well pleased, probably, to have the opportunity of showing it without her husband's help. It was rather small, but well built and convenient; and everything was fitted up and arranged with a neatness and consistency of which Elizabeth gave Charlotte all the credit. When Mr. Collins could be forgotten, there was really a great air of comfort throughout, and by Charlotte's evident enjoyment of it, Elizabeth supposed he must be often forgotten.

She had already learnt that Lady Catherine was still in the country. It was spoken of again while they were at dinner, when Mr. Collins joining in, observed,

"Yes, Miss Elizabeth, you will have the honour of seeing Lady Catherine de Bourgh on the ensuing Sunday at church, and I need not say you will be delighted with her. She is all affability and condescension, and I doubt not but you will be honoured with some portion of her notice when service is over. I have scarcely any hesitation in saying she will include you and my sister Maria in every invitation with which she honours us during your stay here. Her behaviour to my dear Charlotte is charming. We dine at Rosings twice every week, and are never allowed to walk home. Her ladyship's carriage is regularly ordered for us. I *should* say, one of her ladyship's carriages, for she has several."

"Lady Catherine is a very respectable, sensible woman indeed, added Charlotte, "and a most attentive neighbour."

"Very true, my dear, that is exactly what I say. She is the sort of woman whom one cannot regard with too much deference."

The evening was spent chiefly in talking over Hertfordshire

news, and telling again what had already been written; and when it closed, Elizabeth in the solitude of her chamber had to meditate upon Charlotte's degree of contentment, to understand her address in guiding, and composure in bearing with her husband, and to acknowledge that it was all done very well. She had also to anticipate how her visit would pass, the quiet tenor of their usual employments, the vexatious interruptions of Mr. Collins, and the gaieties of their intercourse with Rosings. A lively imagination soon settled it all.

About the middle of the next day, as she was in her room getting ready for a walk, a sudden noise below seemed to speak the whole house in confusion; and after listening a moment, she heard somebody running upstairs in a violent hurry, and calling loudly after her. She opened the door, and met Maria in the landing place, who, breathless with agitation, cried out,

"Oh, my dear Eliza! pray make haste and come into the dining-room, for there is such a sight to be seen! I will not tell you what it is. Make haste, and come down this moment."

Elizabeth asked questions in vain; Maria would tell her nothing more, and down they ran into the dining-room, which fronted the lane, in quest of this wonder; it was two ladies stopping in a low phaeton at the garden gate.

"And is this all?" cried Elizabeth. "I expected at least that the pigs were got into the garden, and here is nothing but Lady Catherine and her daughter."

"La! my dear," said Maria quite shocked at the mistake, "it is not Lady Catherine. The old lady is Mrs. Jenkinson, who lives with them. The other is Miss de Bourgh. Only look at her. She is quite a little creature. Who would have thought she could be so thin and small!"

"She is abominably rude to keep Charlotte out of doors in all this wind. Why does she not come in?"

"Oh! Charlotte says, she hardly ever does. It is the greatest of favours when Miss de Bourgh comes in."

"I like her appearance," said Elizabeth, struck with other ideas. "She looks sickly and cross. – Yes, she will do for him very well. She will make him a very proper wife."

Mr. Collins and Charlotte were both standing at the gate in conversation with the ladies; and Sir William, to Elizabeth's high diversion, was stationed in the doorway, in earnest contemplation of the greatness before him, and constantly bowing whenever Miss de Bourgh looked that way.

At length there was nothing more to be said; the ladies drove on, and the others returned into the house. Mr. Collins no sooner saw the two girls than he began to congratulate them on their good fortune, which Charlotte explained by letting them know that the whole party was asked to dine at Rosings the next day.

# *Chapter 29*

MR. COLLINS's triumph, in consequence of this invitation was complete. The power of displaying the grandeur of his patroness to his wondering visitors, and of letting them see her civility towards himself and his wife, was exactly what he had wished for; and that an opportunity of doing it should be given so soon, was such an instance of Lady Catherine's condescension as he knew not how to admire enough.

"I confess," said he, "that I should not have been at all surprised by her ladyship's asking us on Sunday to drink tea and spend the evening at Rosings. I rather expected, from my knowledge of her affability, that it would happen. But who could have foreseen such an attention as this? Who could have imagined that we should receive an invitation to dine there (an invitation moreover including the whole party) so immediately after your arrival!"

"I am the less surprised at what has happened," replied Sir William, "from that knowledge of what the manners of the great really are, which my situation in life has allowed me to acquire. About the Court, such instances of elegant breeding are not uncommon."

Scarcely anything was talked of the whole day or next morning, but their visit to Rosings. Mr. Collins was carefully instructing them in what they were to expect, that the sight of such rooms, so many servants, and so splendid a dinner might not wholly overpower them.

When the ladies were separating for the toilette. Her said to Elizabeth,

"Do not make yourself uneasy, my dear cousin, about your apparel. Lady Catherine is far from requiring that elegance of dress in us, which becomes herself and her daughter. I would advise you merely to put on whatever of your clothes is superior to the rest, there is no occasion for anything more. Lady Catherine will not think the worse of you for being simply dressed. She likes to have the distinction of rank preserved."

While they were dressing, he came two or three times to their different doors, to recommend their being quick, as Lady Catherine very much objected to be kept waiting for her dinner. – Such formidable accounts of her ladyship, and her manner of living, quite frightened Maria Lucas, who had been little used to company, and she looked forward to her introduction at Rosings, with as much apprehension, as her father had done to his presentation at St. James's.

As the weather was fine, they had a pleasant walk of about half a mile across the park. – Every park has its beauty and its prospects; and Elizabeth saw much to be pleased with, though she could not be in such raptures as Mr. Collins expected the scene to inspire, and was but slightly affected by his enumeration of the windows in front of the house, and his relation of what the glazing altogether had originally cost Sir Lewis de Bourgh.

When they ascended the steps to the hall, Maria's alarm was every moment increasing, and even Sir William did not look perfectly calm. – Elizabeth's courage did not fail her. She had heard nothing of Lady Catherine that spoke her awful from any extraordinary talents or miraculous virtue, and the mere stateliness of money or rank, she thought she could witness without trepidation.

From the entrance hall, of which Mr. Collins pointed out, with a rapturous air, the fine proportion and finished ornaments, they followed the servants through an ante-chamber, to the room where Lady Catherine, her daughter, and Mrs. Jenkinson were sitting. – Her ladyship, with great condescension, arose to receive them; and as Mrs. Collins had settled it with her husband that the office of introduction should be hers, it was performed in a proper manner, without any of those apologies and thanks which he would have thought necessary.

In spite of having been at St. James's, Sir William was so completely awed, by the grandeur surrounding him, that he had but just courage enough to make a very low bow, and take his seat without saying a word; and his daughter, frightened almost out of her senses, sat on the edge of her chair, not knowing which way to look. Elizabeth found herself quite equal to the scene, and could observe the three ladies before her composedly. – Lady Catherine was a tall, large woman, with strongly-marked features, which might once have been handsome. Her air was not conciliating, nor was her manner of receiving them, such as to make her visitors forget their inferior rank. She was not rendered formidable by silence; but whatever she said, was spoken in so authoritative a tone, as marked her self-importance, and brought Mr. Wickham immediately to Elizabeth's mind; and from the observation of the day altogether, she believed Lady Catherine to be exactly what he had represented.

When, after examining the mother, in whose countenance and deportment she soon found some resemblance of Mr. Darcy, she turned her eyes on the daughter, she could almost have joined in Maria's astonishment, at her being so thin, and so small. There was neither in figure nor face, any likeness between the ladies. Miss de Bourgh was pale and sickly; her features, though not plain, were insignificant; and she spoke very little, except in a low voice, to Mrs. Jenkinson, in whose appearance there was nothing remarkable, and who was entirely engaged in listening to what she said, and placing a screen in the proper direction before her eyes.

After sitting a few minutes, they were all sent to one of the windows to admire the view, Mr. Collins attending them to point out its beauties, and Lady Catherine kindly informing them that it was much better worth looking at in the summer.

The dinner was exceedingly handsome, and there were all the servants, and all the articles of plate which Mr. Collins had promised; and, as he had likewise foretold, he took his seat at the bottom of the table, by her ladyship's desire, and looked as if he felt that life could furnish nothing greater. – He carved, and ate, and praised with delighted alacrity; and every dish was commended, first by him, and then by Sir William, who was now enough recovered to echo whatever his son-in-law said, in a manner which Elizabeth wondered Lady Catherine could bear. But Lady Catherine seemed gratified by their excessive admiration, and gave most gracious smiles, especially when any dish on the table proved a novelty to them. The party did not supply much conversation. Elizabeth was ready to speak whenever there was an opening, but she was seated between Charlotte and Miss de Bourgh – the former of whom was engaged in listening to Lady Catherine, and the latter said not a word to her all dinner time. Miss Jenkinson was chiefly employed in watching how little Miss de Bourgh ate, pressing her to try some other dish, and fearing she was indisposed. Maria thought speaking out of the question, and the gentlemen did nothing but eat and admire.

When the ladies returned to the drawing-room, there was little to be done but to hear Lady Catherine talk, which she did without any intermission till coffee came in, delivering her opinion on every subject in so decisive a manner as proved that she was not used to have her judgement controverted. She enquired into Charlotte's domestic concerns familiarly and minutely, gave her a great deal of advice, as to the management of them all; told her how everything ought to be regulated in so small a family as hers, and instructed her as to the care of her cows and her poultry. Elizabeth found that nothing was beneath this great lady's attention, which could furnish her with an occasion of dictating to others. In the intervals of her discourse with Mrs. Collins, she addressed a variety of questions to Maria and Elizabeth, but especially to the latter, of whose connections she knew the least, and who she observed to Mrs. Collins was a very genteel, pretty kind of girl. She asked her at different times, how many sisters she had, whether they were older or younger than herself, whether any of them were likely to be married, whether they were handsome, where they had been educated, what carriage her father kept, and what had been her mother's maiden name? – Elizabeth felt all the impertinence of her questions, but answered them very composedly. – Lady Catherine then observed,

"Your father's estate is entailed on Mr. Collins, I think. For your sake," turning to Charlotte, "I am glad of it; but otherwise I see no occasion for entailing estates from the female line. – It was not thought necessary in Sir Lewis de Bourgh's family. – Do you play and sing, Miss Bennet?"

"A little."

"Oh! then – some time or other we shall be happy to hear you. Our instrument is a capital one, probably superior to – You shall try it some day. Do your sisters play and sing?"

"One of them does."

"Why did not you all learn? – You ought all to have learned. The Miss Webbs all play, and their father has not so good an income as yours. – Do you draw?"

"No, not at all."

"What, none of you?"

"Not one."

"That is very strange. But I suppose you had no opportunity. Your mother should have taken you to town every spring for the benefit of masters."

"My mother would have had no objection, but my father hates London."

"Has your governess left you?"

"We never had any governess."

"No governess! How was that possible? Five daughters brought up at home without a governess! – I never heard of such a thing. Your mother must have been quite a slave to your education."

Elizabeth could hardly help smiling, as she assured her that had not been the case.

"Then, who taught you? who attended to you? Without a governess you must have been neglected."

"Compared with some families, I believe we were; but such of us as wished to learn, never wanted the means. We were always encouraged to read, and had all the masters that were necessary. Those who chose to be idle, certainly might."

"Aye, no doubt; but that is what a governess will prevent, and if I had known your mother, I should have advised her most strenuously to engage one. I always say that nothing is to be done in education without steady and regular instruction, and nobody but a governess can give it. It is wonderful how many families I have been the means of supplying in that way. I am always glad to get a young person well placed out. Four nieces of Mrs. Jenkinson are most delightfully situated through my means; and it was but the other day, that I recommended another young person, who was merely accidentally mentioned to me, and the family are quite delighted with her. Mrs. Collins, did I tell you of Lady Metcalfe's calling yesterday to thank me? She finds Miss Pope a treasure.

'Lady Catherine,' said she, 'you have given me a treasure.' Are any of your younger sisters out, Miss Bennet?"

"Yes, Ma'am, all."

"All! – What, all five out at once? Very odd! – And you only the second. – The younger ones out before the elder are married! – Your younger sisters must be very young?"

"Yes, my youngest is not sixteen. Perhaps *she* is full young to be much in company. But really, Ma'am, I think it would be very hard upon younger sisters, that they should not have their share of society and amusement because the elder may not have the means or inclination to marry early. – The last born has as good a right to the pleasures of youth, at the first. And to be kept back on *such* a motive! – I think it would not be very likely to promote sisterly affection or delicacy of mind."

"Upon my word," said her ladyship, "you give your opinion very decidedly for so young a person. – Pray, what is your age?"

"With three younger sisters grown up," replied Elizabeth smiling, "your ladyship can hardly expect me to own it."

Lady Catherine seemed quite astonished at not receiving a direct answer; and Elizabeth suspected herself to be the first creature who had ever dared to trifle with so much dignified impertinence.

"You cannot be more than twenty, I am sure, – therefore you need not conceal your age."

"I am not one and twenty."

When the gentlemen had joined them, and tea was over, the

card-tables were placed. Lady Catherine, Sir William, and Mr. and Mrs. Collins sat down to quadrille; and as Miss de Bourgh chose to play at cassino, the two girls had the honour of assisting Mrs. Jenkinson to make up her party. Their table was superlatively stupid. Scarcely a syllable was uttered that did not relate to the game, except when Mrs. Jenkinson expressed her fears of Miss de Bourgh's being too hot or too cold, or having too much or too little light. A great deal more passed at the other table. Lady Catherine was generally speaking – stating the mistakes of the three others, or relating some anecdote of herself. Mr. Collins was employed in agreeing to everything her ladyship said, thanking her for every fish he won, and apologising if he thought he won too many. Sir William did not say much. He was storing his memory with anecdotes and noble names.

When Lady Catherine and her daughter had played as long as they chose, the tables were broken up, the carriage was offered to Mrs. Collins, gratefully accepted, and immediately ordered. The party then gathered round the fire to hear Lady Catherine determine what weather they were to have on the morrow. From these instructions they were summoned by the arrival of the coach, and with many speeches of thankfulness on Mr. Collins's side, and as many bows on Sir William's, they departed. As soon as they had driven from the door, Elizabeth was called on by her cousin, to give her opinion of all that she had seen at Rosings, which, for Charlotte's sake, she made more favourable than it really was. But her commendation, though costing her some trouble, could by no means satisfy Mr. Collins, and he was very soon obliged to take her ladyship's praise into his own hands.

# Chapter 30

Sir William stayed only a week at Hunsford, but his visit was long enough to convince him of his daughter's being most comfortably settled, and of her possessing such a husband and such a neighbour as were not often met with. While Sir William was with them, Mr. Collins devoted his morning to driving him out in his gig, and showing him the country; but when he went away, the whole family returned to their usual employments, and Elizabeth was thankful to find that they did not see more of her cousin by the alteration, for the chief of the time between breakfast and dinner was now passed by him either at work in the garden, or in reading and writing, and looking out of the window in his own book-room, which fronted the road. The room in which the ladies sat was backwards. Elizabeth at first had rather wondered that Charlotte should not prefer the dining-parlour for common use; it was a better-sized room, and had a pleasanter aspect; but she soon saw that her friend had an excellent reason for what she did, for Mr. Collins would undoubtedly have been much less in his own apartment, had they sat in one equally lively; and she gave Charlotte credit for the arrangement.

From the drawing-room they could distinguish nothing in the lane, and were indebted to Mr. Collins for the knowledge of what carriages went along, and how often especially Miss de Bourgh drove by in her phaeton, which he never failed coming to inform them of, though it happened almost every day. She not unfrequently stopped at the Parsonage, and had a few minutes' conversation with Charlotte, but was scarcely ever prevailed on to get out.

Very few days passed in which Mr. Collins did not walk to Rosings, and not many in which his wife did not think it necessary to go likewise; and till Elizabeth recollected that there might be other family livings to be disposed of, she could not understand the sacrifice of so many hours. Now and then, they were honoured with a call from her ladyship, and nothing escaped her observation that was passing in the room during these visits. She examined into their employments, looked at their work, and advised them to do it differently; found fault with the arrangement of the furniture; or detected the housemaid in negligence; and if she accepted any refreshment, seemed to do it only for the sake of finding out that Mrs. Collins's joints of meat were too large for her family.

Elizabeth soon perceived that though this great lady was not in the commission of the peace for the county, she was a most active magistrate in her own parish, the minutest concerns of which were carried to her by Mr. Collins; and whenever any of the cottagers were disposed to be quarrelsome, discontented or too poor, she sallied forth into the village to settle their differences, silence their complaints, and scold them into harmony and plenty.

The entertainment of dining at Rosings was repeated about twice a week; and, allowing for the loss of Sir William, and there being only one card-table in the evening, every such entertainment was the counterpart of the first. Their other engagements were few, as the style of living in the neighbourhood in general, was beyond the Collinses' reach. This however was no evil to Elizabeth, and upon the whole she spent her time comfortably enough; there were half hours of pleasant conversation with Charlotte, and the weather was so fine for the time of year, that she had often great enjoyment out of doors. Her favourite walk, and where she frequently went while the others were calling on Lady Catherine, was along the open grove which edged that side of the park, where there was a nice sheltered path, which no one seemed to value but herself, and where she felt beyond the reach of Lady Catherine's curiosity.

In this quiet way, the first fortnight of her visit soon passed away. Easter was approaching, and the week preceding it, was to bring an addition to the family at Rosings, which in so small a circle must be important. Elizabeth had heard soon after her arrival, that Mr. Darcy was expected there in the course of a few weeks, and though there were not many of her acquaintance whom she did not prefer, his coming would furnish one comparatively new to look at in their Rosings parties, and she might be amused in seeing how hopeless Miss Bingley's designs on him were, by his behaviour to his cousin, for whom he was evidently destined by Lady Catherine; who talked of his coming with the greatest satisfaction, spoke of him in terms of the highest admiration, and seemed almost angry to find that he had already been frequently seen by Miss Lucas and herself.

His arrival was soon known at the Parsonage; for Mr. Collins was walking the whole morning within view of the lodges opening into Hunsford Lane, in order to have the earliest assurance of it; and after making his bow as the carriage turned into the Park, hurried home with the great intelligence. On the following morning he hastened to Rosings to pay his respects. There were two nephews of Lady Catherine to require them, for Mr. Darcy had brought with him a Colonel Fitzwilliam, the younger son of his uncle, Lord – and to the great surprise of all the party, when Mr. Collins returned the gentlemen accompanied him. Charlotte had seen them from her husband's room, crossing the road, and immediately running into the other, told the girls what an honour they might expect, adding,

"I may thank you, Eliza, for this piece of civility. Mr. Darcy would never have come so soon to wait upon me."

Elizabeth had scarcely time to disclaim all right to the compliment, before their approach was announced by the door-bell, and shortly afterwards the three gentlemen entered the room. Colonel Fitzwilliam, who led the way, was about thirty, not handsome, but in person and address most truly the gentleman. Mr. Darcy looked just as he had been used to look in Hertfordshire, paid his compliments, with his usual reserve, to Mrs. Collins; and whatever might be his feelings towards her friend, met her with every appearance of composure. Elizabeth merely curtseyed to him, without saying a word.

Colonel Fitzwilliam entered into conversation directly with the readiness and ease of a well-bred man, and talked very pleasantly; but his cousin, after having addressed a slight observation on the house and garden to Mrs. Collins, sat for some time without speaking to anybody. At length, however, his civility was so far awakened as to enquire of Elizabeth after the health of her family. She answered him in the usual way, and after a moment's pause, added,

"My eldest sister has been in town these three months. Have you never happened to see her there?"

She was perfectly sensible that he never had; but she wished to see whether he would betray any consciousness of what had passed between the Bingleys and Jane, and she thought he looked a little confused as he answered that he had never been so fortunate as to meet Miss Bennet. The subject was pursued no farther, and the gentlemen soon afterwards went away.

# *Chapter 31*

COLONEL FITZWILLIAM'S manners were very much admired at the parsonage, and the ladies all felt that he must add considerably to the pleasure of their engagements at Rosings. It was some days, however, before they received any invitation thither, for while there were visitors in the house, they could not be necessary; and it was not till Easter day, almost a week after the gentlemen's arrival, that they were honoured by such an attention, and then they were merely asked on leaving church to come there in the evening. For the last week they had seen very little of Lady Catherine or her daughter. Colonel Fitzwilliam had called at the parsonage more than once during the time, but Mr. Darcy they had seen only at church.

The invitation was accepted of course, and at a proper hour they joined the party in Lady Catherine's drawing-room. Her ladyship received them civilly, but it was plain that their company was by no means so acceptable as when she could get nobody else; and she was, in fact, almost engrossed by her nephews, speaking to them, especially to Darcy, much more than to any other person in the room.

Colonel Fitzwilliam seemed really glad to see them; anything was a welcome relief to him at Rosings; and Mrs. Collins's pretty friend had moreover caught his fancy very much. He now seated himself by her, and talked so agreeably of Kent and Hertfordshire, of travelling and staying at home, of new books and music, that Elizabeth had never been half so well entertained in that room before; and they conversed with so much spirit and flow, as to draw the attention of Lady Catherine herself, as well as of Mr. Darcy. *His* eyes had been soon and repeatedly turned towards them with a look of curiosity; and that her ladyship after a while shared the feeling, was more openly acknowledged, for she did not scruple to call out,

"What is that you are saying, Fitzwilliam? What is it you are talking of? What are you telling Miss Bennet? Let me hear what it is."

"We are speaking of music, Madam," said he, when no longer able to avoid a reply.

"Of music! Then pray speak aloud. It is of all subjects my delight. I must have my share in the conversation, if you are speaking of music. There are few people in England, I suppose, who have more true enjoyment of music than myself, or a better natural taste. If I had ever learnt, I should have been a great proficient. And so would Anne, if her health had allowed her to apply. I am confident that she would have performed delightfully. How does Georgiana get on, Darcy?"

Mr. Darcy spoke with affectionate praise of his sister's proficiency.

"I am very glad to hear such a good account of her," said Lady Catherine; "and pray tell her from me, that she cannot expect to excel, if she does not practise a great deal."

"I assure you, Madam," he replied, "that she does not need such advice. She practises very constantly."

"So much the better. It cannot be done too much; and when I next write to her, I shall charge her not to neglect it on any account. I often tell young ladies, that no excellence in music is to be acquired, without constant practice. I have told Miss Bennet several times, that she will never play really well, unless she practises more; and though Mrs. Collins has no instrument, she is very welcome, as I have often told her, to come to Rosings every day, and play on the piano-forte in Mrs. Jenkinson's room. She would be in nobody's way, you know, in that part of the house."

Mr. Darcy looked a little ashamed of his aunt's ill-breeding, and made no answer.

When coffee was over, Colonel Fitzwilliam reminded Elizabeth of having promised to play to him; and she sat down directly to the instrument. He drew a chair near her. Lady Catherine listened to half a song, and then talked, as before, to her other nephew; till the latter walked away from her, and moving with his usual deliberation towards the piano-forte, stationed himself so as to command a full view of the fair performer's countenance. Elizabeth saw what he was doing, and at the first convenient pause, turned to him with an arch smile, and said,

"You mean to frighten me, Mr. Darcy, by coming in all this state to hear me? I will not be alarmed though your sister *does* play so well. There is a stubbornness about me that never can bear to be frightened at the will of others. My courage always rises with every attempt to intimidate me."

"I shall not say that you are mistaken," he replied, "because you could not really believe me to entertain any design of alarming you; and I have had the pleasure of your acquaintance long enough to know, that you find great enjoyment in occasionally professing opinions which in fact are not your own."

Elizabeth laughed heartily at this picture of herself, and said to Colonel Fitzwilliam, "Your cousin will give you a very pretty notion of me, and teach you not to believe a word I say. I am particularly unlucky in meeting with a person so well able to expose my real character, in a part of the world, where I had hoped to pass myself off with some degree of credit. Indeed, Mr. Darcy, it is very ungenerous in you to mention all that you knew to my disadvantage in Hertfordshire – and, give me leave to say, very impolitic too – for it is provoking me to retaliate, and such things may come out, as will shock your relations to hear."

"I am not afraid of you," said he, smilingly.

"Pray let me hear what you have to accuse him of," cried Colonel Fitzwilliam. "I should like to know how he behaves among strangers."

"You shall hear then – but prepare yourself for something very dreadful. The first time of my ever seeing him in Hertfordshire, you must know, was at a ball – and at this ball, what do you think he did? He danced only four dances! I am sorry to pain you – but so it was. He danced only four dances, though gentlemen were scarce; and, to my certain knowledge, more than one young lady was sitting down in want of a partner. Mr. Darcy, you cannot deny the fact."

"I had not at that time the honour of knowing any lady in the assembly beyond my own party."

"True; and nobody can ever be introduced in a ball room.

Well, Colonel Fitzwilliam, what do I play next? My fingers wait your orders."

"Perhaps," said Darcy, "I should have judged better, had I sought an introduction, but I am ill qualified to recommend myself to strangers."

"Shall we ask your cousin the reason of this?" said Elizabeth, still addressing Colonel Fitzwilliam. "Shall we ask him why a man of sense and education, and who has lived in the world, is ill qualified to recommend himself to strangers?"

"I can answer your question," said Fitzwilliam, "without applying to him. It is because he will not give himself the trouble."

"I certainly have not the talent which some people possess," said Darcy, "of conversing easily with those I have never seen before. I cannot catch their tone of conversation, or appear interested in their concerns, as I often see done."

"My fingers," said Elizabeth, "do not move over this instrument in the masterly manner which I see so many women's do. They have not the same force or rapidity, and do not produce the same expression. But then I have always supposed it to be my own fault – because I would not take the trouble of practising. It is not that I do not believe *my* fingers as capable as any other woman's of superior execution."

Darcy smiled and said, "You are perfectly right. You have employed your time much better. No one admitted to the privilege of hearing you, can think anything wanting. We neither of us perform to strangers."

Here they were interrupted by Lady Catherine, who called out to know what they were talking of. Elizabeth immediately began playing again. Lady Catherine approached, and, after listening for a few minutes, said to Darcy,

"Miss Bennet would not play at all amiss, if she practised more, and could have the advantage of a London master. She has a very good notion of fingering, though her taste is not equal to

Anne's. Anne would have been a delightful performer, had her health allowed her to learn."

Elizabeth looked at Darcy to see how cordially he assented to his cousin's praise; but neither at that moment nor at any other could she discern any symptom of love; and from the whole of his behaviour to Miss de Bourgh she derived this comfort for Miss Bingley, that he might have been just as likely to marry *her*, had she been his relation.

Lady Catherine continued her remarks on Elizabeth's performance, mixing with them many instructions on execution and taste. Elizabeth received them with all the forbearance of civility; and at the request of the gentlemen remained at the instrument till her ladyship's carriage was ready to take them all home.

# *Chapter 32*

ELIZABETH WAS sitting by herself the next morning, and writing to Jane, while Mrs. Collins and Maria were gone on business into the village, when she was startled by a ring at the door, the certain signal of a visitor. As she had heard no carriage, she thought it not unlikely to be Lady Catherine, and under that apprehension was putting away her half-finished letter that she might escape all impertinent questions, when the door opened, and to her very great surprise, Mr. Darcy, and Mr. Darcy only, entered the room.

He seemed astonished too on finding her alone, and apologised for his intrusion, by letting her know that he had understood all the ladies to be within.

They then sat down, and when her enquiries after Rosings

were made, seemed in danger of sinking into total silence. It was absolutely necessary, therefore, to think of something, and in this emergence recollecting *when* she had seen him last in Hertfordshire, and feeling curious to know what he would say on the subject of their hasty departure, she observed,

"How very suddenly you all quitted Netherfield last November, Mr. Darcy! It must have been a most agreeable surprise to Mr. Bingley to see you all after him so soon; for, if I recollect right, he went but the day before. He and his sisters were well, I hope, when you left London?"

"Perfectly so, – I thank you."

She found that she was to receive no other answer – and, after a short pause added,

"I think I have understood that Mr. Bingley has not much idea of ever returning to Netherfield again?"

"I have never heard him say so; but it is probable that he may spend very little of his time there in future. He has many friends, and he is at a time of life when friends and engagements are continually increasing."

"If he means to be but little at Netherfield, it would be better for the neighbourhood that he should give up the place entirely, for then we might possibly get a settled family there. But perhaps Mr. Bingley did not take the house so much for the convenience of the neighbourhood as for his own, and we must expect him to keep or quit it on the same principle."

"I should not be surprised," said Darcy, "if he were to give it up, as soon as any eligible purchase offers."

Elizabeth made no answer. She was afraid of talking longer of his friend; and, having nothing else to say, was now determined to leave the trouble of finding a subject to him.

He took the hint, and soon began with, "This seems a very comfortable house. Lady Catherine, I believe, did a great deal to it when Mr. Collins first came to Hunsford."

"I believe she did – and I am sure she could not have bestowed her kindness on a more grateful object."

"Mr. Collins appears to be very fortunate in his choice of a wife."

"Yes, indeed, his friends may well rejoice in his having met with one of the very few sensible women who would have accepted him, or have made him happy if they had. My friend has an excellent understanding – though I am not certain that I consider her marrying Mr. Collins as the wisest thing she ever did. She seems perfectly happy, however, and in a prudential light, it is certainly a very good match for her."

"It must be very agreeable for her to be settled within so easy a distance of her own family and friends."

"An easy distance do you call it? It is nearly fifty miles."

"And what is fifty miles of good road? Little more than half a day's journey. Yes, I call it a *very* easy distance."

"I should never have considered the distance as one of the *advantages* of the match," cried Elizabeth. "I should never have said Mrs. Collins was settled *near* her family."

"It is a proof of your own attachment to Hertfordshire. Anything beyond the very neighbourhood of Longbourn, I suppose, would appear far."

As he spoke there was a sort of smile, which Elizabeth fancied she understood; he must be supposing her to be thinking of Jane and Netherfield, and she blushed as she answered,

"I do not mean to say that a woman may not be settled too near her family. The far and the near must be relative, and depend on many varying circumstances. Where there is fortune to make the expenses of travelling unimportant, distance becomes no evil. But that is not the case *here*. Mr. and Mrs. Collins have a comfortable income, but not such a one as will allow of frequent journeys – and I am persuaded my friend would not call herself *near* her family under less than *half* the present distance."

Mr. Darcy drew his chair a little towards her, and said, "*You* cannot have a right to such very strong local attachment. *You* cannot have been always at Longbourn."

Elizabeth looked surprised. The gentleman experienced some change of feeling; he drew back his chair, took a newspaper from the table, and, glancing over it, said, in a colder voice,

"Are you pleased with Kent?"

A short dialogue on the subject of the country ensued, on either side calm and concise – and soon put an end to by the entrance of Charlotte and her sister, just returned from her walk. The tête-à-tête surprised them. Mr. Darcy related the mistake which had occasioned his intruding on Miss Bennet, and after sitting a few minutes longer without saying much to anybody, went away.

"What can be the meaning of this!" said Charlotte, as soon as he was gone. "My dear Eliza he must be in love with you, or he would never have called us in this familiar way."

But when Elizabeth told of his silence, it did not seem very likely, even to Charlotte's wishes, to be the case; and after various conjectures, they could at last only suppose his visit to proceed from the difficulty of finding anything to do, which was the more probable from the time of year. All field sports were over. Within doors there was Lady Catherine, books, and a billiard table, but gentlemen cannot always be within doors; and in the nearness of the Parsonage, or the pleasantness of the walk to it, or of the people who lived in it, the two cousins found a temptation from this period of walking thither almost every day. They called at various times of the morning, sometimes separately, sometimes together, and now and then accompanied by their aunt. It was plain to them all that Colonel Fitzwilliam came because he had pleasure in their society, a persuasion which of course recommended him still more; and Elizabeth was reminded by her own satisfaction in being with him, as well as by his evident admiration of her, of her former favourite George Wickham; and though, in comparing them, she saw there was less captivating softness in Colonel Fitzwilliam's manners, she believed he might have the best informed mind.

But why Mr. Darcy came so often to the Parsonage, it was more difficult to understand. It could not be for society, as he frequently sat there ten minutes together without opening his lips; and when he did speak, it seemed the effect of necessity rather than of choice – a sacrifice to propriety, not a pleasure to himself. He seldom appeared really animated. Mrs. Collins knew not what to make of him. Colonel Fitzwilliam's occasionally laughing at his stupidity, proved that he was generally different, which her own knowledge of him could not have told her; and as she would have liked to believe this change the effect of love, and the object of that love, her friend Eliza, she set herself seriously to work to find it out. – She watched him whenever they were at Rosings, and whenever he came to Hunsford; but without much success. He certainly looked at her friend a great deal, but the expression of that look was disputable. It was an earnest, steadfast gaze, but she often doubted whether there were much admiration in it, and sometimes it seemed nothing but absence of mind.

She had once or twice suggested to Elizabeth the possibility of his being partial to her, but Elizabeth always laughed at the idea; and Mrs. Collins did not think it right to press the subject, from the danger of raising expectations which might only end in disappointment; for in her opinion it admitted not of a doubt, that all her friend's dislike would vanish, if she could suppose him to be in her power.

In her kind schemes for Elizabeth, she sometimes planned her marrying Colonel Fitzwilliam. He was beyond comparison the pleasantest man; he certainly admired her, and his situation in life was most eligible; but, to counterbalance these advantages, Mr. Darcy had considerable patronage in the church, and his cousin could have none at all.

## *Chapter 33*

More than once did Elizabeth in her ramble within the Park, unexpectedly meet Mr. Darcy. – She felt all the perverseness of the mischance that should bring him where no one else was brought; and to prevent its ever happening again, took care to inform him at first, that it was a favourite haunt of hers. – How it could occur a second time therefore was very odd! – Yet it did, and even a third. It seemed like wilful ill-nature, or a voluntary penance, for on these occasions it was not merely a few formal enquiries and an awkward pause and then away, but he actually thought it necessary to turn back and walk with her. He never said a great deal, nor did she give herself the trouble of talking or of listening much; but it struck her in the course of their third rencontre that he was asking some odd unconnected questions – about her pleasure in being at Hunsford, her love of solitary walks, and her opinion of Mr. and Mrs. Collins's happiness; and that in speaking of Rosings and her not perfectly understanding the house, he seemed to expect that whenever she came into Kent again she would be staying *there* too. His words seemed to imply it. Could he have Colonel Fitzwilliam in his thoughts? She supposed, if he meant anything, he must mean an allusion to what might arise in that quarter. It distressed her a little, and she was quite glad to find herself at the gate in the pales opposite the Parsonage.

She was engaged one day as she walked, in re-perusing Jane's last letter, and dwelling on some passages which proved that Jane had not written in spirits, when, instead of being again surprised by Mr. Darcy, she saw on looking up that Colonel Fitzwilliam was meeting her. Putting away the letter immediately and forcing a smile, she said,

"I did not know before that you ever walked this way."

"I have been making the tour of the Park," he replied, "as I generally do every year, and intend to close it with a call at the Parsonage. Are you going much farther?"

"No, I should have turned in a moment."

And accordingly she did turn, and they walked towards the Parsonage together.

"Do you certainly leave Kent on Saturday?" said she.

"Yes – if Darcy does not put it off again. But I am at his disposal. He arranges the business just as he pleases."

"And if not able to please himself in the arrangement, he has at least pleasure in the great power of choice. I do not know anybody who seems more to enjoy the power of doing what he likes than Mr. Darcy."

"He likes to have his own way very well," replied Colonel Fitzwilliam. "But so we all do. It is only that he has better means of having it than many others, because he is rich, and many others are poor. I speak feelingly. A younger son, you know, must be inured to self-denial and dependence."

"In my opinion, the younger son of an Earl can know very little of either. Now, seriously, what have you ever known of self-denial and dependence? When have you been prevented by want of money from going wherever you chose, or procuring anything you had a fancy for?"

"These are home questions – and perhaps I cannot say that I have experienced many hardships of that nature. But in matters of greater weight, I may suffer from the want of money. Younger sons cannot marry where they like."

"Unless where they like women of fortune, which I think they very often do."

Our habits of expense make us too dependent, and there are not many in my rank of life who can afford to marry without some attention to money."

"Is this," thought Elizabeth, "meant for me?" and she coloured at the idea; but, recovering herself, said in a lively tone, "And pray, what is the usual price of an Earl's younger son? Unless the elder brother is very sickly, I suppose you would not ask above fifty thousand pounds."

He answered her in the same style, and the subject dropped. To interrupt a silence which might make him fancy her affected with what had passed, she soon afterwards said,

"I imagine your cousin brought you down with him chiefly for the sake of having someone at his disposal. I wonder he does not marry, to secure a lasting convenience of that kind. But, perhaps his sister does as well for the present, and, as she is under his sole care, he may do what he likes with her."

"No," said Colonel Fitzwilliam, "that is an advantage which he must divide with me. I am joined with him in the guardianship of Miss Darcy."

"Are you indeed? And pray what sort of guardians do you make? Does your charge give you much trouble? Young ladies of her age, are sometimes a little difficult to manage, and if she has the true Darcy spirit, she may like to have her own way."

As she spoke, she observed him looking at her earnestly, and the manner in which he immediately asked her why she supposed Miss Darcy likely to give them any uneasiness, convinced her that she had somehow or other got pretty near the truth. She directly replied,

"You need not be frightened. I never heard any harm of her;

and I dare say she is one of the most tractable creatures in the world. She is a very great favourite with some ladies of my acquaintance, Mrs. Hurst and Miss Bingley. I think I have heard you say that you know them."

"I know them a little. Their brother is a pleasant gentleman-like man – he is a great friend of Darcy's."

"Oh! yes," said Elizabeth drily – "Mr. Darcy is uncommonly kind to Mr. Bingley, and takes a prodigious deal of care of him."

"Care of him! – Yes, I really believe Darcy *does* take care of him in those points where he most wants care. From something that he told me on our journey hither, I have reason to think Bingley very much indebted to him. But I ought to beg his pardon, for I have no right to suppose that Bingley was the person meant. It was all conjecture."

"What is it you mean?"

"It is a circumstance which Darcy of course would not wish to be generally known, because if it were to get round to the lady's family, it would be an unpleasant thing."

"You may depend upon my not mentioning it."

"And remember that I have not much reason for supposing it to be Bingley. What he told me was merely this; that he congratulated himself on having lately saved a friend from the inconveniences of a most imprudent marriage, but without mentioning names or any other particulars, and I only suspected it to be Bingley from believing him the kind of young man to get into a scrape of that sort, and from knowing them to have been together the whole of last summer."

"Did Mr. Darcy give you reasons for this interference?"

"I understood that there were some very strong objections against the lady."

"And what arts did he use to separate them?"

"He did not talk to me of his own arts," said Fitzwilliam

smiling. "He only told me, what I have now told you."

Elizabeth made no answer, and walked on, her heart swelling with indignation. After watching her a little, Fitzwilliam asked her why she was so thoughtful.

"I am thinking of what you have been telling me," said she. "Your cousin's conduct does not suit my feelings. Why was he to be the judge?"

"You are rather disposed to call his interference officious?"

"I do not see what right Mr. Darcy had to decide on the propriety of his friend's inclination, or why, upon his own judgement alone, he was to determine and direct in what manner that friend was to be happy. But," she continued, recollecting herself, "as we know none of the particulars, it is not fair to condemn him. It is not to be supposed that there was much affection in the case."

"That is not an unnatural surmise," said Fitzwilliam, "but it is lessening of the honour of my cousin's triumph very sadly."

This was spoken jestingly, but it appeared to her so just a picture of Mr. Darcy, that she would not trust herself with an answer; and, therefore, abruptly changing the conversation, talked on indifferent matters until they reached the parsonage. There, shut into her own room, as soon as their visitor left them, she could think without interruption of all that she had heard. It was not to be supposed that any other people could be meant than those with whom she was connected. There could not exist in the world *two* men, over whom Mr. Darcy could have such boundless influence. That he had been concerned in the measures taken to separate Mr. Bingley and Jane, she had never doubted; but she had always attributed to Miss Bingley the principal design and arrangement of them. If his own vanity, however, did not mislead him, *he* was the cause, his pride and caprice were the cause of all that Jane had suffered, and still continued to suffer. He had ruined for a while every hope of happiness for the most affectionate, generous heart in the world; and no one could say how lasting an evil he might have inflicted.

"There were some very strong objections against the lady," were Colonel Fitzwilliam's words, and those strong objections probably were, her having one uncle who was a country attorney, and another who was in business in London.

"To Jane herself," she exclaimed, "there could be no possibility of objection. All loveliness and goodness as she is! Her understanding excellent, her mind improved, and her manners captivating. Neither could anything be urged against my father, who, though with some peculiarities, has abilities which Mr. Darcy himself need not disdain, and respectability which he will probably never reach." When she thought of her mother indeed, her confidence gave way a little, but she would not allow that any objections *there* had material weight with Mr. Darcy, whose pride, she was convinced, would receive a deeper wound from the want of importance in his friend's connections, than from their want of sense; and she was quite decided at last, that he had been partly governed by this worst kind of pride, and partly by the wish of retaining Mr. Bingley for his sister.

The agitation and tears which the subject occasioned, brought on a headache; and it grew so much worse towards the evening that, added to her unwillingness to see Mr. Darcy, it determined her not to attend her cousins to Rosings, where they were engaged to drink tea. Mrs. Collins, seeing that she was really un-well, did not press her to go, and as much as possible prevented her husband from pressing her, but Mr. Collins could not conceal his apprehension of Lady Catherine's being rather displeased by her staying at home.

# Chapter 34

WHEN THEY were gone, Elizabeth, as if intending to exasperate herself as much as possible against Mr. Darcy, chose for her employment the examination of all the letters which Jane had written to her since her being in Kent. They contained no actual complaint, nor was there any revival of past occurrences, or any communication of present suffering. But in all, and in almost every line of each, there was a want of that cheerfulness which had been used to characterise her style, and which, proceeding from the serenity of a mind at ease with itself, and kindly disposed towards everyone, had been scarcely ever clouded. Elizabeth noticed every sentence conveying the idea of uneasiness, with an attention which it had hardly received on the first perusal. Mr. Darcy's shameful boast of what misery he had been able to inflict, gave her a keener sense of her sister's sufferings. It was some consolation to think that his visit to Rosings was to end on the day after the next, and a still greater, that in less than a fortnight she should herself be with Jane again, and enabled to contribute to the recovery of her spirits, by all that affection could do.

She could not think of Darcy's leaving Kent, without remembering that his cousin was to go with him; but Colonel Fitzwilliam had made it clear that he had no intentions at all, and agreeable as he was, she did not mean to be unhappy about him.

While settling this point, she was suddenly roused by the sound of the door bell, and her spirits were a little fluttered by the idea of its being Colonel Fitzwilliam himself, who had once before called late in the evening, and might now come to enquire particularly after her. But this idea was soon banished, and her spirits were very differently affected, when, to her utter amazement, she saw Mr. Darcy walk into the room. In an hurried manner he immediately began an enquiry after her health, imputing his visit to a wish of hearing that she were better. She answered him with cold civility. He sat down for a few moments, and then getting up walked about the room. Elizabeth was surprised, but said not a word. After a silence of several minutes he came towards her in an agitated manner, and thus began:

"In vain I have struggled. It will not do. My feelings will not be repressed. You must allow me to tell you how ardently I admire and love you."

Elizabeth's astonishment was beyond expression. She stared, coloured, doubted, and was silent. This he considered sufficient encouragement, and the avowal of all that he felt and had long felt for her, immediately followed. He spoke well, but there were feelings besides those of the heart to be detailed, and he was not more eloquent on the subject of tenderness than of pride. His sense of her inferiority – of its being a degradation – of the family obstacles which judgment had always opposed to inclination, were dwelt on with a warmth which seemed due to the consequence he was wounding, but was very unlikely to recommend his suit.

In spite of her deeply-rooted dislike, she could not be insensible to the compliment of such a man's affection, and though her intentions did not vary for an instant, she was at first sorry for the pain he was to receive; till, roused to resentment by his subsequent language, she lost all compassion in anger. She tried, however, to compose herself to answer him with patience, when he should have done. He concluded with representing to her the strength of that attachment which, in spite of all his endeavours, he had found impossible to conquer; and with expressing his hope that it would now be rewarded by her acceptance of his hand. As he said this, she could easily see that he had no doubt of a favourable answer. He *spoke* of apprehension and anxiety, but his countenance expressed real security. Such a circumstance could only exasperate farther, and when he ceased, the colour rose into her cheeks, and she said,

"In such cases as this, it is, I believe, the established mode to express a sense of obligation for the sentiments avowed, however unequally they may be returned. It is natural that obligation should be felt, and if I could *feel* gratitude, I would now thank you. But I cannot – I have never desired your good opinion, and you have certainly bestowed it most unwillingly. I am sorry to have occasioned pain to anyone. It has been most unconsciously done, however, and I hope will be of short duration. The feelings which, you tell me, have long prevented the acknowledgment of your regard, can have little difficulty in overcoming it after this explanation."

Mr. Darcy, who was leaning against the mantelpiece with his eyes fixed on her face, seemed to catch her words with no less resentment than surprise. His complexion became pale with anger, and the disturbance of his mind was visible in every feature. He was struggling for the appearance of composure, and would not open his lips, till he believed himself to have attained it. The pause was to Elizabeth's feelings dreadful. At length, with a voice of forced calmness, he said,

"And this is the reply which I am to have the honour of expecting! I might, perhaps, wish to be informed why, with so little *endeavour* at civility, I am thus rejected. But it is of small importance."

"I might as well enquire," replied she, "why with so evident a design of offending and insulting me, you chose to tell me that you liked me against your will, against your reason, and even against your character? Was not this some excuse for incivility, if I *was* uncivil? But I have other provocations. You know I have. Had not my feelings decided against you, had they been indifferent, or had they even been favourable, do you think that any consideration would tempt me to accept the man, who has been the means of ruining, perhaps for ever, the happiness of a most beloved sister?"

As she pronounced these words, Mr. Darcy changed colour; but the emotion was short, and he listened without attempting to interrupt her while she continued,

"I have every reason in the world to think ill of you. No motive can excuse the unjust and ungenerous part you acted *there*. You dare not, you cannot deny that you have been the principal, if not the only means of dividing them from each other, of exposing one to the censure of the world for caprice and instability, the other to its derision for disappointed hopes, and involving them both in misery of the acutest kind."

She paused, and saw with no slight indignation that he was listening with an air which proved him wholly unmoved by any feeling of remorse. He even looked at her with a smile of affected incredulity.

"Can you deny that you have done it?" she repeated.

With assumed tranquillity he then replied, "I have no wish of denying that I did everything in my power to separate my friend from your sister, or that I rejoice in my success. Towards *him* I have been kinder than towards myself."

Elizabeth disdained the appearance of noticing this civil reflection, but its meaning did not escape, nor was it likely to conciliate her.

"But it is not merely this affair," she continued, "on which my dislike is founded. Long before it had taken place, my opinion of you was decided. Your character was unfolded in the recital which I received many months ago from Mr. Wickham. On this subject, what can you have to say? In what imaginary act of friendship can you here defend yourself? or under what misrepresentation, can you here impose upon others?"

"You take an eager interest in that gentleman's concerns," said Darcy in a less tranquil tone, and with a heightened colour.

"Who that knows what his misfortunes have been, can help feeling an interest in him?"

"His misfortunes!" repeated Darcy contemptuously; "yes, his misfortunes have been great indeed."

"And of your infliction," cried Elizabeth with energy. "You have reduced him to his present state of poverty, comparative poverty. You have withheld the advantages, which you must know to have been designed for him. You have deprived the best years of his life, of that independence which was no less his due than his desert. You have done all this! and yet you can treat the mention of his misfortunes with contempt and ridicule."

"And this," cried Darcy, as he walked with quick steps across the room, "is your opinion of me! This is the estimation in which you hold me! I thank you for explaining it so fully. My faults, according to this calculation, are heavy indeed! But perhaps," added he, stopping in his walk, and turning towards her, "these offences might have been overlooked, had you not your pride been hurt by my honest confession of the scruples that had long prevented my forming any serious design. These bitter accusations might have been suppressed, had I with greater policy concealed my struggles, and flattered you into the belief of my being impelled by unqualified, unalloyed inclination; by reason, by reflection, by everything. But disguise of every sort is my abhorrence. Nor am I ashamed of the feelings I related. They were natural and just. Could you expect me to rejoice in the inferiority of your connections? To congratulate myself on the hope of relations, whose condition in life is so decidedly beneath my own?"

Elizabeth felt herself growing more angry every moment; yet she tried to the utmost to speak with composure when she said,

"You are mistaken, Mr. Darcy, if you suppose that the mode of your declaration affected me in any other way, than as it spared me the concern which I might have felt in refusing you, had you behaved in a more gentleman-like manner."

She saw him start at this, but he said nothing, and she continued,

"You could not have made me the offer of your hand in any possible way that would have tempted me to accept it."

Again his astonishment was obvious; and he looked at her with an expression of mingled incredulity and mortification. She went on.

"From the very beginning, from the first moment I may almost say, of my acquaintance with you, your manners impressing me with the fullest belief of your arrogance, your conceit, and your selfish disdain of the feelings of others, were such as to form that ground-work of disapprobation, on which succeeding events have built so immovable a dislike; and I had not known you a month before I felt that you were the last man in the world whom I could ever be prevailed on to marry."

"You have said quite enough, madam. I perfectly comprehend your feelings, and have now only to be ashamed of what my own have been. Forgive me for having taken up so much of your time, and accept my best wishes for your health and happiness."

And with these words he hastily left the room, and Elizabeth heard him the next moment open the front door and quit the house.

The tumult of her mind was now painfully great. She knew not how to support herself, and from actual weakness sat down and cried for half an hour. Her astonishment, as she reflected on what had passed, was increased by every review of it. That she should receive an offer of marriage from Mr. Darcy! that he should have been in love with her for so many months! so much in love as to wish to marry her in spite of all the objections which had made him prevent his friend's marrying her sister, and which must appear at least with equal force in his own case, was almost incredible! it was gratifying to have inspired unconsciously so strong an affection. But his pride, his abominable pride, his shameless avowal of what he had done with respect to Jane, his unpardonable assurance in acknowledging, though he could not justify it, and the unfeeling manner in which he had mentioned Mr. Wickham, his cruelty towards whom he had not attempted to deny, soon overcame the pity which the consideration of his attachment had for a moment excited.

She continued in very agitating reflections till the sound of Lady Catherine's carriage made her feel how unequal she was to encounter Charlotte's observation, and hurried her away to her room.

# *Chapter 35*

ELIZABETH AWOKE the next morning to the same thoughts and meditations which had at length closed her eyes. She could not yet recover from the surprise of what had happened; it was impossible to think of anything else, and totally indisposed for employment, she resolved soon after breakfast to indulge herself in air and exercise. She was proceeding directly to her favourite walk, when the recollection of Mr. Darcy's sometimes coming there stopped her, and instead of entering the park, she turned up the lane, which led farther from the turnpike road. The park paling was still the boundary on one side, and she soon passed one of the gates into the ground.

After walking two or three times along that part of the lane, she was tempted, by the pleasantness of the morning, to stop at the gates and look into the park. The five weeks which she had now passed in Kent, had made a great difference in the country, and every day was adding to the verdure of the early trees. She was on the point of continuing her walk, when she caught a glimpse of a gentleman within the sort of grove which edged the park; he was moving that way; and fearful of its being Mr. Darcy, she was directly retreating. But the person who advanced, was now near enough to see her, and stepping forward with eagerness, pronounced her name. She had turned away, but on hearing herself called, though in a voice which proved it to be Mr. Darcy, she moved again towards the gate. He had by that time reached it also, and holding out a letter, which she instinctively took, said with a look of haughty composure, "I have been walking in the grove some time in the hope of meeting you. Will you do me the honour of reading that letter?" – And then, with a slight bow, turned again into the plantation, and was soon out of sight.

With no expectation of pleasure, but with the strongest curiosity, Elizabeth opened the letter, and to her still increasing wonder, perceived an envelope containing two sheets of letter paper, written quite through, in a very close hand. – The envelope itself was likewise full. – Pursuing her way along the lane, she then began it. It was dated from Rosings, at eight o'clock in the morning, and was as follows:-

"Be not alarmed, Madam, on receiving this letter, by the apprehension of its containing any repetition of those sentiments, or renewal of those offers, which were last night so disgusting to you. I write without any intention of paining you, or humbling myself, by dwelling on wishes, which, for the happiness of both, cannot be too soon forgotten; and the effort which the formation, and the perusal of this letter must occasion, should have been spared had not my character required it to be written and read. You must, therefore, pardon the freedom with which I demand your attention; your feelings, I know, will bestow it unwillingly, but I demand it of your justice.

"Two offences of a very different nature, and by no means of equal magnitude, you last night laid to my charge. The first mentioned was, that, regardless of the sentiments of either, I had detached Mr. Bingley from your sister, – and the other, that I had, in defiance of various claims, in defiance of honour and humanity, ruined the immediate prosperity, and blasted the prospects of Mr. Wickham. – Wilfully and wantonly to have thrown off the companion of my youth, the acknowledged favourite of my father, a young man who had scarcely any other dependence than on our patronage, and who had been brought up to expect its exertion, would be a depravity, to which the separation of two young persons, whose affection could be the growth of only a few weeks, could bear no comparison. – But from the severity of that blame which was last night so liberally bestowed, respecting each circumstance, I shall hope to be in the future secured, when the following account of my actions and their motives has been read. – If, in the explanation of them which is due to myself, I am under the necessity of relating feelings which may be offensive to yours, I can only say that I am sorry. – The necessity must be obeyed – and farther apology would be absurd. – I had not been long in Hertfordshire, before I saw, in common with others, that Bingley preferred your eldest sister, to any other young woman in the country. – But it was not till the evening of the dance at Netherfield that I had any apprehension of his feeling a serious attachment. – I had often seen him in love before. – At that ball, while I had the honour of dancing with you, I was first made acquainted, by Sir William Lucas's accidental information, that Bingley's attentions to your sister had given rise to a general expectation of their marriage. He spoke of it as a certain event, of which the time alone could be undecided. From that moment I observed my friend's behaviour attentively; and I could then perceive that his partiality for Miss Bennet was beyond what I had ever witnessed in him. Your sister I also watched. – Her look and manners were open, cheerful and engaging as ever, but without any symptom of peculiar regard, and I remained convinced from the evening's scrutiny, that though she received his attentions with pleasure, she did not invite them by any participation of sentiment. – If *you* have not been mistaken here, *I* must have been in error. Your superior knowledge of your sister must make the latter probable. – If it be so, if I have been misled by such error, to inflict pain on her, your resentment has not been unreasonable. But I shall not scruple to assert, that the serenity of your sister's countenance and air was such, as might have given the most acute observer, a conviction that, however amiable her temper, her heart was not likely to be easily touched. – That I was desirous of believing her indifferent is certain. – but I will venture to say that my investigations and decisions are not usually influenced by my hopes or fears. – I did not believe her to be indifferent because I wished it; – I believed it on impartial conviction, as truly as I wished it in reason. – My objections to the marriage were not merely those, which I last night acknowledged to have required the utmost force of passion to put aside, in my own case; the want of connection could not be so great an evil to my friend as to me. – But there were other causes of repugnance; – causes which, though still existing, and existing to an equal degree in both instances, I had myself endeavoured to forget, because they were not immediately before me. – These causes must be stated, though briefly. – The situation of your mother's family, though objectionable, was nothing in comparison of that total want of propriety so frequently, so almost uniformly betrayed by herself, by your three younger sisters, and occasionally even by your father. – Pardon me. – It pains me to offend you. But amidst your concern for the defects of your nearest relations, and your displeasure at this representation of them, let it give you consolation to consider that, to have conducted yourselves so as to avoid any share of the like censure, is praise no less generally bestowed on you and your elder sister, than it is honourable to the sense and disposition of both. – I will only say farther, that from what passed that evening, my opinion of all parties was confirmed, and every inducement heightened, which could have led me before, to preserve my friend from what I esteemed a most unhappy connection. – He left Netherfield for London, on the day following, as you, I am certain, remember, with the design of soon returning. – The part which I acted, is now to be explained. – His sisters' uneasiness had been equally excited with my own; our coincidence of feeling was soon discovered; and, alike sensible that no time was to be lost in detaching their brother, we shortly resolved on joining him directly in London. – We accordingly went – and there I readily engaged in the office of pointing out to my friend the certain evils of such a choice. – I described, and enforced them earnestly. – But, however this remonstrance might have staggered or delayed his determination, I do not suppose that it would ultimately have prevented the marriage, had it not been seconded by the assurance which I hesitated not in giving, of your sister's indifference. He had before believed her to return his affection with sincere, if not with equal regard. – But Bingley has great natural modesty, with a stronger dependence on my judgement than on his own. – To convince him, therefore, that he had deceived himself, was no very difficult point. To persuade him against returning into Hertfordshire, when that conviction had been given, was scarcely the work of a moment. – I cannot blame myself for having done this much. There is but one part of my conduct in the whole affair, on which I do not reflect with satisfaction; it is that I condescended to adopt the measures of art so far as to conceal from him your sister's being in town. I knew it myself, as it was known to Miss Bingley; but her brother is even yet ignorant of it. – That they might have met without ill consequence, is perhaps probable; – but his regard did not appear to me enough extinguished for him to see her without some danger. – Perhaps this concealment, this disguise, was beneath me. – It is done, however, and it was done for the best. – On this subject I have nothing more to say, no other apology to offer. If I have wounded your sister's feelings, it was unknowingly done; and though the motives which governed me may to you very naturally appear insufficient, I have not yet learnt to condemn them. – With respect to that other, more weighty accusation, of having injured Mr.

Wickham, I can only refute it by laying before you the whole of his connection with my family. Of what he has *particularly* accused me I am ignorant; but of the truth of what I shall relate, I can summon more than one witness of undoubted veracity. Mr. Wickham is the son of a very respectable man, who had for many years the management of all the Pemberley estates, and whose good conduct in the discharge of his trust, naturally inclined my father to be of service to him, and on George Wickham, who was his god-son, his kindness was therefore liberally bestowed. My father supported him at school, and afterwards at Cambridge; – most important assistance, as his own father, always poor from the extravagance of his wife, would have been unable to give him a gentleman's education. My father was not only fond of this young man's society, whose manners were always engaging; he had also the highest opinion of him, and hoping the church would be his profession, intended to provide for him in it. As for myself, it is many, many years since I first began to think of him in a very different manner. The vicious propensities – the want of principle which he was careful to guard from the knowledge of his best friend, could not escape the observation of a young man of nearly the same age with himself, and who had opportunities of seeing him in unguarded moments, which Mr. Darcy could not have. Here again shall give you pain – to what degree you only can tell. But whatever may be the sentiments which Mr. Wickham has created, a suspicion of their nature shall not prevent me from unfolding his real character. It adds even another motive. My excellent father died about five years ago; and his attachment to Mr. Wickham was to the last so steady, that in his will he particularly recommended it to me, to promote his advancement in the best manner that his profession might allow, and if he took orders, desired that a valuable family living might be his as soon as it became vacant. There was also a legacy of one thousand pounds. His own father did not long survive mine, and within half a year from these events, Mr. Wickham wrote to inform me that, having finally resolved against taking orders, he hoped I should not think it unreasonable for him to expect some more immediate pecuniary advantage, in lieu of the preferment, by which he could not be benefited. He had some intention, he added, of studying law, and I must be aware that the interest of one thousand pounds would be a very insufficient support therein. I rather wished, than believed him to be sincere; but at any rate, was perfectly ready to accede to his proposal. I knew that Mr. Wickham ought not to be a clergyman. The business was therefore soon settled. He resigned all claim to assistance in the church, were it possible that he could ever be in a situation to receive it, and accepted in return three thousand pounds. All connection between us seemed now dissolved. I thought too ill of him, to invite him to Pemberley, or admit his society in town. In town I believe he chiefly lived, but his studying the law was a mere pretence, and being now free from all restraint, his life was a life of idleness and dissipation. For about three years I heard little of him; but on the decease of the incumbent of the living which had been designed for him, he applied to me again by letter for the presentation. His circumstances, he assured me, and I had no difficulty in believing it, were exceedingly bad. He had found the law a most unprofitable study, and was now absolutely resolved on being ordained, if I would present him to the living in question – of which he trusted there could be little doubt, as he was well assured that I had no other person to provide for, and I could not have forgotten my revered father's intentions. You will hardly blame me for refusing to comply with this entreaty, or for resisting every repetition of it. His resentment was in proportion to the distress of his circumstances – and he was doubtless as violent in his abuse of me to others, as in his reproaches to myself. After this period, every appearance of acquaintance was dropped. How he lived I know not. But last summer he was again most painfully obtruded on my notice. I must now mention a circumstance which I would wish to forget myself, and which no obligation less than the present should induce me to unfold to any human being. Having said thus much, I feel no doubt of your secrecy. My sister, who is more than ten years my junior, was left to the guardianship of my mother's nephew, Colonel Fitzwilliam, and myself. About a year ago, she was taken from school, and an establishment formed for her in London; and last summer she went with the lady who presided over it, to Ramsgate; and thither also went Mr. Wickham, undoubtedly by design; for there proved to have been a prior acquaintance between him and Mrs. Younge, in whose character we were most unhappily deceived; and by her connivance and aid, he so far recommended himself to Georgiana, whose affectionate heart retained a strong impression of his kindness to her as child, that she was persuaded to believe herself in love, and to consent to an elopement. She was then but fifteen, which must be her excuse; and after stating her imprudence, I am happy to add, that I owed the knowledge of it to herself. I joined them unexpectedly a day or two before the intended elopement, and then Georgiana, unable to support the idea of grieving and offending a brother whom she almost looked up to as a father, acknowledged the whole to me. You may imagine what I felt and how I acted. Regard for my sister's credit and feelings prevented any public exposure, but I wrote to Mr. Wickham, who left the place immediately, and Mrs. Younge was of course removed from her charge. Mr. Wickham's chief object was unquestionably my sister's fortune, which is thirty thousand pounds; but I cannot help supposing that the hope of revenging himself on me, was a strong inducement. His revenge would have been complete indeed. This, madam, is a faithful narrative of every event in which we have been concerned together; and if you do not absolutely reject it as false, you will, I hope, acquit me henceforth of cruelty towards Mr. Wickham. I know not in what manner, under what form of falsehood he has imposed on you; but his success is not perhaps to be wondered at. Ignorant as you previously were of everything concerning either, detection could not be in your power, and suspicion certainly not in your inclination. You may possibly wonder why all this was not told you last night. But I was not then master enough of myself to know what could or ought to be revealed. For the truth of everything here related, I can appeal more particularly to the testimony of Colonel Fitzwilliam, who from our near relationship and constant intimacy, and still more as one of the executors of my father's will, has been unavoidably acquainted with every particular of these transactions. If your abhorrence of *me* should make *my* assertions valueless, you cannot be prevented by the same cause from confiding in my cousin; and that there may be the possibility of consulting him, I shall endeavour to find some opportunity of putting this letter in your hands in the course of the morning. I will only add, God bless you.

'FITZWILLIAM DARCY.'

## Chapter 36

IF ELIZABETH, when Mr. Darcy gave her the letter, did not expect it to contain a renewal of his offers, she had formed no expectation at all of its contents. But such as they were, it may well be supposed how eagerly she went through them, and what a contrariety of emotion they excited. Her feelings as she read were scarcely to be defined. With amazement did she first understand that he believed any apology to be in his power; and steadfastly was she persuaded that he could have no explanation to give, which a just sense of shame would not conceal. With a strong prejudice against everything he might say, she began his account of what had happened at Netherfield. She read, with an eagerness which hardly left her power of comprehension, and from impatience of knowing what the next sentence might bring, was incapable of attending to the sense of the one before her eyes. His belief of her sister's insensibility, she instantly resolved to be false; and his account of the real, the worst objections to the match, made her too angry to have any wish of doing him justice. He expressed no regret for what he had done which satisfied her; his style was not penitent, but haughty. It was all pride and insolence.

But when this subject was succeeded by his account of Mr. Wickham, when she read with somewhat clearer attention, a relation of events, which, if true, must overthrow every cherished opinion of his worth, and which bore so alarming an affinity to his own history of himself, her feelings were yet more acutely painful and more difficult of definition. Astonishment, apprehension, and even horror, oppressed her. She wished to discredit it entirely, repeatedly exclaiming, "This must be false! This cannot be! This must be the grossest falsehood!"– and when she had gone through the whole letter, though scarcely knowing anything of the last page or two, put it hastily away, protesting that she would not regard it, that she would never look in it again.

In this perturbed state of mind, with thoughts that could rest on nothing, she walked on; but it would not do; in half a minute the letter was unfolded again, and collecting herself as well as she could, she again began the mortifying perusal of all that related to Wickham, and commanded herself so far as to examine the meaning of every sentence. The account of his connection with the Pemberley family, was exactly what he had related himself; and the kindness of the late Mr. Darcy, though she had not before known its extent, agreed equally well with his own words. So far each recital confirmed the other; but when she came to the will, the difference was great. What Wickham had said of the living was fresh in her memory, and as she recalled his very words, it was impossible not to feel that there was gross duplicity on one side or the other; and, for a few moments, she flattered herself that her wishes did not err. But when she read, and re-read with the closest attention, the particulars immediately following of

Wickham's resigning all pretensions to the living, of his receiving in lieu so considerable a sum as three thousand pounds, again was she forced to hesitate. She put down the letter, weighed every circumstance with what she meant to be impartiality – deliberated on the probability of each statement – but with little success. On both sides it was only assertion. Again she read on. But every line proved more clearly that the affair, which she had believed it impossible that any contrivance could so represent, as to render Mr. Darcy's conduct in it less than infamous, was capable of a turn which must make him entirely blameless throughout the whole.

The extravagance and general profligacy which he scrupled not to lay to Mr. Wickham's charge, exceedingly shocked her; the more so, as she could bring no proof of its injustice. She had never heard of him before his entrance into the —shire Militia, in which he had engaged at the persuasion of the young man, who, on meeting him accidentally in town, had there renewed a slight acquaintance. Of his former way of life, nothing had been known in Hertfordshire but what he told himself. As to his real character, had information been in her power, she had never felt a wish of enquiring. His countenance, voice, and manner, had established him at once in the possession of every virtue. She tried to recollect some instance of goodness, some distinguished trait of integrity or benevolence, that might rescue him from the attacks of Mr. Darcy; or at least, by the predominance of virtue, atone for those casual errors, under which she would endeavour to class, what Mr. Darcy had described as the idleness and vice of many years' continuance. But no such recollection befriended her. She could see him instantly before her, in every charm of air and address; but she could remember no more substantial good than the general approbation of the neighbourhood, and the regard which his social powers had gained him in the mess. After pausing on this point a considerable while, she once more continued to read. But, alas! the story which followed of his designs on Miss Darcy, received some confirmation from what had passed between Colonel Fitzwilliam and herself only the morning before; and at last she was referred for the truth of every particular to Colonel Fitzwilliam himself – from whom she had previously received the information of his near concern in all his cousin's affairs, and whose character she had no reason to question. At one time she had almost resolved on applying to him, but the idea was checked by the awkwardness of the application, and at length wholly banished by the conviction that Mr. Darcy would never have hazarded such a proposal, if he had not been well assured of his cousin's corroboration.

She perfectly remembered everything that had passed in conversation between Wickham and herself, in their first evening at Mr. Philips's. Many of his expressions were still fresh in her memory. She was *now* struck with the impropriety of such communications to a stranger, and wondered it had escaped her before. She saw the indelicacy of putting himself forward as he had done, and the inconsistency of his professions with his conduct. She remembered that he had boasted of having no fear of seeing Mr. Darcy – that Mr. Darcy might leave the country, but that *he* should stand his ground; yet he had avoided the Netherfield ball the very next week. She remembered also, that till the Netherfield family had quitted the country, he had told his story to no one but herself; but that after their removal, it had been everywhere discussed; that he had then no reserves, no scruples in sinking Mr. Darcy's character, though he had assured her that respect for the father, would always prevent his exposing the son.

How differently did everything now appear in which he was concerned! His attentions to Miss King were now the consequence of views solely and hatefully mercenary; and the mediocrity of her fortune proved no longer the moderation of his wishes, but his eagerness to grasp at anything. His behaviour to herself could now have had no tolerable motive; he had either been deceived with regard to her fortune, or had been gratifying his vanity by encouraging the preference which she believed she had most incautiously shown. Every lingering struggle in his favour grew fainter and fainter; and in farther justification of Mr. Darcy, she could not but allow that Mr. Bingley, when questioned by Jane, had long ago asserted his blamelessness in the affair; that proud and repulsive as were his manners, she had never, in the whole course of their acquaintance, an acquaintance which had latterly brought them much together, and given her a sort of intimacy with his ways, seen anything that betrayed him to be unprincipled or unjust – anything that spoke him of irreligious or immoral habits. That among his own connections he was esteemed and valued – that even Wickham had allowed him merit as a brother, and that she had often heard him speak so affectionately of his sister as to prove him capable of *some* amiable feeling. That had his actions been what Wickham represented them, so gross a violation of everything right could hardly have been concealed from the world; and that friendship between a person capable of it, and such an amiable man as Mr. Bingley, was incomprehensible.

She grew absolutely ashamed of herself. – Of neither Darcy nor Wickham could she think, without feeling that she had been blind, partial, prejudiced, absurd.

"How despicably have I acted!" she cried. – "I, who have prided myself on my discernment! – I, who have valued myself on my abilities! who have often disdained the generous candour of my sister, and gratified my vanity, in useless or blameable distrust. – How humiliating is this discovery! – Yet, how just a humiliation! – Had I been in love, I could not have been more wretchedly blind! But vanity, not love, has been my folly. – Pleased with the preference of one, and offended by the neglect of the other, on the very beginning of our acquaintance, I have courted prepossession and ignorance, and driven reason away, where either were concerned. Till this moment I never knew myself."

From herself to Jane – from Jane to Bingley, her thoughts were in a line which soon brought to her recollection that Mr.

Darcy's explanation *there,* had appeared very insufficient; and she read it again. Widely different was the effect of a second perusal. – How could she deny that credit to his assertions, in one instance, which she had been obliged to give in the other? – He declared himself to be totally unsuspicious of her sister's attachment; – and she could not help remembering what Charlotte's opinion had always been. – Neither could she deny the justice of his description of Jane. – She felt that Jane's feelings, though fervent, were little displayed, and that there was a constant complacency in her air and manner, not often united with great sensibility.

When she came to that part of the letter in which her family were mentioned, in terms of such mortifying, yet merited reproach, her sense of shame was severe. The justice of the charge struck her too forcibly for denial, and the circumstances to which he particularly alluded, as having passed at the Netherfield ball, and as confirming all his first disapprobation, could not have made a stronger impression on his mind than on hers.

The compliment to herself and her sister, was not unfelt. It soothed, but it could not console her for the contempt which had been thus self-attracted by the rest of her family; – and as she considered that Jane's disappointment had in fact been the work of her nearest relations, and reflected how materially the credit of both must be hurt by such impropriety of conduct, she felt depressed beyond anything she had ever known before.

After wandering along the lane for two hours, giving way to every variety of thought; re-considering events, determining probabilities, and reconciling herself as well as she could, to a change so sudden and so important, fatigue, and a recollection of her long absence, made her at length return home; and she entered the house with the wish of appearing cheerful as usual, and the resolution of repressing such reflections as must make her unfit for conversation.

She was immediately told, that the two gentlemen from Rosings had each called during her absence; Mr. Darcy, only for a few minutes to take leave, but that Colonel Fitzwilliam had been sitting with them at least an hour, hoping for her return, and almost resolving to walk after her till she could be found. – Elizabeth could but just *affect* concern in missing him; she really rejoiced at it. Colonel Fitzwilliam was no longer an object. She could think only of her letter.

## *Chapter 37*

THE TWO gentlemen left Rosings the next morning; and Mr. Collins having been in waiting near the lodges, to make them his parting obeisance, was able to bring home the pleasing intelligence, of their appearing in very good health, and in as tolerable spirits as could be expected, after the melancholy scene so lately gone through at Rosings. To Rosings he then hastened to console Lady Catherine, and her daughter; and on his return, brought back, with great satisfaction, a message from her ladyship, importing that she felt herself so dull as to make her very desirous of having them all to dine with her.

Elizabeth could not see Lady Catherine without recollecting, that had she chosen it, she might by this time have been presented to her, as her future niece; nor could she think, without a smile, of what her ladyship's indignation would have been. "What would she have said? – how would she have behaved?" were questions with which she amused herself.

Their first subject was the diminution of the Rosings party. – "I assure you, I feel it exceedingly," said Lady Catherine; "I believe nobody feels the loss of friends so much as I do. But I am particularly attached to these young men; and know them to be so much attached to me! – They were excessively sorry to go! But so they always are. The dear colonel rallied his spirits tolerably till just at last; but Darcy seemed to feel it most acutely, more I think than last year. His attachment to Rosings, certainly increases."

Mr. Collins had a compliment, and an allusion to throw in here, which were kindly smiled on by the mother and daughter.

Lady Catherine observed, after dinner, that Miss Bennet seemed out of spirits, and immediately accounting for it herself, by supposing that she did not like to go home again so soon, she added,

"But if that is the case, you must write to your mother and beg that you may stay a little longer. Mrs. Collins will be very glad of your company, I am sure."

"I am much obliged to your ladyship for your kind invitation," replied Elizabeth, "but it is not in my power to accept it. – I must be in town next Saturday."

"Why, at that rate, you will have been here only six weeks. I expected you to stay two months. I told Mrs. Collins so before you came. There can be no occasion for your going so soon. Mrs. Bennet could certainly spare you for another fortnight."

"But my father cannot. – He wrote last week to hurry my return."

"Oh! your father of course may spare you, if your mother can. – Daughters are never of so much consequence to a father. And if you will stay another *month* complete, it will be in my power to take one of you as far as London, for I am going there early in June, for a week; and as Dawson does not object to the Barouche box, there will be very good room for one of you – and indeed, if the weather should happen to be cool, I should not object to taking you both, as you are neither of you large."

"You are all kindness, Madam; but I believe we must abide

by our original plan."

Lady Catherine seemed resigned.

"Mrs. Collins, you must send a servant with them. You know I always speak my mind, and I cannot bear the idea of two young women travelling post by themselves. It is highly improper. You must contrive to send somebody. I have the greatest dislike in the world to that sort of thing. – Young women should always be properly guarded and attended, according to their situation in life. When my niece Georgiana went to Ramsgate last summer, I made a point of her having two men-servants go with her. – Miss Darcy, the daughter of Mr. Darcy, of Pemberley, and Lady Anne, could not have appeared with propriety in a different manner. – I am excessively attentive to all those things. You must send John with the young ladies, Mrs. Collins. I am glad it occurred to me to mention it; for it would really be discreditable to *you* to let them go alone."

"My uncle is to send a servant for us."

"Oh! – Your uncle! – He keeps a man-servant, does he? – I am very glad you have somebody who thinks of those things. Where shall you change horses? – Oh! Bromley, of course. – If you mention my name at the Bell, you will be attended to."

Lady Catherine had many other questions to ask respecting their journey, and as she did not answer them all herself, attention was necessary, which Elizabeth believed to be lucky for her; or, with a mind so occupied, she might have forgotten where she was. Reflection must be reserved for solitary hours; whenever she was alone, she gave way to it as the greatest relief; and not a day went by without a solitary walk, in which she might indulge in all the delight of unpleasant recollections.

Mr. Darcy's letter, she was in a fair way of soon knowing by heart. She studied every sentence: and her feelings towards its writer were at times widely different. When she remembered the style of his address, she was still full of indignation; but when she considered how unjustly she had condemned and upbraided him, her anger was turned against herself; and his disappointed feelings became the object of compassion. His attachment excited gratitude, his general character respect; but she could not approve him; nor could she for a moment repent her refusal, or feel the slightest inclination ever to see him again. In her own past behaviour, there was a constant source of vexation and regret; and in the unhappy defects of her family a subject of yet heavier chagrin. They were hopeless of remedy. Her father, contented with laughing at them, would never exert himself to restrain the wild giddiness of his youngest daughters; and her mother, with manners so far from right herself, was entirely insensible of the evil. Elizabeth had frequently united with Jane in an endeavour to check the imprudence of Catherine and Lydia; but while they were supported by their mother's indulgence, what chance could there be of improvement? Catherine, weak-spirited, irritable, and completely under Lydia's guidance, had been always affronted by their advice; and Lydia, self-willed and careless, would scarcely give them a hearing. They were ignorant, idle, and vain. While there was an officer in Meryton, they would flirt with him; and while Meryton was within a walk of Longbourn, they would be going there for ever.

Anxiety on Jane's behalf, was another prevailing concern, and Mr. Darcy's explanation, by restoring Bingley to all her former good opinion, heightened the sense of what Jane had lost. His affection was proved to have been sincere, and his conduct cleared of all blame, unless any could attach to the implicitness of his confidence in his friend. How grievous then was the thought that, of a situation so desirable in every respect, so replete with advantage, so promising for happiness, Jane had been deprived, by the folly and indecorum of her own family!

When to these recollections was added the development of Wickham's character, it may be easily believed that the happy spirits which had seldom been depressed before, were now so much affected as to make it almost impossible for her to appear tolerably cheerful.

Their engagements at Rosings were as frequent during the last week of her stay, as they had been at first. The very last evening was spent there; and her ladyship again enquired minutely into the particulars of their journey, gave them directions as to the best method of packing, and was so urgent on the necessity of placing gowns in the only right way, that Maria thought herself obliged, on her return, to undo all the work of the morning, and pack her trunk afresh.

When they parted, Lady Catherine, with great condescension, wished them a good journey, and invited them to come to Hunsford again next year; and Miss de Bourgh exerted herself so far as to curtsey and hold out her hand to both.

# *Chapter 38*

On Saturday morning Elizabeth and Mr. Collins met for breakfast a few minutes before the others appeared; and he took the opportunity of paying the parting civilities which he deemed indispensably necessary.

"I know not, Miss Elizabeth," said he, "whether Mrs. Collins has yet expressed her sense of your kindness in coming to us, but I am very certain you will not leave the house without receiving her thanks for it. The favour of your company has been much felt, I assure you. We know how little there is to tempt anyone to our humble abode. Our plain manner of living, our small rooms, and few domestics, and the little we see of the world, must make Hunsford extremely dull to a young lady like yourself; but I hope you will believe us grateful for the condescension, and that we have done everything in our power to prevent your spending your time unpleasantly."

Elizabeth was eager with her thanks and assurances of happiness. She had spent six weeks with great enjoyment; and the pleasure of being with Charlotte, and the kind attentions she had received, must make *her* feel the obliged. Mr. Collins was gratified; and with a more smiling solemnity replied,

"It gives me great pleasure to hear that you have passed your time not disagreeably. We have certainly done our best; and most fortunately having it in our power to introduce you to very superior society, and from our connection with Rosings, the frequent means of varying the humble home scene, I think we may flatter ourselves that your Hunsford visit cannot have been entirely irksome. Our situation with regard to Lady Catherine's family is indeed the sort of extraordinary advantage and blessing which few can boast. You see on what a footing we are. You see how continually we are engaged there. In truth I must acknowledge that, with all the disadvantages of this humble parsonage, I should not think anyone abiding in it an object of compassion, while they are sharers of our intimacy at Rosings."

Words were insufficient for the elevation of his feelings; and he was obliged to walk about the room, while Elizabeth tried to unite civility and truth in a few short sentences.

"You may, in fact, carry a very favourable report of us into Hertfordshire, my dear cousin. I flatter myself at least that you will be able to do so. Lady Catherine's great attentions to Mrs. Collins you have been a daily witness of; and altogether I trust it does not appear that your friend has drawn an unfortunate – but on this point it will be as well to be silent. Only let me assure you, my dear Miss Elizabeth, that I can from my heart most cordially wish you equal felicity in marriage. My dear Charlotte and I have but one mind and one way of thinking. There is in everything a most remarkable resemblance of character and ideas between us. We seem to have been designed for each other."

Elizabeth could safely say that it was a great happiness where that was the case, and with equal sincerity could add that she firmly believed and rejoiced in his domestic comforts. She was not sorry, however, to have the recital of them interrupted by the lady from whom they sprung. Poor Charlotte! – it was melancholy to leave her to such society! – But she had chosen it with her eyes open; and though evidently regretting that her visitors were to go, she did not seem to ask for compassion. Her home and her housekeeping, her parish and her poultry, and all their dependent concerns, had not yet lost their charms.

At length the chaise arrived, the trunks were fastened on, the parcels placed within, and it was pronounced to be ready. After an affectionate parting between the friends, Elizabeth was attended to the carriage by Mr. Collins, and as they walked down the garden, he was commissioning her with his best respects to all her family, not forgetting his thanks for the kindness he had received at Longbourn in the winter, and his compliments to Mr. and Mrs. Gardiner, though unknown. He then handed her in, Maria followed, and the door was on the point of being closed, when he suddenly reminded them, with some consternation, that they had hitherto forgotten to leave any message for the ladies at Rosings.

"But," he added, "you will of course wish to have your humble respects delivered to them, with your grateful thanks for their kindness to you while you have been here."

Elizabeth made no objection; – the door was then allowed to be shut, and the carriage drove off.

"Good gracious!" cried Maria, after a few minutes' silence, "it seems but a day or two since we first came! – and yet how many things have happened!"

"A great many indeed," said her companion with a sigh.

"We have dined nine times at Rosings, besides drinking tea there twice! – How much I shall have to tell!"

Elizabeth added privately, "And how much I shall have to conceal!"

Their journey was performed without much conversation, or any alarm; and within four hours of their leaving Hunsford, they reached Mr. Gardiner's house, where they were to remain a few days.

Jane looked well, and Elizabeth had little opportunity of studying her spirits, amidst the various engagements which the kindness of her aunt had reserved for them. But Jane was to go home with her, and at Longbourn there would be leisure enough for observation.

It was not without an effort meanwhile that she could wait even for Longbourn, before she told her sister of Mr. Darcy's proposals. To know that she had the power of revealing what would so exceedingly astonish Jane, and must, at the same time, so highly gratify whatever of her own vanity she had not yet been able to reason away, was such a temptation to openness as nothing could have conquered but the state of indecision in which she remained, as to the extent of what she should communicate; and her fear, if she once entered on the subject, of being hurried into repeating something of Bingley, which might only grieve her sister farther.

## *Chapter 39*

IT WAS the second week in May, in which the three young ladies set out together from Gracechurch Street, for the town of — in Hertfordshire; and, as they drew near the appointed inn where Mr. Bennet's carriage was to meet them, they quickly perceived, in token of the coachman's punctuality, both Kitty and Lydia looking out of a dining-room upstairs. These two girls had been above an hour in the place, happily employed in visiting an opposite milliner, watching the sentinel on guard, and dressing a salad and cucumber.

After welcoming their sisters, they triumphantly displayed a table set out with such cold meat as an inn larder usually affords, exclaiming, "Is this not nice? is not this an agreeable surprise?"

"And we mean to treat you all," added Lydia, "but you must lend us the money, for we have just spent ours at the shop out there." Then showing her purchases: "Look here, I have bought this bonnet. I do not think it is very pretty; but I thought I might as well buy it as not. I shall pull it to pieces as soon as I get home, and see if I can make it up any better."

And when her sisters abused it as ugly, she added, with perfect unconcern, "Oh! but there were two or three much uglier in the shop; and when I have bought some prettier-coloured satin to trim it with fresh, I think it will be very tolerable. Besides, it will not much signify what one wears this summer, after the —shire have left Meryton, and they are going in a fortnight."

"Are they indeed!" cried Elizabeth, with the greatest satisfaction.

"They are going to be encamped near Brighton; and I do so want papa to take us all there for the summer! It would be such a delicious scheme, and I dare say would hardly cost anything at all. Mamma would like to go too of all things! Only think what a miserable summer else we shall have!"

"Yes," thought Elizabeth, "*that* would be a delightful scheme, indeed, and completely do for us at once. Good Heaven! Brighton, and a whole campful of soldiers, to us, who have been overset already by one poor regiment of militia, and the monthly balls of Meryton."

"Now I have got some news for you," said Lydia, as they sat

down to table. "What do you think? It is excellent news, capital news, and about a certain person we all like."

Jane and Elizabeth looked at each other, and the waiter was told he need not stay. Lydia laughed, and said,

"Aye, that is just like your formality and discretion. You thought the waiter must not hear, as if he cared! I dare say he often hears worse things said than I am going to say. But he is an ugly fellow! I am glad he is gone. I never saw such a long chin in my life. Well, but now for my news; it is about dear Wickham; too good for the waiter, is it not? There is no danger of Wickham's marrying Mary King. There's for you! She is gone down to her uncle at Liverpool; gone to stay. Wickham is safe."

"And Mary King is safe!" added Elizabeth; "safe from a connection imprudent as to fortune."

"She is a great fool for going away, if she liked him."

"But I hope there is no strong attachment on either side," said Jane.

"I am sure there is not on *his*. I will answer for it he never cared three straws about her. Who *could* about such a nasty little freckled thing?"

Elizabeth was shocked to think that, however incapable of such coarseness of *expression* herself, the coarseness of the *sentiment* was little other than her own breast had harboured and fancied liberal!

As soon as all had ate, and the elder ones paid, the carriage was ordered; and after some contrivance, the whole party, with all their boxes, work bags, and parcels, and the unwelcome addition of Kitty's and Lydia's purchases, were seated in it.

"How nicely we are crammed in!" cried Lydia. "I am glad I bought my bonnet, if it is only for the fun of having another bandbox! Well, now let us be quite comfortable and snug, and talk and laugh all the way home. And in the first place, let us hear what has happened to you all, since you went away. Have you seen any pleasant men? Have you had any flirting? I was in great hopes that one of you would have got a husband before you came back. Jane will be quite an old maid soon, I declare. She is almost three and twenty! Lord, how ashamed I should be of not being married before three and twenty. My aunt Philips wants you so to get husbands, you can't think. She says Lizzy had better have taken Mr. Collins; but I do not think there would have been any fun in it. Lord! how I should like to be married before any of you; and then I would chaperon you about to all the balls. Dear me! we had such a good piece of fun the other day at Colonel Forster's. Kitty and me were to spend the day there, and Mrs. Forster promised to have a little dance in the evening; (by the bye, Mrs. Forster and me are *such* friends!) and so she asked the two Harringtons to come, but Harriet was ill, and so Pen was forced to come by herself; and then, what do you think we did? We dressed up Chamberlayne in woman's clothes, on purpose to pass for a lady – only think what fun! Not a soul knew of it, but Col. and Mrs. Forster, and Kitty and me, except my aunt, for we were forced to borrow one of her gowns; and you cannot imagine how well he looked! When Denny, and Wickham, and Pratt, and two or three more of the men came in, they did not know him in the least. Lord! how I laughed! and so did Mrs. Forster. I thought I should have died. And *that* made the men suspect something, and then they soon found out what was the matter."

With such kinds of histories of their parties and good jokes, did Lydia, assisted by Kitty's hints and additions, endeavour to amuse her companions all the way to Longbourn. Elizabeth listened as little as she could, but there was no escaping the frequent mention of Wickham's name.

Their reception at home was most kind. Mrs. Bennet rejoiced to see Jane in undiminished beauty; and more than once during dinner did Mr. Bennet say voluntarily to Elizabeth,

"I am glad you are come back, Lizzy."

Their party in the dining-room was large, for almost all the Lucases came to meet Maria and hear the news: and various were the subjects which occupied them; Lady Lucas was enquiring of Maria across the table, after the welfare and poultry of her eldest daughter; Mrs. Bennet was doubly engaged, on one hand collecting an account of the present fashions from Jane, who sat some way below her, and on the other, retailing them all to the younger Miss Lucases; and Lydia, in a voice rather louder than any other person's, was enumerating the various pleasures of the morning to anybody who would hear her.

"Oh! Mary," said she, "I wish you had gone with us, for we had such fun! as we went along, Kitty and me drew up all the blinds, and pretended there was nobody in the coach; and I should have gone so all the way, if Kitty had not been sick; and when we got to the George, I do think we behaved very handsomely, for we treated the other three with the nicest cold luncheon in the world, and if you would have gone, we would have treated you too. And then when we came away it was such fun! I thought we never should have got into the coach. I was ready to die of laughter. And then we were so merry all the way home! we talked and laughed so loud, that anybody might have heard us ten miles off!"

To this, Mary very gravely replied, "Far be it from me, my dear sister, to depreciate such pleasures! They would doubtless be congenial with the generality of female minds. But I confess they would have no charms for *me*. I should infinitely prefer a book."

But of this answer Lydia heard not a word. She seldom listened to anybody for more than half a minute, and never attended to Mary at all.

In the afternoon Lydia was urgent with the rest of the girls to walk to Meryton and to see how everybody went on; but Elizabeth steadily opposed the scheme. It should not be said, that the Miss Bennets could not be at home half a day before they were in pursuit of the officers. There was another reason too for her opposition. She dreaded seeing Wickham again, and was resolved to avoid it as long as possible. The comfort to *her,* of the regiment's approaching removal, was indeed beyond expression. In a fortnight they were to go, and once gone, she hoped there could be nothing more to plague her on his account.

She had not been many hours at home, before she found that the Brighton scheme, of which Lydia had given them a hint at the inn, was under frequent discussion between her parents. Elizabeth saw directly that her father had not the smallest intention of yielding; but his answers were at the same time so vague and equivocal, that her mother, though often disheartened, had never yet despaired of succeeding at last.

## *Chapter 40*

ELIZABETH'S IMPATIENCE to acquaint Jane with what had happened could no longer be overcome; and at length resolving to suppress every particular in which her sister was concerned, and preparing her to be surprised, she related to her the next morning the chief of the scene between Mr. Darcy and herself.

Miss Bennet's astonishment was soon lessened by the strong sisterly partiality which made any admiration of Elizabeth appear perfectly natural; and all surprise was shortly lost in other feelings. She was sorry that Mr. Darcy should have delivered his sentiments in a manner so little suited to recommend them; but still more was she grieved for the unhappiness which her sister's refusal must have given him.

"His being so sure of succeeding, was wrong," said she, "and certainly ought not to have appeared; but consider how much it must increase his disappointment!"

"Indeed," replied Elizabeth, "I am heartily sorry for him; but he has other feelings which will probably soon drive away his regard for me. You do not blame me, however, for refusing him?"

"Blame you! Oh, no."

"But you blame me for having spoken so warmly of Wickham?"

"No – I do not know that you were wrong in saying what you did."

"But you *will* know it, when I have told you what happened the very next day."

She then spoke of the letter, repeating the whole of its contents as far as they concerned George Wickham. What a stroke was this for poor Jane! who would willingly have gone through the world without believing that so much wickedness existed in the whole race of mankind, as was here collected in one individual. Nor was Darcy's vindication, though grateful to her feelings, capable of consoling her for such discovery. Most earnestly did she labour to prove the probability of error, and seek to clear one, without involving the other.

"This will not do," said Elizabeth. "You never will be able to make both of them good for anything. Take your choice, but you must be satisfied with only one. There is but such a quantity of merit between them; just enough to make one good sort of man; and of late it has been shifting about pretty much. For my part, I am inclined to believe it all Mr. Darcy's, but you shall do as you choose."

It was some time, however, before a smile could be extorted from Jane.

"I do not know when I have been more shocked," said she. "Wickham so very bad! It is almost past belief. And poor Mr. Darcy! dear Lizzy, only consider what he must have suffered.

Such a disappointment! and with the knowledge of your ill opinion too! and having to relate such a thing of his sister! It is really too distressing. I am sure you must feel it so."

"Oh! no, my regret and compassion are all done away by seeing you so full of both. I know you will do him such ample justice, that I am growing every moment more unconcerned and indifferent. Your profusion makes me saving; and if you lament over him much longer, my heart will be as light as feather."

"Poor Wickham; there is such an expression of goodness in his countenance! such an openness and gentleness in his manner!"

"There certainly was some great mismanagement in the education of those two young men. One has got all the goodness, and the other all the appearance of it."

"I never thought Mr. Darcy so deficient in the *appearance* of it as you used to do."

"And yet I meant to be uncommonly clever in taking so decided a dislike to him, without any reason. It is such a spur to one's genius, such an opening for wit to have a dislike of that kind. One may be continually abusive without saying anything just; but one cannot be always laughing at a man without now and then stumbling on something witty."

"Lizzy, when you first read that letter, I am sure you could not treat the matter as you do now."

"Indeed I could not. I was uncomfortable enough. I was very uncomfortable, I may say unhappy. And with no one to speak to, of what I felt, no Jane to comfort me and say that I had not been so very weak and vain and nonsensical as I knew I had! Oh! how I wanted you!"

"How unfortunate that you should have used such very strong expressions in speaking of Wickham to Mr. Darcy, for now they *do* appear wholly undeserved."

"Certainly. But the misfortune of speaking with bitterness, is a most natural consequence of the prejudices I had been encouraging. There is one point, on which I want your advice. I want to be told whether I ought, or ought not to make our acquaintance in general understand Wickham's character."

Miss Bennet paused a little and then replied, "Surely there can be no occasion for exposing him so dreadfully. What is your opinion?"

"That it ought not to be attempted. Mr. Darcy has not authorised me to make his communication public. On the contrary every particular relative to his sister, was meant to be kept as much as possible to myself; and if I endeavour to undeceive people as to the rest of his conduct, who will believe me? The general prejudice against Mr. Darcy is so violent, that it would be the death of half the good people in Meryton, to attempt to place him in an amiable light. I am not equal to it. Wickham will soon be gone; and therefore it will not signify to anyone here, what he really is. Sometime hence it will be all found out, and then we may laugh at their stupidity in not knowing it before. At present I will say nothing about it."

"You are quite right. To have his errors made public might ruin him for ever. He is now perhaps sorry for what he has done, and anxious to re-establish a character. We must not make him desperate."

The tumult of Elizabeth's mind was allayed by this conversation. She had got rid of two of the secrets which had weighed on her for a fortnight, and was certain of a willing listener in Jane, whenever she might wish to talk again of either. But there was still something lurking behind, of which prudence forbade the disclosure. She dared not relate the other half of Mr. Darcy's letter, nor explain to her sister how sincerely she had been valued by her friend. Here was knowledge in which no one could partake; and she was sensible that nothing less than a perfect understanding between the parties could justify her in throwing off this last encumbrance of mystery. "And then," said she, "if that very improbable event should ever take place, I shall merely be able to tell what Bingley may tell in a much more agreeable manner himself. The liberty of communication cannot be mine till it has lost all its value!"

She was now, on being settled at home, at leisure to observe the real state of her sister's spirits. Jane was not happy. She still cherished a very tender affection for Bingley. Having never even fancied herself in love before, her regard had all the warmth of first attachment, and from her age and disposition, greater steadiness than first attachments often boast; and so fervently did she value his remembrance, and prefer him to every other man, that all her good sense, and all her attention to the feelings of her friends, were requisite to check the indulgence of those regrets, which must have been injurious to her own health and their tranquillity.

"Well, Lizzy," said Mrs. Bennet one day, "what is your opinion *now* of this sad business of Jane's? For my part, I am determined never to speak of it again to anybody. I told my sister Philips so the other day. But I cannot find out that Jane saw anything of him in London. Well, he is a very undeserving young man – and I do not suppose there is the least chance in the world of her ever getting him now. There is no talk of his coming to Netherfield again in the summer; and I have enquired of everybody too, who is likely to know."

"I do not believe he will ever live at Netherfield any more."

"Oh well! it is just as he chooses. Nobody wants him to come. Though I shall always say he used my daughter extremely ill; and if I was her, I would not have put up with it. Well, my comfort is, I am sure Jane will die of a broken heart; and then he will be sorry for what he has done."

But as Elizabeth could not receive comfort from any such expectation, she made no answer.

"Well, Lizzy," continued her mother soon afterwards, "and so the Collinses live very comfortable, do they? Well, well, I only hope it will last. And what sort of table do they keep? Charlotte is an excellent manager, I dare say. If she is half as sharp as her mother, she is saving enough. There is nothing extravagant in *their* housekeeping, I dare say."

"No, nothing at all."

"A great deal of good management, depend upon it. Yes, yes. *They* will take care not to outrun their income. *They* will never be distressed for money. Well, much good may it do them! And so, I suppose, they often talk of having Longbourn when your father is dead. They look upon it quite as their own, I dare say, whenever that happens."

"It was a subject which they could not mention before me."

"No. It would have been strange if they had. But I make no doubt, they often talk of it between themselves. Well, if they can be easy with an estate that is not lawfully their own, so much the better. *I* should be ashamed of having one that was only entailed on me."

# Chapter 41

THE FIRST week of their return was soon gone. The second began. It was the last of the regiment's stay in Meryton, and all the young ladies in the neighbourhood were drooping apace. The dejection was almost universal. The elder Miss Bennets alone were still able to eat, drink, and sleep, and pursue the usual course of their employments. Very frequently were they reproached for this insensibility by Kitty and Lydia, whose own misery was extreme, and who could not comprehend such hard-heartedness in any of the family.

"Good Heaven! What is to become of us? What are we to do?" would they often exclaim in the bitterness of woe. "How can you be smiling so, Lizzy?"

Their affectionate mother shared all their grief; she remembered what she had herself endured on a similar occasion, five and twenty years ago.

"I am sure," said she, "I cried for two days together when Colonel Millar's regiment went away. I thought I should have broke my heart."

"I am sure I shall break *mine*," said Lydia.

"If one could but go to Brighton!" observed Mrs. Bennet.

"Oh, yes! – if one could but go to Brighton! But papa is so disagreeable."

"A little sea-bathing would set me up for ever."

"And my aunt Philips is sure it would do *me* a great deal of good," added Kitty.

Such were the kind of lamentations resounding perpetually through Longbourn House. Elizabeth tried to be diverted by them; but all sense of pleasure was lost in shame. She felt anew the justice of Mr. Darcy's objections; and never had she before been so much disposed to pardon his interference in the views of his friend.

But the gloom of Lydia's prospect was shortly cleared away; for she received an invitation from Mrs. Forster, the wife of the Colonel of the regiment, to accompany her to Brighton. This invaluable friend was a very young woman, and very lately married. A resemblance in good humour and good spirits had recommended her and Lydia to each other, and out of their *three* months' acquaintance they had been intimate *two*.

The rapture of Lydia on this occasion, her adoration of Mrs.

Forster, the delight of Mrs. Bennet, and the mortification of Kitty, are scarcely to be described. Wholly inattentive to her sister's feelings, Lydia flew about the house in restless ecstasy, calling for everyone's congratulations, and laughing and talking with more violence than ever; whilst the luckless Kitty continued in the parlour repining at her fate in terms as unreasonable as her accent was peevish.

"I cannot see why Mrs. Forster should not ask *me* as well as Lydia," said she, "though I am *not* her particular friend. I have just as much right to be asked as she has, and more too, for I am two years older."

In vain did Elizabeth attempt to make her reasonable, and Jane to make her resigned. As for Elizabeth herself, this invitation was so far from exciting in her the same feelings as in her mother and Lydia, that she considered it as the death-warrant of all possibility of common sense for the latter; and detestable as such a step must make her were it known, she could not help secretly advising her father not to let her go. She represented to him all the improprieties of Lydia's general behaviour, the little advantage she could derive from the friendship of such a woman as Mrs. Forster, and the probability of her being yet more imprudent with such a companion at Brighton, where the temptations must be greater than at home. He heard her attentively, and then said,

"Lydia will never be easy until she has exposed herself in some public place or other, and we can never expect her to do it with so little expense or inconvenience to her family as under the present circumstances."

"If you were aware," said Elizabeth, "of the very great disadvantage to us all, which must arise from the public notice of Lydia's unguarded and imprudent manner; nay, which has already arisen from it, I am sure you would judge differently in the affair."

"Already arisen!" repeated Mr. Bennet. "What, has she frightened away some of your lovers? Poor little Lizzy! But do not be cast down. Such squeamish youths as cannot bear to be connected with a little absurdity, are not worth a regret. Come, let me see the list of pitiful fellows who have been kept aloof by Lydia's folly."

"Indeed you are mistaken. I have no such injuries to resent. It is not of peculiar, but of general evils, which I am now complaining. Our importance, our respectability in the world, must be affected by the wild volatility, the assurance and disdain of all restraint which mark Lydia's character. Excuse me – for I must speak plainly. If you, my dear father, will not take the trouble of checking her exuberant spirits, and of teaching her that her present pursuits are not to be the business of her life, she will soon be beyond the reach of amendment. Her character will be fixed, and she will, at sixteen, be the most determined flirt that ever made herself or her family ridiculous. A flirt too, in the worst and meanest degree of flirtation; without any attraction beyond youth and a tolerable person; and from the ignorance and emptiness of her mind, wholly unable to ward off any portion of that universal contempt which her rage for admiration will excite. In this danger Kitty is also comprehended. She will follow wherever Lydia leads. Vain, ignorant, idle, and absolutely uncontrolled! Oh! my dear father, can you suppose it possible that they will not be censured and despised wherever they are known, and that their sisters will not be often involved in the disgrace?"

Mr. Bennet saw that her whole heart was in the subject; and affectionately taking her hand, said in reply,

"Do not make yourself uneasy, my love. Wherever you and Jane are known, you must be respected and valued; and you will not appear to less advantage for having a couple of – or I may say, three very silly sisters. We shall have no peace at Longbourn if Lydia does not go to Brighton. Let her go then. Colonel Forster is a sensible man, and will keep her out of any real mischief; and she is luckily too poor to be an object of prey to anybody. At Brighton she will be of less importance even as a common flirt than she has been here. The officers will find women better worth their notice. Let us hope, therefore, that her being there may teach her her own insignificance. At any rate, she cannot grow many degrees worse, without authorizing us to lock her up for the rest of her life."

With this answer Elizabeth was forced to be content; but her own opinion continued the same, and she left him disappointed and sorry. It was not in her nature, however, to increase her vexations, by dwelling on them. She was confident of having performed her duty, and to fret over unavoidable evils, or augment them by anxiety, was no part of her disposition.

Had Lydia and her mother known the substance of her conference with her father, their indignation would hardly have found expression in their united volubility. In Lydia's imagination, a visit to Brighton comprised ever possibility of earthly happiness. She saw with the creative eye of fancy, the streets of that gay bathing place covered with officers. She saw herself the object of attention, to tens and to scores of them at present unknown. She saw all the glories of the camp; its tents stretched forth in beauteous uniformity of lines, crowded with the young and the gay, and dazzling with scarlet; and to complete the view, she saw herself seated beneath a tent, tenderly flirting with at least six officers at once.

Had she known that her sister sought to tear her from such prospects and such realities as these, what would have been her sensations? They could have been understood only by her mother, who might have felt nearly the same. Lydia's going to Brighton was all that consoled her for the melancholy conviction of her husband's never intending to go there himself.

But they were entirely ignorant of what had passed; and their raptures continued with little intermission to the very day of Lydia's leaving home.

Elizabeth was now to see Mr. Wickham for the last time. Having been frequently in company with him since her return, agitation was pretty well over; the agitations of formal partiality entirely so. She had even learnt to detect, in the very gentleness which had first delighted her, an affectation and a sameness to disgust and weary. In his present behaviour to herself, moreover, she had a fresh source of displeasure, for the inclination he soon testified of renewing those attentions which had marked the early part of their acquaintance, could only serve, after what had since passed, to provoke her. She lost all concern for him in finding herself thus selected as the object of such idle and frivolous gallantry; and while she steadily repressed it, could not but feel the reproof contained in his believing, that however long, and for whatever cause, his attentions had been withdrawn, her vanity would be gratified and her preference secured at any time by their renewal.

On the very last day of the regiment's remaining at Meryton, he dined with others of the officers at Longbourn; and so little was Elizabeth disposed to part from him in good humour, that on his making some enquiry as to the manner in which her time had passed at Hunsford, she mentioned Colonel Fitzwilliam's and Mr. Darcy's having both spent three weeks at Rosings, and asked him if he was acquainted with the former.

He looked surprised, displeased and alarmed; but with a moment's recollection and a returning smile, replied, that he had formerly seen him often; and after observing that he was a very gentlemanlike man, asked her how she had liked him. Her answer was warmly in his favour. With an air of indifference he soon afterwards added, "How long did you say that he was at Rosings?"

"Nearly three weeks."

"And you saw him frequently?"

"Yes, almost every day."

"His manners are very different from his cousin's."

"Yes, very different. But I think Mr. Darcy improves on acquaintance."

"Indeed!" cried Wickham with a look which did not escape her. "And pray may I ask?" but checking himself, he added in a gayer tone, "Is it in address that he improves? Has he deigned to add ought of civility to his ordinary style? for I dare not hope," he continued in a lower and more serious tone, "that he is improved in essentials."

"Oh, no!" said Elizabeth. "In essentials, I believe, he is very much what he ever was."

While she spoke, Wickham looked as if scarcely knowing whether to rejoice over her words, or to distrust their meaning. There was a something in her countenance which made him listen with an apprehensive and anxious attention, while she added,

"When I said that he improved on acquaintance, I did not mean that his mind or his manners were in a state of improvement, but that from knowing him better, his disposition was better understood."

Wickham's alarm now appeared in a heightened complexion and agitated look; for a few minutes he was silent; till, shaking off his embarrassment, he turned to her again, and said in the gentlest of accents,

"You, who so well know my feeling towards Mr. Darcy, will readily comprehend how sincerely I must rejoice that he is wise enough to assume even the *appearance* of what is right. His pride, in that direction, may be of service, if not to himself, to many others, for it must deter him from such foul misconduct as I have suffered by. I only fear that the sort of cautiousness, to which you, I imagine, have been alluding, is merely adopted on his visits to his aunt, of whose good opinion and judgement he stands much in awe. His fear of her, has always operated, I know, when they were together; and a good deal is to be imputed to his wish of forwarding the match with Miss de Bourgh, which I am certain he has very much at heart."

Elizabeth could not repress a smile at this, but she answered only by a slight inclination of the head. She saw that he wanted to engage her on the old subject of his grievances, and she was in no humour to indulge him. The rest of the evening passed with the *appearance*, on his side, of usual cheerfulness, but with no further attempt to distinguish Elizabeth; and they parted at last with mutual civility, and possibly a mutual desire of never meeting again.

When the party broke up, Lydia returned with Mrs. Forster to Meryton, from whence they were to set out early the next morning. The separation between her and her family was rather noisy than pathetic. Kitty was the only one who shed tears; but she did weep from vexation and envy. Mrs. Bennet was diffuse in her good wishes for the felicity of her daughter, and impressive in her injunctions that she would not miss the opportunity of enjoying herself as much as possible; advice, which there was every reason to believe would be attended to; and in the clamorous happiness of Lydia herself in bidding farewell, the more gentle adieus of her sisters were uttered without being heard.

# *Chapter 42*

HAD ELIZABETH'S opinion been all drawn from her own family, she could not have formed a very pleasing picture of conjugal felicity or domestic comfort. Her father, captivated by youth and beauty, and that appearance of good humour, which youth and beauty generally give, had married a woman whose weak understanding and illiberal mind, had very early in their marriage put an end to all real affection for her. Respect, esteem, and confidence, had vanished for ever; and all his views of domestic happiness were overthrown. But Mr. Bennet was not of a disposition to seek comfort for the disappointment which his own imprudence had brought on, in any of those pleasures which too often console the unfortunate for their folly of their vice. He was fond of the country and of books; and from these tastes had arisen his principal enjoyments. To his wife he was very little otherwise indebted, than as her ignorance and folly had contributed to his amusement. This is not the sort of happiness which a man would in general wish to owe to his wife; but where other powers of entertainment are wanting, the true philosopher will derive benefit from such as are given.

Elizabeth, however, had never been blind to the impropriety of her father's behaviour as husband. She had always seen it with pain; but respecting his abilities, and grateful for his affectionate treatment of herself, she endeavoured to forget what she could not overlook, and to banish from her thoughts that continual breach of conjugal obligation and decorum which, in exposing his wife to the contempt of her own children, was so highly reprehensible. But she had never felt so strongly as now, the disadvantages which must attend the children of so unsuitable a marriage, nor ever been so fully aware of the evils arising from so ill-judged a direction of talents; talents which rightly used, might at least have preserved the respectability of his daughters, even if incapable of enlarging the mind of his wife.

When Elizabeth had rejoiced over Wickham's departure, she found little other cause for satisfaction in the loss of the regiment. Their parties abroad were less varied than before; and at home she had a mother and sister whose constant repinings at the dullness of everything around them, threw a real gloom over their domestic circle; and, though Kitty might in time regain her natural degree of sense, since the disturbers of her brain were removed, her other sister, from whose disposition greater evil might be apprehended, was likely to be hardened in all her folly and assurance, by a situation of such double danger as watering place and a camp. Upon the whole, therefore, she found, what has been sometimes found before, that an event to which she had looked forward with impatient desire, did not in taking place, bring all the satisfaction she had promised herself. It was consequently necessary to name some other period for the commencement of actual felicity; to have some other point on which her wishes and hopes might be fixed, and by again enjoying the pleasure of anticipation, console herself for the present, and prepare for another disappointment. Her tour to the Lakes was now the object of her happiest thoughts; it was her best consolation for all the uncomfortable hours, which the discontentedness of her mother and Kitty made inevitable; and could she have included Jane in the scheme, every part of it would have been perfect.

"But it is fortunate," thought she, "that I have something to wish for. Were the whole arrangement complete, my disappointment would be certain. But here, by carrying with me one ceaseless source of regret in my sister's absence, I may reasonably hope to have all my expectations of pleasure realised. A scheme of which every part promises delight, can never be successful; and general disappointment is only warded off by the defence of some little peculiar vexation."

When Lydia went away, she promised to write very often and very minutely to her mother and Kitty; but her letters were always long expected, and always very short. Those to her mother, contained little else, than that they were just returned from the library, where such and such officers had attended them, and where she had seen such beautiful ornaments as made her quite wild; that she had a new gown, or a new parasol, which she would have described more fully, but was obliged to leave off in a violent hurry, as Mrs. Forster called her, and they were going to the camp; – and from her correspondence with her sister, there was still less to be learnt – for her letters to Kitty, though rather longer, were much too full of lines under the words to be made public.

After the first fortnight or three weeks of her absence, health, good humour, and cheerfulness began to re-appear at Longbourn. Everything wore a happier aspect. The families who had been in town for the winter came back again, and summer finery and summer engagements arose. Mrs. Bennet was restored to her usual querulous serenity; and by the middle of June Kitty was so much recovered as to be able to enter Meryton without tears; an event of such happy promise as to make Elizabeth hope, that by the following Christmas, she might be so tolerably reasonable as not to mention an officer above once a day, unless by some cruel and malicious arrangement at the war office, another regiment should be quartered in Meryton.

The time fixed for the beginning of their Northern tour was now fast approaching; and a fortnight only was wanting of it, when a letter arrived from Mrs. Gardiner, which at once delayed its commencement and curtailed its extent. Mr. Gardiner would be prevented by business from setting out till a fortnight later in July, and must be in London again within a month; and as that left too short a period for them to go so far, and see so much as they had proposed, or at least to see it with the leisure and comfort they had built on, they were obliged to give up the Lakes, and substitute a more contracted tour; and, according to the present plan, were to go no farther northward than Derbyshire. In that county, there was enough to be seen, to occupy the chief of their three weeks; and to Mrs. Gardiner it had a peculiarly strong attraction. The town where she had formerly passed some years of her life, and where they were now to spend a few days, was probably as great an object of her curiosity, as all the celebrated beauties of Matlock, Chatsworth, Dovedale, or the Peak.

Elizabeth was excessively disappointed; she had set her heart on seeing the Lakes; and still thought there might have been time enough. But it was her business to be satisfied – and certainly her temper to be happy; and all was soon right again.

With the mention of Derbyshire, there were many ideas connected. It was impossible for her to see the word without thinking of Pemberley and its owner. "But surely," said she, "I may enter his county with impunity, and rob it of a few petrified spars without his perceiving me."

The period of expectation was now doubled. Four weeks were to pass away before her uncle and aunt's arrival. But they did pass away, and Mr. and Mrs. Gardiner, with their four children, did at length appear at Longbourn. The children, two girls of six and eight years old, and two younger boys, were to be left under the particular care of their cousin Jane, who was the general favourite, and whose steady sense and sweetness of temper exactly adapted her for attending to them in every way – teaching them, playing with them, and loving them.

The Gardiners stayed only one night at Longbourn, and set off the next morning with Elizabeth in pursuit of novelty and amusement. One enjoyment was certain – that of suitableness as companions; a suitableness which comprehended health and temper to bear inconveniences – cheerfulness to enhance every pleasure – and affection and intelligence, which might supply it among themselves if there were disappointments abroad.

It is not the object of this work to give a description of Derbyshire, nor of any of the remarkable places through which their route thither lay; Oxford, Blenheim, Warwick, Kenilworth, Birmingham, &c. are sufficiently known. A small part of Derbyshire is all the present concern. To the little town of Lambton, the scene of Mrs. Gardiner's former residence, and where she had lately learned some acquaintance still remained, they bent their steps, after having seen all the principal wonders of the country; and within five miles of Lambton, Elizabeth found from her aunt, that Pemberley was situated. It was not in their direct road, nor more than a mile or two out of it. In talking over their route the evening before, Mrs. Gardiner expressed an inclination to see the place again. Mr. Gardiner declared his willingness, and Elizabeth was applied to for her approbation.

"My love, should not you like to see a place of which you have heard so much?" said her aunt. "A place too, with which so many of your acquaintance are connected. Wickham passed all his youth there, you know."

Elizabeth was distressed. She felt that she had no business at Pemberley, and was obliged to assume a disinclination for seeing it. She must own that she was tired of great houses; after going over so many, she really had no pleasure in fine carpets or satin curtains.

Mrs. Gardiner abused her stupidity. "If it were merely a fine house richly furnished," said she, "I should not care about it myself; but the grounds are delightful. They have some of the finest woods in the country."

Elizabeth said no more – but her mind could not acquiesce. The possibility of meeting Mr. Darcy, while viewing the place, instantly occurred. It would be dreadful! She blushed at the very idea, and thought it would be better to speak openly to her aunt, than to run such a risk. But against this, there were objections; and she finally resolved that it could be the last resource, if her private enquiries as to the absence of the family, were unfavourably answered.

Accordingly, when she retired at night, she asked the chambermaid whether Pemberley were not a very fine place, what was the name of its proprietor, and with no little alarm, whether the family were down for the summer. A most welcome negative followed the last question – and her alarms being now removed, she was at leisure to feel a great deal of curiosity to see the house herself; and when the subject was revived the next morning, and she was again applied to, could readily answer, and with a proper air of indifference, that she had not really any dislike to the scheme.

To Pemberley, therefore, they were to go.

# *Chapter 43*

ELIZABETH, AS they drove along, watched for the first appearance of Pemberley Woods with some perturbation; and when at length they turned in at the lodge, her spirits were in a high flutter.

The park was very large, and contained great variety of ground. They entered it in one of its lowest points, and drove for some time through a beautiful wood, stretching over a wide extent.

Elizabeth's mind was too full for conversation, but she saw and admired every remarkable spot and point of view. They gradually ascended for half a mile, and then found themselves at the top of a considerable eminence, where the wood ceased, and the eye was instantly caught by Pemberley House, situated on the opposite side of a valley, into which the road with some abruptness wound. It was a large, handsome, stone building, standing well on rising ground, and backed by a ridge of high woody hills; – and in front, a stream of some natural importance was swelled into greater, but without any artificial appearance. Its banks were neither formal, nor falsely adorned. Elizabeth was delighted. She had never seen a place for which nature had done more, or where natural beauty had been so little counteracted by an awkward taste. They were all of them warm in their admiration;

and at that moment she felt, that to be mistress of Pemberley might be something!

They descended the hill, crossed the bridge, and drove to the door; and, while examining the nearer aspect of the house, all her apprehensions of meeting its owner returned. She dreaded lest the chambermaid had been mistaken. On applying to see the place, they were admitted into the hall; and Elizabeth, as they waited for the housekeeper, had leisure to wonder at her being where she was.

The housekeeper came; a respectable-looking, elderly woman, much less fine, and more civil, than she had any notion of finding her. They followed her into the dining-parlour. It was a large, well proportioned room, handsomely fitted up. Elizabeth, after slightly surveying it, went to a window to enjoy its prospect. The hill, crowned with wood, from which they had descended, receiving increased abruptness from the distance, was a beautiful object. Every disposition of the ground was good; and she looked on the whole scene, the river, the trees scattered on its banks, and the winding of the valley, as far as she could trace it, with delight. As they passed into other rooms, these objects were taking different positions; but from every window there were beauties to be seen. The rooms were lofty and handsome, and their furniture suitable to the fortune of their proprietor; but Elizabeth saw, with admiration of his taste, that it was neither gaudy nor uselessly fine; with less of splendour, and more real elegance, than the furniture of Rosings.

"And of this place," thought she, "I might have been mistress! With these rooms I might now have been familiarly acquainted! Instead of viewing them as stranger, I might have rejoiced in them as my own, and welcomed to them as visitors my uncle and aunt. – But no," – recollecting herself, – "that could never be; my uncle and aunt would have been lost to me; I should not have been allowed to invite them."

This was a lucky recollection – it saved her from something

like regret.

She longed to enquire of the housekeeper, whether her master were really absent, but had not courage for it. At length, however, the question was asked by her uncle; and she turned away with alarm, while Mrs. Reynolds replied, that he was, adding, "but we expect him tomorrow, with a large party of friends." How rejoiced was Elizabeth that their own journey had not by any circumstance been delayed a day!

Her aunt now called her to look at a picture. She approached, and saw the likeness of Mr. Wickham suspended, amongst several other miniatures, over the mantelpiece. Her aunt asked her, smilingly, how she liked it. The housekeeper came forward, and told them it was the picture of a young gentleman, the son of her late master's steward, who had been brought up by him at his own expense. – "He is now gone into the army," she added; "but I am afraid he has turned out very wild."

Mrs. Gardiner looked at her niece with a smile, but Elizabeth could not return it.

"And that," said Mrs. Reynolds, pointing to another of the miniatures, "is my master – and very like him. It was drawn at the same time as the other – about eight years ago."

"I have heard much of your master's fine person," said Mrs. Gardiner, looking at the picture; "it is a handsome face. But, Lizzy, you can tell us whether it is like or not."

Mrs. Reynolds's respect for Elizabeth seemed to increase on this intimation of her knowing her master.

"Does that young lady know Mr. Darcy?"

Elizabeth coloured, and said – "A little."

"And do not you think him a very handsome gentleman, Ma'am?"

"Yes, very handsome."

"I am sure *I* know none so handsome; but in the gallery

upstairs you will see a finer, larger picture of him than this. This room was my late master's favourite room, and these miniatures are just as they used to be then. He was very fond of them."

This accounted to Elizabeth for Mr. Wickham's being among them.

Mrs. Reynolds then directed their attention to one of Miss Darcy, drawn when she was only eight years old.

"And is Miss Darcy as handsome as her brother?" said Mr. Gardiner.

"Oh! yes – the handsomest young lady that ever was seen; and so accomplished! – She plays and sings all day long. In the next room is a new instrument just come down for her – a present from my master; she comes here tomorrow with him."

Mr. Gardiner, whose manners were easy and pleasant, encouraged her communicativeness by his questions and remarks; Mrs. Reynolds, either from pride or attachment, had evidently great pleasure in talking of her master and his sister.

"Is your master much at Pemberley in the course of the year?"

"Not so much as I could wish, Sir; but I dare say he may spend half his time here; and Miss Darcy is always down for the summer months."

"Except," thought Elizabeth, "when she goes to Ramsgate."

"If your master would marry, you might see more of him."

"Yes, Sir; but I do not know when *that* will be. I do not know who is good enough for him."

Mr. and Mrs. Gardiner smiled. Elizabeth could not help saying, "It is very much to his credit, I am sure, that you should think so."

"I say no more than the truth, and everybody will say that knows him," replied the other. Elizabeth thought this was going pretty far; and she listened with increasing astonishment as the housekeeper added, "I have never had a cross word from him in my life, and I have known him ever since he was four years old."

This was praise, of all others most extraordinary, most opposite to her ideas. That he was not a good-tempered man, had been her firmest opinion. Her keenest attention was awakened; she longed to hear more, and was grateful to her uncle for saying,

"There are very few people of whom so much can be said. You are lucky in having such a master."

"Yes, Sir, I know I am. If I was to go through the world, I could not meet with a better. But I have always observed, that they who are good-natured when children, are good-natured when they grow up; and he was always the sweetest-tempered, most generous-hearted, boy in the world."

Elizabeth almost stared at her. – "Can this be Mr. Darcy!" thought she.

"His father was an excellent man," said Mrs. Gardiner.

"Yes, Ma'am, that he was indeed; and his son will be just like him – just as affable to the poor."

Elizabeth listened, wondered, doubted, and was impatient for more. Mrs. Reynolds could interest her on no other point. She related the subject of the pictures, the dimensions of the rooms, and the price of the furniture, in vain. Mr. Gardiner, highly amused by the kind of family prejudice, to which he attributed her excessive commendation of her master, soon led again to the subject; and she dwelt with energy on his many merits, as they proceeded together up the great staircase.

"He is the best landlord, and the best master," said she, "that ever lived. Not like the wild young men nowadays, who think of nothing but themselves. There is not one of his tenants or servants but will give him a good name. Some people call him proud; but I am sure I never saw anything of it. To my fancy, it is only because he does not rattle away like other young men."

"In what an amiable light does this place him!" thought Elizabeth.

"This fine account of him," whispered her aunt, as they walked, "is not quite consistent with his behaviour to our poor friend."

"Perhaps we might be deceived."

"That is not very likely; our authority was too good."

On reaching the spacious lobby above, they were shown into a very pretty sitting-room, lately fitted up with greater elegance and lightness than the apartments below; and were informed that it was but just done, to give pleasure to Miss Darcy, who had taken a liking to the room, when last at Pemberley.

"He is certainly a good brother," said Elizabeth, as she walked towards one of the windows.

Mrs. Reynolds anticipated Miss Darcy's delight, when she should enter the room. "And this is always the way with him," she added. – "Whatever can give his sister any pleasure, is sure to be done in a moment. There is nothing he would not do for her."

The picture gallery, and two or three of the principal bed-rooms, were all that remained to be shown. In the former were many good paintings; but Elizabeth knew nothing of the art; and from such as had been already visible below, she had willingly turned to look at some drawings of Miss Darcy's, in crayons, whose subjects were usually more interesting, and also more intelligible.

In the gallery there were many family portraits, but they could have little to fix the attention of a stranger. Elizabeth walked on in quest of the only face whose features would be known to her. At last it arrested her – and she beheld a striking resemblance of Mr. Darcy, with such a smile over the face, as she remembered to have sometimes seen, when he looked at her. She stood several minutes before the picture in earnest contemplation, and returned to it again before they quitted the gallery. Mrs. Reynolds informed them, that it had been taken in his father's lifetime.

There was certainly at this moment, in Elizabeth's mind, a more gentle sensation towards the original, than she had ever felt in the height of their acquaintance. The commendation bestowed on him by Mrs. Reynolds was of no trifling nature. What praise is more valuable than the praise of an intelligent servant? As brother, a landlord, a master, she considered how many people's happiness were in his guardianship! – How much of pleasure or pain it was in his power to bestow! – How much of good or evil must be done by him! Every idea that had been brought forward by the housekeeper was favourable to his character, and as she stood before the canvas, on which he was represented, and fixed his eyes upon herself, she thought of his regard with a deeper sentiment of gratitude than it had ever raised before; she remembered its warmth, and softened its impropriety of expression.

When all of the house that was open to general inspection had been seen, they returned downstairs, and taking leave of the housekeeper, were consigned over to the gardener, who met them at the hall door.

As they walked across the lawn towards the river, Elizabeth turned back to look again; her uncle and aunt stopped also, and while the former was conjecturing as to the date of the building, the owner of it himself suddenly came forward from the road, which led behind it to the stables.

They were within twenty yards of each other, and so abrupt was his appearance, that it was impossible to avoid his sight. Their eyes instantly met, and the cheeks of each were overspread with the deepest blush. He absolutely started, and for a moment seemed immoveable from surprise; but shortly recovering himself, advanced towards the party, and spoke to Elizabeth, if not in terms of perfect composure, at least of perfect civility.

She had instinctively turned away; but, stopping on his approach, received his compliments with an embarrassment impossible to be overcome. Had his first appearance, or his resemblance to the picture they had just been examining, been insufficient to assure the other two that they now saw Mr. Darcy, the gardener's expression of surprise, on beholding his master, must immediately have told it. They stood a little aloof while he was talking to their niece, who, astonished and confused, scarcely dared lift her eyes to his face, and knew not what answer she returned to his civil enquiries after her family. Amazed at the alteration in his manner since they last parted, every sentence that he uttered was increasing her embarrassment; and every idea of the impropriety of her being found there, recurring to her mind, the few minutes in which they continued together, were some of the most uncomfortable of her life. Nor did he seem much more at ease; when he spoke, his accent had none of its usual sedateness; and he repeated his enquiries as to the time of her having left Longbourn, and of her stay in Derbyshire, so often, and in so hurried a way, as plainly spoke the distraction of his thoughts.

At length, every idea seemed to fail him; and, after standing a few moments without saying a word, he suddenly recollected himself, and took leave.

The others then joined her, and expressed admiration of his figure; but Elizabeth heard not a word, and, wholly engrossed by her own feelings, followed them in silence. She was overpowered by shame and vexation. Her coming there was the most unfortunate, the most ill-judged thing in the world! How strange must it appear to him! In what a disgraceful light might it not strike so vain a man! It might seem as if she had purposely thrown herself in his way again! Oh! why did she come? or, why did he thus come a day before he was expected? Had they been only ten minutes sooner, they should have been beyond the reach of his discrimination; for it was plain that he was that moment arrived, that moment alighted from his horse or his carriage. She blushed again and again over the perverseness of the meeting. And his behaviour, so strikingly altered, – what could it mean? That he should even speak to her was amazing! – but to speak with such civility, to enquire after her family! Never in her life had she seen his manners so little dignified, never had he spoken with such gentleness as on this unexpected meeting. What a contrast did it offer to his last address in Rosings Park, when he put his letter into her hand! She knew not what to think, or how to account for it.

They had now entered a beautiful walk by the side of the water, and every step was bringing forward a nobler fall of ground, or a finer reach of the woods to which they were approaching; but it was some time before Elizabeth was sensible of any of it; and, though she answered mechanically to the repeated appeals of her uncle and aunt, and seemed to direct her eyes to such objects as they pointed out, she distinguished no part of the scene. Her thoughts were all fixed on that one spot of Pemberley House, whichever it might be, where Mr. Darcy then was. She longed to know what at that moment was passing in his mind; in what manner he thought of her, and whether, in defiance of everything, she was still dear to him. Perhaps he had been civil, only because he felt himself at ease; yet there had been *that* in his voice, which was not like ease. Whether he had felt more of pain or of pleasure in seeing her, she could not tell, but he certainly had not seen her with composure.

At length, however, the remarks of her companions on her absence of mind aroused her, and she felt the necessity of appearing more like herself.

They entered the woods, and bidding adieu to the river for a while, ascended some of the higher grounds; whence, in spots where the opening of the trees gave the eye power to wander, were many charming views of the valley, the opposite hills, with the long range of woods overspreading many, and occasionally part of the stream. Mr. Gardiner expressed a wish of going round the whole Park, but feared it might be beyond a walk. With a triumphant smile, they were told that it was ten miles round. It settled the matter; and they pursued the accustomed circuit; which brought them again, after some time, in a descent among hanging woods, to the edge of the water, in one of its narrowest parts. They crossed it by a simple bridge, in character with the general air of the scene; it was a spot less adorned than any they had yet visited; and the valley, here contracted into a glen, allowed room only for the stream, and a narrow walk amidst the rough coppice-wood which bordered it. Elizabeth longed to explore its windings; but when they had crossed the bridge, and perceived their distance from the house, Mrs. Gardiner, who was not a great walker, could go no farther, and thought only of returning to the carriage as quickly as possible. Her niece was, therefore, obliged to submit, and they took their way towards the house on the opposite side of the river, in the nearest direction; but their progress was slow, for Mr. Gardiner, though seldom able to indulge the taste, was very fond of fishing, and was so much engaged in watching the occasional appearance of some trout in the water, and talking to the man about them, that he advanced but little. Whilst wandering on in this slow manner, they were again surprised, and Elizabeth's astonishment was quite equal to what it had been at first, by the sight of Mr. Darcy approaching them, and at no great distance. The walk being here less sheltered than on the other side, allowed them to see him before they met. Elizabeth, however astonished, was at least more prepared for an interview than before, and resolved to appear and to speak with calmness, if he really intended to meet them. For a few moments, indeed, she felt that he would probably strike into some other path. This idea lasted while a turning in the walk concealed him from their view; the turning passed, he was immediately before them. With a glance she saw, that he had lost none of his recent civility; and, to imitate his politeness, she began, as they met, to admire the beauty of the place; but she had not got beyond the words "delightful," and "charming," when some unlucky recollections obtruded, and she fancied that praise of Pemberley from her, might be mischievously construed. Her colour changed, and she said no more.

Mrs. Gardiner was standing a little behind; and on her pausing, he asked her, if she would do him the honour of introducing him to her friends. This was a stroke of civility for which she was quite unprepared; and she could hardly suppress a smile, at his being now seeking the acquaintance of some of those very people, against whom his pride had revolted, in his offer to herself. "What will be his surprise," thought she, "when he knows who they are! He takes them now for people of fashion."

The introduction, however, was immediately made; and as she named their relationship to herself, she stole a sly look at him, to see how he bore it, and was not without the expectation of his decamping as fast as he could from such disgraceful companions. That he was *surprised* by the connection was evident; he sustained it however with fortitude, and so far from going away, turned back with them, and entered into conversation with Mr. Gardiner. Elizabeth could not but be pleased, could not but triumph. It was consoling, that he should know she had some relations for whom there was no need to blush. She listened most attentively to all that passed between them, and gloried in every expression, every sentence of her uncle, which marked his intelligence, his taste, or his good manners.

The conversation soon turned upon fishing; and she heard Mr. Darcy invite him, with the greatest civility, to fish there as often as he chose, while he continued in the neighbourhood, offering at the same time to supply him with fishing tackle, and pointing out those parts of the stream where there was usually most sport. Mrs. Gardiner, who was walking arm in arm with Elizabeth, gave her a look expressive of her wonder. Elizabeth said nothing, but it gratified her exceedingly; the compliment must be all for herself. Her astonishment, however, was extreme; and continually was she repeating, "Why is he so altered? From what can it proceed? It cannot be for *me,* it cannot be for *my* sake that his manners are thus softened. My reproofs at Hunsford could not work such a change as this. It is impossible that he should still love me."

After walking some time in this way, the two ladies in front, the two gentlemen behind, on resuming their places, after descending to the brink of the river for the better inspection of some curious water-plant, there chanced to be a little alteration. It originated in Mrs. Gardiner, who, fatigued by the exercise of the morning, found Elizabeth's arm inadequate to her support, and consequently preferred her husband's. Mr. Darcy took her place by her niece, and they walked on together. After a short silence, the lady first spoke. She wished him to know that she had been assured of his absence before she came to the place, and accordingly began by observing, that his arrival had been very unexpected – "for your housekeeper," she added, "informed us that you would certainly not be here till tomorrow; and indeed, before we left Bakewell, we understood that you were not immediately expected in the country." He acknowledged the truth of it all, and said that business with his steward had occasioned his coming forward a few hours before the rest of the party with whom he had been travelling. "They will join me early tomorrow," he continued, "and among them are some who will claim an acquaintance with you, – Mr. Bingley and his sisters."

Elizabeth answered only by a slight bow. Her thoughts were instantly driven back to the time when Mr. Bingley's name had been the last mentioned between them; and if she might judge by his complexion, *his* mind was not very differently engaged.

"There is also one other person in the party," he continued after a pause, "who more particularly wishes to be known to you, – Will you allow me, or do I ask too much, to introduce my sister to your acquaintance during your stay at Lambton?"

The surprise of such an application was great indeed; it was too great for her to know in what manner she acceded to it. She immediately felt that whatever desire Miss Darcy might have of being acquainted with her, must be the work of her brother, and without looking farther, it was satisfactory; it was gratifying to know that his resentment had not made him think really ill of her.

They now walked on in silence; each of them deep in thought. Elizabeth was not comfortable; that was impossible; but she was flattered and pleased. His wish of introducing his sister to her, was a compliment of the highest kind. They soon outstripped the others, and when they had reached the carriage, Mr. and Mrs. Gardiner were half a quarter of a mile behind.

He then asked her to walk into the house – but she declared herself not tired, and they stood together on the lawn. At such a time, much might have been said, and silence was very awkward. She wanted to talk, but there seemed an embargo on every subject. At last she recollected that she had been travelling, and they talked of Matlock and Dove Dale with great perseverance. Yet time and her aunt moved slowly – and her patience and her ideas were nearly worn ou before the tête-è-tête was over. On Mr. and Mrs. Gardiner's coming up, they were all pressed to go into the house and take some refreshment; but this was declined, and they parted on each side with the utmost politeness. Mr. Darcy handed the ladies into the carriage, and when it drove off, Elizabeth saw him walking slowly towards the house.

The observations of her uncle and aunt now began; and each of them pronounced him to be infinitely superior to anything they had expected. "He is perfectly well behaved, polite, and unassuming," said her uncle.

"There *is* something a little stately in him to be sure," replied her aunt, "but it is confined to his air, and is not unbecoming. I can now say with the housekeeper, that though some people may call him proud, *I* have seen nothing of it."

"I was never more surprised than by his behaviour to us. It was more than civil; it was really attentive; and there was no necessity for such attention. His acquaintance with Elizabeth was very trifling."

"To be sure, Lizzy," said her aunt, "he is not so handsome as Wickham; or rather he has not Wickham's countenance, for his features are perfectly good. But how came you to tell me that he was so disagreeable?"

Elizabeth excused herself as well as she could; said that she had liked him better when they had met in Kent than before, and that she had never seen him so pleasant as this morning.

"But perhaps he may be a little whimsical in his civilities," replied her uncle. "Your great men often are; and therefore I shall not take him at his word about fishing, as he might change his mind another day, and warn me off his grounds."

Elizabeth felt that they had entirely mistaken his character, but said nothing.

"From what we have seen of him," continued Mrs. Gardiner, "I really should not have thought that he could have behaved in so cruel a way by anybody, as he has done by poor Wickham. He has not an ill-natured look. On the contrary, there is something pleasing about his mouth when he speaks. And there is something of dignity in his countenance, that would not give one an unfavourable idea of his heart. But to be sure, the good lady who showed us the house, did give him a most flaming character! I could hardly help laughing aloud sometimes. But he is a liberal master, I suppose, and *that* in the eye of a servant comprehends every virtue."

Elizabeth here felt herself called on to say something in vindication of his behaviour to Wickham; and therefore gave them to understand, in as guarded a manner as she could, that by what she had heard from his relations in Kent, his actions were capable of a very different construction; and that his character was by no means so faulty, nor Wickham's so amiable, as they had been considered in Hertfordshire. In confirmation of this, she related the particulars of all the pecuniary transactions in which they had been connected, without actually naming her authority, but stating it ti be as such as might be relied on.

Mrs. Gardiner was surprised and concerned; but as they were now approaching the scene of her former pleasures, every idea gave way to the charm of recollection; and she was too much engaged in pointing out to her husband all the interesting spots in its environs, to think of anything else. Fatigued as she had been by the morning's walk, they had no sooner dined than she set off again in quest of her former acquaintance, and the evening was spent in the satisfactions of an intercourse renewed after many years' discontinuance.

The occurrences of the day were too full of interest to leave Elizabeth much attention for any of these new friends; and she could do nothing but think, and think with wonder, of Mr. Darcy's civility, and above all, of his wishing her to be acquainted with his sister.

# Chapter 44

ELIZABETH HAD settled it that Mr. Darcy would bring his sister to visit her, the very day after her reaching Pemberley; and was consequently resolved not to be out of sight of the inn the whole of that morning. But her conclusion was false; for on the very morning after their own arrival at Lambton, these visitors came. They had been walking about the place with some of their new friends, and were just returned to the inn to dress themselves for dining with the same family, when the sound of a carriage drew them to the window, and they saw a gentleman and a lady in a curricle, driving up the street. Elizabeth immediately recognizing the livery, guessed what it meant, and imparted no small degree of surprise to her relations, by acquainting them with the honour which she expected. Her uncle and aunt were all amazement; and the embarrassment of her manner as she spoke, joined to the circumstance itself, and many of the circumstances of the preceding day, opened to them a new idea on the business. Nothing had ever suggested it before, but they now felt that there was no other way of accounting for such attentions from such a quarter, than by supposing a partiality for their niece. While these newly-born notions were passing in their heads, the perturbation of Elizabeth's feelings was every moment increasing. She was quite amazed at her own discomposure; but amongst other causes of disquiet, she dreaded lest the partiality of the brother should have said too much in her favour; and more than commonly anxious to please, she naturally suspected that every power of pleasing would fail her.

She retreated from the window, fearful of being seen; and as she walked up and down the room, endeavouring to compose herself, saw such looks of enquiring surprise in her uncle and aunt, as made everything worse.

Miss Darcy and her brother appeared, and this formidable introduction took place. With astonishment did Elizabeth see, that her new acquaintance was at least as much embarrassed as herself. Since her being at Lambton, she had heard that Miss Darcy was exceedingly proud; but the observation of a very few minutes convinced her, that she was only exceedingly shy. She found it difficult to obtain even a word from her beyond a monosyllable.

Miss Darcy was tall, and on a larger scale than Elizabeth; and, though little more than sixteen, her figure was formed, and her appearance womanly and graceful. She was less handsome than her brother; but there was sense and good humour in her face, and her manners were perfectly unassuming and gentle. Elizabeth, who had expected to find in her as acute and unembarrassed an observer as ever Mr. Darcy had been, was much relieved by discerning such different feelings.

They had not long been together, before Darcy told her that Bingley was also coming to wait on her; and she had barely time to express her satisfaction, and prepare for such a visitor, when Bingley's quick step was heard on the stairs, and in a moment he entered the room. All Elizabeth's anger against him had been long done away; but, had she still felt any, it could hardly have stood its ground against the unaffected cordiality with which he expressed himself, on seeing her again. He enquired in a friendly, though general way, after her family, and looked and spoke with the same good-humoured ease that he had ever done.

To Mr. and Mrs. Gardiner he was scarcely a less interesting personage than to herself. They had long wished to see him. The whole party before them, indeed, excited a lively attention. The suspicions which had just arisen of Mr. Darcy and their niece, directed their observation towards each with an earnest, though guarded, enquiry; and they soon drew from those enquiries the full conviction that one of them at least knew what it was to love. Of the lady's sensations they remained a little in doubt; but that the gentleman was overflowing with admiration was evident enough.

Elizabeth, on her side, had much to do. She wanted to ascertain the feelings of each of her visitors; she wanted to compose her own, and to make herself agreeable to all; and in the latter object, where she feared most to fail, she was most sure of success, for those to whom she endeavoured to give pleasure were prepossessed in her favour. Bingley was ready, Georgiana was eager, and Darcy determined, to be pleased.

In seeing Bingley, her thoughts naturally flew to her sister; and oh! how ardently did she long to know, whether any of his were directed in a like manner. Sometimes she could fancy, that he talked less than on former occasions, and once or twice pleased herself with the notion that as he looked at her, he was trying to trace a resemblance. But, though this might be imaginary, she could not be deceived as to his behaviour to Miss Darcy, who had been set up as a rival of Jane. No look appeared on either side that spoke particular regard. Nothing occurred between them that could justify the hopes of his sister. On this point she was soon satisfied; and two or three little circumstances occurred ere they parted, which, in her anxious interpretation, denoted a recollection of Jane, not untinctured by tenderness, and a wish of saying more that might lead to the mention of her, had he dared. He observed to her, at a moment when the others were talking together, and in a tone which had something of real regret, that it "was a very long time since he had had the pleasure of seeing her"; and, before she could reply, he added, "It is above eight months. We have not met since the 26th of November, when we were all dancing together at Netherfield."

Elizabeth was pleased to find his memory so exact; and he afterwards took occasion to ask her, when unattended to by any of the rest, whether *all* her sisters were at Longbourn. There was not much in the question, nor in the preceding remark, but there was a look and a manner which gave them meaning.

It was not often that she could turn her eyes on Mr. Darcy himself; but, whenever she did catch a glimpse, she saw an expression of general complaisance, and in all that he said, she heard an accent so removed from hauteur or disdain of his companions, as convinced her that the improvement of manners which she had yesterday witnessed, however temporary its existence might prove, had at least outlived one day. When she saw him thus seeking the acquaintance, and courting the good opinion of people, with whom any intercourse a few months ago would have been a disgrace; when she saw him thus civil, not only to herself, but to the very relations whom he had openly disdained, and recollected their last lively scene in Hunsford Parsonage, the difference, the change was so great, and struck so forcibly on her mind, that she could hardly restrain her astonishment from being visible. Never, even in the company of his dear friends at Netherfield, or his dignified relations at Rosings, had she seen him so desirous to please, so free from self-consequence, or unbending reserve as now, when no importance could result from the success of his endeavours, and when even the acquaintance of those to whom his attentions were addressed, would draw down the ridicule and censure of the ladies both of Netherfield and Rosings.

Their visitors stayed with them above half an hour, and when they arose to depart, Mr. Darcy called on his sister to join him in expressing their wish of seeing Mr. and Mrs. Gardiner, and Miss Bennet, to dinner at Pemberley, before they left the country. Miss Darcy, though with a diffidence which marked her little in the habit of giving invitations, readily obeyed. Mrs. Gardiner looked at her niece, desirous of knowing how *she*, whom the invitation most concerned, felt disposed as to its acceptance, but Elizabeth had turned away her head. Presuming, however, that this studied avoidance spoke rather a momentary embarrassment, than any dislike of the proposal, and seeing in her husband, who was fond of society, a perfect willingness to accept it, she ventured to engage for her attendance, and the day after the next was fixed on.

Bingley expressed great pleasure in the certainty of seeing Elizabeth again, having still a great deal to say to her, and many enquiries to make after all their Hertfordshire friends. Elizabeth, construing all this into a wish of hearing her speak of her sister, was pleased; and on this account, as well as some others, found herself, when their visitors left them, capable of considering the last half hour with some satisfaction, though while it was passing, the enjoyment of it had been little. Eager to be alone, and fearful of enquiries or hints from her uncle and aunt, she stayed with them only long enough to hear their favourable opinion of Bingley, and then hurried away to dress.

But she had no reason to fear Mr. and Mrs. Gardiner's curiosity; it was not their wish to force her communication. It was evident that she was much better acquainted with Mr. Darcy than they had before any idea of; it was evident that he was very much in love with her. They saw much to interest, but nothing to justify enquiry.

Of Mr. Darcy it was now a matter of anxiety to think well; and, as far as their acquaintance reached, there was no fault to find. They could not be untouched by his politeness, and had they drawn his character from their own feelings, and his servant's report, without any reference to any other account, the circle in Hertfordshire to which he was known, would not have recognised it for Mr. Darcy. There was now an interest, however, in believing the housekeeper; and they soon became sensible, that the authority of a servant who had known him since he was four years old, and whose own manners indicated respectability, was not to be hastily rejected. Neither had anything occurred in the intelligence of their Lambton friends, that could materially lessen its weight. They had nothing to accuse him of but pride; pride he probably had, and if not, it would certainly be imputed by the inhabitants of a small market-town, where the family did not visit. It was acknowledged, however, that he was a liberal man, and did much good among the poor.

With respect to Wickham, the travellers soon found that he was not held there in much estimation; for though the chief of his concerns, with the son of his patron, were imperfectly understood, it was yet a well known fact that, on his quitting Derbyshire, he had left many debts behind him, which Mr. Darcy afterwards discharged.

As for Elizabeth, her thoughts were at Pemberley this evening more than the last; and the evening, though as it passed it seemed long, was not long enough to determine her feelings towards *one* in that mansion; and she lay awake two whole hours, endeavouring to make them out. She certainly did not hate him. No; hatred had vanished long ago, and she had almost as long been ashamed of ever feeling a dislike against him, that could be so called. The respect created by the conviction of his valuable qualities, though at first unwillingly admitted, had for some time ceased to be repugnant to her feelings; and it was now heightened into somewhat of a friendlier nature, by the testimony so highly in his favour, and bringing forward his disposition in so amiable a light, which yesterday had produced. But above all, above respect and esteem, there was a motive within her of goodwill which could not be overlooked. It was gratitude. – Gratitude, not merely for having once loved her, but for loving her still well enough, to forgive all the petulance and acrimony of her manner in rejecting him, and all the unjust accusations accompanying her rejection. He who, she had been persuaded, would avoid her as his greatest enemy, seemed, on this accidental meeting, most eager to preserve the acquaintance, and without any indelicate display of regard, or any peculiarity of manner, where their two selves only were concerned, was soliciting the good opinion of her friends, and bent on making her known to his sister. Such a change in a man of so much pride, excited not only astonishment but gratitude – for to love, ardent love, it must be attributed; and as such its impression on her was of a sort to be encouraged, as by no means unpleasing, though it could not be exactly defined. She respected, she esteemed, she was grateful to him, she felt a real interest in his welfare; and she only wanted to know how far she wished that welfare to depend upon herself, and how far it would be for the happiness of both that she should employ the power, which her fancy told her she still possessed, of bringing on the renewal of his addresses.

It had been settled in the evening, between the aunt and niece, that such a striking civility as Miss Darcy's, in coming to them on the very day of her arrival at Pemberley, for she had reached it only to a late breakfast, ought to be imitated, though it could not be equalled, by some exertion of politeness on their side; and, consequently, that it would be highly expedient to wait on her at Pemberley the following morning. They were, therefore, to go. – Elizabeth was pleased, though, when she asked herself the reason, she had very little to say in reply.

Mr. Gardiner left them soon after breakfast. The fishing scheme had been renewed the day before, and a positive engagement made of his meeting some of the gentlemen at Pemberley by noon.

# Chapter 45

CONVINCED AS Elizabeth now was that Miss Bingley's dislike of her had originated in jealousy, she could not help feeling how unwelcome her appearance at Pemberley must be to her, and was curious to know with how much civility on that lady's side, the acquaintance would now be renewed.

On reaching the house, they were shown through the hall into the saloon, whose northern aspect rendered it delightful for summer. Its windows opening to the ground, admitted a most refreshing view of the high woody hills behind the house, and of the beautiful oaks and Spanish chestnuts which were scattered over the intermediate lawn.

In this room they were received by Miss Darcy, who was sitting there with Mrs. Hurst and Miss Bingley, and the lady with whom she lived in London. Georgiana's reception of them was very civil; but attended with all that embarrassment which, though proceeding from shyness and the fear of doing wrong, would easily give to those who felt themselves inferior, the belief of her being proud and reserved. Mrs. Gardiner and her niece, however, did her justice, and pitied her.

By Mrs. Hurst and Miss Bingley, they were noticed only by a curtsey; and on their being seated, a pause, awkward as such pauses must always be, succeeded for a few moments. It was first broken by Mrs. Annesley, a genteel, agreeable-looking woman, whose endeavour to introduce some kind of discourse, proved her to be more truly well bred than either of the others; and between her and Mrs. Gardiner, with occasional help from Elizabeth, the conversation was carried on. Miss Darcy looked as if she wished for courage enough to join in it; and sometimes did venture a short sentence, when there was least danger of its being heard.

Elizabeth soon saw that she was herself closely watched by Miss Bingley, and that she could not speak a word, especially to Miss Darcy, without calling her attention. This observation would not have prevented her from trying to talk to the latter, had they not been seated at an inconvenient distance; but she was not sorry to be spared the necessity of saying much. Her own thoughts were employing her. She expected every moment that some of the gentlemen would enter the room. She wished, she feared that the master of the house might be amongst them; and whether she wished or feared it most, she could scarcely determine. After sitting in this manner a quarter of an hour, without hearing Miss Bingley's voice, Elizabeth was roused by receiving from her a cold enquiry after the health of her family. She answered with equal indifference and brevity, and the others said no more.

The next variation which their visit afforded was produced by the entrance of servants with cold meat, cake, and a variety of all the finest fruits in season; but this did not take place till after many a significant look and smile from Mrs. Annesley to Miss Darcy had been given, to remind her of her post. There was now employment for the whole party; for though they could not all talk, they could all eat; and the beautiful pyramids of grapes, nectarines, and peaches, soon collected them round the table.

While thus engaged, Elizabeth had a fair opportunity of deciding whether she most feared or wished for the appearance of Mr. Darcy, by the feelings which prevailed on his entering the room; and then, though but a moment before she had believed her wishes to predominate, she began to regret that he came.

He had been some time with Mr. Gardiner, who, with two or three other gentlemen from the house, was engaged by the river, and had left him only on learning that the ladies of the family intended a visit to Georgiana that morning. No sooner did he appear, than Elizabeth wisely resolved to be perfectly easy and unembarrassed; – a resolution the more necessary to be made, but perhaps not the more easily kept, because she saw that the suspicions of the whole party were awakened against them, and that there was scarcely an eye which did not watch his behaviour when he first came into the room. In no countenance was attentive curiosity so strongly marked as in Miss Bingley's, in spite of the smiles which overspread her face whenever she spoke to one of its objects; for jealousy had not yet made her desperate, and her attentions to Mr. Darcy were by no means over. Miss Darcy, on her brother's entrance, exerted herself much more to talk; and Elizabeth saw that he was anxious for his sister and herself to get acquainted, and forwarded, as much as possible, every attempt at conversation on either side. Miss Bingley saw all this likewise; and, in the imprudence of anger, took the first opportunity of saying, with sneering civility,

"Pray, Miss Eliza, are not the —shire militia removed from Meryton? They must be a great loss to *your* family."

In Darcy's presence she dared not mention Wickham's name; but Elizabeth instantly comprehended that he was uppermost in her thoughts; and the various recollections connected with him gave her a moment's distress; but, exerting herself vigorously to repel the ill-natured attack, she presently answered the question in a tolerably disengaged tone. While she spoke, an involuntary glance showed her Darcy with an heightened complexion, earnestly looking at her, and his sister overcome with confusion, and unable to lift up her eyes. Had Miss Bingley know what pain she was then giving her beloved friend, she undoubtedly would have refrained from the hint; but she had merely intended to discompose Elizabeth, by bringing forward the idea of a man to whom she believed her partial, to make her betray a sensibility which might injure her in Darcy's opinion, and perhaps to remind the latter of all the follies and absurdities, by which some part of her family were connected with that corps. Not a syllable had ever reached her of Miss Darcy's meditated elopement. To no creature had it been revealed, where secrecy was possible, except to Elizabeth; and from all Bingley's connections her brother was particularly anxious to conceal it, from that very wish which Elizabeth had long ago attributed to him, of their becoming hereafter her own. He had certainly formed such a plan, and without meaning that it should effect his endeavour to separate him from Miss Bennet, it is probable that it might add something to his lively concern for the welfare of his friend.

Elizabeth's collected behaviour, however, soon quieted his emotion; and as Miss Bingley, vexed and disappointed, dared not approach nearer to Wickham, Georgiana also recovered in time, though not enough to be able to speak any more. Her brother, whose eye she feared to meet, scarcely recollected her interest in the affair, and the very circumstance which had been designed to turn his thoughts from Elizabeth, seemed to have fixed them on her more, and more cheerfully.

Their visit did not continue long after the question and answer above mentioned; and while Mr. Darcy was attending them to their carriage, Miss Bingley was venting her feelings in criticisms on Elizabeth's person, behaviour, and dress. But Georgiana would not join her. Her brother's recommendation was enough to ensure her favour: his judgement could not err, and he had spoken in such terms of Elizabeth, as to leave Georgiana without the power of finding her otherwise than lovely and amiable. When Darcy returned to the saloon, Miss Bingley could not help repeating to him some part of what she had been saying to his sister.

"How very ill Eliza Bennet looks this morning, Mr. Darcy," she cried; "I never in my life saw anyone so much altered as she is since the winter. She is grown so brown and coarse! Louisa and I were agreeing that we should not have known her again."

However little Mr. Darcy might have liked such an address, he contented himself with coolly replying, that he perceived no other alteration than her being rather tanned, – no miraculous consequence of travelling in the summer.

"For my own part," she rejoined, "I must confess that I never could see any beauty in her. Her face is too thin; her complexion has no brilliancy; and her features are not at all handsome. Her nose wants character; there is nothing marked in its lines. Her teeth are tolerable, but not out of the common way; and as for her eyes, which have sometimes been called so fine, I never could perceive anything extraordinary in them. They have a sharp, shrewish look, which I do not like at all; and in her air altogether, there is a self-sufficiency without fashion, which is intolerable."

Persuaded as Miss Bingley was that Darcy admired Elizabeth, this was not the best method of recommending herself; but angry people are not always wise; and in seeing him at last look somewhat nettled, she had all the success she expected. He was resolutely silent however; and, from a determination of making him speak, she continued,

"I remember, when we first knew her in Hertfordshire, how amazed we all were to find that she was a reputed beauty; and I particularly recollect your saying one night, after they had been dining at Netherfield, '*She* a beauty! – I should as soon call her mother a wit.' But afterwards she seemed to improve on you, and I believe you thought her rather pretty at one time."

"Yes," replied Darcy, who could contain himself no longer,

"but *that* was only when I first knew her, for it is many months since I have considered her as one of the handsomest women of my acquaintance."

He then went away, and Miss Bingley was left to all the satisfaction of having forced him to say what gave no one any pain but herself.

Mrs. Gardiner and Elizabeth talked of all that had occurred, during their visit, as they returned, except what had particularly interested them both. The look and behaviour of everybody they had seen were discussed, except of the person who had mostly engaged their attention. They talked of his sister, his friends, his house, his fruit, of everything but himself; yet Elizabeth was longing to know what Mrs. Gardiner thought of him, and Mrs. Gardiner would have been highly gratified by her niece's beginning the subject.

# *Chapter 46*

ELIZABETH HAD been a good deal disappointed in not finding a letter from Jane, on their first arrival at Lambton; and this disappointment had been renewed on each of the mornings that had now been spent there; but on the third, her repining was over, and her sister justified by the receipt of two letters from her at once, on one of which was marked that it had been missent elsewhere. Elizabeth was not surprised at it, as Jane had written the direction remarkably ill.

They had just been preparing to walk as the letters came in; and her uncle and aunt, leaving her to enjoy them in quiet, set off by themselves. The one missent must be first attended to; it had been written five days ago. The beginning contained an account of all their little parties and engagements, with such news as the country afforded; but the latter half, which was dated a day later, and written in evident agitation, gave more important intelligence. It was to this effect:

"Since writing the above, dearest Lizzy, something has occurred of a most unexpected and serious nature; but I am afraid of alarming you – be assured that we are all well. What I have to say relates to poor Lydia. An express came at twelve last night, just as we were all gone to bed, from Colonel Forster, to inform us that she was gone off to Scotland with one of his officers; to own the truth, with Wickham! – Imagine our surprise. To Kitty, however, it does not seem so wholly unexpected. I am very, very sorry. So imprudent a match on both sides! – But I am willing to hope the best, and that his character has been misunderstood. Thoughtless and indiscreet I can easily believe him, but this step (and let us rejoice over it) marks nothing bad at heart. His choice is disinterested at least, for he must know my father can give her nothing. Our poor mother is sadly grieved. My father bears it better. How thankful am I, that we never let them know what has been said against him; we must forget it ourselves. They were off Saturday night about twelve, as is conjectured, but were not missed till yesterday morning at eight. The express was sent off directly. My dear Lizzy, they must have passed within ten miles of us. Colonel Forster gives us reason to expect him here soon. Lydia left a few lines for his wife, informing her of their intention. I must conclude, for I cannot be long from my poor mother. I am afraid you will not be able to make it out, but I hardly know what I have written."

Without allowing herself time for consideration, and scarcely knowing what she felt, Elizabeth on finishing this letter, instantly seized the other, and opening it with the utmost impatience, read as follows: it had been written a day later than the conclusion of the first.

"By this time, my dearest sister, you have received my hurried letter; I wish this may be more intelligible, but though not confined for time, my head is so bewildered that I cannot answer for being coherent. Dearest Lizzy, I hardly know what I would write, but I have bad news for you, and it cannot be delayed. Imprudent as a marriage between Mr. Wickham and our poor Lydia would be, we are now anxious to be assured it has taken place, for there is but too much reason to fear they are not gone to Scotland. Colonel Forster came yesterday, having left Brighton the day before, not many hours after the express. Though Lydia's short letter to Mrs. F. gave them to understand that they were going to Gretna Green, something was dropped by Denny expressing his belief that W. never intended to go there, or to marry Lydia at all, which was repeated to Colonel F. who instantly taking the alarm, set off from B. intending to trace their route. He did trace them easily to Clapham, but no farther; for on entering that place they removed into a hackney-coach and dismissed the chaise that brought them from Epsom. All that is known after this is, that they were seen to continue the London road. I know not what to think. After making every possible enquiry on that side London, Colonel F. came on into Hertfordshire, anxiously renewing them at all the turnpikes, and at the inns in Barnet and Hatfield, but without any success, no such people had been seen to pass through. With the kindest concern he came on to Longbourn, and broke his apprehensions to us in a manner most creditable to his heart. I am sincerely grieved for him and Mrs. F. but no one can throw any blame on them. Our distress, my dear Lizzy, is very great. My father and mother believe the worst, but I cannot think so ill of him. Many circumstances might make it more eligible for them to be married privately in town than to pursue their first plan; and even if *he* could form such a design against a young woman of Lydia's connections, which is not likely, can I suppose her so lost to everything? – Impossible. I grieve to find, however, that Colonel

F. is not disposed to depend upon their marriage; he shook his head when I expressed my hopes, and said he feared W. was not a man to be trusted. My poor mother is really ill and keeps her room. Could she exert herself it would be better, but this is not to be expected; and as to my father, I never in my life saw him so affected. Poor Kitty has anger for having concealed their attachment; but as it was a matter of confidence one cannot wonder. I am truly glad, dearest Lizzy, that you have been spared something of these distressing scenes; but now as the first shock is over, shall I own that I long for your return? I am not so selfish, however, as to press for it, if inconvenient. Adieu. I take up my pen again to do, what I have just told you I would not, but circumstances are such, that I cannot help earnestly begging you all to come here, as soon as possible. I know my dear uncle and aunt so well, that I am not afraid of requesting it, though I have still something more to ask of the former. My father is going to London with Colonel Forster instantly, to try to discover her. What he means to do, I am sure I know not; but his excessive distress will not allow him to pursue any measure in the best and safest way, and Colonel Forster is obliged to be at Brighton again tomorrow evening. In such an exigence my uncle's advice and assistance would be everything in the world; he will immediately comprehend what I must feel, and I rely upon his goodness."

"Oh! where, where is my uncle?" cried Elizabeth, darting from her seat as she finished the letter, in eagerness to follow him, without losing a moment of the time so precious; but as she reached the door, it was opened by a servant, and Mr. Darcy appeared. Her pale face and impetuous manner made him start, and before he could recover himself to speak, she, in whose mind every idea was superseded by Lydia's situation, hastily exclaimed, "I beg your pardon, but I must leave you. I must find Mr. Gardiner this moment, on business that cannot be delayed; I have not an instant to lose."

"Good God! what is the matter?" cried he, with more feeling than politeness; then recollecting himself, "I will not detain you a minute, but let me, or let the servant go after Mr. and Mrs. Gardiner. You are not well enough; – you cannot go yourself."

Elizabeth hesitated, but her knees trembled under her, and she felt how little would be gained by her attempting to pursue them. Calling back the servant, therefore, she commissioned him, though in so breathless an accent as made her almost unintelligible, to fetch his master and mistress home, instantly.

On his quitting the room, she sat down, unable to support herself, and looking so miserably ill, that it was impossible for Darcy to leave her, or to refrain from saying, in a tone of gentleness and commiseration, "Let me call your maid. Is there nothing you could take, to give you present relief? – A glass of wine; – shall I get you one? – You are very ill."

"No, I thank you;" she replied, endeavouring to recover herself. "There is nothing the matter with me. I am quite well. I am only distressed by some dreadful news which I have just received from Longbourn."

She burst into tears as she alluded to it, and for a few minutes could not speak another word. Darcy, in wretched suspense, could only say something indistinctly of his concern, and observe her in compassionate silence. At length, she spoke again. "I have just had a letter from Jane, with such dreadful news. It cannot be concealed from anyone. My younger sister has left all her friends – has eloped; – has thrown herself into the power of – of Mr. Wickham. They are gone off together from Brighton. *You* know him too well to doubt the rest. She has no money, no connections, nothing that can tempt him to – she is lost for ever."

Darcy was fixed in astonishment. "When I consider," she added, in a yet more agitated voice, "that *I* might have prevented it! – *I*, who knew what he was. Had I but explained some part of it only – some part of what I learnt, to my own family! Had his character been known, this could not have happened. But it is all, all too late now."

"I am grieved, indeed," cried Darcy; "grieved – shocked. But is it certain, absolutely certain?"

"Oh yes! – They left Brighton together on Sunday night, and were traced almost to London, but not beyond; they are certainly not gone to Scotland."

"And what has been done, what has been attempted, to recover her?"

"My father is gone to London, and Jane has written to beg my uncle's immediate assistance; and we shall be off, I hope, in half an hour. But nothing can be done; I know very well that nothing can be done. How is such a man to be worked on? How are they even to be discovered? I have not the smallest hope. It is every way horrible!"

Darcy shook his head in silent acquiescence.

"When *my* eyes were opened to his real character. – Oh! had I known what I ought, what I dared, to do! But I knew not – I was afraid of doing too much. Wretched, wretched, mistake!"

Darcy made no answer. He seemed scarcely to hear her, and was walking up and down the room in earnest meditation; his brow contracted, his air gloomy. Elizabeth soon observed, and instantly understood it. Her power was sinking; everything *must* sink under such a proof of family weakness, such an assurance of the deepest disgrace. She could neither wonder nor condemn, but the belief of his self-conquest brought nothing consolatory to her bosom, afforded no palliation of her distress. It was, on the contrary, exactly calculated to make her understand her own wishes; and never had she so honestly felt that she could have loved him, as now, when all love must be vain.

But self, though it would intrude, could not engross her.

Lydia – the humiliation, the misery, she was bringing on them all, soon swallowed up every private care; and covering her face with her handkerchief, Elizabeth was soon lost to everything else; and, after a pause of several minutes, was only recalled to a sense of her situation by the voice of her companion, who, in a manner, which though it spoke compassion, spoke likewise restraint, said, "I am afraid you have been long desiring my absence, nor have I anything to plead in excuse of my stay, but real, though unavailing, concern. Would to heaven that anything could be either said or done on my part, that might offer consolation to such distress. – But I will not torment you with vain wishes, which may seem purposely to ask for your thanks. This unfortunate affair will, I fear, prevent my sister's having the pleasure of seeing you at Pemberley today."

"Oh, yes. Be so kind as to apologise for us to Miss Darcy. Say that urgent business calls us home immediately. Conceal the unhappy truth as long as it is possible. – I know it cannot be long."

He readily assured her of his secrecy – again expressed his sorrow for her distress, wished it a happier conclusion than there was at present reason to hope, and leaving his compliments for her relations, with only one serious, parting look, went away.

As he quitted the room, Elizabeth felt how improbable it was that they should ever see each other again on such terms of cordiality as had marked their several meetings in Derbyshire; and as she threw a retrospective glance over the whole of their acquaintance, so full of contradictions and varieties, sighed at the perverseness of those feelings which would now have promoted its continuance, and would formerly have rejoiced in its termination.

If gratitude and esteem are good foundations of affection, Elizabeth's change of sentiment will be neither improbable nor faulty. But if otherwise, if the regard springing from such sources is unreasonable or unnatural, in comparison of what is so often described as arising on a first interview with its object, and even before two words have been exchanged, nothing can be said in her defence, except that she had given somewhat of a trial to the latter method, in her partiality for Wickham, and that its ill-success might perhaps authorise her to seek the other less interesting mode of attachment. Be that as it may, she saw him go with regret; and in this early example of what Lydia's infamy must produce, found additional anguish as she reflected on that wretched business. Never, since reading Jane's second letter, had she entertained a hope of Wickham's meaning to marry her. No one but Jane, she thought, could flatter herself with such an expectation. Surprise was the least of her feelings on this development. While the contents of the first letter remained on her mind, she was all surprise – all astonishment that Wickham should marry a girl, whom it was impossible he could marry for money; and how Lydia could ever have attached him, had appeared incomprehensible. But now it was all too natural. For such an attachment as this, she might have sufficient charms; and though she did not suppose Lydia to be deliberately engaging in an elopement, without the intention of marriage, she had no difficulty in believing that neither her virtue nor her understanding would preserve her from falling an easy prey.

She had never perceived, while the regiment was in Hertfordshire, that Lydia had any partiality for him, but she was convinced that Lydia wanted only encouragement to attach herself to anybody. Sometimes one officer, sometimes another had been her favourite, as their attentions raised them in her opinion. Her affections had been continually fluctuating, but never without an object. The mischief of neglect and mistaken indulgence towards such a girl. – Oh! how acutely did she now feel it.

She was wild to be at home – to hear, to see, to be upon the spot, to share with Jane in the cares that must now fall wholly upon her, in a family so deranged, a father absent, a mother incapable of exertion, and requiring constant attendance; and though almost persuaded that nothing could be done for Lydia, her uncle's interference seemed of the utmost importance, and till he entered the room, the misery of her impatience was severe. Mr. and Mrs. Gardiner had hurried back in alarm, supposing, by the servant's account, that their niece was taken suddenly ill; – but satisfying them instantly on that head, she eagerly communicated the cause of their summons, reading the two letters aloud, and dwelling on the postscript of the last, with trembling energy. – Though Lydia had never been a favourite with them, Mr. and Mrs. Gardiner could not but be deeply affected. Not Lydia only, but all were concerned in it; and after the first exclamations of surprise and horror, Mr. Gardiner readily promised every assistance in his power. – Elizabeth, though expecting no less, thanked him with tears of gratitude; and all three being actuated by one spirit, everything relating to their journey was speedily settled. They were to be off as soon as possible. "But what is to be done about Pemberley?" cried Mrs. Gardiner. "John told us Mr. Darcy was here when you sent for us; – was it so?"

"Yes; and I told him we should not be able to keep our engagement. *That* is all settled."

"That is all settled" repeated the other, as she ran into her room to prepare. "And are they upon such terms as for her to disclose the real truth! Oh, that I knew how it was!"

But wishes were vain, or at least could only serve to amuse her in the hurry and confusion of the following hour. Had Elizabeth been at leisure to be idle, she would have remained certain that all employment was impossible to one so wretched as herself; but she had her share of business as well as her aunt, and amongst the rest there were notes to be written to all their friends at Lambton, with false excuses for their sudden departure. An hour, however, saw the whole completed; and Mr. Gardiner meanwhile having settled his account at the inn, nothing remained to be done but to go; and Elizabeth, after all the misery of the morning, found herself, in a shorter space of time than she could have supposed, seated in the carriage, and on the road to Longbourn.

## Chapter 47

"I HAVE been thinking it over again, Elizabeth," said her uncle, as they drove from the town; "and really, upon serious consideration, I am much more inclined than I was to judge as your eldest sister does of the matter. It appears to me so very unlikely, that any young man should form such a design against a girl who is by no means unprotected or friendless, and who was actually staying in his colonel's family, that I am strongly inclined to hope the best. Could he expect that her friends would not step forward? Could he expect to be noticed again by the regiment, after such an affront to Colonel Forster? His temptation is not adequate to the risk!"

"Do you really think so?" cried Elizabeth, brightening up for a moment.

"Upon my word," said Mrs. Gardiner, "I begin to be of your uncle's opinion. It is really too great a violation of decency, honour, and interest, for him to be guilty of it. I cannot think so very ill of Wickham. Can you, yourself, Lizzy, so wholly give him up, as to believe him capable of it?"

"Not perhaps of neglecting his own interest. But of every other neglect I can believe him capable. If, indeed, it should be so! But I dare not hope it. Why should they not go on to Scotland, if that had been the case?"

"In the first place," replied Mr. Gardiner, "there is no absolute proof that they are not gone to Scotland."

"Oh! but their removing from the chaise into a hackney coach is such a presumption! And, besides, no traces of them were to be found on the Barnet road."

"Well, then – supposing them to be in London. They may be there, though for the purpose of concealment, for no more exceptionable purpose. It is not likely that money should be very abundant on either side; and it might strike them that they could be more economically, though less expeditiously, married in London, than in Scotland."

"But why all this secrecy? Why any fear of detection? Why must their marriage be private? Oh, no, no, this is not likely. His most particular friend, you see by Jane's account, was persuaded of his never intending to marry her. Wickham will never marry a woman without some money. He cannot afford it. And what claims has Lydia, what attractions has she beyond youth, health, and good humour, that could make him for her sake, forego every chance of benefiting himself by marrying well? As to what restraint the apprehension of disgrace in the corps might throw on a dishonourable elopement with her, I am not able to judge; for I know nothing of the effects that such a step might produce. But as to your other objection, I am afraid it will hardly hold good. Lydia has no brothers to step forward; and he might imagine, from my father's behaviour, from his indolence and the little attention he has ever seemed to give to what was going forward in his family, that *he* would do as little, and think as little about it, as any father could do, in such a matter."

"But can you think that Lydia is so lost to everything but love of him, as to consent to live with him on any terms other than marriage?"

"It does seem, and it is most shocking indeed," replied Elizabeth, with tears in her eyes, "that a sister's sense of decency and virtue in such a point should admit of doubt. But, really, I know not what to say. Perhaps I am not doing her justice. But she is very young; she has never been taught to think on serious subjects; and for the last half year, nay, for a twelvemonth, she has been given up to nothing but amusement and vanity. She has been allowed to dispose of her time in the most idle and frivolous manner, and to adopt any opinions that came in her way. Since the —shire were first quartered in Meryton, nothing but love, flirtation, and officers, have been in her head. She has been doing everything in her power by thinking and talking on the subject, to give greater – what shall I call it? susceptibility to her feelings; which are naturally lively enough. And we all know that Wickham has every charm of person and address that can captivate a woman."

"But you see that Jane," said her aunt, "does not think so ill of Wickham, as to believe him capable of the attempt."

"Of whom does Jane ever think ill? And who is there, whatever might be their former conduct, that she would believe capable of such an attempt, till it were proved against them? But Jane knows, as well as I do, what Wickham really is. We both know that he has been profligate in every sense of the word. That he has neither integrity nor honour. That he is as false and deceitful, as he is insinuating."

"And do you really know all this?" cried Mrs. Gardiner, whose curiosity as to the mode of her intelligence was all alive.

"I do indeed," replied Elizabeth, colouring. "I told you the other day, of his infamous behaviour to Mr. Darcy; and you, yourself, when last at Longbourn, heard in what manner he spoke of the man, who had behaved with such forbearance and liberality towards him. And there are other circumstances which I am not at liberty – which it is not worthwhile to relate; but his lies about the whole Pemberley family are endless. From what he said of Miss Darcy, I was thoroughly prepared to see a proud, reserved, disagreeable girl. Yet he knew to the contrary himself. He must know that she was as amiable and unpretending as we have found her."

"But does Lydia know nothing of this? Can she be ignorant of what you and Jane seem so well to understand?"

"Oh, yes! – that, that is the worst of all. Till I was in Kent, and saw so much both of Mr. Darcy and his relation, Colonel Fitzwilliam, I was ignorant of the truth myself. And when I returned home, the —shire was to leave Meryton in a week or fortnight's time. As that was the case, neither Jane, to whom I related the whole, nor I, thought it necessary to make our knowledge public; for of what use could it apparently be to anyone, that the good opinion which all the neighbourhood had of him, should then be overthrown? And even when it was settled that Lydia should go with Mrs. Forster, the necessity of opening her eyes to his character never occurred to me. That *she* could be in any danger from the deception never entered my head. That such a consequence as *this* should ensue, you may easily believe was far enough from my thoughts."

"When they all removed to Brighton, therefore, you had no reason, I suppose, to believe them fond of each other."

"Not the slightest. I can remember no symptom of affection on either side; and had anything of the kind been perceptible, you must be aware that ours is not a family, on which it could be thrown away. When first he entered the corps, she was ready enough to admire him; but so we all were. Every girl in, or near Meryton, was out of her senses about him for the first two months; but he never distinguished *her* by any particular attention, and, consequently, after a moderate period of extravagant and wild admiration, her fancy for him gave way, and others of the regiment, who treated her with more distinction, again became her favourites."

It may be easily believed, that however little of novelty could be added to their fears, hopes, and conjectures, on this interesting subject, by its repeated discussion, no other could detain them from it long, during the whole of the journey. From Elizabeth's thoughts it was never absent. Fixed there by the keenest of all anguish, self-reproach, she could find no interval of ease or forgetfulness.

They travelled as expeditiously as possible; and sleeping one night on the road, reached Longbourn by dinner-time the next day. It was a comfort to Elizabeth to consider that Jane could not have been wearied by long expectations.

The little Gardiners, attracted by the sight of a chaise, were standing on the steps of the house, as they entered the paddock; and when the carriage drove up to the door, the joyful surprise that lighted up their faces, and displayed itself over their whole bodies, in a variety of capers and frisks, was the first pleasing earnest of their welcome.

Elizabeth jumped out; and, after giving each of them an hasty kiss, hurried into the vestibule, where Jane, who came running downstairs from her mother's apartment, immediately met her.

Elizabeth, as she affectionately embraced her, whilst tears filled the eyes of both, lost not a moment in asking whether anything had been heard of the fugitives.

"Not yet," replied Jane. "But now that my dear uncle is come, I hope everything will be well."

"Is my father in town?"

"Yes, he went on Tuesday, as I wrote you word."

"And have you heard from him often?"

"We have heard only once. He wrote me a few lines on Wednesday, to say that he had arrived in safety, and to give me his directions, which I particularly begged him to do. He merely added, that he should not write again, till he had something of importance to mention."

"And my mother – How is she? How are you all?"

"My mother is tolerably well, I trust; though her spirits are greatly shaken. She is upstairs, and will have great satisfaction in seeing you all. She does not yet leave her dressing-room. Mary and Kitty, thank Heaven! are quite well."

"But you – How are you?" cried Elizabeth. "You look pale. How much you must have gone through!"

Her sister, however, assured her, of her being perfectly well; and their conversation, which had been passing while Mr. and Mrs. Gardiner were engaged with their children, was now put an end to, by the approach of the whole party. Jane ran to her uncle and aunt, and welcomed and thanked them both, with alternate smiles and tears.

When they were all in the drawing-room, the questions which Elizabeth had already asked, were of course repeated by the others, and they soon found that Jane had no intelligence to give. The sanguine hope of good, however, which the benevolence of her heart suggested, had not yet deserted her; she still expected that it would all end well, and that every morning would bring some letter, either from Lydia or her father, to explain their proceedings, and perhaps announce the marriage.

Mrs. Bennet, to whose apartment they all repaired, after a few minutes' conversation together, received them exactly as might be expected; with tears and lamentations of regret, invectives against the villainous conduct of Wickham, and complaints of her own sufferings and ill-usage; blaming everybody but the person to whose ill-judging indulgence the errors of her daughter must be principally owing.

"If I had been able," said she, "to carry my point of going to Brighton, with all my family, *this* would not have happened; but poor dear Lydia had nobody to take care of her. Why did the Forsters ever let her go out of their sight? I am sure there was some great neglect or other on their side, for she is not the kind of girl to do such a thing, if she had been well looked after. I always thought they were very unfit to have the charge of her; but I was over-ruled, as I always am. Poor dear child! And now here's Mr. Bennet gone away, and I know he will fight Wickham, wherever he meets him, and then he will be killed, and what is to become of us all? The Collinses will turn us out, before he is cold in his grave; and if you are not kind to us, brother, I do not know what we shall do."

They all exclaimed against such terrific ideas; and Mr. Gardiner, after general assurances of his affection for her and all her family, told her that he meant to be in London the very next day, and would assist Mr. Bennet in every endeavour for recovering Lydia.

"Do not give way to useless alarm," added he; "though it is right to be prepared for the worst, there is no occasion to look on it as certain. It is not quite a week since they left Brighton. In a few days more, we may gain some news of them, and till we know that they are not married, and have no design of marrying, do not let us give the matter over as lost. As soon as I get to town, I shall go to my brother, and make him come home with me to Gracechurch Street, and then we may consult together as to what is to be done."

"Oh! my dear brother," replied Mrs. Bennet, "that is exactly what I could most wish for. And now do, when you get to town, find them out, wherever they may be; and if they are not married already, *make* them marry. And as for wedding clothes, do not let them wait for that, but tell Lydia she shall have as much money as she chooses, to buy them, after they are married. And, above all things, keep Mr. Bennet from fighting. Tell him what a dreadful state I am in, – that I am frightened out of my wits; and have such tremblings, such flutterings, all over me, such spasms in my side, and pains in my head, and such beatings at heart, that I can get no rest by night nor by day. And tell my dear Lydia, not to give any directions about her clothes, till she has seen me, for she does not know which are the best warehouses. Oh, brother, how kind you are! I know you will contrive it all."

But Mr. Gardiner, though he assured her again of his earnest endeavours in the cause, could not avoid recommending moderation to her, as well in her hopes as her fears; and, after talking with her in this manner till dinner was on the table, they left her to vent all her feelings on the housekeeper, who attended, in the absence of her daughters.

Though her brother and sister were persuaded that there was no real occasion for such a seclusion from the family, they did not attempt to oppose it, for they knew that she had not prudence enough to hold her tongue before the servants, while they waited at table, and judged it better that *one* only of the household, and the one whom they could most trust, should comprehend all her fears and solicitude on the subject.

In the dining-room they were soon joined by Mary and Kitty, who had been too busily engaged in their separate apartments, to make their appearance before. One came from her books, and the other from her toilette. The faces of both, however, were tolerably calm; and no change was visible in either, except that the loss of her favourite sister, or the anger which she had herself incurred in the business, had given something more of fretfulness than usual, to the accents of Kitty. As for Mary, she was mistress enough of herself to whisper to Elizabeth with a countenance of grave reflection, soon after they were seated at table.

"This is a most unfortunate affair, and will probably be much talked of. But we must stem the tide of malice, and pour into the wounded bosoms of each other, the balm of sisterly consolation."

Then, perceiving in Elizabeth no inclination of replying, she added, "Unhappy as the event must be for Lydia, we may draw from it this useful lesson; that loss of virtue in a female is irretrievable – that one false step involves her in endless ruin – that her reputation is no less brittle than it is beautiful, – and that she cannot be too much guarded in her behaviour towards the undeserving of the other sex."

Elizabeth lifted up her eyes in amazement, but was too much oppressed to make any reply. Mary, however, continued to console herself with such kind of moral extractions from the evil before them.

In the afternoon, the two elder Miss Bennets were able to be for half an hour by themselves; and Elizabeth instantly availed herself of the opportunity of making any enquiries, which Jane was equally eager to satisfy. After joining in general lamentations over the dreadful sequel of this event, which Elizabeth considered as all but certain, and Miss Bennet could not assert to be wholly impossible; the former continued the subject, by saying, "But tell me all and everything about it, which I have not already heard. Give me further particulars. What did Colonel Forster say? Had they no apprehension of anything before the elopement took place? They must have seen them together for ever."

"Colonel Forster did own that he had often suspected some partiality especially on Lydia's side, but nothing to give him any alarm. I am so grieved for him. His behaviour was attentive and kind to the utmost. He *was* coming to us, in order to assure us of his concern, before he had any idea of their not being gone to Scotland: when that apprehension first got abroad, it hastened his journey."

"And was Denny convinced that Wickham would not marry? Did he know of their intending to go off? Had Colonel Forster seen Denny himself?"

"Yes; but, when questioned by *him* Denny denied knowing anything of their plan, and would not give his real opinion about it. He did not repeat his persuasion of their not marrying – and from *that*, I am inclined to hope, he might have been misunderstood before."

"And till Colonel Forster came himself, not one of you

entertained a doubt, I suppose, of their being really married?"

"How was it possible that such an idea should enter our brains? I felt a little uneasy – a little fearful of my sister's happiness with him in marriage, because I knew that his conduct had not been always quite right. My father and mother knew nothing of that, they only felt how imprudent a match it must be. Kitty then owned, with a very natural triumph on knowing more than the rest of us, that in Lydia's last letter, she had prepared her for such a step. She had known, it seems, of their being in love with each other, many weeks."

"But not before they went to Brighton?"

"No, I believe not."

"And did Colonel Forster appear to think ill of Wickham himself? Does he know his real character?"

"I must confess that he did not speak so well of Wickham as he formerly did. He believed him to be imprudent and extravagant. And since this sad affair has taken place, it is said, that he left Meryton greatly in debt; but I hope this may be false."

"Oh, Jane, had we been less secret, had we told what we knew of him, this could not have happened!"

"Perhaps it would have been better," replied her sister. "But to expose the former faults of any person, without knowing what their present feelings were, seemed unjustifiable. We acted with the best intentions."

"Could Colonel Forster repeat the particulars of Lydia's note to his wife?"

"He brought it with him for us to see."

Jane then took it from her pocket-book, and gave it to Elizabeth.

These were the contents:

MY DEAR HARRIET,

You will laugh when you know where I am gone, and I

cannot help laughing myself at your surprise tomorrow morning, as soon as I am missed. I am going to Gretna Green, and if you cannot guess with who, I shall think you a simpleton, for there is but one man in the world I love, and he is an angel. I should never be happy without him, so think it no harm to be off. You need not send them word at Longbourn of my going, if you do not like it, for it will make the surprise the greater, when I write to them, and sign my name Lydia Wickham. What a good joke it will be! I can hardly write for laughing. Pray make my excuses to Pratt, for not keeping my engagement, and dancing with him tonight. Tell him I hope he will excuse me when he knows all, and tell him I will dance with him at the next ball we meet, with great pleasure. I shall send for my clothes when I get to Longbourn; but I wish you would tell Sally to mend a great slit in my worked muslin gown, before they are packed up. Goodbye. Give my love to Colonel Forster, I hope you will drink to our good journey.

Your affectionate friend,

LYDIA BENNET.

"Oh! thoughtless, thoughtless Lydia!" cried Elizabeth when she had finished it. What a letter is this, to be written at such a moment! But at least it shows, that *she* was serious in the object of her journey. Whatever he might afterwards persuade her to, it was not on her side a *scheme* of infamy. My poor father! how he must have felt it!"

"I never saw anyone so shocked. He could not speak a word for full ten minutes. My mother was taken ill immediately, and the whole house in such confusion!"

"Oh! Jane," cried Elizabeth, "was there a servant belonging to it, who did not know the whole story before the end of the day?"

"I do not know. – I hope there was. – But to be guarded at such a time, is very difficult. My mother was in hysterics, and though I endeavoured to give her every assistance in my power, I am afraid I did not do so much as I might have done! But the horror of what might possibly happen, almost took from me my faculties."

"Your attendance upon her, has been too much for you. You do not look well. Oh! that I had been with you, you have had every care and anxiety upon yourself alone."

"Mary and Kitty have been very kind, and would have shared in every fatigue, I am sure, but I did not think it right for either of them. Kitty is slight and delicate, and Mary studies so much, that her hours of repose should not be broken in on. My aunt Philips came to Longbourn on Tuesday, after my father went away; and was so good as to stay till Thursday with me. She was of great use and comfort to us all, and Lady Lucas has been very kind; she walked here on Wednesday morning to condole with us, and offered her services, or any of her daughters, if they could be of use to us."

"She had better have stayed at home," cried Elizabeth; "perhaps she *meant* well, but, under such a misfortune as this, one cannot see too little of one's neighbours. Assistance is impossible; condolence, insufferable. Let them triumph over us at a distance, and be satisfied."

She then proceeded to enquire into the measures which her father had intended to pursue, while in town, for the recovery of his daughter.

"He meant, I believe," replied Jane, "to go to Epsom, the place where they last changed horses, see the postilions, and try if anything could be made out from them. His principal object must be, to discover the number of the hackney coach which took them from Clapham. It had come with a fare from London; and as he thought the circumstance of a gentleman and lady's removing from one carriage into another, might be remarked, he meant to make enquiries at Clapham. If he could anyhow discover at what house the coachman had before set down his fare, he determined to make enquiries there, and hoped it might not be impossible to find out the stand and number of the coach. I do not know of any other designs that he had formed: but he was in such a hurry to be gone, and his spirits so greatly discomposed, that I had difficulty in finding out even so much as this."

# Chapter 48

THE WHOLE party were in hopes of a letter from Mr. Bennet the next morning, but the post came in without bringing a single line from him. His family knew him to be on all common occasions, a most negligent and dilatory correspondent, but at such a time, they had hoped for exertion. They were forced to conclude, that he had no pleasing intelligence to send, but even of *that* they would have been glad to be certain. Mr. Gardiner had waited only for the letters before he set off.

When he was gone, they were certain at least of receiving constant information of what was going on, and their uncle promised, at parting, to prevail on Mr. Bennet to return to Longbourn, as soon as he could, to the great consolation of his sister, who considered it as the only security for her husband's not being killed in a duel.

Mrs. Gardiner and the children were to remain in Hertfordshire a few days longer, as the former thought her presence might be serviceable to her nieces. She shared in their attendance on Mrs. Bennet, and was a great comfort to them, in their hours of freedom. Their other aunt also visited them frequently, and always, as she said, with the design of cheering and heartening them up, though as she never came without reporting some fresh instance of Wickham's extravagance or irregularity, she seldom went away without leaving them more dispirited than she found them.

All Meryton seemed striving to blacken the man, who, but three months before, had been almost an angel of light. He was declared to be in debt to every tradesman in the place, and his intrigues, all honoured with the title of seduction, had been extended into every tradesman's family. Everybody declared that he was the wickedest young man in the world; and everybody began to find out, that they had always distrusted the appearance of his goodness. Elizabeth, though she did not credit above half of what was said, believed enough to make her former assurance of her sister's ruin more certain; and even Jane, who believed still less of it, became almost hopeless, more especially as the time was now come, when if they had gone to Scotland, which she had never before entirely despaired of, they must in all probability have gained some news of them.

Mr. Gardiner left Longbourn on Sunday; on Tuesday, his wife received a letter from him; it told them, that on his arrival, he had immediately found out his brother, and persuaded him to come to Gracechurch Street. That Mr. Bennet had been to Epsom and Clapham, before his arrival, but without gaining any satisfactory information; and that he was now determined to enquire at all the principal hotels in town, as Mr. Bennet thought it possible they might have gone to one of them, on their first coming to London, before they procured lodgings. Mr. Gardiner himself did not expect any success from this measure, but as his brother was eager in it, he meant to assist him in pursuing it. He added, that Mr. Bennet seemed wholly disinclined at present, to leave London, and promised to write again very soon. There was also a postscript to this effect:

"I have written to Colonel Forster to desire him to find out, if possible, from some of the young man's intimates in the regiment, whether Wickham has any relations or connections, who would be likely to know in what part of town he has now concealed himself. If there were anyone, that one could apply to, with a probability of gaining such a clue as that, it might be of essential consequence. At present we have nothing to guide us. Colonel Forster will, I dare say, do everything in his power to satisfy us on this head. But, on second thoughts, perhaps Lizzy could tell us, what relations he has now living, better than any other person."

Elizabeth was at no loss to understand from whence this deference to her authority proceeded; but it was not in her power to give any information of so satisfactory a nature, as the compliment deserved.

She had never heard of his having had any relations, except a father and mother, both of whom had been dead many years. It was possible, however, that some of his companions in the —shire, might be able to give more information; and, though she was not very sanguine in expecting it, the application was a something to look forward to.

Every day at Longbourn was now a day of anxiety; but the most anxious part of each was when the post was expected. The arrival of letters was the first grand object of every morning's impatience. Through letters, whatever of good or bad was to be told, would be communicated, and every succeeding day was expected to bring some news of importance.

But before they heard again from Mr. Gardiner, a letter arrived for their father, from a different quarter, from Mr. Collins; which, as Jane had received directions to open all that came for him in his absence, she accordingly read; and Elizabeth, who knew what curiosities his letters always were, looked over her, and read it likewise. It was as follows:

> My dear Sir,
>
> I feel myself called upon, by our relationship, and my situation in life, to condole with you on the grievous affliction you are now suffering under, of which we were yesterday

informed by a letter from Hertfordshire. Be assured, my dear Sir, that Mrs. Collins and myself sincerely sympathise with you, and all your respectable family, in your present distress, which must be of the bitterest kind, because proceeding from a cause which no time can remove. No arguments shall be wanting on my part, that can alleviate so severe a misfortune; or that may comfort you, under a circumstance that must be of all others the most afflicting to a parent's mind. The death of your daughter would have been a blessing in comparison of this. And it is the more to be lamented, because there is reason to suppose, as my dear Charlotte informs me, that this licentiousness of behaviour in your daughter, has proceeded from a faulty degree of indulgence, though, at the same time, for the consolation of yourself and Mrs. Bennet, I am inclined to think that her own disposition must be naturally bad, or she could not be guilty of such an enormity, at so early an age. Howsoever that may be, you are grievously to be pitied, in which opinion I am not only joined by Mrs. Collins, but likewise by Lady Catherine and her daughter, to whom I have related the affair. They agree with me in apprehending that this false step in one daughter, will be injurious to the fortunes of all the others, for who, as Lady Catherine herself condescendingly says, will connect themselves with such a family. And this consideration leads me moreover to reflect with augmented satisfaction on a certain event of last November, for had it been otherwise, I must have been involved in all your sorrow and disgrace. Let me advise you then, my dear Sir, to console yourself as much as possible, to throw off your unworthy child from your affection for ever, and leave her to reap the fruits of her own heinous offence,

I am, dear Sir, &c. &c.

Mr. Gardiner did not write again, till he had received an answer from Colonel Forster; and then he had nothing of a pleasant nature to send. It was not known that Wickham had a single relation, with whom he kept up any connection, and it was certain that he had no near one living. His former acquaintance had been numerous; but since he had been in the militia, it did not appear that he was on terms of particular friendship with any of them. There was no one therefore who could be pointed out, as likely to give any news of him. And in the wretched state of his own finances, there was a very powerful motive for secrecy, in addition to his fear of discovery by Lydia's relations, for it had just transpired that he had left gaming debts behind him, to a very considerable amount. Colonel Forster believed that more than a thousand pounds would be necessary to clear his expenses at Brighton. He owed a good deal in the town, but his debts of honour were still more formidable. Mr. Gardiner did not attempt to conceal these particulars from the Longbourn family; Jane heard them with horror. "A gamester!" she cried. "This is wholly unexpected. I had not an idea of it."

Mr. Gardiner added in his letter, that they might expect to see their father at home on the following day, which was Saturday. Rendered spiritless by the ill-success of all their endeavours, he had yielded to his brother-in-law's entreaty that he would return to his family, and leave it to him to do, whatever occasion might suggest to be advisable for continuing their pursuit. When Mrs. Bennet was told of this, she did not express so much satisfaction as her children expected, considering what her anxiety for his life had been before.

"What, is he coming home, and without poor Lydia!" she cried. "Sure he will not leave London before he has found them. Who is to fight Wickham, and make him marry her, if he comes away?"

As Mrs. Gardiner began to wish to be at home, it was settled that she and her children should go to London, at the same time that Mr. Bennet came from it. The coach, therefore, took them the first stage of their journey, and brought its master back to Longbourn.

Mrs. Gardiner went away in all the perplexity about Elizabeth and her Derbyshire friend, that had attended her from that part of the world. His name had never been voluntarily mentioned before them by her niece; and the kind of half-expectation which Mrs. Gardiner had formed, of their being followed by a letter from him, had ended in nothing. Elizabeth had received none since her return, that could come from Pemberley.

The present unhappy state of the family, rendered any other excuse for the lowness of her spirits unnecessary; nothing, therefore, could be fairly conjectured from *that*, though Elizabeth, who was by this time tolerably well acquainted with her own feelings, was perfectly aware, that, had she known nothing of Darcy, she could have borne the dread of Lydia's infamy somewhat better. It would have spared her, she thought, one sleepless night out of two.

When Mr. Bennet arrived, he had all the appearance of his usual philosophic composure. He said as little as he had ever been in the habit of saying; made no mention of the business that had taken him away, and it was some time before his daughters had courage to speak of it.

It was not till the afternoon, when he joined them at tea, that Elizabeth ventured to introduce the subject; and then, on her briefly expressing her sorrow for what he must have endured, he replied, "Say nothing of that. Who should suffer but myself? It has been my own doing, and I ought to feel it."

"You must not be too severe upon yourself," replied Elizabeth.

"You may well warn me against such an evil. Human nature is so prone to fall into it! No, Lizzy, let me once in my life feel how much I have been to blame. I am not afraid of being overpowered by the impression. It will pass away soon enough."

"Do you suppose them to be in London?"

"Yes; where else can they be so well concealed?"

"And Lydia used to want to go to London," added Kitty.

"She is happy then," said her father, drily; "and her residence there will probably be of some duration."

Then, after a short silence, he continued, "Lizzy, I bear you no ill-will for being justified in your advice to me last May, which, considering the event, shows some greatness of mind."

They were interrupted by Miss Bennet, who came to fetch her mother's tea.

"This is a parade," he cried, "which does one good; it gives such an elegance to misfortune! Another day I will do the same; I will sit in my library, in my night cap and powdering gown, and give as much trouble as I can, – or, perhaps, I may defer it, till Kitty runs away."

"I am not going to run away, papa," said Kitty fretfully. "if I should ever go to Brighton, I would behave better than Lydia."

"*You* go to Brighton! – I would not trust you so near it as Eastbourne for fifty pounds! No, Kitty, I have at last learnt to be cautious, and you will feel the effects of it. No officer is ever to enter my house again, nor even to pass through the village. Balls will be absolutely prohibited, unless you stand up with one of your sisters. And you are never to stir out of doors, till you can prove, that you have spent ten minutes of every day in a rational manner."

Kitty, who took all these threats in a serious light, began to cry.

"Well, well," said he, "do not make yourself unhappy. If you are a good girl for the next ten years, I will take you to a review at the end of them."

# Chapter 49

TWO DAYS after Mr. Bennet's return, as Jane and Elizabeth were walking together in the shrubbery behind the house, they saw the housekeeper coming towards them, and, concluding that she came to call them to their mother, went forward to meet her; but, instead of the expected summons, when they approached her, she said to Miss Bennet, "I beg your pardon, madam, for interrupting you, but I was in hopes you might have got some good news from town, so I took the liberty of coming to ask."

"What do you mean, Hill? We have heard nothing from town."

"Dear madam," cried Mrs. Hill, in great astonishment, "don't you know there is an express come for master from Mr. Gardiner? He has been here this half hour, and master has had a letter."

Away ran the girls, too eager to get in to have time for speech. They ran through the vestibule into the breakfast-room; from thence to the library; – their father was in neither; and they were on the point of seeking him upstairs with their mother, when they were met by the butler, who said,

"If you are looking for my master, ma'am, he is walking towards the little copse."

Upon this information, they instantly passed through the hall once more, and ran across the lawn after their father, who was deliberately pursuing his way towards a small wood on one side of the paddock.

Jane, who was not so light, nor so much in the habit of running as Elizabeth, soon lagged behind, while her sister, panting for breath, came up with him, and eagerly cried out,

"Oh, Papa, what news? what news? have you heard from my uncle?"

"Yes, I have had a letter from him by express."

"Well, and what news does it bring? good or bad?"

"What is there of good to be expected?" said he, taking the letter from his pocket; "but perhaps you would like to read it."

Elizabeth impatiently caught it from his hand. Jane now came up.

"Read it aloud," said their father, "for I hardly know myself what it is about."

*'Gracechurch Street, Monday, August 2.*

'MY DEAR BROTHER,

At last I am able to send you some tidings of my niece, and such as, upon the whole, I hope it will give you satisfaction. Soon after you left me on Saturday, I was fortunate enough to find out in what part of London they were. The particulars, I reserve till we meet. It is enough to know they are discovered. I have seen them both –'

"Then it is, as I always hoped," cried Jane; "they are married!"

Elizabeth read on: "I have seen them both. They are not married, nor can I find there was any intention of being so; but if you are willing to perform the engagements which I have ventured to make on your side, I hope it will not be long before they are. All that is required of you is, to assure to your daughter, by settlement, her equal share of the five thousand pounds, secured among your children after the decease of yourself and my sister; and, moreover, to enter into an engagement of allowing her, during your life, one hundred pounds per annum. These are conditions, which, considering everything, I had no hesitation in complying with, as far as I thought myself privileged, for you. I shall send this by express, that no time may be lost in bringing me your answer. You will easily comprehend, from these particulars, that Mr. Wickham's circumstances are not so hopeless as they are generally believed to be. The world has been deceived in that respect; and I am happy to say, there will be some little money, even when all his debts are discharged, to settle on my niece, in addition to her own fortune. If, as I conclude will be the case, you send me your full powers to act in your name, throughout the whole of this business, I will immediately give directions to Haggerston for preparing a proper settlement. There will not be the smallest occasion for your coming to town again; therefore, stay quietly at Longbourn, and depend on my diligence and care. Send back your answer as soon as you can, and be careful to write explicitly. We have judged it best, that my niece should be married from this house, of which I hope you will approve. She comes to us today. I shall write again as soon as anything more is determined on. Yours, &c.

EDW. GARDINER.

"Is it possible!" cried Elizabeth, when she had finished. "Can it be possible that he will marry her?"

"Wickham is not so undeserving, then, as we thought him;" said her sister. "My dear father, I congratulate you."

"And have you answered the letter?" cried Elizabeth.

"No; but it must be done soon."

Most earnestly did she then entreaty him to lose no more time before he wrote.

"Oh! my dear father," she cried, "come back, and write immediately. Consider how important every moment is, in such a case."

"Let me write for you," said Jane, "if you dislike the trouble yourself."

"I dislike it very much," he replied; "but it must be done."

And so saying, he turned back with them, and walked towards the house.

"And may I ask?" said Elizabeth, "but the terms, I suppose, must be complied with."

"Complied with! I am only ashamed of his asking so little."

"And they *must* marry! Yet he is *such* a man!"

"Yes, yes, they must marry. There is nothing else to be done. But there are two things that I want very much to know:– one is, how much money your uncle has laid down, to bring it about; and the other, how I am ever to pay him."

"Money! my uncle!" cried Jane, "what do you mean, Sir?"

"I mean, that no man in his senses, would marry Lydia on so slight a temptation as one hundred a year during my life, and fifty after I am gone."

"That is very true," said Elizabeth; "though it had not occurred to me before. His debts to be discharged, and something still to remain! Oh! it must be my uncle's doings! Generous, good man, I am afraid he has distressed himself. A small sum could not do all this."

"No," said her father; "Wickham's a fool, if he takes her with a farthing less than ten thousand pounds. I should be sorry to think so ill of him, in the very beginning of our relationship."

"Ten thousand pounds! Heaven forbid! How is half such a sum to be repaid?"

Mr. Bennet made no answer, and each of them, deep in thought, continued silent till they reached the house. Their father then went on to the library to write, and the girls walked into the breakfast-room.

"And they are really to be married!" cried Elizabeth, as soon as they were by themselves. "How strange this is! And for *this* we are to be thankful. That they should marry, small as is their chance of happiness, and wretched as is his character, we are forced to rejoice. Oh, Lydia!"

"I comfort myself with thinking," replied Jane, "that he certainly would not marry Lydia, if he had not a real regard for her. Though our kind uncle has done something towards clearing him, I cannot believe that ten thousand pounds, or anything like it, has been advanced. He has children of his own, and may have more. How could he spare half ten thousand pounds?"

"If he were ever able to learn what Wickham's debts have been," said Elizabeth, "and how much is settled on his side on our sister, we shall exactly know what Mr. Gardiner has done for them, because Wickham has not sixpence of his own. The kindness of my uncle and aunt can never be requited. Their taking her home, and affording her their personal protection and countenance, is such a sacrifice to her advantage, as years of gratitude cannot enough acknowledge. By this time she is actually with them! If such goodness does not make her miserable now, she will never deserve to be happy! What a meeting for her, when she first sees my aunt!"

"We must endeavour to forget all that has passed on either side," said Jane: "I hope and trust they will yet be happy. His consenting to marry her is a proof, I will believe, that he is come to a right way of thinking. Their mutual affection will steady them; and I flatter myself they will settle so quietly, and live in so rational a manner, as may in time make their past imprudence forgotten."

"Their conduct has been such," replied Elizabeth, "as neither you, nor I, nor anybody, can ever forget. It is useless to talk of it."

It now occurred to the girls that their mother was in all likelihood perfectly ignorant of what had happened. They went to the library, therefore, and asked their father, whether he would not wish them to make it known to her. He was writing, and, without raising his head, coolly replied,

"Just as you please."

"May we take my uncle's letter to read to her?"

"Take whatever you like, and get away."

Elizabeth took the letter from his writing table, and they went upstairs together. Mary and Kitty were both with Mrs. Bennet: one communication would, therefore, do for all. After a slight preparation for good news, the letter was read aloud. Mrs. Bennet could hardly contain herself. As soon as Jane had read Mr. Gardiner's hope of Lydia's being soon married, her joy burst forth, and every following sentence added to its exuberance. She was now in an irritation as violent from delight, as she had ever been fidgety from alarm and vexation. To know that her daughter would be married was enough. She was disturbed by no fear for her felicity, nor humbled by any remembrance of her misconduct.

"My dear, dear Lydia!" she cried: "This is delightful indeed! – She will be married! – I shall see her again! – She will be married at sixteen! – My good, kind brother! – I knew how it would be – I knew he would manage everything! How I long to see her! and to see dear Wickham too! But the clothes, the wedding clothes! I will write to my sister Gardiner about them directly. Lizzy, my dear, run down to your father, and ask him how much he will give her. Stay, stay, I will go myself. Ring the bell, Kitty, for Hill. I will put on my things in a moment. My dear, dear Lydia! How merry we shall be together when we meet!"

Her eldest daughter endeavoured to give some relief to the violence of these transports, by leading her thoughts to the obligations which Mr. Gardiner's behaviour laid them all under.

"For we must attribute this happy conclusion," she added, "in a great measure, to his kindness. We are persuaded that he has pledged himself to assist Mr. Wickham with money."

"Well," cried her mother, "it is all very right; who should do it but her own uncle? If he had not had a family of his own, I and my children must have had all his money you know, and it is the first time we have ever had anything from him, except a few presents. Well! I am so happy! In a short time, I shall have a daughter married. Mrs. Wickham! How well it sounds. And she was only sixteen last June. My dear Jane, I am in such a flutter, that I am sure I can't write; so I will dictate, and you write for me. We will settle with your father about the money afterwards; but the things should be ordered immediately."

She was then proceeding to all the particulars of calico, muslin, and cambric, and would shortly have dictated some very plentiful orders, had not Jane, though with some difficulty, persuaded her to wait, till her father was at leisure to be consulted. One day's delay she observed, would be of small importance; and her mother was too happy, to be quite so obstinate as usual. Other schemes too came into her head.

"I will go to Meryton," said she, "as soon as I am dressed, and tell the good, good news to my sister Phillips. And as I come back, I can call on Lady Lucas and Mrs. Long. Kitty, run down and order the carriage. An airing would do me a great deal of good, I am sure. Girls, can I do anything for you in Meryton? Oh! here comes Hill! My dear Hill, have you heard the good news? Miss Lydia is going to be married; and you shall all have a bowl of punch, to make merry at her wedding."

Mrs. Hill began instantly to express her joy. Elizabeth received her congratulations amongst the rest, and then, sick of this folly, took refuge in her own room, that she might think with freedom.

Poor Lydia's situation must, at best, be bad enough; but that it was no worse, she had need to be thankful. She felt it so; and though, in looking forward, neither rational happiness nor worldly prosperity, could be justly expected for her sister, in looking back to what they had feared, only two hours ago, she felt all the advantages of what they had gained.

# Chapter 50

MR. BENNET had very often wished, before this period of his life, that, instead of spending his whole income, he had laid by an annual sum, for the better provision of his children, and of his wife, if she survived him. He now wished it more than ever. Had he done his duty in that respect, Lydia need not have been indebted to her uncle, for whatever of honour or credit could now be purchased for her. The satisfaction of prevailing on one of the most worthless young men in Great Britain to be her husband, might then have rested in its proper place.

He was seriously concerned, that a cause of so little advantage to anyone, should be forwarded at the sole expense of his brother-in-law, and he was determined, if possible, to find out the extent of his assistance, and to discharge the obligation as soon as he could.

When first Mr. Bennet had married, economy was held to be perfectly useless; for, of course, they were to have a son. The son was to join in cutting off the entail, as soon as he should be of age, and the widow and younger children would by that means be provided for. Five daughters successively entered the world, but yet the son was to come; and Mrs. Bennet, for many years after Lydia's birth, had been certain that he would. This event had at last been despaired of, but it was then too late to be saving. Mrs. Bennet had no turn for economy, and her husband's love of independence had alone prevented their exceeding their income.

Five thousand pounds was settled by marriage articles on Mrs. Bennet and the children. But in what proportions it should be divided amongst the latter, depended on the will of the parents. This was one point, with regard to Lydia at least, which was now to be settled, and Mr. Bennet could have no hesitation in acceding to the proposal before him. In terms of grateful acknowledgment for the kindness of his brother, though expressed most concisely, he then delivered on paper his perfect approbation of all that was done, and his willingness to fulfil the engagements that had been made for him. He had never before supposed that, could Wickham be prevailed on to marry his daughter, it would be done with so little inconvenience to himself, as by the present arrangement. He would scarcely be ten pounds a year the loser, by the hundred that was to be paid them; for, what with her board and pocket allowance, and the continual presents in money, which passed to her, through her mother's hands, Lydia's expenses had been very little within that sum.

That it would be done with such trifling exertion on his side, too, was another very welcome surprise; for his chief wish at present was to have as little trouble in the business as possible. When the first transports of rage which had produced his activity in seeking her were over, he naturally returned to all his former indolence. His letter was soon dispatched; for though dilatory in undertaking business, he was quick in its execution. He begged to know farther particulars of what he was indebted to his brother; but was too angry with Lydia, to send any message to her.

The good news spread quickly through the house; and with proportionate speed through the neighbourhood. It was borne in the latter with decent philosophy. To be sure it would have been more for the advantage of conversation, had Miss Lydia Bennet come upon the town; or, as the happiest alternative, been secluded from the world, in some distant farmhouse. But there was much to be talked of, in marrying her; and the good-natured wishes for her well-doing, which had proceeded before, from all the spiteful old ladies in Meryton, lost but little of their spirit in this change of circumstances, because with such an husband, her misery was considered certain.

It was a fortnight since Mrs. Bennet had been downstairs, but on this happy day, she again took her seat at the head of her table, and in spirits oppressively high. No sentiment of shame gave a damp to her triumph. The marriage of a daughter, which had been the first object of her wishes, since Jane was sixteen, was now on the point of accomplishment, and her thoughts and her words ran wholly on those attendants of elegant nuptials, fine muslins, new carriages, and servants. She was busily searching through the neighbourhood for a proper situation for her daughter, and, without knowing or considering what their income might be, rejected many as deficient in size and importance.

"Haye Park might do," said she, "if the Gouldings would quit it, or the great house at Stoke, if the drawing-room were larger; but Ashworth is too far off! I could not bear to have her ten miles from me; and as for Purvis Lodge, the attics are dreadful."

Her husband allowed her to talk on without interruption, while the servants remained. But when they had withdrawn, he said to her, "Mrs. Bennet, before you take any, or all of these houses, for your son and daughter, let us come to a right understanding. Into *one* house in this neighbourhood, they shall never have admittance. I will not encourage the impudence of either, by receiving them at Longbourn."

A long dispute followed this declaration; but Mr. Bennet was firm: it soon led to another; and Mrs. Bennet found, with amazement and horror, that her husband would not advance a guinea to buy clothes for his daughter. He protested that she should receive from him no mark of affection whatever, on the occasion. Mrs. Bennet could hardly comprehend it. That his anger could be carried to such a point of inconceivable resentment, as to refuse his daughter a privilege, without which her marriage would scarcely seem valid, exceeded all she could believe possible. She was more alive to the disgrace, which the want of new clothes must reflect on her daughter's nuptials, than to any sense of shame at her eloping and living with Wickham, a fortnight before they took place.

Elizabeth was now most heartily sorry that she had, from the distress of the moment, been led to make Mr. Darcy acquainted with their fears for her sister; for since her marriage would so shortly give the proper termination to the elopement, they might hope to conceal its unfavourable beginning, from all those who were not immediately on the spot.

She had no fear of its spreading farther, through his means. There were few people on whose secrecy she would have more confidently depended; but at the same time, there was no one whose knowledge of a sister's frailty would have mortified her so much. Not, however, from any fear of disadvantage from it, individually to herself; for at any rate, there seemed a gulf impassable between them. Had Lydia's marriage been concluded on the most honourable terms, it was not to be supposed that Mr. Darcy would connect himself with a family, where to every other objection would now be added, an alliance and relationship of the nearest kind with a man whom he so justly scorned.

From such a connection she could not wonder that he should shrink. The wish of procuring her regard, which she had assured herself of his feeling in Derbyshire, could not in rational expectation survive such a blow as this. She was humbled, she was grieved; she repented, though she hardly knew of what. She became jealous of his esteem, when she could no longer hope to be benefited by it. She wanted to hear of him, when there seemed the least chance of gaining intelligence. She was convinced that she could have been happy with him; when it was no longer likely they should meet.

What a triumph for him, as she often thought, could he know that the proposals which she had proudly spurned only four months ago, would now have been gladly and gratefully received! He was as generous, she doubted not, as the most generous of his sex. But while he was mortal, there must be a triumph.

She began now to comprehend that he was exactly the man, who, in disposition and talents, would most suit her. His understanding and temper, though unlike her own, would have answered all her wishes. It was an union that must have been to the advantage of both: by her ease and liveliness, his mind might have been softened, his manners improved; and from his judgement, information, and knowledge of the world, she must have received benefit of greater importance.

But no such happy marriage could now teach the admiring multitude what connubial felicity really was. An union of a different tendency, and precluding the possibility of the other, was soon to be formed in their family.

How Wickham and Lydia were to be supported in tolerable independence, she could not imagine. But how little of permanent happiness could belong to a couple who were only brought together because their passions were stronger than their virtue, she could easily conjecture.

Mr. Gardiner soon wrote again to his brother. To Mr. Bennet's acknowledgments he briefly replied, with assurances of his eagerness to promote the welfare of any of his family; and concluded with entreaties that the subject might never be mentioned to him again. The principal purport of his letter was to inform them, that Mr. Wickham had resolved on quitting the Militia.

"It was greatly my wish that he should do so," he added, "as soon as his marriage was fixed on. And I think you will agree with me, in considering a removal from that corps as highly advisable, both on his account and my niece's. It is Mr. Wickham's intention to go into the regulars; and, among his former friends, there are still some who are able and willing to assist him in the army. He has the promise of an ensigncy in General —'s regiment, now quartered in the North. It is an advantage to have it so far from this part of the kingdom. He promises fairly, and I hope among different people, where they may each have a character to preserve, they will both be more prudent. I have written to Colonel Forster, to inform him of our present arrangements, and to request that he will satisfy the various creditors of Mr. Wickham in and near Brighton, with assurances of speedy payment, for which I have pledged myself. And will you give yourself the trouble of carrying similar assurances to his creditors in Meryton, of whom I shall subjoin a list, according to his information. He has given in all his debts; I hope at least he has not deceived us. Haggerston has our directions, and all will be completed in a week. They will then join his regiment, unless they are first invited to Longbourn; and I understand from Mrs. Gardiner, that my niece is very desirous of seeing you all, before she leaves the South. She is well, and begs to be dutifully remembered to you and her mother. – Yours, &c.

E. GARDINER."

Mr. Bennet and his daughters saw all the advantages of Wickham's removal from the —shire, as clearly as Mr. Gardiner could do. But Mrs. Bennet was not so well pleased with it. Lydia's being settled in the North, just when she had expected most pleasure and pride in her company, for she had by no means given up her plan of their residing in Hertfordshire, was a severe disappointment; and besides, it was such a pity that Lydia should be taken from a regiment where she was acquainted with everybody, and had so many favourites.

"She is so fond of Mrs. Forster," said she, "it will be quite shocking to send her away! And there are several of the young men, too, that she likes very much. The officers may not be so pleasant in General —'s regiment."

His daughter's request, for such it might be considered, of being admitted into her family again, before she set off for the North, received at first an absolute negative. But Jane and Elizabeth, who agreed in wishing, for the sake of their sister's feelings and consequence, that she should be noticed on her marriage by her parents, urged him so earnestly, yet so rationally and so mildly, to receive her and her husband at Longbourn, as soon as they were married, that he was prevailed on to think as they thought, and act as they wished. And their mother had the satisfaction of knowing, that she should be able to show her married daughter in the neighbourhood, before she was banished to the North. When Mr. Bennet wrote again to his brother, therefore, he sent his permission for them to come; and it was settled, that as soon as the ceremony was over, they should proceed to Longbourn. Elizabeth was surprised, however, that Wickham should consent to such a scheme, and, had she consulted only her own inclination, any meeting with him would have been the last object of her wishes.

# *Chapter 51*

THEIR SISTER's wedding day arrived; and Jane and Elizabeth felt for her probably more than she felt for herself. The carriage was sent to meet them at —, and they were to return in it, by dinner-time. Their arrival was dreaded by the elder Miss Bennets; and Jane more especially, who gave Lydia the feelings which would have attended herself, had *she* been the culprit, was wretched in the thought of what her sister must endure.

They came. The family were assembled in the breakfast-room to receive them. Smiles decked the face of Mrs. Bennet, as the carriage drove up to the door; her husband looked impenetrably grave; her daughters, alarmed, anxious, uneasy.

Lydia's voice was heard in the vestibule; the door was thrown open, and she ran into the room. Her mother stepped forwards, embraced her, and welcomed her with rapture; gave her hand with an affectionate smile to Wickham, who followed his lady, and wished them both joy, with an alacrity which showed no doubt of their happiness.

Their reception from Mr. Bennet, to whom they then turned, was not quite so cordial. His countenance rather gained in austerity; and he scarcely opened his lips. The easy assurance of the young couple, indeed, was enough to provoke him. Elizabeth was disgusted, and even Miss Bennet was shocked. Lydia was Lydia still; untamed, unabashed, wild, noisy, and fearless. She turned from sister to sister, demanding their congratulations, and when at length they all sat down, looked eagerly round the room, took notice of some little alteration in it, and observed, with a laugh, that it was a great while since she had been there.

Wickham was not at all more distressed than herself, but his manners were always so pleasing, that had his character and his marriage been exactly what they ought, his smiles and his easy address, while he claimed their relationship, would have delighted them all. Elizabeth had not before believed him quite equal to such assurance; but she sat down, resolving within herself, to draw no limits in future to the impudence of an impudent man. *She* blushed, and Jane blushed; but the cheeks of the two who caused their confusion, suffered no variation of colour.

There was no want of discourse. The bride and her mother could neither of them talk fast enough; and Wickham, who happened to sit near Elizabeth, began enquiring after his acquaintance in that neighbourhood, with a good-humoured ease, which she felt very unable to equal in her replies. They seemed each of them to have the happiest memories in the world. Nothing of the past was recollected with pain; and Lydia led voluntarily to subjects, which her sisters would not have alluded to for the world.

"Only think of its being three months," she cried, "since I went away; it seems but a fortnight I declare; and yet there have been things enough happened in the time. Good gracious! when

I went away, I am sure I had no more idea of being married till I came back again! though I thought it would be very good fun if I was."

Her father lifted up his eyes. Jane was distressed. Elizabeth looked expressively at Lydia; but she, who never heard or saw anything of which she chose to be insensible, gaily continued, "Oh! mamma, do the people hereabouts know I am married today? I was afraid they might not; and we overtook William Goulding in his curricle, so I was determined he should know it, and so I let down the side glass next to him, and took off my glove, and let my hand just rest upon the window frame, so that he might see the ring, and then I bowed and smiled like anything."

Elizabeth could bear it no longer. She got up, and ran out of the room; and returned no more, till she heard them passing through the hall to the dining-parlour. She then joined them soon enough to see Lydia, with anxious parade, walk up to her mother's right hand, and hear her say to her eldest sister, "Ah! Jane, I take your place now, and you must go lower, because I am a married woman."

It was not to be supposed that time would give Lydia that embarrassment, from which she had been so wholly free at first. Her ease and good spirits increased. She longed to see Mrs. Philips, the Lucases, and all their other neighbours, and to hear herself called "Mrs. Wickham," by each of them; and in the meantime, she went after dinner to show her ring and boast of being married, to Mrs. Hill and the two housemaids.

"Well, mamma," said she, when they were all returned to the breakfast-room, "and what do you think of my husband? Is he not a charming man? I am sure my sisters must all envy me. I only hope they may have half my good luck. They must all go to Brighton. That is the place to get husbands. What a pity it is, mamma, we did not all go."

"Very true; and if I had my will, we should. But my dear

Lydia, I don't at all like your going such a way off. Must it be so?"

"Oh, lord! yes; – there is nothing in that. I shall like it of all things. You and papa, and my sisters, must come down and see us. We shall be at Newcastle all the winter, and I dare say there will be some balls, and I will take care to get good partners for them all."

"I should like it beyond anything!" said her mother.

"And then when you go away, you may leave one or two of my sisters behind you; and I dare say I shall get husbands for them before the winter is over."

"I thank you for my share of the favour," said Elizabeth; "but I do not particularly like your way of getting husbands."

Their visitors were not to remain above ten days with them. Mr. Wickham had received his commission before he left London, and he was to join his regiment at the end of a fortnight.

No one but Mrs. Bennet, regretted that their stay would be so short; and she made the most of the time, by visiting about with her daughter, and having very frequent parties at home. These parties were acceptable to all; to avoid a family circle was even more desirable to such as did think, than such as did not.

Wickham's affection for Lydia, was just what Elizabeth had expected to find it; not equal to Lydia's for him. She had scarcely needed her present observation to be satisfied, from the reason of things, that their elopement had been brought on by the strength of her love, rather than by his; and she would have wondered why, without violently caring for her, he chose to elope with her at all, had she not felt certain that his flight was rendered necessary by distress of circumstances; and if that were the case, he was not the young man to resist an opportunity of having a companion.

Lydia was exceedingly fond of him. He was her dear Wickham on every occasion; no one was to be put in competition with him. He did everything best in the world; and she was sure he would kill more birds on the first of September, than anybody else in the country.

One morning, soon after their arrival, as she was sitting with her two elder sisters, she said to Elizabeth,

"Lizzy, I never gave *you* an account of my wedding, I believe. You were not by, when I told mamma, and the others, all about it. Are you not curious to hear how it was managed?"

"No really," replied Elizabeth; "I think there cannot be too little said on the subject."

"La! You are so strange! But I must tell you how it went off. We were married, you know, at St.Clement's, because Wickham's lodgings were in that parish. And it was settled that we should all be there by eleven o'clock. My uncle and aunt and I were to go together; and the others were to meet us at the church. Well, Monday morning came, and I was in such a fuss! I was so afraid you know that something would happen to put it off, and then I should have gone quite distracted. And there was my aunt, all the time I was dressing, preaching and talking away just as if she was reading a sermon. However, I did not hear above one word in ten, for I was thinking, you may suppose, of my dear Wickham. I longed to know whether he would be married in his blue coat."

"Well, and so we breakfasted at ten as usual; I thought it would never be over; for, by the bye, you are to understand, that my uncle and aunt were horrid unpleasant all the time I was with them. If you'll believe me, I did not once put my foot out of doors, though I was there a fortnight. Not one party, or scheme, or anything. To be sure London was rather thin, but however the little Theatre was open. Well, and so just as the carriage came to the door, my uncle was called away upon business to that horrid man Mr. Stone. And then, you know, when once they get together, there is no end of it. Well, I was so frightened I did not know what to do, for my uncle was to give me away; and if we were beyond the hour, we could not be married all day. But, luckily, he came back again in ten minutes' time, and then we all set out. However, I recollected afterwards, that if he *had* been prevented going, the wedding need not be put off, for Mr. Darcy might have done as well."

"Mr. Darcy!" repeated Elizabeth, in utter amazement.

"Oh, yes! – he was to come there with Wickham, you know. But gracious me! I quite forgot! I ought not to have said a word about it. I promised them so faithfully! What will Wickham say? It was to be such a secret!"

"If it was to be secret," said Jane, "say not another word on the subject. You may depend upon my seeking no further."

"Oh! certainly," said Elizabeth, though burning with curiosity; "we will ask you no questions."

"Thank you," said Lydia, "for if you did, I should certainly tell you all, and then Wickham would be angry."

On such encouragement to ask, Elizabeth was forced to put it out of her power, by running away.

But to live in ignorance on such a point was impossible; or at least it was impossible not to try for information. Mr. Darcy had been at her sister's wedding. It was exactly a scene, and exactly among people, where he had apparently least to do, and least temptation to go. Conjectures as to the meaning of it, rapid and wild, hurried into her brain; but she was satisfied with none. Those that best pleased her, as placing his conduct in the noblest light, seemed most improbable. She could not bear such suspense; and hastily seizing a sheet of paper, wrote a short letter to her aunt, to request an explanation of what Lydia had dropped, if it were compatible with the secrecy which had been intended.

"You may readily comprehend," she added, "what my curiosity must be to know how a person unconnected with any of us, and (comparatively speaking) a stranger to our family, should have been amongst you at such a time. Pray write instantly, and let me understand it – unless it is, for very cogent reasons, to remain in the secrecy which Lydia seems to think necessary; and then I must endeavour to be satisfied with ignorance."

"Not that I *shall* though," she added to herself, as she finished the letter; "and my dear aunt, if you do not tell me in an honourable manner, I shall certainly be reduced to tricks and stratagems to find it out."

Jane's delicate sense of honour would not allow her to speak to Elizabeth privately of what Lydia had let fall; Elizabeth was glad of it; – till it appeared whether her inquiries would receive any satisfaction, she had rather be without a confidante.

# Chapter 52

ELIZABETH HAD the satisfaction of receiving an answer to her letter, as soon as she possibly could. She was no sooner in possession of it, than hurrying into the little copse, where she was least likely to be interrupted, she sat down on one of the benches, and prepared to be happy; for the length of the letter convinced her that it did not contain a denial.

*Gracechurch-Street, Sept. 6.*

MY DEAR NIECE,

I have just received your letter, and shall devote this whole morning to answering it, as I foresee that a *little* writing will not comprise what I have to tell you. I must confess myself surprised by your application; I did not expect it from *you*. Don't think me angry, however, for I only mean to let you know, that I had not imagined such enquiries to be necessary on *your* side. If you do not choose to understand me, forgive my impertinence. Your uncle is as much surprised as I am – and nothing but the belief of your being a party concerned, would have allowed him to act as he has done. But if you are really innocent and ignorant, I must be more explicit. On the very day of my coming home from Longbourn, your uncle had a most unexpected visitor. Mr. Darcy called, and was shut up with him several hours. It was all over before I arrived; so my curiosity was not so dreadfully racked as *yours* seems to have been. He came to tell Mr. Gardiner that he had found out where your sister and Mr. Wickham were, and that he had seen and talked with them both, Wickham repeatedly, Lydia once. From what I can collect, he left Derbyshire only one day after ourselves, and came to town with the resolution of hunting for them. The motive professed, was his conviction of its being owing to himself that Wickham's worthlessness had not been so well known, as to make it impossible for any young woman of character, to love or confide in him. He generously imputed the whole to his mistaken pride, and confessed that he had before thought it beneath him, to lay his private actions open to the world. His character was to speak for itself. He called it, therefore, his duty to step forward, and endeavour to remedy an evil, which had been brought on by himself. If he *had another* motive, I am sure it would never disgrace him. He had been some days in town, before he was able to discover them; but he had something to direct his search, which was more than *we* had; and the consciousness of this, was another reason for his resolving to follow us. There is a lady, it seems, a Mrs. Younge, who was some time ago governess to Miss Darcy, and was dismissed from her charge on some cause of disapprobation, though he did not say what. She then took a large house in Edward Street, and has since maintained herself by letting lodgings. This Mrs. Younge was, he knew, intimately acquainted with Wickham; and he went to her for intelligence of him, as soon as he got to town. But it was two or three days before he could get from her what he wanted. She would not betray her trust, I suppose, without bribery and corruption, for she really did know where her friend was to be found. Wickham indeed had gone to her, on their first arrival in London, and had she been able to receive them into her house, they would have taken up their abode with her. At length, however, our kind friend procured the wished-for direction. They were in —Street. He saw Wickham, and afterwards insisted on seeing Lydia. His first object with her, he acknowledged, had been to persuade her to quit her present disgraceful situation, and return to her friends as soon as they could be prevailed on to receive her, offering his assistance, as far as it would go. But he found Lydia absolutely resolved on remaining where she was. She cared for none of her friends, she wanted no help of his, she would not hear of leaving Wickham. She was sure they should be married some time or other, and it did not much signify when. Since such were her feelings, it only remained, he thought, to secure and expedite a marriage, which, in his very first conversation with Wickham, he easily learnt, had never been *his* design. He confessed himself obliged to leave the regiment, on account of some debts of honour, which were very pressing; and scrupled not to lay all the ill-consequences of Lydia's flight, on her own folly alone. He meant to resign his commission immediately; and as to his future situation, he could conjecture very little about it. He must go somewhere, but he did not know where, and he knew he should have nothing to live on. Mr. Darcy asked him why he had not married your sister at once. Though Mr. Bennet was not imagined to be very rich, he would have been able to do something for him, and his situation must have been benefited by marriage. But he found, in reply to this question, that Wickham still cherished the hope of more effectually making his fortune by marriage, in some other country. Under such circumstances, however, he was not likely to be proof against the temptation of immediate relief. They met several times, for there was much to be discussed. Wickham of course wanted more than he could get; but at length was reduced to be reasonable. Everything being settled between *them*, Mr. Darcy's next step was to make your uncle acquainted with it, and he first called in Gracechurch Street the evening before I came home. But Mr. Gardiner could not be seen, and Mr. Darcy found, on further enquiry, that your father was still with him, but would quit town the next morning. He did not judge your father to be a person whom he could so properly consult as your uncle, and therefore readily postponed seeing him, till after the departure of the former. He did not leave his name, and till the next day, it was only known that a gentleman had called on business. On Saturday he came again. Your father was gone, your uncle at home, and, as I said before, they had a great deal of talk together. They met again on Sunday, and then *I* saw him too. It was not all settled before Monday: as soon as it was, the express was sent off to Longbourn. But our visitor was very obstinate! I fancy, Lizzy, that obstinacy is the real defect of his character after all. He has been accused of many faults at different times; but *this* is the true one. Nothing was to be done that he did not do himself; though I am sure (and I do not speak it to be thanked, therefore say nothing about it), your uncle would most readily have settled the whole. They battled it together for a long time, which was more than either the gentleman or lady concerned in it deserved. But at last your uncle was forced to yield, and instead of being allowed to be of use to his niece, was forced to put up with only having the probable credit of it, which went sorely against the grain; and I really believe your letter this morning gave him great pleasure, because it required an explanation that would rob him of his borrowed feathers, and give the praise where it was due. But, Lizzy, this must go no farther than yourself, or Jane at most. You know pretty well, I suppose, what has been done for the young people. His debts are to be paid, amounting, I believe, to considerably more than a thousand pounds, another thousand in addition to her own settled upon *her*, and his commission purchased. The reason why all this was to be done by him alone, was such as I have given above. It was owing to him, to his reserve, and want of proper consideration, that Wickham's character had been so misunderstood, and consequently that he had been received and noticed as he was. Perhaps there was some truth in this; though I doubt whether *his* reserve, or *anybody's* reserve, can be answerable for the event. But in spite of all this fine talking, my dear Lizzy, you may rest perfectly assured, that your uncle would never have yielded, if we had not given him credit for *another interest* in the affair. When all this was resolved on, he returned again to his friends, who were still staying at Pemberley; but it was agreed that he should be in London once more when the wedding took place, and all money matters were then to receive the last finish. I believe I have now told you every thing. It is a relation which you tell me is to give you great surprise; I hope at least it will not afford you any displeasure. Lydia came to us; and Wickham had constant admission to the house. *He* was exactly what he had been, when I knew him in Hertfordshire; but I would not tell you how little I was satisfied with *her* behaviour while she stayed with us, if I had not perceived, by Jane's letter last Wednesday, that her conduct on coming home was exactly of a piece with it, and therefore what I now tell you, can give you no fresh pain. I talked to her repeatedly in the most serious manner, representing to her all the wickedness of what she had done, and all the unhappiness she had brought on her family. If she heard me, it was by good luck, for I am sure she did not listen. I was sometimes quite provoked, but then I recollected my dear Elizabeth and Jane, and for their sakes had patience with her. Mr. Darcy was punctual in his return, and as Lydia informed you, attended the wedding. He dined with us the next day, and was to leave town again on Wednesday or Thursday. Will you be very angry with me, my dear Lizzy, if I take this opportunity of saying (what I was never bold enough to say before) how much I like him. His behaviour to us has, in every respect, been as pleasing as when we were in Derbyshire. His understanding and opinions all please me; he wants nothing but a little more liveliness, and *that*, if he marry *prudently*, his wife may teach him. I thought him very sly; – he hardly ever mentioned your name. But slyness seems the fashion. Pray forgive me, if I have been very presuming, or at least do not punish me so far, as to exclude me from P. I shall never be quite happy till I have been all round the park. A low phaeton, with a nice little pair of ponies, would be the very thing. But I must write no more. The children have been wanting me this half hour. Yours, very sincerely,

M. GARDINER.

The contents of this letter threw Elizabeth into a flutter of spirits, in which it was difficult to determine whether pleasure or pain bore the greatest share. The vague and unsettled suspicions which uncertainty had produced of what Mr. Darcy might have been doing to forward her sister's match, which she had feared to encourage, as an exertion of goodness too great to be probable, and at the same time dreaded to be just, from the pain of obligation, were proved beyond their greatest extent to be true! He had followed them purposely to town, he had taken on himself all the trouble and mortification attendant on such a research; in which supplication had been necessary to a woman whom he must abominate and despise, and where he was reduced to meet, frequently meet, reason with, persuade, and finally bribe, the man whom he always most wished to avoid, and whose very name it was punishment to him to pronounce. He had done all this for a girl whom he could neither regard nor esteem. Her heart did whisper, that he had done it for her. But it was a hope shortly checked by other considerations, and she soon felt that even her vanity was insufficient, when required to depend on his affection for her, for a woman who had already refused him, as able to overcome a sentiment so natural as abhorrence against the relationship with Wickham. Brother-in-law of Wickham! Every kind of pride must revolt from the connection. He had to be sure done much. She was ashamed to think how much. But he had given a reason for his interference, which asked no extraordinary stretch of belief. It was reasonable that he should feel he had been wrong; he had liberality, and he had the means of exercising it; and though she would not place herself as his principal inducement, she could, perhaps, believe, that remaining partiality for her, might assist his endeavours in a cause where her peace of mind must be materially concerned. It was painful, exceedingly painful, to know that they were under obligations to a person who could never receive a return. They owed the restoration of Lydia, her character, everything, to him. Oh! how heartily did she grieve over every ungracious sensation she had ever encouraged, every saucy speech she had ever directed towards him. For herself she was humbled; but she was proud of him. Proud that in a cause of compassion and honour, he had been able to get the better of himself. She read over her aunt's commendation of him again and again. It was hardly enough; but it pleased her. She was even sensible of some pleasure, though mixed with regret, on finding how steadfastly both she and her uncle had been persuaded that affection and confidence subsisted between Mr. Darcy and herself.

She was roused from her seat, and her reflections, by

someone's approach; and before she could strike into another path, she was overtaken by Wickham.

"I am afraid I interrupt your solitary ramble, my dear sister?" said he, as he joined her.

"You certainly do," she replied with a smile; "but it does not follow that the interruption must be unwelcome."

"I should be sorry indeed, if it were. *We* were always good friends; and now we are better."

"True. Are the others coming out?"

"I do not know. Mrs. Bennet and Lydia are going in the carriage to Meryton. And so, my dear sister, I find from our uncle and aunt, that you have actually seen Pemberley."

She replied in the affirmative.

"I almost envy you the pleasure, and yet I believe it would be too much for me, or else I could take it in my way to Newcastle. And you saw the old housekeeper, I suppose? Poor Reynolds, she was always very fond of me. But of course she did not mention my name to you."

"Yes, she did."

"And what did she say?"

"That you were gone into the army, and she was afraid had – not turned out well. At such a distance as *that*, you know, things are strangely misrepresented."

"Certainly," he replied, biting his lips. Elizabeth hoped she had silenced him; but he soon afterwards said,

"I was surprised to see Darcy in town last month. We passed each other several times. I wonder what he can be doing there."

"Perhaps preparing for his marriage with Miss de Bourgh," said Elizabeth. "It must be something particular, to take him there at this time of year."

"Undoubtedly. Did you see him while you were at Lambton?

I thought I understood from the Gardiners that you had."

"Yes; he introduced us to his sister."

"And do you like her?"

"Very much."

"I have heard, indeed, that she is uncommonly improved within this year or two. When I last saw her, she was not very promising. I am very glad you liked her. I hope she will turn out well."

"I dare say she will; she has got over the most trying age."

"Did you go by the village of Kympton?"

"I do not recollect that we did."

"I mention it, because it is the living which I ought to have had. A most delightful place! – Excellent Parsonage House! It would have suited me in every respect."

"How should you have liked making sermons?"

"Exceedingly well. I should have considered it as part of my duty, and the exertion would soon have been nothing. One ought not to repine; – but, to be sure, it would have been such a thing for me! The quiet, the retirement of such a life, would have answered all my ideas of happiness! But it was not to be. Did you ever hear Darcy mention the circumstance, when you were in Kent?"

"I *have* heard from authority, which I thought *as good*, that it was left you conditionally only, and at the will of the present patron."

"You have. Yes, there was something in *that*, I told you so from the first, you may remember."

"I *did* hear, too, that there was a time, when sermon-making was not so palatable to you as it seems to be at present; that you actually declared your resolution of never taking orders, and that the business had been compromised accordingly."

"You did! and it was not wholly without foundation. You may remember what I told you on that point, when first we talked of it."

They were now almost at the door of the house, for she had walked fast to get rid of him; and unwilling, for her sister's sake, to provoke him, she only said in reply, with a good-humoured smile,

"Come, Mr. Wickham, we are brother and sister, you know. Do not let us quarrel about the past. In future, I hope we shall be always of one mind."

She held out her hand; he kissed it with affectionate gallantry, though he hardly knew how to look, and they entered the house.

# *Chapter 53*

MR. WICKHAM was so perfectly satisfied with this conversation, that he never again distressed himself, or provoked his dear sister Elizabeth, by introducing the subject of it; and she was pleased to find that she had said enough to keep him quiet.

The day of his and Lydia's departure soon came, and Mrs. Bennet was forced to submit to a separation, which, as her husband by no means entered into her scheme of their all going to Newcastle, was likely to continue at least a twelvemonth.

"Oh! my dear Lydia," she cried, "when shall we meet again?"

"Oh, lord! I don't know. Not these two or three years perhaps."

"Write to me very often, my dear."

"As often as I can. But you know married women have never much time for writing. My sisters may write to *me*. They will have nothing else to do."

Mr. Wickham's adieus were much more affectionate than his wife's. He smiled, looked handsome, and said many pretty things.

"He is as fine a fellow," said Mr. Bennet, as soon as they were out of the house, "as ever I saw. He simpers, and smirks, and makes love to us all. I am prodigiously proud of him. I defy even Sir William Lucas himself, to produce a more valuable son-in-law."

The loss of her daughter made Mrs. Bennet very dull for several days.

"I often think," said she, "that there is nothing so bad as parting with one's friends. One seems so forlorn without them."

"This is the consequence you see, Madam, of marrying a daughter," said Elizabeth. "It must make you better satisfied that your other four are single."

"It is no such thing. Lydia does not leave me because she is married; but only because her husband's regiment happens to be so far off. If that had been nearer, she would not have gone so soon."

But the spiritless condition which this event threw her into, was shortly relieved, and her mind opened again to the agitation of hope, by an article of news, which then began to be in circulation. The housekeeper at Netherfield had received orders to prepare for the arrival of her master, who was coming down in a day or two, to shoot there for several weeks. Mrs. Bennet was quite in the fidgets. She looked at Jane, and smiled, and shook her head by turns.

"Well, well, and so Mr. Bingley is coming down, sister," (for Mrs. Philips first brought her the news.) "Well, so much the better. Not that I care about it, though. He is nothing to us, you know, and I am sure *I* never want to see him again. But, however, he is very welcome to come to Netherfield, if he likes it. And who knows what *may* happen? But that is nothing to us. You know, sister, we agreed long ago never to mention a word about it. And so, is it quite certain he is coming?"

"You may depend on it," replied the other, "for Mrs. Nicholls was in Meryton last night; I saw her passing by, and went out myself on purpose to know the truth of it; and she told me that it was certain true. He comes down on Thursday at the latest, very likely on Wednesday. She was going to the butcher's, she told me, on purpose to order in some meat on Wednesday, and she has got three couple of ducks, just fit to be killed."

Miss Bennet had not been able to hear of his coming, without changing colour. It was many months since she had mentioned his name to Elizabeth; but now, as soon as they were alone together, she said,

"I saw you look at me today, Lizzy, when my aunt told us of the present report; and I know I appeared distressed. But don't imagine it was from any silly cause. I was only confused for the moment, because I felt that I *should* be looked at. I do assure you, that the news does not affect me either with pleasure or pain. I am glad of one thing, that he comes alone; because we shall see the less of him. Not that I am afraid of *myself*, but I dread other people's remarks."

Elizabeth did not know what to make of it. Had she not seen him in Derbyshire, she might have supposed him capable of coming there, with no other view than what was acknowledged; but she still thought him partial to Jane, and she wavered as to the greater probability of his coming there *with* his friend's permission, or being bold enough to come without it.

"Yet it is hard," she sometimes thought, "that this poor man cannot come to a house, which he has legally hired, without raising all this speculation! I *will* leave him to himself."

In spite of what her sister declared, and really believed to be her feelings, in the expectation of his arrival, Elizabeth could easily perceive that her spirits were affected by it. They were more disturbed, more unequal, than she had often seen them.

The subject which had been so warmly canvassed between their parents, about a twelvemonth ago, was now brought forward again.

"As soon as ever Mr. Bingley comes, my dear," said Mrs. Bennet, "you will wait on him of course."

"No, no. You forced me into visiting him last year, and promised if I went to see him, he should marry one of my daughters. But it ended in nothing, and I will not be sent on a fool's errand again."

His wife represented to him how absolutely necessary such an attention would be from all the neighbouring gentlemen, on his returning to Netherfield.

"'Tis an etiquette I despise," said he. "If he wants our society, let him seek it. He knows where we live. I will not spend *my* hours in running after my neighbours every time they go away, and come back again."

"Well, all I know is, that it will be abominably rude if you do not wait on him. But, however, that shan't prevent my asking him to dine here, I am determined. We must have Mrs. Long and the Gouldings soon. That will make thirteen with ourselves, so there will be just room at table for him."

Consoled by this resolution, she was better able to bear her husband's incivility; though it was very mortifying to know that her neighbours might all see Mr. Bingley in consequence of it, before *they* did. As the day of his arrival drew near,

"I begin to be sorry that he comes at all," said Jane to her sister. "It would be nothing; I could see him with perfect indifference, but I can hardly bear to hear it thus perpetually talked of. My mother means well; but she does not know, no one can know how much I suffer from what she says. Happy shall I be, when his stay at Netherfield is over!"

"I wish I could say anything to comfort you," replied Elizabeth; "but it is wholly out of my power. You must feel it; and the usual satisfaction of preaching patience to a sufferer is denied to me, because you have always so much."

Mr. Bingley arrived. Mrs. Bennet, through the assistance of servants, contrived to have the earliest tidings of it, that the period of anxiety and fretfulness on her side, might be as long as it could. She counted the days that must intervene before their invitation could be sent; hopeless of seeing him before. But on the third morning after his arrival in Hertfordshire, she saw him from her dressing-room window, enter the paddock, and ride towards the house.

Her daughters were eagerly called to partake of her joy. Jane resolutely kept her place at the table; but Elizabeth, to satisfy her mother, went to the window – she looked, – she saw Mr. Darcy with him, and sat down again by her sister.

"There is a gentleman with him, mamma," said Kitty; "who can it be?"

"Some acquaintance or other, my dear, I suppose; I am sure I do not know."

"La!" replied Kitty, "it looks just like that man that used to be with him before. Mr. what's his name. That tall, proud man."

"Good gracious! Mr. Darcy! – and so it does I vow. Well, any friend of Mr. Bingley's will always be welcome here to be sure; but else I must say that I hate the very sight of him."

Jane looked at Elizabeth with surprise and concern. She knew but little of their meeting in Derbyshire, and therefore felt for the awkwardness which must attend her sister, in seeing him almost for the first time after receiving his explanatory letter. Both sisters were uncomfortable enough. Each felt for the other, and of course for themselves; and their mother talked on, of her dislike of Mr. Darcy, and her resolution to be civil to him only as Mr. Bingley's friend, without being heard by either of them. But Elizabeth had sources of uneasiness which could not be suspected by Jane, to whom she had never yet had courage to show Mrs. Gardiner's letter, or to relate her own change of sentiment towards him. To Jane, he could be only a man whose proposals she had refused, and whose merit she had undervalued; but to her own more extensive information, he was the person, to whom the whole family were indebted for the first of benefits, and whom she regarded herself with an interest, if not quite so tender, at least as reasonable and just, as what Jane felt for Bingley. Her astonishment at his coming – at his coming to Netherfield, to Longbourn, and voluntarily seeking her again, was almost equal to what she had known on first witnessing his altered behaviour in Derbyshire.

The colour which had been driven from her face, returned for half a minute with an additional glow, and a smile of delight added lustre to her eyes, as she thought for that space of time, that his affection and wishes must still be unshaken. But she would not be secure.

"Let me first see how he behaves," said she; "it will then be early enough for expectation."

She sat intently at work, striving to be composed, and without daring to lift up her eyes, till anxious curiosity carried them to the face of her sister, as the servant was approaching the door. Jane looked a little paler than usual, but more sedate than Elizabeth had expected. On the gentlemen's appearing, her colour increased; yet she received them with tolerable ease, and with a propriety of behaviour equally free from any symptom of resentment, or any unnecessary complaisance.

Elizabeth said as little to either as civility would allow, and sat down again to her work, with an eagerness which it did not often command. She had ventured only one glance at Darcy. He looked serious as usual; and she thought, more as he had been used to look in Hertfordshire, than as she had seen him at Pemberley. But, perhaps he could not in her mother's presence be what he was before her uncle and aunt. It was a painful, but not an improbable, conjecture.

Bingley, she had likewise seen for an instant, and in that short period saw him looking both pleased and embarrassed. He was received by Mrs. Bennet with a degree of civility, which made her two daughters ashamed, especially when contrasted with the cold and ceremonious politeness of her curtsey and address to his friend.

Elizabeth particularly, who knew that her mother owed to the latter the preservation of her favourite daughter from irremediable infamy, was hurt and distressed to a most painful degree by a distinction so ill applied.

Darcy, after enquiring of her how Mr. and Mrs. Gardiner did, a question which she could not answer without confusion, said scarcely any thing. He was not seated by her; perhaps that was the reason of his silence; but it had not been so in Derbyshire. There he had talked to her friends, when he could not to herself. But now several minutes elapsed, without bringing the sound of his voice; and when occasionally, unable to resist the impulse of curiosity, she raised her eyes to his face, she as often found him looking at Jane, as at herself, and frequently on no object but the ground. More thoughtfulness, and less anxiety to please than when they last met, were plainly expressed. She was disappointed, and angry with herself for being so.

"Could I expect it to be otherwise!" said she. "Yet why did he come?"

She was in no humour for conversation with anyone but himself; and to him she had hardly courage to speak.

She enquired after his sister, but could do no more.

"It is a long time, Mr. Bingley, since you went away," said Mrs. Bennet.

He readily agreed to it.

"I began to be afraid you would never come back again. People *did* say, you meant to quit the place entirely at Michaelmas; but, however, I hope it is not true. A great many changes have happened in the neighbourhood, since you went away. Miss Lucas is married and settled. And one of my own daughters. I suppose you have heard of it; indeed, you must have seen it in the papers. It was in the Times and the Courier, I know; though it was not put in as it ought to be. It was only said, "Lately, George Wickham, Esq. to Miss Lydia Bennet," without there being a syllable said of her father, or the place where she lived, or anything. It was my brother Gardiner's drawing up too, and I wonder how he came to make such an awkward business of it. Did you see it?"

Bingley replied that he did, and made his congratulations. Elizabeth dared not lift up her eyes. How Mr. Darcy looked, therefore, she could not tell.

"It is a delightful thing, to be sure, to have a daughter well married," continued her mother, "but at the same time, Mr. Bingley, it is very hard to have her taken such a way from me. They are gone down to Newcastle, a place quite northward, it seems, and there they are to stay I do not know how long. His regiment is there; for I suppose you have heard of his leaving the —shire, and of his being gone into the regulars. Thank Heaven! he has *some* friends, though perhaps not so many as he deserves."

Elizabeth, who knew this to be levelled at Mr. Darcy, was in such misery of shame, that she could hardly keep her seat. It drew from her, however, the exertion of speaking, which nothing else had so effectually done before; and she asked Bingley, whether he meant to make any stay in the country at present. A few weeks, he believed.

"When you have killed all your own birds, Mr. Bingley," said her mother, "I beg you will come here, and shoot as many as you please, on Mr. Bennet's manor. I am sure he will be vastly happy to oblige you, and will save all the best of the covies for you."

Elizabeth's misery increased, at such unnecessary, such officious attention! Were the same fair prospect to arise at present, as had flattered them a year ago, everything, she was persuaded, would be hastening to the same vexatious conclusion. At that instant she felt, that years of happiness could not make Jane or herself amends, for moments of such painful confusion.

"The first wish of my heart," said she to herself, "is never more to be in company with either of them. Their society can afford no pleasure, that will atone for such wretchedness as this! Let me never see either one or the other again!"

Yet the misery, for which years of happiness were to offer no compensation, received soon afterwards material relief, from observing how much the beauty of her sister re-kindled the admiration of her former lover. When first he came in, he had spoken to her but little; but every five minutes seemed to be giving her more of his attention. He found her as handsome as she had been last year; as good natured, and as unaffected, though not quite so chatty. Jane was anxious that no difference should be perceived in her at all, and was really persuaded that she talked as much as ever. But her mind was so busily engaged, that she did not always know when she was silent.

When the gentlemen rose to go away, Mrs. Bennet was mindful of her intended civility, and they were invited and engaged to dine at Longbourn in a few day's time.

"You are quite a visit in my debt, Mr. Bingley," she added, "for when you went to town last winter, you promised to take a family dinner with us, as soon as you returned. I have not forgot, you see; and I assure you, I was very much disappointed that you did not come back and keep your engagement."

Bingley looked a little silly at this reflection, and said something of his concern, at having been prevented by business. They then went away.

Mrs. Bennet had been strongly inclined to ask them to stay and dine there, that day; but, though she always kept a very good table, she did not think anything less than two courses, could be good enough for a man, on whom she had such anxious designs, or satisfy the appetite and pride of one who had ten thousand a year.

## *Chapter 54*

As soon as they were gone, Elizabeth walked out to recover her spirits; or in other words, to dwell without interruption on those subjects that must deaden them more. Mr. Darcy's behaviour astonished and vexed her.

"Why, if he came only to be silent, grave, and indifferent," said she, "did he come at all?"

She could settle it in no way that gave her pleasure.

"He could be still amiable, still pleasing, to my uncle and aunt, when he was in town; and why not to me? If he fears me, why come hither? If he no longer cares for me, why silent? Teasing, teasing, man! I will think no more about him."

Her resolution was for a short time involuntarily kept by the approach of her sister, who joined her with a cheerful look, which showed her better satisfied with their visitors, than Elizabeth.

"Now," said she, "that this first meeting is over, I feel perfectly easy. I know my own strength, and I shall never be embarrassed again by his coming. I am glad he dines here on

Tuesday. It will then be publicly seen, that on both sides, we meet only as common and indifferent acquaintance."

"Yes, very indifferent indeed," said Elizabeth, laughingly. "Oh, Jane, take care."

"My dear Lizzy, you cannot think me so weak, as to be in danger now."

"I think you are in very great danger of making him as much in love with you as ever."

They did not see the gentlemen again till Tuesday; and Mrs. Bennet, in the meanwhile, was giving way to all the happy schemes, which the good humour, and common politeness of Bingley, in half an hour's visit, had revived.

On Tuesday there was a large party assembled at Longbourn; and the two who were most anxiously expected, to the credit of their punctuality as sportsmen, were in very good time. When they repaired to the dining-room, Elizabeth eagerly watched to see whether Bingley would take the place, which, in all their former parties, had belonged to him, by her sister. Her prudent mother, occupied by the same ideas, forbore to invite him to sit by herself. On entering the room, he seemed to hesitate; but Jane happened to look round, and happened to smile: it was decided. He placed himself by her.

Elizabeth, with a triumphant sensation, looked towards his friend. He bore it with noble indifference, and she would have imagined that Bingley had received his sanction to be happy, had she not seen his eyes likewise turned towards Mr. Darcy, with an expression of half-laughing alarm.

His behaviour to her sister was such, during dinner-time, as showed an admiration of her, which, though more guarded than formerly, persuaded Elizabeth, that if left wholly to himself, Jane's happiness, and his own, would be speedily secured. Though she dared not depend upon the consequence, she yet received pleasure from observing his behaviour. It gave her all the animation that her spirits could boast; for she was in no cheerful humour. Mr. Darcy was almost as far from her, as the table could divide them. He was on one side of her mother. She knew how little such a situation would give pleasure to either, or make either appear to advantage. She was not near enough to hear any of their discourse, but she could see how seldom they spoke to each other, and how formal and cold was their manner, whenever they did. Her mother's ungraciousness, made the sense of what they owed him more painful to Elizabeth's mind; and she would, at times, have given anything to be privileged to tell him, that his kindness was neither unknown nor unfelt by the whole of the family.

She was in hopes that the evening would afford some opportunity of bringing them together; that the whole of the visit would not pass away without enabling them to enter into something more of conversation, than the mere ceremonious salutation attending his entrance. Anxious and uneasy, the period which passed in the drawing-room, before the gentlemen came, was wearisome and dull to a degree, that almost made her uncivil. She looked forward to their entrance, as the point on which all her chance of pleasure for the evening must depend.

"If he does not come to me, *then*," said she, "I shall give him up for ever."

The gentlemen came; and she thought he looked as if he would have answered her hopes; but, alas! the ladies had crowded round the table, where Miss Bennet was making tea, and Elizabeth pouring out the coffee, in so close a confederacy, that there was not a single vacancy near her, which would admit of a chair. And on the gentlemen's approaching, one of the girls moved closer to her than ever, and said, in a whisper,

"The men shan't come and part us, I am determined. We want none of them; do we?"

Darcy had walked away to another part of the room. She

followed him with her eyes, envied everyone to whom he spoke, had scarcely patience enough to help anybody to coffee; and then was enraged against herself for being so silly!

"A man who has once been refused! How could I ever be foolish enough to expect a renewal of his love? Is there one among the sex, who would not protest against such a weakness as a second proposal to the same woman? There is no indignity so abhorrent to their feelings!"

She was a little revived, however, by his bringing back his coffee cup himself; and she seized the opportunity of saying,

"Is your sister at Pemberley still?"

"Yes, she will remain there till Christmas."

"And quite alone? Have all her friends left her?"

"Mrs. Annesley is with her. The others have been gone on to Scarborough, these three weeks."

She could think of nothing more to say; but if he wished to converse with her, he might have better success. He stood by her, however, for some minutes, in silence; and, at last, on the young lady's whispering to Elizabeth again, he walked away.

When the tea-things were removed, and the card-tables placed, the ladies all rose, and Elizabeth was then hoping to be soon joined by him, when all her views were overthrown, by seeing him fall a victim to her mother's rapacity for whist players, and in a few moments after seated with the rest of the party. She now lost every expectation of pleasure. They were confined for the evening at different tables, and she had nothing to hope, but that his eyes were so often turned towards her side of the room, as to make him play as unsuccessfully as herself.

Mrs. Bennet had designed to keep the two Netherfield gentlemen to supper; but their carriage was unluckily ordered before any of the others, and she had no opportunity of detaining them.

"Well girls," said she, as soon as they were left to themselves, "What say you to the day? I think everything has passed off uncommonly well, I assure you. The dinner was as well dressed as any I ever saw. The venison was roasted to a turn – and everybody said, they never saw so fat a haunch. The soup was fifty times better than what we had at the Lucases' last week; and even Mr. Darcy acknowledged, that the partridges were remarkably well done; and I suppose he has two or three French cooks at least. And, my dear Jane, I never saw you look in greater beauty. Mrs. Long said so too, for I asked her whether you did not. And what do you think she said besides? 'Ah! Mrs. Bennet, we shall have her at Netherfield at last.' She did indeed. I do think Mrs. Long is as good a creature as ever lived – and her nieces are very pretty behaved girls, and not at all handsome: I like them prodigiously."

Mrs. Bennet, in short, was in very great spirits; she had seen enough of Bingley's behaviour to Jane, to be convinced that she would get him at last; and her expectations of advantage to her family, when in a happy humour, were so far beyond reason, that she was quite disappointed at not seeing him there again the next day, to make his proposals.

"It has been a very agreeable day," said Miss Bennet to Elizabeth. "The party seemed so well selected, so suitable one with the other. I hope we may often meet again."

Elizabeth smiled.

"Lizzy, you must not do so. You must not suspect me. It mortifies me. I assure you that I have now learnt to enjoy his conversation as an agreeable and sensible young man, without having a wish beyond it. I am perfectly satisfied from what his manners now are, that he never had any design of engaging my affection. It is only that he is blessed with greater sweetness of address, and a stronger desire of generally pleasing than any other man."

"You are very cruel," said her sister, "you will not let me smile, and are provoking me to it every moment."

"How hard it is in some cases to be believed!"

"And how impossible in others!"

"But why should you wish to persuade me that I feel more than I acknowledge?"

"That is a question which I hardly know how to answer. We all love to instruct, though we can teach only what is not worth knowing. Forgive me; and if you persist in indifference, do not make *me* your confidante."

# Chapter 55

A FEW days after this visit, Mr. Bingley called again, and alone. His friend had left him that morning for London, but was to return home in ten days time. He sat with them above an hour, and was in remarkably good spirits. Mrs. Bennet invited him to dine with them; but, with many expressions of concern, he confessed himself engaged elsewhere.

"Next time you call," said she, "I hope we shall be more lucky."

He should be particularly happy at any time, &c. &c.; and if she would give him leave, would take an early opportunity of waiting on them.

"Can you come tomorrow?"

Yes, he had no engagement at all for tomorrow; and her invitation was accepted with alacrity.

He came, and in such very good time, that the ladies were none of them dressed. In ran Mrs. Bennet to her daughter's room, in her dressing gown, and with her hair half finished, crying out,

"My dear Jane, make haste and hurry down. He is come – Mr. Bingley is come. – He is, indeed. Make haste, make haste. Here, Sarah, come to Miss Bennet this moment, and help her on with her gown. Never mind Miss Lizzy's hair."

"We will be down as soon as we can," said Jane; "but I dare say Kitty is forwarder than either of us, for she went up stairs half an hour ago."

"Oh! hang Kitty! what has she to do with it? Come, be quick, be quick! where is your sash my dear?"

But when her mother was gone, Jane would not be prevailed on to go down without one of her sisters.

The same anxiety to get them by themselves, was visible again in the evening. After tea, Mr. Bennet retired to the library, as was his custom, and Mary went upstairs to her instrument. Two obstacles of the five being thus removed, Mrs. Bennet sat looking and winking at Elizabeth and Catherine for a considerable time, without making any impression on them. Elizabeth would not observe her; and when at last Kitty did, she very innocently said, "What is the matter mamma? What do you keep winking at me for? What am I to do?"

"Nothing child, nothing. I did not wink at you." She then sat still five minutes longer; but unable to waste such a precious occasion, she suddenly got up, and saying to Kitty,

"Come here, my love, I want to speak to you," took her out of the room. Jane instantly gave a look at Elizabeth, which spoke her distress at such premeditation, and her entreaty that *she* would not give in to it. In a few minutes, Mrs. Bennet half opened the door and called out,

"Lizzy, my dear, I want to speak with you."

Elizabeth was forced to go.

"We may as well leave them by themselves you know;" said her mother, as soon as she was in the hall. "Kitty and I are going upstairs to sit in my dressing room."

Elizabeth made no attempt to reason with her mother, but remained quietly in the hall, till she and Kitty were out of sight, then returned into the drawing-room.

Mrs. Bennet's schemes for this day were ineffectual. Bingley was everything that was charming, except the professed lover of her daughter. His ease and cheerfulness rendered him a most agreeable addition to their evening party; and he bore with the ill-judged officiousness of the mother, and heard all her silly remarks with a forbearance and command of countenance, particularly grateful to the daughter.

He scarcely needed an invitation to stay to supper; and before he went away, an engagement was formed, chiefly through his own and Mrs. Bennet's means, for his coming next morning to shoot with her husband.

After this day, Jane said no more of her indifference. Not a word passed between the sisters concerning Bingley; but Elizabeth went to bed in the happy belief that all must speedily be concluded, unless Mr. Darcy returned within the stated time. Seriously, however, she felt tolerably persuaded that all this must have taken place with that gentleman's concurrence.

Bingley was punctual to his appointment; and he and Mr. Bennet spent the morning together, as had been agreed on. The latter was much more agreeable than his companion expected. There was nothing of presumption or folly in Bingley, that could provoke his ridicule, or disgust him into silence; and he was more communicative, and less eccentric than the other had ever seen him. Bingley of course returned with him to dinner; and in the evening Mrs. Bennet's invention was again at work to get everybody away from him and her daughter. Elizabeth, who had a letter to write, went into the breakfast-room for that purpose soon after tea; for as the others were all going to sit down to cards, she could not be wanted to counteract her mother's schemes.

But on returning to the drawing-room, when her letter was finished, she saw, to her infinite surprise, there was reason to fear that her mother had been too ingenious for her. On opening the door, she perceived her sister and Bingley standing together over the hearth, as if engaged in earnest conversation; and had this led to no suspicion, the faces of both as they hastily turned around, and moved away from each other, would have told it all. *Their* situation was awkward enough; but *hers* she thought was still worse. Not a syllable was uttered by either; and Elizabeth was on the point of going away again, when Bingley, who as well as the other had sat down, suddenly rose, and whispering a few words to her sister, ran out of the room.

Jane could have no reserves from Elizabeth, where confidence would give pleasure; and instantly embracing her, acknowledged, with the liveliest emotion, that she was the happiest creature in the world.

"'Tis too much!" she added, "by far too much. I do not deserve it. Oh! why is not everybody as happy?"

Elizabeth's congratulations were given with a sincerity, a warmth, a delight, which words could but poorly express. Every sentence of kindness was a fresh source of happiness to Jane. But she would not allow herself to stay with her sister, or say half that remained to be said, for the present.

"I must go instantly to my mother;" she cried. "I would not on any account trifle with her affectionate solicitude; or allow her to hear it from anyone but myself. He is gone to my father already. Oh! Lizzy, to know that what I have to relate will give such pleasure to all my dear family! how shall I bear so much happiness!"

She then hastened away to her mother, who had purposely broken up the card party, and was sitting upstairs with Kitty.

Elizabeth, who was left by herself, now smiled at the rapidity and ease with which an affair was finally settled, that had given them so many previous months of suspense and vexation.

"And this," said she, "is the end of all his friend's anxious circumspection! of all his sister's falsehood and contrivance! the happiest, wisest, most reasonable end!"

In a few minutes she was joined by Bingley, whose conference with her father had been short and to the purpose.

"Where is your sister?" said he hastily, as he opened the door.

"With my mother upstairs. She will be down in a moment, I dare say."

He then shut the door, and, coming up to her, claimed the good wishes and affection of a sister. Elizabeth honestly and heartily expressed her delight in the prospect of their relationship. They shook hands with great cordiality; and then till her sister came down, she had to listen to all he had to say, of his own happiness, and of Jane's perfections; and in spite of his being a lover, Elizabeth really believed all his expectations of felicity, to be rationally founded, because they had for basis the excellent understanding, and super-excellent disposition of Jane, and a general similarity of feeling and taste between her and himself.

It was an evening of no common delight to them all; the satisfaction of Miss Bennet's mind gave a glow of such sweet animation to her face, as made her look handsomer than ever. Kitty simpered and smiled, and hoped her turn was coming soon. Mrs. Bennet could not give her consent or speak her approbation in terms warm enough to satisfy her feelings, though she talked to Bingley of nothing else, for half an hour; and when Mr. Bennet joined them at supper, his voice and manner plainly showed how really happy he was.

Not a word, however, passed his lips in allusion to it, till their visitor took his leave for the night; but as soon as he was gone, he turned to his daughter and said,

"Jane, I congratulate you. You will be a very happy woman."

Jane went to him instantly, kissed him, and thanked him for his goodness.

"You are a good girl;" he replied, "and I have great pleasure in thinking you will be so happily settled. I have not a doubt of your doing very well together. Your tempers are by no means unlike. You are each of you so complying, that nothing will ever be resolved on; so easy, that every servant will cheat you; and so generous, that you will always exceed your income."

"I hope not so. Imprudence or thoughtlessness in money matters, would be unpardonable in *me*."

"Exceed their income! My dear Mr. Bennet," cried his wife, "what are you talking of? Why, he has four or five thousand a year, and very likely more." Then addressing her daughter, "Oh! my dear, dear Jane, I am so happy! I am sure I shan't get a wink of sleep all night. I knew how it would be. I always said it must be so, at last. I was sure you could not be so beautiful for nothing! I remember, as soon as ever I saw him, when he first came into Hertfordshire last year, I thought how likely it was that you should come together. Oh! he is the handsomest young man that ever was seen!"

Wickham, Lydia, were all forgotten. Jane was beyond competition her favourite child. At that moment, she cared for no other. Her younger sisters soon began to make interest with her for objects of happiness which she might in future be able to dispense.

Mary petitioned for the use of the library at Netherfield; and Kitty begged very hard for a few balls there every winter.

Bingley, from this time, was of course a daily visitor at Longbourn; coming frequently before breakfast, and always remaining till after supper; unless when some barbarous neighbour, who could not be enough detested, had given him an invitation to dinner, which he thought himself obliged to accept.

Elizabeth had now but little time for conversation with her sister; for while he was present, Jane had no attention to bestow on anyone else; but she found herself considerably useful to both of them, in those hours of separation that must sometimes occur. In the absence of Jane, he always attached himself to Elizabeth, for the pleasure of talking to her; and when Bingley was gone, Jane constantly sought the same means of relief.

"He has made me so happy," said she, one evening, "by telling me, that he was totally ignorant of my being in town last spring! I had not believed it possible."

"I suspected as much," replied Elizabeth. "But how did he account for it?"

"It must have been his sister's doing. They were certainly no friends to his acquaintance with me, which I cannot wonder at, since he might have chosen so much more advantageously in many respects. But when they see, as I trust they will, that their brother is happy with me, they will learn to be contented, and we shall be on good terms again; though we can never be what we once were to each other."

"That is the most unforgiving speech," said Elizabeth, "that I ever heard you utter. Good girl! It would vex me, indeed, to see you again the dupe of Miss Bingley's pretended regard."

"Would you believe it, Lizzy, that when he went to town last November, he really loved me, and nothing but a persuasion of *my* being indifferent, would have prevented his coming down again!"

"He made a little mistake to be sure; but it is to the credit of his modesty."

This naturally introduced a panegyric from Jane on his diffidence, and the little value he put on his own good qualities.

Elizabeth was pleased to find, that he had not betrayed the interference of his friend, for, though Jane had the most generous and forgiving heart in the world, she knew it was a circumstance which must prejudice her against him.

"I am certainly the most fortunate creature that ever existed!" cried Jane. "Oh! Lizzy, why am I thus singled from my family, and blessed above them all! If I could but see *you* as happy! If there *were* but such another man for you!"

"If you were to give me forty such men, I never could be so happy as you. Till I have your disposition, your goodness, I never can have your happiness. No, no, let me shift for myself; and, perhaps, if I have very good luck, I may meet with another Mr. Collins in time."

The situation of affairs in the Longbourn family could not be long a secret. Mrs. Bennet was privileged to whisper it to Mrs. Phillips, and *she* ventured, without any permission, to do the same by all her neighbours in Meryton.

The Bennets were speedily pronounced to be the luckiest family in the world, though only a few weeks before, when Lydia had first run away, they had been generally proved to be marked out for misfortune.

# *Chapter* 56

ONE MORNING, about a week after Bingley's engagement with Jane had been formed, as he and the females of the family were sitting together in the dining-room, their attention was suddenly drawn to the window, by the sound of a carriage; and they perceived a chaise and four driving up the lawn. It was too early in the morning for visitors, and besides, the equipage did not answer to that of any of their neighbours. The horses were post; and neither the carriage, nor the livery of the servant who preceded it, were familiar to them. As it was certain, however, that somebody was coming, Bingley instantly prevailed on Miss Bennet to avoid the confinement of such an intrusion, and walk away with him into the shrubbery. They both set off, and the conjectures of the remaining three continued, though with little satisfaction, till the door was thrown open, and their visitor entered. It was Lady Catherine de Bourgh.

They were of course all intending to be surprised; but their astonishment was beyond their expectation; and on the part of Mrs. Bennet and Kitty, though she was perfectly unknown to them, even inferior to what Elizabeth felt.

She entered the room with an air more than usually ungracious, made no other reply to Elizabeth's salutation, than a slight inclination of the head, and sat down without saying a word. Elizabeth had mentioned her name to her mother, on her ladyship's entrance, though no request of introduction had been made.

Mrs. Bennet all amazement, though flattered by having a guest of such high importance, received her with the utmost politeness. After sitting for a moment in silence, she said very stiffly to Elizabeth,

"I hope you are well, Miss Bennet. That lady I suppose is your mother."

Elizabeth replied very concisely that she was.

"And *that* I suppose is one of your sisters."

"Yes, madam," said Mrs. Bennet, delighted to speak to Lady Catherine. "She is my youngest girl but one. My youngest of all, is lately married, and my eldest is somewhere about the grounds, walking with a young man, who I believe will soon become a part of the family."

"You have a very small park here," returned Lady Catherine

after a short silence.

"It is nothing in comparison of Rosings, my lady, I dare say; but I assure you it is much larger than Sir William Lucas's."

"This must be a most inconvenient sitting-room for the evening, in summer; the windows are full west."

Mrs. Bennet assured her that they never sat there after dinner; and then added,

"May I take the liberty of asking your ladyship whether you left Mr. and Mrs. Collins well."

"Yes, very well. I saw them the night before last."

Elizabeth now expected that she would produce a letter for her from Charlotte, as it seemed the only probable motive for her calling. But no letter appeared, and she was completely puzzled.

Mrs. Bennet, with great civility, begged her ladyship to take some refreshment; but Lady Catherine very resolutely, and not very politely, declined eating anything; and then rising up, said to Elizabeth,

"Miss Bennet, there seemed to be a prettyish kind of a little wilderness on one side of your lawn. I should be glad to take a turn in it, if you will favour me with your company."

"Go, my dear," cried her mother, "and show her ladyship about the different walks. I think she will be pleased with the hermitage."

Elizabeth obeyed, and running into her own room for her parasol, attended her noble guest down stairs. As they passed through the hall, Lady Catherine opened the doors into the dining-parlour and drawing-room, and pronouncing them, after a short survey, to be decent-looking rooms, walked on.

Her carriage remained at the door, and Elizabeth saw that her waiting-woman was in it. They proceeded in silence along the gravel walk that led to the copse; Elizabeth was determined to make no effort for conversation with a woman, who was now more than usually insolent and disagreeable.

"How could I ever think her like her nephew?" said she, as she looked in her face.

As soon as they entered the copse, Lady Catherine began in the following manner:–

"You can be at no loss, Miss Bennet, to understand the reason of my journey hither. Your own heart, your own conscience, must tell you why I come."

Elizabeth looked with unaffected astonishment.

"Indeed, you are mistaken, Madam. I have not been at all able to account for the honour of seeing you here."

"Miss Bennet," replied her ladyship, in an angry tone, "you ought to know, that I am not to be trifled with. But however insincere *you* may choose to be, you shall not find *me* so. My character has ever been celebrated for its sincerity and frankness, and in a cause of such moment as this, I shall certainly not depart from it. A report of a most alarming nature, reached me two days ago. I was told, that not only your sister was on the point of being most advantageously married, but that *you*, that Miss Elizabeth Bennet, would, in all likelihood, be soon afterwards united to my nephew, my own nephew, Mr. Darcy. Though I *know* it must be a scandalous falsehood; though I would not injure him so much as to suppose the truth of it possible, I instantly resolved on setting off for this place, that I might make my sentiments known to you."

"If you believed it impossible to be true," said Elizabeth, colouring with astonishment and disdain, "I wonder you took the trouble of coming so far. What could your ladyship propose by it?"

"At once to insist upon having such a report universally contradicted."

"Your coming to Longbourn, to see me and my family," said Elizabeth coolly, "will be rather a confirmation of it; if, indeed, such a report is in existence."

"If! do you then pretend to be ignorant of it? Has it not been industriously circulated by yourselves? Do you not know that such a report is spread abroad?"

"I never heard that it was."

"And can you likewise declare, that there is no *foundation* for it?"

"I do not pretend to possess equal frankness with your ladyship. *You* may ask questions, which *I* shall not choose to answer."

"This is not to be borne. Miss Bennet, I insist on being satisfied. Has he, has my nephew, made you an offer of marriage?"

"Your ladyship has declared it to be impossible."

"It ought to be so; it must be so, while he retains the use of his reason. But *your* arts and allurements may, in a moment of infatuation, have made him forget what he owes to himself and to all his family. You may have drawn him in."

"If I have, I shall be the last person to confess it."

"Miss Bennet, do you know who I am? I have not been accustomed to such language as this. I am almost the nearest relation he has in the world, and am entitled to know all his dearest concerns."

"But you are not entitled to know *mine*; nor will such behaviour as this, ever induce me to be explicit."

"Let me be rightly understood. This match, to which you have the presumption to aspire, can never take place. No, never. Mr. Darcy is engaged to *my daughter*. Now what have you to say?"

"Only this; that if he is so, you can have no reason to suppose he will make an offer to me."

Lady Catherine hesitated for a moment, and then replied,

"The engagement between them is of a peculiar kind. From their infancy, they have been intended for each other. It was the favourite wish of *his* mother, as well as of hers. While in their cradles, we planned the union: and now, at the moment when the wishes of both sisters would be accomplished, in their marriage, to be prevented by a young woman of inferior birth, of no importance in the world, and wholly unallied to the family! Do you pay no regard to the wishes of his friends? To his tacit engagement with Miss De Bourgh? Are you lost to every feeling of propriety and delicacy? Have you not heard me say, that from his earliest hours he was destined for his cousin?"

"Yes, and I had heard it before. But what is that to me? If there is no other objection to my marrying your nephew, I shall certainly not be kept from it, by knowing that his mother and aunt wished him to marry Miss De Bourgh. You both did as much as you could, in planning the marriage. Its completion depended on others. If Mr. Darcy is neither by honour nor inclination confined to his cousin, why is not he to make another choice? And if I am that choice, why may not I accept him?"

"Because honour, decorum, prudence, nay, interest, forbid it. Yes, Miss Bennet, interest; for do not expect to be noticed by his family or friends, if you wilfully act against the inclinations of all. You will be censured, slighted, and despised, by everyone connected with him. Your alliance will be a disgrace; your name will never even be mentioned by any of us."

"These are heavy misfortunes," replied Elizabeth. "But the wife of Mr. Darcy must have such extraordinary sources of happiness necessarily attached to her situation, that she could, upon the whole, have no cause to repine."

"Obstinate, headstrong girl! I am ashamed of you! Is this your gratitude for my attentions to you last spring? Is nothing due to me on that score?

"Let us sit down. You are to understand, Miss Bennet, that I came here with the determined resolution of carrying my purpose; nor will I be dissuaded from it. I have not been used to submit to any person's whims. I have not been in the habit of brooking disappointment."

"*That* will make your ladyship's situation at present more pitiable; but it will have no effect on *me*."

"I will not be interrupted. Hear me in silence. My daughter and my nephew are formed for each other. They are descended on the maternal side, from the same noble line; and, on the father's, from respectable, honourable, and ancient, though untitled families. Their fortune on both sides is splendid. They are destined for each other by the voice of every member of their respective houses; and what is to divide them? The upstart pretensions of a young woman without family, connections, or fortune. Is this to be endured! But it must not, shall not be. If you were sensible of your own good, you would not wish to quit the sphere, in which you have been brought up."

"In marrying your nephew, I should not consider myself as quitting that sphere. He is a gentleman; I am a gentleman's daughter; so far we are equal."

"True. You *are* a gentleman's daughter. But who was your mother? Who are your uncles and aunts? Do not imagine me ignorant of their condition."

"Whatever my connections may be," said Elizabeth, "if your nephew does not object to them, they can be nothing to *you*."

"Tell me once for all, are you engaged to him?"

Though Elizabeth would not, for the mere purpose of obliging Lady Catherine, have answered this question, she could not but say, after a moment's deliberation,

"I am not."

Lady Catherine seemed pleased.

"And will you promise me, never to enter into such an

engagement?"

"I will make no promise of the kind."

"Miss Bennet I am shocked and astonished. I expected to find a more reasonable young woman. But do not deceive yourself into a belief that I will ever recede. I shall not go away, till you have given me the assurance I require."

"And I certainly *never* shall give it. I am not to be intimidated into anything so wholly unreasonable. Your ladyship wants Mr. Darcy to marry your daughter; but would my giving you the wished-for promise, make *their* marriage at all more probable? Supposing him to be attached to me, would *my* refusing to accept his hand, make him wish to bestow it on his cousin? Allow me to say, Lady Catherine, that the arguments with which you have supported this extraordinary application, have been as frivolous as the application was ill-judged. You have widely mistaken my character, if you think I can be worked on by such persuasions as these. How far your nephew might approve of your interference in *his* affairs, I cannot tell; but you have certainly no right to concern yourself in mine. I must beg, therefore, to be importuned no farther on the subject."

"Not so hasty, if you please. I have by no means done. To all the objections I have already urged, I have still another to add. I am no stranger to the particulars of your youngest sister's infamous elopement. I know it all; that the young man's marrying her, was a patched-up business, at the expense of your father and uncles. And is *such* a girl to be my nephew's sister? Is *her* husband, is the son of his late father's steward, to be his brother? Heaven and earth! – of what are you thinking? Are the shades of Pemberley to be thus polluted?"

"You can *now* have nothing farther to say," she resentfully answered. "You have insulted me, in every possible method. I must beg to return to the house."

And she rose as she spoke. Lady Catherine rose also, and

they turned back. Her ladyship was highly incensed.

"You have no regard, then, for the honour and credit of my nephew! Unfeeling, selfish girl! Do you not consider that a connection with you, must disgrace him in the eyes of everybody?"

"Lady Catherine, I have nothing farther to say. You know my sentiments."

"You are then resolved to have him?"

"I have said no such thing. I am only resolved to act in that manner, which will, in my own opinion, constitute my happiness, without reference to *you*, or to any person so wholly unconnected with me."

"It is well. You refuse, then, to oblige me. You refuse to obey the claims of duty, honour, and gratitude. You are determined to ruin him in the opinion of all his friends, and make him the contempt of the world."

"Neither duty, nor honour, nor gratitude," replied Elizabeth, "have any possible claim on me, in the present instance. No principle of either, would be violated by my marriage with Mr. Darcy. And with regard to the resentment of his family, or the indignation of the world, if the former *were* excited by his marrying me, it would not give me one moment's concern – and the world in general would have too much sense to join in the scorn."

"And this is your real opinion! This is your final resolve! Very well. I shall now know how to act. Do not imagine, Miss Bennet, that your ambition will ever be gratified. I came to try you. I hoped to find you reasonable; but depend upon it I will carry my point."

In this manner Lady Catherine talked on, till they were at the door of the carriage, when turning hastily round, she added,

"I take no leave of you, Miss Bennet. I send no compliments to your mother. You deserve no such attention. I am most seriously displeased."

Elizabeth made no answer; and without attempting to persuade her ladyship to return into the house, walked quietly into it herself. She heard the carriage drive away as she proceeded upstairs. Her mother impatiently met her at the door of the dressing-room, to ask why Lady Catherine would not come in again and rest herself.

"She did not choose it," said her daughter, "she would go."

"She is a very fine-looking woman! and her calling here was prodigiously civil! for she only came, I suppose, to tell us the Collinses were well. She is on her road somewhere, I dare say, and so passing through Meryton, thought she might as well call on you. I suppose she had nothing particular to say to you, Lizzy?"

Elizabeth was forced to give in to a little falsehood here; for to acknowledge the substance of their conversation was impossible.

# Chapter 57

THE DISCOMPOSURE of spirits, which this extraordinary visit threw Elizabeth into, could not be easily overcome; nor could she for many hours, learn to think of it less than incessantly. Lady Catherine it appeared, had actually taken the trouble of this journey from Rosings, for the sole purpose of breaking off her supposed engagement with Mr. Darcy. It was a rational scheme to be sure! but from what the report of their engagement could originate, Elizabeth was at a loss to imagine; till she recollected that *his* being the intimate friend of Bingley, and *her* being the sister of Jane, was enough, at a time when the expectation of one wedding, made everybody eager for another, to supply the idea. She had not herself forgotten to feel that the marriage of her sister must bring them more frequently together. And her neighbours at Lucas lodge, therefore (for through their communication with the Collinses, the report she concluded had reached lady Catherine), had only set *that* down, as almost certain and immediate, which *she* had looked forward to as possible, at some future time.

In revolving Lady Catherine's expressions, however, she could not help feeling some uneasiness as to the possible consequence of her persisting in this interference. From what she had said of her resolution to prevent their marriage, it occurred to Elizabeth that she must meditate an application to her nephew; and how *he* might take a similar representation of the evils attached to a connection with her, she dared not pronounce. She knew not the exact degree of his affection for his aunt, or his dependence on her judgment, but it was natural to suppose that he thought much higher of her ladyship than *she* could do; and it was certain, that in enumerating the miseries of a marriage with *one*, whose immediate connections were so unequal to his own, his aunt would address him on his weakest side. With his notions of dignity, he would probably feel that the arguments, which to Elizabeth had appeared weak and ridiculous, contained much good sense and solid reasoning.

If he had been wavering before, as to what he should do, which had often seemed likely, the advice and entreaty of so near a relation might settle every doubt, and determine him at once to be as happy, as dignity unblemished could make him. In that case he would return no more. Lady Catherine might see him on her way through town; and his engagement to Bingley on coming again to Netherfield must give way.

"If, therefore, an excuse for not keeping his promise, should come to his friend within a few days," she added, "I shall know how to understand it. I shall then give over every expectation, every wish of his constancy. If he is satisfied with only regretting me, when he might have obtained my affections and hand, I shall soon cease to regret him at all."

The surprise of the rest of the family, on hearing who their visitor had been, was very great; but they obligingly satisfied it, with the same kind of supposition, which had appeased Mrs. Bennet's curiosity; and Elizabeth was spared from much teasing on the subject.

The next morning, as she was going downstairs, she was met by her father, who came out of his library with a letter in his hand.

"Lizzy," said he, "I was going to look for you; come into my room."

She followed him hither; and her curiosity to know what he had to tell her, was heightened by the supposition of its being in some manner connected with the letter he held. It suddenly struck her that it might be from Lady Catherine; and she anticipated with dismay all the consequent explanations.

She followed her father to the fireplace, and they both sat down. He then said,

"I have received a letter this morning that has astonished me exceedingly. As it principally concerns yourself, you ought to know its contents. I did not know before, that I had *two* daughters on the brink of matrimony. Let me congratulate you, on a very important conquest."

The colour now rushed into Elizabeth's cheeks in the instantaneous conviction of its being a letter from the nephew, instead of the aunt; and she was undetermined whether most to be pleased that he explained himself at all, or offended that his letter was not rather addressed to herself; when her father continued,

"You look conscious. Young ladies have great penetration in such matters as these; but I think I may defy even *your* sagacity, to discover the name of your admirer. This letter is from Mr. Collins."

"From Mr. Collins! and what can *he* have to say?"

"Something very much to the purpose of course. He begins with congratulations on the approaching nuptials of my eldest daughter, of which it seems he has been told, by some of the good-natured, gossiping Lucases. I shall not sport with your impatience, by reading what he says on that point. What relates to yourself, is as follows. 'Having thus offered you the sincere congratulations of Mrs. Collins and myself on this happy event, let me now add a short hint on the subject of another; of which we have been advertised by the same authority. Your daughter Elizabeth, it is presumed, will not long bear the name of Bennet, after her elder sister has resigned it, and the chosen partner of her fate, may be reasonably looked up to, as one of the most illustrious personages in this land.'

"Can you possibly guess, Lizzy, who is meant by this?" 'This young gentleman is blessed in a peculiar way, with everything the heart of mortal can most desire, – splendid property, noble kindred, and extensive patronage. Yet in spite of all these temptations, let me warn my cousin Elizabeth, and yourself, of what evils you may incur, by a precipitate closure with this gentleman's proposals, which, of course, you will be inclined to take immediate advantage of.'

"Have you any idea, Lizzy, who this gentleman is? But now it comes out.

'My motive for cautioning you, is as follows. We have reason to imagine that his aunt, Lady Catherine de Bourgh, does not look on the match with a friendly eye.'"

*"Mr. Darcy,* you see, is the man! Now, Lizzy, I think I *have* surprised you. Could he, or the Lucases, have pitched on any man, within the circle of our acquaintance, whose name would have given the lie more effectually to what they related? Mr. Darcy, who never looks at any woman but to see a blemish, and who probably never looked at *you* in his life! It is admirable!"

Elizabeth tried to join in her father's pleasantry, but could only force one most reluctant smile. Never had his wit been directed in a manner so little agreeable to her.

"Are you not diverted?"

"Oh! yes. Pray, read on."

" 'After mentioning the likelihood of this marriage to her ladyship last night, she immediately, with her usual condescension, expressed what she felt on the occasion; when it become apparent, that on the score of some family objections on the part of my cousin, she would never give her consent to what she termed so disgraceful a match. I thought it my duty to give the speediest intelligence of this to my cousin, that she and her noble admirer may be aware of what they are about, and not run hastily into a marriage which has not been properly sanctioned.' Mr. Collins moreover adds, 'I am truly rejoiced that my cousin Lydia's sad business has been so well hushed up, and am only concerned that their living together before the marriage took place, should be so generally known. I must not, however, neglect the duties of my station, or refrain from declaring my amazement, at hearing that you received the young couple into your house as soon as they were married. It was an encouragement of vice; and had I been the rector of Longbourn, I should very strenuously have opposed it. You ought certainly to forgive them as christian, but never to admit them in your sight, or allow their names to be mentioned in your hearing.' *That* is his notion of christian forgiveness! The rest of his letter is only about his dear Charlotte's situation, and his expectation of a young olive-branch. But, Lizzy, you look as if you did not enjoy it. You are not going to be *Missish*, I hope, and pretend to be affronted at an idle report. For what do we live, but to make sport for our neighbours, and laugh at them in our turn?"

"Oh!" cried Elizabeth, "I am excessively diverted. But it is so strange!"

"Yes – *that* is what makes it amusing. Had they fixed on any other man it would have been nothing; but *his* perfect indifference, and *your* pointed dislike, make it so delightfully absurd! Much as I abominate writing, I would not give up Mr. Collins's correspondence for any consideration. Nay, when I read a letter of his, I cannot help giving him the preference even over Wickham, much as I value the impudence and hypocrisy of my son-in-law. And pray, Lizzy, what said Lady Catherine about this report? Did she call to refuse her consent?"

To this question his daughter replied only with a laugh; and as it had been asked without the least suspicion, she was not distressed by his repeating it. Elizabeth had never been more at a loss to make her feelings appear what they were not. It was necessary to laugh, when she would rather have cried. Her father had most cruelly mortified her, by what he said of Mr. Darcy's indifference, and she could do nothing but wonder at such a want of penetration, or fear that perhaps, instead of his seeing too *little*, she might have fancied too *much*.

## *Chapter 58*

INSTEAD OF receiving any such letter of excuse from his friend, as Elizabeth half expected Mr. Bingley to do, he was able to bring Darcy with him to Longbourn before many days had passed after Lady Catherine's visit. The gentlemen arrived early; and, before Mrs. Bennet had time to tell him of their having seen his aunt, of which her daughter sat in momentary dread, Bingley, who wanted to be alone with Jane, proposed their all walking out. It was agreed to. Mrs. Bennet was not in the habit of walking, Mary could never spare time, but the remaining five set off together. Bingley and Jane, however, soon allowed the others to outstrip them. They lagged behind, while Elizabeth, Kitty, and Darcy, were to entertain each other. Very little was said by either; Kitty was too much afraid of him to talk; Elizabeth was secretly forming a desperate resolution; and perhaps he might be doing the same.

They walked towards the Lucases, because Kitty wished to call upon Maria; and as Elizabeth saw no occasion for making it a general concern, when Kitty left them, she went boldly on with him alone. Now was the moment for her resolution to be executed, and, while her courage was high, she immediately said,

"Mr. Darcy, I am a very selfish creature; and, for the sake of giving relief to my own feelings, care not how much I may be wounding yours. I can no longer help thanking you for your unexampled kindness to my poor sister. Ever since I have known it, I have been most anxious to acknowledge to you how gratefully I feel it. Were it known to the rest of my family, I should not have merely my own gratitude to express."

"I am sorry, exceedingly sorry," replied Darcy, in a tone of surprise and emotion, "that you have ever been informed of what may, in a mistaken light, have given you uneasiness. I did not think Mrs. Gardiner was so little to be trusted."

"You must not blame my aunt. Lydia's thoughtlessness first betrayed to me that you had been concerned in the matter; and, of course, I could not rest till I knew the particulars. Let me thank you again and again, in the name of all my family, for that generous compassion which induced you to take so much trouble, and bear so many mortifications, for the sake of discovering them."

"If you *will* thank me," he replied, "let it be for yourself alone. That the wish of giving happiness to you, might add force to the other inducements which led me on, I shall not attempt to deny. But your *family* owe me nothing. Much as I respect them, I believe I thought only of *you*."

Elizabeth was too much embarrassed to say a word. After a

short pause, her companion added, "You are too generous to trifle with me. If your feelings are still what they were last April, tell me so at once. *My* affections and wishes are unchanged, but one word from you will silence me on this subject for ever."

Elizabeth feeling all the more than common awkwardness and anxiety of his situation, now forced herself to speak; and immediately, though not very fluently, gave him to understand, that her sentiments had undergone so material a change, since the period to which he alluded, as to make her receive with gratitude and pleasure, his present assurances. The happiness which this reply produced, was such as he had probably never felt before; and he expressed himself on the occasion as sensibly and as warmly as a man violently in love can be supposed to do. Had Elizabeth been able to encounter his eye, she might have seen how well the expression of heart-felt delight, diffused over his face, became him; but, though she could not look, she could listen, and he told her of feelings, which, in proving of what importance she was to him, made his affection every moment more valuable.

They walked on, without knowing in what direction. There was too much to be thought, and felt, and said, for attention to any other objects. She soon learnt that they were indebted for their present good understanding to the efforts of his aunt, who *did* call on him in her return through London, and there relate her journey to Longbourn, its motive, and the substance of her conversation with Elizabeth; dwelling emphatically on every expression of the latter, which, in her ladyship's apprehension, peculiarly denoted her perverseness and assurance, in the belief that such a relation must assist her endeavours to obtain that promise from her nephew, which *she* had refused to give. But, unluckily for her ladyship, its effect had been exactly contrariwise.

"It taught me to hope," said he, "as I had scarcely ever allowed myself to hope before. I knew enough of your disposition to be certain, that, had you been absolutely, irrevocably decided against me, you would have acknowledged it to Lady Catherine, frankly and openly."

Elizabeth coloured and laughed as she replied, "Yes, you know enough of my *frankness* to believe me capable of *that*. After abusing you so abominably to your face, I could have no scruple in abusing you to all your relations."

"What did you say of me, that I did not deserve? For, though your accusations were ill-founded, formed on mistaken premises, my behaviour to you at the time, had merited the severest reproof. It was unpardonable. I cannot think of it without abhorrence."

"We will not quarrel for the greater share of blame annexed to that evening," said Elizabeth. "The conduct of neither, if strictly examined, will be irreproachable; but since then, we have both, I hope, improved in civility."

"I cannot be so easily reconciled to myself. The recollection of what I then said, of my conduct, my manners, my expressions during the whole of it, is now, and has been many months, inexpressibly painful to me. Your reproof, so well applied, I shall never forget: 'had you behaved in a more gentleman-like manner.' Those were your words. You know not, you can scarcely conceive, how they have tortured me; – though it was some time, I confess, before I was reasonable enough to allow their justice."

"I was certainly very far from expecting them to make so strong an impression. I had not the smallest idea of their being ever felt in such a way."

"I can easily believe it. You thought me then devoid of every proper feeling, I am sure you did. The turn of your countenance I shall never forget, as you said that I could not have addressed you in any possible way, that would induce you to accept me."

"Oh! do not repeat what I then said. These recollections will not do at all. I assure you, that I have long been most heartily ashamed of it."

Darcy mentioned his letter. "Did it," said he, "did it *soon* make you think better of me? Did you, on reading it, give any credit to its contents?"

She explained what its effect on her had been, and how gradually all her former prejudices had been removed.

"I knew," said he, "that what I wrote must give you pain, but it was necessary. I hope you have destroyed the letter. There was one part especially, the opening of it, which I should dread your having the power of reading again. I can remember some expressions which might justly make you hate me."

"The letter shall certainly be burnt, if you believe it essential to the preservation of my regard; but, though we have both reason to think my opinions not entirely unalterable, they are not, I hope, quite so easily changed as that implies."

"When I wrote that letter," replied Darcy, "I believed myself perfectly calm and cool, but I am since convinced that it was written in a dreadful bitterness of spirit."

"The letter, perhaps, began in bitterness, but it did not end so. The adieu is charity itself. But think no more of the letter. The feelings of the person who wrote, and the person who received it, are now so widely different from what they were then, that every unpleasant circumstance attending it, ought to be forgotten. You must learn some of my philosophy. Think only of the past as its remembrance gives you pleasure."

"I cannot give you credit for any philosophy of the kind. *Your* retrospections must be so totally void of reproach, that the contentment arising from them, is not of philosophy, but what is much better, of innocence. But with *me*, it is not so. Painful recollections will intrude, which cannot, which ought not to be repelled. I have been a selfish being all my life, in practice, though not in principle. As child I was taught what was *right*, but I was not taught to correct my temper. I was given good principles, but left to follow them in pride and conceit. Unfortunately an only son (for many years an only *child*), I was spoilt by my parents, who though good themselves (my father particularly, all that was benevolent and amiable), allowed, encouraged, almost taught me to be selfish and overbearing, to care for none beyond my own family circle, to think meanly of all the rest of the world, to *wish* at least to think meanly of their sense and worth compared with my own. Such I was, from eight to eight and twenty; and such I might still have been but for you, dearest, loveliest Elizabeth! What do I not owe you! You taught me a lesson, hard indeed at first, but most advantageous. By you, I was properly humbled. I came to you without a doubt of my reception. You showed me how insufficient were all my pretensions to please a woman worthy of being pleased."

"Had you then persuaded yourself that I should?"

"Indeed I had. What will you think of my vanity? I believed you to be wishing, expecting my addresses."

"My manners must have been in fault, but not intentionally I assure you. I never meant to deceive you, but my spirits might often lead me wrong. How you must have hated me after *that* evening?"

"Hate you! I was angry perhaps at first, but my anger soon began to take a proper direction."

"I am almost afraid of asking what you thought of me, when we met at Pemberley. You blamed me for coming?"

"No indeed; I felt nothing but surprise."

"Your surprise could not be greater than *mine* in being noticed by you. My conscience told me that I deserved no extraordinary politeness, and I confess that I did not expect to receive *more* than my due."

"My object *then*," replied Darcy, "was to show you, by every civility in my power, that I was not so mean as to resent the past;

and I hoped to obtain your forgiveness, to lessen your ill opinion, by letting you see that your reproofs had been attended to. How soon any other wishes introduced themselves I can hardly tell, but I believe in about half an hour after I had seen you."

He then told her of Georgiana's delight in her acquaintance, and of her disappointment at its sudden interruption; which naturally leading to the cause of that interruption, she soon learnt that his resolution of following her from Derbyshire in quest of her sister, had been formed before he quitted the inn, and that his gravity and thoughtfulness there, had arisen from no other struggles than what such a purpose must comprehend.

She expressed her gratitude again, but it was too painful a subject to each, to be dwelt on farther.

After walking several miles in a leisurely manner, and too busy to know anything about it, they found at last, on examining their watches, that it was time to be at home.

"What could become of Mr. Bingley and Jane!" was a wonder which introduced the discussion of *their* affairs. Darcy was delighted with their engagement; his friend had given him the earliest information of it.

"I must ask whether you were surprised?" said Elizabeth.

"Not at all. When I went away, I felt that it would soon happen."

"That is to say, you had given your permission. I guessed as much." And though he exclaimed at the term, she found that it had been pretty much the case.

"On the evening before my going to London," said he, "I made a confession to him, which I believe I ought to have made long ago. I told him of all that had occurred to make my former interference in his affairs, absurd and impertinent. His surprise was great. He never had the slightest suspicion. I told him, moreover, that I believed myself mistaken in supposing, as I had done, that your sister was indifferent to him; and as I could easily perceive that his attachment to her was unabated, I felt no doubt of their happiness together."

Elizabeth could not help smiling at his easy manner of directing his friend.

"Did you speak from your own observation," said she, "when you told him that my sister loved him, or merely from my information last spring?"

"From the former. I had narrowly observed her during the two visits which I had lately made her here; and I was convinced of her affection."

"And your assurance of it, I suppose, carried immediate conviction to him."

"It did. Bingley is most unaffectedly modest. His diffidence had prevented his depending on his own judgment in so anxious a case, but his reliance on mine, made everything easy. I was obliged to confess one thing, which for a time, and not unjustly, offended him. I could not allow myself to conceal that your sister had been in town three months last winter, that I had known it, and purposely kept it from him. He was angry. But his anger, I am persuaded, lasted no longer than he remained in any doubt of your sister's sentiments. He has heartily forgiven me now."

Elizabeth longed to observe that Mr. Bingley had been a most delightful friend; so easily guided that his worth was invaluable; but she checked herself. She remembered that he had yet to learn to be laughed at, and it was rather too early to begin. In anticipating the happiness of Bingley, which of course was to be inferior only to his own, he continued the conversation till they reached the house. In the hall they parted.

# Chapter 59

"MY DEAR Lizzy, where can you have been walking to?" was a question which Elizabeth received from Jane as soon as she entered the room, and from all the others when they sat down to table. She had only to say in reply, that they had wandered about, till she was beyond her own knowledge. She coloured as she spoke; but neither that, nor anything else, awakened a suspicion of the truth.

The evening passed quietly, unmarked by anything extraordinary. The acknowledged lovers talked and laughed, the unacknowledged were silent. Darcy was not of a disposition in which happiness overflows in mirth; and Elizabeth, agitated and confused, rather *knew* that she was happy, than *felt* herself to be so; for, besides the immediate embarrassment, there were other evils before her. She anticipated what would be felt in the family when her situation became known; she was aware that no one liked him but Jane; and even feared that with the others it was a *dislike* which not all his fortune and consequence might do away.

At night she opened her heart to Jane. Though suspicion was very far from Miss Bennet's general habits, she was absolutely incredulous here.

"You are joking, Lizzy. This cannot be! – engaged to Mr. Darcy! No, no, you shall not deceive me. I know it to be impossible."

"This is a wretched beginning indeed! My sole dependence was on you; and I am sure nobody else will believe me, if you do not. Yet, indeed, I am in earnest. I speak nothing but the truth. He still loves me, and we are engaged."

Jane looked at her doubtingly. "Oh, Lizzy! it cannot be. I know how much you dislike him."

"You know nothing of the matter. *That* is all to be forgot.

Perhaps I did not always love him so well as I do now. But in such cases as these, a good memory is unpardonable. This is the last time I shall ever remember it myself."

Miss Bennet still looked all amazement. Elizabeth again, and more seriously assured her of its truth.

"Good Heaven! can it be really so! Yet now I must believe you," cried Jane. "My dear, dear Lizzy, I would – I do congratulate you – but are you certain? forgive the question – are you quite certain that you can be happy with him?"

"There can be no doubt of that. It is settled between us already, that we are to be the happiest couple in the world. But are you pleased, Jane? Shall you like to have such a brother?"

"Very, very much. Nothing could give either Bingley or myself more delight. But we considered it, we talked of it as impossible. And do you really love him quite well enough? Oh, Lizzy! do anything rather than marry without affection. Are you quite sure that you feel what you ought to do?"

"Oh, yes! You will only think I feel more than I ought to do, when I tell you all."

"What do you mean?"

"Why, I must confess, that I love him better than I do Bingley. I am afraid you will be angry."

"My dearest sister, now *be* serious. I want to talk very seriously. Let me know everything that I am to know, without delay. Will you tell me how long you have loved him?"

"It has been coming on so gradually, that I hardly know when it began. But I believe I must date it from my first seeing his beautiful grounds at Pemberley."

Another entreaty that she would be serious, however, produced the desired effect; and she soon satisfied Jane by her solemn assurances of attachment. When convinced on that article, Miss Bennet had nothing farther to wish.

"Now I am quite happy," said she, "for you will be as happy as myself. I always had a value for him. Were it for nothing but his love of you, I must always have esteemed him; but now, as Bingley's friend and your husband, there can be only Bingley and yourself more dear to me. But Lizzy, you have been very sly, very reserved with me. How little did you tell me of what passed at Pemberley and Lambton! I owe all that I know of it, to another, not to you."

Elizabeth told her the motives of her secrecy. She had been unwilling to mention Bingley; and the unsettled state of her own feelings had made her equally avoid the name of his friend. But now she would no longer conceal from her, his share in Lydia's marriage. All was acknowledged, and half the night spent in conversation.

"Good gracious!" cried Mrs. Bennet, as she stood at a window the next morning, "if that disagreeable Mr. Darcy is not coming here again with our dear Bingley! What can he mean by being so tiresome as to be always coming here? I had no notion but he would go a shooting, or something or other, and not disturb us with his company. What shall we do with him? Lizzy, you must walk out with him again, that he may not be in Bingley's way."

Elizabeth could hardly help laughing at so convenient a proposal; yet was really vexed that her mother should be always giving him such an epithet.

As soon as they entered, Bingley looked at her so expressively, and shook hands with such warmth, as left no doubt of his good information; and he soon afterwards said aloud, "Mrs. Bennet, have you no more lanes hereabouts in which Lizzy may lose her way again today?"

"I advise Mr. Darcy, and Lizzy, and Kitty," said Mrs. Bennet, "to walk to Oakham Mount this morning. It is a nice long walk, and Mr. Darcy has never seen the view."

"It may do very well for the others," replied Mr. Bingley;

"but I am sure it will be too much for Kitty. Won't it, Kitty?"

Kitty owned that she had rather stay at home. Darcy professed a great curiosity to see the view from the Mount, and Elizabeth silently consented. As she went upstairs to get ready, Mrs. Bennet followed her, saying,

"I am quite sorry, Lizzy, that you should be forced to have that disagreeable man all to yourself. But I hope you will not mind it: it is all for Jane's sake, you know; and there is no occasion for talking to him, except just now and then. So, do not put yourself to inconvenience."

During their walk, it was resolved that Mr. Bennet's consent should be asked in the course of the evening. Elizabeth reserved to herself the application for her mother's. She could not determine how her mother would take it; sometimes doubting whether all his wealth and grandeur would be enough to overcome her abhorrence of the man. But whether she were violently set against the match, or violently delighted with it, it was certain that her manner would be equally ill-adapted to do credit to her sense; and she could no more bear that Mr. Darcy should hear the first raptures of her joy, than the first vehemence of her disapprobation.

In the evening, soon after Mr. Bennet withdrew to the library, she saw Mr. Darcy rise also and follow him, and her agitation on seeing it was extreme. She did not fear her father's opposition, but he was going to be made unhappy, and that it should be through her means, that *she*, his favourite child, should be distressing him by her choice, should be filling him with fears and regrets in disposing of her, was a wretched reflection, and she sat in misery till Mr. Darcy appeared again, when, looking at him, she was a little relieved by his smile. In a few minutes he approached the table where she was sitting with Kitty; and, while pretending to admire her work, said in a whisper, "Go to your father, he wants you in the library." She was gone directly.

Her father was walking about the room, looking grave and

anxious. "Lizzy," said he, "what are you doing? Are you out of your senses, to be accepting this man? Have you not always hated him?"

How earnestly did she then wish that her former opinions had been more reasonable, her expressions more moderate! It would have spared her from explanations and professions which it was exceedingly awkward to give; but they were now necessary, and she assured him with some confusion, of her attachment to Mr. Darcy.

"Or in other words, you are determined to have him. He is rich, to be sure, and you may have more fine clothes and fine carriages than Jane. But will they make you happy?"

"Have you any other objection," said Elizabeth, "than your belief of my indifference?"

"None at all. We all know him to be a proud, unpleasant sort of man; but this would be nothing if you really liked him."

"I do, I do like him," she replied, with tears in her eyes, "I love him. Indeed he has no improper pride. He is perfectly amiable. You do not know what he really is; then pray do not pain me by speaking of him in such terms."

"Lizzy," said her father, "I have given him my consent. He is the kind of man, indeed, to whom I should never dare refuse anything, which he condescended to ask. I now give it to *you*, if you are resolved on having him. But let me advise you to think better of it. I know your disposition, Lizzy. I know that you could be neither happy nor respectable, unless you truly esteemed your husband; unless you looked up to him as a superior. Your lively talents would place you in the greatest danger in an unequal marriage. You could scarcely escape discredit and misery. My child, let me not have the grief of seeing *you* unable to respect your partner in life. You know not what you are about."

Elizabeth, still more affected, was earnest and solemn in her reply; and at length, by repeated assurances that Mr. Darcy was really the object of her choice, by explaining the gradual change which her estimation of him had undergone, relating her absolute certainty that his affection was not the work of a day, but had stood the test of many months' suspense, and enumerating with energy all his good qualities, she did conquer her father's incredulity, and reconcile him to the match.

"Well, my dear," said he, when she ceased speaking, "I have no more to say. If this be the case, he deserves you. I could not have parted with you, my Lizzy, to any one less worthy."

To complete the favourable impression, she then told him what Mr. Darcy had voluntarily done for Lydia. He heard her with astonishment.

"This is an evening of wonders, indeed! And so, Darcy did every thing; made up the match, gave the money, paid the fellow's debts, and got him his commission! So much the better. It will save me a world of trouble and economy. Had it been your uncle's doing, I must and *would* have paid him; but these violent young lovers carry everything their own way. I shall offer to pay him tomorrow; he will rant and storm about his love for you, and there will be an end of the matter."

He then recollected her embarrassment a few days before, on his reading Mr. Collins's letter; and after laughing at her some time, allowed her at last to go – saying, as she quitted the room, "If any young men come for Mary or Kitty, send them in, for I am quite at leisure."

Elizabeth's mind was now relieved from a very heavy weight; and, after half an hour's quiet reflection in her own room, she was able to join the others with tolerable composure. Everything was too recent for gaiety, but the evening passed tranquilly away; there was no longer anything material to be dreaded, and the comfort of ease and familiarity would come in time.

When her mother went up to her dressing-room at night, she followed her, and made the important communication. Its effect was most extraordinary; for on first hearing it, Mrs. Bennet sat quite still, and unable to utter a syllable. Nor was it under many, many minutes, that she could comprehend what she heard; though not in general backward to credit what was for the advantage of her family, or that came in the shape of a lover to any of them. She began at length to recover, to fidget about in her chair, get up, sit down again, wonder, and bless herself.

"Good gracious! Lord bless me! only think! dear me! Mr. Darcy! Who would have thought it! And is it really true? Oh! my sweetest Lizzy! how rich and how great you will be! What pin-money, what jewels, what carriages you will have! Jane's is nothing to it – nothing at all. I am so pleased – so happy. Such a charming man! – so handsome! so tall! – Oh, my dear Lizzy! pray apologise for my having disliked him so much before. I hope he will overlook it. Dear, dear Lizzy. A house in town! Everything that is charming! Three daughters married! Ten thousand a year! Oh, Lord! What will become of me. I shall go distracted."

This was enough to prove that her approbation need not be doubted: and Elizabeth, rejoicing that such an effusion was heard only by herself, soon went away. But before she had been three minutes in her own room, her mother followed her.

"My dearest child," she cried, "I can think of nothing else! Ten thousand a year, and very likely more! 'Tis as good as a Lord! And a special licence. You must and shall be married by a special licence. But my dearest love, tell me what dish Mr. Darcy is particularly fond of, that I may have it tomorrow."

This was a sad omen of what her mother's behaviour to the gentleman himself might be; and Elizabeth found, that though in the certain possession of his warmest affection, and secure of her relations' consent, there was still something to be wished for. But the morrow passed off much better than she expected; for Mrs. Bennet luckily stood in such awe of her intended son-in-law, that she ventured not to speak to him, unless it was in her power to offer him any attention, or mark her deference for his opinion.

Elizabeth had the satisfaction of seeing her father taking pains to get acquainted with him; and Mr. Bennet soon assured her that he was rising every hour in his esteem.

"I admire all my three sons-in-law highly," said he. "Wickham, perhaps, is my favourite; but I think I shall like *your* husband quite as well as Jane's."

# Chapter 60

ELIZABETH'S SPIRITS soon rising to playfulness again, she wanted Mr. Darcy to account for his having ever fallen in love with her. "How could you begin?" said she. "I can comprehend your going on charmingly, when you had once made a beginning; but what could set you off in the first place?"

"I cannot fix on the hour, or the spot, or the look, or the words, which laid the foundation. It is too long ago. I was in the middle before I knew that I *had* begun."

"My beauty you had early withstood, and as for my manners – my behaviour to *you* was at least always bordering on the uncivil, and I never spoke to you without rather wishing to give you pain than not. Now be sincere; did you admire me for my impertinence?"

"For the liveliness of your mind, I did."

"You may as well call it impertinence at once. It was very little less. The fact is, that you were sick of civility, of deference, of officious attention. You were disgusted with the women who were always speaking and looking, and thinking for *your* approbation alone. I roused, and interested you, because I was so unlike *them*. Had you not been really amiable you would have hated me for it; but in spite of the pains you took to disguise yourself, your feelings were always noble and just; and in your heart, you thoroughly despised the persons who so assiduously courted you. There – I have saved you the trouble of accounting for it; and really, all things considered, I begin to think it perfectly reasonable. To be sure, you knew no actual good of me – but nobody thinks of *that* when they fall in love."

"Was there no good in your affectionate behaviour to Jane, while she was ill at Netherfield?"

"Dearest Jane! who could have done less for her? But make a virtue of it by all means. My good qualities are under your protection, and you are to exaggerate them as much as possible; and, in return, it belongs to me to find occasions for teasing and quarrelling with you as often as may be; and I shall begin directly by asking you what made you so unwilling to come to the point at last. What made you so shy of me, when you first called, and afterwards dined here? Why, especially, when you called, did you look as if you did not care about me?"

"Because you were grave and silent, and gave me no encouragement."

"But I was embarrassed."

"And so was I."

"You might have talked to me more when you came to dinner."

"A man who had felt less, might."

"How unlucky that you should have a reasonable answer to give, and that I should be so reasonable as to admit it! But I wonder how long you *would* have gone on, if you had been left to yourself. I wonder when you *would* have spoken, if I had not asked you! My resolution of thanking you for your kindness to Lydia had certainly great effect. *Too much*, I am afraid; for what becomes of the moral, if our comfort springs from a breach of promise, for I ought not to have mentioned the subject? This will never do."

"You need not distress yourself. The moral will be perfectly fair. Lady Catherine's unjustifiable endeavours to separate us, were the means of removing all my doubts. I am not indebted for my present happiness to your eager desire of expressing your gratitude. I was not in a humour to wait for any opening of yours. My aunt's intelligence had given me hope, and I was determined at once to know everything."

"Lady Catherine has been of infinite use, which ought to make her happy, for she loves to be of use. But tell me, what did you come down to Netherfield for? Was it merely to ride to Longbourn and be embarrassed? or had you intended any more serious consequence?"

"My real purpose was to see *you*, and to judge, if I could, whether I might ever hope to make you love me. My avowed one, or what I avowed to myself, was to see whether your sister were still partial to Bingley, and if she were, to make the confession to him which I have since made."

"Shall you ever have courage to announce to Lady Catherine, what is to befall her?"

"I am more likely to want more time than courage, Elizabeth. But it ought to done, and if you will give me a sheet of paper, it shall be done directly."

"And if I had not a letter to write myself, I might sit by you, and admire the evenness of your writing, as another young lady once did. But I have an aunt, too, who must not be longer neglected."

From an unwillingness to confess how much her intimacy with Mr. Darcy had been over-rated, Elizabeth had never yet answered Mrs. Gardiner's long letter; but now, having *that* to communicate which she knew would be most welcome, she was almost ashamed to find, that her uncle and aunt had already lost three days of happiness, and immediately wrote as follows:

> I would have thanked you before, my dear aunt, as I ought to have done, for your long, kind, satisfactory, detail of particulars; but to say the truth, I was too cross to write. You supposed more than really existed. But *now* suppose as much as you choose; give a loose to your fancy, indulge your imagination in every possible flight which the subject will afford, and unless you believe me actually married, you cannot greatly err. You must write again very soon, and praise him a great deal more than you did in your last. I thank you, again and again, for not going to the Lakes. How could I be so silly as to wish it! Your idea of the ponies is delightful. We will go around the Park every day. I am the happiest creature in the world. Perhaps other people have said so before, but not one with such justice. I am happier even than Jane; she only smiles, I laugh. Mr. Darcy sends you all the love in the world, that he can spare from me. You are all to come to Pemberley at Christmas. Yours, &c.

Mr. Darcy's letter to Lady Catherine, was in a different style; and still different from either, was what Mr. Bennet sent to Mr. Collins, in reply to his last.

> DEAR SIR,
>
> I must trouble you once more for congratulations. Elizabeth will soon be the wife of Mr. Darcy. Console Lady Catherine as well as you can. But, if I were you, I would stand by the nephew. He has more to give.
>
> Yours sincerely, &c.

Miss Bingley's congratulations to her brother, on his

approaching marriage, were all that was affectionate and insincere. She wrote even to Jane on the occasion, to express her delight, and repeat all her former professions of regard. Jane was not deceived, but she was affected; and though feeling no reliance on her, could not help writing her a much kinder answer than she knew was deserved.

The joy which Miss Darcy expressed on receiving similar information, was as sincere as her brother's in sending it. Four sides of paper were insufficient to contain all her delight, and all her earnest desire of being loved by her sister.

Before any answer could arrive from Mr. Collins, or any congratulations to Elizabeth, from his wife, the Longbourn family heard that the Collinses were come themselves to Lucas lodge. The reason of this sudden removal was soon evident. Lady Catherine had been rendered so exceedingly angry by the contents of her nephew's letter, that Charlotte, really rejoicing in the match, was anxious to get away till the storm was blown over. At such a moment, the arrival of her friend was a sincere pleasure to Elizabeth, though in the course of their meetings she must sometimes think the pleasure dearly bought, when she saw Mr. Darcy exposed to all the parading and obsequious civility of her husband. He bore it however with admirable calmness. He could even listen to Sir William Lucas, when he complimented him on carrying away the brightest jewel of the country, and expressed his hopes of their all meeting frequently at St. James's, with very decent composure. If he did shrug his shoulders, it was not till Sir William was out of sight.

Mrs. Philips's vulgarity was another, and perhaps a greater tax on his forbearance; and though Mrs. Philips, as well as her sister, stood in too much awe of him to speak with the familiarity which Bingley's good humour encouraged, yet, whenever she *did* speak, she must be vulgar. Nor was her respect for him, though it made her more quiet, at all likely to make her more elegant. Elizabeth did all she could, to shield him from the frequent notice of either, and was ever anxious to keep him to herself, and to those of her family with whom he might converse without mortification; and though the uncomfortable feelings arising from all this took from the season of courtship much of its pleasure, it added to the hope of the future; and she looked forward with delight to the time when they should be removed from society so little pleasing to either, to all the comfort and elegance of their family party at Pemberley.

## *Chapter 61*

HAPPY FOR all her maternal feelings was the day on which Mrs. Bennet got rid of her two most deserving daughters. With what delighted pride she afterwards visited Mrs. Bingley and talked of Mrs. Darcy may be guessed. I wish I could say, for the sake of her family, that the accomplishment of her earnest desire in the establishment of so many of her children, produced so happy an effect as to make her a sensible, amiable, well-informed woman for the rest of her life; though perhaps it was lucky for her husband, who might not have relished domestic felicity in so unusual a form, that she still was occasionally nervous and invariably silly.

Mr. Bennet missed his second daughter exceedingly; his affection for her drew him oftener from home than anything else could do. He delighted in going to Pemberley, especially when he was least expected.

Mr. Bingley and Jane remained at Netherfield only a twelvemonth. So near a vicinity to her mother and Meryton relations was not desirable even to *his* easy temper, or *her* affectionate heart. The darling wish of his sisters was then gratified; he bought an estate in a neighbouring county to Derbyshire, and Jane and Elizabeth, in addition to every other source of happiness, were within thirty miles of each other.

Kitty, to her very material advantage, spent the chief of her time with her two elder sisters. In society so superior to what she had generally known, her improvement was great. She was not of so ungovernable a temper as Lydia, and, removed from the influence of Lydia's example, she became, by proper attention and management, less irritable, less ignorant, and less insipid. From the farther disadvantage of Lydia's society she was of course carefully kept, and though Mrs. Wickham frequently invited her to come and stay with her, with the promise of balls and young men, her father would never consent to her going.

Mary was the only daughter who remained at home; and she was necessarily drawn from the pursuit of accomplishments by Mrs. Bennet's being quite unable to sit alone. Mary was obliged to mix more with the world, but she could still moralise over every morning visit; and as she was no longer mortified by comparisons between her sisters' beauty and her own, it was suspected by her father that she submitted to the change without much reluctance.

As for Wickham and Lydia, their characters suffered no revolution from the marriage of her sisters. He bore with philosophy the conviction that Elizabeth must now become acquainted with whatever of his ingratitude and falsehood had before been unknown to her; and in spite of everything, was not wholly without hope that Darcy might yet be prevailed on to make his fortune. The congratulatory letter which Elizabeth received from Lydia on her marriage, explained to her that, by his wife at least, if not by himself, such a hope was cherished. The letter was to this effect:

MY DEAR LIZZY,

I wish you joy. If you love Mr. Darcy half as well as I do my dear Wickham, you must be very happy. It is a great comfort to have you so rich, and when you have nothing else to do, I hope you will think of us. I am sure Wickham would like a place at court very much, and I do not think we shall have quite money enough to live upon without some help. Any place would do, of about three or four hundred a year; but, however, do not speak to Mr. Darcy about it, if you had rather not.

Yours, &c.

As it happened that Elizabeth had *much* rather not, she endeavoured in her answer to put an end to every entreaty and expectation of the kind. Such relief, however, as it was in her power to afford, by the practice of what might be called economy in her own private expences, she frequently sent them. It had always been evident to her that such an income as theirs, under the direction of two persons so extravagant in their wants, and heedless of the future, must be very insufficient to their support; and whenever they changed their quarters, either Jane or herself were sure of being applied to, for some little assistance towards discharging their bills. Their manner of living, even when the restoration of peace dismissed them to a home, was unsettled in the extreme. They were always moving from place to place in quest of a cheap situation, and always spending more than they ought. His affection for her soon sunk into indifference; her's lasted a little longer; and in spite of her youth and her manners, she retained all the claims to reputation which her marriage had given her.

Though Darcy could never receive *him* at Pemberley, yet, for Elizabeth's sake, he assisted him farther in his profession. Lydia was occasionally a visitor there, when her husband was gone to enjoy himself in London or Bath; and with the Bingleys they both